A NOVEL

Carol Soucie

First Edition

NEWMAN SPRINGS PUBLISHING
320 Broad Street
Red Bank, NJ 07701

First originally published by Newman Springs Publishing 2022

ISBN 978-1-68498-538-8 (Paperback)
ISBN 978-1-68498-539-5 (Digital)

Printed in the United States of America

For Frances

The journey has been worth every step of the way.

ONE

That particular Saturday morning of January 23, 1960, in Bel Air, California, the sun was screaming with early morning radiance. It was seven o'clock when Bob rolled over in bed, to find Corey already up and gone from the master suite. He continued to lie there, and the thought of Julie Hayward's funeral that afternoon deeply saddened him. Even though a few months earlier, Bob demonstrated notable prescience, in the knowledge he could not save her, and she showed no resolve in trying to help or save herself.

Bob Richardson was fast approaching the age of twenty-four and was an extremely attractive young man with dark, wavy hair and a beautifully sculpted body of pure muscle. After he graduated from the New England Conservatory of Music, he headed west to Hollywood to make his mark in movies and to find outlets and opportunities to dance and make his music.

He was invited to come to Celebrity Studios to audition and be scrutinized by the head of studio affairs, Jack Windheim, and his warren of studio associates, such as producers, directors, all types of managers, casting directors, choreographers, voice instructors, and any number of people who worked on the production staff of a movie in the making.

Jack Windheim actually saw something pretty amazing in Bob's talent and musical acumen after having met him for the first time. Jack really respected Bob's intrinsic, quiet steadiness and his ingrained confidence in knowing who he was and where he wanted to go.

Bob met Corey his first day at Celebrity as he was exiting Jack's office. Corinth Beth Ann Madrigal was the most renowned dramatic actress in Hollywood, at that time, and the most highly esteemed at Celebrity Studios for the last twenty years. She was handsomely attractive with her auburn hair and those gorgeous big blue eyes. She had a body that was still sexually attractive at her age of forty-six. She carried herself with great dignity, and her professionalism was impeccable. She was the consummate Hollywood star; she never forgot her lines, was always on time, and knew the direction and personality that her character embodied—in every single movie she made.

Upon meeting Bob, Corey took him under her wing after he signed on with Celebrity Studios. She mentored and aided him considerably in his dramatic readings and character portrayals. They became extremely close and spent almost all their free time together. There couldn't have been any other couple who had as much fun, and was so closely bonded in friendship, as Bob and Corey.

Over a short matter of time, Corey had fallen in love with him. However, Bob was extremely reluctant to entertain his real feelings for Corey, for fear if it didn't work out between them, he would lose the remarkable and cohesive magic they shared as close friends.

The rock 'n' roll band that Bob had started while at NEC in Boston, the Night Owls, followed him out to California and took an apartment in Santa Monica, just blocks from the sound studio where they practiced.

Rock 'n' roll was the raucous new musical style at the time that suddenly burst onto the scene in the '50s. Bob was lead electric guitar and lead singer. Len Perry was bass electric guitar and singer and was well-built and stood six feet tall, the same height as Bob. Jimmy Wisner was one of the best beat-keepers around; he was slightly built and smallframed, but could really cook the drums. Doug Peeples, on the alto saxophone, was the group's clown; he had a cheerful disposition, which enhanced his cherubic round face and somewhat stocky physique.

All four of them were close to the same age when they met at NEC. Soon after Bob went west to Hollywood, the three men followed him, and they started writing and producing vinyl 45s; with the help of their agent Nick Marshelder, they soon began to make a name for themselves.

Nick Marshelder was the Night Owls' agent, manager, and legal counsel—all wrapped up into one. He was single and thirty-seven years old. Being five-feet ten-inches tall, he was fairly attractive, with combed-back brown hair, and had been an agent for Bob's sister, Elizabeth, and small-time B movie actors for several years. He lived just west of Hollywood in his own house in beautiful Casa Conejo.

Within four months, the popularity of the band and the three charted songs they wrote allowed Nick to talk to the producers at Dick Clark's *American Bandstand.* They were fortunate to be asked to appear in September of 1958. This was when the Night Owls got their foot in the door, after they performed two of their songs, "Eventual Love" and "Running Wild." The kids on the show loved the group and their upbeat style of rock 'n' roll. They claimed the Owls were a gas and really cool to listen to, and it was fun to watch them perform.

Seven months, one album, *Hanging with the Night Owls*, and ten records later, they appeared on *The Ed Sullivan Show* in April 1959, where they were now enthusiastically and passionately recognized as a very formidable group of young rock 'n' rollers.

Before the band's international fame came into fruition, because of *The Sullivan Show*, Bob had met Julie Hayward at her concert at Carnegie Hall, in New York City, that January of 1959.

Julie was thirty-five years old and a musical icon of the '40s and '50s. She sang big band hits and all the contemporary songs of the time. She was a medium contralto, the lowest female singing voice, with velvety pipes that were recognizable to anyone that knew anything about music.

She was of medium height with black hair that was swept up upon her head in a bouffant. Her beauty was mysteriously provocative and her small crooked smile sensuous. Those full radiant red lips were of beckoning temptation to all men.

The only drawback to this musical genius was the fact she had an addiction to popping barbiturates and consuming large amounts of scotch. Her face began to show the effects of an entire career of pills and booze. Her voice began to show the irreversible laryngeal tissue damage that had presented itself in her thirties.

Bob was initially attracted to her, after meeting her at her after-concert party at Carnegie Hall. They began dating for a short nine to ten weeks, when he realized she was not the person he had envisioned in his teens and early twenties. He initially fell in love with the musical icon who was capable of enrapturing an entire audience and lulling them into a sense of emotional seduction.

He found out he just couldn't stay with a woman who would not allow anyone to help her and who had no intention of ever helping herself with her addictions. They drifted apart with her seeing other men, and also because of the prevalent gloom and doom that was always present in her life.

After Bob had had enough of Julie's fitful behavior, and her rejecting any help he offered her, he just called the whole thing off. Julie never stopped loving him and talked him into appearing on her televised series of shows in late September of 1959.

She would die three and a half months later, from an accidental overdose of poisonous barbiturates. Julie's lifelong addictions finally caught up with her, when she was found dead in her Long Island home in mid-January of 1960. The coroner that performed the autopsy noted that she had cirrhosis of the liver, and had the pills not taken her out, the cirrhosis would have done it in a matter of months.

It took Bob ten months of knowing Corey and loving her as his closest friend for him to realize just how much he was truly *in* love with her.

Corey was always there for him, no matter what the situation or how emotionally damaging the event may have been to her. She was a patient woman who knew exactly what she wanted and was willing to wait for Bob to come to her, and that's exactly what happened on March 20, 1959.

Bob had called Corey the night he had made up his mind about never seeing Julie again, when he realized he needed and wanted Corey in his life forever. He then flew from New York to Los Angeles the day after he talked with her and told her he was in extreme want of her. They both fell irretrievably in love with one another and became absolutely blissful together as a couple.

Bob would propose marriage to Corey in late July of 1959, when he returned from an eventful European tour with the Night Owls. He asked his sister, Elizabeth, if he could give his deceased mother's wedding ring to Corey, and, of course, she gave it to him. He put it on Corey's finger in early August, when he proposed again in front of his sister and her husband, Drake, and Corey's maid and best friend, Haddie. Corey again said she would absolutely marry him.

Then while the Night Owls were performing at the Los Angeles Shrine Auditorium in September 1959, Bob announced onstage that he wanted the group to sing the song "Long Journey Back to You." This was a song that Len, Jimmy, and Doug had written in honor of Bob and Corey getting together. Before they performed the song, Bob announced that night he wanted his fiancée, Corey, to marry him, on the following March 20, the day they finally got together; and both fell totally in love with each other.

Corey then began to look through bridal magazines, talking with friends, and consulting with professional wedding planners about ideas for exactly what she wanted, what venue she wanted, and how she wanted her wedding to look.

In late December of 1958, Bob had moved the Owls back to New York City, where the other three guys were originally from, to perform more of the east coast rock 'n' roll and give Bob the chance to perform in a play on Broadway. After Bob and Corey became a couple, the separation was too much for either to handle, so after the Owls' European tour was over, Bob moved back to Bel Air, and the Owls followed him again, but living in his vacated house in Thousand Oaks, where Bob and his sister grew up together. For when Elizabeth married Drake in September of 1958, she moved into Drake's house in Los Angeles and gave the house to Bob.

Elizabeth had been performing Shakespearean and Elizabethan plays for the last several years. This grew to be her forte, and she loved it. Drake directed most of her plays, which were in and around the Los Angeles area, but mostly at the LA Theater for the Performing Arts.

Elizabeth possessed such natural beauty, with her glossy, black, shoulder-length hair that emanated a beautiful radiance, which was only enhanced by her beautiful eyes of a piercing grayish blue. Her complexion had a flawless silky smoothness that was showcased by her five-foot, seven-inch hourglass figure.

Robert and Margaret Richardson had had two beautiful children in Elizabeth and Bob Junior, before they were killed in a car crash in 1950. Elizabeth stepped up to continue raising her fourteen-year-old brother and encouraged his love for music.

* * * * *

Bob rose from bed and went in to take a shower. When he finished and got dressed in khakis and a polo shirt, he headed out of the master suite and into the long hallway that led to the huge gourmet kitchen. He entered the kitchen, and Haddie, Corey's black fifty-six-year-old maid for almost the last seventeen years, greeted him, "Good morning, Mr. Bob, I've been wanting to tell you how sorry I am about Ms. Julie Hayward. What a shame and what a waste of such talent. May she rest in peace, oh Lord."

Bob respectfully answered Haddie, "Thank you, Ms. Haddie. It was a total waste, but it was an eventuality that everyone had expected. She has to be at peace now. At least, I pray for that."

Trying to unburden his mind, he wistfully asked Haddie if she knew where Corey was. Haddie told him matter-of-factly, "Ms. Corey wanted to take breakfast out by the pool. It was a bit chilly, but she insisted anyway. You go on out there, Mr. Bob, and I'll bring both your breakfasts to you with a carafe of coffee."

"Sounds great, Ms. Haddie. Thank you."

Haddie warned Bob, "I know it's none of my business, but you should know Ms. Corey seems to be caught in the middle of the sad fact of Ms. Julie's death and the beautiful and glorious time she should be having planning for her wedding. She seems kinda melancholy."

Bob looked toward the pool area from the kitchen window and saw Corey, with what looked like a script in her hands, as she lounged in one of the numerous pool chaises.

He assured Haddie, "I've got this. You just hang loose, Ms. Haddie."

"All right, Mr. Bob, it's just that I worry about her. But I know you always take care of her."

Bob resignedly smiled and nodded to her, then turned to go to Corey—out by the pool through the french doors and onto the marbled landing in the back of the house. After walking down the few steps to the pool, he sat down on the side of the chaise lounge facing Corey.

She wearily looked up at him, mildly smiled, then admiringly asked, "Good morning, darling. How did you sleep last night?"

Bob looked deep into those entrancing blue eyes, and concerned, he asked her, "Just fine, doll, but you know, I now think it's time to start putting this wedding together and finalizing some stuff. What do you think, baby?"

Corey's eyes lit up like the sky on the Fourth of July. She was caught off guard by that statement as she imploringly asked, "Do you really mean that, Bob? I thought maybe you'd be upset all day, knowing in New York, it was Julie's funeral."

He looked back at Corey with his irresistible, loving smile and shook his head from side to side and lovingly told her, "No, not at all. Today, I want to spend time with the one woman that makes my heart race, gets me out of bed in the morning, and lures me into bed at night. It's only you, baby."

Corey's eyes moistened as her perpetual loving gaze never left his eyes. Bob leaned over and took her face in his hands, and then slowly and affectionately, he kissed her on the lips. He lowered himself back onto his lounger. Not breaking eye contact with her, he promisingly told her, "And after I get home around twelve-thirty, from the recording studio this afternoon, we can sit down and start puttin' a period behind some of the wedding things."

Corey purred back, "I would love that, darling."

"All right then. I'd like to know your final idea for the venue where you want to hold the wedding at and where you decided to have the reception? I would also want to know what kind of flowers you've locked into place for the tables our guests will be seated at, and that includes your bouquet. I will also want to know what time you decided on and if you wanna hire a band, or a DJ to turn some discs."

Corey was glowing now, but asked, "You didn't mention anything about the honeymoon, darling."

A huge grin came over his face, and those beautiful teeth showed his complete excitement as he instructed her, "The honeymoon? Oh, yeah, well, I have that covered, I've been working on that for the last two months now. You won't need to bother yourself with that, okay?"

Corey threw the manuscript aside and rose from her seat to sitting on his lap, with her arms wrapped around his neck. She stared directly into his glowing green eyes and lovingly told him, "You just never cease to amaze me, Robert Brian. I love you beyond belief, darling."

She leaned into a long and wet kiss, neither one of them wanted to end, when Haddie brought the breakfast tray out and announced, "Okay, all right. We gonna have a time-out now, while the two of you eat some of my flapjacks and sausages. Come on, loosen your grips."

Corey and Bob separated and smiled lovingly at each other, laughed, and then quickly kissed once more before they sat down in different chairs. Haddie placed the tray between them on a small wrought iron table Bob had placed there. As Haddie walked away, she smiled at Bob and nodded her head affirmatively to him. He grinned and winked at her.

As Corey took a sip of her coffee, she kiddingly asked Bob, "So where are we going for our honeymoon, darling, and for how long?"

"You don't worry about that, doll. I have the slate cleared from the Saturday of March nineteenth until Saturday, April 2. No studio, no concerts, no nothing, until that Monday, April 4, at the Academy Awards in LA..."

Corey did not know that the following Saturday after they get back from their honeymoon, Bob had a big birthday bash lined up for her at the estate. Haddie and Elizabeth would handle all the details about that, except for the fact he himself would notify all the people he wanted to be there. So Haddie and Elizabeth would handle the decorations, food, and drinks.

Corey reminded herself about the picture of Bob, her, and Susan Hawthorne, just wrapped up in early January, called *Jumping Off the Deep End*; the movie received five Oscar nominations. So Corey thought that she and Bob probably should attend the event that evening. Corey, being excited for him in his first nomination for best actor, told him, "We really should attend the Oscars that night, darling. I know you must want to, it being your first time and all. It probably won't be as exciting for me since I pretty much know what to expect."

Bob smiled and hastened to tell her, "Yeah, I really would like to go. I've only been able to watch it on television before. It should be a real kick, doll. I'm kinda stoked for it, because I don't know if I'll ever be nominated again. I've been in five movies, and this is my first nomination."

Corey laughed at his young naivete and assuredly told him, "Oh my god, Bob! You're going to have many more nominations, and I'm sure a few Oscars. So let's just plan on attending this year, and just have some fun that night. Okay?"

Bob immediately confirmed that by guaranteeing her, "It'll be another learning experience for me, and I know with you on my arm that night, we'll have an unreal time." Corey was all smiles as she quietly chuckled.

After a minute or two had gone by, Bob and Corey sat and ate their breakfast. Corey almost apologetically mentioned to him, "Bob, would you be terribly disappointed if I just wanted to have the wedding and reception right here at the estate?"

Taken by surprise, he looked up at Corey in wonderment and inquisitively asked her, "Are you sure? No church with a mile-long aisle for me to see you in your beautiful wedding gown flowing high and majestically behind you as you're walking down toward my open arms?"

Then he teased her, "No extremely expensive venue up in the Hollywood Hills? Not even passage on a Japanese whale trawler, out in the middle of the Pacific, with a Shinto priest presiding over the ceremony?" Corey laughed out loud and hard at her broadly smiling fiancé.

She was able to compose herself in several seconds, as she emphatically asserted, "No, no—even as tempting as that trawler may be, I would just as soon have everything right here. After all, darling, this is my fourth time and, may I add, my final time. And my first three were just in front of a justice of the peace. So you see, having the ceremony and reception right here at our estate, which has complete privacy from the outside world—and with the luscious gardens and all the gorgeous trees and flowers—the wedding to me would be like I'm in some kind of Shangri-la—our own paradise, right here on earth."

Bob could see in her beautiful blue eyes just how much she loved her surroundings, and so it wasn't hard for him to acquiesce to her wish. He responded tenderly to her, "Whatever you want, baby. Sunday, March 20, is all about you—and I want you to be the happiest bride ever to walk down any aisle to be married."

Corey's eyes began to moisten as she lovingly shook her head slightly from side to side in disbelief, for she would soon be marrying the man she never thought she would ever find in her lifetime.

Bob rose up and moved over beside her on her lounger and wrapped his arms around her as he gently kissed each eyelid and then her lips. As he pulled away from her and stood up, he exclaimed, "Now that we know where the wedding is going to be, we'll talk this afternoon and tonight about the rest." He moved his left index finger back and forth in front of him. "All except the honeymoon…! Okay, I have to go to the recording studio now and meet up with the guys. We've been working on a couple of songs. We may have enough singles now to put out another album, but we'll see. See you later, doll."

Corey reminded him as he was walking to his '52 Chevy fliptop, parked in the driveway about seventy feet away, "Don't forget, we have three scripts here to read. Then we need to pick one, because that will be the movie we'll be doing together after our wedding, darling. Jack will want that answer sometime this week!"

Bob kiddingly told her as he was walking away, "I want the one that gets me in bed with you, and we're both naked and drinking dry martinis, stirred."

She laughed uproariously as he turned to smile and lightly shook his head, just thinking of how much he loved her. Corey smiled broadly and just studied his entire body as he walked away and got into his car and drove toward the recording studio in Thousand Oaks.

TWO

It only took Bob thirty-five minutes to get to the Thousand Oaks recording studio, where the guys were waiting to rehearse with him. As he walked into the building, his attention was diverted to Len, who was picking at his electric bass guitar. Bob had never heard those chords before in the sequence or the tempo at which he played them.

Bob loudly asked Len, "Hey, man, that run is outta sight! You write that?"

Len, acknowledging Bob's musical perceptiveness, proudly answered, "Yeah, and I think with your help, we can make this song really a badass thing. Something more upscale and more explosive than anything we've done so far."

Bob, really excited about venturing into another aspect of the new genre of rock 'n' roll, told Len, Jimmy, and Doug, "You know, guys, we've seen other groups from here in the States and a few groups from other countries around the world, in person and on television, and we know rock 'n' roll in this coming decade is going to grow exponentially. So I guess what I'm trying to say is, we're going to need to grow with it and step up to the fast-approaching next level or be left behind in the dust."

Doug spoke up and jokingly added, "Yeah, and if we get really exponential, there's just no telling where we'll be headed."

All four guys shook their heads and exhaled a good-sized chuckle as Bob added, "All right, smart-ass, at least you got the message."

At this point, Jimmy, while sitting at his drums and twirling the sticks between his fingers, pointed out, "You guys should know by now there's a group here in California called the Ventures, and they have a song out called 'Walk, Don't Run.' They have three guitarists and one drummer. I guess they really put on a fingerpickin' display. They've been referred to as the new wave of surf rock."

Bob spoke up, answering Jimmy, "Yeah, I've heard of 'em, but they got nothing on us. All of us know that this is a time of growth and rebellion in the youth of this world, and so we need to address that in our future songs. Our songs from now on are going to be more complex and with a more driving beat to 'em. We're gonna give the young kids around the world the music that will stoke the rebellion."

Doug and Jimmy yelled, "Hell yes. Far-out, man!" Len was nodding with determined ardor and satisfaction.

Bob then placed before the guys the question that he knew would change the face of the group; he asked, "What do you guys think about adding a third guitar, maybe an archtop semi-acoustic guitar, and maybe even a trumpet, to the group? That would give us more depth and the orchestral sound of a much bigger group. The third guitar would supply more of the melody. Doug's alto sax already sometimes carries the tune, and it helps to give color and warmth to our overall sound, and he does a great job doing that. But if we added a trumpet, or even a piano, it would add brightness and emphasis in the dramatic passages of the song, while Jimmy's drums are providing the group's rhythmic backbone. The tempo, volume, and balance of the piece would be regulated with the lead-in from our fantastic drummer—well, think about it. This definitely would be world-changing for the group, and our music would change right along with it."

Doug spoke up with little hesitation, "You guys already know I also play trumpet and clarinet. Why would we need another guy for that?"

Bob looked over at Doug incredulously and slowly, but patiently, asked him, "Now you think about that real hard, Doug, and then tell me how you're gonna play those three at the same time."

Len and Jimmy were cracking up, and then Bob joined them. Doug sat bobbing his head, and with his lips pursed, he affirmatively acknowledged Bob by saying, "That's solid, man. Yeah, I get your drift. Well, I'm all for getting a couple more guys. That sounds boss."

Len ambitiously jumped into the fray, reinforcing the addition of another guitar by stating, "I think it's cool if we got the acoustic guitar. That in itself will give the group a lot more depth, but when you add a piece of brass, you're going to put a whole different spin on our tunes. I'm really jazzed about the two extra guys and adding a third guitar and a trumpet—I vote absolutely and unequivocally yes to both of 'em."

Upon hearing Len speak up and give his vote of approval, Doug kiddingly announced, "Yeah, once we get these two new guys, we should really be exponential and unequivocally a real gas—I'm stoked. This should be some real kicks!"

The guys just laughed at Doug, when Bob keenly looked over to Jimmy and asked, "Then I guess I'll start looking for that third guitar and a trumpeter, but only if you, Jimmy, are also on board with that?"

Jimmy looked up and emphatically told them, "As long as you're not looking for another drummer, I'm cool with adding the two other guys."

Bob reassured Jimmy by saying, "Why the hell would we want another drummer? We already have the best beat-keeper in the business?"

Jimmy smiled broadly and then ran a succession of beats on his snare. The guys yelled their approval. Bob then told them they needed to get to work on the two songs that had to be finalized. Then they could get the finished recording to their agent, Nick, and on to the production process.

The Owls were signed to Mercury Records in late September of '58. And in order for the young and upcoming Mercury Records to compete with the likes of RCA Victor, Decca, and Capitol Records, they used an alternative marketing technique to promote their artists' records.

The conventional method of record promotion used by others was dependent on radio airplay. In most cases, the songs played were determined by program directors, who in turn took their orders from station executives and owners who were looking to draw audiences, get sponsors to buy airtime, and make money.

Record companies sought out stations to get their bands played on the radio so that people could have a song, fall in love with it, and then go out and buy the whole album.

But Irving Green, owner of Mercury, decided to promote new records using the jukeboxes, instead of the radio. This lowered promotional costs and enabled Mercury to compete with the more established labels. It eliminated playlists given to DJs by radio execs and advertisers.

This allowed Mercury to land talent like Frankie Laine, Vic Damone, Tony Fontaine, Diahann Carroll, Patti Page, and all the prospective newcomers, like the Night Owls.

There were no voice-overs or reproducible forms such as discs or magnetic tape in 1960, so the music one created was all played and sung at the same time, not done separately or spliced together. However, this period of time would introduce the process of amplification and electric recording.

The Owls' electric up-tempo style had an attitude that resonated with the changing face of rock 'n' roll. Bob knew with the addition of an acoustic guitar and a trumpet, his group would be making a resounding effect on the younger generation, with the group's more orchestral-sounding compositions and arrangements of the newer music they would be producing.

The group used the remaining two and a half hours to finish the fine-tuning on the two songs they were working on, and they ended up recording them. The two songs were called "Not Another Lonely Night" and "Ricochet." The first was a slow dance number, but the second one, "Ricochet," was a song with a tremendously upbeat rhythm, heavy guitar strokes, and a wailing saxophone. This song would trample "Running Wild's" success; it was the second song the group recorded back in May of '58.

After sending them off to their agent, Nick, and the guys all agreed to start pounding out the melodies to the couple of songs Len and Bob had already written lyrics for in their next jam session, on Tuesday, January 26.

Len and Bob talked about finding their two extra members and agreed, when either one had a promising guitarist or trumpeter lined up, they would contact one another and then bring them to meet the group and to audition.

The guys began filing out of the recording studio as they all said they'd see each other on Tuesday. Bob had a thought and excitedly informed them, "Hey, man, when we find these two guys, I'll have all of you, and wives or girlfriends, and Nick and his date, over to the house. That way everyone will be able to meet and talk about the daunting effort of organization, improvisation, and determination that lies ahead of us. We should know that evening how we're going to blend, after we spend the day drinking and partying. Okay?"

All the guys were in total agreement with that. Doug had to add his two cents of humor by shouting out, "Oh, hell yes! I'll have my exponentially daunting-ass there with bells on."

Len warned him, "Look out, man, the three of us are about ready to kick your daunting ass."

They all left for home smiling, with a lot of game-changing information in their heads. Bob arrived back at the estate around one o'clock that Saturday afternoon. He walked from his car, which he had parked in front of the four-car garage, and into the house through the back doors.

The house sounded too quiet until he heard Corey and Haddie in the kitchen talking to each other. He quietly entered the huge gourmet kitchen, and Corey instantly turned to see him walk in and joyously walked to him. He enveloped her in his arms, and they kissed slowly for several seconds.

When Bob pulled his head away from Corey's lips, his smile was brilliantly infectious, and she smiled back with the greatest joy, feeling nothing but the intoxicating passion that ran through her body for him. He leaned his head down again and quickly kissed her on the lips once more.

When Bob pulled his head back, he glanced over at Haddie, who was trying to remain discreet by continuing to clean the countertops. Bob smiled and apologetically told her, "We're sorry, Ms. Haddie. We didn't mean to put you on the spot."

Haddie smiled and turned to tell them, "It don't make me no never mind, Mr. Bob. I know the two of you are just showing the God-given love you have for each other. Not a thing in this world wrong with that—but the instant I see clothes hitting the floor, I'm outta here!"

Bob chuckled, and Corey laughed out loud, as she hadn't released Bob's one arm she still had a hold on when they were kissing.

Corey released Bob's arm, moved toward the coffeepot, and asked him if he would like a cup. He confirmed by stating, "Oh yeah, that sounds primo, and if Ms. Haddie has any more of that honey ham left over, a sandwich would be outta sight."

"Coming right up, Mr. Bob."

Bob added rather matter-of-factly, "Why don't you join us, Ms. Haddie. If you've already eaten, then maybe just some coffee. What do you say?"

Haddie, appreciating the invitation and honestly feeling the warmth of his friendship, replied, "You know, I did just eat, but I could use a cup of coffee right now. So yes, I'll hang around and supervise the two of you lovebirds. No telling what might happen in my kitchen. Uh-huh. That's right."

Bob and Corey just smiled broadly and looked lovingly at each other.

While the three of them sat and drank their coffee, and Bob ate his sandwich, he informed Corey that the band was taking on some major changes—not only in the style of some of their music, but with the addition of two new members.

"Yeah, we're gonna start looking for an acoustic guitar player and a trumpeter. That would give us three guitarists, a drummer, a woodwind, and a brass. We all agreed this move would add depth and width to the band, for more of that orchestral sound of a bigger group."

Bob took a bite of his sandwich and a quick sip of his coffee and added, "Len and I already have the lyrics for a couple more happening songs that deal with the rebellious nature of today's youth around the world. But we'll also deal with peace, heartbreak, upheaval, war, and of course, love."

Corey looked at Bob questioningly and inquired, "Tell me, darling, why would you want to change something that's been working so well for you, for almost two years now?"

Bob took a big breath and tried to explain to her as best he could. "Well, we're in a new decade now. Times are really going to be changing with rock 'n' roll now coming into its own. I mean, all over the world, this is happening. Every one of the Owls seems to feel that the '60s are going to mark the decade when rock 'n' roll will fully take shape as an art form—like jazz, swing, rhythm and blues, big band, country, contemporary vocal, and now rock 'n' roll."

He had Corey's and Haddie's complete attention now, as he continued, "The young people all over the world are feeling the same way. They're fed up with the present generation telling them how they should act, how they should feel, what music to listen to, what music not to listen to, and they're even telling them how and who to love. These kids are drawing the line right now, people, and if we, as a singing group, don't address this emerging explosion, with an answer in our music, we'll just be swept aside and blown away like a pile of yesterday's ashes."

Corey and Haddie just kept staring at Bob and contemplating this new generation.

Bob summed up everything by fatalistically ending his explanation. "The youth of this new decade may just be standing on the precipice of the rebirth of their freedom or the death of their ideals and dreams. Music has always helped people in times of revolt, depression, marginalization, deception, bigotry, discrimination, heartbreak, death, and yes, love. The Owls aren't going to be blown away with the shifting winds of changing moral standards and the ravaging thirst for personal freedoms. We're here to stay and fuel the rebellion."

Corey's eyes began to tear, staring at Bob as her pride and joy and the ultimate reason she now lived for.

Haddie sat in awe, and the only thing she could say was, "Mr. Bob, I don't think anyone could have explained this new rock 'n' roll to us any better or any more eloquently than you just did. You are so talented with words—no wonder you write so many good songs. I just wish you played with the Duke—Mr. Ellington. Oh, my gracious' sake, I know I'd be in my very own heaven at that moment if that were to happen."

Corey rose from her seat and walked over to Bob, bent down, and kissed him, as she sat down on his lap and wrapped her arms around his neck. She murmured into his ear, "Mister, you just drive me crazy with love for you. Don't you ever let go of me."

He hugged her back as he kissed her neck and tenderly answered, "Not on your life, doll. Never ever, ever. Remember? You're stuck with me."

She breathlessly replied, "Thank God!"

Haddie sat sipping her coffee and became very hesitant to mention what she was thinking. After some sudden reluctance, she just looked at Bob and bravely offered, "You know, Mr. Bob, my son, Joshua, has played the trumpet since he was in junior high school."

Bob immediately turned his head toward Haddie and acted like he couldn't believe what she had just said. Corey slid off his lap and remained standing next to him as she stared at Haddie and smiled exuberantly.

Bob was now talking somewhat loudly and implored, "What? I knew you had a son, but you never mentioned the fact he could blow a horn."

Haddie, in trying to justify her reluctance about mentioning it, stated, "Mr. Bob, I raised my boy by myself, after my shiftless, alcoholic husband abandoned the two of us in Stockton just a month after Joshua's birth. We survived by living in a boarding house, and at night, I took in other people's laundry and ironing, and during the day, I was cleaning rooms at Stockton's Grand Meridian Hotel."

Corey's eyes were becoming very moist as Bob sat fixated with Haddie's life story.

Haddie continued with a worn sense of humility, "I got Joshua into an all-Negro school, there in Stockton, when he was five years old in 1929. The Great Depression made it extremely hard on us, but six years later, he attended the all-black junior high school, where he fell in love with music, but most especially the trumpet. The school only had five old, raggedy instruments that the children had to share. When he told me it was the trumpet he loved so much, I moved heaven and earth to save some money to buy a used one for him. I may have gone without dinner a few nights a week, and my clothes were showing the wear and tear of the years, but by God, I bought him that used trumpet, just before he entered the high school."

Now there was a single tear running down Corey's face, and Bob's eyes had formed welled-up tears, with the complete sadness they felt for Haddie and her son. Her story had put everything he had experienced in life into a very stark perspective. He knew he came from white privilege but never really was in a position to feel the direct pain from the Negros' struggle for equality and an end to racism and discrimination. He was feeling the epiphanic effects of experiencing, firsthand, through Haddie's story, the Negros' storied plight of unfavorable treatment based on prejudice and bigotry.

Haddie continued very pridefully with her story, as now a tear ran down her face, "Joshua was always playing that trumpet, and mind you, he was very good at it. When he graduated high school, I'd saved up enough money to get him into the University of the Pacific for Negros, right there in Stockton. He was in their small marching band all four years, and when he graduated valedictorian of his class in 1946, he luckily landed a job with the San Francisco Symphony Orchestra. In a short time, he worked hard to become principal trumpet. He's been with 'em ever since."

Corey walked the few steps over to Haddie and bent down and hugged her. After a few seconds, Corey pulled away and tenderly asked, "Haddie, you never told me all this before. I knew of Joshua, but I had no idea about what you went through before you came here to live and work for me."

Almost apologetically, Haddie answered her, "Well, Ms. Corey, when Joshua went off to work in San Francisco, I answered your ad from the newspaper. It's now been seventeen years I've been here, but I get with him once or twice a year, on my long weekends. He seems happy, but I know for a fact he don't get paid as much as the white musicians there. I guess it's just the way of the world right now."

Bob finally broke the stare he had on Haddie for the last several minutes and emphatically told her, "Listen, Ms. Haddie, you can give me Joshua's phone number, or you can contact him and tell him I most certainly would like to meet him. Tell him to bring his horn, because I would love to hear him play. Lastly, you can tell him I need an experienced trumpeter, and he would be paid one-seventh of everything we clear. The six musicians I will have, and our agent, Nick Marshelder, will all be paid the same. Particularly tell him he'd be making about two hundred times what he's getting there with the orchestra."

Haddie's eyes lit up like she had just won the Irish sweepstakes. Not letting this opportunity slip through her fingers, she excitedly told Bob, "Mr. Bob, thank you so much. I'm gonna go in my bedroom and call Joshua right now. He ain't gonna believe all this till he gets here. God bless you, Mr. Bob."

As Haddie got up from her seat, Bob stood up and leaned over and hugged her; and as he began to let her go, he kissed her on the cheek. "Now you go call your son. Tell him I need a cat that can cook the trumpet and is in the groove when it comes to rock 'n' roll, okay?"

"I'm on my way, and I'll let you know shortly, Mr. Bob."

Bob and Corey both watched her race into her bedroom, and then they turned to embrace one another. Corey whispered up into his face, "I pray to God he's good enough for your band, darling."

He rest assuredly whispered back, and there was something even implicit in his tone, "I feel we have our new trumpeter. I just hope to the heavens he likes rock 'n' roll."

They kissed, and then Corey suggested, "Now, what do you think about us going out to the pool area and talking wedding arrangements? I've been waiting for you to get home, and then we got sidetracked with Haddie's son, for an hour. I have some ideas for you to ponder."

He laughingly asked, "Ponder?"

"Yes, you crazy cat. Now, grab a drink, darling, and I'll meet you outside." Bob chuckled loudly and went and grabbed a beer.

When they each got seated in a chaise lounge, Bob had his bottle of beer, and Corey had her dry martini, stirred, sitting beside them.

Corey started by excitedly reminding him, "As you well know, from our conversation this morning at breakfast, we're going to have the exchanging of the vows and the reception right here in Bel Air. I've always felt this estate is so unique, with its luscious gardens, and it's so professionally landscaped, that no one from any other of the surrounding properties, or from the street, can see anyone or anything that's going on in the backyard. It's such a gorgeous hideaway."

Bob sat facing Corey and was staring at her the entire time, with a cute smile on his face, as he nodded his head in agreement. She noticed his smile and asked adoringly, "Darling, does everything sound all right so far? And what's with that attractive smile, mister?"

Fully smiling now, he confessed in a very sexy tone, "I just love seeing you so happy and excited about everything to do with the wedding, because then, you see, that makes me that much happier and—excited."

Corey romantically asked, "Just how excited are you, darling?"

Bob's heart started racing as he pleasurably answered, "Very."

At that moment and without hesitation, Corey rose from her lounger and, melting Bob with her radiantly sexy smile, tenderly took his hand and began to quietly lead him back into the house and into the master suite.

She shut the bedroom door after he followed her in. Her hand left his hand when she reached up to him and started unbuttoning his shirt. She lifted the polo shirt up and over his head, baring his tremendous pectorals, of which she started kissing and biting at. As she was kissing on him, she loosened and removed his belt and then unzipped his trousers. He helped to lower his pants to the floor, exposing his briefs.

Corey was breathing faster as her heart started racing. Bob wrapped his arms around her and engulfed her in a full-throated kiss, as she placed her hand down the front of his briefs.

Bob made a throaty sound and exhaled loudly. He now was at full attention and quickly got Corey out of her blouse and bra, and as he lowered her slacks, the silk panties went with them.

Not able to wait another second, they both lay down on the bed, after he tore his briefs off and let them fly.

She pulled him onto her and breathlessly begged, "Bob, make love to me. Make love to me, darling!"

He held her hips in his hands as he suckled her breasts, and loving it, she threw her arms back and up against the bed's headboard, moaning loudly, "Oh my god, baby."

His right hand fell between her legs as he lovingly caressed the area. She was crying out now when he gently entered her.

Corey began moving with Bob's thrustful lunges. The tempo hastened, and his veins began to beat with an electric urgency. He couldn't get enough of this woman that he absolutely adored.

She started to orgasm as her body lifted more into him, and she began to seemingly whimper; with full sexual delight, Bob kept moving with her body, and then the moment of fulfillment—so sudden, so jarring, so total.

Corey held him tight and was kissing on his neck, when after several seconds, Bob blew a huge breath of exhilarated contentment and settled down, lying in the warmth of her body. They both lay in each other's arms for a couple of minutes, when Bob rolled off her; and with the sexiness his voice exuded, he remarked, "Yeah, baby, it was to that degree of excitement."

She broadly smiled at him and ran her hand slowly through his beautiful dark hair. Just out of the blue, Bob curiously asked, "You didn't mind me not taking a quick shower beforehand, did you?"

Corey bolted to sitting upright and rolled over on top of him, exclaiming, "You've got to be kidding, darling. I just love the smell of your masculinity, and even after one of your jam sessions. It certainly has always had the power to arouse me—no, I absolutely loved it."

They both looked deeply into each other's eyes, as Bob cupped her face with his hands and pulled her lips onto his. After a long tender kiss, Corey softly reminded him, "All right, darling, now what do you say we give those wedding plans another go at it?"

He broadly smiled and resignedly informed her, "Yes, my love, but right after I get a shower—I really need one now, baby."

Corey laughingly told him, "And I was very happy to help you to that decision."

Bob grinned at her, jumped out of bed, and walked stark naked toward the bathroom. He displayed his full array of muscled physicality, with his chiseled buttocks and his ripped abdominals. Corey was eating up the view of this perfect specimen of the male species and whispered to herself as he turned the shower on, "What a beautiful, beautiful man—and to think this Adonis is all mine."

After Bob showered and changed into some shorts and a tee shirt, he came out of the bedroom and headed toward the back door. Corey popped her head out of the kitchen and asked him, "Darling, would you come into the kitchen for a few minutes? Haddie has an answer for you about her son."

Quite anxious, he answered her with a smile, "Absolutely, doll."

Bob hurried his step, and when he walked into the kitchen, Haddie was standing in the middle, close to the huge island, looking a bit apprehensive.

He inquisitively asked her, "What did he say, Ms. Haddie? I hope it's good news." Haddie, hesitant at first, just told him the truth. "I called and talked with Joshua for a good long time. He seems to think that putting a Negro into an all-white band might not be too wise, with the times we're in, especially for when you have concerts in the South. He said he gets enough disparaging remarks up in San Francisco, being one of the only two black musicians in the orchestra of sixty players. He said he could only imagine how all that would intensify if he was the only black man playing with an all-white band down in Mobile or Natchez."

Haddie's eyes began to glisten, as well as Corey's. Bob walked up close to Haddie and, staring her directly in the eyes, resolutely told her, "You give me his phone number, Ms. Haddie. I'd like to talk with my future trumpeter myself."

Haddie managed a joyful smile and handed Bob her little address book, opened to Joshua's number.

Corey's eyes were glistening with pride as she watched Bob take the address book from Haddie, and determinedly, he headed for the phone in the master suite.

At that moment, Corey reassured Haddie, "You now have nothing to worry about, Haddie. Bob will handle this, and I'll bet you see your son again very soon. Maybe even sometime this week."

Haddie's heart could not have been more full of love for her son and, at the same time, so grateful to Bob for helping to allow her son to play his trumpet with a band that performed all around the world.

It had been nearly an hour when Bob finally emerged from the bedroom. He heard Haddie and Corey talking in the kitchen, and so he headed down the long hallway toward them.

As he slowly walked into the kitchen, both their heads instantly turned to him in a gasping silence of trepidation. Not changing his facial expression at all, Bob walked up to Haddie and leaned over and kissed her on the forehead and comfortingly told her, "Well, Ms. Haddie, I talked with Joshua and tried to make him understand all the great things that were going to happen to him with this group. I also told him there'll be some challenges, but nothing we couldn't face together."

Corey and Haddie were holding their breaths in anticipation as Bob bent his head down sideways and looked into Haddie's eyes and delicately told her, "So… I guess you're gonna see your son this Tuesday evening when we fly him in here from San Francisco."

Haddie instantly started to cry as her hand shot up to cover her mouth. The other hand went around Bob's neck, and she leaned into him, so Bob wrapped his arms around her to steady her as she inaudibly cried, "Oh my god, Mr. Bob. I surely do love you. Thank you, thank you, so much. Oh, thank you, Lord!"

Corey walked over to them and put her arms around both as tears were also flowing freely down her face. Bob's eyes were glistening when he reassuringly said, "Ms. Haddie, this is gonna be so outta sight, with the possibility of you being so close to your son now, and the face of the Night Owls changing so drastically—I mean, literally, the face will be changing. I am so stoked right now, you just wouldn't believe!"

Bob pulled back from Haddie, and Corey's one arm fell to her side, as the other refused to relinquish the hold she had around his waist. Bob informed Haddie, "I've already called Nick, and I have him setting up the plane tickets for Joshua on Tuesday. Nick also said he would be picking him up at LAX that afternoon… And more good news, when I called Len, he was about to call me to tell me he has a guitarist lined up. I guess he actually graduated from NEC a few years ago. His name is Darnell King, and he lives here in Los Angeles—I'm telling you, I just freaked out. This is all really a gas, the unreal way all this has come together."

He looked at Corey's smiling face and those beautiful glistening blue eyes and happily kissed her and then stated to both, Corey and Haddie, "So, what we're gonna do is have a meet-and-greet party here, Tuesday night, with the Owls, and their significant others, Nick, and his date, and Joshua, and his mom."

Bob broadly smiled at Haddie, and she shook her head in rapturous disbelief as he finished, "I believe Joshua's mom's name is Hadda May Chambers—oh, and Darnell King and his wife, Alicia, will also be here. You're not working that night, Ms. Chambers, for I'll have it catered, and we'll have outside help. I just want you to relax with your son and have some quality time with him."

Corey tightened her hold on Bob's waist as she buried her head into his arm and then kissed his sleeve.

Haddie just nodded her head affirmatively, with her eyes sparkling with appreciation. Letting Haddie know, Bob added, "Now I told both Joshua and Darnell to bring their instruments, because we want to see 'em burn it down while they're here."

Haddie cheerfully stated, "That's wonderful, Mr. Bob, 'cause I just love to hear my son play his horn. You won't be disappointed. I promise."

"Rest assured, Ms. Haddie, because I believe I already know that." At that point, Bob turned and put his arm around Corey and happily suggested, "Now I want my beer, and then we're gonna continue talking about the wedding plans—all right?"

Corey admiringly looked up at him and warmly told him, "Yes, sir."

As Bob and Corey turned to walk out of the kitchen, with their arms around each other, Bob looked back at Haddie; and remembering, he lightheartedly tried to allay any fears she may have had with her son joining an all-white band by telling her, "Oh, and by the way, Ms. Hadda May Chambers… Darnell King is a tall, good-looking… black man."

Bob was smiling so brilliantly now as Haddie put both of her hands to her mouth and blew a huge breath of thankfulness. "Yes, oh my lord, bless these young men—bless them, Lord."

In leaving the kitchen, Corey reached up and gently pulled Bob's lips to hers. She ran her tongue over both his lips as a sexual volt ran completely down his entire body, and he whispered, "Now do you want to talk wedding, or do you want to finish what you just started?"

With a toothy grin, Corey mischievously murmured, "Both."

They both ended up sitting themselves in the same lounger together, out by the pool, with their respective drinks on a small table on each side of them.

Corey began the discussion, trying to unburden Bob's mind. "You know, darling, I'm going to go ahead and finalize the flowers, the food, the cake, and the guest list myself. You just have too much on your plate right now, with your band, and I have a lot of free time right now, as I'm between pictures. You've taken care of the honeymoon, and I love that you're interested in helping, but let me handle the rest. After all, I've had a lot of experience with bouquets and receptions."

They both looked at each other and chuckled. Bob, in total agreement, nodded his head and said, "All right, doll, but if you need anything, just tell me. Okay?"

"Absolutely, my love. As a matter of fact, this Monday, I have a floral design specialist coming to the house to help me with the flowers I want outdoors, indoors, and all the arrangements on the tables—I guess just everything to do with flowers for the ceremony, including my bouquet."

That piqued Bob's interest, and so he asked Corey, "What kind of flowers are going to be in your bouquet? You know, I really don't know what flowers you actually love the most."

Excitedly she told him, "I'm sorry, darling, but I can't tell you. I want to surprise you with the color scheme of all the flowers, including my bouquet. This is my surprise to you, as our honeymoon will be a surprise to me. That only seems fair, Robert Brian. Don't you agree?"

He looked at her, and for a few moments, he studied her sexy lips and those beautiful blue eyes that had enraptured many a man throughout the years, and then he leaned in to kiss her, full on the lips, as she pleasurably murmured a faint whimper.

When their lips separated, Bob remained staring at her adoringly and, with great ease, softly and lovingly told her, "Baby, you're so damn easy to love."

Corey sighed heavily and threw her head into his chest. They lay there as Bob held her in his arms, until Haddie came out an hour later to inform them dinner was ready.

THREE

Monday morning arrived at six o'clock for Corey as she slowly got out of bed, leaving Bob to sleep in. She showered as quietly as she could, threw on a handsomely tailored black-and-white, short-sleeved, cotton dress that was pencil-skirted and cut with a modest show of cleavage.

She had coffee in the kitchen with Haddie, as she ate a poached egg on toast that she prepared herself. She and Haddie talked for over an hour about the party that was going to occur tomorrow in the late afternoon, Joshua coming in, and the changes the Owls would be taking on soon enough. Then the doorbell chimed throughout the lower level of the house.

Haddie went to the door and greeted the medium-height blonde with a body and face like Marilyn Monroe. She was probably no older than thirty years, who eloquently told Haddie, "Hello, I'm Abigail Franklin. I'm here on request from a Ms. Corey Madrigal. I will be her floral design specialist for her wedding."

Upon hearing the voices at the front door, Corey came walking down the hall from out of the kitchen. When she first saw the woman, she cased her entire body and the skin-tight flaming-red skirt she wore. Her breasts were screaming to be freed from the low-cut white blouse and matching red jacket she wore. It was at that very minute Corey was convinced she would not be waking Bob up until tomorrow morning.

Extending her hand out to the woman, Corey cordially said, "Yes, I'm Corey Madrigal. How are you this morning?"

Ms. Franklin also introduced herself and, seeming a bit nervous, added, "Of course, Ms. Madrigal, I'd know you anywhere. I'm here to help you with the floral designs you'll want for your wedding. And my congratulations to you and Bob... Is your fiancé going to be working with us on this project today?" Her eyes were scanning the landscape of the house.

Corey now knew this woman must have begged her boss to get this assignment. Everyone in most of the world knew of Bob, and most certainly about his and Corey's engagement.

They were not having the most auspicious start to their business arrangement, but Corey remained cool and confident in the fact that she could handle this from a professional standpoint and with the class that was ingrained in her from birth.

"No, he won't be participating with this aspect of the wedding. So why don't we start out in the back area, where the vows will be exchanged and the reception tables will be located?" Corey directed Ms. Franklin to the french doors.

After a short amount of time, Haddie brought out a pitcher of lemonade on a tray and set it on a table near the pool. She quietly informed Corey that Bob was up and had breakfast and that he said he wanted to come out and take a swim. Corey's head quickly turned to Haddie in alarm, and she asked Haddie loud enough to have Ms. Franklin hear, "You tell Bob I'll be done here in a while and for him to get ready to drive in to the studio with me later. He'll be able to swim all night, when we get home...okay?"

"Yes, Ms. Corey. I'll tell him right away."

When Haddie walked back into the house, Bob was headed out to the pool area. Haddie caught him and informed him, "Ms. Corey is out back with her floral design woman, and you know she wants to surprise you with the flowers for the wedding, so you shouldn't go out there, Mr. Bob. You'd be messing up her surprise if you did. And she said to also tell you she wanted you to go into the studio with her later today, and you could swim all night, when you two get home."

Bob resignedly answered her, "Oh, well, okay. She did want it to be a surprise, so, okay, I'll wait till tonight to swim. I'll just go take a shower and get ready to go with her, when she's done with the flowers and all that."

Out of curiosity, Bob walked over to the french doors and peered out at the woman who came to help Corey with all the flowers for the wedding. When he saw the blond with a body and face to die for, he smiled and looked over at Haddie with a tentative smirk on his face.

Haddie folded under his imploring and scrutinizing eyes and scolded him by stating emphatically, "You should know by now that Ms. Corey doesn't like to share her Christmas candy with nobody. She wouldn't be abiding of you strutting out there in your swimsuit, like a male peacock in heat, with that young and beautiful woman just drinking you in."

"Well, Haddie, Corey should know by now that I would never touch another woman but her. I'm sure you've heard the saying 'Look all you want, but once you touch, you've crossed the point of no return.' All I know is that she and I are going to have a sit-down tonight, if not sooner, and then I'll finally take my swim."

Bob turned and went into the master suite, showered, and casually dressed in some slacks and a short-sleeve shirt, and then went in to sit in the library while he wrote some lyrics for a couple of new songs.

After two and a half hours, Corey and Ms. Franklin wrapped up their business for the day.

As soon as Ms. Franklin walked out the front door, Corey raced into the kitchen and asked Haddie where Bob had gone. Haddie answered her, "I'm not sure, but I know he didn't go outside. You should know, Ms. Corey, the jig is up. He figured out what was going on, and he plans to have a talk with you."

Dreading having to explain herself, and somewhat ashamed of her possessive behavior, she went looking for Bob. After a few minutes, she poked her head into the library and saw him sitting at the desk writing on a sheet of paper; she slowly started walking over to him.

Only Bob's eyes moved to look at Corey standing there. He laid down the pen and got up and walked over to her and hugged her around the waist.

She started to explain what she was thinking. "Darling, I just—" Then Bob cut her off by shaking his head a couple of times as he mouthed the word *no*.

He pulled his body slightly away from her to look her directly in the eyes, and as he still held his arms around her, he lovingly told her, "I know exactly what you were thinking, baby, and it's not like that. I wasn't planning on trying to put the make on her. I just wanted to take a swim and then go back into the house and shower and get dressed."

After hesitating for a moment, he assured her, "Corey, there will never be any other woman for me besides you. I don't care if they stare or flirt with me or even ask me to dance with them—it won't mean anything, unless it's you staring or flirting or asking me to dance."

He smiled broadly at this point as her eyes filled with unshed tears. Looking very affectionately into her eyes, he finished, "I'm so in love with you that really no other woman even interests me. There isn't one quality about you that I don't love. You're everything to me, doll, so you don't need to explain anything. I get it, and I'll try to be more respectful about how you feel at times like that."

Corey pulled his body into hers, and with her hands, she pulled his head down and kissed him tenderly and for several seconds. When their lips parted, she looked up at him with her moistened eyes and proclaimed, "Our life together will never be long enough for me. I adore you, Robert Brian—my life's love."

They stood hugging each other for another minute when Corey, feeling more comfortable with him, cheerfully asked, "Now, darling, are you ready to drive in with me to the studio? I want to talk with Jack about the finalization of our picture in early April and also see if I can spot anyone on lot that's working with us on that project."

"I'll be right beside you, doll," he assured her as they quickly kissed and then headed for the garage for her to drive her black '57 T-Bird into Hollywood.

Driving into the main entrance to Celebrity Studios, Corey and Bob waved at Morgan, the front gate's security guard. It seemed he always had an appealing air about him—of someone perpetually on the verge of laughing.

Corey pulled the T-Bird into her very own reserved parking spot, which wasn't but a few steps to Jack's office building.

As the two of them ascended the stairway to the office, Bob looked at Corey and, smiling like a schoolboy, mischievously asked her, "Remember these stairs, babe?"

Corey's eyes, looking over at Bob, were just beaming and radiating the love she felt for him. She remembered very vividly that first day she had literally bumped into him as he was descending the stairway and she was coming up. She hooked her arm through his and pulled him down to kiss her as she tenderly told him, "How could I ever forget, darling?"

Bob and Corey entered the waiting area of Jack's office as Corey just kept walking past the receptionist toward the door to Jack's office. Bob stopped to ask the same receptionist, Deloris, that had been there for almost the last two years, "Yes, hi, Deloris. Is Jack free right now to talk with us?"

The receptionist answered Bob as Corey entered Jack's office, "Well, hi, Bob. Nice to see you, honey. Jack's free for the next hour, but then I don't think that would have made any difference anyway," as she glanced over at Corey.

Bob looked over at Jack's door, which was left open for him by Corey; and when he turned back to Deloris, all he could do was grin and fatalistically throw his hands face-up beside him. She smiled back and just shook her head.

When Bob entered, Jack was right there to shake his hand and welcome him into his office.

Corey was already seated in one of the chairs facing Jack's desk.

Jack loudly but cheerfully asked, "Well, it's good to see you two. It's been a couple of weeks now since I've talked with either one of you. So tell me, what's up?"

Corey immediately spoke up, "I believe the last we talked was at the wrap party for Bob and my last picture, *Jumping Off the Deep*

End. But, Jack, what we came to talk with you about was the picture we both will be working on the first week of April. I know you've lined up Robert Ryan and Jack Carson, but have you filled the part of the seductive mistress?"

It seemed to Jack that Corey came to approve the producer's choice for the open role of the mistress, which Bob would be having some pretty heated scenes with in the picture.

So Jack looked through some papers on his desk and answered Corey straight out, "Yes, the producer, Trent Voight, wanted Rita Hayworth, and so there you go. She's been assigned to the project."

Corey, smiling with transparent amusement, looked over at Bob as he was trying very hard not to smile or make eye contact with her. He pulled the front of his shirt up over his mouth to mask his comical facial expression.

Jack smiled and inquisitively asked, "All right, what's so funny? Let me in on it."

Corey answered Jack straight-faced and dead serious, "Before I even get married, I'm going to file for divorce."

Jack was still in bewilderment as Corey implored, "You've allowed Bob's seductive mistress to be the hot-bodied, male-seeking redhead Rita Hayworth. Thank you so much, Jack. Bob and I just discussed me trying to curb my possessive and jealous tendencies, and then you give Rita a blank check and a bottom birth with him."

Jack looked Corey directly in her eyes and, with his formidable presence and commanding demeanor, reminded her, "Now look, Corey, we're all acting and playing a part here. This isn't me setting Bob up with a date to the prom. You do remember how a picture is shot, don't you?"

Bob was laughing so hard, he almost fell out of his chair. Corey and Jack were now beside themselves laughing at Bob's infectious and youthful foolishness.

After they all composed themselves, Jack presumptuously stated, "I guess now the next time I see the both of you will be at the wedding, March 20. I know you were going to invite me, so I just saved you an invitation."

Bob smiled and Corey laughed at him and confirmed, "Why, of course, we want you there, Jack. You're much too good a friend to not have been invited to come and drink our liquor and eat to your heart's content."

"Great! I'll see you in less than two months."

Tuesday morning, January 26, was the day Bob was to meet his two new prospective band members at the party he was throwing at the estate. He was on the phone and confirming the arrival of the caterer, the two servers, and the bartender.

Nick called that morning and informed Bob he would not only be picking up Joshua Chambers at the airport, but Joshua would be bringing his girlfriend, Deidra, with him; he'd been going with her for the last four months. He also told Bob he would drive to Darnell King's apartment in LA and pick up him and his wife, Alicia, on his way to Bel Air.

Nick told Bob he would be arriving with the four of them and his own steady date, Charlotte, at around three thirty that afternoon.

After getting everything confirmed and in order, Bob got ready to go to the recording studio in Thousand Oaks. He had a cup of coffee and two pieces of toast for breakfast and promised Corey he would be home at no later than one o'clock.

Corey asked him, out of curiosity, as he was heading toward the french doors to get his car from the garage, "Darling, are you as anxious as I am about you adding two new members to your band this year?"

Bob looked at her, and with his ebullient disposition, he chuckled a bit, answering, "Not at all, doll! I'm really jazzed about this move. It's going to complicate the composition of our songs, but it'll be so worth the extra work. Oh, and have I told you lately how foxy you are?" He looked down at the small amount of cleavage she was displaying, with her top two buttons to her blouse undone.

"Uh, uh, uh," he hummed and then leaned in to kiss her lovingly. He stood admiring her for a few seconds, smiled, shook his head, and winked. She was very sexy when she slowly winked back at him. Bob then comically ran dancing to his car, throwing his arms into the air and turning a couple of pirouettes. Corey laughed out loud, and her smile was enormously full of pride for him as she watched him back his car down the long driveway and head for Thousand Oaks.

When Bob met with the guys and reminded them that the party was set for three o'clock and that Nick would be having six people with him coming in at three thirty. Doug's buoyant attitude assured Bob the guys would all be there, when Doug jokingly remarked, "I think this party is going to be a blast and so far out with all the skirts that are gonna be there."

Len spoke up and implied, "You do know that every skirt that's gonna be there will be with some hunk. All I'm saying is, I don't want to see you get your ass kicked tonight because you're sniffing around the wrong tree."

Jimmy scolded Doug by asking, "You're gonna bring a date, aren't you? I have Jessy, from here at the recording studio, coming with me. So if you don't have a girl, it's gonna be a lonesome night for you, man."

Doug laughed and allayed their fears by saying, "Yeah, yeah, I'm bringing a girl I met at the grocery store the other day, and I guarantee you by the end of the night, I'll know her name."

Bob just shook his head in disbelief and seriously looked at Doug and, reproving sharply, told him, "You know, man, if you honestly respected the women you dated, you'd one day find that woman you truly loved, and you'd thank God every night if she felt the same way towards you. All I'm saying, Doug, is, man...women want to feel needed and loved, not used and convenient. You know what I mean?"

Doug looked at Bob with obvious hurt in his eyes and, with heartfelt feelings, explained, "I do respect women, and I know every one of the names of the women I have ever dated. I just joke around with you guys, trying to make you laugh and make you think I have all kinds of women around me—I'm not tall and good-looking like you fellas."

Doug hesitated and tried not to let his voice crack as he continued to pour his heart out, "I just made up that girl at the supermarket, but I'll ask someone to come with me after our session here today. Don't worry, I won't come stag."

Bob was crushed that he even brought the subject up to Doug about respecting women, but he had an idea and ran it by Doug, "You know what, Doug? I know a young woman at Celebrity that just might want to be your date tonight. She's turning twenty this year, and she was with me in the picture *Living for Now*, made in August of '58. She's a quiet, good-looking redhead that's still available, as far as I know. Let me see what I can do. All right?"

Doug shrugged his shoulders and softly agreed, "Sure. Why not?"

Bob immediately went into the office of the studio and called home to Corey. He explained the situation to Corey and asked if she would call Ann Margaret to see if she would attend the party and meet a blind date when she arrived at three. Bob knew Corey had the power of persuasion and could move mountains, if she was called on to do that. He asked her to call him back at the studio with Ann's response.

When Bob returned to the group, they started rehearsing the last two songs they had just recorded and sent off for marketing a few days ago.

It wasn't even fifteen minutes when Jessy called Bob to the phone. "Hey, doll, did you get a hold of Ann? Go ahead and lay it on me."

Corey happily informed Bob that Ann would love to come and meet Doug and be his date for the evening. Corey cheerfully added, "Ann told me it would be wonderful to date someone that wasn't affiliated with Celebrity Studios. So you tell Doug to be on his best behavior tonight, because I don't want this coming back on me if he can't be a gentleman to Ann."

Bob agreed and assured her, "I've got this, babe. See you in a little while. Oh, and, Corey? Thanks, beautiful. Love you always, doll."

Corey told him earnestly before he hung up, "Drive home carefully, and I'll see you shortly. Just wanted to tell you I'm madly in love with you, darling."

He retorted playfully, "Madly in love or just mad?"

She purred back in her most sexy tone, "Come home early, and I'll show you which one."

Bob was caught breathless for a moment and very excitedly yelled, "All right, and outta sight! I'll be bookin' and laying down some rubber when I bug out of here. Oh, yeah!"

The phone was hung up at this point, with Corey loudly laughing and throwing her head back, as she exhaled heavily and was dreaming only of the love that consumed her for this man.

Bob returned to the guys inside the studio, and he looked at Doug and, smiling, warned him, "You have a date with one of the most attractive and sexy newcomers at Celebrity. Ann said she's anxious to meet you because you don't work at Celebrity. She is stacked, man, and if I remember her rightly, she'll be decked out and dressed to the nines. Wear your best threads, and no pegged pants tonight, man. Have fun, but keep it aboveboard—got it?"

Doug's eyes showed anticipated excitement and yet a disquieting unrest. "Thanks a lot, man. You won't even know me because I'll be so cool and behaving myself with a choice skirt like that."

"Behaving? I wasn't even sure you had that word in your vocabulary!" Bob retorted.

The guys finished their rehearsal of their two most recent songs and split the scene a little before twelve noon. Bob reminded them again to be at the house at three so all the present band members and their dates would be there when the newbies arrived at three thirty.

Bob arrived back home at twelve forty-five that afternoon, and Corey met him at the french doors in back of the house. She kissed him for several seconds, took his hand, and never losing eye contact with him, led him over to the master suite. He was so sexually aroused at this point, his eyes were fixed on her lips, her eyes, her cleavage—her body. His face radiated the want he had for her at that moment, and without either one saying a word, they entered the master suite.

Haddie came walking down the hall from the kitchen and heard the door close to the master suite. All she could do was boldly smile, shake her head from side to side, and chuckling, she quietly stated, "Lord, I think they gonna wear themselves out before the honeymoon, but I think Mr. Bob got enough ammunition in that young body to keep both of 'em going full throttle."

At close to two o'clock, Corey and Bob emerged from the master suite, already showered and changed into the clothes they'd be wearing for the party. Bob dressed in an open-collared white shirt and a pair of trim blue khakis. He rolled the sleeves up to just below his elbows. He was as slim as a male model, and better-looking. Corey decided a sleek, formfitting, lemon-yellow silk dress that had an inviting cut to the cleavage would be fun to wear for a party at her and Bob's estate.

The caterers arrived at two fifteen that afternoon to set up a buffet table outside, twenty feet from the side of the pool, and in the shade of the orange trees. They also brought the tables in for the guests to sit at and a bar for the beverages. They had the table spread with sliced roast beef, oven-roasted turkey, and some BBQ'd pork ribs. There were three different salads, two different sliced breads, and desserts of lemon meringue and strawberry/rhubarb pies. There was also a delicious-looking Kahlua-marbled pumpkin cheesecake and a strawberry carrot cake with a strawberry ganache glaze.

To keep everything fresh, a lot of the food was placed on trays of ice and covered for now. The guests today would be hard up not to leave the party full, drunk, and very happy.

Bob walked up to the food table that was covered in what looked like fine linen tablecloths set beneath the enticing display of beautifully prepared food. He was shaking his head and looked up smiling and told the headwaiter, "This is just spectacular. I'll bet you've been quite busy preparing all this. Thanks so much for your attention to detail." The waiter nodded his head and thanked Bob for his appreciation.

The full bar of hard liquors, wines, and six varieties of local and imported beers were set in the shade more closely to the sixty-foot marbled landing leading down from the house.

Haddie came strolling out of the house close to three o'clock, dressed in a colorful cotton, short-sleeved, purple-paisley silk dress, accented with a silky lavender neck scarf. Bob looked over and saw her come walking down the few steps from the landing. He smiled and gave out a cat whistle. Haddie smiled broadly as Bob complimented her, "Lady, you're burning it down today! You are a righteously choice fox." She chuckled and thanked him.

At that moment, Corey brought Ann Margaret out through the french doors, and they walked down to Haddie and Bob as Corey introduced Ann to Haddie. "Ann, this is our friend Haddie, and of course, you must remember Bob."

Ann shook Haddie's hand and politely told her, "It's so nice to meet you, Haddie." She then turned to Bob and walked over and hugged him, saying, "Why, of course, I remember Bob from our movie we made over a year and a half ago. We had a lot of fun, and I learned quite a lot from everyone on that set. I remember I learned from Bob how to chug a beer and holding the last mouthful to gargle my name."

The three ladies all laughed uproariously, as Bob, trying to jokingly play down the event, stated, while experiencing a feeling of awkwardness, "Are you sure that was me?"

He smiled as Ann put her hand on his arm and, nodding and laughing, confirmed, "Yes, it was you. I'll always remember that shoot. You made me feel very comfortable and self-assured. Thank you so much, Bob." He just bowed his head saying, "You're welcome. You're a lady and should be treated with respect even when you're being taught how to chug a beer."

Corey just stood staring back and forth at both Bob and Ann, as she had always taken so much pride in his inherent moral uprightness. All she knew was that Bob was raised by two parents and a sister, who all possessed impeccable integrity and flawless principles.

Suddenly the roar of a car engine caught everyone's attention over in the driveway. It was Len and Valerie, Jimmy, with his date, and Doug. They arrived right on time in Doug's new bright-red '59 Cadillac DeVille that had thick white walls and rear fins that looked like they were cut off of a two-ton, twenty-five-foot great white shark.

They all piled out of the DeVille and walked the seventy feet over to the pool area. Doug was looking at the woman standing beside Bob and knew it had to be Ann. He immediately became entranced.

Bob yelled out, "Nice to know you guys clean up pretty good."

Jimmy answered in return, "Yeah, this shindig better be good. I put on clean underwear."

Everyone lightly laughed or chuckled. Bob told everyone to get themselves a drink and make themselves at home. There were fifteen people expected, so Bob had the caterers place four tables close to the pool, with tablecloths and flowers adorning them.

Corey led Ann over to Doug, and smiling, she introduced them, "Ann, I would like you to meet Doug Peeples, and, Doug, this is Ann Margaret. Ann, Doug is the saxophone player for the Night Owls. And, Doug, Ann has been an actress at Celebrity Studios for almost two years. And now I'll let you two get acquainted." Corey gracefully stepped away.

Doug extended his hand and shook Ann's hand as she lifted it to him. He was very nervous and hoped his hand wasn't sweating because when he saw her up close, with those soft and sexy eyes, long shiny red hair, and that cute one-sided smile, he was her prisoner.

Ann was dressed to the nines, as Bob said she probably would be, in a tight, formfitting, brilliantly colored orange taffeta dress that had a white-and-orange accent neck scarf. Her stiletto heels were white and made her five-foot, three-inch frame look four inches taller.

Doug managed to choke out, "Hi, Ann. I'm glad to meet you."

Ann responded smiling and sensing his discomfort, "Hi, Doug. It's my pleasure meeting you. Would you like to go over and get a drink, and then maybe we can just sit and talk and get to know one another. That sound all right?"

Doug was only able to shake his head and mumble, "Wow, yeah, that would be outta sight."

Ann started to walk toward the bar area, when Doug turned to the guys, with his eyes wide open, and with a terrified look on his face, he shook his right hand hard three times and mouthed the word *whoa*. Everyone who saw his gesture tried to contain their laughter but chuckled hard to themselves anyway.

Bob was still smiling and laughing to himself when Corey came over to him and put an arm around him. He reciprocated by putting his arm around her. He was cupping her shoulder and pulling her into him. He slightly leaned over and kissed her on the forehead and lovingly told her, "Thanks again, doll, for setting that up. That oughta be a show within itself tonight."

Bob looked her directly in the eyes and asked, "Let's go get a drink and relax, until Nick gets here. How about that?"

She purred, "I'd love that, darling."

Bob put his free arm around Haddie and invited her to get a drink with them. She happily agreed but was acting very anxious for the arrival of her son, Joshua.

On their way to the bar, both Corey and Bob introduced themselves to Jimmy's date, Jessy, and then introduced Haddie to all the guys and gals that she didn't have prior knowledge of before the party.

After a few minutes with everyone talking, drinking, and getting to know one another, a black stretch limousine pulled in behind Doug's DeVille. It was Nick's driver behind the wheel, as all six of the passengers exited on the house-side of the limo. It was almost three thirty, and now everyone who was coming to the party had arrived.

Nick and Charlotte led the group toward the nine other people waiting to meet them. Haddie rose from her seat and started to walk slowly toward Joshua. As he saw her coming to him, he darted toward her, leaving Deidra behind. When he reached her, he put his arms around her and hugged her as he lifted her into the air. They were both shedding tears of joy, as you could hear Haddie tell him, "Oh, Joshua, my baby boy, I love you, and I'm so glad you could come here tonight, baby."

Joshua told her after he set her back on the ground, "I just pray this all works out, Mama, 'cause I would love to live closer to you." They kept hugging for several more seconds and then began wiping the tears from their eyes.

Joshua was an attractive six foot, thirty-five-year-old man who wore a small patch of facial hair just below his lower lip. The hair on his head was neatly combed back and shined like that of Nat King Cole's. His eyes were bright and were now filled with the loving tears he was sharing with his mother.

Nick started to introduce everyone he brought to everyone that was already there. Bob introduced Corey and Ann to the newcomers and told everyone to get themselves what they wanted to drink. He added, "We'll all sit and talk for a while, and then we're gonna have some dinner, and believe me, there is a fantastic spread laid out on the buffet table for you tonight."

When everyone got comfortable in their respective seats, Len started the group talk by asking Darnell, "Now I know Joshua is from here in Stockton, California, but where are you from, Darnell?"

Darnell was a tall drink of water, at six feet, three inches, and had a thin mustache that ran down from his nose, on both sides of his mouth, to his chin. He had a great smile, and his hair was short and parted on one side, looking like one of the guys from the Ink Spots, an R&B group.

Darnell seemed just a bit anxious, but calmly told everyone, "I'm originally from Philly. I graduated from NEC, in Boston, in '52, with a degree in music performance and music history. I then came down to LA in '56, following a lead on a job, at the nightclub called Raisin' the Roof. It's a predominantly black-patronized club in south LA—two floors, and I played on the rooftop level. I've been there the last four years playing my guitar, with two other guys—one on drums, the other on the keys. That's where I met Alicia. She sang there when we met, and we were married six months later. That was seven months after I started playing there."

Bob followed that by asking Darnell, "That's outta sight, man. So cool. Now let me ask you, what kind of guitar do you play, Darnell?"

He was quick to answer, "I can play a classical or a steel-string acoustic." Bob inquisitively asked him again, "What do you think about playing an archtop semi-acoustic?"

Darnell answered without hesitation, "I'm sure I wouldn't have any problem transitioning. Is that what you had in mind for the addition to your band?"

Bob told him straight out, "Yeah, Len and I thought adding an acoustic guitar, and a trumpet would add more depth and the orchestral sound of a much bigger band. The acoustic would supply more of the melody that Doug's sax would already be kickin' out."

Darnell nodded affirmatively and agreed, "That's solid, man—really, boss."

Doug spoke up just out of curiosity and asked, "Joshua? We heard you're the principal trumpet for the San Francisco Symphony Orchestra. What exact trumpet do you play for them, man?"

Answering Doug as honestly as he could, Joshua expressed to him, "That really depended on what piece of music we were playing. I'm not trying to skirt your question, or anything like that, but there are thirteen different trumpets, and I've played all but the flugelhorn. Most of the time I play the B-flat or the C trumpet, because they're the most called for. I also enjoy playing the bass trumpet, because it's pitched one octave below the standard B-flat or C. It really speaks to me."

At this point Joshua lapsed into his own beautiful musical jargon by dramatically and articulately expressing, "And the bass sounds like a beautiful woman dolefully crying with prolonged wailing for her lover to come back to her. It makes me whisper softly with the trumpet's valves, 'I'm on my way, my love. Please wait for me.'"

The entire fourteen other people sat mesmerized with the thought Joshua had just instilled in them with his beautiful analogy.

Haddie sat with her eyes welling up with the ultimate pride in her heart that she felt at this moment for her son. The other ladies all sat with moistened eyes, caught in trancelike stares fixed on Joshua.

Bob was studying Joshua, and also watching in amusement, as Doug squirmed with Joshua's answer. Bob looked over at Len, and he looked like he was fighting back the laughter he wanted to release because of Doug's painful lack of ease.

Joshua finished by telling Doug, "I guess I could play the B-flat, C, B-flat pocket, the F, D, E, E-flat, G, A, or the piccolo trumpet or even the coronet. You tell me what you want 'cause I got 'em all floating around inside of me."

Doug smiled and admitted, "You have an incredible rapport and history with the trumpet, but we just need you to play the horn you're going to feel most comfortable with in playing rock 'n' roll."

Bob tried to help Doug out and suggested to Joshua, "You know, man. The horn that will add that brightness and emphasis in the dramatic passages of our songs."

"All right then, guys. I guess I'd go with my main mistress, the bass trumpet, and maybe have my C trumpet handy for when the bass wanders away, looking for its midnight lover."

Bob started cracking up, and then Len got into the mix. Bob, still laughing, walked over to Joshua and put his hand out to him, saying, "Gimme some skin, man. You're really too smooth, Joshua… outa sight, man. Now I'm stoked to hear you play, but we'll get to that after dinner."

Joshua put his hand out and smoothly stroked his hand over Bob's and suavely assured him, "Then I will beckon my lady out of hiding, to come forth and reveal her true heart to all."

Bob couldn't stop laughing at Joshua's allegorical and extremely witty reference to his instruments. "Damn, man, I love it! You shoulda been a Shakespearean actor on Broadway."

Then calming himself, Bob more seriously asked, "Now, are you sure you want to kick some rock 'n' roll with us and burn some concert halls down? Or do you wanna stay fixated on your concertos and sonatas and your obvious obsession with your horns?"

Haddie looked at Joshua in concern and waited anxiously for his answer to Bob. Corey even looked worried about whether Joshua wanted to play rock 'n' roll, as she looked at Bob and then turned to listen to Joshua.

Joshua, with a gently skeptical expression on his face, admitted, "I do have a garrulous nature, and I apologize for trying to be cute and entertaining. But when I think about the problems we're gonna face, with mixing black artists with white ones, and the hatred and fear it foments, I've got to admit, it's just very disconcerting."

Darnell sat nodding his head in agreement. Haddie began to tear up; and Bob, Len, and Nick, nodded back to Darnell, agreeing.

Joshua fatalistically continued, "I know I'd prepare for every contingency, but it only takes one incautious moment to wipe out everything you worked for. I would love to play for your band, Bob, and besides what you might think, I would find it a total gas and so unreal to crank my sizzling horn to some smokin' hot rock 'n' roll. So, if after you hear me play, you decide you want me, I'd be stoked to give it a go with you cats."

All the other guests started yelling, "Yes!" "All right, man!" "Yes, Lord!" There was even applause and a lot of handshaking going on. Haddie even jumped up to hug her son, and from the bottom of her heart, she told him, "Oh, Joshua, I'm just so proud of you, I could just burst! I'm sure you'd have the time of your life with Mr. Bob's Night Owls. They're so good!"

"I know, Mama. I've listened to 'em, and that's why I'm here." Then Joshua kissed her on the cheek and smiled broadly into her face.

After everyone calmed down and became more at ease, Bob pensively approached Joshua and Darnell, who were sitting close to one another.

Bob, seriously looking at both of them, promised, "I know I told you on the phone, Joshua, that Nick would see to it that security would be ramped up threefold at our concerts. And we would demand the concert venue to have their own guys around the entrances, stage-side, and throughout the parking areas. Yeah, there's a lot of hate out there. It's based in ignorance and taught at an early age. When people don't understand something, they tend to fear it, and with that fear comes anger and rage. Just know, that anything you go through out there with us, that we've got you covered. One of us goes down…all of us goes down. You'll find this is a brotherhood of trust and mutual respect for one another, and you two would be treated no differently. We're gonna make this happen, and it's gonna be an ass-kickin', righteous time."

Corey started to tear up, along with all the women and a few of the guys.

Everyone yelled and clapped their approval to what Bob had told Joshua and Darnell.

They both stood up and shook Bob's hand, and there were even some shoulder bumps thrown in.

Then Bob smiled at both of them and kiddingly told them, "And now, on a more lighter and happier note, I only hope you two can play your damned instruments like you know what you were born to do!"

Everyone was smiles, and there were hugs exchanged throughout the entire group. Doug then announced, "Let's eat, I'm starved."

FOUR

All the party guests began to fix their plates from the buffet table after Bob proclaimed to everyone, "Okay, I agree with Doug. Let's eat dinner, have some dessert, and get some fresh drinks to go with that, and then we're gonna hear these two cats burn the place down."

Amid the cheers and din of the gathering, Doug and Ann seemed to be getting along famously, as he led her hand in hand up to the long buffet table. Everyone seemed to be in the same flowing line and standing with their spouse or date beside them.

Bob stood emboldened by his words, for he knew the group would stand by Joshua and Darnell, and he could foresee the unmitigated triumph that was coming from this serendipitous journey the band of brothers were about to venture into together.

Corey quietly walked up to him and slid her arm through his as he stood with his hands in his pant pockets. Startled, but always happy to see her smiling face, he softly said, "Hey, baby. How are you holding up to all this? Or is this one great big boring time for you?"

Corey affectionately scolded, "Darling, I'm with you, and it really wouldn't matter what we were doing. I just love to spend my time with and near you...however, I will say, I really enjoyed your talk to the two guys. It was so moving and heartfelt. I like both of the men you've found for your band, darling. They both seem very knowledgeable—and not just in music, and they're so nice and personable. I think you've really struck pay dirt with these two."

"We'll see how that plays out when we hear 'em in a short while. Although, you know deep down, I don't have a worry in the world that these guys can't cook it. I can't wait for them to crack it open." Bob laughed to himself.

Corey and Bob were last to fix their plates and sit down to eat. The waiters were bringing around coffee for anyone who wanted some, to accompany their desserts. There were a lot of exchanging of thoughts and ideas among the group, and a lot of laughter and drinking.

Doug and Ann were up walking around the pool area with their drinks in hand. They were talking and staring into the blue lights that illuminated the bottom and sides of the swimming pool. Occasionally they would laugh, and it seemed they were generally just having a good time together.

It was almost six o'clock that evening when Len and Nick came up to Bob, and Len asked inquisitively, "I think it's time to hear some guitar and trumpet. I'm gonna ask Darnell and Joshua to get themselves ready, and Nick and I will get their instruments, that we left somewhere behind the buffet table."

Bob leaned over and kissed Corey on the lips as he rose up and announced, "All right, ladies and gentlemen, and anyone else, we're now going to hear Darnell 'B.B. King' and Joshua 'Dizzy Gillespie' Chambers lay down some tunes for us."

There were some chuckles as Nick carried Darnell's acoustic guitar case over to him, and after he removed it from the case, he immediately started to tune and tighten the strings. Len handed Joshua his black carry-case with his C trumpet enclosed.

Bob purposely asked, "Darnell, would you mind starting us off?"

Then in jest and melodramatically, Bob softly spoke, "Joshua still has to tenderly lift his lady out of the case and calm her fears by stroking her curvaceous body and then lament over the passing of his love for her while yearning for his bass."

Everyone started laughing loudly. Joshua was beside himself in laughter and wobbled over to Bob, swaying from side to side, and put his hand out to Bob still laughing uncontrollably, slipped Joshua some skin, and then pulled him in to bump shoulders.

Haddie and Corey were laughing hard enough to bring tears to their eyes. Even the waiters and the caterer were laughing as Bob looked over at them and nodded his head smiling. The partygoers seemed to be having a blast, and the liquor was still flowing.

Finally, when the merriment subsided and the guests quieted, Darnell pulled his guitar strap over his shoulder and readied himself as he smiled. "All right, I'm gonna start by playing John Lee Hooker's 'Boom Boom.'"

Joshua, Deidra, Bob, and Len all responded with, "All right now, yes, sir."

Darnell started out slow and methodical as he stroked the beginning chords. After about thirty seconds into it, he started singing some of the lyrics, which caught the Owls off guard.

His voice was a soulful lower-case baritone that melted the words:

> Boom Boom Baby
> I say to you Boom Boom Baby
> I be comin' back to you, my Boom Boom Baby
> Yeah, oh yeah

Corey looked over at Bob and saw he was studying Darnell's finger placements on the frets and his picking and stroke play on the strings. She felt he was lost in the performance.

When Darnell hit the finishing chord, everyone started clapping and whistling. Bob nodded affirmatively while he clapped his hands.

Darnell, trying to inject a little humor, announced, "And now I'd like to play a song after my namesake B.B. King that was written by Roy Hawkins, 'The Thrill Is Gone.' There was some inward chuckles and a lot of amused smiles because of the reference to B.B. King. Then Darnell hit the opening chords and started to rhythmically and sadly sing the lyrics:

> The thrill is gone
> The thrill is gone away

The thrill is gone baby
The thrill is gone away
You know you done me wrong baby
And you'll be sorry some day

The thrill is gone
It's gone away from me
The thrill is gone baby
The thrill is gone away from me
Although I'll still live on
But so lonely I'll be

The thrill is gone
It's gone away for good
The thrill is gone baby
It's gone away for good
Someday I know I'll be open-armed baby
Just like I know a good man should

You know I'm free, free now baby
I'm free from your spell
Oh, I'm free, free, free now
I'm free from your spell
And now that it's all over
All I can do is wish you well

The last chord of the song was still resonating through the air when everyone was applauding and shouting, "Yeah, man, oh yeah." Bob looked over at Len and Nick, and they returned his stare with one quick nod of the head. He then looked at Jimmy as he was shouting, "Right on, B.B.!" Doug's face was lit up like a Christmas tree, as he was jubilant, and stoking his fist in the air triumphantly at Darnell.

Bob then walked up to Darnell from his seat next to Corey, and the silence was almost immediate. Not having changed his facial expression at all, Bob extended his hand out to him and officially stated before everyone, "Welcome to the Owls' nest, man!"

Corey smiled fondly and clasped her hands in front of her, clapping them once in a while. Darnell took the guitar strap off his shoulder and laid the throat of the instrument leaning into a chair and then gleefully took Bob's hand and shook it. Everyone jumped up to congratulate him by patting him on the back, slapping hands, and hugging him. His wife, Alicia, put her arms around his neck and then kissed him long and joyfully.

Bob then stepped back to Corey and hugged her. She put her arms around his waist and buried her face in the chest of his shirt. He kissed her on the top of her head and then turned around and helped her back into her seat as he sat down and stated, "Okay, everyone, we have a new member to the Owls, so now let's see if we've found our horn."

The party calmed down, and Joshua stepped up with his C trumpet in hand. Haddie was tentatively smiling at her boy because she was nervous for him. However, she knew, with stark certainty, he was going to softly and tenderly coax his horn to lay down the sweetest and yet the most kickin' notes it was capable of playing.

Joshua, seeming comfortable and self-assured, announced, "I also have two songs for trumpet this evening. The first is by my man Dizzy Gillespie. This is his 'Desafinado,' and the last one is 'Take the A Train' by my mama's man, Mr. Duke Ellington."

He put his lips to the mouthpiece and started a loud upbeat run of fast notes that crescendoed into a piercing roar that reeked of the trumpet's bright, metallic thunder. The clarion was rousing and brilliant and also dark in the lower register. He was projecting the cleanness of the notes through the purity of its timbre.

Everyone present was mesmerized by the genius of his bright, penetrating tone. Corey took one look at Bob's face and knew he was witnessing a brilliant trumpeter.

Joshua brought the last notes home as his trumpet whispered the closing notes with such purity; it seemed they kept floating through the air, like mist on the Scottish moors.

Every person there, even the waitstaff, was loudly applauding and shouting their verbal approval. Haddie just sat crying, with her face in her hands, as she rested them on her lap. Joshua bent down to her and kissed her on the head and consolingly told her, "It's all right, Mama, my lady and I got this covered."

It quieted once again, and Joshua simply stated, "'Take the A Train.' He put the horn to his lips again and slowly rolled into the notes that the Duke had written. He started to ramp up the intensity of the beat, and soon he was sizzling in a heat of great excitement. The notes were combustible at this point and soon barking the powerful and stately sound of the raging C trumpet, which happened to be Joshua's second mistress-in-waiting.

Two minutes later he brought the piece to a soft whispering end, and then he lowered the trumpet and took a breathless bow to everyone. Haddie jumped out of her chair and quickly moved to him and wrapped her arms around his waist as she placed her head on his fast-beating heart.

The entire group of listeners couldn't stop clapping, whistling, and shouting. Bob was still seated, for it was an experience of transcendence for him. He knew what he had just heard, but he knew it wasn't an experience of normality or one of the physical level; it felt eerily providential.

When Bob finally got out of his seat, he slowly walked toward Joshua, and the silence of the group became deafening. He came face-to-face with Joshua, and not even blinking his eyes, Bob affectionately shared with him, "You know, Joshua. Your mama once told me that I sang like an angel, when we sang 'Amazing Grace' together, oh, about six months ago now."

Corey took a short gasp of breath, with tears copiously filling her eyes. She remembered that morning in the kitchen, soon after Bob's head surgery he needed after taking a fall in London, the last night of the Owls' world tour last summer.

Bob continued, "Well, I can honestly tell you, you make that trumpet sing like an angel." Bob put out his hand and announced, "I believe we've filled the nest with this Owl."

Joshua kissed his mama on the forehead and shook Bob's hand at the same time. Everyone moved in to congratulate the two guys and welcomed them to the Night Owls.

Bob stepped over to Haddie and gave her a big hug, and in kissing her on the cheek, Haddie honestly whispered in his ear, "See, Mr. Bob, I didn't lie... I told you Joshua could really play that trumpet."

Bob smiled broadly at Haddie and assured her, "Ms. Haddie, I knew Joshua was gonna cook that horn when I saw the gleam in your eyes Saturday, after I talked with him on the phone, and I told you he was coming today."

Haddie proudly answered back, "You've got to know, Mr. Bob, I love that boy like I love life itself. I know you won't be disappointed with Joshua in your band. He's just brilliant!"

At that moment, Corey came up and hugged Joshua and congratulated him and then hugged Haddie, happily telling her, "I know Joshua will do well with the Owls, and you can sleep at night knowing the band, and Nick, will take very good care of him and Darnell. I don't want you worrying about them. They couldn't be in better company than with these guys."

While still hugging Corey, Haddie thankfully stated, "Why oh why, Lord, can't there be so many more people like you and Mr. Bob? The world would be so much better off."

Everyone at the party kept a drink in front of them, and the caterer kept the dessert table open. It was now seven thirty in the evening, and there were people sitting around the pool in couples, either one in a lounger, two in a lounger, or they were seated at one of the dinner tables. Bob had music playing from a radio that was sitting up on the landing. The music was slow instrumentals, with some vocals, from a lot of the big bands of the forties and fifties.

Bob asked Corey to dance with him to "The Masquerade Is Over," with a very young twenty-two-year-old Nancy Wilson singing with the Cannonball Adderley Quintet. The song was a very slow and mellow jazz number that was perfect for lovers to move to, and with the silky and crisp contralto chords Ms. Wilson was laying down, every couple got up to dance.

There were couples dancing on the huge marble landing. Others just danced close to the pool, by the ten feet of marble, rolled-edge coping that surrounded the entire seventy-five feet of the pool.

Corey had her arms around Bob's neck as he held his arms around her waist and lower back. They were barely moving to the song as he kissed her ear then the side of her neck. She was melting into his body, and after having three dry martinis, stirred, she would have let him take her at that moment, right there by the pool, if it wasn't for their party guests.

The next song that played was "Satin Doll" by Duke Ellington and sung by Ella Fitzgerald. Joshua led Deidra back to her seat, and then he grinned at his mama and approached her and asked, "Come on, Mama…let's cut a rug with the Duke."

Haddie jumped up, and they were dancing a medium-speed swing by the poolside. She kept up with him, and the guests were clapping and whistling their approval. They were having the time of their lives as both were unmistakably lost in the excitement of the moment.

When the evening was wearing down, people were just sitting and talking around the lit pool, and only accent lights softly showed the outline of the huge back area. Bob walked over to the caterer and waitstaff, thanked them for a great job, and paid them with a check and a two-hundred-dollar cash tip. He asked them to leave the bar platform and supplies, and they could pick that up tomorrow. They were good with that.

Bob then returned to his guests and kicked back with Corey in her lounger. At that exact moment, he heard Doug yell encouragingly, "Okay, everyone, in the pool!"

The next thing everyone witnessed was Doug cannonballing into the fifteen-foot-deep end. Ann, totally taken by surprise, was wide-eyed and screamed in amusement, "Oh, no, Doug, you're kidding!" Her hand went over her mouth, covering her laugh.

Everyone was laughing with Ann and was amused with Doug's antics. Corey was in shock and was staring at Ann's reaction. Bob glanced over at Corey and read the alarm on her face. So in trying to allay her fears, he told her, "He's not being an ass, baby, he's just having fun. No one seems upset about it, okay? Now, don't freak out because—"

Bob immediately jumped up after taking his shoes off, and then he dove into the pool with Doug. They were splashing each other and trying to dunk one another as the entire group of guests were laughing out loud and cheering them on. Corey sat smiling and just shaking her head fatalistically at their exuberant display of youthful mischievousness.

Darnell was laughing so hard, it was difficult for him to pull his cashmere sweater up over his head to remove it, before he jumped in. Alicia tried to stop him, but after he removed his shoes, he went racing to jump into the water. Bob and Doug slapped Darnell's high-hand and then splashed him in the face. He returned the favor.

Haddie was looking at Joshua and hoping he wouldn't jump in with them. He caught her looking at him worriedly and assured her, "Don't worry, Mama, I still don't know how to swim. If I jumped in there with 'em, it'd be like a rock tied to another rock that was anchored by a big cement brick—at that point, you might as well just kiss me goodbye."

Everyone chuckled at Joshua, and Haddie was greatly relieved.

When Jimmy and Jessy followed Darnell into the pool, Haddie rose up and told Corey, "I'll go in the house and grab some towels for these crazy kids, 'cause I'm convinced it's just their young blood—it's poisonous to their brains at this age."

Corey thankfully told Haddie, "You do that, Haddie, before they all catch their death of pneumonia."

Corey remained lying back in her lounger as she was drinking in the sexy way Bob's wet dress shirt clung to his muscled chest and powerful abdominal muscles. She took another sip of her drink, and her mind wandered away thinking, with the band at four members, she at least saw Bob at home, or when they were making movies together; with two more guys and their partners, she felt her and Bob's time together would now be vastly diminished, with all the extra composing, practice sessions, and recording of the new songs.

About a half hour later, everyone started filing out of the pool. Haddie made sure that the five that had jumped in got a towel when they exited the pool.

Ann was laughing at Doug and whimsically told him, "Doug, you're a gas! That cannonball of yours was outta sight. You'll have to teach me that some other time." Doug's face lit up with pure satisfaction, and his smile was infectious to everyone.

Bob was toweling himself down as he walked toward Corey. She was smiling with unusual delight as she studied his body coming toward her. She charmingly said to him, with her smile strengthening, "I hope you don't get pneumonia, darling. Even though I could see all of you had a great time in the water."

Bob bent over Corey then kissed her as he cautiously spoke softly into her ear, "That was great fun. I just hope you're not upset at Doug for being himself. You've got to know, he wouldn't do anything to spoil his date with Ann. I think he's really stoked with this fox."

He stood upright, as Corey looked puzzled, and asked imploringly, "Well, does that mean he really likes her?"

Bob smiled brilliantly and silently mouthed the word *yes!*

It was now a few minutes past nine o'clock. Bob turned to the group and announced, "I just want everyone this evening to know how much of a kick this has been for me tonight. I mean, the Night Owls have found their two owlets, and both of 'em are so in the groove and can really burn it down. I'm just so jazzed to start working with these guys. So, in knowing how good I knew they'd be, I had Nick secure us some studio time tomorrow. With Darnell, Alicia, Joshua, and Deidra staying the night, I thought this would give us something to do tomorrow, and also Thursday."

Nick held up his drink and dutifully stated, "Noon, tomorrow, until three o'clock—I will briefly be there, just to see how close you are to having a couple of new songs ready."

Len inquisitively asked Nick, "Why? What's cookin', Nick? Where do you have us jetting off to next?"

Nick smiled and informed them, "Well, I was going to tell you at the studio tomorrow, but I'll lay it on you now. You do remember last April, when you were on *The Ed Sullivan Show*? Well, Mr. Sullivan would like you to return to do the show next month. We're looking at February 21. How's that sound to you cool cats?"

Darnell looked at Joshua with shocking disbelief. Len, Doug, and Jimmy, and their ladies, started yelling and hugging one another. Joshua slapped hands with everyone and then hugged his mama, exclaiming into her face, "*The Sullivan Show*, Mama? What a blast that will be. This is just unreal."

Corey rose from her lounger and hugged her very happy fiancé. They kissed, and when Bob pulled his head back, he cutely told her, "Well, I guess now I can make rent next month!"

Corey laughed out loud and just stood hugging him. She loved his sense of humor. She also knew Bob made ten times the money she did—with his marketed vinyls and LPs, the band's concert appearances, his motion pictures, and the once-in-a-year Broadway play he insisted on doing; soon he would be rich, way beyond the point of vulgarity.

When Bob moved in with Corey, in late July of last year, after he returned from the Night Owls International Tour, he immediately had all his earned revenue transferred to her personal investment firm. Any money he made from that point on was directly sent into Corey's account, which now was in both their names. Bob really didn't care about the amount of money he made, for the love of the arts overrode everything in his life, except for his deep and abiding love he had for Corey.

Still hanging on to Corey, Bob turned to Nick and informed him, "Nick, I think we need to get Darnell and Joshua under contract, and then we're gonna renegotiate your contract." Nick was bewildered with what Bob said, and so he asked, "What do you mean, man? I was locked in through this year."

Bob happily explained to him, "Well, Nick, the guys and I talked it over, and we feel you're worth far more than what you get paid."

Jokingly, Nick responded, "Well, I could have told you that over a year ago, but I was content to take the peanuts you guys threw at me! Just kidding, man."

Bob then emphatically told him, "All the new contracts will read that every one of the seven of us will receive one-seventh of all record receipts, performance fees, and the sales from our paraphernalia—such as tee shirts, mugs, hats, and everything else that's out there." Nick knew that the new contracts would increase his salary exponentially. He walked over and shook Bob's hand, and then Len's, Doug's, and Jimmy's.

Very emotionally, Bob resolutely added, "We're a band of brothers, Nick. We'll stand together, or we'll go down together—no middle ground."

Nick moved toward Bob and then hugged him like he was his own brother.

FIVE

That January 27, Wednesday morning, unfurled a brilliant blue sky, with not even a wisp of a cloud hanging above. Haddie, Corey, Joshua, and Deidra were already in the kitchen at six thirty, drinking their morning coffee and conversing about the previous evening.

There was a pervasive excitement in the air, a kind of electricity that ran through each person's veins. They radiated those emotions within the excitement that shone in their eyes.

In the upstairs bedrooms of Bob and Corey's estate, where Darnell and Alicia and Joshua and Deidra stayed the night, Darnell and Alicia walked out of their room after they showered and dressed. As they walked toward the vast and curving stairway, which was lined with beautiful mahogany railings and the steps covered with soft, Cajun-red carpeting, Darnell looked into Alicia's eyes and swore to her, "Someday, baby, I'm gonna buy us a place like this. A huge house that we'll fill with all of the kids we gonna have. I'll work hard at it, baby."

Alicia stopped before the stairway, pulled Darnell's head toward hers, and kissed him. She then softly told him, "I know you will, sweetie, and I'll be right there beside you helping." They continued down the stairway and into the kitchen, where they heard voices. As they entered, everyone greeted each other and asked how they had slept. Haddie brought them some coffee, but Alicia wanted orange juice.

A few minutes later, Bob walked into the kitchen, bemused by the fact everyone was ready for breakfast and sat waiting for him.

"Had I known everyone was going to be up and at 'em with the rooster's call, I would have set my alarm clock last night." He chuckled a little bit while others were laughing with him.

Corey walked over to him and kissed him tenderly and then announced to all, "Now that we have a full contingency"—she ran her hand playfully through Bob's hair—"Haddie and I are going to make breakfast for you. Now, what does everyone want?"

At that moment, Alicia and Deidra popped out of their chairs, with Deidra exclaiming, "Corey? Alicia and I would love to help you and my future mother-in-law make everyone breakfast."

Deidra and Joshua looked at each other smiling and then looked back at Haddie. Corey was taken by surprise, with her mouth gaping open, while Bob was waiting in anticipation of Haddie's reaction.

When Haddie realized what Deidra had said, and it had sunken into her brain, she quickly jerked her head toward Deidra and threw a quick glance at Joshua. Haddie instantly covered her mouth with her hand and began to cry. She managed to draw air in convulsive gasps and asked with broken sentences, "You two gonna get…married? You gonna…marry one another? Oh my god! Hallelujah, praise the Lord. Oh, sweet Jesus!"

Deidra was nodding her head affirmatively when Haddie grabbed her with both hands and pulled her into her body for a tight hug. Joshua rushed over to them and put his arms around both and joyfully told Haddie, "Yeah, Mama. We gonna get married this summer sometime. I asked Deidra last night in bed, and she said, 'Are you kidding? I would love to marry you, Joshua.' And so, there you have it… Bob and Corey hitching up in March, and Deidra and I, probably sometime in July or August."

Everyone was hugging everyone. The kitchen was filled with congratulatory wishes, laughter, joyful tears, and exciting conversation.

Everyone ate a fine breakfast right there in the middle of the kitchen, sitting at the huge island, on the leather-backed stools that surrounded it.

After breakfast, all seven of them took their coffee mugs into the massive living area. Corey had the fireplace roaring, and Haddie brought in a tray with a fresh pot of coffee and a plate of mixed-fruit Danish.

Until a little bit after eleven o'clock, they all spent time talking about everything that had been happening in their lives. Bob then suggested to the ladies that maybe everyone could meet up for dinner that early evening at the house in Thousand Oaks. They would order in. "I'll drive us three guys over in my Chevy, and then you ladies could have Curtis bring you to the house around three thirty this afternoon. How's that sound?"

Corey, showing interest, mentioned tentatively, "Maybe some of the gals would like to sit in on your session and just observe. If we get tired or bored, we'll just take off to the house and ready it for our early dinner."

The three guys were good with that, so they all met at the studio shortly before noon. Len, Doug, Jimmy, and Nick were already there when Bob, Joshua, and Darnell came walking in with instruments in hand.

Bob told the four guys that were already there about Joshua and Deidra's engagement. They congratulated Joshua, and then they waved at Deidra, in the soundproof booth with Haddie, Corey, and Alicia, as the ladies entered the booth to sit down. Nick then went in the booth and sat down by Corey.

Businesslike, Bob spoke to the guys and said, "Okay, let's get this in motion. Len says he has lyrics for a song and has pounded out some melody for it. He needs all of you to collaborate with him on the harmonic movements that will be underlying the theme your instruments would be laying down or any riffs you may want to run. I have also written a song with the basic arrangement and the time signature, but right now we're not going to be playing whole songs but simply producing runs of melody, along with some feeling for the notes and key signatures, registered by the horn and the sax. Then, I think, we'll throw it all together and do some roughing out of the chords and, perhaps, even rework the melody, where needed."

Up in the soundproof booth, Alicia, Deidra, and Haddie just looked at Corey in puzzled amazement. Corey looked back at them with a prideful smile and turned back to look at Bob and boasted, "I know…handsome and intelligent. What a stunning combination!" The three women just smiled back at her and chuckled.

Bob began running an upbeat run of notes to Joshua's melodious trumpet riff. It was magical for all to listen to. The pace was fast, and the volume was loud.

Nick, sitting by Corey, interjected with some introspective thoughts he had about the group. "Ladies?" All three turned to face Nick. He tried to explain as best he could. "There's a sound of a sound. The sound inside of a sound. Just listen to that—every note is a different coloration. And at this insanely loud and fast tempo, if this doesn't make your ears bleed, it isn't doing its job. *Ears* are jazz-speak for the capacity to hear what is going on in music as it unfurls across the air. With Bob's and Joshua's good ears, they soon memorize the songs and the arrangements they may be asked to play. They pick up, or already know, the harmonic movement underlying the theme, and then they follow the transformations and substitutions to that pattern, introduced by their fellow musicians."

Nick looked at the three ladies, and they were either entranced by what he was saying or they were hopelessly lost within the musical jargon.

Either way, he continued, "But whether or not they can accurately read notes written on a staff, a musician with great ears learns melodies and arrangements the first time he hears them. He grasps the harmonic intricacies through flawless intuition and immediately identifies the notes and key signatures registered by the horn or the sax. These special people inhabit a world defined by the particularities of individual sounds. Bob, Len, and Joshua are three of them. Ladies, these men are in a class by themselves."

Corey had tears in her eyes, and when she turned back to face Bob, she blinked, and a single tear fell from each eye as she smiled brilliantly.

Nick told Deidra, trying not to be patronizing, "Look, Darnell, Doug, and Jimmy are all great musicians and are a tremendously valuable part of the band, but when I heard Joshua play that horn last night, I knew instantly he was a natural and had the gift. I've been aware of Bob's and Len's gift for the last year and a half. It's just been amazing how fast they could create a song of great quality and substance. I just feel blessed to be a part of this unbelievable warren of such talented and brilliant musicians."

Deidra nodded her head in agreement and affirmatively stated, "They most certainly are a magical mix of great guys."

At that point, Corey knew she had to leave to get some fresh air. She felt if she stayed, she would want to go into the sound studio and kiss Bob long and hard. So she suggested, "Why don't we go over to the house now, and the two of you can familiarize yourselves with your new crib." Alicia and Deidra just laughed at Corey, saying, "All right. Right on, Corey!"

Haddie just looked at Corey surprisingly and stated, "Look at your bad-self, Ms. Corey. You be in the groove and outta sight, you choice skirt."

The four ladies were now all laughing out loud as they headed for the door. Corey asked Nick as she put her hand on his shoulder, "We're going to see you at the house, aren't we, Nick?"

Nick turned and informed them, "I'll be leaving here shortly before the guys are done. I'm going the three miles home to Casa Conejo to pick up Charlotte. So, why don't I just stop and pick up a bunch of Italian food from Fontana's, right there in town? Then we'll see all of you around four o'clock at the house, okay?"

All four ladies agreed that would be wonderful.

When Corey, Alicia, Deidra, and Haddie arrived at the Thousand Oaks house, Valerie began showing Alicia, Deidra, and Haddie around. Valerie also let it slip that she and Len were in the process of buying a new home.

Deidra asked Valerie, "I hope we didn't make you feel like we were coming here to squeeze anyone out?"

Valerie emphatically told her, "Oh, for goodness' sakes, no! Len and I have been looking for a place of our own since the middle of October. We found a great four-bedroom, triple-garage, three full baths in Burbank, in the Magnolia Park area. It's twelve miles from

LA and eighteen miles from you, Corey, and only twenty-seven miles for Len to go to the recording studio. We just love it!"

Corey, being excited for Valerie, enthusiastically told her, "It sounds wonderful. Now you let us know when the house warming party is. Bob and I will absolutely be there."

The guys called it a day a few minutes after three o'clock. Joshua and Bob had written down some raw notes for the melody, and Len and Bob had roughed out the chords to Len's song "Stronger than You Think."

When the guys arrived at the house in Thousand Oaks, Nick and all the ladies were there, with all of the food laid out on the table in buffet-style. Corey quickly kissed Bob and then kept her arm around his waist the whole time he fixed a plate of food for each of them.

After dinner, Len, Joshua, and Bob were discussing their music with an inordinate degree of enthusiasm. Darnell, Jimmy, and Doug sat listening and added to the conversation when they felt they had something to offer.

This band of brothers were venturing emboldened into this new form of rock 'n' roll. They all were intrinsically in tune with one another, and they called upon every bit of the knowledge, skill, expertise, and seat-of-the-pants inspiration at their disposal to accomplish their goals.

The 1960s was a time when the world was changing. Music was changing, politics was changing, fashion and hairstyles were changing, and people were changing. There was one problem that seemed to remain in society: racism. The racist segregation did not subside, even with the new era of the baby boomers. Most people went along with it and didn't seem to mind the effects that it had on the victims.

The year 1960 was the start of a decade of tumultuous counterculture protests and the civil rights movement.

The civil rights movement and the dismantling of Jim Crow laws, in the '50s and '60s, just deepened existing racial tensions in much of the Southern United States.

Riots broke out from the frustration of blacks demanding their civil rights; the police would use any method necessary to exert their power to stop them. They would use clubs or physical force or spray the blacks with large fire hoses, and police dogs were released on the demonstrators when they tried to enter an all-white facility or march in the streets demanding equality.

The 1950s rock 'n' roll had broken the race barrier. Whites were getting into the soulful style of black rock as they enjoyed listening to Fats Domino, Jackie Wilson, Chuck Berry, Harry Belafonte, the Drifters, the Isley Brothers, the Ink Spots, the Mills Brothers, Little Anthony and the Imperials, the Platters, and Little Richard—just to name a fraction of the many black entertainers that were out there singing the rudimentary, beginning roots of soulful black rock 'n' roll.

However, none of the black or white groups were racially integrated, so that made what the Night Owls were doing just that much more substantial, significant, and daring, as far as race relations went.

The movies, and most especially the music of the '50s, were only a pre-shock of a genuine earthquake to come in the '60s.

The next morning at the sound studio, the band continued to give Bob's song, "Raging Fire," a going-over, by reworking the melody a few times, to give it a clearer shape. It now had a good mix of repetition and variation while preserving the original idea of the lyrics.

The guys knew they could finalize this song with a couple more sessions, but Darnell and Joshua had to leave that afternoon when the session ended. Both men had to get back to their apartments to give notice of their impending departures and to notify their employers they would no longer be working for them.

Nick's limousine picked up Darnell and Joshua at exactly three o'clock to take Joshua and Deidra to the airport and deliver Darnell and Alicia back to their apartment in LA. They informed Nick they both would be returning next Monday with everything they owned and ready to move into the house in Thousand Oaks.

Len told all the guys, after the session ended, that Valerie and he would be moving into their new home that weekend. The guys were all stoked about having the entire band members not farther away from one another than thirty-five minutes.

Bob jokingly asked Len, "Hey, man. You need any help moving? I know Jimmy and Doug would be more than willing to help you out this weekend." All the guys began laughing loudly when Len answered Bob, "No, really, we don't have all that much. I mean, all the furniture and beds were furnished for us. We're going out today to buy furnishings and, of course, a bed."

"Then we'll see you Saturday at noon, or would you just want to cancel the session, because I know you two are gonna be busy getting the house arranged?"

Len spoke up enthusiastically, "Oh, hell no. I thought we could get busy on my lyrics and, perhaps, lay some badass melody on it and work on giving it the right pitch. I want it to have some good intonations and vocal placements. So, I'll be here Saturday. We've got some work to do. Then when we have all the guys here, we'll buff it and smooth out the rough spots."

Bob left the studio around three thirty and headed home to Bel Air. When he arrived and walked through the french doors, Haddie ran into him.

She asked Bob about Joshua to make sure Deidra and he made their flight home. Bob assured her that they made their flight.

She then informed him, "And, Mr. Bob, Corey is in the living room, talking on the phone to one of her best friends. I was told by Ms. Corey that her name is Alexandria—oh, something, something. She lives in Florida."

"All right, thank you, Ms. Haddie. This gives me time for a swim before dinner." He turned to walk away, and with urgency, Haddie told him, "I've been wanting to thank you, Mr. Bob, from the bottom of my heart for getting Joshua here and having him join your band. I'll never be able to repay you for all this. It's just so unbelievable, and it has made me so very happy."

Bob smiled and hugged her then kissed her on the cheek, saying, "Ms. Haddie, you just repaid me in full, knowing the joy this has brought you. Just remember, the Night Owls are really benefitting from this also. We're gonna make some earth-shattering music, and Joshua is going to be right there in the middle of it all. So, I really must thank you!"

Bob then walked away to change clothes, and Haddie boastfully said, "I warned you. I told you that boy could blow a horn, and ain't nobody in this world better than him."

"You won't get an argument from me, Ms. Haddie." He disappeared into the master suite.

After a few minutes, Bob went out to the pool and jumped in. Corey finally hung up the phone after speaking with Alexandria for almost an hour. She walked to the kitchen and asked Haddie, "Is Bob home yet? Have you seen him, Haddie?"

Cleverly, Haddie answered, "Well, if the two of you aren't together in the bedroom, where do you think you might find him, Ms. Corey?"

Corey smiled broadly and then laughed out loud. "Thank you, Haddie." She immediately headed for the pool area.

When she reached the pool, she watched his smooth, sleek body moving through the water as he swam his laps. She sat down in a lounger she had pulled up close to the water's edge. Within minutes, Bob finished his laps and pulled himself up and onto the coping of the pool. When his eyes caught the presence of Corey so near to him, he shook the water from his head and started walking the few steps toward her.

She was mesmerized with his physicality, and visually, she drank up every bit of him as she sexily asked him, "Are you out here working away some sexual tension, darling?"

Bob kept staring at Corey, casing her entire body with the look of wanton desire in his eyes. He quickly toweled off and then lay down beside her on the lounger, with one leg lying between both of her legs.

He placed one hand on the side of her face as he tenderly told her, "No, I thought I'd let you do that for me." He slowly started to kiss her lips, and then suddenly, they were engulfing each other while tasting the other's cravings. He ran his hand over her entire body and started breathing heavily as his excitement started to physically show.

Corey hurriedly told him, "Darling, I need you to come with me into the bedroom."

Bob quickly nodded affirmatively and then helped her out of the lounger. He wrapped the towel around his waist, and they walked into the house with arms around each other.

When Corey passed Haddie in the hallway to the bedroom, she told her, "You might—" But Haddie was way ahead of her by stating, "Yes. I'll hold dinner for another hour. If you can't make it to the table by that time…then I need to tell you 'bout the express route."

Corey whimsically chuckled and then smiled as she and Bob entered the bedroom.

Bob tore the towel off of him and flung it to the floor. He began to undress Corey by unbuttoning her blouse and then sensually kissing her cleavage. He unhooked her bra with one hand and slowly removed it as his salivating mouth found her naked breast with his tongue.

She began to breathe more rapidly as she softly moaned with delight. Her slacks flew open, and his fingers found the way in. He then lowered her slacks and panties to the floor as she stepped out of them. He lay down in bed and guided her on top of him.

They kissed feverishly while his hands roamed her naked torso. He took her in his arms and held her tight as he quickly and dominantly rolled her over, with him now lying between her open legs. Bob lowered his head down and moved to taste the nectar she had emitted during her subdued and passionate murmurs.

Corey was crying out for him as his hands were fondling her nipples. She was now begging him, "Please, darling. Oh, please."

Bob raised himself up onto her as he eagerly entered her. She instantly was moving her pelvis with his thrusts, as she had a firm hold onto the bed's headboard. She began to climax, and the orgasm forced her back to arch. He wrapped both of his arms around her and kept the thrusts penetrating her until he reached his orgasm. Holding on to her tightly, he loudly exclaimed, "Oh my god. Uh-uh-uh!" He then became motionless.

Both of their breathing was labored, but with an element of complete physical satisfaction, it was justified. Bob lay on her for another couple of minutes, just kissing her neck and telling her,

"Baby, I just love you so damned much! I will never be able to get enough of you. You're such a sexy fox!"

Corey kissed him on the lips again, and as her eyes slightly moistened, she breathlessly and adoringly whispered, "Darling, I just love being with you. I wish I could take you with me everywhere I go. I can't stand it when we're separated, not even for a day. Just hold me, sweetheart. Just hold me."

Bob rolled off of her and then pulled her body over next to him. Corey lay her head on his shoulder as he enveloped her with his arms. He managed to pull the sheet up with one hand and covered them as he kissed her on the forehead.

Several minutes had passed when Corey mentioned to him, "Maybe we'd better go and take a quick shower and then get to dinner. I wouldn't want Haddie to come looking for us."

Bob propped himself up on one elbow, and looking her in the eyes, he jokingly stated, "We're going to have to tell Haddie it was no express route, but not a long, cross-country trip either."

Corey smiled radiantly and lovingly told him, "It was exquisite, darling."

As both of them got out of bed and were moving toward the bathroom, Corey matter-of-factly stated, "Oh, and by the way, darling, I want to talk to you about my good friend Alexandria Amani Buchanan. She's the person I was on the phone with when you arrived back home today."

Bob told Corey as he turned the shower on, "Okay. I'd like to hear about her...but now, why don't we take a shower together, and then maybe I can still take that cross country-trip?"

Corey laughed loudly and affectionately as she led him into the shower and then shut the door. They began making love immediately, and it lasted another forty-five minutes.

When Bob and Corey walked into the kitchen, two hours after they initially went into the bedroom, Haddie turned to them with a broad smile on her face. "Did you two get lost on the express route?"

Bob spoke up with his youthful vivaciousness, "No, not at all, Haddie. We just took a couple different routes. That's all."

Corey dropped her head back and was looking up at the ceiling and chuckling loudly. She was only breathing out of her nostrils when she brought her head forward again. She sat shaking her head at Bob in amusement.

Haddie laughed at Bob and added, "Yeah, I remember those days. Nowadays, I'd be afraid I'd be too doggone tired just walkin' to the car!"

They all laughed out loud.

When Haddie put dinner in front of them, Corey remembered to tell Bob, "Bob, I want to tell you about my friend Alexandria."

"Yeah, go right ahead. I'm all ears."

Corey cutely came back at him, "Don't sell yourself short, darling."

Bob gushed with laughter, and Haddie cautioned, "Oh, Lord. Do I want to hear this?"

Corey giggled and then continued, "Alex called me this morning. We hadn't talked in probably close to a year. Well, now I know why. She was divorced a year ago, and she told me it was a messy one. I guess it all boiled down to her wanting to get back to work in the business of making motion pictures."

Bob looked at Corey in surprise as she continued explaining, "She started with MGM Studios about the same time I signed with Celebrity. Celebrity bought her contract from MGM, after Alex became disgruntled with Louis B. Mayer. She actually was one of the premier postwar vocalists around. She had a strikingly pure voice. She was a part of American music's glamorous era back in the forties and early fifties. Alex was also one of the most prolific actresses of that time—present company excluded."

Bob nodded his head in agreement, asking inquisitively, "Do you have any pictures of her? What does she look like? That name, Alexandria Buchanan, doesn't ring a bell."

Corey explained to him, "*Buchanan* was her married name. She told me she was going back to her maiden name: Alexandria Katherine Amani. In the credits of her movies, she was known as Alex Amani."

"Oh, yeah. Now, that name rings a bell. She was in that movie *I Gave It All* in fifty-two or fifty-three. I remember seeing that picture in my midteens, before I left to go to NEC in fifty-four."

Corey playfully admonished him by facetiously noting, "All right, darling. You don't have to remind us how old we are." He chuckled, bowed his head, and remorsefully exhaled very loudly.

Haddie was working at the cutting board with some vegetables when she giggled out loud. Corey shot a look of amused scorn at her, when Haddie, having fun with her, stated, "Ms. Corey, my goodness, woman, by now we all thought you'd have come to terms with that. 'Cause you know that ain't never gonna change."

Corey quickly raised her eyebrows up and down and conveyed a look of resignation at Haddie, as she told her, "Every day I wake up, I am painfully aware of that, Haddie."

Corey turned to Bob and finished telling him, "I do believe that could have been her last picture of any significance. That was probably 1952, because after she got married, her husband whisked her off to West Palm Beach, Florida. He was an entrepreneur in the textile business. I guess Alex never lost her love for motion pictures, causing their marriage to last less than six years."

Bob sat staring at Corey, then told her, "Maybe you should invite her to the wedding?"

"That's what I was getting at, darling. Alex called, and asked me, that if she moved back here again to work in Hollywood, could she move in with us temporarily, until she found her own place. She told me she had read somewhere about our engagement, so, naturally, I had already invited her to our March wedding. So, I guess, what I'm asking you, are you going to mind having her staying with us for a little while?"

Bob didn't have to think long at all when he honestly answered her, "Baby, you know I won't mind having a friend of yours staying with us as she tries to put her life back together. Of course she's welcome here."

Corey leaned over and quickly kissed him, saying, "I promise, she won't be here long enough to become a nuisance, to either one of us. She told me she'd probably be ready to move in within the next few weeks."

Bob surprisingly exclaimed, "Wow, okay. You know, you haven't yet shown me a picture of…Alex. What does she look like? How old is she? How tall? White? Black? Fat? Sassy? You need to give me some kind of idea about her before she gets here."

Haddie piped in by playfully directing her comment to Bob. "Mr. Bob, I'll bet she's at least two or three of those." Bob and she just giggled at each other.

Corey left the kitchen; she acquiesced to his curiosity. She returned in a few minutes, holding three pictures. She laid the pictures down in front of Bob on the island's marbled surface. She pointed at the top picture. "Now, this first one is from seven years ago, just before she left Hollywood. The second is a couple of years ago, and the third, she said, was taken two months ago, around Thanksgiving."

The pictures indicated to Bob that Alex was a handsomely attractive woman, of medium build, brown hair, and a body that looked as if she had worked at maintaining it through the years.

Corey added, trying not to sound too harsh or jealous, "Alex is forty-one years old and turning forty-two this September. She's very mild-mannered, polite, easygoing, and five feet, six inches tall. I don't foresee any problem with her staying here for a while—unless, she starts trying to undercut me for some of the pictures I'm looking at." She nervously laughed. Bob could see some worry and tension written across her face.

He tried to reassure her, "There's no one on lot that could undercut you for any role you wanted, baby. You're still the most choice actress at the studio. You are so awesome and way cool. I can't wait for us to start working on *Love's Wicked Lies* in a couple of months. I'm really looking forward to that, Corey."

"So am I, darling. So am I."

On Monday night, February 1, Nick contacted Bob and told him that Darnell and Joshua had moved into the Thousand Oaks house. He told Bob they seemed to be really cranked about working at the recording studio the next day and redressing those two songs.

Nick also told him, "Joshua has the lyrics for one more song that he wanted the group to look at. Then after the Owls get the other two songs completely done, and ready to record, maybe they could start working on his song, or any other song, that was waiting for the development stage."

"All right, Nick. That sounds fantastic. Really boss, man! But, Nick, do you actually realize the magnitude of this life-changing wind blowing down here from San Francisco? Joshua is so intrinsically good at creating music."

"I've got to tell you, Bob. This group, the Night Owls, has been blessed with an enormous array of great musicians. However, I happen to know that Joshua, you, and Len exceed even that level. The three of you are just pure genius, man. It's just so unreal! Really." Bob was so flattered with Nick's compliment, he became a little flustered. "Hey, thanks, man. I appreciate that. So, I guess I'll see you for a little while tomorrow, okay?"

"Absolutely. Tomorrow, man."

The next afternoon, when all the guys, including Nick, got together and were studying both of the songs they had been working on, Nick announced to them, "We've only got three and a half weeks until we play *Sullivan*. I'd really like you to crank out at least two new ones by then. We could then showcase the Owls new stuff to the entire world that Sunday night."

Nick left the studio a half hour later, after he got Darnell and Joshua signed to their contracts. Then the guys rolled up their shirtsleeves and dove headlong into the process of finishing the two songs they had waiting for them.

The group really got down to finalizing the melody on "Raging Fire," giving the choruses more energy and urgency; the words were pitched higher, the pace made faster, and the volume was cranked with an edge that would make your ears bleed.

The entire session, which ran over by an hour, was masterfully chorded by Bob, Len, and Darnell. Joshua and Doug worked on the arrangements for the trumpet and saxophone. They all understood this process on some deep level. It all seemed so naturally ingrained in them.

These six guys were truckin' as they seemed to work together with seamless efficiency. They had "Raging Fire" and "Stronger than You Think" finished and recorded by the following Tuesday, February 9.

This made Nick extremely happy, because now the Owls fans, and the soon-to-be fans, would be looking forward to the performances of the group's new songs. And having bought the 45 rpm already, they would know the lyrics and have listened to the entire song plenty of times before *The Ed Sullivan Show*.

It was just amazing, and unimaginable to Nick—the frightening rapidity that these guys exhibited in writing, adding melody, figuring out what pitch to use, volume, pace, and rhythm the songs needed. This group of Night Owls was most definitely in a class by themselves.

SIX

Bob arrived home later than he usually did, after he had worked at the recording studio. Corey was reading a script in the living room, as she was hunkered down in one of the massive leather chairs adjacent to the couch, in front of the fireplace. The chair was in perfect view of the french doors in back of the house.

As he moved wearily down the long hallway, toward the master suite, Corey intercepted him. She approached Bob; seeing the fatigue in his face, she affectionately asked, "Are you all right, darling?" She then put her arms around his neck, leaned into him, and kissed him softly on the lips.

Bob smiled at her loving gaze, exhaled loudly, and feeling mentally exhausted, he told her, "I'm fine, baby. I just feel like someone's kicked my ass, dragged me behind a car for a couple of miles, and then peeled out, leaving me with tire tracks across my forehead. Other than that, I'm really just fine, doll."

Corey sympathetically smiled and tenderly suggested, "Why don't you go stand in a hot shower for a while and then come out and eat dinner with Haddie and I? I've missed you today, and especially because of the extra time you spent at the studio."

"All right, I'll be out in a while. We'll talk then, okay?"

"Absolutely, darling." She watched him walk farther down the hallway and into the suite, as she thought to herself, *I knew this larger group was going to be more time-consuming and more physically exhausting, so, I guess, I may as well start getting used to it.*

At dinner, an hour later, Corey and Bob sat at the huge island in the kitchen as Haddie was putting ladlefuls of vegetable soup into three bowls.

Corey excitedly told Bob, "Well, today you missed the bakery-lady. She came with several samples of different cakes for the wedding. I liked one in particular, but let's see which one you would want."

"Samples? Where are those? Haddie, I won't be eating too much for dinner tonight," Bob joked.

Corey and Haddie laughed heartily as Corey playfully reprimanded him, "You'll eat your normal dinner and then try the samples for dessert. You'll only need a nibble to tell which kind you like or not."

"We'll see. I'm not making any promises," he quipped.

Corey also told Bob, "And, darling, I've already sent out the wedding invitations this past Saturday. You know, the wedding is less than six weeks away, but everything seems to be falling into place, for now."

Concerned, Bob asked, "You did invite my group of brothers and their significant others, didn't you?"

She incredulously answered, "You've got to know, I invited all eleven of your band people and, of course, Nick. The other eighty-nine invitations went out to my people, in Hollywood and LA.

Bob stated comically, "Well, as long as I got half the invitations, I guess I'm cool."

Corey smiled brilliantly, leaned over and kissed him, and placatingly murmured to him as she ran one hand through his hair, "I'm thrilled you're happy, darling."

Haddie just smiled and ate her soup as she shook her head back and forth in amusement.

Bob was still smiling at Corey when she reminded herself to tell him, "Oh, and before I forget, for your birthday on Saturday, February 20, I would like to take you out to dinner at an exclusive french restaurant. We'll be eating at Tu Es Mon Monde. It's that suit-and-tie, high-class french restaurant in the Hollywood Hills. The name, literally translated, means, 'you are my world.' You probably remember last fall the cast from *Jumping Off the Deep End* met our director, Rennie Whitmore, there, and we discussed the production aspects of the movie."

"I most certainly do. That was with Susan Hawthorne, wasn't it? Yeah, too cool."

"I had a feeling you'd remember that little thing. Anyway, darling, I've already reserved the entire restaurant that night just for us and all of our friends."

Bob looked at Corey in total disbelief. He was caught completely unaware of her plans.

Her big, beautiful blue eyes were radiating that dazzling ray of adoring love she had for him. He took her face in his hands and kissed her on each eyelid, and then he kissed her full-on on the lips. After several seconds, he pulled back, and with heartfelt emotion, he softly told her, "Thank you, baby. It should be a real gas."

Corey emphatically stated, "And I want the first dance with you that evening, sweetheart. Okay?"

"I wouldn't have it any other way, doll."

Corey leaned over and sweetly kissed him.

After Bob finished his soup, Haddie placed a dinner plate in front of Bob; it had the sample pieces of all the cakes they were to choose from. He looked at the colorful array and excitedly uttered, "Whoa! These look far-out!"

Haddie agreed and told him, "They do, Mr. Bob, and they taste even better. I had a go at 'em this afternoon with Ms. Corey."

"Oh yeah? Well, okay then. Let's have a go at 'em." He then started tasting each one. Corey, remembering the phone call she received two hours ago, anxiously stated, "Oh, I wanted to tell you, darling, Alex is coming to stay with us this Saturday, the thirteenth. She said her plane would arrive in LA at noon. I told her I'd send Curtis to meet her at the airport. She's coming a little earlier than I thought she would, but now, she'll be here to help us celebrate your birthday, darling. So, I guess things are looking good right now."

With his mouth full of cake, Bob nodded affirmatively, and then after he swallowed, he answered, "That sounds outta sight, babe. You mean, she'll be shakin' with us at my righteous birthday blast? This oughta be some primo kicks, doll."

Haddie and Corey both stared at him questioningly. Corey then looked at Haddie, shrugged her shoulders, shook her head, and numbly stated, "Well, I hope it's close to that, darling."

Haddie also answered Bob, "Yeah, Mr. Bob, Ms. Corey be digging that scene with her choice self." Corey and Haddie started laughing loudly, and Haddie grabbed Corey's hand and slipped her some skin, which made them laugh even louder.

Bob just sat there, with his mouth surrounded with frosting, and mumbled, "I think I like the chocolate one with chocolate frosting the best."

Corey ran her hand through his hair, and then rubbing his head, she implicitly told him, "Well, then I guess it's the spice cake, with the caramel panache…by a long shot."

Haddie just chuckled.

That Saturday, at one o'clock in the afternoon, Curtis delivered Alexandria Katherine Amani to the front entrance of the estate. Alex exited the Cadillac while Curtis held the door open for her. Corey met her at the front door.

They fell into a full body hug and then kissed each other's cheeks. Corey happily told her, "Alex, it's so nice to see you again. It's been much too long. But then I guess you've been busy lately. Please, come on in."

On the way through the door, Alex told Corey, "It seems like centuries since we've seen each other, but we'll make up for that. Won't we?"

"Of course, we will." Corey, looking at Curtis, asked him, "Curtis, you just set the luggage inside the door, and I'll have Bob take them to Alex's room later, when he gets home."

"All right, Ms. Corey."

When Corey and Alex eventually wandered into the living area to talk and relax, they took a pot of coffee and some finger sandwiches with them.

Alex was an attractive, soft-spoken woman who was from an upper-class background. Her parents were rich, lived in New Canaan, Connecticut, and were bathed in old money, made from real estate in and around New York City. The money had been in the family for over a hundred years.

Alex attended the Juilliard School of Performing Arts from 1936 to 1940. She left home for Hollywood, on an invitation from MGM Studios. Starting out, Alex didn't get the roles she felt she was more suited to play, so after two years with MGM, she talked to and worked with Jack Windheim, at Celebrity, to buy her contract from MGM. Having confidence in her, he did just that—and was never sorry.

When Alex came to Celebrity Studios in 1942, she struck up a close friendship with Corey. The two became instant best friends. Alex was there for her when Corey's second husband was killed in World War II in 1944. Then in 1952, Alex was by her side in Corey's bitter divorce from producer/director Michael Sutton.

When Alex's first marriage crumbled, after being married to actor Rex Downing, from 1943 until 1951, Corey stood by her and helped her put the pieces in her life back together. They continued their friendship, long-distance style, by writing each other, occasionally calling, and once Corey flew down to West Palm Beach, Florida, to stay with Alex for a few days.

Alex gave Corey the rundown of her marriage and her messy divorce. Corey talked about Bob and how she met him and how and when they got together.

Alex alluded to the subject of Bob's age by asking Corey, "Bob's pretty young. Was that ever a problem between the two of you when you got together with him? How did that happen to come about?"

Corey sensed not only her obvious curiosity, but a definite trace of jealousy in her voice. She tried to be honest with Alex in answering her, "It wasn't Bob's age that was so attractive to me. It was his whole persona: his strength of character, the quiet steadiness he possessed, the compassion he had for others, his incredible musical talent, his intense acting ability, and I've got to tell you…his beautiful face and body sealed the deal."

They both laughed out loud and then took another sip of their coffee. They talked and laughed until three-thirty, when Corey heard the french doors open. She excused herself to Alex and swiftly moved toward the back of the house.

Corey smiled adoringly at Bob and quickly threw her arms around his neck and kissed him. As their lips separated, he flirtatiously said, "I like this kind of welcoming home. Let's try to do this more often. Okay?"

She lovingly chuckled at him and then grabbed his hand, saying, "I'll work on that, darling. Right now I want you to come into the living room and meet my friend Alex. She's been here for a couple of hours now, and we've just been sitting and talking and laughing the whole time."

"Oh, yeah. That's right. She was flying in today, wasn't she?" He nervously stated the obvious.

They started walking back and into the living room hand in hand. As Corey and Bob entered the room, Alex rose to her feet and was instantly struck by the masculine beauty of this man. She stayed focused on his youthful and flawless face.

Bob unpretentiously smiled at Alex as he extended his hand to her and sincerely said, "I'm so glad to finally meet you, Alex. Corey has only had great things to say about you."

Trancelike, she held her hand out to him and warmly smiled, saying, "It's my pleasure meeting you, Bob. You seem like a fine young man." Bob graciously thanked her.

Again, Corey felt the sharp insinuation about his age. She wanted to remain impervious to her reference, but she needed to say something. So she answered calmly, but with a drop of venom, "Now, Alex, you really shouldn't focus on one's age—you do realize it's only a number."

"Why, of course, Corey. I really meant nothing by it."

Bob, now feeling the small twinge of tension in the air, decided discretion is the better part of valor. He told the ladies, "Well, I'm going to go in and take a shower and clean up before dinner. I'm glad to have met you, Alex. I'll see you at dinner."

"We'll talk more at dinner, Bob."

The two songs the Owls finished and recorded Thursday, February 18, were already on their way to the mixer in New York the day after they were given to Nick for processing.

The group no longer had to venture into LA, where their record label, Mercury Records, used to send them to record. Recently, the recording studio in Thousand Oaks had updated their equipment to state-of-the-art.

Nick worked expeditiously on getting "Raging Fire" and "Stronger than You Think" to the mixer in New York and then on to the pressing plant for the end product of the two 45 rpm's. The two songs were soon in jukeboxes and record stores throughout the country, and they both began enjoying very brisk sales the same day they hit the market.

That Saturday, February 20, the guys were working on Joshua's lyrics. They were trying to put a melody to it that had a downbeat rhythm Joshua wanted to ascribe to the song. Joshua had named it "Let Me Lay within Your Arms."

They also started another new song, with lyrics pounded out by all six of the guys. The collaboration between the six talented and musically gifted men was a process of melodious intricacy. They wrote the song to a guitar groove, and not drums, because it was a slow romantic song, which spoke to all of them.

Bob asked Doug to name the song. Doug thought about it for a minute and then comically said, "She's Right for Me, Right Now."

Len, Jimmy, Joshua, and Darnell just started laughing loudly. Bob just stared at Doug and, smiling, shook his head. "Okay. All right. I just hope you weren't thinking about Ann when you named it that. Darnell, why don't you give us a title for this song. This ROMANTIC song about love." Bob looked at Doug, smiling, but feigned a wisp of hardheartedness toward him.

Doug apologetically told the guys, "Hey, I was just kiddin'. There's no way in hell I was thinking about Ann. Sorry, guys."

Bob, allaying Doug's guilt trip, asked again, "Okay, do you have a cool title for it, or not? Because I'm sure Darnell will step up with one if you don't."

"I do have one, and it's about Ann. 'Looking for a Lifetime with You.'" Doug proudly smiled.

All the other five guys simultaneously screamed, "Yeah, man. That's boss. We can dig it, Doug. Truly, unreal." Every one of them slipped Doug some skin.

Bob was proud of Doug at this point, but pointed out, "That's great, Doug, and I think we can work that title into the chorus somewhere."

Bob looked at his watch, and it was close to three o'clock. "All right, let's call it a day. We'll pick up again Tuesday. Now don't any of you forget about tonight. Corey is expecting all of you to show up, with your ladies, to my birthday dinner. I'm looking forward to seeing all of you at six o'clock tonight at Tu Es Mon Monde. Okay?"

They all confirmed they'd be there. Even Doug said he'd be there, with Ann.

When Bob arrived home at almost four o'clock, he heard voices coming from the huge living room. The resonance of these voices all seemed to blend into one continuous echo.

He sauntered down the hallway and peeked into the room, seeing Corey, Alex, and Haddie dressed to the nines in beautiful evening gowns. Corey's silk gown was a deep red, with a black stole draped around her shoulders. Alex had on a dazzling gray-silk gown with sequined gray lines running through it. It was complemented by a white fox stole thrown over her shoulder. Both gowns had an ample cut of cleavage, and he couldn't take his eyes off either woman. Haddie's was a gorgeous melon-orange silk gown, with no cut of cleavage, but was cut a foot down her back. She had a black mink stole, Corey had given her, draped over her shoulder.

Corey and Alex had their hair in beautiful coiffures gathered on top of their heads, with waves and curls scattered about, adorning them.

All the ladies' makeup was exquisitely applied and was heavily steeped with sophistication.

Bob walked into the living room, interrupting their conversation. He immediately said with an enthusiastic tone, "Wow! You ladies are just beautiful. Now you know this is just my birthday, not an inaugural ball." His eyes went from one lady to the next, and just kept going back and forth.

Corey carefully lifted herself from her chair to go over to Bob and put her arms around his neck. He told her as he held her hips, "You smell like we're not gonna be on time for the party, baby!"

She purred in his ear, "It's all for you, darling. Happy birthday. I'll give you your present when we get home."

His face burst into the biggest smile, and breathing harder, he exclaimed, "Whew, man. Someone needs to throw me into a cold shower—and I mean now!"

Corey tenderly kissed him on the lips and then told him, "You really should go in and shower and shave. If you don't mind, darling, I have your tux hanging from your closet hook. I would just love to see you in that tonight. Would that be all right, sweetheart?"

Staring into those beautiful blue eyes of hers, he happily answered, "Anything for you, doll. You do know that I'll be wearing that tux four times in the next two months. So do you know how special this makes you?"

She lovingly smiled at him and then giggled, telling him, "Welcome to Hollywood, darling."

An hour later, Bob came strolling into the living area, wearing his very stylish black tuxedo. Alex was captured by how dashing Bob looked, with a red cummerbund around his waist and a red kerchief in his left breast pocket.

Corey was taking it all in and told him, "Oh my god! You really need to wear that tux more often, Robert Brian. You are a beautiful man."

Haddie, agreeing with Corey, stated, "You certainly are, Mr. Bob. You make a good-looking birthday boy." Bob smiled and thanked her.

Alex was almost afraid to give any compliment to him, for fear it might expose her untenable attractiveness to him. She simply told him, "You look so handsome tonight, Bob."

Bob bowed and thanked her.

However, Corey felt deep down, with her practical ingenuity, that Alex found Bob inviting.

At five-thirty, Corey asked Bob to drive them to the restaurant, in one of the two Cadillacs she had. Bob was more than willing, but couldn't figure out why Curtis wasn't driving.

At almost six, the four of them walked into Tu Es Mon Monde; it seemed that every table was full of people, except the one table that was Bob's table. That table was fifteen feet from the black-satin-finished parlor grand piano up in the heart of the restaurant.

Of the seven tables that sat six people at each, there were three out in front of Bob's table that formed an arc. There were two tables beside him, a little to the side, and the last table was to his left, a small distance behind his table. The thirty-square-foot dance floor was located just behind the arc of the three tables.

Bob, Corey, Alex, and Haddie started walking to their table, and everyone began standing and applauding. The three ladies were all smiles as they led the procession from the front door to their table, thirty-feet away, which was the first one they came upon. Bob was brilliantly smiling and was trying to wave at everyone.

When they reached their table, Bob held the chairs out for the three ladies. He then went to hug his sister, Elizabeth, and Drake, who were standing and clapping and were assigned to sit at his table.

Bob motioned for everyone to sit as he remained standing. After everyone was seated, and the room became silent, he looked around the tables and just shook his head in seeming disbelief and playfully stated, "Wow! I didn't know I knew this many people." Everyone laughed loudly. The five at his table were beside themselves with laughter.

He continued, "I want to tell all of you how grateful I am that you could make it to my cool birthday blast. I hope to be shakin' it with every one of you as we kick it tonight." That brought some mild laughter.

Corey just chuckled, throwing her head back and gently biting her lower lip. She brought her head back down, facing the table, and lightly shook her head, attributing the new rock jargon to his exuberant youthfulness.

Bob pointed out, "As I look around the room, I see all these primo actors and actresses that I've had the privilege to work with—

or will one day be able to work with. I see Stanley Kabrinski and his lovely wife, Eve. I can't believe you flew all the way in from New York City. What's going on? Do I owe you some money?" The room roared with laughter.

"Of course, as most of you must know, Stanley is one of the most intrinsically talented Broadway directors and producers I've had the honor to work with. But then, I've only been in one Broadway play, so, there you go." There was more laughter.

All of a sudden, Stanley yelled out, "I'd like to change that fact, Mr. Richardson."

Bob laughed and joked back, "I'm not sure. Have we even met, Mr.... Kabrinski?"

Everyone was laughing again.

"Well, all I'd like to say now is I want to circulate the room and talk to each and every one of you before we order our dinner. So, drink up, but try not to get blitzed before dinner." There was a mild applause, as Bob leaned over and kissed Corey and told her he'd be back shortly.

He headed out to the tables and shook hands with director Rennie Whitmore and producer Cameron Thompson, sitting with their wives. Also, actors Richard Carlson, Lee J. Cobb, Lew Ayres, Cornel Wilde, Richard Widmark—all with their wives or dates.

The women he hugged and talked with were Debbie Reynolds, Susan Hawthorne, Shirley Jones, Dorothy Malone, and Martha Hyer. This also included the wives or dates the Night Owls, and Nick, brought with them.

At around seven o'clock, Bob returned to his table to order his dinner, along with the rest of his guests. He hugged Corey and asked the five at his table what they were having. Elizabeth said, "It seems the four of us women are going to start with the lobster bisque, and then the entree, that will be the coq au vin—the chicken braised in red wine, with bacon and mushrooms. It just sounds delicious."

Bob looked at Drake, and all Drake could say was, "Sorry, ladies, I like my red meat. I'll be having the soup and then the boeuf bourguignon."

"Well, I think you have great taste, Drake. I'll be joining you with the beef dish." He then caught a waiter and ordered a couple of bottles of Dom Perignon for every table at the party.

After the food was served, and everyone had eaten, the partygoers were now enjoying an after-dinner drink. Then suddenly, the lights were dimmed to a very subtle tone, and the doors to the kitchen opened, throwing a narrow tunnel of light onto the guests.

A three-layered birthday cake was rolled out of the kitchen on a cart, and the cart was placed in front of Bob's table. The twenty-four candles atop were blazing like a barbecue that had been doused with gasoline and was left unattended.

Corey, smiling with such satisfaction, stared at Bob's face for his reaction. He laughed out loud with pleasure as he rocked his head and body back and forth while still seated in his chair.

Bob then looked at Corey with such a look of love that he had to turn his body to her; he took her in his arms and then kissed her straight on the lips. He whispered in her ear, "I just love you to the moon and back, Alice."

Corey laughed out loud as he brilliantly smiled. Then he lost the smile. He stared at her and seriously told her, "There is just no end to my love for you."

Her eyes started moistening as he kissed her again. Everyone in the room witnessed the enormous amount of love Corey and Bob had for each other. Even Alex could see they were strong and unaffected by outside influences of any kind.

Most of the women in the restaurant were overwhelmed with delight that a man would show in public so much of his emotional side before so many people.

Bob very attractively smiled at Corey as her face radiated the immense love she had for him. Then he rose from his chair and headed for the cake.

He stood before it and acted like he was going to make a wish, but he came to the realization of which he stated aloud to the room, "You know, I really don't need to make a wish."

He turned around to face Corey and, with great affection, told her, "I already have everything that I have ever wanted."

Corey's eyes immediately began to fill with loving tears. She slowly rose from her seat, and not losing eye contact with Bob, she sexily walked toward him. When she reached him, as he anxiously awaited her, she put her hands on the sides of his face, stared deep into his soul, as two tears fell from her eyes, and then passionately kissed him, as though no one was watching.

After several seconds, and a few cat whistles from the Owls, Bob took Corey by the hand and then looked at the cake and then back at her and invitingly gestured his head toward the cake again.

She knew exactly what he was silently asking, as she excitingly answered, "All right, mister. Let's go!" At the same moment, they both lurched at the lit candles, and within three seconds, they had blown out all twenty-four of them. The entire room was amused by this, and applause broke out, along with much laughter.

Bob still had not relinquished his hold of Corey's hand, and after he leaned into her lips to kiss her, he lovingly led her to the dance floor. On the way, he motioned to the maitre d' to turn on some music and start cutting the cake up for his guests.

When they reached the dance floor, he tenderly told her, "I saved this first dance just for you, baby."

Corey purred, "Thank you, darling."

Then the opening notes to "At Last" by Etta James came over the public address system as the radio was sitting next to the turned-on microphone of the PA system.

After wrapping his arms around her, Bob kept Corey as close to his body as he could. He kissed her ear and then softly sang the song, along with Etta, into Corey's ear:

> At last, my love has come along
> My lonely days are over, and life is like a song.
>
> At last, the skies above are blue
> My heart was wrapped in clover
> Ever since the night I looked at you.

And I found a dream that I could speak to
A dream to call my own.
I found a thrill to press my cheek to
A thrill I'd never known.

When you smiled, the spell was cast
And here we are in heaven.
I found my love, at last.

As the song slowly came to an end, Bob placed his right hand behind her neck and slowly pulled Corey's face toward him, and they kissed very sensually.

When they looked up, there were a handful of other couples that had been dancing near them, but Bob and Corey hadn't noticed, or didn't want to.

Bob tried to dance with all the ladies as the night moved along. Doug even tried to cut in on him, as Bob danced with Doug's date, Ann Margaret. When Bob started to step away, Doug grabbed Bob's hands, and not Ann's, and began to dance. The people on the dance floor around them were shaking their heads and laughing.

Bob playfully laughed, and then Doug motioned for Bob to go away as Doug took Ann's hands and began to dance, while she was still smiling and chuckling at both of them.

Corey had a few dances with some of the men, but when Bob danced with Alex, Corey preferred to stay at her table and observe. There didn't seem to be any inappropriate behavior by Alex; they just talked most of the time they were on the dance floor, and Bob kept a comfortable distance between them.

Bob soon returned to his table and sat down beside Corey. He took a mouthful of his wine when his sister, Elizabeth, asked him, "Bobby, I want to ask you something."

Bob smilingly answered her, "Anything, big sister. What's ya got cookin'?"

Elizabeth pointed out, "You know that big beautiful parlor grand piano they have right over there?" She looked and pointed it out to him. "Could you play something for your big sister and your guests?"

Len heard Eizabeth's question as his table was just a couple of feet away and the closest one to Bob's table. He spoke up and asked Bob, "Yeah, Bob. Go and kick it loose on the ivories!"

Len then asked the maitre d', "Would it be all right for the birthday boy to play your piano?"

He answered Len, "Why, of course, monsieur."

Len then announced to the room, "Would everyone here tonight like to hear Bob play the piano? Let me hear it!" The room erupted into a thunderous applause, with a few whistles.

Corey was excited and, yet, nervous for Bob. She had never heard him play the piano and knew he hadn't been practicing on one since she met him almost two years ago.

Bob was caught off guard by his sister's request, but he felt he needed to try to play something, just for her.

He smiled and rose from his seat. There was a welcoming applause from the room. He leaned over and kissed Corey. She could sense his nervousness.

He then kissed Elizabeth on the cheek as she sat on the other side of his chair.

Alex sat watching Bob with a sense of amazement, now knowing just how gifted a musician this man really was. She looked at Corey and saw the absolute and unmistakable pride she had running through her veins for Bob.

Bob walked slowly to the piano and then sat down on the piano bench and adjusted his distance from the instrument. He started to rub his opened hands together as he studied the eighty-eight-note keyboard.

He instantly began playing "Chopsticks," and three bars into it, the room erupted into laughter. He seriously looked over at Debbie and Susan, who were seated close by, and inquisitively asked, "No?"

Debbie sat laughing and jovially clapping her hands together. Susan was playfully smiling at him and delicately shaking her head as her lips formed the word *no*.

Bob, cutely smiling, quickly looked toward his table, and Corey was smiling brilliantly and lovingly shaking her head.

He then seriously looked out at his guests, and then back to Elizabeth and Corey as he tentatively stated, "I just want you to know it's been about two years since I've played the piano, but I'll give it the old college try. This piece I'll be playing is called 'Clair de Lune' by Claude Debussy. To use the poetic and romantic jargon of my friend and fellow Owl Joshua Chambers, I would say of 'Clair de Lune': It is a journey my lady travels, to find the lover that, in her past, had eluded her, and whom she ultimately discovers, had been lying next to her the entire time, it's truly a journey of emotion and intensity. I hope you enjoy it."

Joshua smiled at Bob then looked over at Darnell, and both were taken by surprise that Bob had the making of a classical pianist and hadn't mentioned a word about it to them.

Bob fell silent, and the look of very serious concentration shrouded his face. He took one breath a second, steeling himself, getting ready.

He placed his hands on the opening keys and started out with the smooth, slow-noted legato. Then the notes turned into a beautiful staccato, with the quicker motions of light rolling strokes that were tempered by the dulcet tones of the higher notes. He crossed his bass hand over the treble hand to play the higher notes that the treble hand could not play because it was holding four fingers down, continuing the resonating sound of the previous high notes.

Bob's complete and unabbreviated emotions were put on display, with just the simple wave of his hands on the keys, as he closed his eyes, and his body moved to the beautiful notes.

It was as if he were making love to his audience with the sweet intensity of the melodic strokes he compassionately conveyed with his sophisticated and expressive dolce.

Bob looked over at Elizabeth and Corey, and each had tears in their eyes, with a few that had run down their cheeks. He smiled and winked at Corey. She lightly shook her head with loving admiration and then winked back.

The piece returned to the opening notes of sweet enrapture he had started with. The wistfulness of the notes hung in the air, with the crisp, yet soft, dulcet tones of the higher notes that were exquisitely soothing to the senses. He then softly stroked the few remaining high notes with his treble hand and slowly closed out the piece with the remaining three notes that were rolled to the ending high note.

Bob lifted both his hands into the air and slowly closed them to fists and turned his head to his guests. The entire room gave him a standing ovation. Corey was standing up, with her hands in praying position and holding them to her mouth as another tear fell from her eye.

Bob took a couple of short, quick bows and looked at Debbie and Susan. Both ladies were standing and then walked over to Bob and gave him a kiss on the cheek and then hugged him, saying, "That was just exquisite, Bob! Just beautiful!"

Before they could walk away, he told them, "Thank you, ladies. It really is all about the woman, and how beautiful she is—just like the two of you." They smiled and thanked him.

He walked back to his table, and Elizabeth hugged him tightly and kissed him on his cheek. Corey threw herself into his arms, and all she could say was, "Oh my god, darling. Oh my god! I just love you, Robert Brian!"

Moments after Corey pulled away from Bob, he lightly kissed her on the lips and then held her chair so she could sit back down, while she dabbed her eyes with her handkerchief.

Joshua, Len, Darnell, Jimmy, and Doug all came over and slipped Bob some skin as they congratulated him. Joshua emphatically told him, "We gonna talk, brother. You ain't getting away with that, no sir." Bob smiled brilliantly.

The evening ended around eleven o'clock. All of the guests seemed to have had a great time as they filed out of the restaurant, again bestowing birthday wishes on him. Some guests were more than tipsy from the free liquor that had circulated all evening. Those guests, fortunately, had a driver taking them home.

Since Bob had only two glasses of wine, he drove Corey, Haddie, and Alex back to Bel Air. On the way home, he was excitedly telling Corey, "You know, doll, Debbie and Susan mentioned the fact they would love to make another movie with me. And Stanley Kabrinski told me, this fall, he wanted to revive the musical *Oklahoma*, and he instantly thought of me as his lead actor, Curly McLain. Then, I was talking to the Owls, and they told me what Nick had already suggested to me a few days ago. He was working hard at putting a US tour together for us. He says he's already booking places in twenty-one different cities from June into August. That's when Joshua spoke up and suggested maybe I should play piano for a couple of our next new songs. He said Darnell would be all right playing lead guitar for just a couple songs each night. What do you think of all that, baby?"

Corey remained silent and simply sat in a kind of absorbed silence, taking it all in. After a few moments, she placatingly told Bob, "That's wonderful, darling. It sounds like you're going to be quite busy this year." Her face, showing plenty of unease, spoke differently.

SEVEN

Arriving home shortly before midnight, Corey, Alex, and Haddie entered the estate through the back french doors, of which Bob was holding open for them. When Bob finally entered, Corey took his hand in hers and softly said to him, "Come with me, darling. I want your opinion about something."

She led him into the huge living area, with Haddie and Alex in tow. After she felt she had him placed perfectly in the room, she let go of his hand and excitedly asked him, "Well, what do you think of it?"

Bob was perplexed and started looking around the enormous room. He was looking at everything, starting from left to right. He didn't notice anything different, until he took a double take of a beautiful ebony satin-finished Steinway concert grand piano enveloping the entire right corner of the room.

His jaw dropped open, and he became speechless by the very sight of its resplendent stateliness. He slowly turned his head toward Corey as his eyes moistened a bit. She stood next to him with tears that had welled in her eyes and anxiously awaited his honest reaction.

Bob stared at her with no emotion on his face at all. Then suddenly, and loudly, he yelled, "That's why you wanted me to drive tonight!"

Corey just laughed out loud and brilliantly smiled at him.

His face was resonating the ebulliency of his joyous heart as he stooped over a little and then cupped his arms around her buttocks and lifted her into the air, moving her head higher than his face.

Corey was thrilled beyond belief with his reaction and radiated a loving smile to Bob. She looked down upon his face, which she had cupped in her hands, and very affectionately told him, "Happy birthday, my darling man."

Bob lowered her just enough so their faces were almost touching, and he kissed her passionately, and for several seconds. When he finally brought her down on her feet, he lovingly spoke into her exquisite blue eyes, "Thank you, baby. I just love it. I am so jazzed!"

Haddie stood nearby and jokingly stated, "Well, I could be wrong, but I think Mr. Bob kinda likes it, Ms. Corey."

Alex, standing next to Haddie, remarked, "I think that's unmistakable, Haddie."

Corey, smiling, informed, Bob, "You know, I had Curtis stay here tonight to take delivery of the piano. I paid a little more for the night delivery, but now I know it was worth it." Bob just smiled at her and shook his head in disbelief. Then he slowly walked over to the concert grand, admiring every aspect of the brilliant workmanship it displayed.

As he sat down on the piano bench, Alex had followed him over and asked, "Maybe sometime soon you'll play us another beautiful piano concerto."

He looked up at her and smiled and answered, "I may just do that, Alex. Is there any particular composer or composition you'd prefer, Ms. Juilliard?"

Alex responded to his humor with an alluring smile and lightly chuckled. Then she pondered his question for a moment, and standing to the side of the keyboard, she earnestly answered, "I have always been partial to Johannes Brahms, with his violin and piano concertos and symphonies. But I also enjoy Franz Schubert and Claude Debussy—true romanticists."

"So you were actually awake when you were in those music classes at Juilliard, huh?" Bob remarked jokingly to her. Alex smiled at him lustrously with intrigue that was imbued across her entire face.

Corey stood a few feet from the end of the piano, as it ate at her that Alex's musical acumen was so defined by having spent four years at Juilliard. There were twinges of jealousy she was feeling, but she was not going to let them overwhelm her. Not yet.

Haddie stood a foot back and to the side of Corey. She slyly looked over at Corey and knew exactly what was happening: Alex was baiting and teasing Bob, inviting him into her game.

Bob resignedly told Alex, "Well, I think I'm going to call it a day. Maybe we can play around with one of those composers another time?"

"That sounds wonderful, Bob. Good night now. And I'm so glad you had so much fun at your birthday dinner tonight. It was a truly enjoyable evening."

He thanked her and then turned his attention to Corey. She was still standing by the end of the piano as she told Alex, "Good night, dear. Sweet dreams." There was a wisp of facetiousness to Corey's voice. Alex remained impervious to her tone and continued to walk out of the room.

Not moving her head, Haddie raised her eyebrows, making her eyes look comically big and round. She stared at Corey in nervous anticipation and then excused herself by anxiously stating, "Well, I'm gonna mosey along to bed now and let you two remember just how much you love and care for each other. I hope I don't hear Mr. Bob's head rollin' down the hallway later tonight. Y'all take care now, and remember, I'm a light sleeper."

Bob gave Corey a puzzled look and asked after Haddie had left the room, "What was that all about, doll?"

"In a roundabout way, she was just telling me I have nothing to be jealous about. She saw Alex flirting with you. I saw and heard Alex flirting with you. Where were you the whole time? Darling, you're just too trusting of people. I guess your naivete and your youth is just part of your charming personality, and you tend to remain oblivious to other women's flirtations."

Bob innocently retaliated, "I really don't think she was flirting. She's just trying to be a friend to not only you, but everyone else she's met. I treat her like a friend, Corey. I have no design on this woman, at all."

"Well, I've felt, from what I've witnessed and heard this week, that she has interest in you, and she most certainly has some kind of design for you." Corey took a deep, cleansing breath.

She looked him straight in the eyes and exclaimed, "Darling, you're modest, honorable, compassionate, and responsible. And no matter what you may think you are right now, I trust you implicitly. But you've got to know that no woman on the face of this earth is going to allow her man to be tempted or played with, without putting up some form of resistance. I won't say another word about this because I know you'll handle it when the time is right."

Bob stared in bewilderment at Corey as she walked away toward the master suite. Still, he was not convinced there was anything that had to be handled, but out of respect, he would definitely take a closer look at things.

The Monday of February 22, Corey had Curtis drive Alex into Hollywood to meet with Jack Windheim, the head of operations at Celebrity Studios. She was scheduled to talk with Jack the first day he had returned from his winter getaway week in Aspen—the reason he was not at Bob's birthday dinner the previous Saturday.

Alex told Jack, now that she was single again, she was excited and interested in getting back into the business of making motion pictures.

Jack told her with his bellowing, ubiquitous voice, "Well, Alex, you've been out of the business for almost seven years now. Trying to break back in with all the new, younger faces might prove to be rather daunting. There's just not a lot of roles for a forty-two-year-old woman who will, literally, be starting all over."

She tried to defend herself by adding, "I can still carry a note, Jack. I haven't lost my voice. Albeit, my lower register is more pronounced now, but the tonal quality remains. I could start out in a B movie musical, and we could see where that takes me."

Jack ended up having to tell her he would let her know if anything came up. Jack had Alex sign a one-year-minimum two-picture contract, but nothing long term for now.

At the estate, Corey was meeting with the caterer that worked the party Bob had to audition his two new Owls. She had to plan the menu for the wedding reception, the tables that would be needed, with tablecloths and cutlery, along with the assortment of liquors that would be needed, for slightly over one hundred guests.

Bob was in the living area and tinkering with his new piano. He could not believe the crispness of the notes and how the new Steinway grand piano gave him better control over the keys.

The size of the soundboard and the length of the strings influenced the tonal quality of the concert grand's fuller sound, over any other kind or size of piano. It was simply the best you could own.

The man from the catering company heard the piano music coming from inside the house and asked, "That's a great recording you have playing in there. Is that Johannes Brahms playing his Fourth Symphony?"

Corey smiled and pridefully told him, "No. That's my fiancé playing with his birthday present."

He emphatically stated, "Even better. Wow!"

As Bob was still playing Brahms's Fourth Symphony, Curtis was helping Alex out of the Cadillac in front of the house. She entered the house, having heard the piano from the driveway, and now was walking slowly into the living area. The sound of Johannes Brahms was sublime. The notes were floating in the air, and as she approached the piano, she saw Bob entranced with the melody as he blended romantically with the chords.

Alex stood studying him as he sat erect on the piano bench. His body and eyes were moving with every stroke his hands made, and she could sexually envision herself with him, for he was extremely fascinating and multitalented, which was very attractive to her. The temptation was certainly there.

Bob played the last notes and finally looked up and into the room. When he saw Alex standing and watching, he smiled and asked, "Well? How did you like Mr. Brahms?"

Alex threw her head back in joyful enthusiasm and started to walk toward him as she broadly smiled. "That was beautifully played, Bob. Just exquisite!"

She then leaned over onto the piano, with her elbows supporting her and her head balanced on her cupped hands. There was an ample display of cleavage showing from the low-cut blouse she had worn to the studio. As she leaned over, her breasts were showcased through the triangle her arms had made. Seductively, she asked, "It looks like you're enjoying your new toy. Do you like playing with toys, Bob?"

If Bob didn't know what Corey and Haddie were referring to Saturday night, he most certainly was able to figure it out now. He sat staring at only her face and thought, *This woman has me lined up in her crosshairs. Now how do I tell her to back off and stop disrespecting Corey?*

What neither Bob nor Alex knew was that Corey had seen Curtis pull the car into the garage without Alex in it. At that point, Corey curiously walked into the house, and the piano stopped playing. She stayed behind the wall to the entrance of the living area and had heard everything.

She was ready to pounce on Alex when she heard Bob start to talk.

He was still staring at Alex as he stood and moved a few feet from the piano. When he turned to her, he tactfully admonished her, "You know, Alex, the woman I love has invited you back into her life by letting you stay here with us until you find your own place. I would have sworn you had better breeding than what you've just shown to me. The fact that you would even think you had a chance with me proves you haven't been watching and listening to Corey and I when we're together. There is no one that will ever come between that lady and myself. You should perhaps try looking somewhere else."

Corey's eyes began welling with tears as her heart became exhilarated with the love she had for this man. She remained behind the wall, but was leaning up against it now.

Alex was feeling rebuffed, and listening to Bob scold her, she innocently apologized, "Bob, I'm sorry if I said something to offend you. I meant nothing by what I said. I was just joking and having a little fun with you. Again, I apologize."

She turned and started to walk to the staircase to go to her room, when Bob asked inquisitively, "Alex? We can still be friends, can't we?"

Alex turned and exhaled loudly. Then she smiled and happily told him, "Of course, we can." She continued up the stairs as Bob remained standing and feeling guilty for what he felt was an attack he made on her.

Then Corey came around the corner of the hallway wall and slowly walked toward him. He had his head down, staring at the floor. When she was a few feet from him, his attention was drawn to her. Bob started to tell Corey the whole story. "Hey, baby. I had a talk with—"

Corey instantly stopped him by putting her index finger over his lips. She looked deep into his eyes and placed her hands on the side of his face and then pulled his lips to hers. She kissed him long and passionately. His arms immediately wrapped themselves around her body as he felt the intensity of her love.

* * * * *

That Tuesday, February 23, all the Night Owls met at the recording studio. They were going to practice the five songs they'd be taking in their cache to *The Ed Sullivan Show*. There would be two slow songs and three more that were more upbeat rock 'n' roll. They would have with them the last five songs they had recorded.

Nick came to the studio to fill the new guys in on the trip to New York and what the *Sullivan Show* would be wanting from them. He had them sitting down before they could even tune their instruments and warm up.

He informed them, "We'll be flying out of LAX at eight o'clock this Saturday morning. The show has given us a six o'clock rehearsal time that night. All the instruments will be delivered to the Ed Sullivan Theater after we touch down at LaGuardia airport at four o'clock, New York time. We'll have enough time to check into our hotel and then catch something quick to eat."

Nick anxiously waited for the moment when he could tell them, "Now, I want to run something by you guys. Corey told me she would be very happy to let us use her penthouse suite over on the East Side, on Park Avenue, if we wanted to do that."

The guys all started cheering, excitedly laughing, and slipping one another some serious skin. Darnell yelled with force, "Damn! This is boss, man! Just too unreal!"

All the guys started bumping shoulders and slapping hands again. Bob, not knowing Corey had set this up, looked at Nick and just smiled as he shook his head in loving disbelief.

Nick excitedly added, "Well, I guess that's a yes! Well, it's a four-bedroom, with two long couches, so you can take your pick Saturday night. Oh, and by the way, Corey said she would have Rodney, the concierge, order in a complete buffet for you before you go to the theater to rehearse."

The group was again yelling and dancing around, slipping skin to everyone.

Joshua turned to Bob and gratefully told him, "Hey, man. You thank Corey from all of us. She is really just too much!"

Bob broadly smiled and laughingly told him, "Yeah, man. I'll be thanking her, all night long!"

All the guys just started roaring with laughter.

When the laughter subsided, Nick added, "All right, I'll be canceling the hotel rooms. That will put a little more money back in our pockets. And, Bob, I'll have you bring the cache of songs with you because the producer, Mario Lewis, will have us perform which ones he wants to see. He'll then tell us which ones we'll be playing on the show. Our airtime will be seven forty, Sunday night. They run live footage, so be prepared to start playing as soon as they open that curtain in front of all of you."

Doug added, "Yeah, man! We unload as soon as Jimmy gives us that four-count on the snare. The noise from the audience is just going to blow you away, man. I can't wait!"

Darnell turned to Joshua, quickly nodding his head with a huge smile. Joshua slipped him some skin and was nodding back at him.

Nick continued, "I'll be picking you four guys up at the house in Thousand Oaks at six o'clock Saturday morning. Bob, we'll see you at LAX, at the American Airlines counter at roughly six forty-five."

Joshua, out of curiosity, asked the group, "Hey, we never discussed what we were going to wear. Is there any specific clothing or colors we should have with us?"

The four original Owls just chuckled as Bob explained, "No, not really, Joshua. We've just always worn what we wanted to. We've never felt our band should be judged by the pretty, matching suits or sweaters that almost all bands wear. Just no sweat suits, pajamas, or swimming trunks, okay?"

All the guys got a kick out of that statement and laughed heartily.

In leaving, Nick told the guys as he walked out, "Then I'll see all of you Saturday morning, bright and early. Set your alarm clocks—I don't want any delays."

The guys then got down to business and practiced each song at least four times before they called it a day.

Bob arrived home in Bel Air close to four o'clock. He heard women's voices coming from the kitchen as he entered the house from the back. Cautiously, he slowly walked down the hall to the kitchen and could make out Corey's, Alex's, and Haddie's voices. They all seemed to be getting along famously. He couldn't hear tension in any of their voices.

Bob continued on into the kitchen. He told everyone hello as Corey moved to him and quickly kissed him on the lips. He raised his eyebrows to her, silently asking why everyone was getting along so well.

Corey pleasantly told him, "Everything is just fine, darling. Alex and I had a long talk today, and we've worked things out. We're going to find her a lover at Celebrity, and if that doesn't work out, I'll just hook her up with Louis B. over at MGM."

Everyone laughed at that prospect.

Bob whimsically looked over at Alex and bent over and asked, "Are you okay with that, Alex? Because I really think you can do better."

Alex smiled at him and stated, "It will be nice getting back to work and meeting new people. So, who knows? I just might get lucky."

Bob turned to face Corey as he brilliantly smiled at her and then took her in his arms and whispered in her ear, "Thanks loads, babe, for putting us up in your New York crib this Saturday night. You are so choice, lady. I just love you."

He kissed her softly for a few moments.

When they separated, Corey lovingly told him, "Listen, mister. That crib, as you describe it, is ours. No longer just mine. Got it?"

Bob smiled and graciously nodded his head slowly and toward her.

"And that was the very least I could do for the men in my life. I was happy to do it, darling."

Haddie was curiously watching Alex stare at the romantic interaction between Bob and Corey. She noticed Alex resignedly turning her head away as they kissed. Haddie thought to herself, *That's right, you take notes...and don't you dare try to make a mess around here again.*

That night, Bob and Corey made some very sensual love. Their bodies moved in unison as they lost themselves in each other's passion. They seemed to never get enough of each other as the sexual fervor between them continued on past midnight.

The rest of the week went uneventful; Jack Windheim sent Alex a few scripts to look over, but they were nothing as juicy as the ones he sent Corey.

The Owls' last practice session on Thursday went flawlessly. The guys were really kicking their five songs and could not have sounded better. Corey kept busy with the wedding arrangements and, Thursday morning, had Curtis take her into LA, to Santini's, a dressmaker who would be creating her wedding dress.

Saturday morning, February 27, everyone met at LAX on time. Their plane landed in New York, at LaGuardia, at four o'clock that afternoon. Nick had a limousine waiting for them, as it whisked them over to the island of Manhattan.

The guys were in awe of the penthouse suite. They couldn't get over the view from the front full ceiling-to-floor window. It showcased Park Avenue in both directions.

After all of them, except Nick and Bob, were done admiring the spacious penthouse, they dug into the buffet that was spread out over the kitchen's twelve-foot counter.

Doug boastfully said, with his mouth half full of his roast beef sandwich, "Damn, man! This is how I'm gonna live in another year or two. A mellow place like this on each side of the country. Ain't nobody gonna stop us now!"

The guys all chimed in with, "Yes, sir! You got that right, brother! Ain't nobody!"

It was almost five thirty in the evening when Nick told the guys to start heading down to the car he had waiting for them. They arrived at the Ed Sullivan Theater, with twenty minutes to check out their instruments and get them in tune.

As they were readying themselves, the producer of the show, Mario Lewis, came up onstage to greet them. With an air of authority, he asked the guys, "How are you all doing this evening?"

The guys all answered in unison, "Great, man. We're cool."

Mario continued, "Nice seeing your group again, Bob. However, it does look a little bit larger this year. What prompted that?"

Bob defensively got slightly fresh with him, saying, "I needed two more guys that could really kick it and teach us the righteous way to lay down some soulful rock 'n' roll. Darnell and Joshua are our new guys, so don't flip your wig, Mr. Lewis, but they're gonna burn it down tonight and tomorrow night."

Mario's stare was fixated on Bob as he suddenly flipped up his eyebrows and pursed his lips. "Okay, whatever you just said. Let's hear what you brought, and we'll take it from there."

The Night Owls began with "Ricochet." It was the last song the original four Owls recorded, but was rewritten to accommodate the harmonies of the trumpet and the third guitar. It was a rousingly upbeat song that had far more rock than roll.

The group played all five songs they brought with them. Mario came up onstage and called Nick up from the audience seats to talk to him also. Mario told all of them, "Good work, guys. They were all well put-together songs."

Then, with his businesslike efficiency, he stated, "All right, tomorrow night, I want you to open with 'Let Me Lay within Your Arms.' Then you're going to talk a little bit with Mr. Sullivan and finish with 'Stronger Than You Think.' Now you do know Mr. Sullivan could have you back up onstage before the show is over for a show-ending song. That's all up to him. I have nothing to do with that. So, if that should happen, I want to hear that really powerful rock 'n' roll song 'Raging Fire.' Okay, that's all for now. I want you here, behind the right curtain, with your instruments ready to go by six thirty tomorrow night. See you then…and good luck, guys. You're going to have a rough road ahead of you, and I think you know what I mean."

Mario looked over at Darnell and then back to Joshua and sincerely told them, "Just keep your focus on the great work you're doing—not the ones who are trying to undo you."

Bob's eyes began to glisten as he put his hand out to shake Mario's hand. Mario shook Bob's hand and then continued around the entire group, shaking theirs.

All the guys were pridefully looking at each other, and every one of them began to smile.

Doug spoke up with determined fortitude, "Tomorrow night, and every night after that, let's kick some righteous ass. We're the badasses here. Nobody else—and like I said before, ain't nobody gonna stop us. Right, guys?"

There was more than just Bob's eyes that began to glisten that evening.

That night, in the penthouse, Bob called Corey from the master suite's bedside phone; it was nine o'clock in New York, but only five o'clock in Bel Air.

Corey was in the living area reading scripts, but when the phone rang, she raced to the one sitting on the end table at the foot of the couch she was sitting on. She optimistically answered, "Hello? Is that you, Robert Brian?"

Bob chuckled into the receiver of his phone then playfully told her, "It had better be me and not anyone else, my love."

She smiled brilliantly and anxiously asked, "Well, how did the rehearsal go for you tonight, darling? Did all of you just blow their socks off?"

"Well, doll, they want us to start with the song Joshua wrote the lyrics to, 'Let Me Lay within Your Arms.'"

Corey cut in, "Oh, that sounds exquisite! Sing it to me, baby."

Bob continued, "Now don't start something you can't finish." She giggled sexily.

He playfully exhaled into the receiver then told her, "Then we close with the more upbeat song Len wrote the lyrics to, 'Stronger than You Think.' That's the first song we recorded that addresses a lot of what the younger generation is experiencing now."

Corey asked, "Then it's the first song you recorded that's speaking to the rebellion of our young people today?"

"Yeah, and if Mr. Sullivan invites us back out onstage to sing again, they want us to perform the song I wrote, 'Raging Fire.' That one will literally blow the first row of audience seats into the lobby. So, let's pray that happens."

"I'll keep my fingers crossed, darling." Corey, concerned, asked, "You got into the penthouse all right, didn't you, Bob? And was the buffet enough for all of you? I told Rodney that there would be seven big, burly, muscled men eating, so I had him load it up."

He assured her, "Oh, yeah. We're still eating what's left of it tonight. And speaking of tonight, I'm really gassed, babe, so I'll have to call it a night. I guess Joshua is the only one who's not familiar with the Big Apple, so tomorrow, we're going to show him around Times Square and Central Park. I promise, no one will be picking up any hookers." He laughed into the receiver.

Corey emphatically told him, "You pick up a hooker, you might as well stay there and set up house with her, because I would not want your smelly ass back here."

Still laughing, Bob tenderly told her, "I'll see you tomorrow night, around eleven o'clock. You tell Curtis I'll find him at LAX around ten thirty, he doesn't have to come looking for me. And,

Corey, when I sing 'Let Me Lay within Your Arms,' I'll be singing that to only you, baby. Good night, baby girl. Sleep tight."

Corey lovingly told him, "When you sing Joshua's song directly into the camera, I'll feel like you'll be making love to me, darling. I love you so much, that sometimes, it hurts. Good night, my beautiful man."

"Night, doll."

The next morning, all seven guys drank ordered-in coffee and was finishing off the buffet they removed from the refrigerator. They all agreed to eat dinner out on their way back from showing Joshua a little bit of the Big Apple.

The guys were all showered, dressed, and ready to leave by six o'clock that Sunday night for the *Sullivan Show*. When in the theater, they all moved toward their instruments behind their appointed curtain.

Each guy checked out his own instrument, and the three guitars had to be tuned before Ed came out onstage to start the show at seven o'clock.

Back in Bel Air, Corey had at least two dozen people over to watch the program out in the living area. She had her Motorola TV situated just right and all the furniture turned to face it so no one had a bad seat.

Almost all the people that were there worked at Celebrity, including Jack Windheim. It was almost four o'clock, Sunday afternoon—probably the best time for getting working actors and actresses together to party. All of the Owls' and Nick's significant others welcomed Corey's invite to come over and watch the show. Elizabeth and Drake also thanked Corey for asking them to come. Corey introduced the guys' ladies, Haddie, Elizabeth, Drake, and Alex to everyone by getting the guests' attention and then just announcing them one at a time.

It was minutes from four o'clock, and everyone settled down and took a seat and became instantly glued to the set.

Corey's group had been there since three that afternoon, drinking and eating the food she had catered in for the party. Some were already getting slightly inebriated and started to demand *The Ed*

Sullivan Show had better start soon. They were all very curious about seeing the new faces of the Owls and anxious to see Bob perform.

At exactly four o'clock, a commercial for Fab, a laundry detergent, came on the channel everyone was focused on. Then Mario Lewis's voice followed the commercial, saying, "Welcome to *The Ed Sullivan Show*, coming to you tonight from the Ed Sullivan Theater, in New York City. Now here's Ed Sullivan."

The audience was prompted to applaud until Ed decided he wanted to start talking. Then the applause died down to a tomb-like silence.

The guys were set up behind the curtain but had to wait forty minutes for their turn. They all seemed calm and ready to kick out some tunes—all but Darnell. He was the only one who had not experienced playing in front of hundreds of people, and on nationwide TV. The nightclub he worked in, Raisins on the Roof, he played five nights a week to a couple dozen people, who most of the time were talking, drinking, and basically just trying to get lucky that evening.

Darnell was fidgety and sweating up a storm. His heart was thrumming in anticipation, and he kept taking deep breaths, trying to calm himself.

Bob looked over at Darnell, and his nervousness was very noticeable. Bob had his guitar strapped to his shoulder and ready to start, when he moved over to Darnell and stood beside him. He spoke in low tones, as not to be heard by the stage manager. "Hey, B.B.? We're cool, man. You be that badass guitarist that we know you are. We got this all night long, man. Okay?"

Darnell nodded his head affirmatively and reassured Bob, "It's okay, man. Once I play that first chord, this shit is in the groove."

Bob and Len both smiled at Darnell and slipped him some skin. The band members were now slipping skin to each other and pumping their heads defiantly.

Out in front of the curtain, the Owls could hear a moderate applause coming from the audience, in response to a female opera singer. They knew it would only be twenty more minutes until that curtain would fly open for them.

Haddie was talking out loud to herself, and to anyone who wanted to listen—from the anxiety she was feeling in waiting for the band to start playing. "Why do these shows play on your last nerve? They show all this other stuff that no one nohow has any sane desire in watching. I just want to yell at that TV and tell 'em to bring out my boy and his brothers. Now that would be worth all the time and money in the world for me."

A handful of the partygoers all yelled and cheered Haddie's little speech. Corey was sitting by Elizabeth and loudly stated, "Hear! Hear!" Elizabeth and Drake lightly applauded.

Jack made his presence known when with his loud and ubiquitous voice warned, "All right, I think everyone here knows about the Night Owls. And if you haven't, you most certainly know Bob Richardson, anyway."

Corey beamed with pride and with an enormous smile that warmed the entire room.

Jack finished his statement. "This group is phenomenal, and only better, I've heard, since they've added two new guys to the mix. With a musical wizard like Bob running the band, of course, they're not going to put these guys on until they've showed you every sponsor's commercial they have—they have to pay the bills, too. It's probably only another few minutes. Hang in there, people."

While the audience was still applauding the second-to-the-last act, Ed Sullivan walked out onstage, and the applause died away. Ed asked the audience inquisitively, "Well, wasn't that a good juggling act? Let's hear it for the Rudolph family!"

The audience mildly applauded, and Ed added, "However, I really don't think they're related to Santa Claus." There was slight laughter coming from the audience.

Ed then got serious and announced to the audience and into the cameras, "Now, we have for the last performance of the night a group who has come to us from the Los Angeles area." The young women in the audience started screaming, and there was appreciable applause from most everyone.

Ed waved his arms up and down, and the din of the studio started to lower, but never completely disappeared. He then added,

"This band has been around professionally for almost two years. I understand they just added two new members in the last five weeks. They have toured Europe and will be touring the US starting this June. They have two albums and twenty-four singles out, with a handful of them climbing the charts. So, tonight, here they are, the Night Owls."

The young women started screaming, and the boys were cheering, before the curtain was fully opened. As the curtain flew completely away from the band, Jimmy started with the four-count beat of his drumstick on the snare's rim.

Immediately, Len and Darnell started the bass notes as Bob started to play the melody lines. The slow, romantic song was written to a guitar groove. Before Bob started the vocal passages, Joshua tenderly entered in with his whispering mistress, the bass trumpet. Doug was running a melodic riff with his alto sax, complimenting Joshua's beautiful and passionate notes of love.

The triumphal opening chords were glorious and the very basis of the harmony. Bob then started to vocalize the lyrics very provocatively, with his very gifted sense of melody and his perfectly pitched baritone. He was lovingly looking straight into the number 1 camera and sang:

> Let our souls blend tonight,
> For what we have seems so right.
> Make me tell you, "I'll never let you go,"
> An eternity with you is all that I know.
>
> (Chorus)
>
> Let me lay within your arms,
> Let me feel your warming touch.
> You'll always have my love with you.
> It seems a dream to me, but not much.
>
> I'm drawn into your look of love,
> It's not wrong with powers from above.

You give me happiness and joy.
Love me, but don't treat my heart like a toy.

(Chorus)

You touch my soul with those eyes.
Don't pierce my heart with any lies.
Tell me you'll love me till the end of time.
For loving me would make you mine.

(Chorus)

Magic is what happens when I'm with you.
How you talk and touch me is always new.
Melt together with me, as we dance,
As I will lose myself in your loving trance.

(Chorus)

As the last word of the chorus was sung, the entire theater exploded into a controlled frenzy. The young women were screaming with delight, and the young men were clapping loudly and cheering. The theater was filled with excitement and wildly appreciative fans.

Bob, Len, and Darnell took a synchronized step forward and bowed together to the audience, with guitars still strapped to their shoulders. Bob then raised his right arm and, with an opened hand, pointed toward Doug, Joshua, and Jimmy. The applause was almost deafening to the guys.

Bob was smiling at a group of young women sitting in first row, left. He suddenly lifted his right hand, and with his index finger, he pointed directly at one of them and smiled broadly. The young woman slapped her hand to her heart and gasped for air as she fell back into her seat with tears rolling down her cheeks.

Ed came out onstage, smiling, and started to fan his arms up and down to quell the noise coming from the audience. After another ten seconds, the theater became somewhat quiet. At that point, Ed started interviewing the band. "That was great, guys. You seem to have some fans here tonight."

The screaming and applause flared again.

Ed then asked Bob, "Bob, tell me about your two new members to the group. I remember last April, you were only four. And now you've grown."

Bob laughed lightheartedly and smiled, explaining, "Yes, Mr. Sullivan. We've added two new Owls to the nest."

Ed smiled and chuckled at the reference.

"We felt we needed another guitar and a piece of brass to give us that more orchestral sound. So when we began writing more progressive music, these two fantastic musicians were going to fill those passages for us. And by the way"—Bob pointed to Darnell—"that's Darnell King, alias B.B. King, on the semi-acoustic guitar"—then pointed to Joshua—"and that's Joshua Chambers, alias Dizzy Gillespie, with his smokin'-hot bass trumpet."

The audience applauded enthusiastically, and there were a few women that screamed. Some guys yelled, "Yeah, man. Cool!"

Ed started talking again. "That's really something to be commended for, guys…but now I'm sure everyone wants to hear your next song. So, now let's hear it for the Night Owls!"

As the guys opened up on the more upbeat song, "Stronger than You Think," Corey sat before the TV, not moving, but with her eyes filled with prideful tears of joy. She was still so emotionally moved by Bob singing the Owls' love song into the camera to her that she seemed paralyzed and lost in her love for him.

All her guests were commenting on the fact the Owls were so intrinsically talented and ahead of their time; there really was no other group so inextricably joined together as these young men seemed to be.

Everyone in the room quieted down as Bob started singing the group's last song. The audience received this song almost as well as the first, but not quite. There was still screaming and loud applause, and the cameras kept rolling as the curtain slowly closed in front of the group.

Ed came walking back out onstage as the audience was still applauding.

Corey pleaded into the TV, "Call them back out. Please, just call them out there again!"

Haddie heard Corey's plea and boisterously stated, "You need to call my boys back out there, Mr. Sullivan, or I'll be out there quicker than you can shut your mouth on those big old teeth of yours!"

Everyone in the room just started howling with laughter. Corey looked over at Haddie and just loudly chuckled at her as her attention immediately went back to the TV.

Ed spoke to the audience, "Well, that was a really big show! I want to thank our guests for coming tonight and all our sponsors that help make this show possible."

Elizabeth threatened, "Don't you dare say good night, you turkey!"

Ed added, "My producer, Mario Lewis, tells me we have four more minutes to fill. So, I'm going to bring the poodle act back out."

The audience started booing, and all of Corey's guests just screamed their disappointment. Ed started laughing and explained, "Oh, that's right, we didn't have a poodle act tonight."

Corey sarcastically spewed, "Very funny, you little gnome."

Ed then shouted, "Of course, let's have those Night Owls back out here! And now let's hear it for the Night Owls!"

The theater's audience and Corey's guests joyfully yelled their approval as the curtain flew open once again in front of the group.

Jimmy gave the four-count on his snare and then just started punishing it with a time signature that could melt steel. The bass drum entered in as he hit the crash cymbal in almost every bar. Len and Darnell started to lay down heavy strokes on their strings when Bob followed them with his lead guitar screaming a run of melodic chords that would captivate the audience as it made their ears bleed.

All three guitars were synchronizing themselves to the chord progressions when Joshua's C trumpet opened up with a loud and spiteful riff. He was trying to push the first row of seats in the theater out into the lobby. Doug then started to wail on his alto sax with some heavy and foreboding notes that screamed of the defiance for the man.

After a minute of this aggressive instrumental musical blending, it eventually led Bob into his impassioned vocal entrance of "Raging Fire."

> They come at us with loaded guns that are held
> on shoulders high.
> I start bleeding hard and turn to tell all my friends
> goodbye.
> No one can stop the fury they show in their eyes,
> And now I see it's my own kind puttin' out the
> lies.
>
> (Chorus)
>
> We can't last long now, the end is really near.
> Believe me, brother, we've lost everything that's
> dear.
> We pray to keep our lives to God, who's watching
> from above,
> But the man has taken away our peace, our youth,
> and now, our love.
>
> Help me rein this terror in and change the raging
> fire.
> No one seems to listen to us, because every gun's
> for hire.
> We wish we knew why there's always a top gun
> in the world,
> As strangers shoot at our flying flag, as it remains
> unfurled.
>
> (Chorus)

The load just becomes too much for our youth
to carry,
But we'll show them, as they place our bodies
down to bury.
We didn't give up our innocence, just asked for
so much more.
For we all know, the consummate evil in this
world is war.

(Chorus)

Bob was practically screaming the last two lines of the chorus as his eyes welled up with tears. The band ended the song on the same crashing note, and everything, and everyone, became still and frozen in their last position as they held that note.

The theater exploded, once again, into a thunderous eruption of applause, screaming, screeching, whistling, and yelling voices. No one could hear the person talking next to them. The galvanic effect the group had on this audience was unspeakable. Some of the younger people in the audience had tears in their eyes and kept sympathetically staring at Bob as they perceived the significance of the song.

Bob was so emotional at this point because he was convinced the weeks of planning and preparation for this moment had borne their first fruit. He was absolutely sure that this generation was on the precipice of earth-shattering change.

The camera ran a close-up shot of Bob's face as a tear streamed down his left cheek. It showed him trying to fight back further tears as he pursed his lips and exhaled deeply. The band took their final bow, all together, at the same time. They all smiled and waved to the audience; some were blowing kisses to the young women. Then the curtain slowly descended upon them as the cameras cut away to a commercial.

Corey sat in front of the TV with tears flowing freely down her face after seeing Bob so noticeably moved by his song.

Haddie handed her a tissue and consolingly told her, "Now, Ms. Corey, all our boys were just spectacular tonight. Those were tears of joy racing down Mr. Bob's face. He knew what that group of men accomplished tonight. Ain't no doubt about it!"

Corey just smiled at her and nodded her head affirmatively. She lightly blew her nose into the tissue and went back to her delightful thoughts of him.

Many people came up to Corey and told her how incredible the Owls were. Jack moved in front of her as she stood dabbing her eyes with her tissue. He loudly exclaimed, "Corey, you have an unbelievable man there in Bob."

Her heart was so filled with pride and love for Bob, she could only answer, almost inaudible and breathily, "I know, Jack."

Jack, being concerned, asked, "With all this fame and fortune coming his way, with this band, I hope he doesn't have any ideas of stopping his work in motion pictures. That would be a great loss to the studio, you know."

Corey immediately reassured Jack, "Yes, it would be, Jack. But I happen to know he enjoys making pictures, and especially with me. So, I know we'll be ready to start up again five weeks from now. You can count on it."

Several people stayed past the dinner hour, just talking and drinking. However, all Corey could think about was Bob coming home to her in a few hours.

As her guests started to file out, Corey reminded each and every one of them about the wedding in three weeks. All of them gave her a thumbs-up and said good night.

At the front door, Susan Hawthorne was the last to leave. Susan stood by the door and tentatively told Corey, "If you remember last fall, at our wrap party for *Jumping Off the Deep End*, I told Bob I was happy he had found the right music for dancing. I know now, beyond all reasonable doubt, I was absolutely right."

Susan leaned over and kissed Corey on the cheek and lightly hugged her, gladly saying, "Good night, Corey, and thanks for inviting me over. Now you take care of that man. There's going to be women around him and after him from this moment on."

"Don't worry, Susan. I've been beating them back for almost a year now." Corey chuckled.

At ten thirty, Haddie told Corey, "I'm gonna go on to bed, Ms. Corey. I'll talk with Mr. Bob in the morning. Now you two keep the volume down. You know how sounds echo in this house." She laughed teasingly and kept on walking back to her room off of the kitchen. Corey just smiled mischievously and headed for the master suite.

Corey showered and put on her most seductive and low-cut, light-blue silk negligee. She was determined to stay awake until he came home. She propped herself up in bed, on two of the pillows, and began to read a book.

She read for over two hours when at eleven thirty, she heard Bob coming through the french doors and then walking toward the bedroom.

Corey's heart started racing with intense anticipation as she immediately closed the book and set it on the nightstand.

Bob walked into the room and instantly focused his brilliant smile upon her. Corey got up and stood beside the bed as her breathing became labored. She started to walk toward him, and he asked her, lifting one hand up, "Just stand still, baby."

Bob stood in place after setting his suitcase down. He expelled all the air from his lungs. Still staring at her and wanting her beyond belief, he finally remembered to breathe.

Now his breaths were in short gasps as he sensually confessed to her, "Corey, I need to tell you that every time I look at you, you have always been able to take my breath away. I just can't love you enough."

After hearing that, she raced into his arms. Bob wrapped his arms around her, and they fell into a deep, passionate kiss. He was moving his hands up and down her body as she stood running her hands around his neck and through his hair.

Several seconds later, Corey began to unbutton his rolled-sleeve dress shirt. She then started to kiss his chest, rubbing her hands over the nipples, and then lovingly biting at them.

Bob couldn't contain himself any longer. He bent down and placed one arm behind her back and the other under her legs. He then lifted her up into his chest and carried her over to the bed.

He softly laid her down on the sheets after he tore the comforter from the bed with just one hand. He quickly removed his belt and unzipped his pants. With great haste, he stepped out of the pants, and his underwear went with them, along with his socks.

Corey was now staring at his beautiful naked body as he climbed into bed and straddled her one leg. They were both breathing quite heavily when Bob lowered the top of her negligee. His mouth and tongue discovered her right breast as his hand moved tenderly over the left one. He was running his tongue over the nipple and then began sucking as much of the breast that he could get into his mouth.

After he moved totally on top of her, Corey was moving her pelvis into his excitement. She ran her hand down to rub and stimulate him. They both began to moan and move together as neither could wait any longer.

Bob, with no further thought, entered her and into the wetness of her awaiting love.

As they began to move together, Bob breathily whispered into her ear, "Oh my god, baby. I will love you till the end of time."

Corey's eyes were moistening when she threw her arms around his neck and lovingly responded, "Darling, you will always be mine. I love you so damned much."

They savagely kissed each other as he moved to kiss and suck at her neck. Bob continued moving his hips into hers when he climaxed with what seemed like a strong electrical current that ran through his body. He continued moving with Corey's body until she exploded into a huge vaginal orgasm. She pulled him very tightly into her body, and they kept moving with his continued thrusts.

Soon, they were just lying still, with him on top of her. Both were now breathing very hard and labored. They again kissed deeply and passionately, and for several seconds.

When their kiss ended, Bob lowered himself so his head was lying between her breasts. He moved his hands up and under her shoulders, cupping the back of her collarbone with his open hands.

Corey held his head, with one hand stroking his hair and the other gently caressing the side of his face. They ended up falling asleep for several hours lying just like that.

EIGHT

The next morning of February 29, Haddie was already out in the kitchen at seven o'clock, getting things ready for a breakfast of waffle and eggs for the four of them.

She got the waffle iron out of the cupboard and then jokingly said out loud, "I don't know what on earth I'm doing here. Them lovebirds ain't gonna fly the nest for 'nother day or two."

So Haddie decided to just go into her room and call Joshua, until she could hear Corey and Bob making some noise out in the kitchen. When Deidra answered the phone, Haddie asked, "Hey, daughter-to-be, how's my boy? What'd he say 'bout last night on the show?"

Deidra giggled a little bit and told her, "He was just beside himself with pride and excitement for this band. He more than once said he couldn't wait for that US tour in June and July to start. He sounded like he had a great experience working with those guys."

Haddie was joyful hearing that and told Deidra to have him call her when he finally rolled out of bed. Deidra told her she would do just that.

Alex had dressed and came down to breakfast, but she only had coffee for now. She wanted to wait for the four of them to eat together, so she took her coffee and went out and sat by the pool.

Corey had asked Alex, a week after she arrived in Bel Air, to be one of her attending bridesmaids. Of course, Alex told her she would be honored. Her remaining three bridesmaids were Elizabeth,

Debbie Reynolds, and Susan Hawthorne. Corey particularly wanted Haddie to be her maid of honor, and Haddie was absolutely thrilled to be the steeped-in-tradition, unmarried lady who would be attending to the queen. Haddie and Corey had a special bond. They seemed like sisters to each other, for Haddie had worked for Corey for over seventeen years now; and to Corey, she really seemed like a roommate to her. Albeit a paid roommate.

It was another two hours Before Corey and Bob came strolling hand in hand into the kitchen. Haddie comically told them, "By the look on your faces, it seems like all the heavens opened up last night and showed you the glorious face of our Savior. 'Cause I thought I heard a few 'Oh my god's' coming from in there."

Corey, knowing Haddie was kidding, laughingly admonished her, "Oh, Haddie, you didn't hear anything like that. I don't think, anyway. However, I think there was something transcendent between Bob and I last night."

Corey, smiling brilliantly, looked at Bob, and his face reflected only his unending love for her. Then he facetiously told Haddie, "Yeah, Haddie, you know that chandelier in the master. Well, it's gonna need some repair after last night."

All three of them laughed out loud as Haddie joked, "That probably happened at the same time those tremors were shakin' my bedroom walls like crazy."

They began to laugh again when Haddie happily told Bob, "Being serious now, I wanted to tell you, Mr. Bob, that the band was fantastic last night on *The Sullivan Show*. You were really puttin' down the beat! Yes, sir."

"Thanks, Haddie. We had a blast, and things couldn't have gone any smoother than they did."

Haddie, kidding with Corey, told Bob, "Yeah, couple of times, I almost threw Ms. Corey a lifejacket. I thought she was gonna drown herself in those tears she was shedding for you."

Corey looked at Haddie slightly embarrassed and then changed the subject purposefully. "Well, anyway, darling, I want you to know, that when you're at the recording studio tomorrow, I'm having Curtis take Haddie, Alex, and I into LA to my dressmaker, Santini's. I'm going to have a fitting for my wedding dress, and Debbie and Susan are coming in to have their bridesmaid dresses fitted, along with Haddie and Alex. You did know the wedding is in just two weeks and five days, didn't you?"

Surprised by that, he told her, "Wow, it's fast approaching, isn't it? I can't wait, doll." Corey beamed in answering him, "I can't wait either, sweetheart."

Bob asked out of curiosity, "So, Haddie? Corey told me you're to be her maid of honor. I think that's so cool."

Haddie boastfully answered, "Yes, Mr. Bob. Ms. Corey knows who her best girl is. And besides, it's my honor to take care of the bride-to-be."

At that moment, hearing what Corey had said, Alex continued on into the kitchen. She excitedly asked Corey, "Corey? I'm so anxious to see your dress, and to actually see it on you is going to be wonderful."

Corey instantly answered her, "I know, Alex. I can't wait either. Tell you what. We'll make a morning of it with the ladies and do some shopping at some of the boutiques in LA."

"That sounds great. I'll be ready in the morning when you and Haddie are."

At the recording studio the next morning, Bob had the guys working on the song he would sing to Corey at the wedding. The Owls would be playing their instruments and would be Bob's vocal backup. He had written the lyrics and could hear the melody he wanted, but he now wanted the guys to give him their ideas about the pitch, pace, volume, and rhythm.

They worked on the wedding song for over an hour, and they all agreed it was very smooth. So smooth, that they would record it later and add it to the playlist that would be on their third album this summer. It was actually a great song that many people would want to have sung at their own wedding ceremony.

The rest of the studio time was spent looking at and working on a song Joshua and Darnell had scratched out in the plane Sunday as they returned from New York. It dealt with the racial strife and the unanswered concerns of the colored man in America. It was called "Courage for the Fight."

That same Tuesday, March 15, Corey had received all the responses to her wedding invitations. A total head count was now one hundred and twelve people. No refusals, but an additional twelve people that would be coming as a friend of a friend. She reported this to the caterer and the floral designer so she would have enough food and the extra flower arrangements for the extra tables.

Bob was at the recording studio practicing his song to Corey for the wedding. The song "Knowing You Were Mine" would be sung to her right after their solo dance together, to "Long Journey Back to You."

The guys were really stoked about performing Bob's song at the wedding; for when he sang it, there were some misty eyes in the group.

Corey's gardener and his two helpers had been working on the backyard space for almost two weeks now. They had been trimming, fertilizing, planting, and watering every inch of the two acres the wedding would be taking place on. Her remaining third acre was filled by the orange trees she had and her spacious four-car garage.

Every kind of bush and tree known to Mother Nature and God surrounded her wrought iron fence line. There were the beautiful blue Chinese wisteria trees, three red crape myrtles and three white ones, two elegant mimosa trees with their pink powder puff flowers, and the gorgeous jacaranda tree with the exquisite purple blossoms it displayed year-round.

At the base of all the trees, there were many red and pink flowering rosebushes. These were centered among bunches of radiant African blue lilies, blue verbena, and yellow and crimson bush snapdragons.

A blanket of deciduous ferns encompassed the beautiful year-round blue and lavender hydrangeas that sat nestled under two of her gorgeous cypress trees. The deep-blue-to-white California lilacs and the five rockroses with their pink hibiscus-like flowers that attracted hummingbirds into the yard formed their own retaining wall, fifteen feet back, from the end of the seventy-five-foot-long, rectangular pool.

This enclosed acreage was truly the Shangri-la Corey loved most about this property. She knew she had made the right decision in having the wedding here in her very own paradise, with her very own prince charming.

The Thursday morning of March 17, just three days to the wedding, Corey sat with Bob in the kitchen sipping at her coffee as he ate his breakfast.

She warningly told him, "You know, darling. You're going to have to leave the house tomorrow morning and not come back until the wedding on Sunday."

Bob shot her a look of disbelief and asked, "What? What are you talking about, doll?"

Corey tried to explain to him. "It's an old tradition for the groom to stay away from the bride the night before the wedding. Well, I want you to stay away two nights before the ceremony, because I'm going to have all the flowers delivered Friday and Saturday. I really want the look of the back area to be a surprise to you. The flowers will all be put in place Friday and Saturday, along with the tables. The tablecloths and the flower arrangements on each table will be done Saturday."

Bob incredulously stated, "Two nights? Wow! This is going to be a real challenge. I can't be with you until we have our honeymoon in—whoa! I mean, till our honeymoon?"

Corey lovingly pleaded to him, "Oh, darling. I know this sounds like I'm asking so much of you, but I want everything to be just perfect when we become husband and wife. Would you do this just for me, Bob?"

After he resignedly smiled at her, he then acquiesced to her wishes. "Okay. All right. I'll stay away, but I'm not going to like it."

Haddie chuckled out loud and kiddingly said, "Oh, Mr. Bob, you should have such a reserve of playtime stored up in you, you could make it till the Fourth of July, and you'd still have some time left over."

Corey and Alex playfully laughed, but Bob humorously looked at Haddie and joked, "Well, I can see I'm outnumbered here. So,

I'll just get my things in the car tonight and move out tomorrow morning."

Alex smiled at him, and putting her hand on his arm, she tried to soothe him. "It really is a time-honored tradition, Bob. For when you see her walking down that aisle after you've not seen her in two days, your heart will race, and you'll fall in love with her all over again."

Corey showed an appreciative smile to Alex and then lovingly looked at Bob for a response.

He slightly nodded his head at Alex then looked at Corey with a loving smile. "I'll just get studio time for Friday to keep me busy." Then as he started to leave the kitchen, he softly kissed Corey on the lips and walked toward the door and turned to state to all three women, "And just so you know. I could watch Corey eating cornflakes, and my heart would be racing." He turned and left for the studio.

Haddie and Alex smiled tenderly to him. Corey bowed her head, exhaled loudly, and closed her eyes, knowing, all in all, it came to her, Bob was far and away the coolest human being she had ever been privileged to encounter in her almost forty-eight years of living.

At the recording studio, the guys practiced the wedding song and "Journey" half a dozen times, before Bob informed them they would also have studio time on Friday, from three o'clock until six that night. He told them Corey didn't want him near the house for Friday or Saturday because of flower delivery and setup and how she wanted that to be a surprise.

The caterers would arrive at noon, and the Owls instruments would be taken over and set up by Nick after their Saturday jam session. There was going to be a disc jockey spinning some 45s on a huge stereo record player after the Owls performed "Knowing You Were Mine."

Doug facetiously asked Bob, "You mean Corey kicked your ass out of the house? I always knew that woman had a good head on her shoulders!"

Bob bit his lower lip and, in jest, balled his fist up and pumped it at Doug. "Yeah, I guess it's some kind of tradition. All I know is that it's some kind of sadistic ritual. But then I guess I would do anything for that woman. All she would have to do is ask."

All the guys chuckled and smiled at Bob, knowing how crazy in love he was with Corey.

Curiously, Len asked Bob, "So, let me get this straight, man. You want us there at one o'clock to help Joshua and Darnell usher the guests to their assigned tables and then just visit with some of the people. Is that it?"

Bob informed all of them, "Yeah, because there'll be waiters getting drinks for the guests, and then close to the two o'clock ceremony time, you four groomsmen will head out to the pool house in the back of the yard. That's where Corey and all her bridesmaids will be. Corey didn't want a rehearsal, because then there would be no element of surprise to anything, for her and I. Nick is going to set up the instruments on the marbled landing outside of the french doors. After I dance with Corey to 'Journey,' and Len and Darnell sing the lyrics, you guys will also play and sing backup for me to 'Knowing You Were Mine.'"

Jimmy asked, "When we gonna pick up our tuxedos for the wedding? I haven't had one of those monkey suits on since Len's wedding in September of last year."

Bob comically snorted. "Our studio time isn't until three o'clock tomorrow. So all of us are going into Santa Monica, to the tailor Georgio's, who's custom-made the tuxedos, and we're going to try 'em on. Then we'll bring them back with us. We've already had a fitting, so they should be ready for us to take home."

Darnell spoke up and asked Bob, "So where you staying tomorrow and Saturday night, man? We can squeeze you in if you want."

Bob nodded his head and smiled at Darnell. "No, man, but that's cool of you to ask. I'll be driving from here, after our session, to stay with Elizabeth and Drake in LA. They'll be leaving for the wedding way before I have to, so I'll be driving into Bel Air around one thirty by myself, just before the ceremony."

Before they left the studio that afternoon, Bob reminded them, "Then I'll see all of you, including Nick, tomorrow morning at ten o'clock in Santa Monica."

Bob arrived home in the late afternoon, leaving his car parked out in front of the estate. He entered through the front door and went straight into the master suite to start packing the clothes he would be taking with him to Italy. For at eight o'clock of the wedding night, he and Corey would be leaving for the airport. They would be flying out at nine thirty that night to Italy for their honeymoon.

He also packed a small valise to take to Elizabeth's for the next two days.

Corey came into the house after sitting out by the pool for the last hour, waiting for Bob to come home. She went into the kitchen and asked Haddie if she had seen him.

Haddie told her she thought she had heard the front door open and close. So Corey moved toward the master, and upon entering, she didn't understand why Bob had two large suitcases packed and was working on one smaller one. It frightened her; it felt like her heart was pushed way up into her throat as she watched him packing.

Alarmed, she asked, "What are you doing, darling? You shouldn't need that much clothing for the next two days. What's going on?"

Bob quickly turned to her and could see the panic in her eyes. He sympathetically smiled at her and tried to placate her by flirtatiously inviting her, "Come here."

Corey moved slowly toward him and felt more reassured as she kept eye contact with him. This swarm of emotion that had been threatening to undo her started to dissipate when Bob gave her a loving smile.

He took her in his arms and kissed her warmly on the lips. She responded to him by tightly wrapping her arms around his neck and then pressing into him as she kissed him passionately, arousing her own sexual fervor.

Bob tenderly pulled away from her and explained, "Baby, I'm just packing for our honeymoon. There's just not going to be any time later to do it besides right now. The smaller bag is for the next two days while I'm away from you."

"Oh, Lord, thank you. I never thought of that. Oh my god, I can now start breathing again." Corey was now so much more relaxed as she studied the clothes in his suitcases.

Bob warned her, "You're going to need clothes for warm and cooler weather. So don't say I didn't give you some heads-up."

She jokingly told him, "Well, that would lead me to believe we could be going anywhere in the world. I need more information, mister."

Playfully, he added, "And if you don't take the right clothing, we'll just have to go shopping for you. That's all."

She played with him again, stating, "Well then, I guess we're not going to the Arctic Circle or the Sahara Desert." Bob chuckled to himself.

After dinner, Bob wandered into the huge living area and sat down at his piano. Within minutes, he began playing Chopin's rippling Waltz no. 2 in C-sharp minor. Corey, Alex, and Haddie all filtered into the room and sat quietly listening to Bob as he moved his hands softly and smoothly over the keys. He looked up and smiled at each lady and then returned his attention to playing the rest of the piece.

Alex pleasingly told him, "That was exquisite, Bob. I don't know why you don't become a true piano virtuoso. You have a beautiful inflection of tone, and your technique is very nuanced. Just incredible."

Bob just smiled at her and then quickly winked at Corey. He looked at Alex again and then glanced at Corey as she lovingly winked back at him. He was instantly all smiles.

Bob then informed them, "I think I'll play one more piece by Debussy called 'Sunken Cathedral,' then I'm going to go and take a swim. If any of you foxy chicks would like to join me, that would be a gas."

Corey radiantly smiled as Alex and Haddie looked at her face beaming with her love for her fiancé.

After Bob had hit the ending run of notes for 'Sunken Cathedral,' he arose from the piano bench and excused himself, "Thank you for listening, ladies, but now I'm going to change into my swimsuit, grab a brew, and then do some laps. Excuse me."

Alex suggested to Corey and Haddie, "Why don't we fix ourselves a drink and go out and talk by the pool? That would be nice, just sitting and sharing our thoughts."

Haddie sat looking out of the corner of her eyes at Corey and waited for a sharp rebuttal to Alex's idea, but there was no immediate response.

Corey looked at Alex with a suspicious nature; there was something evasive, and maybe even adamant, in her friend's affability. However, Corey felt a firm belief in the truth when Alex told her she would not make Bob the target of her affections anymore. Corey would have to trust her, even knowing how Alex was attracted to him.

Corey resignedly answered her, "That sounds like fun, Alex. Haddie, could you bring all of us dry martinis? We could just sit and talk about the fine subtleties of the wedding and pray we have them all covered."

Bob was already doing laps when Corey and Alex came out and sat in the loungers closest to the water. They both watched Bob swimming the front crawl, when after a few minutes had passed, Haddie brought out the three martinis and sat the tray down on the table between their chairs. Haddie took her drink and sat beside Corey and tried to listen to their conversation.

Alex started the conversation by sincerely asking Corey, "Have you ever thought about encouraging Bob to get serious about his piano? He would make such a tremendous piano virtuoso."

Corey just smiled while still watching Bob swim. She turned to look at Alex, and it seemed she possessed both confidence and an air of authority when she informed her, "Bob is his own man. He decided long before I came into the picture that his love for writing and performing rock 'n' roll, working in live theater, and making movies was his premiere interests. He has always remained impervious to the suggestion of anything else."

Alex exhaled heavily, took a sip of her drink, and stated, "It just seems he's been blessed with this prodigious musical gift, and all he really wants to do with it is play rock 'n' roll. It's just very tragic. That's all."

Haddie had heard enough when she spoke up challenging Alex's criticism of Bob. "Ms. Alex, I think you'd be wrong pushing someone away from somethin' they love, just so they're doing somethin' you might love. If I had told Joshua I would rather have had him play the piano because my main man, Mr. Duke Ellington, played it, it would have broken his heart. He was in love and totally possessed with playing the trumpet. He would have just died if I had pushed him into any other instrument. No one should ever take away someone's dreams because of their selfish nature. To this day, every time I see my boy, I can see the brilliant light of love in his eyes when he speaks about his trumpets. I would die if he ever lost that light."

With moistened eyes, Corey looked at Haddie with even more respect for her than she already had—and smiled.

Alex had to relent to this logic and yield to her compassion. "I suppose you're right. I'm sorry if I seemed harsh or severe. I guess it's just something I do love about music. A piano virtuoso is what I wanted to be, but didn't possess the full range of what that precisely demanded of a person. But you're right, I would just be living vicariously through that person I had pushed in a direction they originally did not want to go."

At that moment, Bob lifted himself out of the pool and grabbed his towel. All three ladies were intently watching him and his extremely attractive masculine physicality, when he asked, "No one wants to get wet?"

Alex couldn't take her eyes off of him as Corey lightheartedly suggested, "No, darling, but why don't you come and sit with us and talk?"

After Bob had toweled off, he slipped his T-shirt on and wrapped the towel around his hips, in respect for Corey. He knew she would not appreciate him parading around in front of Alex in just his bathing suit. He took a seat next to Alex, which made her happy.

Alex asked him, just trying to make small talk, "Do you swim every day, Bob?"

Matter-of-factly, he answered, "I'd like to, but some days I'm just too busy, or Corey and I are too busy, or we're working. So, I swim when I can."

Alex pursued the topic of playing the piano by asking, "You know, Bob, we were talking about your piano playing. I wondered if Corey had suggested to you that maybe you'd want to study to become a piano virtuoso? Have you ever thought about that possibility? She told me you probably would not. Now I must ask, why? You'd make an incredible virtuoso."

Bob looked at Haddie and then Corey, knowing they both understood him, but now he felt he needed to explain that to Alex. So with a waning degree of tolerance, he exhaled deeply and began to explain, "Well, Alex, if Elizabeth hadn't told me that I would probably need piano skills if I wanted to pursue a degree in music, I would not have learned to play at all. The piano has always been a blast and always helped me to take my mind off of things when I needed to, but I have never been in love with it."

He looked around the yard for several seconds, exhaled loudly, and continued, looking right into Alex's eyes. "You can just tell by the sound of the notes that are floating in the air if a musician is truly in love with their instrument. With my personal musical acuity, I would cite the analogical comparison to how you make love to a woman. How you touch her, how you treat her, how you care and protect her—just how deeply you love her. All that should be felt by the audience, and not just by you. So you see, I have always loved the guitar from an early age, and would never have picked any other instrument in its place."

Alex was fascinated with his whole persona and enthralled with his musical acumen. She now knew she was not only attracted to him, but she may very well be in love with him.

NINE

Friday morning, March 18, Bob was in the kitchen eating his breakfast, but was soon to leave Corey for the next two full days. Alex and Corey were also having their breakfast with him, knowing they wouldn't be seeing him until the ceremony on Sunday.

Corey was staring at Bob because he seemed somewhat pensive in his demeanor. Concerned, she asked him, "Are you all right, darling? You seem very quiet. I hope you're not upset about having to leave the house until Sunday."

Bob immediately answered, "Oh, no. Not at all. Anything for you, baby. I was just lost in thought about how much everything is going to be changing this year. I mean, we're going to be married and then jumping right into a picture together when we return from our honeymoon. The Owls will be performing everywhere with six guys now, instead of the starting four, and I'll be playing the piano for a couple of our songs at each performance. I'm looking forward to making a picture in late summer, then I'll be doing a Broadway musical revival this fall, and Stanley is lining it up to take it into London for a few weeks after that. That would take me right into next year. I mean—*boom!* Then I'll be starting another year, just like that. I really don't want to play hit-'n'-run with you, like we had to when we first got together. I may just have to sit down with Nick and shuffle some things around."

Corey took a hold of Bob's arm and pulled herself into his body as she earnestly tried to soothe him by saying, "My darling man.

Why don't we take some time when we're on our honeymoon to discuss everything that's bothering either of us. I know that's not what honeymoons are for, but they'll be no outside interference. It'll be just you and I, and we'll only talk of this matter when we have nothing else to do. Got it, mister?" She smiled brilliantly.

Bob looked at her with a huge loving grin. "I got it. That's cool."

Haddie was standing over by the sink and giggled, saying, "I'd put my last money down that there's not gonna be much talking on this honeymoon." She giggled again.

Bob laughed and said, "Let's just play it by ear."

Again, Haddie laughed out loud this time and jokingly stated, "You sure that's the body part you'd pick, Mr. Bob?"

All four of them were really laughing now as Bob stood up and facetiously announced, "Well, this has been fun! But I have to be in Santa Monica by ten o'clock. So if you ladies will excuse me. I'll see you Sunday—at the most righteous day of my life."

Corey walked with him out to his car. They kissed and hugged each other for a few more minutes when Bob told her, "Thank you for last night, baby. It was fantastic! Maybe now, I'll be able to make it until Monday night." He smiled, then seriously told her, "I can't wait until Sunday, when I first see you walking down that aisle toward me. I adore you, Corey."

Corey looked up into his eyes and tenderly whispered, "We don't need a wedding to promise to be together forever. That happened on those stairs at Jack's office, almost two years ago. You were mine at that moment, and I was yours the first time you smiled at me. I'll be counting down the minutes from now until the ceremony. Darling, I can't even tell you how much I love you. It's that much."

They kissed one last time, and as they separated, Bob passionately told her, "I just can't get enough of you, baby." Bob then slipped into his car as Corey watched the car back out of the driveway and then watched it disappear out of sight. Her eyes were misty, and her heart raced with the love for him that consumed her.

* * * * *

All seven guys picked up their tuxedos after having tried them on. They encountered no problems, and so they headed to the house in Thousand Oaks, until their studio time of three o'clock came around.

While they were all sipping on some beers, Doug suggested, "Hey, why don't we throw a bachelor party for Bob tomorrow night. I'll get a keg, we'll order some pizza, and maybe if Jimmy wants a girl, I can look for that, too."

Jimmy was the first to speak up, by warning Doug, "Hey, man. Don't go getting me any chick. Jessy and I are getting pretty tight, it's all cool, man."

Bob also warned Doug, "Don't you dare hire any strippers, either. Let's just have an all-guys bachelor party. More simply put, let's just watch football on TV, drink some beer, and eat some pizza. I want to be all put together and not bummed out with a hangover for my wedding. You dig?"

Len spoke up and let everyone know, "Yeah, Deidra, Alicia, and Charlotte are going to spend the day with Valerie over in Burbank, at our new home. So it'll be outta sight tomorrow afternoon. We'll have some kicks."

At the estate in Bel Air, Corey was working with her floral design specialist, Abigail Franklin. They were discussing where each huge pot of flowers would be placed. There were ten pots in all; a couple had the beautiful pink-to-red hibiscus, surrounded by the purple sensation allium, which drew butterflies and bees into the yard. Other pots held the spiderflowers, which had incredibly flamboyant flowers of white, pink, and red on this evergreen shrub. Two pots held the California holly, an evergreen shrub that has red Christmas berries on it all year long. One pot that had to be carried on a hand dolly, with two men assisting, contained the Coast sunflower, which bloomed year-round, and the double-white angel trumpet flowers that were surrounded by the dramatic multicolored protea flowering plant.

However, the most beautiful displayed pot had the deep purple of the Douglas iris, blended together with the hummingbird sage, which was a dark rose lilac that was just opening its March blooms.

All around the edge of that was the grandiflora petunia that grew year-round and was grown in the rarest of its colors, of deep purple.

There was indeed a wealth of luxuriant flowers in these pots that painted an incredible mosaic throughout the entire area. Every color of the rainbow was represented in this magnificent display of Mother Nature's gifts to humankind.

After getting all of the flowered pots in their places, Abigail told Corey she would see her early tomorrow morning. She would be arriving with the caterer to place the tables in a strategic pattern to create the aisle the wedding party would be walking down.

That aisle would then be covered with thousands of purple, pink, and white rose petals. These would not be dropped until just before the guests began arriving.

She also said every one of the nineteen tables, sitting six people at each, would be covered in Irish white-linen tablecloths, and there would be different floral arrangements scattered amongst all of them.

Some tables would have the fluffy red and white roses with sprigs of greenery, which would bring a look of stately sophistication. Other tables would have the florals that were reminiscent of an enchanting backyard garden. The pastel arrangement would bring the best of the blush-toned roses and the ethereal ferns, along with the more pillow-like ranunculus, and would be but one of the stems in this garden design; this arrangement showcased nature's true beauty.

The floral arrangement for the last tables, where the bridal party and wedding party would be seated, would have a brilliant mosaic of amethyst, citrine, and ruby-colored florals, which took its color inspiration from the many dazzling gemstones.

The twelve-foot-high vine arbor on the sixty-foot landing, where the vows would be exchanged, and where the wedding party would be standing, would have coral and white roses, with purple African orchids cascading down both sides and running across the top. Intermingled with the roses and orchids, there would be the fragrant white trumpet-shaped lily of the valley.

The long table, which would be just off the front of the landing area, would have the same floral design on their tables as the vine arbor. This is where the groom, bride, best man and his guest, maid of honor and her guest, would be sitting.

Before she left for the day, Abigail told Corey, "I'll be bringing your bouquet the morning of the ceremony. I want it to be the freshest that we can give you. It will be made that morning."

Corey thanked her and walked her to the door.

The Owls were at the studio and rehearsing "Journey," "Knowing You Were Mine," and Joshua and Darnell's song, "Courage for the Fight." Nick was there and told the guys the last two songs they played sounded like they could be recorded. For "Long Journey Back to You" was still bringing in many thousands of dollars almost a year after its release.

So Nick asked the soundman to be in the recording studio that Saturday morning to run the recording tape so they could get those two songs on the market after the wedding.

Each song had to be performed three times to get the most perfect-sounding copy to send to New York for the mix-down. Nick knew these songs would be in record stores in Europe, Australia, and here in the US within the next few weeks.

Before the group bugged out at noon, Nick asked them to hang for a couple minutes longer. When he had all their attention, he told them, "Look, guys. Bob and Corey's wedding is tomorrow, then they honeymoon until April 2. Bob then starts his movie with Corey, April 6. So, I'm giving you notice that you'll be playing the six thousand seats at the Los Angeles Shrine Auditorium, April 16 and 17."

The guys were very excited about that as they started slapping hands and bumping shoulders. Darnell excitedly yelled, "The LA Shrine Auditorium? That place is monstrous, man. This is so far-out and way too cool!"

Doug jumped in and told everyone, "Yeah, man. We played that in late September of last year. It was an incredible time. That's when Bob told Corey, in front of thousands of people, the date of their wedding. It was such a gas! I can't wait."

Joshua just shook his head in an excited disbelief and softly said, "That sounds solid, man. I guess I'll be taking my three lovely ladies with me: my jealous mistress, the C trumpet; my most romantically entwined midnight lover, the bass trumpet; and my gorgeous and spirited fiancé, Deidra. But, mind you, not necessarily in that order."

All the guys were cracking up and telling him that they weren't finks and that they wouldn't let Deidra know she was third on his list.

Bob drove in to the recording studio from Elizabeth and Drake's place, where he would also be spending the last night before the wedding. That Saturday morning, the group was trying to create the melody for a song Len and Bob had already written lyrics for. Before they left to go to the house, they practiced "Journey" and "Knowing" two more times.

At the house in Thousand Oaks, all seven of the guys were there watching football, eating pizza, and drinking beer, when Nick called Bob aside and asked him to go out by the pool and talk with him. Bob became somewhat concerned, but he told Nick he'd be right there.

When Bob walked up to Nick, standing by the pool, he inquisitively asked, "What's crackin', man? I'm starting to freak out here."

Nick looked back at the house to make sure none the guys had followed Bob outside. He then said to Bob in a hushed tone, "When the Owls played *The Sullivan Show* in New York City, almost three weeks ago, I came home, but I went back to New York two weeks later on an invite. Well, I was asked to come to the Birdland jazz club over on Broadway, just West of Fifty-Second Street, by an anonymous benefactor. So, not having anything to lose, I went. That night, Duke Ellington and Ella Fitzgerald were the headers at the club."

Bob's eyes got huge, his face froze, and it seemed like he wasn't breathing after hearing that.

Nick continued, "Now don't flip your wig. But like that wasn't enough to watch two of the greatest jazz performers of our time, I was told after their performance I was requested to come backstage and talk with Mr. Ellington."

Bob's facial expression hadn't changed, and his body still remained rigid. He did let out a high-pitched sound, like he had just seen a ghost. Then not believing what he had been hearing, Bob nonsensically stated, "You're shittin' me, man!"

Nick declared, "Hell no, I'm not. But I will tell you, I went backstage and met, not only, Duke Ellington, but also, Ms. Ella Fitzgerald. It was like I was floating high above my body, that was sitting down below me, and I was talking with the two of them. It was just surreal."

Bob insisted, "Well, what the hell did you talk about? He's not looking to take Joshua away from us, is he?"

Nick reassured him, "No, no. It was nothing like that. Both of them told me they had seen us perform on Sullivan's show, and they wanted to meet us. They told me what we were doing as a band should be applauded—not just for our bravery, but the acceptance we showed to one another and the diversity we conveyed to all of America. They also said that what we've showed to the entire world is that times are changing, and now small steps like this will turn into leaps and bounds later."

All Bob could say was, "Wow, that's heavy, man."

Nick, more excitedly, told Bob, "Well, I'll cut to the chase. The Duke Ellington Band, with Ms. Ella Fitzgerald, will be playing the Hollywood Bowl, Friday, May 6, and Saturday, May 7. He would like me to set up a meeting with the band early that Friday, before his concert that night, at eight o'clock."

Bob was talking loudly now. "Holy shit, Nick! Tell me you're not hanging me out to dry? The guys are going to be so jazzed about this. I can't wait!" Bob was pumping his fists very quickly close to his chest and imagining meeting these two icons of the jazz world.

Nick then asked, "Do you think you and Corey…"

Instantly Bob interrupted, "Why, hell yes, Nick! Corey and I would be in seventh heaven having Mr. Ellington and Ms. Fitzgerald over to the house for lunch and drinks. And oh my god! Haddie is going to lose her mind. When she sees those two musical icons walking up to her, she's going to melt into a puddle of nothin'. I know for a fact she will never be the same person after that."

Nick shook Bob's hand, saying, "Thanks, man. I'll set this up, immediately. Now, not a word to anyone. I want this to be a complete surprise to everyone."

Not hesitating, Bob added, "I've got to tell Corey. She's really good at keeping secrets. Hell, when you two surprised me at the end of my run in *Casual Affair* last June…when she showed up at my cast party, at Sardi's—now that was a well-kept secret."

Nick shot back, "That sounds solid, man. Just none of the guys or Haddie."

Bob couldn't contain his excitement anymore and, in a subdued manner, yelled, "Wow!"

They went back inside to sit with the guys. A couple of them asked what was going on. Nick simply told them it was business pertaining to a future commitment. The guys seemed all right with that and kept drinking and watching football on the TV.

At seven o'clock, Bob decided it was time to head back to Elizabeth and Drake's house for the night. He wanted to spend a few hours talking with them about the wedding.

He told the guys he'd see all of them tomorrow at the wedding. As he was exiting out the front door, Doug kiddingly shouted, "You better stay up late, man. This is your last night of bachelorhood."

Bob turned and was all smiles when he happily told Doug, "I know, man. And I'm loving everything that's coming."

Darnell, Len, and Joshua all agreed. "Yes, sir. Amen. Gonna be a happy day, brother."

When Bob arrived at his sister's house, he walked in, and Elizabeth told him, "Corey had called, and she said she didn't want to disturb you while you were with the guys, but she wanted to talk with you when you came in."

Bob sat and visited with Elizabeth and Drake for another hour, and then he excused himself for the evening around nine o'clock. He went to his bedroom and showered and got ready for bed when he dialed up Corey a half hour later.

The phone rang at the estate, and Corey picked it up before the ringtone had dissipated into the air. "Hello, darling. How are you tonight? Did you have a good time with the guys?"

When he first heard her voice coming through the phone receiver, Bob's heart began racing with the irretrievable love he felt for this woman. "Hey, baby. I'm doing all right, considering I haven't held you in my arms for over thirty-six hours."

Corey purred, "It seems like so much longer than that. But just try to remember, we'll be together, forever, in just sixteen hours from now. Are you ready for this life-changing event?"

He tenderly answered her, "Baby, I married you exactly one year ago, tomorrow. The only thing that's going to be life-changing is that we'll be wearing rings, and we'll have a piece of paper reminding us of the day. Other than that, you've been mine for the last year."

With tears welling in her eyes, Corey exclaimed, "Oh my god. I love you beyond belief, Robert Brian. When I see you tomorrow, I will never be letting you go."

"I'm counting on that, doll. Now I'm gonna sit here in bed… alone, and write some music or lyrics or something, to keep me occupied, so I don't drive up to Bel Air to be with you."

Corey exhaled heavily as she contently smiled and closed her eyes. "You know, darling, we'll have to spend the first few days of our honeymoon in bed. We'll live off our love."

Bob kidded with her, "The first few? We may not leave that bed until the morning we fly back to LA!"

Corey laughed out loud and assured him, "Whatever you want, my love."

He didn't want to hang up the phone, but he knew tomorrow would come much faster if he kept busy writing tonight, until he fell asleep. So he regretfully told her, "I'll see you tomorrow, my foxy skirt. And I know, you'll be the most captivating lady of all the women that will be there tomorrow."

Corey sexily whispered back, "Well, I know, for a fact, you'll be the most incredibly drop-dead gorgeous man in the whole state of California."

"What? Just California?" After Corey stopped laughing, Bob lovingly told her, "Good night, my baby girl. I love you to the moon and back, Alice."

She giggled with the nuanced sexiness that Bob had always loved since the day that he had bumped into her at the Celebrity Studio.

After a moment of silence, Corey softly told him, "Good night, my darling man. I'll never be able to tell you how much you mean to me, how much I'll always want you, or how much I absolutely adore you. I can't wait to see you tomorrow, my darling."

"Good night, my sweet, baby," Bob whispered to her.

* * * * *

The back area of the estate looked incredible, with all the magnificent colors of the flowers that were placed throughout the yard. They were in beautiful huge pots and also planted in beds around the edges of the yard. The dazzling table arrangements, that showcased the brilliance and importance of the event, were steeped with every color of the rainbow and had fifteen different flowers and stems mixed throughout them.

At twelve o'clock noon, Corey had her bridesmaids and maid of honor help her to move everything she was going to be needing to the pool house. Haddie and she had transformed the building into her dressing room on Friday. They would all be staying in there until the ceremony, and if Corey needed anything, one of her ladies would leave to get it for her.

At twelve-thirty, the guys and their ladies from Thousand Oaks arrived in Doug's DeVille. Nick and Charlotte pulled in right behind them, and not even a minute later, Len and Valerie pulled in behind Nick.

The women were all decked out in beautiful silk and taffeta dresses of all colors. They wore matching gloves and carried clutch purses that complimented the dresses accordingly. Every one of them wore their hair up, with a french twist in the back or curls cascading down the entire coiffure, with very small flowers adorning a couple of the hairstyles.

The men wore their custom-made black tuxedos that had a sky-blue cummerbund, matching bow tie, and chest-pocket handkerchief. They all looked amazing and clean-shaven for their brother Bob's wedding.

The prelude music for the guests' arrival and seating began to be played over the sound system. The music was "Clair de Lune" by Debussy. The same classical piece Bob played for his guests at his birthday party in February.

The floral designer Abigail Franklin arrived next with Corey's bouquet, the bridesmaids' wrist corsages, and the boutonnieres for the men in the wedding party, along with the two ushers.

She was told to take the bouquet and corsages back to the pool house, where the bride would be waiting for their arrival. The guys were busy having their ladies pin the boutonnieres to their lapels, when at almost one o'clock, guests started to arrive.

The caterer was trying to keep the food warm until two thirty. His tables were located more closely to the grove of orange trees near the garage. The eight waiters and the two bartenders situated behind the fully-stocked bar were waiting for the first guests to be seated before they would begin to take drink orders. All drinks and dinners would be taken directly to each table. No one would have to wait on themselves today.

All six of the guys had a copy of the seating arrangements for the guests. So as each set of guests arrived, one of the guys would immediately take them to their table. The waiters were fast and efficient in taking the drink orders and then delivering them to the correct table.

Nick asked Len, as they were waiting for someone else to seat, "Len, have you seen Bob yet?"

Len quickly looked around and shook his head, saying, "No, but he'll be here soon. Don't sweat it, man."

The many guests kept filing in, and all were dressed to the nines. There were many tuxedos, but the majority of men wore beautifully tailored suits that screamed of extreme expense. Some of the ladies wore floor-length gowns, bedazzled with expensive-looking jewelry, and long, over-the-elbow gloves. Most of the gowns worn today had some degree of a cut in the cleavage.

Doug was studying and appreciating the varying degrees of exposed cleavage, when he leaned over and jokingly told Darnell and Jimmy, "Some of these dresses are cut so low, that their breasts look like they're ready to escape the corral. They must have to glue those in place. I mean, there's so many breasts flying around the yard, that someone might mistake the wedding for a Kentucky Fried Chicken restaurant." The guys just laughed out loud and tried not to make their perusal over the guests' breasts so obvious to everyone.

The makeup on each lady looked as if a makeup artist at Celebrity had applied it on their face, and the sparkling lipstick they wore looked as if it was from Ardennes of Paris.

The yard area was audaciously bedecked with Hollywood stars; directors, producers, and even two CEOs of studio affairs were in attendance; Jack Windheim of Celebrity and Henry Tremont from Command Studios.

Present was Richard Carlson, Anne Baxter, Dorothy Malone, Connie Stevens, Shirley Jones, and Joel McCrea, Lee J. Cobb, Martha Hyer, and Cornel Wilde, Richard Widmark, Ann Sheridan, Rita Hayworth, Robert Ryan, and Hope Lange. These were just a handful of the show business luminaries from Celebrity in attendance today. They all attended with their spouses or their dates for the event.

Jack Windheim attended with Ann Margaret on one arm and Deloris on the other.

Jack found out they were assigned to the same table, so he asked Ann if she wanted to ride in with Deloris and him.

Ann was decked out in a very sophisticated, formfitting pink silk dress with white sequins running around the bodice. There was a generous cut to the cleavage, and most people could not take their eyes off of her.

Doug met Ann and Jack as they approached the tables, and with a loving grin, Doug remarked, "You look so choice, Ann. It's really cool you could come today. We're gonna have some kicks."

Ann happily replied, "I wouldn't have dared missed it. I've been looking forward to this wedding for some time. Yes, I think we'll have a good time today, Doug."

Then Doug showed her to their table down in front of the bride and groom's table while Jack headed for the pool house.

It was now one fifteen in the afternoon when Jack lightly knocked on the door. Alex opened the door and ushered him in. Corey was completely dressed by this time, and Haddie was helping her to apply her makeup. Corey's beautiful long, auburn hair was gathered on her head and interweaved with strands of glorious winter-white french lace, and very small groupings of baby's breath flowers were added for accent. Corey had her regular hairstylist at Celebrity, Nina, style her hair there at the house early that morning.

Resoundingly, Jack asked, "Well, are we ready for this? How you holding up, Corey?"

Corey looked at Jack in her mirror and nervously smiled. "We just about have everything in place. How you doing, Jack? Are you ready for this?"

What Bob didn't know was Corey asked Jack to walk her down the aisle and then give her away. Her parents had separated years ago. Her mother had died in her late forties from breast cancer, and she had never seen her father again after her mother's death.

This was going to be a very emotional surprise for Bob because he viewed Jack as a father figure and had complete and unmitigated respect for him since the day they met almost two years ago at Celebrity Studios.

Curiously worried, Corey asked Jack, "Did you happen to see my dashing young fiancé out there? I bet he looks amazing in his new tux."

Jack suspiciously looked at all four bridesmaids as Corey watched his expression in her mirror. He tried not to alarm her when he said, "I really don't know, Corey. I just arrived a few minutes ago with Deloris and Ann. I didn't look around for Bob. I just knew I had to come back here before the start of the ceremony."

This didn't help Corey's anxiety. Susan saw the way Corey was working herself up and went to her. She bent down to look at Corey in the mirror, and in trying to allay her fears, she self-assuredly told her, "Corey, you know Bob loves you beyond belief. There is not a force in this world strong enough to keep him away from you, ever. Now I'm going to go out there and find him, and then I'll be back here to tell you, you have nothing to worry about. Okay?"

Debbie spoke up at this time. "Yeah, honey. I've seen men in love many times before, and I can honestly tell you, Bob's love for you surpasses any I've ever seen. He's just lost in his love for you."

Corey managed a very nervous smile.

Alex was uncomfortable hearing all this but knew Corey's love for Bob would always be more significant in meaning to him than what she felt for him.

After several minutes, and it being almost one thirty, Susan came back into the pool house. She hurriedly told Corey, "Bob's not here yet, but…"

Corey, now fearfully uneasy, closed her eyes and exhaled heavily, saying, "Oh my god! Something has happened to him. My heart tells me he would never do this to me."

Susan calmly finished saying, "He's not here yet, but they called his sister's house, and there's no answer. This tells me he's on his way and is probably walking in right now."

Just then, there was a knock on the pool house door. Corey held her breath. Haddie went to the door and opened it, and it was the groomsmen coming to get ready for the start of the ceremony.

Haddie very nervously asked Len, "Is Mr. Bob here and ready to start the ceremony? People say they haven't seen him yet."

Len apprehensively told Haddie, "We're pretty sure he's on his way. My guess is he got caught up in traffic. Don't any of you worry. I know this guy, and he would give his right arm before he missed his marriage to Corey."

Corey sadly smiled as Debbie came up to her and gave her an encouraging hug.

Doug chimed in, "Oh, he'll be here. No way in hell he would burn you, Corey. Just no way. I'll go out and ask Joshua or Darnell to go out front and watch for him. *When*—not *if*—he gets here, I'll tell 'em to bust their butts to get back here and let us know. Then we can kick this ceremony into gear. Okay?" Doug then raced out of the pool house.

It was now one forty-five, and it even seemed all the guests were beginning to question Bob's conspicuous absence.

Just two minutes had passed when Joshua and Bob came running in from the driveway entrance to the back area. They were moving at breakneck speed as Bob ran up to the waiting minister, who was on the landing in front of the beautifully adorned vine arbor trellis. Although, Joshua kept moving toward the pool house to notify everyone that things were cool.

All the guests stood and were shouting their approval and applauding the fact he had made it in time for his wedding. Bob had a tremendously broad smile on his face. He was breathing heavily and pumping his right fist affirmatively at everyone.

Joshua knocked once on the door, opened it, and in a raised voice of jubilation, announced, "He's here, and yes, there was an accident on the Northbound 405. Now we can unscrew this lid and let the amazing out!"

Corey was beside herself. She was thankful and totally relieved as her eyes were now filled with unshed tears.

Haddie took Corey's hand and warned her, "Now don't you cry, Ms. Corey. We spent too much time getting your makeup on, and there's no time now to fix it. Everything's gonna be all right now. You're gonna be married to the love of your life shortly, and this is gonna be a truly beautiful happening today after all."

Bob was talking with the minister and trying to describe the mess that was on the 405. When they finished talking, it was two o'clock and time to start the ceremony. The minister turned to the DJ and had him start the recorded processional music, which would have the bridesmaids and groomsmen walking down the aisle—the aisle that was covered with the thousands of fluffy purple, pink, and white rose petals.

The classical piece was "Arioso" by Johann Sebastian Bach. The soft piano channels were pure elegance and sophistication.

Bach would lead up to the wedding march for the bride to come down the aisle.

When the bridesmaids and groomsmen heard the music start, they began to pair themselves together, with Debbie and Doug starting out of the pool house first.

As Doug led Debbie, with her right arm through his bent left elbow, the two of them kept a slow, staggered pace down the flowered aisle toward Bob and the minister.

Debbie looked very attractive in her full-length, light-blue bridesmaid dress; it was made of silk and elegantly banded under the bosom with a strand of light-pink silklike material. There was also a slight cut of cleavage. Her hair was piled high on her head in an amazing french twist that had two spirals of hair falling to surround her face. Her wrist corsage was five miniature roses of light blue and deep pink, coupled with a sprig of white baby's breath.

Doug looked very stately in his black tuxedo with the light-blue cummerbund, matching bow tie, and pocket handkerchief. The men's boutonnieres were one single African blue orchid, coupled with a sprig of baby's breath.

As Doug and Debbie approached the landing with the flowered trellis, Bob was pridefully smiling at both of them. Both were broadly smiling at him. Then when Debbie stepped up onto the landing to move to her spot, Bob moved to her and hugged her. He then kissed her on the cheek and gratefully told her, "Thank you for wanting to be a part of our day. I'll always remember you doing this for us."

Debbie was taken off guard but hugged and kissed him; as her eyes moistened, she told him, "Of course, Bob. I love both of you so much."

Bob then moved toward Doug and quickly reached out his hand to him, saying, "Thanks, man. I love you, brother."

Doug shook his hand and hugged Bob and told him, "You're a lucky man, brother." Bob nodded his head then returned to his place in front of the minister when he noticed Jimmy and Alex halfway down the aisle.

Bob was also happily smiling at them. When Alex moved toward her spot on the landing, Bob was there to hug and kiss her on the cheek. She returned the cheek-kiss. He told her, "I'm so glad you're here to be at our wedding. I appreciate everything you do for Corey."

Alex would have given quite a bit to trade places with Corey, but she knew that was not to be. She answered, "This has been a wonderful time. Thank you for having me."

Bob smiled and then walked over to Jimmy. He shook his hand and then also told him, "Thanks for wanting to do this, Jimmy. I love you, brother."

Jimmy answered quickly, "Yeah, man. We're all family here. No doubt about it."

Bob broadly grinned and walked back to his place by the minister. His attention was then drawn to Nick and Susan walking down the aisle toward him.

Bob was staring at Susan only, and he managed to grin with a sparkle in his eyes. Susan Hawthorne was definitely a woman Bob would have pursued had he not met Corey when he did. She was now forty-two years old, and she was radiant with spirit and inner grace. She was a compassionate, intelligent woman whose strength glowed in her eyes. She was also married when Bob started work at Celebrity Studios, so the chances of any relationship between them would have been nullified at that point anyway.

When Susan reached the landing and stepped up, Bob met her and wrapped his arms around her and then kissed her on the cheek. She responded by kissing him long, but on his cheek. He was only inches from her face when he softly told her, "I was thrilled when I found out you'd be in the wedding party. Thank you for always being so kind to me."

Susan looked into his eyes and wanted to kiss him on the lips, but she knew better; Corey was a very good friend, and so many people were watching, including her husband.

She simply told Bob, "This was my pleasure, and being kind to you was my way of showing my love for both of you."

They both shared another kiss to each other's cheeks, and then Bob went over to Nick and shook his hand. They shared a mutual hug, and as Bob pulled away, he seriously told Nick, "You, my man, have been such an instrumental part in my career, my business, and my life. I don't know how I'm ever going to repay you. Love you, brother."

Nick nodded and earnestly answered, "I just thank God I knew your sister. Because these past couple of years would never have happened for me if it wasn't for Elizabeth. This has been absolutely a blast for me. I love all you like brothers, man."

Bob hugged him again and patted him on the back a couple of times and then moved the few feet back to his place on the landing.

When Bob looked up the aisle, he now saw his sister, Elizabeth, being escorted by her husband, Drake. Elizabeth was a stunning beauty; her black hair was swept up and truly enhanced her gorgeous face. She was all smiles as Drake guided her up onto the landing. Bob took her in his arms and just held her for several seconds, until he kissed her on the cheek and tenderly told her, "I thank God you're here with me today. I just wish Mom and Dad could have known Corey."

Elizabeth began to tear when she consolingly told Bob, "Mom and Dad are here today, Bobby. They're surrounding you through my love for you and through Corey's love for you. And yes, they would have adored Corey, just as we all do."

Bob was now fighting back the tears as he hugged and kissed Elizabeth again. He then walked over to Drake and hugged him, then shook his hand, telling him, "Drake, thank you for being here today, and thank you so much for loving Elizabeth the way you do. I will never be able to tell you how much that means to me."

Drake leaned over and into Bob's ear; he pledged, "Elizabeth will always be loved by me, and I will always take good care of her. She means the world to me, Bob."

Bob nodded his head to him and grinned with complete satisfaction.

Bob looked up the aisle, and Len was leading Haddie arm in arm toward him and the minister. Bob smiled joyously as his eyes began to glisten. Len and Haddie were both grinning from ear to ear. They were having the time of their lives; Len being part of one of the biggest moments in his best friend's life was monumental, and he was gaining another good friend with Corey. Haddie could feel the love Bob was exuding through his eyes. She knew Corey would be taken care of, protected, and always loved by this incredible man that both she and Corey had fallen in love with. Both in different ways, of course.

As Haddie stepped up onto the landing, Bob took her in his arms and hugged her and then kissed her on her cheek. Haddie wrapped her arms around him, and with tears welling in her eyes, she kissed him on his cheek.

Bob leaned in to Haddie's face, and heartfelt, he told her, "Haddie, I will always be indebted to you for taking care of my lady so thoroughly and so lovingly. And I will always cherish our friendship and be grateful you're my singing buddy when I need it."

Haddie began to drop single tears down her face, and as her voice broke a few times, she told him, "Mr. Bob, I have always liked you a lot, and I knew the first time we met...that you were goin' to fall in love with Ms. Corey... I just thank God that it finally happened."

Bob nodded and smiled at her then kissed her on the cheek and quickly hugged her again. He then turned to Len and hugged him while patting his back. Bob pulled back and shook Len's hand while saying, "This has been one hell of a journey, brother, and you know, I think we're just beginning this trip. Thanks for supporting me throughout the years and helping to make this band what it is today. Love you, brother."

Len smiled, still shaking Bob's hand; he answered, "I couldn't have asked for a better friend than what you've been to me through the years. I'm just glad we actually liked each other when we met at NEC. You are definitely my brother, and I love you, man."

They shook hands again and then bumped shoulders as they cheerfully smiled at each other while nodding their heads in unison.

Finally, the music signaled the wedding march of the bride. "Ave Verum Corpus" by Mozart started to play, and it made everyone feel they were transcending to the altar. Everyone at the wedding stood up and watched for Corey to start her walk down the aisle.

Bob turned to watch for his bride. The entire wedding party was looking toward the pool house. The guests were all focused on the opened door, and suddenly, Jack Windheim and Corey walked through the door and commenced to start the slow tempo of the bride's walk to her awaiting groom.

A lot of guests were surprised to see Jack walking Corey down the aisle to be married.

Bob was caught off guard when he saw Jack arm in arm with Corey. Bob tried to refocus his eyes; he didn't believe what he was seeing. When he finally reconciled himself to believing what was actually happening, he started to form tears in his eyes. He really wanted his father to be the one walking his bride down the aisle, but Jack had become like a father to him since the day they met at Celebrity almost two years ago. So Bob was thrilled seeing Jack do this for Corey and him.

It took several seconds for Bob to catch his breath. He smiled brilliantly as he watched Corey walking toward him. She was the picture of perfect love to him; her wedding dress was a full-length, winter-white silk gown that had staggered, thin, offset rows of light-blue and light-pink silk inserts. The dress was beautiful and elegantly hung on Corey's gorgeous body. The slight cut of cleavage was just enough to get Bob's attention and was dignified enough to wear at her wedding. The bridesmaids' dresses also had the same cleavage cut to them.

Corey's winter-white veil was draped over her face and surrounded her head and finished at her shoulders. Her bouquet was full-size blue and sunset-pink roses. The bouquet took all the colors from the coastal waters of the Pacific. There was an array of stems, from ranunculus to mini calla lilies to delphiniums, to create the high-end beauty of this magnificent floral piece.

Corey was watching Bob's reaction to Jack and to her. She saw his beautiful smile and how resplendently handsome he was in his wedding tuxedo. She absolutely knew how his intelligence, resolve, and dependability had shaped the cast of his features so deeply that their attractiveness was irrelevant to their meaning. All these things abruptly, magically coalesce into a vision of earthly beauty that brought tears stinging into her eyes. In fact, Bob would be an anomaly anywhere in this world, because he was such a beautiful person, and vanity never had played a part in his character.

All Bob could see when he looked at Corey was her inner self. Her abundant capacity to love and to be loved. Her moral uprightness, her honesty, wholeness, and soundness; her integrity went unquestioned, and her principles and standards were impeccably ingrained within her soul.

Corey's beauty was not put on in front of a mirror, but it grew, with breathtaking simplicity, straight from her innermost being; what you see is only the small, visible portion of a far greater, more comprehensive, radiant, and formal quality within. She had mastered the art of dramatic acting; no one could tell her the way any character should be portrayed. She was beautiful, smart, gutsy, and unpretentious; for when she knew what direction she was taking with any role, she just locked in and inhabited the part.

When Jack and Corey reached the step to the landing, Bob put out his hand to her and guided her to her place in front of the minister. He couldn't take his eyes off of her. She looked so captivating, and she glowed with the most perfect aura of transcendence.

Bob quickly turned to look at Jack, and before Jack turned to go to his table, Bob wrapped his arms around the plumpish frame of a man hardened by the industry of making money off of other people's hard work and sweat. Although, Bob knew by now that Jack Windheim was the exception to all the ruthless, cutthroat, and demanding studio directors there were in Hollywood. Jack actually had a heart; he was very astute in assessing the qualities, talent, and ambition in his people. He knew who was at Celebrity to further their careers and who would work with him to do that, and those who just came to blow smoke up his ass and expect to climb the ladder without putting in the effort.

Jack hugged Bob tightly, like a proud father would. They both had welled-up tears in their eyes as they patted each other on the back several times. The entire wedding party had not a dry eye amongst them. Corey watched the tender display of love exchanged between Bob and his "adoptive" father, Jack. Tears had formed in her eyes and then slipped down her cheek.

Bob then kissed Jack on the cheek and, quickly but heartfelt, told him, "Straight from my heart, Jack… I love you, man. Thank you."

All Jack could do was smile and gently but affirmatively nod his head, trying not to cry.

Bob turned back to Corey as both of them had tearstained eyes. Len handed Bob a tissue. Bob smiled at Len, took the tissue, and began dabbing at his eyes and face. He stuffed it in his coat pocket, after he felt he had everything under control.

When he looked at Corey's face, he took the light-blue handkerchief from his coat's breast pocket and carefully began to dab her cheeks, but did not go near her gorgeous eyes, for fear of smudging the mascara on them.

Bob tenderly told her, "There…now you're even more mesmerizing to me."

Corey wanted so much to kiss him, but she stopped herself and lovingly told him, "Thank you, darling."

Her voice had always had the power to paralyze and then melt him. He just stood staring into those glorious eyes, with such a heart filled with love.

The minister felt it was time to begin the vows when he spoke up and into the microphone placed in front of him, "Dearly beloved, we are gathered here today to join this man and this woman in holy matrimony. I ask today, who gives this woman to be married to this man?"

Bob stood wondering who this would be when he heard Jack's deep, ubiquitous voice proclaim, "I do."

Bob looked at Corey, and she was brilliantly smiling at him. Bob then turned, with one single tear running down his cheek, and smiled at Jack. As Jack sat back down, Bob turned back to the minister and just shook his head approvingly.

The minister continued, "If there is anyone here today who objects to this union, speak now or forever hold your peace."

Both Alex and Susan had fleeting thoughts of stopping the ceremony, but each woman knew their thoughts were just that—fleeting.

The ceremony moved along to where the minister asked Corey, "Corinth Beth Ann Madrigal, do you take Robert Brian Richardson to be your partner in marriage—to live together in holy matrimony, to love, honor, comfort, and keep in sickness and in health, forsaking all others, for as long as you both shall live?" Corey and Bob were now facing each other and holding hands. Already crying, Corey said, as her voice was breaking, "I do."

The minister followed by asking Bob the same question. Just before he answered, another single tear dropped from one of his eyes. He swallowed heavily and swore, "I do."

The minister now told Corey, "Place the ring on Bob's finger and repeat the following: I give you this ring as a token and pledge of our constant faith and abiding love."

Corey turned to Haddie, who handed her the ring, and then Haddie hugged her, whispering in her ear, "Bless you, Ms. Corey."

Corey, with a tear falling from each eye, could only smile at Haddie. She turned to Bob and slid the ring on his left ring finger. She then said, "I give you this ring as a token and pledge of our constant faith and abiding love." She looked up at him and saw his eyes glistening, and she began to cry even harder.

The minister asked Bob, "Now you place the ring on Corey's finger and repeat the phrase." Just before Bob turned to Len, a single tear dropped from one of his eyes. He swallowed heavily. He was trying to keep it together when he turned to Len and saw a tear in his eye. At that point, Bob lost it. Len wrapped his arms around Bob as Bob was outwardly weeping. After several seconds, Bob straightened himself, wiped his face with the tissue from his coat pocket, and then took the ring from Len. Bob sincerely told Len, "Band of brothers, right?"

Len grabbed Bob's hand and lifted it to shoulder height and staunchly told Bob, "We are your band of five brothers. That will never change, man!"

Bob nodded his head several times, very quickly, and then turned back to Corey. She was a mess, with her tears falling down her chest and moistening her cleavage.

All five of her bridesmaids were wiping tears off their faces, and many of the guests were quite moved by the touching emotionalism that both Corey and Bob were showing.

Bob took Corey's left hand with his left hand and then slipped the beautiful banded ring onto her ring finger. He then told her, "I give you this ring as a token and pledge of our constant faith and abiding love."

They both were lost in each other at this point; they just stared at each other as their hearts were beating almost uncontrollably.

The minister finally said, "Would you both join hands?" They immediately took the other's hands in theirs.

"By virtue of the authority vested in me and in accordance with the laws of the state of California, it is my honor to now pronounce that you are husband and wife. You may now kiss the bride, young man."

Bob slowly moved the two steps to Corey, and not losing contact with her eyes, he carefully lifted her veil and peeled it back on top of her head. He softly told her, "I love you to the moon and back, Alice... I just adore you, baby."

Corey smiled and exhaled heavily when he said "I just adore you, baby." She handed her bouquet to Haddie, and then she threw her arms around Bob's neck and whispered into his ear, "You are my entire world, darling. You gave new meaning to my life."

Bob started to tear up again as he moved to kiss her. She met his lips as he lovingly moved them on and around hers. Their lips parted and came back together again, another three times, when they both parted and began to smile and wave to the applauding guests.

Corey began hugging and cheek-kissing her bridesmaids and thanking them for being a part of her special day. Bob shook hands with his groomsmen and threw in a couple of shoulder bumps before he left the landing and went down to where Joshua and Darnell were seated. They were still standing and applauding when Bob came up to them and shook hands and hugged each of them. He kissed Deidra and Alicia on their cheeks and thanked them for wanting to come to the wedding. They both said it was their pleasure being there.

Bob appreciatively told Joshua and Darnell, "I want to thank both of you for being a part of this today. I feel like we've known each other far longer than the two months we actually have. I know the two of you will become even closer brothers to all of us as we go down this road together. You're both very special to me and to the other guys."

Joshua honestly answered Bob by stating, "I gotta admit, man, when Darnell and I started with this band, the thoughts of touring became scary. Now that we've settled in somewhat, it's been a badass time. We really have a blast with all the guys, Nick, and all the choice skirts that come with the group...and by the way, congratulations, and we all wish you a smokin'-hot honeymoon and a solid lifetime of love."

Bob smiled broadly at that last remark and replied jokingly, "I've got both those covered, man. No sweat, brother. It's all right on."

Bob then turned and went back up on the landing and announced into the microphone to everyone, "Corey and I really appreciate everyone that made time today to come to our wedding. You are truly appreciated and acknowledged as almost good friends." Everyone laughed, and Bob told them, "Now we'll have your dinner brought to you, and if you are a member of Alcoholics Anonymous, we'll have apple cider for you. The rest of you drink to your heart's content…as long as tonight, you have a ride home."

The laughter and talking started back almost immediately as the waiters were buzzing around the yard taking dinners to tables and refilling drink orders.

Bob then turned to the bridesmaids, who were getting ready to have pictures taken, by themselves with Corey and some with the bride and groom. The photographer wanted the vine arbor to be the background for the wedding party pictures.

Bob went down the line of bridesmaids and hugged each one and cheek-kissed them again. After he finished with Debbie, he turned to find Corey. She was standing by the vine arbor, looking at him and waiting for him to come to her.

As Bob walked to her, his face was aglow with the love he felt for her. When he reached her, he startled her by wrapping his arms around her hips and then picking her up so her head was towering over him. He turned her around in a circle and then carefully set her back down on the landing. Their lips came together as he slowly let her body slide down his chest.

Corey laughed and playfully scolded him, "All right, darling. We need to get these pictures taken so we can talk to our guests."

Bob whispered into her closest ear, "You know, there's this huge bedroom in this house, and to my surprise, no one's using it right now. What do you say, doll?"

Corey loved the fact that Bob was so sexually drawn to her. She knew he was young and very masculinely virile, but he always made her feel so much younger than what she was.

At that moment, the photographer started lining the wedding party up by the arbor, to get his pictures taken, so he could then wander around the yard taking pictures of everyone else.

After all the pictures were taken, each one of the Owls walked up to the landing area. They moved the vine arbor all the way over to the right edge of the marbled floor. Then they brought Jimmy's drums up six feet closer to the middle of the landing. All the instruments were originally up close to the house, way in back of the vine arbor, where Nick had placed them Saturday after the Owls' studio session.

Most of the guests were watching the guys set up. They knew they were in for a treat, most especially when Bob walked up to the Owls and asked, "You guys ready to turn it on?"

Doug yelled, "Hell, yes."

Joshua affirmed, "Yes, sir. Let's burn it down."

Darnell determinedly warned, "We are stoked and ready to shake it with ya, brother." Bob contently smiled and then stepped up to the microphone as Corey was visiting with Jack's table of Deloris, Ann Margaret, Susan Hawthorne and husband, Alex, and her date, Robert Ryan.

Bob announced into the mic, "I hope everyone is enjoying their dinner. Corey and I will have some cake ready for you in a little while."

Corey's attention went immediately to Bob at the microphone. She pridefully stared at him with a very alluring smile enhancing her face.

Bob continued speaking into the microphone, "Maybe some of you noticed, and for those who did not, the Night Owls will be playing a couple of songs tonight."

There was a welcoming applause from all, with a few yells and whistles thrown in.

"The first song, 'Long Journey Back to You,' was written by Len, Jimmy, and Doug. They dedicated this song to Corey and I when we were trying to work through some stuff last year. As you can tell, we worked it out." A small amount of nervous laughter from the guests. Corey closed her eyes, lowered her head, and exhaled the air of complete content.

Bob then tenderly spoke into the microphone, "Now, I would love to dance with my new bride, to our song, if she'll join me."

Corey immediately moved toward the landing, briskly took the two steps up, and then placed her hand into his hand that he was holding out to her. The guys started with the slow notes of the first bar. Bob took Corey romantically in his arms and drew her body very close to him.

When the point came in the song for the vocal lead-in, Len, Darnell, and Jimmy started singing the lyrics. Together, they sounded pretty good, but they knew they could never sing this song with the beautifully and perfectly pitched baritone that Bob possessed.

Corey felt like she was floating on a cloud, the way Bob held her and led her around the dance floor. It was sublime, as she once in a while looked up into his face and she drew his lips down to hers. Corey was experiencing wonder and pleasure; almost a kind of rapture had enveloped her entire being.

Most of the women in attendance this day could only swoon as they were witnessing what true love was actually all about. Alex and Susan would have given anything to have a man like Bob; he was attentive, not afraid to show his emotions, fun to be with, but most of all, he was a very passionate man. They could only venture a guess, but probably knew, he was also an incredible lover.

Toward the end of the song, Bob had his arms around Corey, and his hands covered her lower back up to her shoulder blades. Her arms were around his neck, with one of her hands slowly moving through his hair. They were barely moving at this point. They locked into a kiss; everyone thought they acted like they never wanted it to end.

When the music stopped, everyone applauded the newlyweds. Bob and Corey were holding hands at this point and smiling at everyone. They exchanged some very sexy looks at each other, when Corey placed Bob's face in her hands and pulled him down and kissed him.

She told him, "I'm going out now and visit with some of our guests."

Bob hastily told her, "No, no. You stay here for just a couple more minutes. Okay?"

Corey was confused, but she trusted him implicitly, answering, "All right, darling. If that's what you want. I'm not moving."

Bob smiled at her, and then Joshua brought a high stool over and sat it in front of Corey. She now knew what was going on and put one hand to her mouth, and this brought dazzled tears to her eyes.

Bob helped her onto the stool by picking her up and carefully placing her on the seat. He kissed her again and then went to the microphone. An immediate quiet descended over the entire yard as Bob lovingly announced, "Today is a day I thought would never happen to me: marrying the absolute love of my life; having five brothers, all of whom would risk their lives for any guy in our band; having a stage and motion picture career; and last but not least, having a man with such a high standard of scruples and an impeccable character who has become my adopted father. Thank you, Jack."

Jack's eyes became a little misty, along with Corey's. Bob breathed heavily and swallowed, trying not to tear up again. "Now with all that aside, I wrote the lyrics to this next song, with the guys having kicked in the melody, the volume, the pace, and the rhythm. You know, all that incidental stuff."

He looked back at the guys' reaction, and they were all laughing. The guests enjoyed a good laugh also. Bob was smiling brilliantly at Corey and found he couldn't take his eyes off of her.

He shook his head in disbelief and turned back to the yard of people and stated, "Have you ever seen anything so ravishingly beautiful?"

There was an appreciative applause along with some whistles and catcalls.

Bob finally said into the microphone, "This song was written strictly for Corey and to be sung by me, to her, at our wedding. It's called 'Knowing You Were Mine.' So here goes."

Bob turned to the side of the microphone so he'd be looking straight at Corey. Jimmy started in on the snare with the loose-hair sticks as Len came in with the bass guitar, and then Darnell began playing the melody lines with his lead semi-acoustic guitar. Doug was soon adding some slow jazzy notes, and then Joshua started running a riff on his muted bass trumpet. After Joshua ran his first riff, the song called for Bob's vocal entrance:

> Your loving soul is all my heart can feel.
> For you are the best part of me that remains so
>   real.

Love is eternal in our souls, so I'm told,
And time will only strengthen my hold.

(Chorus)
I would give up my life so that you would live.
The only other thing would be my love to give.
You are the starting point, and you are the finishing line.
The only thing I've ever wanted was to love you, knowing you were mine.

To have found your love waiting for me,
It was so clear it was meant to be.
Baby, I was born late to love you like this.
You must have known I was coming for your kiss.

(Chorus)

You have eyes that reach deep into my heart.
I knew there was something magical with us from the very start.
So take me deep into the night and let's never return.
Let your heart consume me with its passion to burn.

(Chorus)

With the ending words, "knowing you were mine," Corey was crying almost uncontrollably. The song had raised the hairs on her arms and the back of her neck. Her heart was beating with an immediate urgency.

Bob went to her and gave her his handkerchief. He kept his arms around her and kissed her on top of her head. She wrapped her arms around his waist as she buried her head in the front of his shirt. She looked up at him with eyes that were so filled with love, it made

Bob want to cry with her. Corey, almost inaudibly but softly, said to him, "Oh my god! I love you beyond belief, Robert Brian. Don't you ever let go of me, darling!"

Bob's eyes began to tear as he looked her straight in her eyes and swore, "Not in this lifetime, baby."

Corey slowly rose to her feet and wrapped her arms around his neck as he took her in his arms, and they kissed long and hard. After several seconds, Bob left one hand around her waist, and then he announced into the microphone, "I think on that note, we're gonna take a break now…"

Bob pursed his lips and humorously blew a "Whoa!" into the microphone and then took a few fingers to loosen his collar and fan his face with that same hand.

Most people were laughing when Bob turned to the Owls and lifted his hands on high with the thumbs and forefinger joined in the gesture of perfection. "Thank you, brothers. That was better than at rehearsals. You kicked it!"

Doug jokingly answered, "Yeah, we don't like to work too hard at rehearsals. It might set a precedent."

Bob just laughed and then led Corey down to their seats at the long front table, just a few steps from the landing. He held Corey's seat for her and then went to Valerie, who was already seated and waiting for Len to join her. Bob hugged her and kissed her on the cheek, saying, "Thank you for coming, Val. We don't get to see you much these days. We'll have to change that."

Valerie, agreeing with him, said, "I'd like that, Bob. It just always seems like everyone is so busy living, that they don't stop long enough to smell the flowers."

Bob nodded to her and agreeably stated, "That's the God-honest truth, but let's work on that, okay?"

When Bob turned to look down at the other end of the table, he saw Haddie seated next to her date, Curtis Bell, Corey's chauffeur for the last eighteen years.

Curtis was of medium height, sixty years old, a black man who was a little rotund and unassuming. He learned very young, through experience, you kept any disparaging comments about white people in general to yourself for fear of losing your life. Being born in Natchez, Mississippi, in 1900, you learned quickly, or you could be hanging from your front apple tree by morning. He was an innocuous man that kept to himself and was a widower just five years ago. He lived in a small two-bedroom apartment just a few miles from Bel Air, in West Hollywood.

Corey met him when he was hired to drive her to the Academy Awards ceremony in 1942. She asked him if he would become her full-time chauffeur, and she would pay him as much as the white drivers were getting, and ended up paying him much more. They became lifelong friends, and he never had to worry about a job or money again.

Bob quickly moved to shake Curtis's hand. When Curtis offered his hand, Bob just put his arms around him and hugged him, proclaiming, "Curtis, my man. How are you? This is cool. You and Haddie together. Are we gonna have another wedding soon?"

Curtis blushed, and Haddie just laughed. Curtis shyly told Bob, "Mr. Bob, your wedding was beautiful. I want to thank Ms. Corey and yourself for inviting me, and Ms. Haddie here, for asking me to sit with her. I wish the two of you a long and loving life together."

Bob was touched by this and hugged Curtis again and patted him on the back. "Thanks, man. I appreciate that."

As Bob began to walk to his seat on the other side of Corey, he grabbed Haddie by her shoulders and leaned over and kissed her again on the cheek, saying, "Thanks again for everything, Ms. Chambers. You were a showstopper today."

Haddie was beside herself from that compliment, and her eyes just beamed with the love she had for both Bob and Corey.

Bob returned to his seat next to Corey and tenderly kissed her on the lips. She had heard the whole conversation with Curtis and Haddie, for she was seated on Haddie's right side.

Corey told him, "You're just so gracious, darling. That's what I love about you: you are gallant, you have courage, and you are markedly attentive to women. I do love that, especially when I'm the woman."

Bob could only smile and laugh to himself, when Len stood up in front of his seat, next to Bob, and clanged his fork on his drink glass.

The din of laughter and conversation ceased at the high-pitched sound of the glass being tapped on by Len.

Len announced to the entire nineteen tables, "I guess now is the time for Bob's best man to toast the newly wedded couple."

Bob sat quietly smiling and then looked up at Len and facetiously said, "This had better be good, man." He then looked at Corey, and she was smiling as broadly as Bob was.

Len laughed to himself, and then he continued, "I met Bob at the New England Conservatory of Music, just six years ago, and as I recently told him, it's a good thing we liked each other from the start, or he'd be sitting here listening to some stranger toasting him and his bride. I never thought he'd meet anyone as classy as Corey, let alone falling in love with her. She's so obviously above his class. I mean, she's clearly too good for him."

The yard instantly filled with laughter, and Bob was laughing just as loud as anyone. Corey played along and leaned over and kissed Bob on the cheek and then ran her hand through his hair. Bob was rocking back and forth in his chair with uncontrolled laughter.

Len began again, more seriously this time, "You know, a guy like Bob Richardson is someone a person may never meet in their entire lifetime, but those that do meet him know how truly blessed they are to be able to call him a friend. This is a man who has that potent mixture of ambition and belief—in himself and in his dreams. He's had no practice in failure, and he has no intentions of starting now. He took this band of brothers—into his heart and then straight to the top of the music charts. He wasn't going to settle for anything less than worldwide acclaim. He's such a multifaceted guy. I know that if he had chosen any other profession, other than a professional musician, an incipient dramatic actor, or a Broadway performer, he would be the best badass, top-drawer, groovy, son-of-a-bee-hiver in that profession." The wedding goers were just cracking up with laughter.

"The fact that he just happened to run into Corey, his first day at Celebrity Studios, just speaks to this man's karma. He's the most happy-go-lucky person I know. He's easy to talk to, and he's just relentlessly and, at times, aggravatingly upbeat."

Everyone was laughing again, as Bob was staring at Corey, as she was enjoying herself. Len finished, "I look at Bob as my brother, and Corey as my sister. I, and the four other Owls, just love these two people. I have no doubt in my mind that this family will always be together, and what goes down with one will go down with all. Now, let's raise our glasses to this beautiful couple. With all the love vested in these two, we toast their happiness, good fortune, and a lifetime of sharing, caring, and always loving."

The entire yard was drinking to Len's toast. There were many "Hear, hear's" from the crowd.

Bob stood up and hugged Len. They patted each other on the back, and Bob jokingly told him, "That was all right, but just work on it for the next wedding you go to, okay?"

Len bumped shoulders with Bob then happily told him, "Congratulations, man."

Bob remained standing; as Len took his seat, Bob told his wedding guests, "Corey and I are now going to eat our dinner, drink some champagne, and then cut the cake. We would really appreciate all of you having some of our spice cake with the caramel panache. Only because what's not eaten won't fit into our suitcases."

The guests had a good laugh, along with the wedding party, but especially Corey.

At that moment, everyone heard Jack's genial bellow rising and directed toward Bob. And with Jack's quick, efficient gestures, he loudly asked, "Where are you two going on your honeymoon, anyway?"

Bob laughed heartily, looked at Corey's questioning happy face, and answered Jack, "Wouldn't you like to know, Mr. Windheim?"

Everyone started clapping and yelling for Bob to reveal where the honeymoon nest was. Bob looked at Corey and then acquiesced to everyone's request. "Well, I wasn't going to tell anyone, for fear of it getting back to Corey, but I guess I can pop that lid and tell her now."

The guests applauded. Bob smiled and disclosed, "Last July, I told Corey, over the phone and 4,850 miles away from her, that I promise I would take her back to one of the countries the Owls were performing in that night. It just happened to be Italy."

Many people yelled their excitement for them, and there was clapping and whistles. Corey gasped a short breath of air and then placed her closed hand to her mouth and began to tear up. She distinctly remembered Bob telling her about Rome, but she didn't think he would want to go back so soon. However, she was thrilled with the idea.

"We leave tonight at nine thirty, out of LAX, to Rome, Italy, with one touchdown for refueling. We'll spend two days in Rome and the remaining ten days on top of the beautiful mountaintop village of Anacapri, on the Isle of Capri."

Corey and most of the women in attendance this day were romantically fixated on the thought of being alone with the person they loved—and on top of an island, no less.

Bob finished with his description. "Corey and my suite will be seated atop the five other suites and the other thirty-eight rooms that are scattered across a beautiful labyrinth of three different levels. We'll have the most spectacular views on the planet, from every window that surrounds the suite. We'll be looking out onto the Gulf of Naples. Oh yeah, and there's a private balcony for sunbathing." Bob sexily looked over into Corey's eyes. "Swimsuits are not required."

A lot of the men started their cat-whistles, yelping, and yelling their approval.

Bob was still looking at Corey, with her tearstained eyes, when she stood up and wrapped her arms around his neck; she then kissed him with such heartfelt emotion.

As they separated lips, they tightly hugged, when Bob turned to the guests and added, "And I already have a standing order for an endless supply of martinis—stirred, not shaken. They are to be delivered to our room the moment we arrive."

Corey could not relinquish her hold on him while their dinner started to get cold.

TEN

After Corey and Bob had finished their dinners, Bob took Corey's hand and escorted her over to the table that held the five-tiered wedding cake. The two of them together picked up the knife sitting beside the cake and began to cut on the second smallest tier.

Bob removed a small piece of the spice cake and placed it in Corey's mouth. She began to daintily eat at it, when Bob started eating the same piece from the other end. When their mouths met in the middle of the piece, they began kissing and allowed the cake to just melt in their mouths, as they enjoyed each other's lips.

Everyone cheered, and Bob motioned to the waiters to come over and cut the cake up and then take some to every table.

Jokingly, Bob told everyone, "Now I want all of you to eat cake until it's coming out of your ears. Got it?"

The waiters were instructed to wrap the small top tier and then give it to the newlyweds. Haddie took the wrapped cake into the kitchen and placed it into the freezer, for next year's first wedding anniversary.

The DJ started to spin the vinyl discs, as Glenn Miller's "In the Mood" began to play. Bob asked Corey if she wanted to cut a rug. Corey, unsurprisingly, told him, "Oh, Lord no, darling. I'll wait for something a lot more tame."

Bob kissed her and left her at Jack's table as he moved toward his sister, Elizabeth. She smiled radiantly as he put his hand out to her.

She grabbed his hand, and they quickly moved to the dance floor on the landing. Bob untied his bowtie and unbuttoned his shirt a little. He then removed his jacket and threw it to Len, at their table.

Bob and Elizabeth immediately started to jitterbug. He took her hand and quickly pulled her into him and then returned her to arm's length. After he led her into a couple pirouettes, he grabbed her by the waist and shot her into the air. Bringing her down, he slid her through his legs. Turning at the speed of light, he grabbed her under her arms and threw her body completely around and caught her again and then set her feet gently on the floor.

Elizabeth was smiling brilliantly, laughing, and loving every minute of dancing with her brother. She kept up with him extraordinarily well, considering she was in a floor-length gown and high-heeled pumps. They had danced together many times as they grew up. Big band music and jazz were always being played in the house by their father.

Everyone was enjoying the exuberant display of talent between the two of them. Corey was laughing and amusingly screaming when she saw Bob throw Elizabeth into the air. When he landed her perfectly onto the dance floor, Corey then clapped and was filled with the pride she had always felt for him.

When the song was over, Elizabeth hugged her brother, and arm in arm, Bob escorted her back to her seat next to Drake.

The next song was a slow one, by Artie Shaw, with Helen Forrest singing "Do I Love You." Bob headed toward Corey, when he abruptly stopped, after seeing her being led to the dance floor by the thirty-one-year-old Lew Ayers. Lew had been in the epic movie, of mammoth proportions, with Corey in May of last year. At the movie's wrap party, Lew had helped Bob sneak into the restaurant to surprise Corey, for at the time, Bob was living in New York City and wanted badly to see her. That wasn't even a month after Bob and Corey got together as a couple.

Bob just stood watching Lew and Corey walk onto the dance floor. He had an uncomfortable twinge of jealousy, but he knew his feelings were unsubstantiated. He'd met Lew almost a year ago at Celebrity, and he seemed like a good guy.

Before Bob started for his seat, he heard a woman's voice behind him ask, "How would you like to dance with me, Bob?"

He recognized the rich, mellowed, sweet tone of the voice and turned and smiled at Susan Hawthorne and happily said, "Why, of course. Thanks, Susan."

Bob put his hand to her lower back and let her lead him to the landing. The dance floor already had many couples dancing. Bob took Susan's right hand into his left as he kept his right hand firmly planted at the base of her spine.

They began moving slowly to the music and made small talk, as they occasionally looked up and into the other's eyes. Corey spotted them while she looked over Lew's shoulder. She didn't seem entirely comfortable watching them; she was remembering the movie she had just finished in early January, where Susan had two steamy romantic scenes with Bob. It just all seemed a bit unsettling.

Susan then pulled Bob closer so she could press her right cheek against his. He went along with this but kept talking to her about the probability of making a movie together in August or September. Susan demurely answered him but remained caught up in the moment while she was in his arms.

When the song ended, Susan kissed Bob on the cheek and thanked him for the dance. He reciprocated and told her, "Thank you for asking me. Now, let's work on getting that picture deal together for the end of this summer."

Susan agreed and started for her seat, when Richard Widmark, already on the landing, asked her to dance. She smiled and took his hand, and they remained on the dance floor.

Corey quickly moved to Bob and put her arms around him and lovingly purred, "I've got you now, and I'm not letting go."

Bob, purposely showing a slight hint of jealousy, pretended to scold her, saying, "Well, if you weren't so busy with other men, I would have grabbed you earlier."

"I will never be busy with any other man but you, darling."

Bob took her in his arms, kissed her for several seconds, and they began dancing.

Bob and Corey danced to the Owls' "Let Me Lay within Your Arms" and "Not Another Lonely Night." They seemed lost within each other, like there wasn't anyone else around.

When the music was over, Bob looked at his watch. It was seven o'clock, and he knew they had to leave for the airport in one more hour. Bob asked Corey, "Do you want us to go in and change clothes now, or just before we leave?"

"Why don't we go in now, and then I can throw the bouquet just before we leave."

At that exact moment, Duke Ellington's "Cottontail" started playing, and Debbie grabbed Bob by the hand as she apologetically told Corey, "Sorry, honey. I just need him for a couple of minutes."

Corey smiled then graciously backed away toward the french doors. She stood there the whole time Debbie and Bob danced the jitterbug, and she enjoyed watching them doing what came naturally.

Debbie and Bob joined hands and started to bob their heads at each other, moving from one side of their face to the other. Then as one kicked their foot to one side, the other kicked opposite. That happened three times. Bob then grabbed her and spun her entire body, twice around his body. She was flying free-form around him, until he grabbed both her hands and slid her between his legs. The heels on Debbie's white high-heeled pumps scraped across the marbled landing. When she righted herself, with Bob's help, she found one of her heels had snapped off.

She quickly kicked both pumps off and returned to Bob. Trying to make her feel less embarrassed, he ripped both his shoes off and tossed them off the landing.

Everyone was laughing and applauding at the same time. Corey stood laughing so hard, she was bent over holding a hand to her chest, with tears of laughter running from her eyes.

Bob grabbed Debbie's hands again and spun her into three consecutive pirouettes. As he released her body, they both strutted around each other, holding one hand in the air and shaking the index finger back and forth, like Minnie the Moocher.

Their hips were swerving in time to the music, and they seemed undaunted by the very upbeat tempo of the Ellington band.

As the song ended, Bob dipped Debbie and held her for several seconds, with his right arm under her and his left hand around her waist.

The two then bounced up into each other's arms. They were winded, but they managed to kiss on the lips ceremoniously and then hugged each other one more time. The guests were applauding, yelling their appreciation, and there were even some loud whistles.

After Debbie and Bob found their shoes, she headed back to her table, and he quickly moved up to the doors of the house. He secured his arm around Corey, and they headed for the bedroom.

As they were changing, Bob sexily hinted to Corey, "Just look at that big bed, and not a person using it…what a shame."

Corey's eyes were sparkling with the love she had for him as she said, appearing mysteriously attractive and seductive, "Robert Brian, there just isn't enough time right now, and I don't want a 'slam, bam, thank you, ma'am' either. I want us to make love slow, and lasciviously, and for days at a time. Then when we come home, we'll begin all over again, darling."

Bob slowly walked over to her and took her face in his hands and kissed her very steamily. He pulled away smiling then spoke directly into her eyes, "That is exactly why I love you so much. You really get me."

At almost seven thirty that evening, Bob and Corey returned to the reception. He was dressed in a short-jacketed blue suit, and Corey had on a blushing-pink two-piece, skirted suit.

Corey had Haddie bring her bouquet to her, and she announced, as she stood above the two steps of the landing, "I'm ready to toss my bouquet."

Bob stood a few steps to her side when several women started walking up and formed a small group in front of Corey; there was Ann Margaret, Debbie Reynolds, Haddie, Alex, Shirley Jones, Hope Lange, Anne Baxter, and Ann Sheridan.

Corey was giggling to herself as she studied the group, and then she happily announced, "Okay, here goes."

She turned her back to the women, and after a few seconds, she threw her bouquet over her shoulder.

All of them grabbed for it and were screaming, but the successful and believed-to-be future bride that came up with it was Ann Margaret. All the women congratulated her, and there was mild applause from the guests.

Corey stepped down from the landing and hugged Ann then told her, "Good luck, Ann. I hope you find whom you're looking for."

Doug was certainly happy to see Ann catch the bouquet. Maybe now he could pop the question to her.

Bob and Corey had one arm around each other when Bob got the guests' attention after hitting a fork against one of the glasses at his table.

He told everyone, "Corey and I will always be grateful to all of you for coming today. This day was made extra special by everyone of you being here with us. We're going to be heading to the airport in about twenty minutes. We'd like to tell all of you goodbye on our way out, but if we miss anyone, just know that we'll catch up with you sometime, somewhere, when we get back. Please, stay and enjoy yourselves the rest of the evening. Just remember to help yourselves to all the cake you want to eat and all the liquor you'll need to wash it down. Thanks again for sharing our day with us."

There was a calming applause, and everyone wished the lovers happiness and good fortune.

Bob and Corey made their way through most of the guests, and Bob specifically told Susan they would see her at the Academy Awards on April 4. She told them she wouldn't miss it.

Close to eight o'clock, Bob shook hands and shoulder-bumped all his guys and cheek-kissed their wives and girlfriends. Corey and Bob both hugged Jack and thanked him for stepping up to help Corey with her bridal march down the aisle.

As they left the yard, Bob and Corey were both waving and blowing kisses to everyone. Some of the guests were throwing the rose petals from the aisle. They eventually made it to the Cadillac that Curtis had parked out in front of the house that morning. Their luggage was already loaded before Curtis backed the car out.

They both stepped into the back seat, and Curtis, who had been waiting for them, whisked them off to the airport just a few minutes after eight o'clock.

Most of the thirteen hours of Bob and Corey's flight to Italy, they slept in their huge first-class seats, horizontally. Corey was lying between his legs, with her head on his upper chest, while Bob held her in his arms after draping a blanket over the two of them.

The remaining other fourteen first-class customers knew exactly who Bob and Corey were. They also guessed that their honeymoon must be in Italy. Everyone had a peek at them and felt lucky to be on the same plane with these two renowned and highly acclaimed stars. No one bothered them for an autograph, but gave them their privacy.

It was 8:30 p.m., Monday, when the plane touched down at the Leonardo da Vinci Airport in Rome, Italy. This was actually a good time to come to Italy; March was one of the best months to visit because most of the tourist crowds had dissipated, the rates were lower (not like that mattered), and the temperature was in the high sixties to low seventies.

After Bob tipped a man for their baggage pickup, it was delivered to the limousine he had ordered to be waiting for them at arrivals. The driver had advanced notice to take them to the Hotel Villa Borghese, near the Barerini Gardens.

The hotel was a nineteenth-century villa, with a beautifully landscaped garden area, where the newlyweds would have their meals served to them.

Out of the bedroom windows, they had perfect views of the lush garden, which had a high-rising water feature. They were told by the concierge that the water clock in the middle of the Villa Borghese Gardens actually worked.

The beautifully crafted clock was based on using the force of the water that flowed beneath it to move the pendulum and wind the clock.

In 1867, a friar of the Dominican Order, Giovanni Battista Embriaco, made two of the clocks to show at the Paris Expo.

In 1873, one of these clocks was placed in the Villa Borghese Gardens, on top of the fountain designed by architect Gioacchino Ersoch. The idea of the water clock was to show a harmony between technology and nature.

Both Corey and Bob were taken aback by the natural splendor of the almost-hundred-year-old clock sitting amongst the exquisite beauty of the gardens.

There was also a giant sauna and a small swimming pool for their enjoyment. The entire area was covered with floating sheets of beautiful silk materials that hung lazily in the breeze. The many large white-material-covered umbrellas protected the seating area from the sun. Everything was surrounded by a teakwood deck that encased many round, globular lights.

After Corey walked through the villa, and then experienced their magnificent private garden area, she walked up to Bob, and with the entrancing look of total and complete rapture in her eyes, she placed her arms around his neck and kissed him long and hard.

Bob was ecstatic with Corey's reaction to the villa. He then felt he could begin to relax and enjoy himself in knowing he chose the right place for them to stay their first two nights.

He asked her, "Would you like me to order in some dinner or maybe just something to munch on to get us through to breakfast tomorrow morning?"

Almost immediately, Corey answered him with a seductive tone to her voice, "The only thing I want to munch on right now is you, darling."

Bob leaned over her, put his hand behind her back, and then the other hand under her knees, and picked her up and carried her into the bedroom.

He set her down and went and turned the shower on as they began to undress each other. Bob then led Corey into the walk-in shower area They immediately stood under the spray from the show-erhead and began kissing.

When they ended the prolonged and sensual kiss, Bob reached for a body sponge that sat next to a bottle of foaming shower gel. After he got the sponge foaming wet, he began to run it up and down

Corey's body. When he moved it around her back, he was kissing all over her neck. She had her arms around his neck and was thoroughly enjoying his touch.

While taking the sponge up and down her legs, he gently brought it through her buttocks, and began to move the sponge, with firm pressure, over the surface between her legs. Bob let the sponge fall to the shower's floor and started to suckle the nipples of her breasts while he ran his hands around her backside. Corey was whimpering and breathing quite hard as she gasped when he entered her.

Bob held her by the cheeks of her buttocks as he worked at moving deeper into her. He was thrusting himself into her as Corey yelled with abandon, "Oh my god, baby. Oh my god, how I love you."

She was moving with him, and she could feel her body start to convulse with the galvanic effects of an extremely intense climax. Corey kept pushing her pelvis into him. She never wanted this feeling to end. Her arms wrapped themselves around his waist as she stood tightly holding him. Her face fell into his chest as Bob tenderly kissed her on top of her head.

Corey again began to move herself with his body when Bob lifted her with his hands while cupping her buttocks. He turned her back to the shower wall and began his rhythmical thrusts into her with his hips. Bob was breathing like he had just finished dancing the jitterbug as Corey surrendered every part of herself to him. His head fell to her shoulder when he held his breath and gasped heavily as he began to climax.

They held each other in that same position for another minute or so. They were both breathing hard when Bob then withdrew and released his hold of her.

The water continued to cascade down upon them as Corey relaxed her hold on him, and then she picked up the sponge. After she got it foaming again, she turned Bob around and began to soap his back. She loved running the sponge over his chiseled buttocks.

He turned back to Corey as she sponged his chest and then worked her way down his groin and then his legs. Bob started to breath heavily again as Corey dropped the sponge and started to kiss every part of him. She tenderly held the back of his thighs as her tongue played with his body. Bob was holding his breath as he fell into complete sexual abandonment to this woman. He started gasping for air when his second orgasm totally overwhelmed him. He struggled for air and breathlessly pleaded to Corey, "Oh, baby! My god! Come to me, baby!"

Corey immediately stood up and put her arms around his waist. Bob tightly held her to his chest. He lifted her head with one hand and softly kissed her on each eyelid. He then buried her in an intense kiss, where they were probing each other's mouths with their tongues and nibbling at each other's lips.

They then stood holding each other until they calmed themselves down. They then began rinsing each other off under the spray of the shower.

Bob turned off the shower, and as he stepped out, he grabbed a towel and began to dry Corey's entire body. After he dried each part of her, he would kiss it and run his tongue over it. Corey closed her eyes in complete ecstasy. Hurriedly, they brushed their teeth and quickly ended up in bed. When they started kissing again, Bob took a deep breath and exhaled heavily as he could hear Corey quietly yawning. Within minutes, they both had fallen fast asleep in each other's arms.

From the time they got up Sunday morning for their wedding, and the thirteen hours it took to get to their villa from LA, Bob and Corey were up for almost twenty-eight hours straight. The few hours of on-and-off sleep on the plane helped but did not fully erase the fatigue they had built up before, during, and after their wedding.

At six o'clock, Tuesday morning, the sun was brilliantly shining through the several windows of Bob and Corey's villa. When Corey arose from bed, she grabbed her robe, which was draped across the foot of the bed, and threw her arms into it then tied it around her waist. She lovingly looked at Bob and let him sleep. She walked to the window that overlooked the Villa Borghese Gardens, and between the fresh morning air streaming into the room and the view of one of the biggest, most exquisite gardens in the world, both just took her breath away.

As she stood admiring the beauty of Italian ornamental gardening, Bob came up behind her and wrapped his arms around her stomach, just below her breasts.

Corey pulled in a little gasp, and in her surprise, she saw it was Bob. She dissolved into a huge smile, and the beauty of her face was lit by the love in her heart. They kissed, and then Corey turned back to the window, placing Bob's hands on her breasts.

Bob stood for a minute, kissing her neck and nibbling on her earlobes. Corey affectionately turned her head a little toward Bob's head and slowly closed her eyes, enjoying the moment.

She then whispered to him, "Just look at that big bed, and no one using it. Isn't that just a shame?"

Bob smiled brilliantly, knowing Corey was using his own words against him. He swooped her up and quickly moved toward the bed. They made some very passionate love for the next hour and a half.

Before they got out of bed, Bob had ordered some coffee, eggs, and toast. They jumped into the shower and then got dressed. They had until nine o'clock to eat their breakfast, because Bob had set up a tour guide to introduce them to the wonders of Rome.

They met their tour guide, Giovanni, down in the lobby minutes before nine o'clock. He commenced to drive them away in a midsize, red vintage Porsche.

Within the three-hour tour, Giovanni led Bob and Corey around Rome; they toured the Colosseum, which dated back to AD 80, where the Romans enjoyed the chariot races and the gladiators fight to the death as pure entertainment.

They visited the Vatican, the smallest country in the world; they were shown Michelangelo's masterpiece, the Pieta, and the magnificent frescoed ceiling in the Sistine Chapel, which was his most famous work.

They witnessed the Roman Forum, which was the center of Roman life and government two thousand years ago. The ancient remains mark the old Rome, which butted up to the modem Rome of today.

They also visited the seventeenth-century masterpiece the Trevi Fountain, the Spanish Steps, and one of Rome's most majestic churches, Santa Maria Maggiore.

Santa Maria Maggiore had stood since the fourth century. Mass has been celebrated there every day since the fifth century.

Corey was just awestruck with the Romans' stunning two-thousand-year-old architecture. They were an advanced civilization and extremely gifted with the brilliant masterfulness of the arts and the unified design of their Baroque architecture.

The entire city of Rome was historically steeped in antiquity, with the beautiful mosaics and frescoes in their structures on the streets, in their columns, and in the fountains.

At noon, Bob asked his tour guide, "Giovanni? Would you mind dropping us off at a good out-of-the-way restaurant not far from our hotel? I think we'd like to walk back to the villa."

Giovanni obliged and dropped Corey and him off at Verona Piazza, just six city blocks from the Villa Borghese Hotel.

The interior of the restaurant was weathered and dark. It appeared like a mom-and-pop eatery you'd find within the confines of Brooklyn. There were tablecloths and cloth napkins, but the crowning touch was the portrait of the Mother Mary hanging on the wall in the back of the bar.

Corey looked at Bob with boding trepidation. He sensed her anxiety and smiled at her, and with an adventurous tone, he said, "Oh, come on, doll. Let's try it. Don't freak out on me, 'cause this is gonna be outta sight. I can just tell."

Corey answered reluctantly, knowing she was placing the well-being of her intestinal tract in his hands, "I think I would prefer it was out of sight."

Bob laughed to himself as an old Italian woman, dressed in a worn plaid dress covered by a stained and greasy apron, came to show them to a table. She laid a menu in front of each of them and asked in very broken English, "You hava drink or what?"

Bob knew by looking at Corey's worried face he would have to do the ordering. He told the woman, "Two iced teas, *per favore*."

The woman looked at him puzzled and asked, "You wanna ice in some tea?"

Bob answered, nodding his head, "Si." The woman walked away.

Amazed, Corey asked him, "You know some Italian, along with your French?"

"I studied a little bit before the wedding. I didn't want to be totally rude to these people. After all, we are in their country."

Corey acquiesced to his logic, "Yes, I guess we are."

Bob studied Corey, and it seemed like she couldn't wait to get out of there. He smiled at her, holding back his laughter, and told her, "Don't worry, babe. I've got this."

When the woman brought them some hot tea, in a tall glass, with two small melting ice cubes floating helplessly in the tea, the woman asked, "You eatta food now?"

Bob looked at Corey, and she was biting at her lower lip, wanting to laugh, and looking at her watch.

Bob concealed his smile and told the woman, "Noi mangiare ilpollastro panmigiano, si?"

The woman responded, "Oh, you be happy tonight, no problems."

Bob answered her, "Grazie."

Corey looked at Bob and inquisitively asked, "What did you order, darling? Whatever it is, it sounded wonderful."

Bob laughed out loud and told her, "The hell if I know. It just sounded good." When Corey started laughing, he started laughing with her.

They were drinking their room temperature tea, when ten minutes later, the woman returned with their meals. She placed a plate down in front of each of them that had the most beautiful and sumptuous-looking chicken parmesan either one of them had ever seen. And the aroma wafting up into their nostrils was making their mouths water. The woman also left a sliced baguette and a large bowl of salad in the middle of the table.

Corey almost apologetically remarked, "Oh my god. This looks and smells divine."

Bob had already cut into his dish and was thoroughly enjoying it.

In a few minutes, the woman returned to their table with a small plate in her hands and asked, "You like the *il pollastro parmigiano*?"

Both of them, with a full mouth of food, nodded. Then the woman put the small plate down on the table and told them, "Here some Maritozzi. You no buy. They free Italian *creama* buns. *Saluti*."

Bob told her, "Grazie, grazie."

Bob smiled broadly at Corey, and she giggled, knowing she wouldn't have room to eat all the food that was on the table. Bob just laughed, then he facetiously asked, "And you were having your doubts about this place. What do you think now, doll?"

"Well, I've learned to never judge a book by its cover and to trust my darling husband."

Bob, grinning at her, lovingly told her, "I love you too, baby."

After they finished eating what they could, they managed to convey to the woman to wrap the rest, and they'd take it with them.

Bob generously tipped her, and when she told him, "Grazie, signore," he immediately answered, "Prego, signora."

When Bob and Corey returned to their villa, they walked in and around the gardens that surrounded the hotel. They lay out together in one chaise lounge for a couple of hours, just holding each other and napping on and off.

They returned to their villa that late afternoon and enjoyed some very tender and amorously attentive lovemaking.

The last full day they would be in Rome, Bob and Corey just took off walking. The thought of being adventurous was exciting to them. They walked for hours and saw beautiful churches dating back to the Dark Ages, magnificent fountains, majestic thousand-year-old buildings, streets of cobblestone—probably laid down two millennia ago by Greek slaves. The entire day was awe-inspiring and truly a lesson in historical Italian antiquity.

Early Wednesday morning, March 23, Bob and Corey were driven to Naples by a private driver he had hired months ago. The drive was one hour south of Rome. They departed from Molo Beverello in Piazza Municipal on a ferry that would take them forty minutes to the Isle of Capri.

The only way to reach Capri was by sea or helicopter; there was no airport. Capri was 130 miles from Rome and was a magnificently beautiful island that was located in Italy's Bay of Naples.

Bob and Corey stood against the forward deck railings of the ferry, and he held her tightly as the salt water lightly sprayed them with every wave the ferry encountered. He occasionally kissed Corey on her cheek, her forehead, and on top of her head; she responded by turning to face him and then kissing him on the lips very affectionately.

They were both caught up in the tremendous views of the bay and the rugged landscape of Italy's cove-studded coastlines and Capri, with its picturesque grottoes and breathtaking gardens.

Bob was just staring at Corey as they approached Capri. He was absolutely thrilled with her reaction to the island; she seemed mesmerized by the unbelievable views she was taking in of the coastline.

As the ferry neared the docking area, the entire cove was lined with brilliantly colored small homes, many small docked boats, and the beautiful pops of blues and deep-peach colors of the thousands of flowers that comprised the entire shoreline.

After they debarked the ferry, a driver met them and escorted them to a luxury sedan that would then drive them up to Anacapri. The island had two towns: Capri and, high above it, at an elevation of 1,932 feet above sea level, was Anacapri. Its peak was Monte Solaro.

There were many upscale hotels on the island, but Bob wanted to indulge his new bride. The driver delivered them to the Anacapri Hotel—Punta Tragara; this was where luxury was personified. The hotel embodied the island's glamour and panache. It exemplified an era marked by aristocratic opulence.

Punta Tragara had the 1920s vintage patterns and colors that were inspired by the gorgeous rose gardens on the island. Their room overlooked these fragrant rose gardens and the Bay of Naples in the distance.

The concierge at the front desk informed Corey and Bob about the hotel's beauty rituals and relaxing massages that could be had at the Roman Fabrizio Narducci's boutique, if they were able to tear themselves away from the hotel's staggering vistas and pampering environs.

Bob and Corey's suite was seated atop the labyrinth of the three levels of the hotel. No two rooms were alike; the decor in their suite was classic—with imperial marbled bathrooms, sculptured ceilings, and an ostentatious display of ornate paintings and drapery.

They had the most spectacular views on the planet, from all their windows, onto the Bay of Naples. It was a masterpiece of million-dollar views and 1920s sophistication.

They were lofted so high above the iconic *faraglioni* pinnacles that they could have reached out and touched them.

The concierge informed them, "Our executive chef, Luigi Lionetti, will be preparing your meals in the window-lined dining room of Le Monzu. The bar area of Monzu, called Gin and American Bar, you can sip on a fizzy or fruity cocktail, or you can have a classic martini—stirred, not shaken."

Corey turned her head slowly, and with a sexy look on her face, she grinned at Bob. He smiled back at her and lovingly told her, "I've got to keep my best girl happy."

"You do that very well, darling," Corey purred.

With a huge smile, he said to her with the Italian flair, "Grazie, cara mia."

Before Corey could ask, Bob explained, "Thank you, my beloved."

After the concierge showed them into their suite and had their luggage brought in, he left the key with Bob. Bob tipped him and then shut the door after the men walked out.

Before Bob could turn around completely, Corey had her arms wrapped around his neck, pulling his lips toward hers. She pulled her head away and looked deep into his eyes as she swore to him, "Robert Brian, you really know how to love a woman. Love me now, darling."

Bob started to unbutton her blouse. He then leaned over and tenderly kissed the side of Corey's neck as he unfastened her bra and her skirt. She was feeling overwhelmed with her love for Bob, and her entire body cried out for the want of this man.

They ended up in bed past lunchtime. Suddenly, there was a knock on their door. Bob kissed Corey once more then got up and tied a robe around himself and opened the door. The waiter brought in a silver tray that had a pitcher of dry martini—stirred, not shaken.

The waiter left, and Bob poured two martini glasses full, with one olive in each glass.

He took them into the bedroom and sat on the edge of the bed closest to Corey. She sat up, and Bob handed her one glass, saying, "I have a standing order for a pitcher of these to come to the room every afternoon and evening. So, my beautiful lady, drink up."

Corey took the glass from Bob's hand and sipped at the rim of the drink. After they both had a short sip, she leaned into him for a kiss. He met her halfway, and they engaged in a respectfully short kiss while holding their glasses out of the way.

Corey lovingly told him, "Thank you, darling. Capri has been exquisite, and I've not even been out of the room yet."

Bob broadly smiled and asked her, "What do you say about going down to the main dining room and having lunch. Then we can wander around the many different stores and boutiques the island has. Then come back and get ready for an unreal dinner down in Le Monzu?"

"That sounds unbelievably exquisite, sweetheart," Corey purred.

After their delicious lunch, they went from store to store looking and buying. Corey bought a beautiful full-length, black evening gown. It possessed many flowing layers of silk that wrapped around the entire gown and finished at the bodice. The cut of cleavage was extremely seductive and sexy. She told Bob this would be the dress that she would wear to the Academy Awards in a week and a half. Corey had the dress shipped back to Bel Air.

Bob and Corey returned to the hotel around six o'clock and showered and changed into a casual dress. They enjoyed a wonderful dinner of *lasagna al fruitti di mare* (fruits of the ocean or seafood lasagna).

When they finished their meal, and were having an after-dinner drink of a peach liqueur, the headwaiter approached their table and asked, "We don't meana to bother, but Signore Richardson, woulda you mind singing for us anda our guests? And it'sa pleasure meeting you, Signora Corey Madrigala. Your movies, wonderful, and you *bellissima*."

Corey was thrilled they were translating her movies for the Europeans' enjoyment. After hearing Bob use the word, she graciously told the waiter, "Grazie."

That made Bob very proud upon hearing they knew her and of her movies; all he could do was look at Corey very admiringly and with eyes that radiated his love for her.

Corey was all smiles from ear to ear and encouraged Bob to go up and play. Bob was flattered and asked the waiter, "I see you have a baby grand over in the corner. How about I use that for my song?"

"*Magnifico*, Signore Richardson."

Bob graciously told him, "Prego, signore," as he rose from his seat and walked over to the baby grand. The guests gave him a warm, welcoming applause.

He sat down on the piano bench, and smiling, he looked over at Corey and then began to play "My Foolish Heart."

> The night is like a lovely tune
> Beware my foolish heart
> How white the ever constant moon
> Take care, my foolish heart

Corey was just mesmerized by his beautiful baritone, but then she always was. The dinner guests in the restaurant seemed to be enjoying the song as they smiled. There were even two couples who got up and slow danced while Bob kept singing and playing the piano. Bob finished out the song with the last two stanzas:

> Her lips are much too close to mine
> Beware my foolish heart
> But should our eager lips combine
> Then let the fire start
>
> For this time it isn't fascination
> Or a dream that will fade and fall apart
> It's love, this time it's love
> My foolish heart

The ladies and gentlemen stood and clapped loudly for him. Corey clapped dreamily as she glowed with the pride and love she would always feel for him.

As Bob walked back to his table and shook hands with some of the people, he told them, "Grazie…Grazie."

Bob and Corey finished their drink, and as they stood up to leave, a gentlemen asked, "E` tua moglie?"

Bob smiled and proudly told him, "Mia moglie, nozze quattro giorni fa. Mio cara mia."

The entire room applauded now with some whistles.

Bob told everyone, "Grazie, miei amici." Then they slowly walked out of the restaurant.

When they started walking to the elevator, Bob told Corey, "The gentleman asked me if you were my wife. I told him you are my wife and that we were married four days ago. Then I introduced you as my beloved."

Corey took Bob's arm and pulled it between her breasts. She then lay her head on his arm and took a deep, cleansing breath and exhaled loudly.

Bob looked down at Corey and told her, "Sei bella, cara mia." She peered up at him, and he lovingly told her, "You are beautiful, my beloved."

There was a fresh pitcher of martinis waiting for them when they returned to their room, of which they bathed themselves in. Then they took their time and made some very sensual love that evening.

The next morning, Corey had scheduled a day at the boutique, with Bob's prompting. She really didn't need any prompting, but she allowed him to think he convinced her.

Starting after breakfast, Corey had a rejuvenating hot stone and oil massage, a facial, a mud pack, a manicure, pedicure, full-detoxifying body scrub, organic body wrap, and a haircut with a world-class hairdresser. All this was very calming to her. It promoted a state of total relaxation within her and improved her bodily tension.

The compresses used in the facials and wraps were incorporated with plants from their own hotel gardens, and the fragrances from those were simply intoxicating to Corey.

Bob had spent this time getting his hair trimmed and a shave right there in the hotel's boutique. The hairdresser ended his shave by splashing some sandalwood-scented aftershave on his face and neck. He actually liked the smell of that and hoped Corey would like it also.

Bob went back to their suite and put on his bathing suit. He then headed for the private balcony off of the bedroom, which had the incredible views of the bay. He reclined on one of the oversized chaise lounges, trying to soak up some sun.

Bob had left the door to the suite unlocked so the waiter could bring in another of their endless pitchers of martinis, and also Corey would be able to have easy access when she returned.

A couple of hours later, Corey came waltzing into the suite, a renewed woman. She felt fabulous and looked even better. She looked around and didn't see Bob, but when she walked into the bedroom, she noticed the doors to the balcony were opened.

Corey moved with excitement to the opened doors and found Bob sleeping on the lounger. She stood admiring his masculine physicality, and with his bathing suit on, she started to breathe just a little bit harder, and her heart beat just a little bit faster.

She turned back into the bedroom and decided she would change into her two-piece bathing suit and join him.

Minutes later, Corey came out onto the balcony wearing her bright-yellow bathing suit that had an accented black trim around the edges. She slowly and quietly sat down beside him as he remained asleep. When she lay down beside him and tenderly stroked his chest muscles, Bob awoke to Corey's touch.

He yawned and was bleary-eyed, but when he noticed it was Corey, he exhaled a breath of loving desire for her. "Hey, baby. You smell and look *magnifico, cara mia*."

She raised herself up to where she could put both her arms on Bob's chest and run her hand through his beautiful hair.

Corey could now smell the scent of the sandalwood on his face and amorously exclaimed, "Oh my god, Robert Brian. Your hair looks so handsome, and that aftershave is delicious!"

Within minutes, Bob had both of their swimming suits off and Corey lying on top of him.

His arms were wrapped around her as she had her arms lying on his shoulders, with her hands stroking the side of his face. Corey's breasts lay full and voluptuously on Bob's chest, revealing the alluring cleavage that had always raised his body temperature.

They looked into each other's eyes, and Corey sensed some mild trepidation in Bob. As she held his face in her hands, she concernedly asked, "Darling, what is it? What's on your mind, sweetheart?"

Bob kept staring at her as his eyes began to moisten. Corey really became worried now.

"Tell me, baby. Remember? We said we would talk over here in Italy because we would be absolutely alone and away from everyone. So tell me, what is it, darling?"

Bob exhaled heavily, and still looking into her eyes, he confessed to her, "Baby, when I fell in love with you, it was like I had my own heaven right here on earth. You were exactly the woman I had ever dreamt about."

Corey's eyes were now glistening as she was fixed on his eyes and what he was saying.

He then told her, "I don't ever want to lose you, Corey. For whatever reason, it wouldn't matter. I would not be able to function without you. You've become a big part of me. Promise you'll never let me go, baby."

A single tear ran down the side of his face, and she softly wiped it away.

Corey wiped her own tears away and consolingly looked directly into Bob's eyes, and with the burning passion that she held in her heart for him, she irrevocably told him, "Oh my god, baby. I can't even imagine letting you go. I've told you before, and I'll keep telling you, you are my life, Robert Brian. That will never change, darling."

Instantly, Bob reached up and took Corey's head in his hands and pulled her lips down to his. They kissed each other savagely as they were rubbing their pelvic areas together and becoming quite sexually aroused.

The cool late afternoon breezes began sweeping in from the bay. That's when Bob carried Corey into the bedroom, and upon laying her on the bed, Corey pulled him onto her. They continued making some very torrid love for well over an hour. When their passion subsided, they ordered in their dinner that night and ate it in bed. They spent the rest of the evening there—drinking, talking, playing, and making love on and off all night.

Bob and Corey spent the next six days roaming the island, shopping, eating, enjoying the vistas of an absolutely gorgeous island retreat, and the whole time loving each other and enjoying each other's company.

On the last evening of their stay on the Isle of Capri, April 1, they ordered their dinner to be brought to their room again. After eating their rigatoni carbonara, along with drinking a copious amount of martinis, they relaxed for a while out on the balcony. They were taking in their last views of the Bay of Naples and smelling the pure and clean saltwater mist that hung in the air.

Bob turned and invitingly asked Corey, "What do think about me giving you a full-body massage, tonight?"

Without hesitation, Corey took him by the hand and led him into the bedroom. She began undressing herself, as Bob was out of his clothes within seconds. He watched her lower her panties and remove her bra; his mouth began salivating, and he could feel his heart beating outside of his chest.

She climbed into bed as she lay on her stomach. Bob straddled her body with his legs, and after grabbing the Moroccan argan body oil that he bought in the hotel's boutique, he began to rub it into her shoulders and arms.

After he worked the oil into her muscles, he started to kiss her skin as he went along. While he slowly rubbed the oil all over her lower back, he was kissing the oiled areas and running his tongue lightly over her skin.

Corey was loving this. This massage was far more pleasurable to her than what the masseuse gave her down in the boutique. Having the man she adored kissing on her and tasting her skin with his tongue may have been the major difference between the two.

When Bob was done massaging Corey's legs and buttocks, he gently rolled her over and immediately started to oil her arms and breasts. When he kissed and ran his tongue over her nipples, her chest was heaving with breathless expectancy.

Bob began softly rubbing the oil around her stomach and then down her groin area and onto her thighs. He lowered himself to where he was kissing and suckling her. When he placed his tongue in and around her, Corey started to beg him to enter her.

He was fully engorged and moved up to kiss her on the lips and let the taste of the oil from his lips meet hers. At that instant, he penetrated her, and she totally surrendered her entire body to him.

Bob began to work himself deeper into her as she rhythmically moved her pelvis with his thrusts. It was pulse-pounding and pure erotic pleasure they were experiencing.

Corey held on as long as she could, and then she exploded into a very intense orgasm. Her body became rigid as she whimpered with total sexual satisfaction. She continued to move with Bob as she kissed his neck and upper chest area. He suddenly grabbed her around her shoulders and breathed in short, gasping breaths as he was reaching orgasm.

Corey held him tight to her body as he began to relax and calmly exhale. After a minute or two, Bob withdrew from her, and then he collapsed his head onto her chest.

She ran one hand through his hair while the other lay on his shoulder. There was complete silence for several minutes, until Corey said dreamily, "In all the world, there is no heart for me like yours. In all the world, there is no love for you like mine. Maya Angelou."

When Bob heard this, he raised his head and moved his body up to kiss Corey ever so tenderly on the lips. Bob then pulled the covers up over them as they fell asleep in each other's arms.

The next morning, they showered and washed the oil off of their bodies. After they were dressed, packed, and had breakfast down in the dining room, they had to leave their Italian Shangri-la. They took one more look out over the bay, from the outside of the hotel, as they held each other and then kissed one last time.

Their plane left Rome at noon and was scheduled to land in LA, Saturday, April, 2, at four o'clock in the afternoon. The time change allowed them to take back the hours they had lost flying to Italy.

After Bob and Corey retrieved their luggage, they met Curtis out in front of the arrival's terminal. Haddie was excited about them coming home, so she hitched a ride with Curtis to the airport.

When Haddie saw Bob and Corey, she gave each one a big bear hug and excitingly asked Corey, "Well, did you have the time of your life? You don't need to tell me. I can see it in your eyes and your face."

Corey, with a mammoth smile on her face, exclaimed, "Oh, Haddie, it was exquisite! Absolutely enthralling! We could not have gone to a more perfect and romantic place."

After they were all in the car and on their way home, Haddie inquisitively asked Bob as she was looking over her shoulder into the back seat, "Mr. Bob, did you enjoy your honeymoon?"

Bob was all smiles when he answered Haddie, "More than I could have ever imagined, Haddie." He gazed over at Corey and then turned back to Haddie and told her, "Mia moglie e' solo delizioso!"

Corey moved close to Bob, and he put his arm around her as he tenderly kissed her lips.

Haddie didn't understand what he said, so she remarked, "Okay, now you gotta quit talking those spaghetti-os and tell me what you just said."

Bob kissed Corey on top of her head and then softly translated, "My wife is just delicious!"

Happily, Haddie answered, "All right, now we gettin' somewhere. I'll talk with Ms. Corey another time about all that. I'll get the scoop on that deliceo-o-o-o stuff."

Bob took his free hand and moved Corey's face toward him as he kissed her lips for several seconds.

Haddie saw them locked in a kiss, and Curtis saw them in his rearview mirror. They looked at each other and mischievously smiled. Curtis then took his right hand and turned Haddie's face back around to the front of the car.

Haddie quietly exclaimed, "Oh, you old fool. I'm just enjoying the scenery."

ELEVEN

At dinner that Saturday night, Haddie told Corey and Bob about everything that had been happening since they left to go on their honeymoon.

Haddie informed them, "Ms. Corey, your package from Italy arrived yesterday, it's in your bedroom closet. And your studio sent over two copies of the motion picture manuscript, you and Mr. Bob will be starting this Wednesday. And last, but not least, Ms. Alex has found a house in Beverly Hills, just five miles east of here. She said to tell you welcome back, and she would be by sometime tomorrow to pick up her remaining things."

Corey mentioned out loud, "I knew Alex was interested in a place over in Beverly Hills, but I find it intriguing she couldn't wait to move until we got back."

Bob offered his take on the situation and surmised, "She probably felt it would be an impingement for her to stay here and interfere with the newlyweds' privacy."

Haddie facetiously added, "It'd be hard for me too to watch someone dipping into the cookie jar that I wanted to get some goodies out of but knew I couldn't."

Bob was baffled by Haddie's metaphorical reasoning. "What? You don't mean—"

Immediately, Corey interjected, "Alex is in love with you, darling! A woman knows these things." She then quipped, "It's an inherent quality we possess from birth."

Bob stared at Corey ambivalently and casually stated, "It doesn't really matter, does it? Because, as we know, it takes two to tango… now, I'm gonna go for a swim. How about you?"

Corey offered an alternative idea, suggesting, "How about I come out, and we throw some lines back and forth after your swim?"

Bob jokingly shot back, "How about we do that in bed, tonight?"

Smiling very seductively, she answered, "Because I'm afraid you'd have a diminished interest in just running some lines, darling."

Haddie could be heard chuckling as she was washing the dinner dishes.

He questioningly asked, "Okay, but I'm not seeing the problem."

Corey smiled broadly and saucily answered, "Ah-ha."

After Bob swam his laps and then ran some lines with Corey out by the pool, he showered and gave Jimmy a call. Jimmy welcomed him back home and asked, "All right, lay it on me, man. What's crackin'?"

Bob asked Jimmy if he could get Jessy, his girlfriend, who worked at the recording studio, to open it up Sunday so the Owls could rehearse.

Jimmy told him he would ask Jessy and then get back to him.

Corey came out of the bedroom as Bob hung up the phone in the front hallway. She was moving eloquently across the hardwood floors, draped in her new evening gown she had bought and sent home from Capri.

Bob whistled the two high notes of sexual arousal. Corey smiled and chuckled with content as Haddie came walking down the hall to find out what was going on.

Corey asked Haddie, anticipating her reaction, "How do you like it, Haddie? This is what I sent home from Capri. I'm going to wear it Monday night to the Academy Awards."

Haddie took a look at the black silk evening gown and excitedly told Corey, "Oh, Ms. Corey! You gonna be the foxiest, badass skirt ever at the Academy Awards! It's just beautiful!"

Bob stood studying Corey, and as she looked at him for his verbal approval, he enticingly told her, "You look absolutely stunning, doll. And that low neckline—you're gonna have guys falling all over you Monday night."

Corey seductively told him, "The only man I want falling all over me is you, darling."

Bob had to grin at her, and then the phone rang. Bob picked it up, and it was Jimmy telling him Jessy would open the studio to them at nine o'clock tomorrow morning. They could stay and use it as long as they wanted to.

When Bob hung up the phone, he informed Corey, "Jimmy secured the recording studio for us tomorrow morning and, if we feel we need it, the afternoon also. You know, we're playing the LA Shrine Auditorium two weeks from tonight? And I haven't touched my guitar in the last two weeks." Bob added playfully, "I've touched many other things, but not my guitar."

Haddie started cracking up with laughter as Corey stood smiling, and then she joined in laughing with Haddie.

Right after breakfast the next morning, Bob left for the recording studio. Shortly after Bob was gone, Alex showed up at the estate. Corey welcomed her in and offered her some coffee.

While they drank their coffee, seated at the island in the kitchen, Alex asked Corey, "I wanted to ask you and Bob about your honeymoon. Where did he go this early in the morning? It must be related to his music."

Corey knew there was only one reason Alex would have come so early in the morning, and that was so she could see and talk with Bob.

Corey told her, "Yes, he went to the recording studio to rehearse with his band. I guess they're performing at the Shrine Auditorium in less than two weeks, and he needed to get their program in order for the concert. Alex, I'm sure if he had known when you were coming, he may have stayed for a while longer. But then who knows? He's just so busy right now."

Alex stayed another hour talking with Corey about her and Bob's honeymoon, Corey and Bob's new picture coming up, and about her new house in Beverly Hills. She took her remaining two boxes of clothes with her and mentioned to Corey before she left about having people over for cocktails and finger food soon. Corey reservedly told her she and Bob would enjoy that.

When Bob arrived at the recording studio, the guys all shook his hand, patted him on the back, and asked funny—and even lewd—questions about what kept him occupied on his honeymoon.

Bob simply answered, "Wouldn't all of you like to know? So just kiss off! Corey and I had a blast. It was just a gas in both Rome and Capri. I would recommend that trip to anyone. Now, why don't we start producing some music?"

At that moment, Joshua spoke up and informed Bob, "Hey, man. While you were really stoked out on Corey and in that groovy marriage state of mind, we kicked out rough forms of two more songs. They're both upbeat and ass-slapping, man."

Joshua handed Bob the rough draft of both songs, and Bob sat reading them as he moved his head to the beat and to the early stages of the development of the melody. Joshua had even written in a part for piano on one of the songs.

When Bob was done reading the songs that were still in their infancy, he nodded his head affirmatively and told the guys, "I think with some work, these two songs are going places. I like the piano addition to the one. Yeah, these are solid. So, let's get to work."

The guys spent the next four hours pounding out the melody, rhythm, pitch, and the volume for the two new songs: "Conviction" and "Makin' Roads Inland."

The songs were now taking on the more oblique and the more cutting edge of the new rock 'n' roll. Bob, Joshua, and Len reworked the melody as they went along to give it a clearer shape.

Len mentioned to the group, "You guys know it's the lead guitar that makes the record. In 'Conviction,' the guitar riff needs to be surprisingly sophisticated, and I know the best you can hope for is that your instrument is in tune. So, Bob, you're going to be painting pictures in the audience's mind and trying your damnedest to mentally engage them. I know you can kick ass with these chords, but this song needs you to burn the auditorium down, blow away the first five rows of seats, and walk away unapologetically."

Bob smiled and chuckled at Len, saying, "Every time I play this song, believe me, I will be igniting a fire under every seat in the house and destroying everything that anyone ever felt they thought they knew about rock 'n' roll. I'm gonna give the audience a chance to feel what we're feeling. I mean, the face of rock 'n' roll is going to be changing now with every song that's written."

The guys all shouted out words of assent, and Darnell reassured the guys by stating, "Hell yes! We're gonna redefine the word *badasses!* Ain't no one, nohow, gonna walk away from our music and feel we didn't speak to the many people who are ignored by the man! Those discriminated against, those held down by an unjust system, and those trying to make their lives better, and then run into the red-taped wall of resistance."

Doug yelled out, "Right on, B.B.!"

Right at that moment, Nick came walking into the recording studio. Bob had called Nick and told him about their impromptu session, and Nick told him he would drop by.

Nick sat down on one of the stools in the recording room and began updating the guys about everything pertaining to the Night Owls. He told them, "All right, guys, I just wanted to remind you about the Shrine Auditorium two weeks from yesterday. Get your program in order, and I'll get the instruments down there after your last rehearsal that Thursday, April, 14. I want you there a couple of hours before the concert, Saturday, at eight o'clock. You're gonna need to tune up, check out your instruments, and then we'll run a sound check."

Len excitedly told Nick, "We've been working all day to get the two songs we wrote polished and ready to go while Bob was on his honeymoon. We're pretty sure they can be part of the program those two nights."

Nick grinned and told them, "That would really help to sell 'em after you perform them. Yeah, try to do that, guys. And, by the way, Bob starts his motion picture this Wednesday, so your recording sessions will be moved, starting on April 7, to six o'clock until nine o'clock in the evening."

Doug jumped in and facetiously told everyone, "Oh-h-h, our Hollywood star is making another movie." He wrapped his arms around his shoulders and started making kissing sounds and moaning sensuously.

All the guys laughed heartily. Even Nick got a kick out of Doug's melodrama. Bob just laughed and facetiously blew Doug a kiss.

Nick added one more thing before he left. He told the guys, "Now keep May 6 open. I'll explain it to you later." Bob looked at Nick and smiled, for he knew that was the night all of them and their ladies were going to the Hollywood Bowl to listen to Duke Ellington's band, along with Ms. Ella Fitzgerald. All this was only after everyone met the Duke and Ms. Ella at Bob and Corey's estate earlier that day.

Before Nick made it to the door, he turned and told the guys, "All of you need to think about a name for the new album you'll be releasing in May. It wouldn't hurt if you had two more songs along with these two here. Okay? I hope to see all of you at Corey's surprise birthday party next Saturday. See you guys later."

Jimmy spoke up and asked Bob, "How are you gonna keep this birthday a secret, when Corey lives right there where you're having it?"

Bob answered, "Well, Jack is gonna call Corey at two o'clock and get her to drive in to the studio for some lamebrain reason. That's when the people Haddie and I've invited will show up. Everyone should be there by three o'clock. Jack will cut Corey loose at that time."

Darnell asked, "I'm gonna be wearing my swimsuit under my pants, is that all right?"

"Oh, hell yes! I think most of us will be playing in the pool," Bob excitedly answered. "And don't forget…no presents. Haddie and I also have a caterer coming who will be furnishing not only food, but a full bar of beer and liquor. So, plan on having some fun!"

Bob arrived home at almost three o'clock that Sunday afternoon. Corey was lounging out by the pool and studying her manuscript for Wednesday's script read-through.

When Bob pulled into the opened garage, Corey's attention went to him. As he walked from the garage toward the house, her eyes were fixated on his every move. When he spotted her on the lounger, he smiled broadly, and then in his strolling cadence, he headed straight for her.

He immediately kissed her on the lips and noticed the manuscript on her lap. "Well, do you have all your lines memorized, doll?"

"A good portion of them, but I have a ways to go," Corey answered sleepily. Bob then lowered himself next to Corey onto her lounger. She tossed the manuscript on the ground and wrapped her one arm around his waist as she lay her head on his chest. She lovingly asked, "How did your session go today, darling? Is the band ready to play the auditorium?"

"A good portion of them, but I have a ways to go." He laughed, after echoing her answer.

Corey smiled smartly and then chuckled a couple of times as she brought her hand up and directed his lips onto hers.

When they quit kissing, Corey informed him, "I should tell you, sweetheart. The director, Victor Trudeau, and the producer, Trent Voight, who are working our picture, want us in early this Wednesday for a preproduction conference on the Celebrity lot. This picture will be my first ever that some of the scenes will be shot on location rather than all of the picture being shot on a soundstage."

By 1960, the "state of the art" had advanced to the point where a set and soundstages were becoming nearly obsolete. The set of reality was changing; films had made available shooting a picture in natural light perfectly possible.

Also, the Motion Picture Production Code had unraveled by 1960. The code had further marginalized oppressed minorities, and it determined how women, sexuality, and people of color were cinematically portrayed. The old studio system for almost the last thirty years was breaking down, and restrictions on sexual content, obscenity, and violence had loosened.

The Dream Factories, as the Hollywood motion picture studios were referred to for more than four decades, finally had to start evolving with the times.

"That sounds like a lot of fun and adventure," Bob told her, showing his youthful naiveté.

"Yes, of course, darling, but it will also take more time to finish a picture if you're jumping around from one location to another," Corey added, with a little apprehension.

Before Bob could say anything else, she asked, "Tomorrow night, for the Academy Awards ceremony, are you going to wear a black jacket with your tux, or are you going with a white dinner jacket? I think we'd look exquisite with me in my new black evening gown and you in your all-black tuxedo. What do you think, darling?"

"I would love to look exquisite while walking alongside of you on the red carpet." Bob just smiled brilliantly and then kissed Corey tenderly.

Monday night, Curtis drove Bob and Corey the thirteen minutes to the RKO Pantages Theatre, which was located on Hollywood Boulevard and Vine in LA.

It was five fifteen in the afternoon, and the ceremonies would be starting at six o'clock. Since this was Bob's first nomination for Best Actor in a Leading Role, and his first Academy Awards ceremony, Corey felt she should school him on the Academy's protocol.

While still riding in the car, Corey told him, "Now when Curtis drops us off in front of the theater, darling, you stay close to me, walk slowly up the red carpet. You want to give the press and the fans that will be lining the carpet some time to take pictures and let them feel they're part of the ceremony."

Bob excitedly exclaimed, as they pulled up close to the front of the theater and behind the three limos that were already lined up, "This is just some crazy stuff. The cameras must like all this pomp and circumstance. It looks like there's an army of them out there."

"Believe me, darling, there will be a lot of press, and a lot of our fans will be there. Just try to smile and wave. We need to keep moving along, unless we're asked to come over to a microphone for a couple of short questions from one of the interviewers or a critic." Corey was trying to set firmly in his mind the procedural process.

A few moments later, Curtis pulled the Cadillac up to the red-carpet entrance after their car had been waiting in line for five minutes. Curtis got out of the car and went around to ceremoniously open the back door for Bob and Corey.

Bob stepped out first and held his hand out to Corey as she ducked her head, as not to mess up her hair. She then slowly stuck one leg out of the car and then the other.

When the press saw Bob step out, a few of them yelled, "It's Richardson and Madrigal." The flashbulbs started lighting up the front of the theater, and the young female fans in the side bleachers began screaming and waving for Bob to come over to them.

Bob shook hands with Curtis and slyly told him, "Good job, Curtis. You looked very professional tonight. I bet you hope you don't have to do this again."

Curtis proudly told him, "I just hope you have to do this again. Good luck, Mr. Bob."

"Thanks, man." Bob smiled and then turned back to Corey.

Bob immediately put his right arm around Corey's waist, and they began their slow walk up the red carpet. The noise and the flash of the cameras, and the gallery clapping, screaming, and yelling questions to them, was exhilarating to Bob. He kept smiling and waving his free left hand to both the cameras and the bleachers of fans.

Corey grinned and smiled for the cameras with a prideful look in her eyes; she knew she had the most handsome, youngest, and most talented husband in Hollywood—who just happened to have his arm around her. She kept looking up into Bob's face for his reaction to everything that was going on. She felt he was carrying himself extremely well, until she felt his arm leave her waist.

Bob was taken so much by all of this public adulation, he felt the need to personally let a lot of his fans know how much he appreciated them being there.

After Bob dropped his hold of Corey's waist, he quickly ran over to the bleachers and began shaking hands and blowing kisses to most of the young women who were screaming with delight. A couple of them looked as though they might faint.

Corey stood totally taken by surprise but remained impervious to the situation. She actually thought Bob's gesture to his fans was quite attractive, even if they showed his youthful exuberance and fervent emotions.

One of Hollywood's most renowned film critics, Army Archer, watched Bob abandon Corey. Army felt he needed to rescue her and instantly asked Corey over to talk with him on camera.

Haddie was watching the ceremonies on TV in her bedroom. When she saw Bob leave Corey standing alone on the red carpet, her eyes became as big as silver dollars. She blurted out, "Oh, my goodness. I'm sure that wasn't in the script for tonight."

Army jokingly asked Corey, "Well, good evening, Corey. You look sensational."

"Thank you, Army. We're excited to be here tonight. It's been a few years for me," Corey stated.

At that moment, Bob briskly walked up and put his arm back around Corey's waist. "Oh, I guess I didn't lose him after all," Corey fondly said.

Army playfully tried to scold Bob, "We thought you got lost over there by the bleachers, young man. Glad to see you here tonight, Bob."

Sensing a little bit of animosity, Bob determinedly answered back, "Yeah, I was over thanking the people that enabled me to be here, to speak with critics like you."

Corey knew at that point it was time to go into the theater. "Well, thank you, Army, but we need to get inside now and find our seats."

"Yes, you do. And good luck to everyone involved with your picture, Corey," Army added.

Walking into the theater, Corey sensed Bob's agitated demeanor and tried to calm him by saying, "Darling, someday you may need a critic like him on your side. So it might serve you well if you just ignore him as a person and accept him for the job he does."

Bob knew there was a lot of politics being played in Hollywood, as there was in any big private business, but he never liked politics, and really didn't want to start playing them now.

He made it known to her, "If it ever comes to me needing someone like that, I'll just throw in the towel. I think I do fine on my own, with Nick and I both handling the critics and the PR."

Corey just took a big breath and exhaled loudly. "We'll talk another time, darling."

Seconds later, they were shown their seats: second row, two on the aisle. Susan Hawthorne and her husband were already seated. Corey took the seat next to Susan, leaving Bob on the aisle. Corey hugged and air-kissed Susan after shaking her husband's hand and greeting the picture's director and producer, Rennie Whitmore, who was seated on the other side of Susan's husband.

Bob made his way down to shake Rennie's hand and Susan's husband's hand. He then embraced Susan and kissed her hard on the cheek, as she returned the affection by kissing him close to his mouth but kept it low on his cheek.

Corey watched all of this and made no noticeable facial expression at that moment.

Bob returned to his seat, and the opening music started to play as the curtain went up, and out walked the master of ceremonies, Bob Hope.

After Hope's opening monologue, he started to introduce presenters to read the nominees and announce the winners. The Supporting Actress was Shelley Winters in *Diary of Anne Frank*. The Supporting Actor was Hugh Griffith in *Ben Hur*. The first award of a record-breaking eleven for that picture.

An hour later, the top awards began to be announced. David Niven, who won last year in *Separate Tables*, came out and read the nominees for Best Actress in a Leading Role. "The nominees are Doris Day in *Pillow Talk*. Katharine Hepburn in *Suddenly Last Summer*. Corey Madrigal in *Jumping Off the Deep End*. Susan Hawthorne in *Jumping Off the Deep End*. Simone Signoret in *A Room at the Top*, and Audrey Hepburn in *The Nun's Story*. And the winner is"—the envelope was handed to David, and he smiled and said, after ripping the envelope open, "Simone Signoret."

The audience started to applaud. Susan, Corey, and Bob applauded, as Bob looked over at both of them sympathetically. At this point, he stopped applauding.

Susan Hayward was announced to present Best Actor next because she had won in 1959 for *I Want to Live*. Susan announced,

"The nominees for Best Actor in a Leading Role: Lawrence Harvey in *Room at the Top*. Jack Lemmon in *Some Like It Hot*. Bob Richardson in *Jumping Off the Deep End*. James Stewart in *Anatomy of a Murder*, and Charleston Heston in *Ben Hur*. And the winner is…" The envelope was handed to Susan. She ripped it open and unsurprisingly announced, "Charleston Heston. *Ben Hur*."

Bob smiled and started applauding. Corey took his hand in hers and clenched it, giving him a prideful look of admiration. Presciently, he turned his head toward her, smiling affectionately, then lifted her hand and gently kissed her palm.

The last two awards went exactly the same way. Best Director went to William Wyler for *Ben Hur*, and Best Picture was *Ben Hur*'s eleventh award for the evening.

Bob Hope came back out one last time and congratulated all the winners and told everyone to have a good night and get back to work tomorrow and start working on next year's Oscar.

Everyone started standing up and filing out of the theater. Walking up the theater's aisle, Susan Hawthorne caught Bob and Corey and asked them, "You know, win or lose, I was still going to have that after-Oscar party at my house. It's only eight o'clock. What do you say? Are you two going to join me and another couple dozen other people in drowning our sorrows with cocktails and seafood?"

Bob looked at Corey grinning, and she hesitantly told Susan, "It should be fun to drink and dance the night away. We all have something to drink about, don't we?"

"Wonderful! Then I'll see you at the house," Susan excitedly told them.

At Susan's after-Oscar party, Bob and Corey danced to every slow song. They were both drinking, but especially Corey. She was enjoying her double martinis.

The motivating factor for her excessive drinking seemed to be the thought that had haunted her all night; she may never get another Best Actress nomination and, even more importantly, win another Academy Award.

The possibility of losing Bob had corrupted her normally logical brain. She felt that if she became washed-up in Hollywood, he wouldn't find her desirable anymore. She was moving quickly to her fifties, whereas Bob was so youthful, multitalented, and would always be incredibly handsome and highly desired by many beautiful women.

An hour into the party, Corey was "feeling no pain" and got up in Bob's face and impetuously asked him, "Darling? Would you play a song on the piano…for me?"

He put his arms around her and softly answered her, "Of course, I would. You know I would." He was being patient and meticulously attentive to her. Bob knew there had to be something major going on with Corey to make her drink and act like this.

Corey then turned to Susan and asked, "Can Bob play your piano, for me? I need to have my husband sing 'But Not for Me.'"

Susan, realizing how blown away Corey was, acquiesced to her request. "Why, of course, Corey. Bob can play the baby grand in the great room."

Bob looked at Susan and mouthed the words *thank you.*

Bob then took Corey by the hand and headed for the great room. As they both sat on the piano bench, Bob told her, "Now, there's only one thing I want, doll. I want you to sing with me. Okay?"

Many people followed them into the room and sat down or stood by the piano watching.

"All right, darling, but just know, I'm not a singer," Corey warned.

Bob just grinned and told her, "You'll do fine, babe."

Bob started out with the opening notes. As he readied himself to sing, he looked at Corey and nodded his head and mouthed the first words:

> They're writing songs of love, but not for me
> A lucky star's above, but not for me
> With love to lead the way, I've found more clouds
> of gray
> Than any Russian play could guarantee.

Bob decided to keep the song at just two stanzas. He didn't think Corey would make it to the end of the song.

> It all began so well, but what an end
> This is the time a feller needs a friend
> When every happy plot ends with a marriage knot
> And there's no knot—for—me.

Bob ran the last few notes to the song, and some people quietly clapped their hands. He looked over at Corey, and she had her head resting on his shoulder. Her eyes were closed, and someone had already taken her glass from her limp hand.

Bob smiled at her lovingly and quietly told the partygoers, "I think we're going to call it a night." He stood up and caught Corey in his arms. He placed an arm around her back and the other under her knees and began to carry her out to their awaiting car with Curtis driving.

As Bob walked past Susan, he apologetically whispered to her, "It was fun. We'll see you Saturday."

Susan leaned over and kissed Bob lightly on the lips and affirmatively told him, "I'll see both of you Saturday. Okay?"

Bob was caught off guard by the lip-kiss but acted like it was a common gesture between them. He smiled at Susan and then left the party.

The next morning, Corey didn't wake up until eight o'clock. The sun shining into the bedroom was blinding her. She deeply moaned and turned over in bed, putting the sun at her back. When she slightly opened her eyes, Bob was sitting on his side of the bed, staring and smiling at her.

He had gotten out of bed two hours previously, taken a shower, dressed, and opened the drapes in the master suite, then went into the kitchen to get her some coffee.

Haddie was there, preparing breakfast for them, when she asked Bob, "How's my girl looking this morning? She certainly wasn't doing that beautiful evening gown any favors when I saw you carry her into the bedroom last night."

"She'll be all right, Haddie. Something's going on, but I'll get to the bottom of it."

Corey saw his smiling face as he sat staring at her. She remorsefully closed her eyes and rolled on her back, still moaning and groaning. She took a deep breath and then exhaled, sorrowfully telling Bob, "I can't even begin to tell you how sorry I am for drinking so much last night, in so little time, darling. I just felt compelled to do it. I hope I didn't embarrass you."

Bob was touched by her expiatory frame of mind, but told her, "Baby, you could never embarrass me. It wouldn't matter what you did or said. I love you and know you extremely well. Well enough to know that something is eating at you, and I want you to tell me what it is. Let me try to help. Let's iron this out."

Corey sat up in bed, bracing herself against two pillows. Bob handed her the mug of coffee. She sat for a few moments sipping on it and finally began pouring her heart out to him.

"Firstly, you well know I've been nominated ten times for the Oscar, and have won twice. I'm having my forty-eighth birthday in four days, and the roles for me are thinning. I don't want to ever quit making pictures, darling. It's been my whole life, up to now."

Bob kept watching her intently, not taking his eyes off of her. Not saying a word.

Corey then looked him straight in the eyes; as her eyes began to moisten, she worriedly told him, "And secondly, you're so young, and there's so many different women wanting to be with you. Sometimes it just scares the hell out of me if you would tire of me and just leave me one day. I remember what the great poet Yeats had written: 'Man is in love, and loves what vanishes.'"

Bob's mouth dropped open, and a surprised look of disbelief came over his face.

Corey earnestly told him, "Bob, I'm absolutely sure Susan Hawthorne has designs on you. She may be married, but that has never stopped a woman who is in love with another man other than her husband."

Bob sat for a few moments, puzzled by everything she had mentioned. He finally looked up and, being deeply moved, told her,

"Corey, you are the most talented dramatic actress of our time. There is just no way they would run out of scripts for you. And I don't care how old you are, no one can hold a candle to you. You make me so damn proud every time I watch you at work, doing what you love doing. Your movies are still grossing several hundred thousand to several million dollars with every release. And this picture we're working on together will be no different. Maybe even bigger than we think."

Corey sat with welled-up tears in her eyes, intently listening to Bob speak.

Bob's voice became low and suffused with empathy as he tried to explain, "Corey, there is nothing, at least in my mind, going on with Susan Hawthorne. I really like Susan, but that's the extent of it. She's a gracious, talented, and compassionate human being. I'm not going to play upon these innate feelings of your paranoia, because if I did, I would never be able to talk to, work with, or even socialize with another woman. Corey, that's just not possible."

Corey sat thinking about everything Bob had said and took a deep breath, nodded her head affirmatively, and resolutely answered, "You're right, darling. I think I just need to get back to work tomorrow and keep my mind more focused on that."

Bob grinned and leaned over and kissed her. He then hurriedly said, "I need to get to the recording studio now, but believe me, we're gonna talk more when I get home. I'm running late right now, so I'll probably be home a little later than normal. Okay? Are you gonna be all right, baby?"

Corey assured him, "Oh, I'll be fine. Go on now. Get out of here, and drive careful."

"Absolutely, doll. Later." Bob kissed her again and then quickly moved out of the bedroom.

Corey's most secret and fundamental heart, the part of her that assures the rest of her that everything is fine, had to trust her total and complete love for him. She really had no other choice.

* * * * *

Bob arrived at the recording studio about twenty minutes late, and when he walked in, all the guys told him how sorry they were Corey or he didn't win an Oscar.

Bob simply said, "Maybe next year. We'll work really hard on winning one of those dust collectors next time. We'll see."

Doug spoke up and asked, "Hey, man, you're late. You're never late. What gives? Did you and Corey start your second honeymoon, or what?"

All the guys chuckled inwardly.

Bob smiled and, in fun, told him, "Damn, I wish." Bob then turned and picked up his guitar and threw the strap over his shoulder and stated, "Now, let's get to work on our last two songs. We need to rework the melody on 'Conviction.' I think a more slightly rising melody to a guitar groove would kick it up a few degrees."

All the guys agreed with the changes as their heads bobbed affirmatively in unison.

When Bob spoke, he was precise and vivid. One believed what he said; one wanted to do what he proposed.

Looking at Joshua, Bob inquisitively asked, "Yeah, man. Which one of your ladies are you bringing to this dance?"

Joshua smiled, and having fun with the guys, he spoke in his poetic prose, "The lady that will be so eloquently floating across the dance floor with me will be the downhearted and repeatedly scorned C trumpet. She awaits our nocturnal rendezvous with bated breath."

Everyone started laughing out loud. Joshua stood emotionless for a few seconds, and then he laughed along with the guys.

Bob, still laughing, remarked, "Smooth, man. Okay, Joshua. Let's hear your scorned lady come into 'Conviction' after the lift between the first verse and the first chorus. I'll lead you in, and then you take over at that point. Here we go."

Jimmy gave them the four-count beat on the snare, then Bob started out on his guitar, playing the chords leading into the lift. Joshua then opened up on his C trumpet with the powerful peal of a loudly ringing bell. The clarion was clear, with a rousing sound of the melodious, metallic intensity of the C trumpet.

Bob had only known Joshua for a few months—long enough to form some favorable opinions, but not long enough to realize how really extraordinary he was. He was a musical genius.

When they finished working on "Conviction," they moved on to reexamine their second newest work, "Makin' Roads Inland." This song would have Bob on the piano, playing for the first time ever in one of their songs.

The recording studio had only a small upright piano. Bob informed the Owls, "When we go on to record this song, I would recommend the piano to be a concert grand piano or, in the least, a baby grand. Nothing else."

Doug spoke up and mentioned, "Well, you have a concert grand at the house."

Bob smiled then chuckled, jokingly saying, "Yeah, man. I'll just put the top down on my car and load that badass grand into the back seat. That's cool."

The guys were all laughing again when Len told them, "I guess we'll just have to go into LA and record those songs that call for a piano. We had to record in LA when we first signed with Mercury Records. It's not that big a deal."

As their rehearsal came to an end, at almost three thirty that afternoon, Bob reminded the guys that starting Thursday, their studio time would be six to nine o'clock at night.

When Bob arrived home, he went straight toward the concert grand in the enormous front room. He started playing the piano part of "Makin' Roads Inland."

He was listening to the brilliant singing and sustaining tone quality of the grand. He was focusing on the rhythm, pitch, tempo, and note duration.

Corey and Haddie were in the kitchen, preparing dinner, when they heard the piano being played. Corey turned to Haddie and just smiled. She knew there could only be one person that would be playing the piano like that; it had to be Bob.

Both Corey and Haddie slowly walked into the front room and took a seat near the piano. Bob saw them and looked up and smiled.

He continued playing, completely enthralled in the upbeat melody of the song.

To Corey, it seemed Bob had fireworks going off in his brain. He was tapping his one foot to the pulsating beat, and the other foot was working the piano's pedals.

As he finished the piano run, he turned to the two ladies and determinedly stated, "See? I knew the octave stretch would retain the harmonic balance, even when I aligned the treble notes to a harmonic produced from three octaves below. The grand has such a fuller sound to it, and the tonal quality is far superior to any other size piano."

Corey stood up and walked toward Bob as he remained seated. She jokingly told him, "You might as well be speaking Italian, darling, because you lost me at 'See?'" She leaned over as her lips met his.

Haddie started to walk out of the room when she told Bob, "I knew you were a little bit bilingual, Mr. Bob, but I didn't know that included the piano, too."

Bob just laughed to himself and then, concerned, looked at Corey and asked, "Are you feeling better, doll? You look and sound pretty good to me."

"Really, I'm just fine, darling. Last night, everything seemed to hit me all at once: losing the Oscar, watching Susan flirting with you all evening, and then thinking about my birthday coming up this Saturday. I guess it was an emotional overload. I'm sorry I didn't handle it better, because I usually am able to stiff-arm my way through anything. It just wasn't meant to be last night."

Bob thought, *I'm not going to deepen the preoccupation by continuing to entertain the issue*. He could not help but radiate a persuasive authority, and so he suggested, "You know what? Why don't we go out and sit by the pool, with a cup of coffee, and run some lines that we'll be scrutinizing tomorrow at the studio? What do you say, doll?"

Corey smiled brilliantly at him and purred, "Anything you say, mister."

Bob stood up to the side of the piano bench and wrapped his arms around her, and they kissed for several seconds. When he pulled away, he continued to lovingly look into her beautiful big blue eyes. Then with a low, subdued voice, he softly said, "Come on, baby."

Bob led Corey into the master suite, where they would make some very passionate love for the next hour and a half. They never made it to the pool that evening.

Haddie came out of the kitchen at six o'clock to tell them dinner was ready, but she saw the bedroom door closed, which was always the precursor to "stay the hell away." She just mumbled to herself, "Honeymoon: act two, scene one, action."

TWELVE

Wednesday morning, April 6, came very early for Bob and Corey. It had been three months since they had to get up at six in the morning to go to work.

However, Curtis was able to drop them off at seven o'clock at the Celebrity Studio for their preproduction conference that director Victor Trudeau had called.

Bob and Corey entered the soundstage, where dozens of people were already seated in several rows of folding chairs. As they walked toward the crowd, there was a welcoming applause from all the production staff and the handful of actors that were present, including Rita Hayworth, Robert Ryan, and Jack Carson.

As they were shown to their seats down in front with the other actors and producer Trent Voight, Corey graciously smiled and nodded her head to everyone. Bob shook hands with Robert and Jack and then introduced himself to Rita, shook her hand, and slightly hugged her.

Victor stood up and asked everyone if they got some coffee and rolls from a table full of breakfast items because he was ready to get started on the production of the picture.

After everyone was seated, Victor affably stated, "I'm Victor Trudeau, the director of this film, for those of you who are thinking, 'Who the hell is he?'" That got a quiet chuckle out of everyone. "Well, I've been around different studios for several years, but was specifically asked by Jack here at Celebrity if I was willing to take a brilliant screenplay, work with a very successful producer in Trent Voight, and direct actors like Madrigal, Richardson, Hayworth, Ryan, and Carson. I promptly asked Jack, 'What the hell do you need me for?'"

Jack Windheim was standing off to the side of the rows of chairs, laughing at this point. When the laughter died down from the crowd, Victor told everyone, "Yes, I've read the script a few times and feel this could be right in the mix for the Oscar next year. And I'll tell you why...because Jack, Trent, and I have hired probably the best set director in the business, Marvin Halstead. He, in return, has hand-selected his production design team, who have all been in the business for over twenty years or more. That would include our costume designer for this film, Ms. Edith Head."

There was a lot of applause, along with shouts expressing excitement. Bob looked over at Corey and Rita and lipped, *Whoa!* Corey chuckled at him, but kept smiling.

Victor continued, "Ms. Head has just finished a movie with Sophia Loren, when she agreed to take on *Love's Wicked Lies*. She will be the lead costume designer, overseeing the outfitting of all our characters, but she will also be collaborating with Hubert de Givenchy to create Audrey Hepburn's costumes in *Sabrina*."

Victor then asked Trent Voight, the producer, to come up and speak. After a polite applause, Trent started out saying, "Yeah. I'm that producer no one has heard of, because I was hiding out with Victor all this time."

After the laughter subsided, Trent continued, "Actually, this will be the first time I've been on a picture that will have several scenes shot on location in and around the LA area. We're really proud to be able to shoot this in Technicolor. So remember when you're in front of the cameras, smile, because this movie will be costing the studio a badass amount of money." The soundstage erupted in laughter, and when Bob looked over at Jack, he was laughing so hard, he was coughing the thirty years of cigar smoke into a handkerchief.

Victor cut in at that point, telling everyone, "Now, today we're going to get this powerful film started. Right now, I want all my actors meeting me in the conference room of building 1. We're going to have a complete cast script read-through to check and see if we need to keep our writers busy with corrections or rewrites."

The script read-through went uneventfully, and the actors were told to be in earlier than normal on Friday morning because Ms. Edith Head would be there all day. She would be working at taking people's measurements, envisioning which color would blend well with which actor, and gathering any suggestions from the director as to what he felt the costumes should be portraying.

On the way home from the studio that Wednesday evening, Bob asked Corey, "Are you excited about having Edith Head dressing you for this movie?"

Corey unsurprisingly answered, "Well, of course, I am, darling. I've never had the chance to work with her, because she had always been at Universal. So now that she's freelancing, I'm thrilled to have her outfitting me for our picture."

Thursday's read-throughs went so well, that Victor told the cast they would start running rehearsals on Monday. At this rate, they would start shooting film in a couple of weeks.

After having a quick dinner, Bob left for the recording studio. When he arrived ten minutes early, Nick was already inside talking with the guys.

Bob walked in, and Nick summoned him over to sit and listen to what was going down.

Nick started out telling the guys, "Okay. First, I want all of you to know Bob and I had talked here Tuesday, after your session, and both of us agreed that I'm going to need an assistant. The Night Owls are getting so popular and in demand that I find myself just chasing my tail most of the time, trying to keep up with everything. This assistant will help to keep the books balanced, assist me in scheduling appearances, handling publicity, and really just being my gopher. What do you guys think?"

Every one of the guys agreed with this move. Bob informed them, "This assistant will get a salary, not a percentage of anything.

His pay will be twenty-five thousand a year. That's gonna be about thirty-five hundred out of each of our takes."

Len spoke up and confirmed, "That's cool. Sounds okay to me."

All the rest of the guys were nodding their heads affirmatively.

Nick then stated, "I think I've found the right guy. Our attorney recommended Truman Atwater. He's a paralegal, a CPA, and a great office manager. I'll introduce you to him sometime before we play the Shrine Auditorium."

To reassure the guys this move wasn't going to financially hurt anyone, Bob gladly told them, "Nick and I just wanted all of you to know our 21-City Tour coming up in June, our two nights at the LA Shrine Auditorium this month, the two nights in mid-May at the Fillmore Auditorium in San Francisco, and the two nights in late May at the Las Vegas Convention Center Rotunda, in Winchester, Nevada, will bring in over half a million dollars for each one of us. And this is only up until the middle of August."

The guys stared at Bob as if he was insane—most especially Darnell and Joshua; they looked at each other like they were caught in a dream. Joshua's eyes became misty, thinking how he could get a house, marry Deidra, and move his momma in with them. She would finally be able to retire and quit keeping other people's houses clean.

Darnell slapped Joshua on the back, and then they gave each other some skin, as Darnell yelled, "Holy shit, man. What the hell is happening here?"

Len, Jimmy, and Doug started giving skin to Darnell and Joshua, and then everyone was jumping around and yelling like small children on a playground.

When the guys quieted down, Joshua excitedly told everyone, "The Fillmore Auditorium in San Francisco? Oh my god! That place is a classy outfit, man! This is gonna be huge for me. I went there once while I was in the philharmonic, where I saw a young James Brown tear up the stage in 1952. That place is probably the most innovative rock music venue anywhere. They're always booking fast-emerging artists and in-demand groups. It seats about thirty-seven hundred people…my god, I can't wait!"

Bob interjected, "All right, everyone knows now what we're doing up until the end of the 21-City Tour, August 14. So now, I think we need a name for the album we're going to record sometime in May. Len, Nick, and I liked *Shakin' It with the Night Owls*. What do you guys think?"

Doug spoke up and jokingly proposed, "How about *Nesting with the Night Owls*?"

All the guys laughed loudly at Doug.

Bob facetiously told him, "We're not suggesting to our fans to sleep with us. We simply want them to dance and sing with us."

Doug innocently answered, "I really don't see the problem."

The majority of the guys agreed with *Shakin' It with the Night Owls*.

After a couple of hours working on their two newer songs, the guys called it a night. Because of Corey's birthday party Saturday, they all agreed to rehearse that morning at nine o'clock instead of the now later time of six at night.

Bob reminded everyone that they needed to be at the house by three o'clock. Jack was instructed to hold Corey at the studio until, at least, three o'clock. All of the eighteen guests were told to park down the street or be dropped off.

When Bob and Corey arrived at the studio six o'clock Friday morning, they were instructed by the set director, Marvin Halstead, to meet with Edith Head in the costuming department of building 3.

Corey walked in first, followed by Bob. At that time, Rita Hayworth was being measured by Edith Head, so they continued in, sitting beside the already seated Robert Ryan and Jack Carson. Edith's attention was drawn to Bob and Corey, so she went to introduce herself and shake their hands.

Smiling, the diminutive, dark-haired, red-lipsticked, dark-rimmed-glassed woman of sixty-three years put her hand out to Corey and said, "Corey Madrigal. I'd know you anywhere. What a great honor it is for me to be able to dress you for this picture."

Corey was extremely flattered and smiling brilliantly as she revealed to her, "Ms. Edith Head. You just don't know how many years I've wished for this moment—when you would be my personal costume designer. This is just thrilling!"

"Oh, please. Just call me *Edith.*" She then looked over at Bob and asked, "This must be Bob Richardson. I've heard a lot about you in the last year or so. I'm happy to meet you, Bob. I look forward to dressing you also."

Bob shook Edith's hand, and he thought to himself, *Wow! Doug would really have had fun with her last line.* But Bob grinned and cordially answered her, "It's my pleasure meeting you, Edith. I never thought I'd be working on a picture you would be costuming. It's unreal."

"Well, thank you, Bob." Edith turned and addressed all five of the actors in the film, "Today, I'm here to take all of your measurements. And I mean the length of your fingers down to the circumference of your thighs and ankles. I don't want to leave any stone unturned. So then in a couple of weeks, I'll be fitting, tucking, tearing, and re-pinning every costume made for your character."

Edith looked directly at Corey and informed her, "Corey, your director, Victor, and I talked for almost an hour on the phone last night, and he mentioned to me that the color palette for you should be in the black or blue family. We'll have to play with that as we go along. Okay?"

"Yes, Edith, but it does capture the demeanor of my character. Those colors would resonate the most." Corey agreed with Victor on the color of her costumes.

The motion picture *Love's Wicked Lies* was the story of a couple (Bob and Corey); because of his weaknesses, she could no longer trust him. He was drawn to a nightclub singer (Rita). His wife (Corey), at the same time was fighting the temptation to be with her married brother-in-law, Robert Ryan. She still wanted her husband, right up until the end of the picture, and then events become inextricably entwined.

At almost eleven o'clock, Edith was done getting the measurements she needed for all five actors when Victor came in and asked everyone to grab some lunch, and then they'd meet again in the conference room for their last script read-through.

Bob was talking with Robert Ryan; while they were just outside the wardrobe area, Corey told Bob she would meet him outside. She said she wanted some fresh air.

As Corey was standing outside and leaning up against the building, enjoying the pleasant warmth of the sun on her face, her third ex-husband, Michael Sutton, approached her.

Michael casually strolled up to her and affably asked, "Well, Corey. How have you been these last several years? I haven't seen you lately."

Corey was completely caught off guard and was startled by the familiar but unsettling voice of the man that cheated on her, with more than one woman, in the year and a half they were married; one of those women was the now-deceased Julie Hayward.

He gave her a deep abiding chill as she sarcastically told him, "Michael. I can't say I'm happy to see you, but how have you been?"

Trying to make amends, he told her, "I asked around the studio, and they told me I could find you getting fitted in wardrobe. It's good you're keeping busy. Right now, I'm an associate producer on a B movie, being shot here on one of the back lots. It doesn't pay a whole helluva lot, but it does pay the bills."

Corey feigned pride for him by stating, "Well, good for you, Michael."

At that moment, Robert Ryan and Bob came walking out of the building. Ryan told Bob he'd see him at lunch, as not to say anything about being there tomorrow for Corey's birthday party.

Corey stood knotted with anxiety, not knowing what reaction Bob would have in seeing one of her ex-husbands.

Bob walked up to Corey and put his arm around her, staring questioningly at Michael the whole time. Michael was around six feet tall, had dirty-blond hair, with that mediocre look of someone who was now over fifty and still didn't know what he wanted out of life.

Hesitantly and with trepidation, Corey introduced Michael to Bob, "Bob, this is my ex-husband Michael Sutton. Michael, this is my..."

Michael cut her off by facetiously saying, "Your newest and fourth husband. Congratulations to both of you."

Michael put his hand out to Bob to shake, but Bob just kept staring at him with contempt and couldn't believe this jerk had the temerity to be flip with Corey.

Bob took his arm out from around Corey and took two steps toward Michael, putting him only inches from his face. Corey took a tight hold of one of Bob's arms.

Bob kept staring at him with extreme reproach and finally told him, "So you're the disloyal and unfaithful asshole? By now, I'm sure you know how big a mistake you made in cheating on, most likely, the best woman that could ever have happened to a schmuck like you."

Bob inched even closer, almost touching noses with him, and threateningly told him, "Now, you get out of here, and if I ever see or hear of you being around Corey, I will tear your head off and feed it to your ass. Got it, you son of a bitch?"

Michael, knowing he was outgunned by youth and muscle, just turned and walked away. After a couple of steps, he turned and mockingly told Corey, "I'll see you around, Corey."

Bob bolted toward him, and in surprise, Michael tripped over his own feet trying to get away and went hard to the ground. Bob didn't have to touch him but warned him, "You do that, you bastard, and it'll be the last thing in this world you'll ever see."

Corey was uncharacteristically flustered, but she took Bob by the arm and pulled him back away and toward the studio's cafeteria. She was extremely proud of what he did and because of the constraint he showed, but she was more proud of the fact he wanted to protect her from someone who had hurt her six years ago.

As Corey walked with Bob to get some lunch, they had their arms around each other. Corey looked up at him; as Bob was still a little hot under the collar, she pridefully boasted, "Thank you, darling. I didn't think I'd ever run into him again. He's not doing well, and I almost feel sorry for him."

Bob was able to joke about the encounter and sarcastically inferred, "The only thing I feel sorry about is that ten-dollar suit he was wearing."

They exchanged a small bit of tepid laughter between them and continued on to lunch.

Saturday morning, April 9, Corey's birthday, Bob woke Corey early, as he was already dressed to leave the house, and gently kissed her on the forehead. She responded by blinking her eyes several times as she very contently smiled into his face. He then lowered his head down to her, where he kissed her on the lips, and she then warned, "Darling, you didn't give me a chance to fully wake up this morning."

Bob, having fun with her, quipped, "For better or for worse, until both of us part ways and can brush our teeth...birthday girl."

Corey chuckled and then stretched her arms out. Bob kissed her again and then told her, "I'm sorry, baby, because I would love for this morning to be a little more romantically prolonged, but I have to leave for a morning session at the recording studio. I promise to make this up to you, my birthday girl. Now don't forget our birthday dinner tonight We'll be dining with three other couples at seven o'clock."

Bob smiled to himself knowing the dinner date was a ruse, as he darted from the room. He couldn't wait to see Corey's face when she'd walk into the backyard coming home from Celebrity Studios and see the balloons and decorations along with the eighteen other friends that would be there.

Corey, still in bed, shouted, "Yes, darling, and I'm holding you to that, mister."

At the recording studio, the Owls felt after three hours of playing, rearranging, polishing, and finishing the two songs, they were ready to record both of them.

Bob told them, "Nick's new assistant, Truman Atwater, already has contacted the recording studio in LA, and they've given us a late recording time this Wednesday night, from seven o'clock until ten o'clock. They usually don't stay open that late, but for the Owls, they said they'd be happy to accommodate us. And they have a baby grand there, so it's all cool, guys."

It was almost one o'clock in the afternoon when Bob arrived home, and Corey was out by the pool reading a book. She saw him pull his car into the garage, and she closed her book and laid it on the small iron table beside her chaise lounge.

Bob strolled over to her and leaned over and kissed her. "Hey, baby. How's your special day been going for you?"

Corey pulled him down to lie in her lounger beside her. "Rather uneventful, but it's been very calming and restful. How was your session today, darling?"

"Well, we wrapped up our two songs, and now late Wednesday night, we're gonna record them in a bigger, more-well-equipped studio in LA. I need to use at least a baby grand piano in one song, and they have that in LA. So I'll be driving myself into Celebrity Wednesday morning and probably won't be home until eleven o'clock or even midnight that night."

Corey seductively told him, "I'll keep the home fires burning, sweetheart."

Bob widely grinned and leaned in to kiss her, when they both heard the phone ring. A minute later, Haddie came out onto the landing and told Corey she had a phone call from Jack Windheim.

Corey exclaimed, "What could Jack possibly want on a Saturday?"

Bob helped her out of her lounger and watched her go into the house. Haddie and he just stood broadly smiling at each other, knowing they would now have to quickly transform the back area—get the caterer in, set up about ten tables, and call to have the two-tiered birthday cake delivered. Elizabeth, Susan, and Debbie were coming over at two o'clock to help with the decorations and tables, along with Alex, who also wanted to help.

Corey returned within five minutes and disappointedly told Bob and Haddie, "Well, I guess I have to go into the studio and talk with Jack about something. He couldn't explain to me over the phone what it was about."

Bob feigned his wonderment at this occurrence by questioningly stating, "It must really be something important."

"Would you like to drive in with me, darling? I would love your company."

Bob sadly told her, "No, I don't think so, doll. I still need to wrap your present."

Corey's sly response to that was, "Then I'll expect you to be wrapped when I get home."

Bob was all smiles as he sexily entertained the thought. "Okay, then."

At two o'clock, Elizabeth, Alex, Susan, and Debbie arrived and started right in on decorating the landing with a huge birthday banner and many balloons they had brought that were already inflated with helium.

Bob and Haddie were helping the caterer set up the tables with festively colored tablecloths and a simple vase containing three beautiful blushing pink roses, which were placed on each table.

The Owls and their ladies arrived shortly after two o'clock, except Doug, who had to come stag because Ann couldn't make it to the party. Doug wasn't quite sure why she couldn't be there, and he was afraid to ask.

Nick and Charlotte were unable to attend, for they would be at Charlotte's mother's birthday, and Susan's husband was away on business, so she would be alone. Elizabeth came by herself, for Drake would be busy directing an afternoon matinee of *The Tempest*.

The backyard was beginning to look almost as beautiful as it did for Corey and Bob's wedding. Everything was in bloom for this early spring party. The colors were magnificent, and the air smelled of a warming wind sweeping in from the ocean.

All of Corey's closest friends at Celebrity had already arrived and were standing around the tables with a drink in their hands, talking and laughing.

At almost three o'clock, Bob raced into the house and showered, shaved, and changed into a pair of tan linen pants and a light-blue dress shirt with an opened collar and rolled sleeves.

Bob returned outside to his guests and grabbed a bottle of beer when Corey drove up the driveway and into the garage with her black '57 T-Bird.

Corey didn't look toward the backyard when she pulled in, so she didn't notice the fanfare that was awaiting her. As she exited the garage and began to walk toward the house, she was startled when everyone shouted, "SURPRISE!"

Corey broke into a brilliant smile as she removed her dark sunglasses. She continued walking toward the gathering of people as she chuckled and pointed and shook her index finger at everyone in feigned admonishment.

She began hugging people as she passed them. Corey began looking for Bob, when she noticed him standing back close to the pool and beside Haddie. They were both smiling and laughing at Corey's total surprise.

Corey told everyone kiddingly, "All right, you got me. I was not expecting this." She looked over toward Bob and slowly and seductively kept her eyes on him as she approached and wrapped her arms around his neck.

She lovingly told him, "Thank you, darling. This is wonderful. And I was anticipating you to be wrapped as my birthday present."

Bob kissed her, and then he told her, "You'll be able to unwrap that one later."

Haddie just chuckled and then hugged Corey, telling her, "Happy birthday, Ms. Corey." Another car came roaring into the driveway at that moment. It was Jack Windheim. Corey now knew Jack was in on the surprise.

As Jack started walking toward the party, Corey yelled, "You'd better start running, Jack. I'm going to skin you alive, Windheim."

Jack laughed out loud and yelled back, "Well, at least I now know how to get your undivided attention: just tell you there's something I can't divulge over the phone."

The partygoers laughed, and Corey even laughed out loud.

Everyone was told by Bob, "Just relax, drink, eat, and laugh to your heart's content, as we celebrate my new bride's birthday. I want to thank everyone for coming today...and especially for coming early enough, so as not to spoil the surprise for Corey."

The yard was roaring with laughter and conversation. Corey sat talking with her guests while soft dance music played in the background, by the new amplification system Bob had installed.

Doug, Len, Darnell, and Jimmy were all in the pool after they had dinner and three beers. Bob went in the house and changed into a swimsuit and tee shirt and then came out and jumped into the pool with the guys.

After seeing all the guys in the pool, Lew Ayers, Robert Ryan, and Richard Widmark all took off their shoes and jumped in. The rest of the guests just watched as the guys were jumping off the diving board and cannonballing each other.

Jack sat talking with Corey when Bob heard him say to her, "You came blowing into the studio this afternoon like the wind from a sandstorm that was racing across the Mojave Desert. I've never seen you move as quickly as the wind like you did today."

Immediately, Bob got all the guys in the pool to help him sing the song "Mariah," but putting *Cor-ee*, in place of *Mariah*. Bob got them lined up in the shallow end as he started to loudly sing the song:

> Away out here, they got a name for rain, and
> wind, and fire.
> The rain is Tess, the fire's Joe. They call the wind,
> Cor-ee.
> Cor-ee blows the stars around, and sends the
> clouds a flyin'.
> Cor-ee makes the mountains sound, like folks
> were up there dyin'.
> Cor-ee, (crescendo) Cor-ee. They call the wind,
> Cor-ee.

Corey and Jack were howling with laughter. The rest of the guests not in the pool were just laughing at Corey's and Jack's infectious laughter.

> Out here they got a name for rain, for wind, and
> fire only
> But when you're lost and all alone, there ain't no
> word for lonely.

And I'm a lost and lonely man, without a star to guide me.
Cor-ee blow my love to me. I need my girl beside me.
Cor-ee (crescendo), Cor-ee. They call the wind, Cor-ee.
Cor-ee (louder crescendo), Cor-ee. Blow—my—love—to—me.

As the song ended, everyone was applauding, and the guys in the pool congratulated each other by slapping hands and yelling victoriously. Corey and Jack had tears running down their cheeks from laughing so hard, and it was hard for them to compose themselves.

When Corey's laugh was under control again, Bob smiled and looked over at her. He then blew her a kiss and winked at her. She slightly shook her head in loving disbelief, and very seductively, she blew him a kiss and winked back at him.

Around six o'clock, everyone started to just sit around and talk and drink. Some couples were up on the landing, slow-dancing to the mellow instrumentals of Dorsey, Miller, Ellington, and Harry James.

While Bob was sitting with Corey and talking with Jack, Susan had just returned from the dance floor after dancing with Robert Ryan. She approached Bob and asked him, "Bob, would you mind dancing with me?"

Bob turned and smiled and obligingly answered, "Absolutely, Susan."

Immediately, he stood up and escorted her to the dance area, with his hand on her lower back, guiding her.

When they started dancing, Susan, in jest, smilingly said, "I'm glad you changed clothes and put some shoes on, because I wouldn't want to step on your bare feet."

Bob laughed and told her, "If you step on my feet, Susan, it would be my fault, not yours. I'm supposed to be leading you…not trying to confuse you."

Susan just smiled and put both of her arms around his neck as she moved with him. Bob kept his hands on the side of her hips, not wanting to wrap his arms around her, in respect for Corey.

Bob was now convinced she was trying to seem alluring with her attractiveness and that very enticing quality she always seemed to demonstrate.

Corey sat studying the two of them dancing, and she unsurprisingly kept a vigilant watch as they moved in unison together.

Jack noticed Corey staring at Bob and Susan and felt he needed to speak up, "Corey, you know you don't have anything to worry about when it comes to Bob. And Susan and Bob are both married, for God's sake."

Corey shot back at Jack, "When has a wedding ring ever stopped a woman from going after what she really wants? Believe me, Jack, I've known for years when a woman is on the prowl. And although Susan is a good friend, I know her interest in Bob tells me her marriage is something less than what she wants or needs. I'm just protecting what's mine, Jack. If any woman makes a move on my man, I'll nip it in the bud early, before she has a chance to unbutton her blouse."

Jack chuckled to himself and reassured her, "Well, you know best, Corey."

At around seven o'clock, everyone was gathered in a roundish circle. Chairs had been pulled together, and there were couples in each of the chaise lounges, and all had drinks or were still nibbling at the birthday cake.

Doug could be heard talking to Jimmy, "Well, you know darned well Eisenhower has already sent military personnel over to Vietnam. They're supposedly consulting with the South Vietnamese and helping to train their forces to fight the North Vietcong. If this becomes a war, you know we'll be called up to go over there."

Jimmy answered, sounding agitated, "All this is nothing but an intervention in a foreign civil war, just exactly what Korea was all about. It just lacks clear objectives and appears to be an unwinnable conflict."

Joshua spoke up, commenting, "Yeah, it just seems like this country tries to police the entire world. Since this country was established, not even two hundred years ago, we've been in a helluva lot of wars. Just fifteen years ago, we returned from the Second World War. Over three hundred thousand Americans died, twenty million Russians, over six million Jews, and millions more from many different countries. This has to stop somewhere, people."

Darnell added, "I lost two uncles in World War II. A lot of families can identify with that. How about you, Len? Did the Second World War affect your family?"

Len solemnly told Darnell, "Yeah, my dad lost his best friend and a brother on D-Day in June of 1944… What about you, Bob? What impact did the war have on your family?"

Bob looked over at Elizabeth, and the moment he saw her tearing up, his eyes also became moistened. With great hesitancy, he quietly began explaining, "My dad wasn't called up. He joined when he was thirty years old, in 1941. He had a five-year-old and a ten-year-old at home, and a wife who vehemently screamed at him not to sign up. His passion to fight for his country overrode every sane thought he had about home and family. He told me he knew his family would be all right, and he deeply felt he would come home alive to them. He just felt he had to exercise his patriotic duty and help free the world from tyranny."

Corey had never heard Bob talk about his father's military service. Her eyes started to fill with empathetically unshed tears.

"So he left and joined the army, just days after Christmas. He was assigned to the First Battalion of the 383rd Infantry, and he saw action in the South Pacific; on Leyte, Guam, and in the Philippines. He was fighting in the Philippines when he stood up in full view of the enemy and emptied three Browning automatic rifle clips into the Japanese; along with grenades, he used his bayonet and trench knife in hand-to-hand combat. He ended up killing twenty-one of them. My dad was the only survivor of six men, who earlier in the day had knocked out a spigot mortar. It was a huge gun, but the six of them took care of it with two satchel charges."

The guests were entranced with Bob's story of his dad, and Corey and other men and women had very misty eyes at this point.

"The First and Third Battalion of the 383rd Infantry lost 126 men that long morning and early afternoon. The battalions had to retreat under cover of a smoke bomb, carrying their wounded with them. The First Battalion was at half strength and was considered ineffective after that morning. The regiment had gained no ground but did kill 420 of the enemy. The First Battalion's executive officer was ordered to relieve the battalion's commander of his duties. Because the commander was told to hold the ridge 'at all cost,' but he knew everyone would have been slaughtered if they remained. So he retreated with as many men that he had left. That day he had saved dozens of lives that would have surely been killed."

Bob was choking up, and his eyes glistened as he finished, "My dad was one of those men that made it back to camp. Later, my dad was awarded the Bronze Star. The other five men he started out with received them posthumously. My dad told this story only once to me, because, he said, it just caused him too much pain to keep reminding himself of the war."

There were tears running down a handful of faces now, and Corey was one of them. She never once thought Bob's dad was in the military because Bob and Elizabeth would have been very young at that time. It had never occurred to her to ask Bob about any involvement his parents had in the war.

Corey put her arms around Bob and hugged him as he sat with her in her lounger. He felt much better with Corey's arms around him. He turned his head and looked at her lovingly. He resignedly smiled at her, then he looked away, with his gaze now fixed on the still water of the swimming pool.

Jack reached over from his chair to pat Bob on the back of his shoulder, consolingly saying, "You had one helluva dad there, Bob. You should be extremely proud of him for putting his life on the line for this country—even willing to leave a young family back home. Now that's true patriotism, by God."

"I'm very proud of my dad, but now I think we need to talk about something a little more happy or joyful. What do you think?" Bob stated in a more uplifting tone.

Darnell spoke up and cheerfully told everyone, "Well, Alicia and I would like to announce to everyone here that we're pregnant."

Instantaneously, everyone present started applauding and cheering for them. Doug yelled, "All right, man. You're gonna have your very own ankle biter."

Bob jumped up and went over and shook Darnell's hand then hugged and kissed Alicia. All the rest of the band members were shaking hands and hugging both Darnell and Alicia. Corey moved quickly to hug Alicia and then Darnell. She was all smiles, along with everyone else at the party.

Then all of a sudden, Len spoke up and confessed to the partygoers, "There's gonna be more than one new baby owlet this year in the Owls' nest. Valerie and I are expecting a little goblin around Halloween."

Then everyone clapped even louder, and the screams of excitement and smiles were everywhere. Len and Valerie were swarmed by well-wishers at that point. Everyone was hugging and kissing Darnell, Alicia, Len, and Valerie; and the ambient noise in the yard was of jubilation and great happiness.

When the noise began to settle, Elizabeth raised her wide-opened hands in the air and asked, "Could I have your attention, please?"

Corey looked at Elizabeth and instantly knew what she was going to say, and under her breath, she stated the prophetic significance to a good omen. "Oh my god! You're kidding."

Emboldened now after hearing about the other two women, Elizabeth unflinchingly began to unburden herself by stating, "I was going to hold off giving my news until my husband, Drake, would be around to share it with me, but I'll add even more gas to the bonfire by telling everyone that Drake and I are due with a child in the middle of November."

There were now loud screams and unbelievable shouts of excitement to go along with the loud applause. Everyone was laughing with joy and the unbelievability of all this happening.

Bob's face was immediately lit up with surprise and the pride he felt for his sister. He slowly walked toward Elizabeth, and the people congratulating her saw him coming and backed away to make room for him. With slightly glistening eyes, he hugged her tightly and then kissed her on the cheek. His smile couldn't be contained, for it was enormous and consumed his entire face.

With pure and uncontrolled emotions, Bob screamed, "I'm gonna be an uncle! Hot damn!" He hugged and kissed Elizabeth again. Corey was standing behind him, and when he noticed her, he kissed and hugged her. Corey then hugged Elizabeth and said her congratulations into her ear. They both kissed each other on the cheeks as Bob was strutting around the yard boasting, "Uncle Bob. Yeah, man. Just call me *Uncle Bob*. Whoa, we got baby booties coming!"

Corey stood watching Bob prancing around the yard, slapping hands with all the guys and hugging the women. Susan and Alex both hugged him and congratulated him with the prospect of becoming an uncle in the fall.

Corey wanted to give Bob a child of their own, but she had great trepidation in telling him what she thought was going on with her lately; she had missed her last two menstrual cycles and was sick with worry that maybe she was pregnant also.

Bob was done strutting and boasting, and when he happily walked back to Corey, he could sense something about her demeanor that wasn't quite right. She stood staring at him, and her expressionless face triggered the reactions that were visceral to him; she looked worried and afraid. His mind was floundering with whatever was going on with Corey.

Almost scared, Bob approached her and put his arms around her waist. Looking deeply into her eyes, he pleaded with her, "Please, doll. Tell me what's going on. Lay it on me, babe."

Corey looked into Bob's troubled eyes, and tearing up, she told him, "We'll talk later tonight, after everyone is gone. All right, darling?"

Bob was really worried now. It took several seconds, but Bob was able to get control of his worry and anxiety. He kissed Corey on the forehead and acquiesced to her wishes. “Okay, we’ll talk about it later, baby.”

He walked away from her and grabbed another beer and then sat on the side of the pool with his feet in the water, after he had kicked off his shoes and socks, again.

Haddie walked over to him and sat on the side of the pool next to him and also dangled her feet in the water after she slipped her sandals off.

Bob quickly looked over at Haddie, smiled, and facetiously asked, “Don’t tell me you’re pregnant, too. I’ve had enough surprises tonight.”

Haddie took ahold of Bob’s arm that was next to her with both her hands. She was staring down into the clean, sparkling pool water, just like Bob was, when she bared her soul to him. “You know, Mr. Bob, Ms. Corey has been my friend for many years now. I was there when her third marriage blew up. I helped her get herself back together and move on with it all. I was her sounding board when she came home from the studio at night bitching about anyone and everything. And I was the one who had to peel her off the ceiling after she met you. She’s been crazy in love with you since she first laid eyes on you, Mr. Bob. There is probably nothing more in this world that she would want to do than to give you a child from her own body.”

Haddie’s rational explanation was met with an incredulously piercing stare from Bob. He had no idea it was even possible for Corey to get pregnant at her age.

Corey sat talking with Jack, Susan, and Alex but kept an eye on Haddie talking with Bob. She noticed Haddie was doing most of the talking, which increased Corey’s level of anxiety.

Haddie continued, “And now tonight, these three young women told the world they’re all gonna have a baby this year. How do you think that made Ms. Corey feel, considering she once told me that she would make the ultimate sacrifice to give you a child of your own?”

Bob instantly became choked up, with tears forming in his eyes.

"The good Lord knows I never want to lose Ms. Corey, but she loves you beyond human comprehension, and she never ever wants to lose you. I truly believe she would die of a broken heart if she didn't have you by her side. So you see, Mr. Bob, I know deep down in my heart she wants to make you even happier. She thinks giving you a baby would make you happier than what you are with just her." Haddie forlornly looked over at Bob as a single tear ran down the front of his face.

Devastated, Bob looked back at Haddie and inquisitively asked, "Is she pregnant, Ms. Haddie?"

Haddie sadly answered, "She thinks she is, but I think it's the beginning of her change of life—you know, her menopause, Mr. Bob. And she's afraid to go to her doctor because she don't wanna hear she's not pregnant."

Bob determinedly told Haddie, "Well, we're certainly going to find out Monday, when I get her into her doctor in LA. Now don't you worry your head, Ms. Haddie. Everything is going to be all right, okay?"

"I certainly am praying for that, Mr. Bob."

"I'll talk with her tonight… Thank you, Ms. Haddie, for sitting with me and giving me a heads-up on all this. I deeply appreciate that."

Haddie smiled and just nodded her head while sadly looking up at Bob.

THIRTEEN

The party started to break up around nine o'clock, and Corey and Bob told all the guests good night and thanked them for coming.

Bob walked Elizabeth to her car and hugged and kissed her again and told her, "Thanks, sis, for letting us in on the outta-sight news about the little one coming. I can't wait."

Elizabeth excitedly informed him, "When the baby is born, Drake and I both agreed to name it Robert Brian or Margaret Robin—after our parents."

Bob was so touched by this, his eyes began to glisten as he smiled and hugged her again, happily telling her, "That sounds perfect, sis. Thank you. Tell Drake he's a great guy." Elizabeth kissed him on the cheek and then got in her car and drove home to LA.

As Bob was walking back to the house, he noticed Jack was starting to get into his chauffeured car, which sat in front of the estate. Bob ran toward him, yelling, "Jack, wait a minute. I need to talk to you."

Jack stood outside the car and shut the door in anticipation of what Bob had to say. When Bob reached Jack's car, Bob entreatingly asked, "Listen, Jack, before you go, I have to tell you Corey and I have to go into LA Monday morning. We may be a couple of hours late for rehearsal, but this is something very important. We need to straighten something out right away."

Jack was alarmed with this news and inquisitively asked, "What in the hell is going on, Bob? Tell me. Maybe I can help you two."

"Thanks, Jack, but we'll talk after Corey and I resolve this issue. I don't think I should talk about anything until after Monday morning. I'm gonna go in now and make a call to set up an appointment. Believe me, Jack, as soon as I find out something, you'll be the first to know, okay?" Bob shook Jack's hand and headed up the driveway.

"You remember, if you need anything—let me know." Jack watched Bob nod his head.

When Bob entered the house, he headed straight for the library and located Corey's gynecologist, Dr. Todd, and found his home number. Her doctor was gracious enough to talk with him as Bob explained everything that was going on. Dr. Todd told Bob to have Corey at his office at eight o'clock, Monday morning—one hour before his scheduled appointments would start arriving.

At this point, Bob started looking for Corey. He found her in the master suite, lying on the bed, fully clothed. She had the back of her left arm resting on her forehead, and her eyes were wide open, just seemingly staring into space.

Bob slowly approached her, and the closer he got to her, he could see she had been crying, quite a bit; her beautiful eyes were red and slightly puffy, and she held a crumpled handkerchief in one of her hands.

He quietly sat down on the bed beside her. His apprehension was insurmountable as he placed one arm on the other side of her, balling his fist into the comforter, not touching her.

Bob waited for her to start talking. Instantly, her torso popped up toward him as she threw her arms around his neck. Corey started to cry so hard, she was actually sobbing. Bob held her, and after a couple minutes, she was able to compose herself.

Bob sympathetically whispered into her ear, "It's okay, baby. We're gonna work this out. Whatever you're going through, we're both gonna go through it together. I love you so much, Corey. I hate to see you like this. Let me help you, baby."

Corey pulled her head back enough to look directly into Bob's eyes. Devastating sorrow was written all over her face as she anguished in trying to explain herself. "Oh, Bob, I want to be able to give you a child. And right now, I don't know if I'm pregnant or not, and I'm terrified to find out."

He just kept staring at her with his saddened eyes. Bob thought for a moment and then tried to console her with his impassioned plea. "All right. Now we need some answers. I'm going to take you into LA Monday morning to see Dr. Todd. We'll find out one way or another about your condition. Then we'll handle it from there, okay?"

"All right, darling. But I know Haddie talked to you about this, didn't she?"

Bob earnestly answered her, "Don't blame Haddie about any of this. She loves you, and she was worried beyond belief about you. The better question would be, why didn't you come to me about this, Corey?"

"I thought I could handle it myself. I didn't want to bother you. You have so much going on right now, and Haddie being another woman, I thought I could bounce all of this off of her."

Bob nodded his head, trying to understand. "Corey, there is nothing in this world that is more important to me than you. I would give up everything if it meant I could keep something bad from happening to you."

She wrapped her arms around his neck again, but this time she was tightly hugging him as she kissed his neck.

Bob decided to try and appease her in another way. "Okay, baby, let's decide that we'll deal with this Monday morning, all right?"

He then put his hand into the back pocket of his pants and came out with a small, rectangular jewelry store box. "I really wanted to give you this under much more happier circumstances. But, anyway—happy birthday, baby."

Bob softly pulled her one arm from around his neck and placed the box in the palm of that hand. Then he smiled lovingly at her.

Corey looked at the box and instantly started to tear up again. She pulled him toward her with the one arm that was still around his neck. Overcome with the all-encompassing love she had always felt for him, she breathlessly shouted, "Oh my god!" Then their lips met, and she couldn't drink in enough of him with that one kiss.

When they separated lips, Bob softly coaxed her, "Go on, doll. Open it up."

Corey started to open the box, without her eyes leaving Bob's smiling face. When she looked down at the box, she saw a magnificently sparkling diamond bracelet with matching earrings. The inside of the box read Tiffany's.

Bob helped her to fasten the bracelet onto her wrist. She admired it by turning her wrist back and forth.

Corey looked him straight in the eye and practically screamed, "What on God's green earth did I ever do to deserve you?"

They hugged one more time, and both fell onto the bed locked in a passionate kiss. Bob then undressed Corey and put her nightgown on her. He pulled the covers back and slipped her into bed. He then took his clothes off, except his boxers, and climbed in next to her. They fell asleep in each other's arms and remained like that until morning.

Monday morning, Curtis had the car out front waiting for Bob and Corey to take them into LA to see Dr. Todd. They arrived right on time, and Corey was immediately taken back to the lab to have a couple of tests done.

After about thirty minutes, Dr. Todd sat Corey and Bob down in his office. He told them, "While we're waiting for your test results, I thought I should warn you that a woman at your age of forty-eight has only a one percent chance of having a successful biological pregnancy. The risks increase with your maternal age. You'll have a distinct possibility for miscarriage, chromosomal abnormalities such as retardation and other complications, gestational diabetes, high blood pressure, and bleeding. Women over forty are at higher risk of experiencing the sudden death of their fetuses. Data has shown that pregnancies in older women are infrequent and must be considered as high risk. You'll have a higher risk of complications such as preeclampsia. That is a pregnancy disorder that can cause high blood pressure and swelling. This can lead to serious, and even fatal, complications for the mom and baby. You are at a very advanced maternal age, Corey, and the risks will be compounded exponentially for you."

Corey started to cry, so Bob moved his chair closer to her and put his arms around her. He showed a very worried look on his face as he handed Corey a handkerchief.

The doctor's nurse walked in and placed a thin folder in front of Dr. Todd. He opened it and studied Corey's test results. Corey and Bob sat racked with tense anxiety.

The doctor looked directly at Corey and told her, "Well, Corey, you're not pregnant. What you're experiencing is perimenopause. Perimenopause is the transition to menopause, which starts a year or two before menopause begins. This is the time where the ovaries gradually slow down its estrogen production. It starts when a woman reaches her forties. At the stage of menopause will be the point where your body no longer releases eggs for the function of reproduction. This can last a few years or as long as ten years. Once you've reached the point where you haven't had a menstrual cycle in a full year, then you'll be full-blown menopausal. Do either one of you have any questions?"

Corey was so upset that her whole body slightly trembled. She looked seemingly devastated at Bob and stoically whispered, "Now I'll never be able to give you a baby."

Bob had huge unshed tears in his eyes as he kept a firm hold of Corey.

The doctor cautiously interrupted, "Corey, it's extremely unfortunate you can no longer have children, but the risks you would be running right now if you were pregnant could put your very life on the line, along with the baby. The risk of spontaneous abortion increases to about 75 percent for women over forty. The chances of you conceiving in your late forties of spontaneous conception is likely less than 1 percent. I'm just so sorry."

Bob thanked the doctor for seeing them on such short notice and then shook his hand. He turned back to Corey and helped her out of her chair and into a standing position.

It was a long, quiet trip back home from LA. Curtis felt that something really bad was happening, so he didn't say a word the whole twenty-five minutes back to Bel Air.

When they got home, Bob explained everything to Haddie after he helped Corey to lie down in the bedroom. Bob asked Haddie to watch over her while he was gone to the studio to talk with Jack and to try to work some rehearsal time into the day.

Bob talked with Jack immediately after he arrived at Celebrity. Jack told him to tell Corey she could take as much time as she needed. Jack informed the director, Victor Trudeau, that Corey may be taking a few days off. Victor was disappointed because he knew he'd be losing precious production time, but he totally understood.

After Bob was able to rehearse a handful of scenes with Rita Hayworth, Robert Ryan approached him and asked about Corey. "Bob, I hope everything is all right with Corey. It's not anything serious, is it?"

Bob played the whole situation down and tried to allay any worries that anyone had about Corey by casually answering, "Oh, no, she just isn't feeling well right now. Believe me, she'll get back as soon as she can. She loves her work."

When Bob arrived home at five o'clock, he found Corey sitting out by the pool, simply sunning herself and drinking some coffee. After he garaged his car, he walked over to her and began to sit in the lounger next to her, when Corey scooted over and patted the seat of her lounger with her hand. "Come and sit with me, darling. Won't you?"

Bob immediately moved in and lay beside her as he softly kissed her lips.

Corey tried a faint stab at humor by asking Bob, "Are those the lips that was just kissing Rita not long ago at rehearsal?"

Bob started smiling brilliantly and then laughed as he jokingly told her, "I'm sorry to say, but no, they're not. We're saving all that hot stuff for when the cameras start to roll later next week."

Corey chuckled and smiled back at him.

"That's what I love to see. My best girl laughing and smiling. You feeling better, babe?"

Corey took a deep breath and exhaled loudly as she stared at the pool. "I'll be just fine, darling, it just took a dose of reality to remind me of my limitations at this age."

Incredulously, Bob spoke up and told her, "Limitations? What do you mean *limitations*? You are probably the most formidable person I have ever known. You can move mountains, Corey, and anything that gets in your way, you have this prodigious capability of demanding respect, and even inspiring fear in whomever."

Corey was fixated on Bob's face. She had never felt so close to him as she felt at that moment. He was, emphatically, her pride and joy—absolutely and unequivocally the love of her life. There would be no other.

"Corey, you're a daunting force. You're always trying to push the limits of what you're able to do within the parameters that you have. I fervently disagree with you. You have no limitations, but for the fact that you can't have children anymore. Corey, I told you, when we were in New York a year and a half ago, I've never thought about having kids. There were just too many things I wanted to do, and children would be a tie-down. Baby, I just want you. Please believe me." With a short chuckle, Bob said, "I love you to the moon and back, Alice."

Corey instantly began to cry and pulled his body into her as she buried her face into his chest and just held him.

Corey decided to go back to work Tuesday morning. She simply told everyone she just wasn't feeling well the previous day.

After Bob and Corey returned home that evening, he grabbed a quick sandwich and was out the door to the recording studio to rehearse with the guys.

Bob ran out the back door, and Haddie yelled at him, "Mr. Bob? You're gonna start sounding like a bag of bones rattling together if you don't slow down and eat somethin'."

Corey's smile broadened as she proudly told Haddie, "He'll be all right, Haddie. He knows exactly what he wants, what he's doing, and where he's going."

Bob reached the recording studio fifteen minutes late. When he walked in, he apologized and explained to them how rehearsal ran over. He then congratulated Len and Darnell again on expecting a baby this fall. He did find out that Alicia, Darnell's wife, was expecting in the middle of October; then at Halloween, Valerie was due; and in mid-November, it would be Elizabeth and Drake's turn. Bob knew all this news about three of the gals being pregnant really didn't help Corey's disposition at all.

The guys then got down to the business of making music. Joshua had brought in another song he roughly scratched out on a piece of paper as he was watching a baseball game on TV. Len had another song he'd been working on for a few days, and Bob brought in the lyrics to a song he had just started to add some melody to.

Bob noticed Doug was not his flamboyant, joking self. Doug was quiet, reserved, and almost melancholy in nature. Bob walked over to Len and, whispering, asked, "What's up with Doug? He's not acting right."

Len just shook his head with disappointment and slyly whispered back to Bob, "Ann."

Bob knew at that exact moment that Ann had dumped Doug.

Trying to keep things upbeat, Bob suggested, "Okay, why don't we start with playing our latest recordings tonight and then again on Thursday night. We're going to play the Shrine this Saturday and Sunday, so I'd like our last four new songs to be embedded in our minds for those two nights."

Len added, "Yeah, and don't forget our seven o'clock appointment tomorrow night at the recording studio in LA. We'll be cranking on 'Conviction' and 'Makin' Roads Inland.'"

A couple of hours into rehearsal, Nick walked in with his new assistant, Truman Atwater. Nick introduced Truman to each guy, and surprisingly, Doug didn't have anything funny to say.

Truman was a thirty-four-year-old five-and-a-half-foot-tall redhead that maybe weighed 130 pounds soaking wet. He wasn't a bad-looking man, but he wasn't handsome either.

Truman nervously told the guys, "I'll be here Thursday night, when you're done rehearsing, to take all the instruments over to the Shrine Auditorium in LA and get those set up for Saturday night. I'll try my best to do whatever Nick and you gentlemen would want me to do."

Darnell smiled and jokingly told Truman, "Gentlemen? You really don't know us, do you, man?"

Everyone laughed a little, and Darnell added, "Welcome to the nest, Truman. You're gonna be cool, man. Really tight."

Nick spoke up and asked the guys, "If any of you need tickets for either night, I've got the entire third-row orchestra reserved."

After Len, Darnell, Jimmy, and Joshua asked for a few apiece for each night, Bob asked, "How many does that leave, Nick?"

Nick did the math and told Bob, "That would leave ten tickets for opening night and fourteen for when we close it down on Sunday."

"Sell the ten on opening night, and give me the fourteen for Sunday, okay?"

"You got 'em, man." Nick left shortly before the guys got back to rehearsing.

At nine thirty, the guys called it a night. Truman started to load the instruments into a large van, and Jimmy helped him with the drums.

Bob caught Doug outside by Jimmy's car. Bob told Jimmy, Darnell, and Joshua to just go on home to the house, and he'd drive Doug home in a little while.

Concerned, Bob started by asking Doug right away, "What's going on with you, man? You just haven't been acting like the Doug we all know."

Doug, embarrassed, but trusting in Bob's friendship, sadly told him, "Well, I felt I was in love with Ann, so I asked her to marry me. She turned me down. She told me she really liked me, but she'd also been seeing some other guy for the last three weeks. Then she dumped me, and I haven't heard from or seen her since Corey and you went on your honeymoon."

Bob could see Doug was crestfallen, and his every word was filled with heartbreaking tenderness. Trying to console him, Bob said, "It's good she was honest with you, man. You now can make tracks and move on, knowing Ann is going to be happy. You'll find someone else. Someone you totally didn't expect to walk into your life at that time. Just like the way I met Corey. Fate just happened to have me in the right place at the right time that day. And I'll be grateful to God the rest of my life for that, and for her. So, you hang tough now. In a few days at the Shrine, they'll be women throwing themselves at you. All you'll have to do is pick and choose."

Bob grinned and started chuckling as he patted Doug on the shoulder. Doug started acting like his old self by telling Bob, "Then I'm gonna have to play the guitar this weekend so I'll be closer to 'em."

Bob laughed and put his hand out. Doug slapped it and slipped Bob some skin.

Bob got home close to ten o'clock that night, and Corey was sitting up in bed reading.

He walked into the bedroom, and he smiled the instant he saw her. He quickly kissed her and then took a shower and brushed his teeth.

When he came out of the bathroom, Corey had already placed her book on the nightstand and was waiting for him, seductively holding the covers up so he could slip in.

Bob revealed to her a toothy smile, and in a low, very suggestive voice, he sexily said, "I see how this evening is going to go."

Corey's heart was racing, seeing him in pajama bottoms, and nothing covering his beautiful chest. She was drinking him in, and her desire for him was all-consuming.

Bob slid under the covers and slowly took her in his arms and began kissing her on the neck. As he lowered her torso down onto the sheet, he moved his right leg between her legs and whispered, "Tonight, I'm going to take my time with you, baby."

Corey began to breathe heavily as her chest was rapidly moving up and down. Bob kissed her very deeply, with his tongue probing her entire mouth. He then ran his tongue over her lips and began kissing and probing her ear with his tongue. She started moving her pelvis into his lower stomach as she moaned, "Oh my god. Yes, baby."

Bob lowered himself enough to start kissing her breasts. He started nibbling and suckling her nipples until they were hard and erect. As he was enjoying her breasts, he started to run his hand around her lower stomach and then her upper thighs.

Corey was breathing so hard, she breathlessly begged Bob to enter her. After he was kissing on her torso and running his tongue over her soft skin, he pulled his body up to where he was now lying on her. He could feel her getting close to her climax, so with both his legs between her widely spread legs, he entered her.

She cried with delight and started moving with his deep-thrusting undulations. When Bob moved more rapidly, he felt Corey's sexual excitement as she jerked and tightened her body in orgasmic spasms.

Bob was still kissing on her neck as he kept rapidly moving his pelvis into her. He had a hold of her hips now, and the thrill of his climax now overwhelmed him. His head vaulted into the air as he gratifyingly breathed in short, quick gasps.

Corey tightly held him and still moved her hips to where she could still feel him inside her. He kept moving deeper into her, and she screamed with the eruption of her second orgasm. "Oh, baby, I love you so much. Oh my god!"

Bob withdrew from her after a couple more minutes went by, but it took several minutes before he wanted to leave the warmth of her body. He lay his head just below her breasts, and with his hands, he felt the softness of her shoulders and upper arms.

Corey started to breathe a little more slowly as she ran one hand through his hair, and the other over his muscled arms and shoulders.

Bob started to fall asleep; when Corey sensed this, and she began to pull him up toward his pillow, saying, "Come on, darling. Come up and put your head on your pillow."

Bob was barely awake from the fatigue of the long day, but he managed to get to his pillow and lie on his side, facing Corey. He pulled her into him, and he cupped her body. She held his one arm between her breasts, and they both fell asleep like that, until the six o'clock alarm went off Wednesday morning.

Curtis drove Corey to the studio, but Bob drove his own car because of the need to be in LA at seven o'clock that night to record the Owls' two newest songs.

When Bob and Corey reached the studio the next morning, Bob and Rita were whisked off to a location near the Santa Monica pier. The two were going to have a blocking rehearsal, with the director, Victor Trudeau, a handful of the camera crew, and Marvin Halstead's production design team. Victor wanted to talk to them about the love scene they would be shooting at this location the following week.

Marvin was collecting all the information with his cameraman that they would need to run "light shooting."

The '60s marked an era of forward-thinking artistry, experimentation, and cutting-edge filmmaking. Out of the studios and into the streets went production companies.

New handheld cameras were a tremendous change from the big stationary cameras that were heavy, bulky, and hard to set in place. The new jump cuts, with the portable equipment and smaller sound devices, enabled quicker location shoots, saving valuable production time, and lowered expenses. There was a shift in the style and themes that could now be explored in films, because real light and real scenery allowed far more freedom in movement, space, and story lines.

Victor had Bob and Rita lying on the beach next to each other. The crew was measuring the length and width of different angled shots where the sun would be at different times of the day and the shading or added light that would be added for the crucial close-ups.

When Victor and Marvin felt they had everything they needed, everyone headed back to the studio for lunch around noon.

Bob and Rita were walking between two of the soundstages, behind everyone else that were with them that morning. They were headed for the cafeteria; and as they were talking, Rita saw Corey, Robert Ryan, and Jack Carson walking from the cafeteria toward them.

When the three of them were within twenty feet of Bob and Rita, in jest and acting jealous, Rita hopped in front of Bob so he supposedly wouldn't see Corey. Rita held her arms up and loudly announced, "I'm here all alone. Where are you three headed in such a hurry?"

Robert Ryan and Jack got a kick out of Rita's crazy behavior, but Corey was not amused. She had already seen Bob from a distance and was anxious to hug him.

Bob hadn't noticed Corey walking toward them until Rita drew his attention to them. When Bob did finally notice Corey, he smiled brilliantly and picked up Rita with his two arms wrapped around her waist and then set her down in back of him.

Rita screamed with surprise, but Corey, Robert Ryan, and Jack Carson were laughing quite loudly now. Bob then quickly moved toward Corey, and as she widely held her two arms out to him, he wrapped his arms around her waist, and they tightly embraced each other. Bob lifted his head, looked into her eyes, and lovingly asked, "How you doing, baby?"

"Right now, I'm doing wonderful, darling." Corey's eyes were sparkling as she looked at him.

They kissed for a few seconds, and then he told her, "Don't forget, I'll see you late tonight, doll." He then gave her an even longer kiss this time.

Corey answered him as he began to walk to the cafeteria with Rita, "All right, darling. Be careful tonight."

* * * * *

Bob arrived at the recording studio in LA with time to spare. All five of the guys were there, and Doug was starting to act like his old self, making jokes and wisecracking with everyone.

Truman got the instruments there without any trouble, and he would be there at the end of the recording session to take them back to Thousand Oaks for tomorrow's last rehearsal before the Shrine Auditorium concerts.

The guys finished recording the songs by ten o'clock, with perfect versions of "Conviction" and "Makin' Roads Inland." Truman loaded the instruments into the van and took the two recordings to be sent to New York for the first step in pressing them into vinyl.

Bob arrived home at eleven thirty and found Corey fast asleep. She obviously had a long day also. He quickly showered and brushed his teeth and then climbed into bed with her at midnight.

Corey, feeling him get into bed, rolled over to him. Bob was on his back, and she put her arm around him as she lay her head on his shoulder and upper chest. He lifted her head with his free hand under her chin, and they kissed. He softly placed her head back down as she moaned with complete satisfaction.

* * * * *

All the guys arrived at the LA Shrine Auditorium at six o'clock Saturday night. They tuned their instruments and ran a sound check on them. The guitars were then placed in the front three guitar stands behind the three microphones.

Jimmy checked the tautness of his skins, and Doug and Joshua made sure the spit-valves on their saxophone and trumpet were cleaned out. It was going to be a long night.

The doors were opened to ticket holders at seven o'clock. The guys were backstage talking with Nick and Truman. Nick felt he had to remind the guys of something, and he warningly told them, "I just wanna tell you guys this is the first time you'll be playing to people who may or may not have a problem with the integration of black and white. I feel here in LA, it probably won't be an issue, but I have security standing by at every exit, just in case. Let's just pray they've come to listen to your music and not to stir up some shit."

Joshua stood contemplating the possibility of trouble, and a fierce conviction washed over him as he authoritatively expressed, "I've known from an early age what I wanted to do with my life. I worked hard getting myself through school while playing the hell outta my horn. I believed no one was gonna stop me from fulfilling my dreams, and I'll be damned if I'm gonna let some assholes put up more barriers for me now." Tears were forming in his eyes as he emphatically added, "I love what I do, and I most especially love what this group of my brothers do, because I love each and every one of you. We're not gonna let someone else tell us what we can and cannot do. Like Bob said, when Darnell and I joined forces with the Owls, 'one of us goes down, all of us goes down.' Now let's get out there and kick some ass!"

Bob knew this was something Joshua would never say in the ordinary course of things. So he walked up to him and grabbed his hand with both of his. Looking directly into his face, Bob pumped Joshua's hand twice and determinedly expressed, "Amen, brother."

All the other six men were now yelling with fearless encouragement for the group.

When the guys started to quiet down, the stage manager came by and told them, "Five minutes, guys."

Because of the inherent strength of Bob, he emboldened the guys with further words of encouragement. "All right, guys. We've put a lot of time, hard work, and sweat into our music, just for moments like this. I want you to dig down deep within your souls as you play tonight. Because together, we're gonna tear down age-old prejudices, enlighten those people who think you should stay within the boundaries they set for you, and then we're gonna torch this son-of-a-bitchin' auditorium with music our fans will find that frees their hearts to experience their own personal freedoms."

Everyone was yelling with galvanized energy as they were slapping hands and bumping shoulders. Doug screamed, "Come on, guys, let's burn it down!"

The Owls entered stage right, as they were met with thunderous applause, screaming, and loud whistles. They all smiled to the audience and waved until they reached their spot on the stage. As the guitar straps were lifted over shoulders, drumsticks were picked up, and trumpet and saxophone were placed in hand, there was electricity rolling through their bloodstreams.

When each man looked ready, Bob nodded to Jimmy. Then with the four-count from Jimmy's stick to the snare, he started to beat the snare, with the accompaniment of his kick drums and the bass drum. When he hit the crash cymbal, Len's electric bass guitar came in, followed by Darnell, and then Bob on the lead guitar.

They were opening with "Raging Fire," and the audience knew this song very well as they wildly applauded, and the young women screamed with excitement.

Doug started wailing on the alto sax with some rockin' notes that eventually led into Bob's vocal entrance. He sang the upbeat lyrics with true conviction as Joshua jumped in with the C trumpet howling its doleful cries.

The sound of Joshua's trumpet was intense, powerful, and brilliantly played. He was convincing the audience of his love for his instrument by running a riff of brassy notes that defined the embodiment of "Raging Fire."

The entire performance was imbued with sparkle and elan. The Owls were demonstrating their powerful musical delivery in convincing fashion.

The exquisitely loud sound system of the auditorium screamed the deep, thunderous ending notes of the song as the Owls ended together perfectly on the closing synchronous vibrating beat. The resonance that echoed through the speakers was impeccable.

The crowd went wild with applause, screams, and loud yells of encouragement. They embraced the Owls with open arms, hearts, and minds.

Haddie was in the audience, sitting next to Deidra, her future daughter-in-law, and Darnell's wife, Alicia. There were a lot of prideful tears being shed by the three ladies as they loudly applauded.

As Alicia looked around the auditorium at the crowd of over six thousand people, who were applauding and shouting their approval, she was exhilarated to see many people of color in the waves of Owl fans.

The two key personnel changes with the addition of Joshua and Darnell definitely strengthened the band. Their impact on the Owls sound was so profound, that their relatively brief tenure was drawing more and more fans of color to the group's music.

Suddenly, Jimmy hit the four-count on the snare, and the applause began to die down, but the young people, most especially the women, kept up the screaming.

The Owls ripped into their latest recording, "Conviction," with Jimmy punishing the drums with an opening run of fifteen seconds of continuous and thunderous beat time. Then all three guitars exploded with the innovative chord structure of the song.

Doug jumped in and absolutely blew the valves off of his saxophone as he was running the notes tenaciously and with tremendous volume.

Joshua threw some backup into the mix with some raging notes on his mistress-in-waiting, the C trumpet.

After a minute of the loud and raucously composed song of rebellion, Bob and Len both sang the mutinous lyrics into the same microphone. The audience was loving it, as they cheered them on, shaking their fists in the air to the rhythmic beat.

The Owls knew this recently recorded song was going to sell as soon as it hit the record stores and jukeboxes because of the amazing reaction of the young people in the audience that night.

Almost three hours later, the guys brought the concert to an end by closing with Len's lyrical composition, "Stronger than You Think." It was the first song the Owls recorded with Joshua and Darnell as members of the band.

As the last note evaporated into the air, the huge crowd broke into uproarious applause with screeching, screaming, and high-pitched whistles. Bob, Len, and Darnell placed their guitars in the guitar stands and walked out to the front of the stage. The young girls in the first ten rows of the auditorium charged the stage. Bob signaled for Joshua, Doug, and Jimmy to join them. They immediately moved to the front of the stage and joined them, where together they all took a synchronized bow.

The guys started shaking hands with the young women. As they smiled and blew kisses to as many of them as they could, a handful of the women put their hands to their hearts, held their breath, and feigned absolute rapture. A couple of the women actually had to lower themselves to the floor, acting like they were going to faint. At that point, security raced to them and helped them into a seat.

The women were pushing and shoving each other just to reach Bob and be able to touch one of his hands. Hands down, he was the most popular band member to the young women. Bob was smiling brilliantly at them as he pulled Doug over. He got Doug out in front, where the women started to swarm him, and Bob, enjoying all this, yelled into Doug's ear, "See, man, they're all yours."

Doug yelled back to him, "I'm cool with that, man."

After about ten minutes of this fan-appreciation time, Bob signaled to the guys to pull back. They took one last bow, and the deafening roar coming from the auditorium was reassuring to them; there was no sign of trouble, and LA loved the Night Owls.

Bob didn't get home until after midnight. He crept into the master suite, trying to be quiet, but Corey rolled over in bed and threw the covers off of her. Unhesitating, she slowly walked over to him, placed a hand on each side of his face, and pulled him into her kiss.

He leaned into her warm and enveloping lips, and as they released from each other, Bob apologetically told her, "I'm sorry if I bummed out your zees, doll. I'm still trying to turn the thermostat down, baby."

With a broad, happy smile, Corey said, "Well, if that means you awakened me, no, you did not, darling."

Corey then anxiously asked, "So, I take it the evening went very well for you guys?"

"It was phenomenal, babe. We had no glitches or trouble of any kind, it was a blast. And now I'm stoked about tomorrow night, when you and your entourage of thirteen will be there."

Corey excitedly told Bob, "Well, Jack will be there, along with Susan, whose husband is out of town, as usual. However, it does make me wonder. Of course, Elizabeth and Drake wanted to see the new face of your band in concert. Alex will be with Robert Ryan. Debbie is coming with a man she met in Hollywood named Harry something or other. Richard Widmark and his wife will be coming, and Lew Ayers is bringing Ann Sheridan. And last but not least, Rita Hayworth asked me if I could secure a seat for her. So there you go. All fourteen tickets booked for the Madrigal entourage."

Bob just stared at Corey with a silly smirk on his face. She chuckled at him as his face turned into a broad smile as he told her, "Baby, you're just magical."

He kissed her once more, and on his face, he wore the same soft languor as always after playing a long concert. Bob tenderly whispered, "I'm gonna take a shower now and brush my teeth, but when I get into bed, I want you to hold me and then gently rock me to sleep. Will you do that for me, doll?"

"You know there isn't anything I wouldn't do for you, mister. I'll be waiting for you, darling."

After Bob climbed into bed, he lay between her legs, face up with the back of his head between her breasts, and Corey wrapped her arms around his chest. Within seconds, she could hear him heavily breathing as he quietly fell asleep.

Sunday morning, April 17, Corey was awake at seven o'clock and went into the kitchen to get some of Haddie's fresh coffee, which she had smelled all the way from the bedroom.

As Corey entered the kitchen, Haddie was squeezing some oranges into juice. Corey inquisitively asked Haddie, "Well, good morning, Haddie. How did you like the concert last night? Did you have fun?"

Haddie, surprised Corey was out of bed so early, turned and smiled, answering, "Morning, Ms. Corey. Oh, yeah. The concert was somethin' else. My Joshua was blowing that horn like there wasn't gonna be any tomorrow. I just thank God that I've been given the chance to see my boy so happy. It's like a dream come true for both of us."

Haddie brought a glass of orange juice over and sat it down in front of Corey along with a cup of coffee. She added very confidently, "And you got to know, Ms. Corey, Mr. Bob had a hold of the whole concert by the loose hairs. He was in the groove with his guitar and piano playing, and for sure, he was melting those young women who were sitting in those first few rows of seats with his angelic voice. I thought a couple of them women were gonna go up onstage and kiss him."

Corey chuckled out loud and prodigiously smiled, saying, "And I wouldn't have blamed them for doing that. I may just do that myself tonight."

"Well, Ms. Corey, you better be prepared to stand in line."

Several minutes later, Bob came strolling into the kitchen, dressed in sweatpants and a Night Owls tee shirt. His eyes still showed some fatigue from the previous night.

When he sat down next to Corey, they quickly kissed, then Haddie set a cup of coffee in front of him. Bob thanked Haddie and then looked at Corey amorously and playfully told her, "Yeah, last night, baby, I had these two beautiful soft pillows comforting my head, and before I knew it, I was wiped out."

Haddie immediately warned, "Oh, no, no, no. Do I wanna hear this?"

Bob, acting guileful, incredulously asked Haddie, "Whatever do you mean, Ms. Haddie? I was just talking about the warm and soft pillows Corey has on our bed."

Corey smiled and laughed to herself as she turned her head away, drawing her lips tightly together.

Haddie smirkingly told him, "Oh yeah, Mr. Bob. You a cool cat, that's for sure. But you ain't pulling my wig down over my eyes this time. I can dig it. You a bad dude, Mr. Bob."

All three of them laughed heartily together as they drank their coffee.

That evening, Bob drove into the LA Shrine Auditorium at five fifteen, giving him some leeway if the traffic was heavy.

Jack was coming by to pick up Corey and Haddie at seven o'clock, and he would have Susan and Rita riding with him.

There were tickets held at the box office for each guy's lady, and fourteen tickets specifically for Corey's Hollywood grouping.

Close to showtime, at eight o'clock, Nick peeked out at the audience and saw the entire third row was filled with all very familiar faces.

The Owls were going to change up the program for their closing night concert. They added a couple of songs and planned on playing as many of their older songs that time allowed.

After the Night Owls were introduced over the loudspeaker system, all six guys came out from backstage. The audience erupted in an extremely loud and boisterously welcoming applause, with screaming and high-pitched whistles thrown into the mix.

Bob, Len, and Darnell were all securing the guitar straps over their shoulders when Bob, brilliantly smiling, threw his arms in the air and pumped his closed fists three times.

The audience loved this, and the roar of the crowd heightened.

Corey stared at Bob with such a wealth of pride; she absolutely knew his music was the most important aspect of his career. She felt his blood was imbued with musical notes.

Excitedly, Bob looked back at Jimmy and gave the nod. Jimmy struck the rim of his snare with the four-count, and all three guitars opened up playing "Ricochet," the last song the Owls recorded before Joshua and Darnell joined them.

Doug rolled in some smooth sax while Joshua ran an opening riff on his main mistress, the bass trumpet.

The Owls used a lot of head arrangements to see what timing and progressions they could improvise on in all their performances.

Bob and Joshua reworked the song to add trumpet and another guitar into the melody. The song was up-tempo, but not as fast and driving as "Raging Fire."

When the song's ending notes were still resonating, the six thousand fans in the auditorium started cheering and aggressively applauded the new version of the song.

As the applause died down, Bob stepped up to the microphone by himself. The young women in the audience started screaming. He smiled his approval to them as he began to talk into the mike, "I just want to mention to you that tonight, the Owls are going to play a song that our two brothers, Joshua and Darnell, have written the lyrics for."

After pointing his hand at each one of them, Bob introduced them, and the crowd applauded loudly, along with some whistles.

"This is a song for the changing times we're entering into. This is a song to call all souls together in the fight for equality. And this is a song that promises everyone must have the strength and courage for the fight."

There was louder applause, along with yells and screaming.

Lastly, Bob proclaimed, with loud enunciation, "This is 'Courage for the Fight.'"

There were a lot of *amens* and *yes sir's* coming from the audience; they could be heard throughout the auditorium. These people were ready for the changing times.

After the four-count, Jimmy started beating his drums with vigor and determination. The thump and bray of the electrical guitars were kickin' it down, as Doug unloaded a loud and fast run on his saxophone. Then Joshua's C trumpet came thundering in as his horn was sizzling in a state of great heat and excitement.

Bob turned sideways and looked up at Joshua as the man was setting fire to the air around him. His trumpet was combustible at this point, and the notes were melting in the air from the heat of that fire.

Bob couldn't help but to smile with tremendous respect for Joshua's brilliance on that horn.

At the same time, Darnell, Len, and Bob stepped up to Darnell's microphone; and on cue, all three began to sing "Courage for the Fight":

> Our journey has been long and still remains
> I can still feel your whip and all the chains
> You can't hold me down like that anymore
> I can see the light, and I'm goin' walk through
> that door.
>
> (Chorus)
> Don't bother helping me up, I was born carrying
> the weight
> I'll learn to fight for myself, and bury your hate
> Lord, keep me brave and give me courage for the
> fight
> 'Cause I'll be standing tall and praying to God,
> for him to make it right.
>
> You beat me down and hold me to the floor
> But I'm goin' to rise up, not take any more
> I bleed just like you, brother, but I can't forget
> the past.
> I can't figure out why you hate, but I know the
> dye is cast.

(Chorus)

Why can't we share the love of life we've been
given
But you seem to teach the hate, for which you
are driven
I'm not asking anymore, but demand from you
The equality you stole from me, and the respect
I'm due.

(Ending Chorus)

On the prolonged last note of the song, it became controlled bedlam in the auditorium as the applause became thunderous, and the screams and yelling were of an enormous magnitude. The entire crowd was standing, and the noise was deafening as it filtered down onto the stage from every level of the auditorium.

The heart of the song was the introspective lyrics, and it would soon become an instant showstopper at every one of their concerts.

Bob threw kisses to the entire third row and then singled Corey out, and beaming with pride and self-satisfaction, he slowly winked at her.

Corey was beside herself with excitement as she seductively winked back at him. Her eyes were glistening, but she kept clapping and remained standing until most of the audience began to sit down.

Then Joshua started playing some soft and sophisticated notes on his main mistress, which danced with such a romantic flair to them that the audience instantly knew he was introducing "Let Me Lay within Your Arms."

After Joshua's lead-in, Jimmy began the smooth teasing of the snare with his drums wire brushes, which were used to infuse a softer effect to the melody.

Doug threw in some lazy background runs as Len and Darnell began playing the slightly downward melody. Bob took the top of the microphone from its bass and began moving out toward the front of the stage close to the audience.

With the opening lyrics to the song, he was looking squarely at Corey:

> Let me lay within your arms
> Let me feel your loving touch
> Tell me that you'll never leave
> Knowing how I love you so much.

Bob moved seductively toward a group of young women as he smiled at them. That entire section of the audience began to scream with delight, and many of the women grabbed for his hand. He touched some of their hands, and those women screamed and started to cry as they held their hands to their heart, now thinking they would never wash away the feel of his hand on theirs.

Corey, Elizabeth, Susan, and Alex were all smiles, watching the women loving him like they loved him, each in their own particular way.

Bob kept singing in his beautiful baritone voice:

> Come whisper your secrets to me
> Then kiss me till my body melts
> You'll be mine for all of tonight
> With the love I've always felt.
>
> Your magic touch is all I need
> It sets off fireworks and alarms
> So give yourself to me, and
> Let me lay within—your—arms.

Bob's voice cried out with surprising strength to the last three words as he held the final note for thirteen seconds.

The crowd erupted with applause, screaming, and whistles; young women jumped toward Bob and surged toward the stage. He touched as many hands that he could reach. A couple of the women grabbed his hands, but he escaped unscathed.

Corey stood with the rest of the crowd clapping and cheering, but when the young women grabbed Bob's hands, she became alarmed, and her hand came up to cover her mouth.

The rest of the concert went smoothly. The Owls experienced great fan backing in LA and were resolute in their thoughts; they felt their eclectic music collection of romance and revolution was entertaining and exactly what the youth of this new generation was begging for.

After almost three hours of nonstop performing, all the Owls came together at the front of the stage and took a final bow. Everyone in the audience was standing and applauding, screaming, and whistles sounded from all directions.

Then the Owls quitted the stage. As the audience was filing out, Truman began to collect their instruments for transport back to the Thousand Oaks recording studio.

Nick was talking with the Owls backstage when Corey came racing up to Bob with her arms held wide open to him. Bob happily smiled and put his arms around her waist as she wrapped her arms around his neck and head.

Corey exclaimed, "Your new songs were magnificent, darling! I just love to watch your band performing them, and you singing! It was truly marvelous!"

They kissed deeply and unapologetically in front of the guys.

Doug howled like a coyote on the prowl as the other guys just laughed to themselves.

Bob and Corey didn't mind the kidding; as they separated, Bob boasted, "Yeah, but now I get to go home with this lady."

Corey chuckled and lovingly stared at Bob.

Corey rode home with Bob in his '52 Chevy that evening with her hands around his right arm and her head on his shoulder.

FOURTEEN

Even with the fatigue still clinging to Bob's body Monday morning, he was able to roll out of bed, get dressed, and go into the studio, with a little bit of coaxing from Corey.

The director, Victor Trudeau, of Bob and Corey's picture *Love's Wicked Lies* was going to commence shooting film today. Victor was traveling with Bob and Rita on their location shoot; there was going to be two steamy love scenes filmed, with the two actors on a secluded beach near Santa Monica.

Rita was playing Bob's mistress in the picture; her screen persona always challenged respectability and the loosening moral codes of the time.

The bathing suit she was wearing for the first scene had an extreme cut to the cleavage. Victor informed Edith Head that all of Rita's costumes should be very provocative and with a very sexy cut in cleavage to each one. He wanted to portray her as irresistible to any man and exploit her beautiful breasts and body, supposedly, for the integrity of the story line.

After the handheld cameras were set to go, and the sun was to the cameras' backs, the scene began with a few lines of dialogue as Rita and Bob lay on a blanket in the sand. Bob placed his one leg between her legs and started to kiss her neck. He then moved down to kiss the area between her breasts. They enveloped each other's lips in a very sensual and long kiss as he lowered the straps to her bathing suit.

All the scenes that would be shot on a beach would be shot this day. Then these close-ups would be evaluated by Victor later tonight at the studio, as either keepers or scheduled for a reshoot at a later date.

Corey was back at the studio rehearsing scenes with Robert Ryan and Jack Carson that would be shot today and tomorrow.

All Corey could think about was Bob making love to Rita in the warmth of the Southern California sun. She had to tell herself to believe that it was just a job and nothing else.

Later that afternoon, when Bob was through with his location shoots, he snuck into the soundstage where Corey would be shooting some of her scenes. He stood way in the back, off camera, and behind all set design.

Victor shouted, "All right, action."

Corey attacked the scene determinedly, and with fire and intelligence in her eyes, she delivered her lines with true conviction and from a deep part of her soul.

Few people were privy to the original motivation behind the intensity of her drive. Bob was one of those few who knew; making motion pictures was Corey's absolute obsession in life—besides him. She would most likely still be making pictures right up until the time she died. She loved the work; and working with fellow actors she respected and cared for just made it more exhilarating for her.

When Victor yelled, "Cut. That's a take. Good job, Corey. Let's take ten, people."

Corey went to sit down in one of the canvas-backed chairs when she caught a glimpse of Bob standing behind the cameras. He noticed she had seen him, and he grinned at her. Corey's eyes lit up as she excitedly moved toward him.

Corey couldn't help but notice his taut, angular face, with those square shoulders, and that shy cast he had to his gorgeous green eyes. The eyes alone were enough to drive her crazy as they deliberately provoked her sexual desire for him.

When she reached him, she placed her hands on the sides of his face and pulled him down to kiss her. As they separated, Corey playfully asked, "Well, I see you still have some lips left for me. Thank you, darling."

"I'll always have lips for you, baby." They kissed once more with great feeling. Then Corey very reluctantly left him to go and shoot the next scene.

At dinner that same night, Corey mentioned to Bob, "You know, darling, Alex has asked us over this Wednesday evening to a cocktail party she'll be hosting. She seems to think there will be about fifteen other people. I told her I would talk it over with you."

Bob facetiously answered, "Well, we have picture shoots every day this week, I have recording studio sessions Tuesday and Thursday nights, and we're flying to New York for the Tony Awards, Friday night. So, I think we can make an appearance but not make a night of it. How does that sound to you, doll?"

Corey delightfully smiled at him and sexily responded, "Perfect. Just perfect, darling."

Wednesday evening came around very quickly, as Bob and Corey arrived home from the studio late and then had to rush to get ready to go to Alex's party.

Bob drove them in his Chevy flip-top, and they arrived inadvertently, but fashionably, late. Alex welcomed them in as they told her how beautiful her six-bedroom, five-thousand-square-foot house looked.

Alex had Corey's dry martini, stirred, and Bob's chilled beer brought to them by the hired waiter, almost as soon as they began looking the place over.

Within the hour, Alex asked Bob if he wanted to go out on the back veranda so he could take in the beautiful views of her impeccably manicured back acre of property.

As he stood and looked over the space that was lit with soft accent lights—some mounted on trees, others on trellises of beautifully colored perennials—he exclaimed, "This really is quite a nice yard you have here. It looks very peaceful."

Alex took Bob by the hand and led him over to a wrought iron table surrounded by six chairs. They sat down next to each other as Bob experienced some nervous trepidation.

Alex explained, "I've wanted to talk to you for quite some time now. I want to apologize if there has ever been anything I have said or done that would make you uncomfortable being around me. I will admit, Bob, that I am attracted to you, but I would never act on that as long as you're with someone else."

Bob was perplexed about this entire disconcerting conversation because he thought everything had been ironed out before she moved out weeks earlier from Corey and his estate.

"Alex, I really don't think we have a problem here. Corey is my wife now, and there's just no possibility anything would ever happen between some other woman and I. I thought we understood that we could be friends."

Corey finished talking with Anne Baxter and her new husband, Randolph Galt, and looked around the room for Bob. When she didn't see him or Alex anywhere, she thought maybe she should peruse the house, until she found them.

Corey eventually ended up at the entrance to the back acreage and could see Alex and Bob sitting and talking to each other. She remained at the door but stood listening to their conversation, praying it had only to do with business.

Alex looked directly into Bob's eyes, and with subdued fascination, she softly made clear to him, "Bob, you're a good man, of course, you're also charming, but charm and decency don't always go together."

Corey almost rushed to rip into Alex, but with great constraint, she held back and continued to listen.

Bob sat fixed on her next words to him.

"But in your case, they certainly do. Your good looks haven't made you vain. You're not shallow, and that might have something to do with it. Mainly though, you had the gift of a good upbringing. I'd say you had a wonderful mother. You know how that shows? In the way you treat other people. I'm pretty sure you come from a background people only know from the movies, but it hasn't gone to your head. It's obvious your mother did a great job."

Bob was greatly relieved to hear Alex complimenting him on his upbringing and not lashing into him for the unrequited love she had for him but he was not able to give her.

Bob gratefully told her, "Thank you, Alex. And yes, my mother was fantastic, and she loved Elizabeth and I more than anything in the world."

Corey started a slow walk over to the table they were seated at. She was looking only at Alex, and she gave her a brilliant, dangerous smile. The message of that smile was clear: you're on the verge of having your face scratched off and your throat ripped out.

It was obvious to both Bob and Alex that Corey had heard their conversation. Bob instantly stood up and put his arm around Corey, because he knew her well, and that smile was not meant to be a pleasurable greeting to anyone.

Bob tried to placate Corey by telling her, "Hey, doll, Alex was just complimenting me on the wonderful way my mother raised me and how it shows. I thought it was really cool."

Corey's eyes were still fixed on Alex as she sarcastically blurted out, "Peachy. Just peachy."

Alex felt Corey's wrath and tried to explain, "Corey, I've always wanted to apologize to Bob for any times that I may have made him uncomfortable and made even you upset with me. I hope you know that I respect your relationship and marriage and that I would never cross that line."

Corey, now getting her bearings on things, almost apologetically told Alex, "I know you wouldn't, Alex, but there just seems to be a lot of push and pull when you're around him. I do know, however, you're too smart of a woman to go fishing for something that you know you could never catch."

Bob knew at this point it was time to leave the party, so he spoke up, "Alex, we have to get up pretty early tomorrow, so I think we're gonna call it a night. Thank you for inviting us to your new home. It's really outta sight. Good night, and I hope we see you again soon."

Alex quickly added as Corey and Bob turned to leave, "And good luck this Sunday at the Tony Awards, Bob. I really hope you win."

"Thanks, Alex. I appreciate that."

Friday night, April 22, 1960, Bob and Corey flew out to New York City as soon as they finished their work at Celebrity. They were going to spend all day Saturday and Sunday, up until six o'clock Sunday evening, doing whatever they wanted to do.

After they greeted Rodney in the large foyer of their penthouse building, they dragged themselves into the elevator at almost one o'clock Saturday morning.

They took a warm shower together as they kissed each other's wet bodies, and after each had washed and rinsed the other with a sudsy loofah sponge.

When Bob climbed into bed naked, Corey quickly slipped off her negligee she had hastily put on after their shower. She softly laid her warm and yielding body on top of him. He ran his hands over her back and hips as she kissed him with great fervor.

Corey excitedly ran her hands through his hair and around his head as he gently held her body and rolled her over on her back. Her hand went down between his legs as she began to lustfully fondle his excitement. They both started panting with loving desire when Bob bent his upper body down to suckle at her breast.

He began to lick and bite at her nipple; Corey always found this intoxicating. She was now breathing in short, quick gasps when suddenly Bob entered her. She started to slowly move with him as his body powerfully surged forward, and then back, regaining strength to go even deeper into her.

Within a couple minutes, Bob started to reach orgasm but kept up the heavy forward-and-upward motion of his hips into Corey. With a soft cry, and then whisperingly Corey whined, she began to climax, "Oh my god. Baby, don't stop. Please, don't stop."

Bob continued until Corey wrapped her arms around his neck, and in a total state of exhaustion, she started to cry, saying, "I just can't believe how much I love you, darling."

Bob kissed her again and adoringly told her, "It will always be only you, baby."

They kissed one more time and then fell fast asleep in each other's arms.

Bob woke up that Saturday morning at nine o'clock to find Corey was already out in the front room waiting for him with a pot of coffee.

He walked out into the living room with just the bottoms to his pajamas on. After he walked over to Corey, sitting in one of the chairs, he leaned down to kiss her. She purred with delight.

The room was warmed from the gray stacked-stone gas fireplace Corey had turned on after she ordered their pot of coffee.

Bob then questioningly asked, "What do you think about going tonight to see *Bye Bye Birdie* at the Martin Beck Theatre and, before the play, some dinner at Coppola's?"

Corey happily told him, "Anything you want, darling. This weekend is all about you."

Bob smiled and said, "Good. Then tomorrow, we'll catch the matinee to *Flower Drum Song* and dinner at Tessa's, okay?"

"Absolutely, my darling man."

He kiddingly asked, "Are you patronizing me, lady?"

"Absolutely, my darling man."

Bob reached over and quickly grabbed her by the waist with both his hands. When he began tickling her, Corey screamed with delight. She ran her hands up his muscular arms, and smiling seductively, she pulled him into her kiss.

The weekend went by quickly for them as they arrived a half hour early at the Grand Ballroom of the Astor Hotel for the Tony Awards.

Corey was exquisitely dressed in a fabulous deep-cobalt-blue ball gown, with elbow-length matching gloves and clutch purse. Her hair was pulled up onto her head and styled by the famous hairstylist Ted Gibson, who had his own salon right there in New York City.

Bob was dressed in one of his black tuxedos, and the bow tie, cummerbund, and handkerchief matched the cobalt blue of Corey's dress. They were very stylish, for 1960, and made a beautiful-looking couple.

They sat at their table with his costar in *A Casual Affair*, Natalie Moore, and her husband, along with the director, Stanley Kabrinski, and his wife, Eve.

There were twelve hundred people seated at individual tables in the ballroom when Eddie Albert, the master of ceremonies, came walking out right on cue.

It was customary to start the awards show with the national anthem. After everyone was seated again, they started presenting the awards. Over an hour and a half later, the awards had been presented for scenic design, costume design, choreographer, producer, and actor and actress in a featured role.

Now Harry Gardino walked out and read the nominees for Best Actress in a Play. After the envelope was handed to him, he read, "Anne Bancroft, *Miracle Worker.*"

Bob looked over at Natalie with a saddened disappointment on his face as he lightly shook his head in disbelief.

Anne's acceptance speech was commendable as she thanked everyone, including her husband, Mel Brooks.

Corey sat in twisted anxiety as Bob seemingly stayed somewhat calm, both knowing the next award was for Best Actor in a Play.

Helen Hays walked out onto the stage as the next presenter of the Best Actor in a Play Award. The audience applauded her with great respect, for she was an already seasoned Broadway and Hollywood star of great notoriety.

When the applause died down, Bob looked over at Corey and just smiled brilliantly and then sexily winked at her.

Corey took his hand and nervously smiled back as she returned the wink.

Ms. Hays then began to read the nominees: "For Best Performance by a Leading Actor in a Play, there is Lee Tracy, *The Best Man*; Jason Robards, *Toys in the Attic*; Sidney Poitier, *Raisin in the Sun*; Bob Richardson, *A Casual Affair*; and George C. Scott, *The Andersonville Trial.* And the winner is…"

Corey intently watched Helen take the envelope and tear it open. Her heart was pounding even louder than Bob's was as Helen smiled and read, "Bob Richardson, *A Casual Affair*."

Bob's jaw dropped as he sat paralyzed in his seat.

Corey yelled so loud, Bob startlingly looked at her, and the already unshed tears in her eyes made his eyes start to glisten. They grabbed each other in an enormous embrace and kissed explosively. When they separated, Bob movingly told Corey, "I love you to the moon and back, Alice!"

She reluctantly let go of him as he hugged each and every person at their table, and then in hastened excitement, he ran up to the stage, jumping upward on every other step of the stairs, showing his youthful exuberance.

Bob smiled uncontrollably at Ms. Hays, with his eyes now glistening; they appeared to be very close to becoming tears.

As he was handed the Tony, it just felt so surreal to him that he had to tell her, "Ms. Hays… I find this an honor to have this presented to me from such a tremendous actress of your caliber. Thank you so much."

Helen leaned into him, and he bent down to listen to her, when surprisingly, she kissed him on the cheek and graciously said, "Thank you, Bob. I thought you were wonderful in the play."

There were tears streaming down Corey's face as Bob enthusiastically began his acceptance speech. "I want to tell all of you how big a surprise this is to me, because of the powerhouse actors I was up against. My god! I have always had great respect and admiration for the four gentlemen who were nominated along with me. If I could, I would cut this up into five pieces and give each man their part."

Bob seriously stated, "I do want to thank Natalie Moore for helping me and guiding me throughout this whole process. She was invaluable to me. And to Stanley Kabrinski, for proving to me that if you're willing to put your heart and soul into your performance, there will be an end reward for you. And lastly, but absolutely by no means least, I want to thank my mentor, my friend, my wife, and my life's love, Corey."

Corey's eyes were now seriously dropping full tears down her face.

"She has been the inspiration in my career, the motivation to my drive, and the absolute love of my heart." Bob looked directly at Corey and lovingly stated, "Just thinking of you keeps me awake. Dreaming of you keeps me asleep. But being with you keeps me alive." Bob held the Tony in the air and pointed it at Corey as his voice started to break, proclaiming, "This would never have happened…if it weren't for your love for me. Thank you, baby."

Bob was choking back the tears then walked off the stage with Helen Hays's arm locked in his arm.

The audience applauded loudly, giving appreciative recognition to Bob's theatrical talent. They also fell in love with the heartrending way he professed his undying love to his wife.

Corey was absolutely sobbing now as Stanley, sitting beside her, put his arm around her and tried to calm her.

Fifteen minutes later, Bob returned to his table in the ballroom, after having his picture taken alone and then with Best Actress Anne Bancroft and briefly being interviewed by *Playbill* and *Broadway World* magazines.

Corey saw him making his way to their table, and from her seat, she bolted toward him. Bob was a table away when Corey flew at him with open arms. They embraced so tightly that some thought they'd never let go of each other. Then they kissed, and still holding on to each other, they slowly moved back to their own table.

Bob had missed the presentation of Best Producer in a Play while he was backstage. That award went to Andrew McNichols for *The Miracle Worker*.

Now was the presentation for Best Director in a Play. Lauren Bacall, the legendary Hollywood and Broadway actress, walked out to introduce the nominees.

She read, "The nominees for Best Director in a Play are Joseph Anthony, *The Best Man*; Tyrone Guthrie, *The Tenth Man*; Elia Kazan, *Sweet Bird of Youth*; Lloyd Richards, *Raisin in the Sun*; and Stanley Kabrinski, *A Casual Affair*. And the winner is…"

The envelope was handed to Ms. Bacall, and she ripped it open and turned to smile at Stanley, excitedly saying, "Stanley Kabrinski, *A Casual Affair*."

Bob jumped from his seat, yelling, "Yes! Yes!" He quickly moved to hug Stanley after he had kissed his wife, Eve. Bob embraced Stanley with a huge bear hug and then patted him on the back several times. Stanley hugged Natalie and Corey also as Bob stood pumping his hands in the air and cheering loud praise for him.

Corey watched Bob in all his excitement and could see how he absolutely glowed with pride for his friend Stanley. Her smile was brilliant, and her pride for Bob was to the highest degree of extreme.

Stanley and Ms. Bacall exchanged cheek kisses as she congratulated him. They were very good friends, as he had directed her in two Broadway plays within the last five years.

Stanley spoke into the microphone, "I can't remember when I had so much pleasure in directing a play as I had with *A Casual Affair*. My two leads were probably the most magical combination of any two people I have ever had the opportunity to work with. Natalie, you've always been an extremely good actress, and, Bob, you have such a future in theater—I can't even imagine. And I can tell all of you now Bob and I will be working together again this fall in a musical. It should be an incredibly good time!"

The audience sounded their delightful surprise with their applause and many approving cheers.

Stanley finished his acceptance speech, thanking the whole production staff and his wife, Eve, for putting up with his long work days and the lonely nights.

Before all the people sitting at Stanley's table went out for drinks to celebrate the two big wins for *A Casual Affair*, the award for best play went to *Miracle Worker*.

Bob and Corey flew back from New York to LA late that evening. However, in LA, it was only midnight when Curtis picked them up from the airport to take them home.

Even having slept on the plane for almost the full five hours, they were still pretty tired when the six o'clock alarm screamed at them to get out of bed and get to the studio.

When Bob walked into the soundstage at Celebrity, the Monday morning after Corey and he had returned from New York, he was met with applause and kudos for his Tony Award win from the night before. Bob thanked everyone as Rita walked up and kissed him on the cheek, saying, "Congratulations on your award, Bob."

She then seductively looked at him and added, "Loved your acceptance speech, it was quite moving. Corey's a lucky girl, isn't she?"

Corey walked up behind Rita after hearing what she had told Bob and facetiously reminded Rita, "Yes, Rita. Lucky, married, and in love with my husband. Maybe one day you'll be able to say that, sweetie."

The evening of Tuesday, April 26, while at the recording studio, and before the Owls started work on their two newly written songs, Nick told the guys, "I want you to wrap up these new songs within the next two weeks. We need this album released before we play the Fillmore in San Francisco on May 13. I really wanna see the fan reaction to these before that next concert."

So the guys really dug their heels in and worked tenaciously at putting the right melody, pitch, volume, pace, and rhythm to the already written lyrics of Bob and Joshua's "Time Is Ours to Change" and Bob and Doug's "Maybe Another Time, Another Place."

The last Friday in April, Bob was shooting scenes with both Corey and Rita. Victor felt these close-up scenes had to be shot on a soundstage at the studio because he wanted the refraction of light to be at just a certain angle when it showcased his actor's eyes to the cameras.

In one of the most intense scenes of the movie, Bob's character was pleading with Corey's character to take him back into her life after he betrayed her with Rita. Bob was full-out crying as Corey didn't find it difficult to cry on cue after seeing him begging her for another chance.

In these close-ups, Corey's eyes dominated the scenes. It was their sheer strength, confidence, and expressiveness that Bob had always been drawn to. She had a nuanced manner of speech and posture that evinced wisdom, while still communicating her deep and brilliant delivery of every line she had in the picture.

The movie still had five more weeks of production time; there were more location shoots, reshoots of already presumed takes, rewrites, and script changes ahead of them.

The producer, Trent Voight, was never worried about Victor bringing the movie in on time and under budget. With the outstanding actors in the picture, the brilliant script, and the genius of Victor Trudeau's directing, Trent knew this picture was going to be mind-blowing and electrifying to the moviegoers around the world.

The Tuesday evening of May 3, the guys finished and recorded the two new songs. Nick's assistant, Truman Atwater, was there to collect the recordings and remind the guys that it was planned that their third album, *Shakin' It with the Owls*, would now be released early next week. The arranger and mixer in New York would use the taped recordings of the Owls' last twelve songs to create the album.

Before everyone left the studio, Bob asked the guys and their significant others to come over to his and Corey's place at three o'clock that next Saturday afternoon. He told them, "I really can't tell you right now why I want you there, but trust me, it'll be worth all of your time and totally outta sight, man."

Doug boisterously chimed in, "Oh, man. Why can't you tell us what's goin' on? We have to wait until Saturday afternoon? What's shakin', man? You got the New York City Rockettes comin' in, or what?"

Bob smiled and simply said, "Even better."

What no one knew, except Nick, Bob, and Corey, was that this Saturday was the day Ms. Ella Fitzgerald and Mr. Duke Ellington were to come to Bob and Corey's estate to spend a few hours with everyone affiliated with the Night Owls. Then that night, at Duke and Ella's concert, Duke had arranged for fifteen seats in the second row of the Hollywood Bowl to be reserved for Bob's group.

Saturday, May 7, Bob arrived back home from the recording studio early to get cleaned up and help Corey and Haddie meet with the caterer at two o'clock. All the food would be brought into the kitchen area, and drinks would be served from the wet bar in the massive living room.

While Haddie was overseeing the safe storage of the sandwiches, ribs, grilled chicken wings, and salads, she inquisitively asked Bob, "Mr. Bob, I want to know why you and Ms. Corey can't tell me what's goin' on here today? How is this affecting me, anyway?"

Corey playfully looked at Bob as he answered Haddie, "You're just going to have to trust me, Ms. Haddie. And believe me, you won't be sorry you're a part of this."

"All right then. Now I can't wait, Mr. Bob. This sounds like somethin' special."

Bob smiled broadly at Haddie and then at Corey as he winked at her.

After the front doorbell rang, he left the kitchen to go and let the guys and their ladies in. By two thirty, everyone who needed to be there had arrived. Doug came stag because he didn't want to bother to find a date. Nick, his girlfriend, Charlotte, and Truman came together in Nick's car.

The two servers that Bob had hired to wait on the get-together was getting everyone a drink before the two jazz icons' arrival at the house.

Bob stood up and got everyone's attention by snapping his middle finger with his thumb four times against his glass of beer. Excitedly, he began by saying, "Okay, all you guys and dolls. It's almost three o'clock, and now we're close to having one of the most thrilling days in our lives, so far. I want all of you to brace yourselves and take some deep breaths, because you're gonna need 'em."

At that exact moment, the front doorbell rang again, and Bob warned, "Here we go."

Bob turned and went to the door, accompanied by Nick, who was the arranger of this meeting today. When Bob opened the huge mahogany door, Nick stepped forward to welcome in Mr. Duke Ellington, Ms. Ella Fitzgerald, and Duke's lead trumpeter, James "Bubba" Miley.

Nick shook hands with all three of them, and then Bob followed suit, exclaiming, "You just don't know how electrifying this whole experience is to me. Welcome to my home. Please, come in and meet everyone."

The door had been blocking the view of everyone in the living room. Doug and Darnell tried to lean toward the door, but Bob was blocking their view.

Joshua was sitting, with his arm around his mother, and the anticipation was almost too much for either one to bear.

Duke explained to Nick and Bob, "Bubba, my main man trumpeter, wanted to come and meet this group of guys. Those guys that are helping to remove the racial barriers in this country and fight the racial injustices that exist. So, Bob, I hope you don't mind Bubba stringing along."

Bob approvingly stated, "Absolutely not. It's our honor to have all of you here today visiting with us. Nick will take you in, and I really don't think you'll need an introduction."

Nick led them into the living area, where everyone was seated but Corey. She stood behind the people sitting down in chairs and on sofas because she felt this meeting was more for the band members and Haddie.

When Duke, Ella, and Bubba came walking into the room, every single person's eyes became twice their size, their mouths dropped open uncontrollably, and their entire bodies were frozen in time.

Nick, knowing it was unnecessary, still introduced the three of them. "I want all of you to meet the greatest jazz legions of our time: Mr. Duke Ellington, Ms. Ella Fitzgerald, and Duke's trumpeter, Mr. James 'Bubba' Miley."

Haddie put both hands to her face and instantly started to weep. She made a loud inarticulate utterance of joy, saying, "Oh magod! Magod! Oh lawd enheaven!"

Joshua slowly lifted himself from the loveseat that he was sitting on with his mama and couldn't take his eyes off of Duke and Ella. He began to walk, without memory of this, toward the threesome and just stood smiling at them, seemingly entrapped in another dimension of time.

Duke put out his hand to Joshua and said, "You've got to be the horn for this mellow group of cats."

Joshua heard his voice, and something clicked in his head. He came floating back down to earth and realized this wasn't a dream. As chills were still running through his body, Joshua put his hand out to Duke and expressed to him, "This is so righteous and way cool! I'm totally blown away, Mr. Ellington. I'm thrilled to meet you and Ms. Ella and Bubba Miley. Oh my lord! I now know that I've died and gone to heaven."

He then shook Ella's hand and then Bubba's. Joshua then told them, "I really want you to meet your number one fan—my mama, Ms. Haddie Chambers."

Duke and Ella walked over to Haddie, because they didn't think she was able to lift herself from her chair and stand up on her own. When Duke put his hand out to Haddie, she had tears running down both cheeks of her face, but managed to shake hands with him and Ella, anyway.

Through her tears, Haddie uttered whimperingly, "Oh my god! Nice meeting both of you."

Feeling sympathetic toward Haddie, Ella sat down next to her and hugged her and, in her soft, soothing voice, reassured Haddie, "That's all right now, Haddie. We really appreciate you liking our music and following our orchestra. We enjoy number one fans like you, honey."

Haddie hugged her back, and again, in an almost incoherent whimper, Haddie told her, "Thank you, Ms. Lady Ella."

Darnell was not so shy but was definitely moved by meeting these living icons of music. He walked up to Duke and Bubba and introduced himself, "I'm thrilled to meet you two. I'm Darnell King, and I play semi-acoustic guitar for the Owls. This is really far-out, and meeting someone I've only seen on TV or in a magazine just blows my mind."

Bubba jokingly answered back, "We could say the same thing about all of you, man. And now it's our pleasure meeting your band and your people."

Darnell just smiled and laughed, saying, "I can dig it, man." They exchanged hand slaps.

Bob had his arm around Corey as he walked her over in front of the threesome and introduced her to them. "Duke, Ella, and, Bubba, I would like to introduce you to my wife, Corey. She really loves dancing to your music."

Ella spoke out, saying, "Corey Madrigal. Of course, the Hollywood movie star. I have always loved your movies, Corey. And I've heard you have a very compelling picture coming out in June, and Edith Head is designing all your costumes? I'm jealous. I can't wait for its release."

Corey smiled widely and answered proudly, "Yes, thank you, Ella. Bob plays my cheating husband, and Rita Hayworth, his mistress. I can't tell you the ending, but the picture will be worth the theater ticket."

Bubba was intrigued by the story line Corey had described, and smilingly, he exclaimed, "Wow! I bet that cat's number is up."

The small group all laughed in amusement, nodding their heads in agreement.

For the next half hour, everyone sat talking about the monumental changes that the Owls took on by racially integrating an all-white rock 'n' roll band with two black musicians.

Duke explicitly addressed the band members by commending them, "You six men have shown the world that it takes courage, determination, and a camaraderie of unyielding adhesiveness amongst you to make this undertaking successful. And what I've seen and heard about your band—you certainly have been very successful. All of you Owls should be applauded."

All at once, everyone in the room started to clap their hands. Bob smiled brilliantly as he mouthed the words *thank you* to everyone, but especially at Duke.

Corey was bursting with pride as she got up on her toes and gave Bob a big cheek-kiss.

Doug piped up and inspiringly stated, "Yes, sir, Mr. Ellington. We've all agreed that if one of us goes down, all of us goes down. That's a promise, sir."

Duke grinned and answered back, "That's very admirable, Doug. Absolutely too cool!"

When the din of the room died down, Bob showed everyone to their dining room, which was across from the gourmet kitchen. Their pecan dining table could seat twenty people, and the two hired servers had placed all the food on the table.

As everyone sat down and placed their drinks out in front of them on the table, Bob remained standing at the end of the table.

When they saw him, everyone quieted down and inquisitively looked his way.

Bob smiled and proudly announced, "We all know the Third Annual Grammy Awards were over three weeks ago, and we would like to congratulate Ms. Lady Ella for winning two that night."

The entire table applauded her as she nodded gratefully to everyone.

"Yes, Ms. Lady Ella won for Best Vocal Performance by a Female for a Single Record with 'Mack the Knife.' And she also won for Best Vocal Performance by a Female for her album *Mack the Knife—Ella in Berlin*." Bob started the applause again.

Bob started to announce again, after the applause died down, "And we would also like to congratulate Mr. Duke Ellington for winning three Grammy Awards that same night."

Before anyone could applaud, Bob quickly added, "The master of jazz won for Best Score for a Soundtrack. He also won for Best Instrumental Composition and the third Grammy for Best Performance by an Orchestra. All three Grammys were for the movie *Anatomy of a Murder*."

Everyone was impressed as they applauded, along with some oohs and aahs.

Then everyone dug into the diverse selection of foods that was being served for dinner. There was a lot of dinner conversation, along with laughs and some very intense listening, especially when Duke, Ella, or Bubba had a story to tell.

When everyone was done eating, and they were just talking and drinking, Duke gave Bob the signal that he wanted to announce something.

Bob stood up and tapped his glass of beer with his knife, and after he got everyone's attention, he announced, "Thank you. Right now, Duke would like to talk with all of you. So, listen up."

Duke, being at the opposite end of the table from Bob, stood up and began to profess, "I need to tell the Night Owls that music, of course, is what I hear and something that I more or less live by. It's not an occupation or profession, it's a compulsion. Saying that, I feel deep down in my heart that for all you Owls, this isn't just a job or a means to making money. It's all of you feeling that your comprehensive collective is to express yourself and your life through your music. No one will be able to take that from you, for this is something ingrained in your brains and in your souls. You're untouchables."

Darnell and Doug slipped each other some skin as they concurred, saying in unison, "Yes, sir. Right on, brother."

Duke smiled and agreed, "Amen, my young brothers. But now I would like to tell everyone at this table: my band, with Bubba on the main horn, and Ms. Lady Ella's beautiful voice out front are going to be appearing at the Hollywood Bowl tonight at eight o'clock. And everyone here will have a seat in the second row for our performance. We just hope all of you can come and share the evening with us."

All the guys jumped out of their seats, yelling, "Oh my god! For crying out loud. What's going on here?" They were hugging each other, bumping shoulders, and slapping hands.

Bob sat laughing with joy, watching their elation and excitement. Corey laughed along with Bob as she saw Haddie begin to cry again, but Joshua was there to hug her; even in his excitement, he loudly told her, "Mama, what you crying for? We gonna see the king of jazz and his first lady perform tonight? Mama, you need to be happy 'bout this."

Haddie looked Joshua directly in the eyes and kiddingly stated, "I am happy, baby. Can't you tell? These are tears of complete joy and rapture!"

Everyone at the table began to laugh, including Duke, as he told the group, after the laughter died down, "Well, this has been our pleasure coming here today to meet all of you. But most especially, the six courageous guys that have been making monumental changes in the unjust and prejudicial treatment of people, purely on the grounds of race."

Bubba could be heard saying, "Yes, sir. Amen."

Duke added, "And now, before we leave to get ready for our concert tonight, I want all of you to remember the memorable quote from the great African American Baptist minister Martin Luther King: 'In the end, we will remember not the words of our enemies, but the silence of our friends.' So stay strong, and stay inspiringly powerful."

Everyone was struck by the words and began nodding their heads in rousing compliance.

At that same moment, Doug raised his glass of beer into the air, professing loudly, "To all our brothers—black, white, yellow, purple, or polka-dotted. Prejudice be damned!"

All glasses were raised as Darnell shouted, "Hear, hear!"

Shortly before eight o'clock, all fifteen seats were filled in the middle of the second row at the Hollywood Bowl by the Owls' entourage. Duke Ellington and his Orchestra, featuring Ms. Ella Fitzgerald, were only minutes away from taking the stage.

The Hollywood Bowl was known for its band shell; a distinctive set of concentric arches graced the site. The shell was set against the backdrop of the Hollywood Hills and the famous Hollywood sign to the northeast.

The Hollywood Bowl was built in 1922 and seated 17,500 concertgoers. It was a natural amphitheater; it had a shaded canyon that was chosen for its natural acoustics and its proximity to downtown Hollywood.

Bob looked down the second row of seats to his left and told them, "Take a good look. We'll be playing this venue August 12 and 13—the last two concerts of our summer tour."

Corey, sitting next to Bob, stared at him with a dark foreboding look. All she could feel about the Owls' summer tour was that they would be separated for a lot of the time when he was on the road and that there, more than likely, was going to be trouble in some of those cities.

The entire group knew there would be factions of intolerant, prejudiced people scattered about the country, but not as pronounced as in the Southern regions.

Then suddenly, the curtain flew open onstage, and Duke's orchestra began playing "22 Cent Stomp." It was a medium-paced number, with only piano and drums starting out, and then trombone and trumpets threw in the jazzy melody of a slightly upbeat song.

After the song ended, Duke Ellington walked up to the microphone Ella would be singing at. He waited for the applause to die down, and then he spoke to the audience, "Tonight, I would like to bring out here onstage the most popular jazz singer in the United States. The one and only Ms. Ella Fitzgerald."

The audience applauded loudly, mixed with whistles and cheering. Ella moved to center stage, beside Duke and the microphone. She thanked the audience for the warm reception, and as soon as Duke got back to his piano, the music began to play.

Everyone in the second row was greatly anticipating having Ella sing. Haddie was staring a hole through Ella, feeling like all this was just part of her dream; she never wanted to wake up from this experience.

Joshua and Darnell were filled with pride and much hope for the future when they listened to the racially diverse orchestra strike up "I'm Beginning to See the Light." It was set to a drum groove, and the pronounced screeching of Bubba's C trumpet was ripping into it as Ella began to sing:

> I never cared much for moonlit skies
> I never wink back at fireflies
> But now that the stars are in your eyes
> I'm beginning to see the light

I never went in for afterglow
Or candlelight on the mistletoe
But now when you turn the lamp down low
I'm beginning to see the light

Ella Fitzgerald was known for her purity of tone, impeccable diction, phrasing, timing, intonation, and a hornlike improvisational ability. Particularly in her scat singing. Her voice was flexible, wide-ranging, accurate, and ageless. She was forty-three years old when she toured with Duke's orchestra in 1960.

I never made love by lantern-shine
I never saw rainbows in my wine
But now that your lips are burning mine
I'm beginning to see the light

When the song was over, the audience cheered, as they loudly clapped their hands. Before the applause died down, the orchestra started in on "Satin Doll," with Duke opening up with a slow tempo on the piano, accompanied by soft and mellow horns.

After an hour and a half of the orchestra playing all of Duke's favorite hits: "Do Nothin' till You Hear from Me," "Take the 'A' Train," "I Got It Bad and That Ain't Good," "Sophisticated Lady," "It Don't Mean a Thing (If It Ain't Got No Swing)," they ended the evening with "Cottontail."

Before they started to play their final song, Duke stepped up to the microphone; and after the audience quieted, he announced, "This has been a stone-cold gas tonight, but before we end our evening with one more song, I'd like you to meet six of the most courageous men I've met in this music industry. They are challenging the barriers of prejudicial treatment of performers in the rock 'n' roll genre. They are stating, 'No more unfairness, direct discrimination, or unequal treatment to people on the grounds of the color of their skin.' Their success is a measure of their determination. I am proud to present to you the Night Owls."

Motioning to the Owls to stand, Duke raised his open-faced hands slowly into the air.

All six of the guys stood and waved hands, blew kisses, and returned the applause to the audience. A lot of the audience stood in respect for the guys as they clapped their hands and yelled encouragingly to them for a couple of minutes.

Corey sat with unshed tears in her eyes as she watched the rousing acceptance the people from Southern California had for the band. She wondered, with great trepidation, how all this would change when the Owls toured different cities, especially throughout the Southern states.

FIFTEEN

The next morning, Corey let Bob sleep in because she knew yesterday he had been on the run for almost fifteen straight hours.

She had gotten out of bed at seven o'clock and sat in the kitchen replaying yesterday with Haddie one of the most memorable days Haddie would ever experience in her lifetime.

Haddie told Corey, while pouring them another cup of coffee, "Ms. Corey, I still can't believe I actually touched, talked, and had dinner with my two musical idols, and didn't wake up in the hospital this morning having suffered a heart attack and hallucinations. All I know is ever since Mr. Bob moved in here and started messin' with you, our lives have changed so much for the better."

Corey just laughed at Haddie's description of her and Bob's relationship and then answered her, still chuckling, "I'll give you no argument there, Haddie. You see Joshua more now in a single month than you saw him the entire time after he moved to San Francisco. You've met many celebrities and, most especially, your lifetime idols. Your life must now be more fulfilling for you."

Haddie just nodded her head and whispered, "Praise the Lord."

Corey then confessed to her, "As for me, I found my most perfect partner. Actually, the love of my life. Now with him by my side, I've found such blissfulness every single day since I met him. I absolutely love working with him, traveling with him, and loving him. He makes me smile just looking into his eyes. His seductive smile makes my heart race, and when we make love, I never want him to let go of me."

Haddie was staring at Corey with a frozen look on her face and just had to say, "All right, Ms. Corey. You keep this up, I'm goin' have to put on some boots. All this mush is startin' to stack up in here."

"Oh, Haddie, I just pray you meet someone one day that just turns your life around. Your feet will never be touching the ground again because you'll be walking on air from that moment on."

Haddie jokingly answered, "I hope I do too, Ms. Corey, 'cause these shoes has been killing my feet for months now."

Corey just shook her head and chuckled.

At that moment, Bob came walking into the kitchen, asking, "What's so funny, you two?"

Corey's face lit up, seeing him walking toward her. She opened her arms to him, and he hugged her and then tenderly kissed her on the lips. "Good morning, darling. I thought I should let you sleep in today after such a full day for you yesterday."

Bob's smile was huge as he agreed, "Ah, yeah. It was a great day. Wasn't it, Haddie?"

Haddie's face sparkled with the memory of having met Duke Ellington and Ella Fitzgerald as she turned to Bob. With such graciousness, she told him, "Mr. Bob, I will always be thankful to you and Nick for arranging yesterday to include me. Now I can truly die happy."

Corey watched Bob smiling enormously at Haddie when he told Haddie, "It was my absolute pleasure surprising you yesterday, Haddie. Oh my god, yes! They're the two biggest names out there. And I gotta say, I thoroughly enjoyed the experience myself."

Haddie responded, "But, Mr. Bob, you've made your mark, and that's only gonna get bigger as time passes."

"Well, thank you, Haddie. I may be making my mark, but those two have already written the book."

Tuesday, at the recording studio, Bob told Nick and the guys that he and Corey would be flying up to San Francisco from LA after they finished their shoot at Celebrity that Friday.

It was 350 miles from LA to San Francisco, and they'd be cutting it close, arriving at the hotel around seven that evening.

The concert was scheduled for eight o'clock, and at seven-thirty, all six guys were behind the curtain tuning up their instruments. Corey, Haddie, Alicia, Valerie, and Deidra were all sitting in the third row, center orchestra.

The Fillmore Auditorium, built in 1912, launched a music movement like no other musical venue in the country. At the Fillmore, some of the most innovative rock music emerged there. It was continually booking in-demand artists because, quite simply, it was one of the best-sounding "rooms" in the world. It always carried its mythical status as being San Francisco's most illustrious rock concert venue; it was just a very classy outfit. From its inception, every ticket holder, while exiting the Fillmore, received a free apple at the door.

At two minutes after eight o'clock, the Owls were introduced over the sound system, and then the stage curtain slowly was drawn open. As soon as the audience saw their first glimpse of the Owls, there was a thunderous applause, and the young ladies started to scream when the curtain exposed Bob. Hands down, he was the most popular band member, just as any of the lead singers were in any band in the country.

The Owls opened with "Courage for the Fight," and the audience responded with cheers, whistles, and more screaming.

When the song ended, Bob placed his guitar in the stand and walked back to his microphone. The young women went crazy, and there was a deafening uproar as he took the handheld mike from the stand and walked to the front of the stage.

The teenage women who had seats down in front began reaching for him and screaming that much louder. Bob smiled enthusiastically as he looked at Corey and just laughed. He shook his head in disbelief, as Corey just gave him a toothy grin and winked at him. When he winked back at her, the women felt he was winking at them, and the noise became that much more pronounced.

Bob knew he needed to just start talking to quiet them down. "Tonight, we'd like to play one of our newest songs." The bedlam in the auditorium finally died down. "We'd like to play one of our newest songs called 'Maybe Another Time, Another Place.' The lyrics were written by Doug, my saxophone guy, and myself."

The audience all knew this was a very sad but romantic song, so they showed their excitement by applauding, and the young women began yelling "I love you." They were swooning and swaying to the slow beat Jimmy was putting down with his metal-brushed drumsticks as he massaged the skin of his snare drum.

Bob stayed at the front of the stage but out of reach of any of his fans, and after the saxophone and Joshua's main lady, the muted bass trumpet, entered in, he began to slowly sing the lyrics with his beautiful baritone voice:

Meeting you may have been too late in the game
But I knew you were the one, even before I knew your name
I let you in my heart, for which I had no right
So I'll just dream about our love, every single night

(Chorus)
I watch you as you pass, and your smile is what I love
You'll be mine one day, with some help from up above
But if I can't have you now, I'll always still see your face
Because I know we'll meet again, maybe another time, another place

I will always love you, even though we've never touched
You'll be in my heart forever, because I love you so much
Because we belong to others, we may never speak again

So if you ever need me to hold you, just tell me
where and when

(Chorus)

As the last note dissipated into the air, the audience cheered with a tremendous sound of approval. The applause was loud, and the screaming was unbelievable. Bob quickly glanced at Corey, and she was wiping away her tears and dabbing at her nose with a tissue.

Bob started to touch some of the hands of the young women down in front who were grasping for him. They screamed with excitement after touching his hand, and some were crying in disbelief.

The concert went on for another two hours, and the Owls had played eighteen songs, except for the last of their two newest ones, "Time Is Ours to Change."

With his guitar now strapped around his shoulder, Bob loudly announced into his mike over the prevailing din in the auditorium, "We'd like to close our show tonight"—and the audience yelled and moaned disapproval to that—"with our second newest song, 'Time Is Ours to Change,' which appears on our latest album."

Seconds later, Jimmy started to blister the skins to his drums, the guitars started to wail, as Bob ran a high-pitched riff on his lead guitar, and then Joshua came in screaming with the C trumpet howling its doleful cry. The time signature was fast, and the loud, raging tempo of their song had people standing in the aisles moving to the upbeat rhythm.

Suddenly Doug opened up on his alto saxophone with a sizzling run of notes as he moved his fingers with lightning speed over the saxophone's keys. He was a master of his instrument.

After a full minute of the explosive beginning instrumental, the song turned to something different, giving the track a fuzzed-out guitar vibe that led to Bob's loud vocal entrance:

We don't know where you're comin' from
So we're marching to a different drum

You take our young off to war
You said that would never happen, so you swore

(Chorus)
You're going to fight and die, were your last words
spoken
That gesture of your truth, leaves me betrayed
and broken
We know truth and honesty is out of your range
But we're the country's youth, and time is ours
to change

Leave me in another country, bleeding or dead
I do know you'll be sleeping safe tonight, in your
own bed
Clean this mess up and let your children live
We'll make amends one day, and maybe learn to
forgive.

(Chorus)

When Bob screamed the last five words of the chorus into the mike, the guys' instruments all hit the last note of the song with such loud synchronicity, there was an explosion as the song ended; the screaming, screeching, whistling fans (especially the young women) jumped from their seats, and they were surging toward the stage.

The entire audience in the auditorium was on their feet, thunderously clapping and were loud in their praises for the Owls.

The song was an unapologetic pop showcase that took on a life of its own after they performed it. This song would become an indelible part of all their concerts to come.

Bob placed his guitar in the stand and motioned to all five guys to come to the front of the stage and join him.

The fans loved that they were willing to share a few moments, shaking hands, blowing kisses, and just being grateful for the fans' patronage for almost the last two years.

Bob caught sight of Corey amongst the controlled chaos, as she was still clapping and smiling at him. He smiled proudly as he blew her a kiss and sexily winked at her.

Corey's eyes started to moisten as she blew him a slow, sexy kiss and winked back.

Bob started to do a crazy dance from all his excitement. Corey laughed out loud, but his fans started to yell for more.

He was dancing because he absolutely knew his fans loved the two newest songs, and he also felt this talented group of guys were ready for a lengthy summer tour.

Saturday morning in San Francisco, the six Owls, Nick, and the five ladies spent some time seeing the city. They all ventured down to the Fisherman's Wharf—Pier 39 for lunch. Then they took a ride over the Golden Gate Bridge into Sausalito and shopped around for a while. When they returned to San Francisco, they found the views of the bridge to be more beautiful from Nob Hill, where there were some exquisite posh old mansions to view.

The group decided to have an early dinner in Chinatown before they headed back to their hotel to rest and freshen up for the night's final concert at the Fillmore.

The second night's concert went just as smooth and was just as successful as the one on Friday—with one exception.

As the band packed their melodies back inside their cases and had quitted the stage, they were met, out in back of the Fillmore, by eight guys that were looking for trouble. They were bunched close together by the van and limousine that was to take the Owls' entourage to the airport.

If the Owls eyes and mouths displayed any recognizable expression, it was that of mild surprise. Nick's face was showing plenty of unease as he walked back into the Fillmore and called for security.

One of the eight troublemakers, probably the ringleader, shouted out, "Why don't you boys take your two Negroes and get the hell outta town? You're stinking up the place!"

Doug and Darnell started to move toward the loudmouth, but Bob put his arm out and stopped them. With an outward calm and precision that did not reflect his inner apprehension, Bob warned them, "You guys need to leave right now. We're not gonna put up with this bullshit. So if you don't wanna sleep tonight with your front teeth still in your mouth…just keep on talking shit."

More than one of them started for Bob, Darnell, and Doug, while another one of them shouted, "Don't you two monkeys try to rise above your station. You hear me, boys?"

Doug, Darnell, and Bob moved toward the three guys coming at them from the front of the van. The first guy took a swing at Darnell, and he dodged the flying fist as he counterpunched the guy hard to the jaw, with all of his six foot three inches. The guy hit the ground and appeared to be unconscious.

As Bob was staring at the guy on the ground, another of the three guys clipped him by his left eyebrow with a sucker punch. Doug immediately jumped the guy and started pounding him in the face. Len, Joshua, and Jimmy started for the other men who were coming at them pretty quickly.

It was at that moment Nick and four security officers came running from the auditorium.

When the eight guys saw security coming, they took off, almost dragging the guy that Darnell had laid out on the ground. The guy Doug pummeled ran away as he held his hand to his face. Doug yelled at him, "Hey, man! I think I plugged your mother the other night!"

The guy turned and flipped Doug the bird. Doug comically told him, "No, thanks."

The security men chased the eight men while Nick asked his guys if they were all right. Doug told Nick, "One of them got a sucker punch in on Bob. You might want to take a look at his eye. I nailed the son of a bitch, though. He should feel real good tomorrow morning!"

Nick went to Bob and asked how he was. He noticed a little blood trickling down the side of his face, but it didn't appear to be anything that would need stitches.

Bob told him, trying to maintain his cool, "I'm okay, man. He caught me with a ring, or brass knuckles, or something. I didn't see it coming. That was my fault…but I'll be fine."

The Owls' ladies eventually made their way backstage to catch their ride to the airport with the guys. They were informed by the Fillmore staff about what had happened out back. This information quickened their step to get to the limo they would all be riding in.

Deidra and Haddie ran to Joshua, and Joshua told them, "Everyone is cool, Mama, except for maybe Bob. He got caught by a sucker punch."

Corey heard Joshua say that, and she began to move toward the vehicles with extreme haste. She didn't spot Bob right away until she saw Nick standing and talking with him.

Corey immediately grabbed Bob by the arm, and scared to death, she loudly asked, "Darling, are you—" When he turned to face her, she alarmingly got the full view of the blood running down the side of his face and the redness of an already-swelling eye.

She gasped and put her free hand over her mouth. Bob tried to calm her by saying, "It's okay, babe. I'll be just fine. The guy got lucky, and I got stupid for just one second."

Corey shouted with uncontrolled anger, "This can't keep happening! You're obviously not okay...oh my god, Bob!"

The incident in London last summer on the Owls' international tour flashed through her mind; Julie Hayward showed up, and supposedly, she accidentally caused Bob to trip, and he suffered a very traumatic head injury requiring surgery.

Corey turned to Nick and demanded, "Nick, you've got to ramp up the security for these guys. I will lose my mind with worry with every concert they have if this isn't stopped now!"

Nick defended himself by telling her, "Corey, all of us agreed that we felt we'd be all right here in San Francisco. Now we know that no venue can be without extra security no matter where we travel."

Bob put his arm around Corey's waist and told her, "That's true, Corey. We really didn't think this far north we'd have any problems. We'll be a lot more cautious now... Come on, let's go inside and clean me up. We have a plane to catch at the airport in an hour."

As Bob and Corey walked by Haddie, Haddie took a sharp intake of breath, and her hand went to cover her mouth in horror as she saw the blood that had run down the side of Bob's face.

They caught their plane on time, and everyone returned home ecstatic about how the two concerts turned out; but now they each shared a fundamental belief in their hearts that this journey they were about to take was not going to be an easy one.

Nick called Bob the next morning, and Corey answered the phone. Nick informed her the San Francisco police caught five of the men that initiated the confrontation Saturday night. They wanted to know if Bob wanted to press charges against them for assault.

Bob was out sitting by the pool when Corey went out and asked him what he wanted to do about the men they had arrested. Bob awoke from his deep thoughts as he answered her, "Nothing… I'd be spending too much time up there in court. Just let it go. I'll have my ass covered next time knowing now what I'm going to be dealing with."

Corey relayed the message to Nick and then went back outside to sit with Bob. She carried her mug of coffee out with her and sat in the lounger next to him.

Bob looked up and saw Corey and smiled, and with his head, he motioned her over to him. She didn't hesitate as she moved slowly into the lounger with him and was careful not to bump the side of his head. She laid one leg between his legs and rested her head on his chest as she put her arm around his waist. He then enveloped her with both of his arms.

Nothing was said between them for several minutes.

Corey always watched and admired Bob. She had admired his personal qualities from the moment she had met him; he was diligent, respectful, insightful, and intelligent enough to grasp immediately the scope of this situation…and the potential for danger. She now knew that every time his band was in concert, or on his 21-City Tour, she would experience extreme trepidation and a prodigious amount of anxiety for the safety of the band; she actually feared for their lives.

After a short while, Bob kissed Corey on top of her head and whimsically asked, "I hope there's someone good enough at the studio in makeup to hide my bruising."

Corey lifted her head to look at his eye and slowly closed her eyes as she heavily exhaled, shaking her head in disgust. She earnestly told him, "Bob, I can't live like this—you having this tour in God knows what cities of the country, and me not knowing if you and the guys are going to finish each concert unscathed or seriously hurt, or even worse… It's not even four weeks away when you start your tour, and I'm now beside myself with worry and anxiety."

His reaction was one of quiet, of resignation, of a slow-moving contemplation.

Bob moved from his lounger to stand up. He slowly walked a few steps toward the pool and stopped and turned back to look at Corey. She was now sitting on the edge of the lounger and waiting for him to say anything.

He stared intently at her, and saddened by the matter, he told her, "You know, I never thought I'd be with a woman that would put restrictions on me—"

Corey immediately spoke up, emphatically stating, "Bob, I would never put—"

Bob put one hand up to her and demanded, "Just hear me out.

"All us guys decided from the start we were going to bring to the forefront of America's conscience the unjust and prejudicial treatment the African Americans had been suffering with for centuries now. We knew this wasn't going to be a cakewalk from day one. The only thing we did wrong was to not add extra security in a city we took for granted. We thought that maybe there wouldn't be people in San Francisco who were intolerant, ignorant, and prejudicial…we guessed wrong, that's all."

He stared down at the ground for several seconds, and when he brought his head up, Corey could see the unshed tears in his eyes. She still remained silent, until she knew he was through talking.

Bob, in a constrained manner, told her, "Corey, I would be devastated if I had to quit my music…but if I lost you, I would die."

At that exact moment, Corey ran to him and threw her arms around him. She lifted her head, and looking him directly in the eyes, she deliberately and forcefully told him, "Oh my god, darling! I would never ask you to quit playing your music. I would have no right or reason to do that...and, baby, you will *never* lose me. I didn't mean I couldn't live with you if you were still playing with the band. You just need more security everywhere to lessen my worry and anxiety... My life begins and ends with you, Bob. There's no me without you. Now, do you understand what I, obviously, had trouble conveying to you?"

Bob took a deep breath and then exhaled deeply. He pulled Corey into his body and slowly kissed her all over her face, ending with a forceful kiss to her lips. Several seconds later, when the kiss ended, he just stood holding her as a single tear ran down his cheek.

As they stood still holding each other, Haddie came walking down to them; and being Haddie, she humorously quipped, "Now that the two of you are done swabbing each other's tonsils, you need to get in the house and have at my western omelet. It ain't gonna stay hot too long...oh, and, Mr. Bob, watch that french door—it may take a swing at you while you're not looking."

Haddie giggled under her breath as she walked back into the house. Bob and Corey laughed out loud as Bob shook his head and jokingly told Corey, "I've given her way too much material to work with, haven't I, babe?"

Corey gave him a huge toothy grin. They laughed again; as they headed in to have their breakfast, Bob momentarily stopped them, and with one hand, Bob lifted Corey's chin to his face, and looking directly into her eyes, he tenderly kissed her once more.

They had one arm around the other as they continued on into the house.

Monday morning, at Celebrity, the buzz was all about Bob's band being assaulted by a group of thugs in San Francisco.

Corey tried to play it down to the inquiring people, but when they saw Bob's eye, they knew it was hate-mongers just showing their asses.

Makeup was able to hide most of the bruising, but Victor, the director, knew there would be no rushes or close-ups involving Bob for at least a week.

Jack Windheim even dropped over to the soundstage from his office for a few minutes. When he walked up to Bob, he kiddingly said, "Whoa, man! Do I have to teach you how to box and pop 'em with the jab followed by the old uppercut?"

Bob bit his lower lip and shook his head while he disconcertedly assured Jack, "No, that's all right, Jack. I just won't turn my head next time. Not that there'll be a next time, because we're really gonna ramp up the security now no matter where we go."

Corey was within earshot of Jack and Bob's conversation as she smiled then brought her closed fist up to her chin and leaned into it. She was expressionless now as she stared down at the wooden floor of the soundstage.

Tuesday, May 24, the Owls met Nick and his assistant, Truman, at the recording studio. Nick wanted to carefully go over their plans for their Las Vegas concerts that coming Friday and Saturday.

The six guys were sitting around them before they started their practice session. Nick began by reassuring them, "You're gonna fly out of LAX late Friday afternoon. It'll only take you forty-one minutes to get there. If you guys would rather drive, it takes almost six hours."

All the guys echoed the same sentiment, "Oh, hell no!"

"Okay, that's what I figured when I booked your flights. Now, I want all of you to know there will always be from this moment on extra security at all your concerts around the country and internationally. The venues have all agreed they will be furnishing all their own security, along with any private security we hire. I don't want to see any more of the shit we experienced in San Francisco. I do want to tell you, though, Truman will be accompanying you guys to Vegas for those two nights. You'll be playing the ninety thousand square feet of the Convention Center Rotunda in Winchester, Nevada. That's just outside of Vegas."

There would be no rock 'n' roll on the Vegas strip until the early 1970s.

"The Rotunda will have 6,300 seats for you to play to, and the place is fairly new. It just opened in April of last year. It's only seven miles from the longest single-level facility strip in the world. So you could venture into Vegas and have some fun during Saturday afternoon. I'll see you guys again next week, and we'll discuss the tour in depth. And by the way, this 'twenty-one cities' tour was labeled months ago for publicity reasons and ticket-printing, *Shakin' It with the Night Owls*. Okay? Have fun and burn it down, man."

In Las Vegas, the audiences were great, and the money was enormous. If the Owls could have played any hotel on the Strip when Vegas started booking rock 'n' roll groups in 1970, with only a four-week stint, they would have earned enough money to buy a Third World country. The money coming in for their two shows at the Rotunda was still very impressive and resulted in $75,000 every night the Owls appeared there.

They arrived in Las Vegas with enough time to catch dinner and still check out the venue and the instruments.

The guys heard from Truman that a forty-eight-year-old Nat King Cole was performing at the Thunderbird Casino. But all of them became disheartened and angry when Truman also informed them, "Yeah, Nat King Cole is good enough to entertain the audience at the Thunderbird, but he isn't allowed to gamble in the hotel, only because of his race."

That Friday night, it was a packed house at the Convention Center Rotunda. All 6,300 seats were filled with loud, roaring fans who obviously loved the Owls and their music.

Security was noticeable throughout the Rotunda. Every entrance or exit was covered with security who regularly worked at the venue or with one of the private security force Nick had put in place.

The two concerts went spectacularly, and when the Owls quitted the stage, there were only a few small groups of ruffians out in back of the Rotunda. They were screaming accusations of betrayal to their own race and denunciations of the group for not adhering to the unwritten code of blatant and deliberate discrimination. Of course, their language was very hateful and most hurtful, especially to Darnell and Joshua. Yet it wasn't anything they hadn't heard before.

However, the security force that had gathered in back when the Owls exited the Convention Center Rotunda had everything under control, and there were no instances of violence.

Bob had called Corey Friday night and then again Saturday afternoon. And to allay her fears, he convinced her of the safety of the band and the swarm of security that had already been present at the concert Friday night.

Bob reminded her he would be arriving home at around one o'clock, Sunday morning, and told her not to wait up for him.

It was one thirty in the morning when Bob entered the house through the back french doors and walked down the long hallway to the master suite, where, unsurprisingly, he found Corey in bed and reading a book.

She laid her book down on the nightstand, threw back the top sheet that had been covering her from her waist down, and moved quickly to him. Corey opened her arms wide to Bob, and they tightly embraced and then kissed.

As she looked into his eyes, she could see the insurmountable fatigue that plagued his face. She told him, unhesitatingly, "Welcome home, darling. Why don't you go in and take a shower, and then when you return, I'll rub your back and shoulders until you fall asleep. How's that sound, mister?"

Bob resigned himself to the fact that he was worn-out, absolutely dead worn-out. The worry he had demonstrated for the safety of the band over the last nineteen hours while they were in Las Vegas had taken a lot out of him. Then you factor in two very physically demanding concerts at the same time, and you have the maximum degree of mental and physical exhaustion.

When Bob returned from his shower, he climbed into bed with only his pajama bottoms on and then rolled onto his stomach. Corey instantly began to massage his shoulders and back. She lightly kissed his back after every slow stroke she made with her hands. He fell asleep within minutes, but she continued to run her hands over him from his neck to his buttocks for several more minutes, just enjoying the feel of his body.

Bob and Corey spent the entirety of Sunday out, in, and around the pool area. Together, they had their meals, their drinks, and their naps out there—in the same lounging chair.

Monday morning, May 30, when Bob and Corey arrived at Celebrity, Victor informed everyone that the last scenes of the picture would be shot this week, hopefully before Bob had to leave for New York City to be at the closing curtain for *A Casual Affair*.

The movie had picture-perfect moments, thanks to the brilliant costuming by Edith Head. She had set the tone by outfitting Bob and Corey and the rest of the cast in sharp 1960s fashions.

She had designed glamorous and sexy gowns pushing the envelope of sex appeal. There were dreamy gowns with sophisticated designs that were fabulous and flamboyant. Her looks consisted of suits to feminine gowns. They ranged from more casual to full-on ball gowns.

The stunning wardrobe from the film *Love's Wicked Lies* was memorable and outstanding in design. Victor and producer Trent Voight were absolutely convinced Edith would earn the nomination for Best Costume Design next year for the 1961 Academy Awards, and would probably win.

The remaining outdoor scenes were finished up by midweek, leaving Corey to shoot the final scene that she would have with Bob on the main soundstage.

Edith Head dressed Corey in what soon would become the iconic midnight-blue gown she wore when she shot and killed her cheating husband. It was a magnificent full-length evening gown of beautiful proportions. The satin dress streamlined her sexy body, and the sleeveless top of the dress played perfectly into the seductive cut to the cleavage.

This was a time when Corey felt age was catching up with her, somewhat limiting the roles she could agree on with her studio, Celebrity.

Although she was at the beginning of something, too, she was putting the pieces together for a second act—one that capitalized on her skill at framing herself in the right light.

The movie *Love's Wicked Lies* would relaunch her as a grande dame of the screen. This role used what was best of Corey's star persona, but refracted it through cinematic style of the time, putting hauteur and intellect in an Edith Head gown.

Thursday evening, Nick and Truman met the guys at the recording studio. It was almost nine o'clock that night after the guys had finished their session. Nick gathered them up into a circle and began reminding them, "All right, guys. You're all aware that the 'twenty-one cities' tour starts one week from tonight, but we'll be leaving the night before, on June 8, to spend the night at our first venue, in Albuquerque, New Mexico."

All the guys were yelling, "Hell yeah! All right!" They were slapping hands and shaking fists into the air as every one of them was excited to start the new and improved group's first tour.

Nick proceeded to explain to them with complete reassurance, "Every single venue you are going to be playing from now on will be blanketed with security guards. The venues have guaranteed security of their own, and I have arranged to have private guards assisting in that matter at every concert."

All the Owls were slightly nodding their head in agreement, most especially Joshua, Darnell, and Bob.

Nick continued by adamantly adding, "We just cannot let what happened at the Fillmore to happen again! And coincidentally, we'll be starting our tour with our first twelve concerts in six of the Southern states."

The guys looked at each other with a noticeable amount of anxiety and trepidation.

At that exact moment, Bob explosively shouted out, "There's no one or nobody who's gonna ruin this tour for us and, more importantly, ruin it for our fans! We've been together now for over four months—writing songs, finalizing those songs, playing our own music, performing on TV, appearing in concerts—generally, just kickin' ass, and that's not gonna change because of some ignorant assholes out there who are just trying to control the narrative and won't accept the changing times."

All the guys yelled their approval to what Bob had said, slipping each other some skin as they fervently nodded their heads and rocked their bodies back and forth.

"We're gonna rock this tour with our message of brotherhood and our music of revolution, romance, and the moral and ethical reclamation of our black brothers!" Bob's words were packed with meaning, edged with menace, but nonetheless optimistic.

Nick jumped to his feet and then shook Bob's hand. They both nodded their heads in complete agreement to one another.

As the guys quieted down, Nick instructed them, "There will be no more studio sessions before we leave because Bob will be in New York this Saturday at the final curtain for *A Casual Affair*. Bob's part in his motion picture should be over tomorrow. Then I want you to have some free time until we leave Wednesday. So tonight, Truman and I will load up all your instruments for transport to LAX. Okay?"

Darnell gave a rousing "Yes, sir. Now we're talking, Nick, my man!"

Nick smiled amusingly and informed them, "I'll pick up all of you in Thousand Oaks, because I'm so close by, but I want the rest of you to meet us at the airport at three o'clock, Wednesday afternoon. We fly out at four and arrive in Albuquerque one hour and forty-five minutes later, just in time for dinner."

Nick jokingly told them, "I don't think that any of you would want to drive, it being eleven and a half hours, so I booked all our airfares."

Doug pointed out to Nick in his smart-ass demeanor, "Man, you can quit mentioning any of us to drive anywhere 'cause you know that just ain't gonna happen, brother. We really dig being chauffeured around."

All the guys rolled their eyes at Doug. Jimmy admonished him by saying, "Doug, man, you're a drag. Don't you realize it's because of Nick, our tireless manager, that we're at where we're at right now?"

"Damn, man. I was just horse-assing around. Crap!"

Laughing to himself, Jimmy smiled at Doug, and then Nick told everyone he'd see them again Wednesday afternoon, when they would be flying out to Albuquerque.

Bob got home around ten thirty that evening. Corey was in bed carefully studying a few new scripts that Jack had sent her. She felt that while Bob was on tour, she could pass a lot of the time making another picture.

Bob walked into the master bedroom, and after seeing Corey sitting up in bed, he ran to her, feeling like he wanted to try to make her laugh. When he reached the bed, he dove onto the mattress from a couple of feet away and landed with his hands around her waist.

Corey was caught off guard by this, but she delighted in his antics. She playfully screamed when he started to tickle her ribs and stomach. As they laughed at each other, Corey placed her hands on each side of his face and began to pull his head down toward her lips. He immediately stopped tickling her as he began staring into her entrancing blue eyes. Those eyes had that familiar mind-blowing look of sexual want for him.

Bob ripped off his shirt and moved in on her for a very deep-throated kiss. They were both breathing heavily as each was running their hands all over the other's body.

He slowly removed Corey's silk nightgown, kissing every part of her body as it became exposed to him. He tore his slacks off, along with his briefs and socks. They both were completely naked now; as Bob was at full attention, he moved methodically slow to lie between her gorgeous legs.

Corey's head lurched back, and she closed her eyes when he placed his hand between her thighs. Bob started to stimulate her as two of his other fingers entered her. Corey was moaning and crying for him, "Oh my god, baby. How I want you!"

He kept kissing and running his tongue over her breasts, occasionally biting at the nipples. Within minutes, her body froze as she started to experience her climax. She kept moving her hips into his hand, when Bob removed his hand and then gently entered her wetness with his hips already pulsating into her. After he slowly penetrated her, Corey moved with his thrusts as he held her hips within his hands.

After a short time, Corey could not help but to feel another orgasm building. Her arms flew back over her head, hitting the bed's headboard, and Bob kept up a hurried thrust going even deeper into her.

Corey exploded into an electrifying orgasm of mammoth proportions. She loudly yelled, "Oh, baby! Oh my god! I love you so much!" Corey kept moving her hips with the rhythm of his thrusts until Bob reached orgasm. He was breathing quite heavily at this point as he lowered himself and gently lay his head between her breasts, with his hands still holding her hips.

Corey slowly ran her one hand through his hair, and her other hand held him tight to her body. There were no words spoken for several minutes; they were basking in the intoxicating love they felt for each other.

A short time had passed, and Bob felt Corey's warm breath on his shoulders. She had fallen off to sleep. He gently and slowly raised himself up and away from her so he could go in and take his shower and brush his teeth. After he was out of bed and on his feet, he covered her with the bedsheet. She quickly drew a deep breath and exhaled loudly with complete satisfaction. She settled back into her pillow and quickly fell back to sleep.

Bob just stood staring at her and smiled broadly. He loved this woman with his entire being and knew he was going to miss her tremendously after he left in just six days to go on the 21-City Tour with the Owls.

The Friday morning of June 3, Bob and Corey busied themselves at the studio trying to get their last scenes shot in the picture, for Corey was to go with Bob to New York the following day for the closing curtain of *A Casual Affair*.

The final scene that Corey would have with Bob was the coup de grace of the picture. The finishing stroke and the resolution to the conflict of emotions she had playing in her character's mind throughout the picture.

The scene called for Corey to shoot and kill Bob after having called him over to their house to talk about her taking him back and forgiving him of his past indiscretions.

After they exchanged their few lines, Corey shot him three times with a fake rubber handgun that appeared real but was just a prop. As

Bob grabbed his wounded chest, he released a handful of fake blood encased in very thin plastic, which broke open the instant he hit it on his chest. He took one last surprised look at Corey and then fell to the carpeted floor.

She raced to him after she dropped the gun. He exhaled one last breath as he died in her arms. Bob was told to hold his breath for the remainder of the scene, which would only be another ten to fifteen seconds. Corey had absolutely no trouble crying real tears while holding on to him. She was so convincing and seemingly devastated by what she had done that Victor held the shot for a full twenty seconds.

Then Victor yelled, "Cut! That's a take. Well done, you two."

At that exact moment, Bob opened his eyes and took an enormous breath. Corey, still holding him in her lap, looked down on him with her wet, sympathetic eyes and then quickly proceeded to kiss him long and hard. The crew began to applaud and whistle.

At the end of the day, Bob had finished his scenes and reshoots, but Corey had at least a half day left of scenes with Rita, Robert, and Jack.

She was beside herself with disappointment, but Victor knew Corey wanted to go to New York with Bob, so he told her to be in at six o'clock tomorrow morning, and they would try to finish up by lunch.

Bob reassured her he would move their flight time to early afternoon, and they would still get into New York with plenty of time for the eight o'clock curtain that Saturday night. Corey calmed down at this point but quietly told Bob, "I was going with you, darling, no matter what. I don't know why we couldn't have just finished it up on Monday?"

Bob, trying to alleviate her agitation, told her, "I'm sure it has to do with bringing the picture in early, and not three days later. You know it's all about money, babe. This is a business. It survives by making lots of money. My god, woman! How long have you been doing this?"

Corey looked at him and snorted a quick breath as she began to smile at him. She knew he was patronizing her, so she swatted him in the pants and then resolutely said, "Come on. Let's go home, darling."

Bob smiled broadly as he wrapped one arm around her and walked her to the car.

It took until almost eleven o'clock on Saturday for Corey's finishing scenes to be shot and okayed for edit. Bob hung around the studio talking with Jack, among others, while Corey was wrapping it up.

For a couple of hours, Bob just stood in the back of the sound studio studying Corey's formidable screen persona. He delighted in her impeccable timing and her powerful delivery. All he could do was shake his head in reverential wonder as he proudly smiled.

Bob called Curtis to come to the studio and pick them up as soon as he knew Corey was finishing her last scene. He whisked them off to the airport, where they flew out of LA exactly at eleven twenty that morning.

Bob and Corey had only a half hour to freshen up and change into the clothes they were going to wear to the closing curtain for the Broadway play that had kick-started the theatrical aspect of Bob's career: *A Casual Affair*.

They picked up their tickets at the will call window that Stanley had secured for them.

They walked down the long aisle with the usher to be seated in the third row, when a handful of people started to clap their hands. Bob looked around the theater but could not figure out why the clapping began to swell in nature.

Bob and the Night Owls were so well-known as to be instantly recognizable. Adding his incredible performance in *A Casual Affair* to the equation, and he was now known everywhere he traveled.

Corey pointed out to him, "Darling, they're clapping for you. These people know and remember you, and most especially you winning the Tony for this play."

Bob looked back around the audience and just began to brilliantly smile as he waved his hands to them. He then looked toward the mezzanine and raised his arms and started to wave at them as he crossed his hands back and forth.

People then started to cheer for him. While still standing, he raised his arms again and shouted out loud, "Thank you. Thank you very much." He then bowed his head and took his seat next to Corey. She looked at him with such admiration in her eyes. When he proudly looked at her, he shook his head in disbelief, saying to her, "There is no other audience on the face of this earth that is more endearing than a Broadway show audience. I just love it!"

Moments later, the theater lights dimmed, and the theme for *A Casual Affair* began to be played. The overture played after the lights went down and before the curtain went up as an introduction to the show. The term *overture* came from the French, which meant "opening."

Bob and Corey sat through the play and enjoyed every minute of it all over again.

When the final curtain came down, and after Natalie and her male costar were still taking bows minutes later, Stanley came walking out. The applause grew louder as Stanley took his bows and then motioned for the audience to quiet.

Stanley then began his closing night speech, "I just want to thank everyone in the cast and the crew, but most especially all of you." He pointed both index fingers toward the audience.

"This play has been such fun from start to finish, and I can't tell you how much the year and five months' run on this is because of this woman." Stanley put his arm around Natalie Moore and smiled into her face. She was crying with pent-up emotions over the closing of the play.

The audience started applauding for her.

"Although we've had four different leading men for her in this play, I have to say, Alan has been a good match." Stanley then put his arm around Alan and smiled back at the audience while nodding his head.

"Now I'm not going to brag, but winning the Tony for best director, on the same night my first leading man in this play won for Best Actor in a Play, was just one of the most remarkable evenings, I think, in both of our lives." The audience applauded their approval.

Corey looked at Bob with proud and glistening eyes as she softly took his hand in hers. Bob looked over at her with loving eyes of his own as he quickly leaned over and kissed her.

Stanley sincerely added, "Having said that, I would now like to have that talented young actor, with a lifetime of good things ahead of him, to come up onstage and share with us the closing curtain of *A Casual Affair*—Mr. Bob Richardson."

Bob rose from his seat, leaned over and kissed Corey again, and then headed for the stage. The people in the theater thunderously applauded him. There were screams and whistles as Bob walked up and hugged Stanley for several seconds. Bob shook Alan's hand and then happily went over to Natalie and brilliantly smiled at her as they hugged for several more seconds. As Bob pulled away from her, she placed her hand on his cheek and leaned in to ceremoniously kiss him on the lips.

Still smiling, Bob turned to stand by Natalie, with she and Stanley in the middle of the foursome.

Corey did not let the kiss that Natalie provocatively pulled Bob into bother her, for she knew Natalie was a seasoned Broadway actress, and she was just playing to the audience—or so Corey wanted to believe.

Stanley handed Bob the handheld microphone, and as the applause died down, Bob gratefully stated, "I thank everyone who has ever bought a ticket to *A Casual Affair*, and especially to those of you who have seen it more than once. Come on, show of hands. How many of you are there?"

About half the audience raised their hands. Bob laughed out loud along with Natalie, Alan, and Stanley.

"Seriously now, I guess I can tell you it had always been my childhood dream to be an actor on a Broadway stage. Of course, I knew it wouldn't happen until after I had at least turned ten, but still."

The audience started laughing, along with Corey and the three onstage.

"Stanley Kabrinski gave me the break I needed to get my foothold into theater, and I will always be indebted to him for that."

There was mild applause as Stanley reached in front of Natalie to shake Bob's hand.

"I just want everyone to know what a great experience this was for me. Not just working for one of the greatest directors and producers around, but working with some of the most talented people in theater. Thanks to all of you, and keep coming and supporting the shows on and off Broadway. Thank you very much." The applause was loud and long.

Stanley took the microphone, and before the final curtain was to come down, the theater quieted, and he announced, "Tonight I just want the world to know that Bob and I are going to open another play on Broadway this November 1, in a musical revival of *Oklahoma!*"

The audience gave a thunderous applause, with shouts and whistles.

"This will be an eight-week limited engagement run, and then we'll be taking it over to London for a couple more weeks just after Christmas. Bob will be costarring with Ms. Debbie Reynolds, and the three secondary roles will be played by Doris Day, Angela Lansbury, and Arthur Stuart. We'll be appearing at the St. James Theatre on Forty-Fourth Street, so look for us, because it's going to be a phenomenal show and lots of fun. Good night to everyone, and thank you for your patronage."

After the final curtain came down, Bob went back out onstage and waved Corey to come up and leave with him out the back of the theater and into Stanley's limo.

Stanley had invited Bob and Corey to come and celebrate the closing of the play at Sardi's, with he and his wife, Eve, and the full cast of the play.

At Sardi's, there was a lot of talk about the revival of *Oklahoma!* Stanley stated to Bob matter-of-factly, "I was able to secure Doris Day three days ago. I caught her in between pictures. She's just coming off of shooting *Midnight Lace* with Rex Harrison, and her next project in late July is a movie with David Niven called *Please Don't Eat the Daisies*. She informed me that would only be a ten-week shoot and that she would be free for the ending months of this year."

Bob was excited about working with such a prolific singing and dancing actress that he exclaimed to Stanley, "I can't wait to work with her. She seems as seasoned a performer as Debbie. This should be a blast, and we're gonna get some kicks outta this!"

Stanley answered affirmatively, "Yeah, when I told her I had Debbie Reynolds playing the part of Laurey Williams, Angela Lansbury playing Aunt Eller, Bob Richardson playing Curley McLain, she abruptly told me, 'Say no more. I'm yours from early October until January 10.' So naturally, I signed her to a contract just yesterday. I wasn't letting any grass grow under my feet on that one."

Corey sat listening to all this when she turned to Bob with spurious bravado and, barely smiling, told him, "Oh, darling. It does sound like a lot of fun. I'm going to be happy for you."

He leaned over and kissed her, but he sensed the temperament of her mood and knew they would talk about it later that night or tomorrow. They weren't flying home until Monday morning, the day of their picture's wrap party, so there would be time to resolve the issue.

Shortly after midnight, Bob was tired and knew Corey had to be worn-out, having started the day at getting up at five in the morning, finishing her shoot on the picture, flying to New York, sitting through a complete play, and then going out for dinner and drinks afterward. So he told the table of Stanley, Natalie, and Alan and their spouses that Corey and he were exhausted and needed to leave, but told Stanley he was thrilled that he had asked them back for the closing of *A Casual Affair*.

When they arrived by cab back at the penthouse, Corey just fell into bed when she reached the master suite. Bob undressed her and put a nightgown on her, as she immediately fell deeply asleep. He stood admiring her, feeling bad for her, but always loving her.

Bob knew what was eating at Corey; a week after he would return from his 21-City Tour, he would start script-reads for his picture with Susan Hawthorne and Alex. Then one day after the presumed wrap on that picture, he would fly to New York to start rehearsals for Stanley's musical revival of *Oklahoma!* That project would not be completed until after four weeks of rehearsals and eight weeks of performances at the St. James Theatre. Then the company would finish with two weeks in London on January 10, 1961.

Bob was out of bed early that Sunday morning and out in the living area drinking a cup of coffee and perusing the Sunday edition of the *New York Times*.

Corey awoke at nine o'clock and got up and quietly walked out of the bedroom. She noticed Bob reading in a chair close to the front window wall. She walked toward him in her nightgown, and when he spotted her, he instantly threw down his newspaper and just smiled at her. She could only smile back at him.

Bob sensed her mood had not changed from last night, and so he sexily ordered her, "Come here. Come sit on my lap and tell me all about it."

When Corey reached him, he turned her around and placed his arm behind her back as she settled onto his thighs. He then pulled her legs and hips close to him and tenderly kissed her and then asked, "Now I wanna know what's going on with you. Something last night obviously didn't sit well with you. If it's because Stanley added Doris to the cast, then believe me, baby, you've got nothing to worry about. She's married with a child, and I'm also married to this gorgeous creature who just happens to be needlessly jealous at times. So what is it, doll?"

Corey sadly looked into Bob's eyes, then looked away and exhaled loudly as she started to explain to him despairingly, "I knew as we were driving home from your birthday party at Tu Es Mon Monde, back in February, that you were going to be very busy all of this year. None of this comes as a surprise to me. It's just that we haven't had big chunks of time together since our exquisite honeymoon in Italy. I'm just missing you all the time, and when you leave for your 21-City Tour, I'm not only going to dreadfully miss you, but I'm going to worry my head off for you and the guys' safety."

Bob tried to reassure her by reminding her, "Corey, you now know that at every concert we have, there will be security everywhere. I don't want you worrying about that at all. And just three and a half weeks into our tour, you're gonna fly into New York on the morning of July 3 and stay with me until July 10. Then don't forget, just three weeks later, you meet up with me again in San Diego after our concerts and you continue on to Honolulu with us, and then we don't come back home until August 10. Our tour then ends with two concerts at the Hollywood Bowl on August 12 and 13. So you see, my foxy chick, you'll be spending seventeen out of sixty-six days with me. That's almost twenty-five percent of the time we'll be together. I've already cleared with Jack the times you'll be spending with me, no matter what picture you pick next. So don't even let that enter your head. Now isn't that really outta sight? And you gotta know we'll have it made in the shade, baby."

Corey's entire perspective changed after Bob laid it all out for her. She ended up with a very buoyant disposition for the rest of the day, after having heard what exactly was on the itinerary for most of their summer.

They ended up in the shower together, each one washing the other's body and running their hands all over each other. They made slow, lascivious love to each other as the warm water from the shower enveloped them and danced over and off their heads. There could not have been two other people more in love than Bob and Corey.

After spending a relaxing Sunday together, they flew back to Los Angeles Monday morning and were relieved that the only thing they had to do was to show up for the *Love's Wicked Lies* wrap party at D'Angelo's that night at eight o'clock.

Bob and Corey spent the afternoon and early evening just lying out by the pool. They always loved to share one of the big loungers together.

Haddie knew not to bother them when they were out in the same lounger, unless they called to her. This was a very special time for them because of the time restrictions of both their careers; their free hours and days were spent as a very intimate experience for them.

Haddie was told to come out and tell them when it was six o'clock, so that would give Bob and Corey enough time to get ready for the wrap party.

Haddie approached them with caution, as she jokingly announced when she was just a few feet away, "Here I come, ready or not. I hope y'all are decent."

Corey could be heard chuckling as Bob kiddingly shouted, "Oh, Ms. Haddie! Don't look. I'm in my birthday suit!"

Corey then began to laugh out loud, and Bob started to laugh with her as he leaned over and kissed Corey on the forehead.

Haddie kept walking to where she could see they were both wrapped separately in their own robes. She then teased Bob by saying, "That better not be the case, Mr. Bob, or you gonna start waking your own ass up from now on. Of course, if I did accidentally see your pride 'n' joy, I'd wait a minute or two, but I'd let you know 'bout it!"

Bob and Corey started to laugh uncontrollably as Haddie herself couldn't contain a very high-pitched laugh of her own.

Still laughing, Bob choked out, "I bet you would, Ms. Haddie. I bet you would."

When Bob and Corey arrived at D'Angelo's, Mario greeted them. "I miei amici. So nice to see you, Signora Corey and Signore Bob."

Bob answered his friend Mario, "Buona sera, mio amico, Mario."

This put a broad smile on Mario's face, as he gladly took them into the back room of the restaurant and showed them to their table. Corey was smiling at Bob with loving pride for his acumen with foreign languages.

Mario started to walk away as Bob thanked him, "Grazie, Signore Mario."

Corey nodded her head to Mario as he answered Bob, "Prego, Signore Bob."

Rita was seated at Bob's and Corey's table, with her date. Robert Ryan and Jack Carson were seated with their wives. Corey took notice of Rita's extremely low-cut red dress and knew the only way her breasts didn't pop out had to be for the fact that she had glued them in place.

Bob looked at the dress only after he said good evening to everyone, and then he tried not to give it any more attention, out of respect for Corey. He did lean over to whisper into Corey's ear, "And by the way, I really like what you have on tonight, doll. And I most certainly would like to help you out of that at our earliest convenience."

Throwing her head back, Corey smiled at him brilliantly and then sexily told him, "Later, darling. Later."

Bob started to move in his chair, like he was listening to a romantic song, and smoothly replied, "All right! I can deal with that. Yes, ma'am!"

Corey started to laugh at him as he continued to move to the imagined rhythm of the song.

Victor Trudeau now spoke up and into the microphone out on the dance floor, "All right, everyone—I'd like to bring our producer, Trent Voight, up here with me."

Trent moved quickly to Victor's side, and then Victor began telling everyone, "I've got to tell all of you directing this picture was such a pleasure for me. Don't get me wrong, it was a lot of work, but working with the actors and actresses that I had in this picture made it a lot easier on everyone. Jack and Robert, you two were great in your supporting roles and were very easy to work with."

The room applauded this remark from Victor.

"And, Rita, your portrayal of our strikingly pretty, strikingly foulmouthed home-wrecker was right on target. You were very convincing, so we know you must have done some fine acting."

More applause and mild laughter followed that.

"Now, Corey. How does one sum up a performance like you gave us? I can tell you with one word: magnificent!" There was a lot of applause and a few "Yeah's."

Victor continued. "I was always aware of your talent, but finally directing you in this picture has shown me the incredible ability you have to make your character come to life. You were just amazing!"

The entire room started to applaud as Bob stood up, and smiling brilliantly, he started clapping his hands with such fervor, that everyone stood up while still applauding. His face beamed with the absolute love he had for her.

Corey's eyes began to fill with unshed tears, and when she looked into Bob's glowing eyes, a tear escaped down her cheek. Bob, having seen the tear fall, leaned over and hugged her. As he slightly pulled away, he gazed into her moistened eyes and then kissed her on the lips.

After the applause and cat whistles had dissipated, Victor remarked into the microphone, "Now that was a well-earned kiss!" There were a few more shouts and whistles. Bob's and Corey's smiles were incandescent at this point.

Victor continued, "I have to describe our leading man as a cad, a louse, and a complete heel." There was laughter and even some boos from the partygoers. Bob threw his arms into the air and facetiously yelled, "Thank you, thank you so much. My heart goes out to you."

Corey laughed out loud, as well as most in the room.

Victor added, "Bob, your character was very intriguing and yet imbued with all the wrong qualities to lead a life of content and pleasure. This just shows how great a job you did in portraying this man, because you, my friend, are the complete opposite of this character."

There were a few "Hear, hear's." Bob nodded his head in appreciation.

"Your performance was hardly unexpected—as men with the energy, ambition, and the intelligence you possess usually find their place in this world. You, sir, I think, have always known who you were and where you were going. Thanks for an unbelievable job!"

The applause and shouts were now quite loud. Corey leaned over and put her arms around his neck. Bob turned his head to meet her lips with his.

Victor then let Trent have the mic, and he thanked the cast and crew for bringing the picture in early and flawlessly making his job just that much more easy.

Everyone kept drinking and eating when the music began to play. Corey heard "Knowing You Were Mine" start to play. It was the song Bob wrote and sang to her at their wedding.

Corey immediately grabbed Bob's arm and leaned in and lovingly asked him, "Dance with me, darling, it's our wedding song."

Bob didn't hesitate by answering, "Of course, baby." He took her hand and led her to the dance floor. He wrapped both his arms around her waist and pulled her as close to him as he could. Corey placed her arms around his neck and laid the side of her head on his chest. Bob softly sang the entire song into her ear.

When the song ended, Bob and Corey remained on the dance floor just holding each other. Bob moved one hand to the small of her back and the other hand between her shoulder blades. He then pulled her body up so he could passionately kiss her. She responded enthusiastically by running both of her hands through his beautiful head of hair, as they were lost in each other and really didn't care who was watching.

They returned to their table a few moments later, and looking down at his watch, Bob hurriedly told the people at his table, "Well, I think Corey and I are going to call it an evening. It's almost eleven o'clock, and we only have till noon Wednesday to be together for a while before I have to leave on tour. So, good night to all of you, and it's been a fantastic experience and a lot of fun."

Rita felt bad about the fact she didn't get a chance to dance with Bob that evening, but she knew she would see him around the studio from time to time. She lamented in the fact that he did not become one of her fleeting affairs. She would always regret that.

When Bob and Corey returned home to Bel Air, they ended their night in bed making some very passionate love. Corey was primed for this, especially after Bob sang their wedding song to her and they danced to the music of "Knowing You Were Mine."

The last full day, Tuesday, June 7—before the next three and a half weeks of separation they would experience—they, of course, spent together out by the pool.

SIXTEEN

Tuesday morning, June 7, Bob and Corey were out by the pool eating breakfast and drinking their coffee. They were both very aware this would be the last full day for weeks that they would be able to spend together.

Corey, swallowing and then taking a drink of her coffee, matter-of-factly told Bob, "You know, darling, both Jack and I agreed on my next picture I'll be making while you're on your tour."

This caught Bob's attention, for he was curious as to what the picture was about and who Corey would be working with. He turned his head to her with an inquiring curiosity and asked, "That's great, doll. What's the title, and whom are you going to be working with?"

"It's called *Beneath the Sullen Sky*, and I'll be working with Herbert Marshall, Teresa Wright, Richard Carlson, and Hope Lange. I guess Lloyd Patterson will be directing it. It's about dark intrigue and the irascible forces of covert double agents risking the possibility of capture and their own death."

Bob looked at Corey incredulously for a few seconds, and with great uncertainty, he asked, "Wow! That's some heavy-duty material, doll. Whatever made you choose a role like that? I guess I'm just not used to you playing a dark, villainous character…and who's this director Lloyd Patterson?"

Corey chuckled and smilingly answered, "I guess I just needed a good challenge, darling. It'll help me to focus more on my work, and maybe not have so much time worrying about how your tour is going...and Lloyd has been around Hollywood for many years. He's come over from Paramount to shoot this picture. Jack asked him if he would work this project because Lloyd is so good with this particular genre. He's maybe six two, still with a pretty good head of salt-and-pepper hair, and around fifty years old."

This spurred a twinge in Bob's fiercely protective nature. He sat on the side of his lounger tapping one foot on the cement, and giving Corey a suspiciously playful smile, he then pursed his lips.

Corey laughed out loud because she knew exactly what he was thinking. She threw her head back and laughingly informed him, "My precious man, you have *nothing* to worry about. Lloyd is a homosexual, and his thirty-year-old live-in boyfriend skates with the Ice Capades. So you see, you can put your saber back into its scabbard."

Bob instantly started to laugh as Corey continued to chuckle. She quickly moved over to join him in his lounger.

He put his hands around her waist and guided her on top of him. She lay between his legs with her hands running up his chest to grip his shoulders. Bob's hands were feeling her buttocks. Then he ran them up her torso and the sides of her breasts. They both fell into a very deep kiss, with one of his hands now holding the back of her head and enabling him to run his tongue around and over her tongue.

They were moving their pelvises together slowly at first, and then it became an intense reaction as Corey could feel Bob's erection through his bathrobe. She placed one hand down the front of him when she lowered herself to start fondling his privates.

Bob was beside himself enjoying the avid sexual fervor of the moment when he felt Corey put her entire mouth into the job. He immediately began to climax as Corey continued to gently massage his manhood. The release was incredibly overwhelming to him as he loudly moaned and exhaled a breathy, "Oh my god, baby!"

He tried to catch his breath as he pulled Corey up to him and tenderly turned her over on her back. He tore her bathrobe open as he was on his knees between her legs. Bob stared at her incredibly sexy body for a few seconds as both of them were breathing heavily and their hearts were pounding with the extreme sexual want of the other.

Bob lowered himself to kissing the inside of her thighs. Corey was panting loudly and almost screaming for him to put his mouth on her. When he ran his tongue over her, she began to breathe extremely heavy gasps of air. Corey moaned a high-pitch sound that was almost like she was crying.

Bob then pulled himself up to suckle the nipple of her left breast as he slowly entered her. Corey threw her arms up and back, surrendering every part of her body to his movements and his sexual cravings.

She was now moving with his methodical thrusts, but he kept kissing at her neck. Suddenly her back arched, as she was overcome with the euphoria of a massive orgasm. She screamed and raised her pelvis hard into his hips. "Oh my god! Baby, I love you!"

Corey held him tight to her body and wouldn't allow him to move from on top of her. She breathlessly told him, "Just hold me, darling! Never let go of me."

Bob held her as he kissed her neck and then the side of her face. He slowly raised his head and looked her directly in the eyes, and breathlessly he promised, "Corey, I could never let you go. You are just pure magic to me, baby."

Corey's luminous eyes shone more brightly than usual from the unshed tears of joy that were inundating them. Bob smiled adoringly at her, and then he slowly leaned over to kiss her. Their kiss was unending until Haddie came to the french doors and announced, "Sorry to bother you, Mr. Bob, but Jack Windheim is on the phone for you."

Bob and Corey both looked puzzled by the fact Jack needed to talk with him the day before he left on tour. Bob gently lifted himself up off of Corey and rearranged his bathrobe around himself. He sexily drew Corey's robe up and around her, kissed her, and then apologetically said to her, "I'm sorry, baby. I'll be right back."

Corey slightly moved her head and flirted with him by teasing, "You'd better be."

He smiled at her and then told Haddie, "I'm coming, Haddie."

Haddie kiddingly answered, "I thought you already had announced that once or twice, Mr. Bob?"

Bob smiled brilliantly, and you could hear Corey loudly laughing. Looking at Corey, he jokingly quipped, "See? I just give her way too much material to work with."

All Corey could do was chuckle and lovingly smile at him as she blew him a sexy kiss. Bob then hurried into the house with a worried look on his face.

He reached the phone still smiling. He tentatively picked up the receiver and responded, "Hello, Jack. What's crackin', man?"

"Yeah, Bob. Sorry to bother you and Corey today, but I thought you should know about the switch in leading ladies you're gonna have in that picture you're signed on to do in August. You know, the one you're working on shortly after you return from your tour?"

Bob inquisitively asked, "What do you mean *switch*? What's brewing, Jack? Go ahead and lay it on me, man."

Jack hesitated for a moment and then informed Bob with the details: "Alex has pulled out of the picture, for personal reasons I'm told, but we immediately got a replacement from an actress over at Columbia Pictures. I'm sure you've heard of Kim Novak. She started with Columbia in 1954 and made her mark in '55 with Bill Holden in *Picnic*. She's twenty-seven years old and was one of the biggest box office draws in '57 and '58."

"Of course, I've heard of Kim. You had to have had your head under a pillow for the last six or seven years not to have knowledge of her. She's a really good actress, and beautiful on top of all that."

"Yeah, well, now after making *Vertigo* with James Stewart, you know, Hitchcock's picture, then *Bell, Book, and Candle*, again with Stewart, and finishing late last year in *Middle of the Night* with Fredric March, her contract is up with Columbia. She's been shopping around the last few months for a good script, and her agent got wind of Alex leaving our picture *Hidden Desire*. Well, I was told when she heard it was Susan Hawthorne and yourself in the picture, she immediately tried to sign onto it. Of course, I didn't hesitate in getting her signature to a contract...so you see, my boy, this might all be for the better. She's so much more of a box office draw than Alex would have been."

Bob stood with the phone still to his ear as he was puzzled. So he questioningly asked Jack, "That all sounds great, man, but Alex was in her early forties, and the role called for that. So how are you going to work replacing her with Kim, who's only twenty-seven?"

"Don't you worry about a thing, Bob. I have the writers on it as we speak. Did you know that Columbia's hierarchy and studio head, Jackson Schneider, thought that Kim was Columbia's answer to Marilyn Monroe over at Twentieth Century Fox? Kim was also intended to be Rita Hayworth's successor, who was one of the biggest stars of the '40s for Columbia. That was all before she stormed out on them and before she started making a few pictures for me here at Celebrity. I guess Kim made quite a mark at Columbia Studios, but now she's not under contract and is still going gangbusters."

Nodding his head, Bob agreed by saying, "Yeah, it's strange sometimes how things work out, isn't it? Well, thanks for the heads-up, Jack. I think the picture will be a blast. Can't wait for it to happen. I'll talk with you again, man, when I get back from the tour. Later."

Jack signed off, "You young men be careful, and, Bob, remember that uppercut I showed you. You may need to have that ready at all times."

Bob snorted a chuckle and then placed the receiver back down on the phone.

As Bob turned to walk back out to the pool area, Corey was walking toward him from the french doors. Her prescience in any given situation was always impressive, as she knew this was something of a momentous nature, a portent.

She asked concernedly, "Whatever did Jack want, darling? It must be important. It took you forever in talking with him."

Matter-of-factly, Bob informed Corey, "Oh, there's been a personnel change in my picture. I guess Alex has withdrawn from her role, due to personal reasons, and Jack has replaced her with Kim Novak. He told me her contract was up with Columbia late last year, so I guess she's freelancing these days."

Corey knew exactly who Kim was, and a tremendous jolt of possessiveness washed over her. She mockingly cocked her head a little and facetiously smiled at Bob, smartly saying, "I see. How nice for you, darling."

Bob just chuckled, smiled brilliantly, and then picked her up in his arms and started to carry her back outside while playfully telling her, "I just love it when your blood starts to boil and your face looks like it's going to explode…kiss me, you gorgeous creature!"

They were locked in a long and involved kiss all the way out to the pool area as Bob romantically carried Corey to their lounger and placed her down beside him.

It would have taken a paragon of virtue not to feel viciously jealous at this moment, but Corey trusted Bob unequivocally and unquestioningly.

The morning of June 8, the day the Owls were to leave to start their 21-City Tour, Bob and Corey spent the morning making soft, sweet love, with a lot of pillow talk ensuing.

Haddie knew this was the day Bob was to leave on tour, so she left them alone until they decided it was time for them to get up.

At around eleven o'clock that morning, Bob and Corey came meandering into the kitchen, where Haddie was prepping for Corey's dinner that evening. They had showered and were fully dressed, because Corey was going to ride with Bob to the airport to see him off at four o'clock that afternoon.

Haddie looked up from her cutting board and saw them walking in. She instantly chuckled and jokingly stated, "Well, well, you did remember where the bedroom door was, huh?"

Bob answered in a low and romantic voice; he slowly, kiddingly told her, "Yeah, Ms. Haddie, we remembered where *everything* was. It was outta sight and some real kicks, baby!"

Corey was laughing out loud as she smiled at Haddie and then lovingly looked at Bob.

Haddie, acting embarrassed, warned, "All right. Okay! Say no more… I deserved that. Yeah, I'm gonna miss you, Mr. Bob. That's for sure." Haddie chortled.

Corey, still smiling, inquisitively asked Haddie out of concern, "Did you get a chance to see Joshua once more before he leaves today with the Owls' tour?"

Haddie answered her assuredly, "Oh, certainly, Ms. Corey. Joshua and Deidra came and picked me up Monday night. They took me to dinner at Lacey's Place in West Hollywood. It was just wonderful."

"Well, I'm glad you were able to see your son before he flies away this afternoon. Did you give him any words of encouragement he'll need while performing in concert for the next three weeks in the deeply segregated Southern states?"

Haddie expressed determinedly and with great emotional fervor, "I told him like a lovin' mother would that's trying to help her son to raise himself up for the storm that's fast approaching, 'There will be fear in the guys' eyes that will represent a God-given opportunity for focusing their collective concentration on each other. And because of their remarkable solidarity, their concentration will be formidable.' Then I swore to him that this solidarity will be the assurance that someone will always have his back."

Corey's eyes began to glisten when Bob lovingly smiled at Haddie and reassured her, "I'll take good care of your son, Ms. Haddie. We're all family, and family takes care of family." Bob walked over to Haddie and nodded his head reassuringly and then hugged her for a few seconds. As he pulled away from her, he kissed her on the cheek and then promised her, "No worries, Ms. Haddie."

That sent a chill running through Corey's body. She would swear that Bob would sacrifice himself to save someone he loved from endangering peril.

At three forty-five that afternoon at LAX, the Owls, Nick, and Truman began boarding their airplane. Bob stood close to the opened door of the jetway with his arms around Corey. They were tightly hugging each other after having kissed very affectionately.

Corey lovingly whispered to Bob, "Oh god, how I'm going to miss you, darling! But I will see you in New York in three and a half weeks. Okay, sweetheart?"

Bob looked into Corey's moistening eyes and promised her, "I'll absolutely be waiting for you, baby. We'll make up for lost time all of that week you're with me. I'll see you now… I love you to the moon and back, Alice."

"You…are…my…heart," Corey whispered. "Be careful and take care of one another," she pleaded.

Bob quickly kissed her once more and then moved quickly through the door of the jetway as they began to close it.

Within fifteen minutes, Corey watched their plane back away from the terminal and then race down the runway, slowly lifting itself into the air. The jet contrail rose behind the aircraft, stealing the love of her life away from her, even if it were only for a short while.

After Corey was driven home by Curtis, she thought about Alex pulling out of the picture with Bob and Susan. She felt Jack was trying to get Alex into a top-billed feature film with two very bankable stars in Bob and Susan, but this was a mystery to her why Alex wanted out.

Corey went right to the phone and dialed Alex's number. When Alex picked up the receiver, Corey pleasantly said, "Alex, this is Corey. How are you doing? Are you feeling all right?"

Alex was caught off guard by Corey's call. She felt it couldn't just be a neighborly call from one friend to another. She figured Corey already knew she had withdrawn from the picture. "Well, hello, Corey. How are you doing? I'm just fine, thanks."

Curiously, Corey asked, "I ask if you're feeling all right because Jack informed Bob you had wanted out of their picture. Now I know it's none of my business, but, Alex, this was a great opportunity for you to get back into A-list movies. Is it your health or what?"

Alex knew the moment had come that she needed to be honest with her friend. After exhaling resignedly, Alex unburdened herself to Corey. "Corey, I was going to have a sit-down with you, but since you needed to know now, I can tell you it's not because of my health I'm not doing this picture. It's because of Bob."

Corey's eyes widened, and she was taken aback with surprise. She remained silent and didn't move a muscle, waiting for Alex to explain.

"We both know I love your husband. I'm sure that's been no secret for some time now...right now I'm absolutely sure I would not be able to handle a love scene with him. I know we're all professional actors, and we should be able to just play the part and leave our personal feelings at the door. But I wouldn't be comfortable in doing that, and it might affect the quality of my performance and the picture. So, I guess what I'm saying is, I need some time and space to handle this situation. I'm so terribly sorry to tell you this, but both of you should really know what's going on. I hope you understand and know that I would never attempt to come between you two. And after seeing how truly in love you two were at your wedding, I knew I didn't stand a chance anyway."

Instead of Corey having a bitter jealousy of Alex, she now gained an admirable amount of respect for her. She actually gave solace to her by saying, "Yes, Alex, I've known your feelings for Bob since you were living here with us. And I do understand how you may need time to come to terms with the fact you will never have him. So I thank you for being honest with me, and I sincerely hope you're able to shoot a picture with us both somewhere down the line."

"Sounds wonderful, Corey. I'll see you two around the studio hopefully."

"Absolutely, Alex. Now, take care. Goodbye."

"Goodbye, Corey."

* * * * *

An hour and forty-five minutes later, the Owls landed in Albuquerque, New Mexico. They were shuttled to their hotel by a rented van Truman would be driving for them.

Upon arriving at the hotel, Nick was informed by the elderly desk clerk, who had beard stubble of at least a week on his face, and his shoddy clothes barely covered his corpulent mass, "The six white men will have three rooms together in front of the building, but the two Negroes will be in back of the hotel on the lower level. That room will not be as expensive 'cause it's so much smaller."

Nick just stared at the old white clerk disbelieving what he just heard. Bob was standing behind Nick when he heard the room assignments and was incredulously in shock from what the clerk said. To both Nick and Bob, this struck them as both ridiculous and utterly untenable.

Bob sternly advised the clerk, "This is not acceptable. Now you give us four rooms all the same and together. Do you understand?"

The old guy stood his ground and firmly stated, "That can't happen, sir. Rules are rules."

All the other guys now realized what was going down, and Doug, being extremely agitated by the situation, screamed, "These two men aren't any different from the rest of us except for the color of their skin. Now give them a suitable room next to us and learn to show a little bit of respect while you're at it!"

Joshua could see how upset everyone was getting and spoke up, trying to assuage the problem at hand. "All right, guys. We had to realize that this far South, we were gonna have some problems...let's just go with the flow. It's only for two nights."

Darnell, pretty pissed at the whole situation, pugnaciously bellowed, "Joshua, brother! It's not just two nights. We're down here in the land of cotton for fourteen nights. We can give in to ole Jim Crow, or we can find a way to work around it."

Bob was a man who saw the world in light and dark colors with little shading in between. He had a capacity for outrage at injustice and wrongdoing; this was one of his guiding motivations.

At that exact moment, Bob had an idea. He turned to Joshua and Darnell and winked at them, indicating he had figured out a ruse to handle the problem. Bob turned to the hotel clerk and nonchalantly said, "Okay, we'll take the four rooms we were assigned. It's obvious that all the hotels down here are going to be the same."

Pompously, the clerk agreed, "You'd better believe it, boy!"

The clerk handed Nick the keys to the three rooms in front and then handed Joshua the key to his and Darnell's room in the rear of the building. When the eight of them went out front to get their luggage out of the van, Bob quietly tried to explain to Joshua and Darnell how the situation was going to be handled.

Bob instructed Joshua and Darnell to leave what clothes they were going to wear tomorrow and their nightclothes with him. They could then carry their suitcases back to their room. He added, "That'll give the clerk and any security something to see. When it gets dark, I'll come back and escort both of you to my room. It'll have to be a very quiet, covert operation, but I know your room is probably not habitable, so it's worth the risk…just make sure you make the room look like you've slept there—even though we know it probably already does."

Darnell offered the guys, "You know, man. We can just sleep in the van."

Doug began to freak out but kept his cool by calmly saying, "There is no flipping way you guys are gonna sleep in the van, because if you do, we all do!"

African American performers of the late fifties and early sixties had to contend with all the Jim Crow absurdities; it was just standard operating procedure in the Southern states, and some of the Northern ones as well.

Often they couldn't stay at hotels and were served rotten food at white restaurants and were outright banned from others.

This was a time when black performers found themselves on the front lines of the battle over segregation; the clashes at lunch counters, schools, and on buses for starters.

Rock 'n' roll, with its mixture of white country music and black rhythm 'n' blues, arrived just as segregationists were tightening Jim Crow laws in response to the culminating civil rights movement. Entertainers throughout the South were forced to participate in a crowd-separation ritual. Venues could be unofficially classified black or white. Blacks were usually in the balcony, and whites on the floor; other times, a painted line ran down the center of the theater, or a rope separated the audience.

Joshua thought to buy the latest copy of *The Negro Motorist Green Book* before they left California. When he pulled it out of his suitcase, he informed the guys, "I have a guidebook here for African American travelers. It's been around for over twenty years, it's an exhausted directory of every business in the country that is open to people of color. Nick, Truman, and I did check it out for hotels here in Albuquerque, but the few they had were just too far away from our concert venue. Maybe we can change that at our next gig in San Antonio."

Len spoke up this time, suggesting, "Well, let's find a place in the *Green Book* to go and eat some dinner tonight. I'm starved."

After the group found a barbecue place that served white as well as people of color, they chowed down on pork ribs and Pabst Blue Ribbon beer.

Around eleven o'clock that night, Bob cautiously snuck over to Joshua and Darnell's room and spirited them over to his and Len's room. Len and Bob slept in the same big bed, and Joshua and Darnell slept together in the other clean, white-sheeted bed.

When they awoke in Bob and Len's room at around nine o'clock that Thursday morning, of June 9, all four guys showered and changed into the clothes they would wear to their first concert that night.

The guys found a restaurant out of the *Green Book*, not far out of the way, that served breakfast to all colors of people. After they finished eating, Truman drove all the guys to the concert venue at Tingley Coliseum in downtown Albuquerque. The coliseum seated almost twelve thousand ticket holders, so they'd be opening their tour to a large crowd the first night.

The guys ran a sound check on the instruments and inspected them for any damage that may have occurred in transit. A private company was hired by Truman to transport the instruments to all their concerts until they reached Montgomery, Alabama. They would then be flown to Raleigh, North Carolina, and driven up the East Coast from venue to venue after that.

The entire group agreed from that day on they would only be staying at a hotel that was recommended by Joshua's *Green Book*. So before their concert that night, they booked one of the hotels that was twenty-five miles away from the coliseum. They returned to their original hotel, collected their luggage, and checked out a day early.

The old, white-haired desk clerk tauntingly asked, "You boys unhappy 'bout somethin'?"

Nick turned to him and, with extreme reproach, warned, "Subhuman people like you are just beneath contempt...but one day you'll get yours. Just don't be surprised when equality and everyone's civil rights kick you so hard in the ass, that you're chewing on your own balls that night!"

The old guy behind the desk shot Nick a very dirty look and then just chuckled to himself.

The concert that night went uneventfully. The omnipresence of the security was noticeable, both with the venue's staff and the private force Nick had secured.

The thousands of fans and new groupies were in abundance at the coliseum. They were enjoying themselves immensely as the whites were sequestered to one side of the white line and the colored to the other side.

Surprisingly enough, there was a tremendous show of black faces in the audience. They eagerly wanted to witness the first ripple of the changing times by giving their support to a mixed musical group of black and white musicians alike. The new fans now felt they were a small part of the movement.

The Owls played over half of their original songs, but they kept for last the songs pertaining to the civil rights of coloreds and the power the youth of America was demanding.

They finished their concert with "Makin' Roads Inland," in which Bob played the piano; "Raging Fire"; "Courage for the Fight," one of their signature songs; and their second signature song, "Time Is Ours to Change."

When they closed with the loud and defining note to "Time," there was a thunderous applause and screams and whistles of approval.

The din in the coliseum was so amplified and prolonged, that Bob yelled at the guys, "Conviction."

At that very moment, Jimmy began to punish his drums, and the guys tore into one of their more upbeat songs of the time, "Conviction." The audience cheered their deafening approval, and when the song ended, the guys quitted the stage after waving and blowing kisses to the ladies on both sides of the line.

That night after their first concert, all the guys got settled into their new hotel. It was a bit of a drive, but they also knew it was absolutely necessary.

When Len left the room to go and talk with Nick, Bob took advantage of the moment and dialed home to talk with Corey. It was almost midnight in Albuquerque, and almost eleven in Bel Air, when he decided to take a chance on her still being awake.

The phone rang just once when Corey, feeling it was Bob, picked up the receiver, "Hello, darling. How did your first concert go this evening?"

Hearing her voice instantly shot a loving warmth throughout his entire body. Bob closed his eyes and sexily answered, "Hey, baby. How's it going with you tonight?"

Corey seductively answered, "I've been studying my script for the start of my picture Monday, and reading anything else I can get my hands on. And because I don't have you to put my hands on, I just try to stay busy."

Bob took a huge breath and exhaled loudly, exclaiming, "Oh, baby, don't do that! Now I'm tempted to fly home and put my hands on you."

"I'll leave the light on, sweetheart."

Feeling like he needed to change the subject, Bob chuckled then said, "Okay, doll, you do that... But I did want to tell you we had no trouble at all at the venue tonight. Everything went smoothly. However, at the hotel, Joshua and Darnell were treated pretty badly by being given a small, dirty, and unkempt room far in the back and away from us."

Corey shot back, "That's disgusting! I hope you guys left that place! That's reprehensible!"

Bob explained what they did the first night and then how they changed hotels after that. He told her about *The Green Book* that Joshua had and how that would be the only places they would fraternize for the rest of the tour.

"Well, my baby girl, I have to say good night to you now. I'll call you again after we drive over to San Antonio and are in an acceptable hotel. Good night, doll. I love you."

"Please be careful! I love you to pieces, darling! Good night."

That Friday night, the second concert in Albuquerque was just as good, just as loud, and just as segregated.

In moving on to San Antonio, they would now find out in more depth, in entering the fringe of the Deep South, about the discrimination and the incongruities of the practice of Jim Crow.

The Owls' hotel was only five miles from the Freeman Coliseum in downtown San Antonio, but their rooms were together, and they were clean and well-kept.

They would be playing to 11,700-capacity seating. This was a music venue built in 1949 that hosted thousands of events, including the San Antonio stock show and rodeo, trade shows, motor sports, circuses, and professional bull riding.

The night of their first concert, the two vans that carried their instruments and the eight guys were met before entering the Freeman Coliseum with protesters and signs reading, "Take your black asses back to Africa" and "No niggers—No kidding!" There was even a couple of ripe tomatoes thrown at the vans.

The exterior security forces were able to disperse the small group and allow clear entrance to the venue for the guys. This small demonstration of about two dozen people was caught on a portable TV camera by one of the local stations that had guessed right about the biracial concert running into some trouble.

Just before the doors were to open for the ticket holders, four of the maintenance guys for the coliseum came out and roped off the seating. They used white window cord, which they looped and tied to each seat down the center aisle, making it an off-limits zone that neither colored nor white could tread.

Throughout the fifties and early sixties, the South began to mobilize these forces of massive resistance in a much more concerted way: the laws tightened up, coinciding with federal law decisions.

The Night Owls fans stayed loyal and supportive to the band, however. Kids of both colors got out of their seats during the first concert and danced up and down the aisle, but, of course, only on the side of the aisle they were designated to sit. No one wanted to be thrown out of the coliseum, but they were still having fun and loving the music and the messages it was sending to them.

After the second night's concert, the same hate groups still met them outside the coliseum, but the seats were still full of their fans—black and white together, yet separate.

The group moved up to Norman, Oklahoma, June 13. They played the McCasland Field House, which was built in 1928 and held five thousand fans. They were told Frank Sinatra and Elvis Presley had played the Field House not too long ago. There was no trouble either of the two concert nights, because security was swarming the entire area and busted up anything that looked like future trouble.

The night before they were to leave for New Orleans, Bob called Corey from his room while Len was in the shower.

It was Wednesday night when Corey picked up the phone after only one ring. The trepidation in her voice was quite noticeable as she stifled whatever sounds her shivering heart might cause her to utter. "Oh, baby. I'm just so relieved you called me tonight."

"I know, Corey, but things here have been pretty tentative lately. It seems we're all so uptight and always scrambling to ensure the safety of the band. Nick told us before this tour started to never be complacent and reminded us constantly of the sheer unpredictability of these hate groups and of the necessity for total vigilance at all times… It just always seems pretty tense with the blatant discrimination and the horrific segregation at these concerts."

Corey's eyes began to moisten as she tried to console Bob. "It must be absolutely horrible for you guys. Just try to remember I'll meet up with you in New York in just two and a half weeks. The time will not go fast enough for me, darling."

Bob was mentally exhausted, and with disjointed thoughts blundering through his head, he managed to let Corey know, "I don't know when next I'll be talking with you, doll, but I know there will be many moments I'll be jazzed just thinking of you."

"Oh, Bob…I love you so much and miss you so badly. You call me anytime, even if I'm at the studio. Do you hear me, darling?"

Bob answered with what little energy he had left in his body, "Good night, sweet lady. I'll always love you, Corey."

Corey was now worried beyond belief after hearing the way he said his good nights. She couldn't seem to reach him, as she pledged to him with unshed tears in her eyes, "You be ready for me to come to you in New York in just a short while, baby. I will never be able to tell you how much I love you, Bob. Please be careful and take every precaution… Good night, sweetheart."

She could hear the receiver click down from the other end of the line, and she began to cry. She was convinced this tour was having a profound psychological impact on him. Her only worry was she wasn't quite sure if he'd return as the same person that left her.

The Owls arrived in New Orleans late Thursday evening, June 16, after Truman drove them the entire way from Norman, Oklahoma. They were not to perform until Friday night, so everyone hit the sheets pretty early at their *Green Book* hotel Nick had booked yesterday.

The next morning, after breakfast at a "welcoming restaurant," the guys drove the ten miles into City Park in New Orleans to check out the venue and their instruments. They tuned the guitars and then ran a sound check. They were ready to go for tonight's concert.

The Tad Gormley Stadium could seat 26,500 ticket holders and was a multipurpose outdoor stadium for not only concerts, but sporting events and any event requiring a huge area with ample seating.

That evening, driving into the stadium's vomitorium (the passage below a tier of seats in a stadium that's the pathway for performers to enter and leave the stage), the Night Owls van was met by dozens of audacious protesters and hate-mongers holding foully-worded signs and yelling filthy and disgusting racial slurs at the entire van.

Amongst the eight guys, there was notable evidence of a rebellious ebullience on the surface, but it was sedately undercut by crosscurrents of fear and mistrust.

Hell-bent on confrontation, Doug stood up in the van and screamed, "You shitheads need to get your head out of your asses… you're no better than us, you damned fools!"

Bob stood and moved to Doug; as he put his hand on Doug's back, he calmly told him, "Even if they could hear you, they're not gonna listen to you, no matter what you say. Save your energy for the concert, brother. We need all of your life force with us the next five days."

Doug looked at Bob's convincing face, and he knew that he had allowed his own will and better judgment to come into conflict with one another. Doug nodded and quietly sat back down in his van seat.

Bob had hoped the guys could maintain their cool in the face of the steady abuse, yet molten anger also bubbled underneath his own skin just the same.

However, Bob absolutely knew deep down in his soul that he would guard his band assiduously, even if it meant sacrificing his own safety.

The concert went on with no noticeable trouble inside the stadium. The Night Owls fans were all in attendance; black on one side of the venue, and white on the other.

The security forces were all in place—at the stairs emptying to the higher seats, all the exit doors, in the parking lots, and most especially up and around the stage area where the Owls were performing.

The Owls were met with a resounding acceptance and thunderous applause after each song. They had performed several songs, and when the audience had calmed down a bit, Bob stepped up very close to his own microphone. The young girls, black and white, started to scream, while there were many loud whistles and shouts of encouragement coming from their fans on both sides of the aisle.

After Bob waited several seconds, holding his opened hands in the air, the din inside of the stadium died down to a deafening silence.

Never more serious in his life, Bob began to speak to everyone within hearing distance. "Whether all of you know it or not, we're all playing the same tune. We may be different on the outside, but inside, we all laugh, we all play, and certainly we all love."

There was applause and whistling from the audience.

His voice rose with more fullness to the tone as he continued, "Believe me, we are all in this together, people. No one is above anyone else. No one calls all the shots, and no one is better than any other color of person on the face of this earth."

The crowd went crazy with applause and screaming. The appreciative uproar became deafening within the stadium, and it took another minute for the crowd to quiet.

There were prideful smiles on all the guys as a tear slowly slipped down Joshua's cheek, and Darnell became choked up as his own eyes welled up with tears.

Bob now spoke with great fervor in his voice. "A great man once said, 'All men are created equal.' And I believe the greatest of all men said it first…and that was Jesus Christ!"

Again, the applause was tremendously loud, with shouts and whistles.

Bob's cadence ran through his sentences when he spoke; it was his underlying rhythm, like your own personal drummer.

With the silence of the crowd, and Bob's eyes filled with unshed tears, he continued even though his voice was choked with the vehemence of his feelings. "Let's celebrate our differences, not crucify them. Love one another, and make a difference in this world. Don't remain silent about anything you know is wrong. Let's come together tonight and pray for equal rights, freedom for all, and an end to this absurd discrimination."

Bob took a step back from his microphone as the complete stadium of people rose to their feet, applauding loudly, screaming approval, and yelling at the top of their lungs.

It was this instant that Bob yelled to the guys, "Courage for the Fight!"

Jimmy gave them the four-count on his snare, and the Owls tore into the song composed by Joshua and Darnell that spoke of showing your courage and bravery for the long struggle still ahead. This song was the first of the Owls' signature songs, along with "Times Are Ours to Change," a song they would be known for and one that they would always have to perform at every concert.

The remaining hour of the concert went fabulously, with no show of trouble, as the huge security force covered the stadium like a sealed drum.

What Nick and the Night Owls didn't know was that just weeks before they came to perform at the Tad Gormley Stadium, the cops interrupted a biracial jam session at New Orleans Preservation Hall and arrested all the musicians. The black musicians were playing to an unseparated, mixed crowd of black and white people, and that was greatly frowned upon. The judge told an assembled courthouse crowd, according to several who were in the audience, "We don't want Yankees coming down to New Orleans mixing cream with our coffee."

There was only the New Orleans famous Dew Drop Inn that catered to an exclusively African American crowd. But in all other cases, police and promoters physically separated the audiences.

The next concert the Night Owls would be performing at was in Baton Rouge, Louisiana, June 19, and then on to Birmingham, Alabama, June 22. The band of brothers would now be piercing the heart of the Deep South and Ole Dixie.

SEVENTEEN

The bright morning hours of Saturday, June 18, the Owls made their way up to Baton Rouge, Louisiana; it was only one hour and eighteen minutes from New Orleans.

The group arrived and checked into their *Green Book* hotel and then found a suitable restaurant to eat breakfast.

An hour later, they drove to their concert site, the Varsity Concert Hall, which was built in 1924 and was located in the heart of Baton Rouge. The Owls would be playing to the 5,600 seats of the bi-level concert venue. Looking around the hall, there didn't seem to be a bad seat in the house. There was an upstairs balcony, which overlooked the stage area, and they figured this would be where the coloreds would be sequestered.

As the guys got their instruments set up and ran a sound check on them, they witnessed the impeccable sound quality along with the great acoustics that resonated throughout this long-in-use concert hall.

The Owls were adding to their already huge fanbase in the United States a lot of fans from within the colored communities. Their music was reaching the disenfranchised black youth that was getting on board with the new genre of rebellious rock 'n' roll. This only added to the far-reaching European and Australian popularity they already enjoyed.

That night, the eight guys were all in Nick and Truman's hotel room enjoying some beers and a couple of large pizzas and discussing tomorrow's concert; suddenly their attention was drawn to the front window of the room.

All of them saw a huge flash of light just outside the window and to the one side of the room. They looked at one another with alarm and compelling protectiveness.

Nick and Doug raced for the door with abandoned caution and ripped it open while the other six guys ran up to poke their heads out from behind them. The light was blinding but could plainly be seen as a huge flaming white cross that was placed into the grassy area next to their van. The room they were all in was at the end of the hotel's bottom floor and only about twelve feet from the burning cross.

Bob called the front office and screamed to them, "Call the fire department and police. There's a huge burning cross just outside of our door!"

The black night manager complied by yelling, "I'll call right now, but don't expect them to come too quickly."

The news media must have been tipped off about what was going down that night. Because minutes after the flame was ignited, a portable news cameraman and reporter emptied out of a small sedan and ran to set up a good shot of the burning cross. As the reporter looked into the camera, with the flames surging behind him, he excitedly announced, "As you can see behind me, there has been a burning white cross placed near the door of the biracial rock 'n' roll band the Night Owls."

Doug and Darnell dashed out of the room and toward the reporter. Doug was first to rip into the reporter as he became defensive toward him in trying to protect his brothers. "Get the hell outta here, you vulture. You're no better than the son of a bitch that placed this damned thing here to begin with!"

Darnell held Doug back with one hand and then commenced to rip a little ass himself: "Go ahead, get your story! Put the damned thing on TV if you gotta! This only helps us to be stronger and more determined to put an end to this shit! You don't scare us. You only make us more resolute in our purpose and so much more bold with our music. So go and take a flyin' leap, you asshole."

Bob raced out of the room with the van keys in his hand. He eyeballed the reporter with contempt in his eyes and then jumped into the van and quickly moved it to a safer parking space.

When he came walking back toward the hotel, he saw the night manager bringing a water hose from around the side of the building closest to the guys' room. He already had the water running from it, so Bob instantly grabbed it from his hand and moved toward the flaming cross. As he directed the water flow to the top of the flames, a crackling, sizzling sound consumed the previously tranquil night. The smoke started bellowing skyward into the darkness of the sky. Within a couple of minutes, he had extinguished all the flames.

The reporter had told the cameraman to keep the tape rolling.

Bob stood staring at the smoldering, burnt wood of the one religious symbol that had reminded him of the sufferings of the Christ.

Bob was not a religious man, but he was a spiritual one. He knew for certain that it was understood Christ's death on the cross was completed by God raising him from the dead three days after he was entombed. The resurrection was a sign of Christ's victory over sin and death. The symbol of the crucifix had always reminded him of the redeeming benefits of his passion and death.

As he became enthralled by the situation, Bob loudly shouted out, "This is just pure, unmitigated blasphemy! Why on earth would a hateful, evil person use this symbol to strike fear and intimidation into someone? This just isn't right!"

Quietly, Joshua walked over to Bob and gently took the water hose from his hand. Bob didn't even show notice of Joshua standing next to him.

Joshua began to explain to Bob resignedly and with great morose, "You know, man, these hate groups have been around since just after the civil war. They believe the white man is this unconquerable race and should be the most powerful race on earth. The burning cross wasn't originally intended to intimidate, but instead to honor the traditions of past Scottish clansmen. They used it as a symbol of faith for their journey into battle and also to warn enemies who brought battle to them. Yeah, man, after the civil war, the burning of the cross was intended to intimidate and warn those minorities, especially the black man, not to go against the Klan. It very quickly became a symbol of hate and represented the ignorance of the people of the South, at that time. It was meant to strike fear into blacks through violence and intimidation. So you see, Bob, it had a religious meaning centuries ago, but now all that has been so grossly distorted, just to spread their evil and make a statement."

At the same time, the fire department and the Baton Rouge police arrived, with full lights and sirens.

As the two officers approached Bob and Joshua, Bob shot visual daggers at both of them and snidely remarked, "Good timing, guys, but you missed the show."

Bob walked away and back into Nick's room, as Nick, Joshua, Darnell, and Len started to give their story of the cross burning to the officers.

The fire department watered down the burnt cross until it was cooled completely, and then they removed it from the property. The police simply told them, because there was no eyewitness to the event, it was going to be hard to find the ones responsible for the event.

Not surprised at all, Joshua and Darnell turned and went back to the room.

That same night in Bel Air, Haddie was watching the nightly news, which she had always done before she turned the TV off and went to sleep. To her surprise, the story of a burning cross at a hotel in Baton Rouge came on. The news story was picked up by every major station in the country and went nationwide that same night.

Haddie gasped and instantly started yelling for Corey to come to her room, which was off the back of the kitchen. "Ms. Corey! Come quickly! On the TV! Oh, hurry, Ms. Corey! Oh my god. It's the band!"

Corey came running through the kitchen to where Haddie's room was. Her heart was racing, and she was frantic with fear. When she heard it was about the band, terror was struck in her heart as she hurriedly made her way to sit at the end of Haddie's bed, watching the TV.

She saw the reporter standing in front of the burning cross, and she fatalistically whispered, "Oh my god. This can't be happening!"

They both sat watching Doug and Darnell yelling at the reporter. Corey, now worried beyond belief, thought to herself, *Where's Bob? What's happened to him? Come on, show me Bob. I know he's there!*

Then the camera switched angles and caught Bob moving quickly to take the van to a safer spot. Corey breathed a huge sigh of relief but never took her eyes off of the TV.

The camera followed Bob as he took the water hose from the night manager and began to extinguish the flames shooting from the top of the cross.

Corey held her breath, while nervously running her index finger continually over her bottom lip, as Haddie tried to calm her by stating, "Don't worry, Ms. Corey. It looks like Mr. Bob's got everything under control… I just wish I knew where my boy was."

Then the news footage of the event showed Joshua walking up to Bob and talking with him. Haddie joyously yelled out, "There's Joshua! There's my boy. He's okay. Thank you, Lord, for that! Thank you!"

Corey had a single tear run down her cheek as she forlornly told Haddie, "I haven't talked with Bob since Wednesday, and it's now Saturday, the night before their concert in Baton Rouge. That just isn't like him to not call me, especially if they're having trouble of any kind."

Haddie tried to console Corey and reassured her, "I know he'll call you, Ms. Corey. Mr. Bob won't like you worrying about the band like this. Maybe he'll call tomorrow before their concert. Them having to get these new hotels down South has really made it difficult on everyone. Don't worry, Ms. Corey, I know they have control of this, because they're all young, strong, and intelligent young men. And besides, they only have two more concerts in the Deep South, and then they start moving north after Alabama."

Corey's faculties became numb and unresponsive as she was terrified with fear; she then answered Haddie, "Two more down there is what I'm afraid of."

The Owls had mentally readied themselves for the concert that Sunday night at the Varsity Concert Hall in Baton Rouge, Louisiana. Every one of them maintained their cool but knew the strength and numbers of their security force was going to be tested this night.

Bob tried to assure the guys by discussing the matter in a commendably responsible fashion, while traveling to the concert hall, "We are not going to give these hate-mongers any more of our time. I want every one of you to just do your thing out there tonight, and don't be bummed out. We have a lot of good people out in the audience, and by God, we're going to show them a great time. Now, are you with me, brothers?"

Every guy shouted, "Hell yes! We're ready! No sweat! Let's go."

When the van reached the concert hall, Joshua and Darnell wanted to get out in front of the hall and take a look at the marquee; they hadn't yet seen the name of the band in lights on a venue's front marquee.

Truman stopped the van, and Joshua and Darnell got out and was admiring "The Night Owls, June 19, 8 p.m. SOLD OUT."

Darnell put his hand out to Joshua, and in a very soulful and prideful gesture, both men slipped each other some skin.

Two of the hall's maintenance men came out and boldly stepped up to the two black men admiring the marquee and ordered, "Hey, you two darkies. You need to use the back entrance. There's a separate door for all y'all coloreds."

Darnell looked at the two husky, unkempt white men with disgust and audaciously told them while pointing at the marquee, "Listen, man, we're members of the Night Owls, and we'll go in any damned door we want!"

The guys began to pile out of the van after having heard the verbal exchange out in front of the hall. Len inquisitively asked the men, "What's the problem here, guys?"

The taller of the two men, with a shaggy beard and a cigarette hanging from his mouth, daringly stated, "The two coloreds have to enter through their own door in back. Rules are rules. Got it?"

Bob and Len had to hold Doug and Darnell back from knocking these two guys on their ass. Then mockingly, Bob smirked at them while shaking his head from side to side and told the Owls, "All right, guys. Let's go in through the back. You know, rules are rules."

Nick told Truman, "Drive the van to the back, but the other seven of us will walk, and we'll all enter through the back door with our pride and brotherhood intact."

The maintenance man took the cigarette from his mouth and directed his comment to Bob, "Hey, you white boys can go in through the front. It's only the darkies that go around back."

Joshua stepped up and admonished the two men by stating, "The renowned social activist and Baptist leader, Martin Luther King, Jr., has said, and will keep saying, 'It's not possible to be in favor of justice for some people and not be in favor of justice for all people.' You men will find that hate is too great a burden to bear… We're all brothers deep down in our souls, guys."

Len swung his arm around Joshua's shoulders and then turned him to start walking around to the back of the building and out of sight of the two maintenance men.

The two men seemed a bit disgruntled and then just shrugged their shoulders and laughed to one another.

After all eight of the guys went in through the "coloreds only" door, they began to check out their instruments and ran another sound check on them.

Ticket holders were starting to fill the seats; of course, the coloreds were seated up in the balcony and the whites on the main floor. All the guys were still ticked off about that, and their anger remained constant.

By eight o'clock that Sunday night, the seats in the concert hall were filled. Security was thick and surrounding the interior of the hall. There were just a few security men out back maintaining the safety of the two vans.

Jimmy, sitting at his drums and who was now behind the curtain with the rest of the guys, grew anxious and fearful. Instead of his fear receding from last night's cross-burning experience, it seemed to be intensifying. He was the shortest and closest to not being physically or athletically prone to self-defense, so he was praying there would be no trouble tonight of any kind.

All of a sudden, a commanding voice came over the loudspeaker, and the din of the audience quieted as the voice announced, "Tonight, here at the Varsity Concert Hall, we're bringing you a very popular and talented group from LA—the Night Owls!"

When the curtain went up, Jimmy's inherent musical ability kicked into high gear, when he sounded out the four-count with his sticks attacking the snare.

The crowd gave them a thunderous welcoming. There was a resounding din of cheering, whistling, and applause through the concert hall as all the Owls now tore into the song "Raging Fire."

The concert went remarkably well, and the Owls played all of their newest material. After two and a half hours, they quitted the stage, but were cheered to come back out and play two more songs. When they finished their encores, they were exiting the stage waving their hands and throwing kisses to the young ladies, both white and black.

After the final curtain came down and the instruments were loaded into the waiting van, the eight guys were met in the back of the concert hall by a couple dozen guys looking to break open a few heads.

The few security guards that were in the back watching over the vans tried their best to get the crowd dispersed, but to no avail. At that point, one of the concert hall security men ran inside and called for the police.

The crowd was pushing toward the seven guys, for Nick had told Truman to get into the van with the instruments and just take off toward Birmingham, Alabama. As the tires squealed on the asphalt, Truman quickly accelerated the van and was headed out and onto the main street leading into the downtown area of Baton Rouge.

The hate-mongers kept making their way closer to the guys who were blocked from getting into the passenger van. The crowd was all screaming accusations and offensive denunciations and still moving closer to the band members.

Only dimly aware of the sound of a police siren, Bob suddenly saw Darnell wade into the crowd and knock out the first three men he could reach. Being young, strong, and six foot three certainly helped Darnell lay his fist into these men.

Nick yelled at Darnell, "What the hell do you think you're doing? You're gonna get yourself killed!"

Darnell said something to the effect, "It's them or us, man!" Then the siren whooped again, but was much closer and pulled into the drive behind the guys' van.

Although Bob and Doug were trying to assist Darnell, in Bob's subconscious mind, this was distantly playing out like they were still in high school; and ineffectually and ordinarily, they just played their instruments and then, after class, ended up at the corner malt shop putting moves on the skirts.

However, this night they possessed the determination of gladiators, but were terrified by the chaos around them. Bob and Doug still went into the crowd swinging. Some people went to the pavement bloodied, and Bob and Doug were no exceptions. They quickly got up and back on their feet and continued to knock men out of their way.

Len and Joshua told Jimmy to go back inside the hall. They'd come and get him when they cleared a path to the van. That's when Len and Joshua strode into the screaming mob and shoved a few people aside on their way to help and rescue Darnell, Bob, and Doug.

Darnell, Bob, and Doug looked shaken, but not injured, except for a few scratches and minor cuts.

All Darnell could yell at Bob was "I'm sure as hell glad to see you guys!"

At the concert hall's rear entrance, it seemed like a war zone, as the two cars of police officers emptied out and ran into the crowd of men, handcuffing a few and pushing the bulk of the crowd away from the hall's back entrance.

The Owls and Nick managed at last to squeeze out of the crowd of men. The sound level of the raucous assault decreased with the appearance of the police, or maybe it was just from the Owls breaking heads open or the fact of Nick constantly screaming for the guys to get into the waiting van.

The moral ugliness of all this just infuriated Bob; galvanized by loathing, he started to move away quietly to the van, but as he turned, his voice rose, and he yelled, "Is this shit for real?"

The local BR police chief, Lyle Douglas, called his battalion sergeant over to him and asked him earnestly, "I believe we've seen enough here. Is this what you call securing an area?"

His young subordinate sergeant showed his frustration in his expression of futility, "I did everything in my power to make this area secure."

Chief Douglas addressed his sergeant, "Let's handle first things first, sergeant. What do you intend to do with the knuckleheads and his friends you have in handcuffs? Are you gonna charge them with inciting a riot? Or are you going to let them stink up the county jail for a couple of nights?"

The besieged sergeant answered dutifully, "Probably just let 'em get themselves under control by gracing our lockup for a few nights. That is unless these band members want to press charges."

Nick, Bob, and Darnell looked at one another, and out of pure exasperation, Darnell turned toward the van and quickly threw his opened hand toward the sergeant. He walked away feeling helpless and always the underdog.

Nick looked at Bob for an answer, and all Bob could do was throw both his hands in the air; and trying to ascribe meaning to the event, he frustratedly told them, "Do what you want with them. We really don't give a damn."

One of the hotheaded, discriminating, and foulmouthed young men yelled out, "Yeah, how about you charge these monkeys and their monkey-lovers with assault? You just can't let that one big nigger go free. He knocked out cold two of my boys."

The chief sarcastically answered him, "Then maybe it might have been a good idea if you boys would have just stayed home tonight instead of inciting a riot and disturbing the peace."

Chief Douglas turned his focus on the band members and resolutely told them, "I'm not going to charge you fellas with anything, so go on and get out of here. I hope you have better luck down the line, but I wouldn't count on it until you drive north of the Mason-

Dixon." The chief turned to his sergeant and yelled, "Throw 'em into lockup, and charge 'em with disturbing the peace...a week in jail might take a little bit out of 'em, but I'm not sure."

The guys all got in the van for the drive of five and a half hours and four hundred miles to Birmingham, Alabama.

There was a deafening silence amongst the guys, when Doug spoke up and angrily stated, "We should have cracked a few more heads than we did. They had it coming!"

Bob looked at Doug in a disquieting manner and quietly scolded, "Then we would have been just as evil and ignorant as they were."

Bob then sat back in his van seat and knew now he had to call Corey, because he felt this incident would also end up on the nightly news. He wasn't trying to scare her or conceal what had been going on by not keeping in touch with her, but only trying to take instinctive and immediate measures to ensure the safety of his brothers.

Truman met up with the other seven guys in Birmingham, as the new *Green Book* hotel was written into his book he had in the van, along with the instruments the van carried.

It was almost seven o'clock Monday morning, and too early to check into their rooms, so the guys found an acceptable restaurant on the south side of the city to catch some breakfast.

After breakfast, they ventured over to the Birmingham Music Hall, where they would be performing the Tuesday, June 21, concert. After dropping off their instruments and running a sound check on them, they checked out the beautiful multitiered concert venue, for which they'd be playing to 6,200 fans tomorrow night. Satisfied with everything, they drove the twenty miles back to their hotel.

Being able to check in, they all took showers, doctored their wounds from the previous night, and lay down to take a well-deserved nap. That is, all except Bob. He left Len napping on his bed to go to the office and make a phone call to Corey. It now being after nine o'clock that morning, he only hoped Corey had not yet left for the studio.

The phone rang four times, and to Bob's delight and surprise, someone picked up the receiver. Haddie's voice came through loud and clear, "Hello, this is Ms. Madrigal's residence. How may I help you?"

Sad and in need of Corey's love and attention, Bob depressingly asked Haddie, "Hello, Ms. Haddie. This is Bob calling from Birmingham, Alabama. How are you doing this morning? I thought maybe I could catch Corey and you up on what's been going on with the band."

Haddie didn't hesitate in telling him, "Oh, Mr. Bob, I'm so glad to hear your voice. We've seen the news stories on the trouble you young men have had along the way. I know Joshua must be all right, or you woulda told me by now."

"Oh, Haddie, Joshua is just fine, and what a brave man you have there as your son… No one is hurt, except for maybe a few scratches and minor cuts, but we as a band of brothers are looking out for each other and trying our damnedest to keep everyone safe."

Haddie, feeling greatly relieved, reminded Bob, "Just one more concert down there in the land of hate and bigotry, and then you young men can push your way up to the North."

"You're so right, Haddie. Now will you tell Corey for me that everyone is fine and I look so forward to having her fly into New York to be with me on July 3. Okay?"

"All right, Mr. Bob. I know she'll just be crazy glad you called and that everyone is fine."

Before Bob hung up, he quietly told Haddie, "You tell Corey I love her more than my own life, and I'll be holding her, kissing her, and loving her before she knows it… Thanks, Haddie."

Haddie's eyes started to fill with unshed tears when she sweetly told him, "I'll tell her everything, Mr. Bob. Now all of you, please, take care."

"Absolutely. Now goodbye, Ms. Haddie."

"Goodbye, Mr. Bob. God bless all you young men."

"Thank you so much, Haddie." He then softly replaced the receiver.

Haddie hung up the phone and immediately tried to get in touch with Corey at the studio. She thought she could relieve a lot of

Corey's worry and trepidation if she let her know things were not as bad as what was shown on the TV news station.

Corey was in wardrobe, getting fitted by Orry-Kelly for the stylish outfits she'd be wearing in her intriguing movie, *Beneath the Sullen Sky*, when the production manager entered the room and told Corey, "Corey? Your maid is on the phone for you. She says it's important that you take this call. It's in the director's room."

Terror could be seen in Corey's eyes as she ran from wardrobe, not caring she only had on her undergarments and her slip. The phone in the director's room was one door down, and she prayed no one else would be in the room with her.

When she raced into the room, she was alone. She could see the phone receiver was laid sideways on the desk. She stared at it for a couple seconds, with her heart pounding so loud she thought she could actually hear it over the silence of the room. After taking the few steps over to the receiver, Corey picked it up and hurriedly put it to her ear; and silently praying, she begged Haddie, "Oh, Haddie, please tell me something that's going to make my day, please!"

Haddie tried to calm her fears by explaining to Corey, "Ms. Corey, everything is all right. All the young men are just fine. Mr. Bob said there was only a few scratches and minor cuts, but it's not as bad as the news stories that are being released to the networks."

"Oh, thank God for that! Why didn't he call me sooner than this? I need to talk to him myself, or I'm going to go crazy!"

Knowing this would placate Corey, Haddie gave her the rest of Bob's message. "Ms. Corey, he told me to tell you something."

Corey anxiously and loudly asked Haddie, "Oh my god! What else did he tell you, Haddie?"

"Mr. Bob told me he couldn't wait for when you came to meet him in New York, and then he whispered to me to tell you he loves you more than his own life. And he'd be holding you, kissing you, and loving you before you know it…and then we said our goodbyes. Lord, Ms. Corey! I'd wet myself if a man ever told me that! You got yourself a good one, Ms. Corey!"

There was a deafening silence on the other end of the phone as Haddie kept listening for Corey's response.

Finally, when Corey answered back, Haddie could hear her voice breaking as she confirmed, "No, Haddie. I have the best… there is!"

After Bob hung up the phone having talked with Haddie, he walked slowly back to his room, contemplating and yearning for the second he would have Corey back in his arms again.

The rest of Monday and most of the day on Tuesday, the guys just hung out at the hotel, except to go out and eat. Nick told them, "You guys are just too recognizable to be hanging out around the city of Birmingham. There might just be people who would be looking for you, and I absolutely know that trouble would ensue."

All the guys, except Doug, called their wives, fiancées, or girlfriends sometime during the remainder of Monday or on Tuesday, before they had to leave for the concert.

Bob decided he would wait to call Corey after the Birmingham concert and the group had driven to the airport to fly on to their next venue up in Charlotte, North Carolina. For she would still be at the studio when the Owls were scheduled to take the stage.

The evening of the concert, the two vans pulled up in front of the music hall, and they were met by a row of thirty to fifty police officers holding rifles and billy clubs and waiting for them.

The officers escorted the six-member rock 'n' roll group to its dressing room and gave strict instructions: The black performers were to make eye contact with only the black fans, who were confined to the balcony, and not with whites on the floor.

The police would be all over the main floor of the hall and making sure the two black members of the band did not look at any white person, most especially the white women.

It was a rule they were told by the police sergeant, as he lectured the guys. "I don't want to see either of you two darkies looking at the white women out there. If you do, and you're caught, your ass is mine!"

Bob looked at Nick incredulously and, upset beyond belief, screamed, "Let's just get the hell out of here! This is just a bunch of shit!"

Nick walked over to Bob and calmly told him, "Don't think I hadn't tried to cancel this concert after what we'd gone through in Baton Rouge. The sad fact of the matter is we're irrevocably committed to perform tonight—it's in our contract. Only an act of God or Mother Nature could cancel this show."

All the guys had a great amount of apprehension written across their faces as they exchanged tentative stares with one another.

It was at this point Bob yelled to them with boldness, "By the grace of God, we've made it this far, and with the grace of God, we're gonna perform this concert to the best of our abilities! Remember, guys? If one of us goes down, all of us goes down. And tonight, none of us is going anywhere but to the airport after we finish burning down this son-of-a-bitchin' stage."

The guys were all yelling loudly and agreeing with Bob as they raised their clenched fists all in unison and began slapping hands together and slipping skin to each other.

There was fire in Bob's eyes as he was hell-bent in awaiting the threatening trouble but was ready to just spit in the devil's face. "Now, my brothers, let's go give 'em hell."

A few minutes before the start of their performance, the Owls were readying themselves backstage for the curtain to open. There was an atmosphere of heightened tension amongst the guys. Most especially Darnell and Joshua.

Nick apologetically told Darnell and Joshua before he had to vacate the stage, "I know this is a frontal assault on everything you know to be good and decent, but just remember, guys, this will be the last time you'll ever have to put up with this evil anymore. Believe me!"

Darnell reassured Nick, "It's cool, my brother. That's why we're here, man. To make a dent in this shithole and give 'em an idea about what's going down."

The curtain then opened, as Nick just got off the stage in time. There was a loud and tumultuous roar from the fans, both black and white. They were screaming, whistling, and applauding their approval for the Owls, as Jimmy hit the four-count on his snare. The guys instantly ripped into "Stronger than You Think."

All of their fans were keeping beat either with their bobbing heads, their stomping feet, or clapping their hands together to the rhythm of the song.

The Birmingham police were placed around the stage area as well as up the sides of the lower-level walls. They seemed to be fixated on Darnell's and Joshua's eye movements, but the two of them had already agreed they would only be looking at each other during every song. Darnell was turned sideways, so he stared at Joshua the whole time while, when playing his trumpet, Joshua was only looking at Darnell.

By the start of their second song, "Ricochet," Bob had noticed the police had squeezed out almost all the security forces on the main floor. There was no security men at the front of the stage between the band and the audience. This seemed to negate the whole concept of safety.

Bob looked over at Len, and with a nod of his head, he pointed it out to Len the absence of a security force down in front. When they ended their song, Len took the guitar strap off his shoulder and placed his guitar in a guitar stand. As the audience was very noisy, and giving the Owls an uproarious applause, along with screeching their assent, Len casually walked off stage directly toward Nick.

Len and Bob absolutely knew that logic demanded it, and intuition screamed it, that security had to be stationed at the front of the stage at all times.

Nick immediately ran to find his twelve-man privately hired security force.

Len returned to the stage and was strapping his guitar once more over his shoulder. He checked out every band member's face, and all he could read from their eyes was a very disquieting tension that had blanketed the band's demeanor.

These six men derive the old, primitive reassurance from one another's company that four of them have enjoyed since college; if anything makes them a touch uneasy, it would be for a good cause.

Bob saw Len nod his head once affirmatively toward him, so he gave the guys a guitar lead-in to "Let Me Lay within Your Arms." Joshua was unleashing his favorite mistress, the bass trumpet. The roll of her loud, deep rage moaned and echoed throughout the hall. Bob's vocal entrance into the song was very provocative, and with that beautiful baritone voice, all the young women in the audience were swooning, and some sat crying with tears running down their cheeks.

Nick was told by his private security force that they wouldn't be needed because of the numerous police officers inside the building. Nick then told them to post themselves around the vans in back of the hall. Out back was where all twelve of them headed.

The entire concert was going very well, and when it ended, their fans called them back out onstage to play two more encores.

Not even thirty minutes later, there was relative silence in the hall. The instruments were loaded into the one van, with Truman driving them directly to the airport.

The Owls all started out the back door of the hall and saw their own security force standing around the vans and up close to the exit door.

It was at that moment a mob of at least twenty to thirty guys came from around the corner of the back of the hall and rushed at them. It looked to the Owls like some were carrying clubs and knives. The security men tried to push and beat the crowd of men back, but a couple of them were knocked to the ground, and the mob just walked by them.

Nick yelled to Truman, "Get the hell outta here! We'll meet up with you later!"

Truman gunned the engine, and the wheels spun in place squealing for a second, and then the van took off out onto the main drag and flew out of town like a bat out of hell.

Doug and Darnell, with the foolishness and bravery of their youth, met the crowd head-on. They were both knocking down some of the men in the mob but caught a few punches upside their own heads and bodies.

Bob's heart took a sudden hard leap in his chest, seeming to knock against the left side of his rib cage like a fist. The beads of sweat on his forehead had swelled and broken and gone running down his face like tears.

Bob advanced slowly, but not hesitantly, into a group of about five disgusting, narrow-minded bigots; a few were missing the full complement of teeth, but seeming incompetent and outright dangerous, nonetheless.

One in the small group took a swing at Bob, and even though Bob preferred to break his nose, he contented himself with a hard punch to the guy's stomach. The big awkward idiot clutched his gut and folded in half and then fell to the ground. His face had turned a blushing red, and he gasped and struggled for breath. His face registered shock and disbelief.

The security men mixed with the Owls' attempt to thwart this attack, and they worked at getting themselves the hell out of there. There were a lot of men dropping to the pavement, but mostly they were the attackers hitting the ground.

After Len joined Bob, they both began to knock some heads together in the crowd. They were both receiving glancing blows from a few of them, but nothing monumentally damaging.

A jarring chill ran through Bob as he heard a scream that was so guttural, it was almost like a moan. It came again, a cry of pure agony. He turned, leaving Joshua to help Len.

Bob screamed at the top of his lungs, "And what about Jimmy?"

His voice still tempered, he loudly exclaimed to anyone that would listen, "Where the hell is he? Where is Jimmy?"

Instantly, Bob saw his small, thin, and innocent brother Jimmy slumped to the ground with two huge-muscled men hovering over him. Witnessing this, Bob went on full throttle.

Bob could feel blood running down his own chin after he had bitten into a fount of blood. He still continued to quickly move to Jimmy as he leapt at both men. He knocked one down and started hammering the other's face with his right fist balled up tightly. With all the ferocious anger that was running through his veins like electricity, he jumped the other man on the ground and began pummeling him with both fists simultaneously. The man was rendered unconscious and bleeding profusely from his face.

The next thing Bob could remember was being hit in the back of the head with some kind of small pipe or stick. He fell off the unconscious man and crumpled to the ground. There was now blood running down his shirt and saturating his back. His lip was split and was bleeding down his chin. There was also a laceration on his cheek that had smeared his entire face; he was hurt, but not out of it yet.

Managing to surmount his trauma, Bob slowly opened his eyes as the sounds of struggle reached him with angry shouts from the small bunches of men. His initial response was a deep, sharp intake of breath while he resolutely ignored his own mental voice, which told him he was being dangerously stupid.

As he looked around him, he could see Doug was in need of help. With a supreme act of will, Bob got himself up and staggered over to help Doug.

Upon reaching Doug, Bob knocked two men out cold—one with Jack's suggested uppercut to the underside of his chin, and the other with a hard right cross to his temple, aside his head. Bob then helped Doug up and walked him over to the van. Two security guys took over Bob's and Doug's places.

After Bob got an obviously injured Doug into the van, he noticed someone had already put Jimmy into the van. He was lying unconscious on the back floor. Alarmed, this struck terror into Bob's heart. He knew they had to get to a hospital soon.

When Bob saw one of the security men, he screamed, "Jesus Christ, this is intolerable!"

The security man yelled back, "We're doing the best we can!"

Bob screamed back with infuriated rage, "Your best isn't worth a shit. This is an emergency. I want you to make your son-of-a-bitching security men move and help us get the hell outta here!"

Bob was not used to giving verbal lashings to anyone, unless they deserved it, but this was an unprecedented situation.

Joshua could see Bob gritting his teeth, the redness of the rage in his face merging into the redness of the sunburn on his neck, and the veins in his neck bulging from the fury within him.

The entire situation was so precarious.

There were indeed daunting considerations, although hardly more formidable than getting all the guys out of this alive.

The police had finally moved out in back of the music hall with a glacial lack of haste. They began putting the cuffs on a handful of the mob. Bob saw they had handcuffed a big, robust guy with blond hair who had the relatively insolent grin that showcased his face. It was the man that was standing over an injured Doug just seconds ago. Bob slowly walked over to him. When he reached him, the guy just laughed in Bob's face. That's when quickly and with full force, Bob swung his iron fist into his face and watched him plummet to the ground, moaning loudly, as his bleeding nose started to form a puddle of blood in front of him.

One cop walked up and looked at the big guy on the ground and then turned to Bob, and very impressed, he commendably remarked, "Damn! Good one, man!"

With great animosity in his voice, Bob looked at the officer and firmly stated, "That was nice of you guys to finally do your job and quit hawking my two black brothers, who were just doing their job!"

The cop answered defensively, "Hey, man. We were told to secure the interior and front of the structure. Then we heard the ruckus out here and came running."

Indignantly, Bob added, as he started to walk away, "Yeah, I get it, man. Don't worry, I know exactly what you were doing. You cops are just all show and no go. You're wasted!"

By the time the TV news cameras made it to the scene of the conflict, there were just a few isolated incidents here and there. The police and security detachment almost had control of the situation when Bob noticed Joshua struggling with two men by the back door of the hall. They were getting the best of him as Joshua was trying to block their punches.

Bob's heart started beating hard again—hard enough to start the prominent vein in the center of his forehead pulsing. But with wet terrified eyes, and his indomitable courage under fire, Bob immediately bolted to where Joshua was, and he barreled into the man that was ready to knife Joshua in the stomach.

Bob screamed, enraged with anger, "YOU SON OF A BITCH! I'LL KILL YOU!"

When Bob hit the man with his shoulder, the knife flew out of his hand, cutting Bob on the upper arm. Bob, without constraint or any self-control about him, kept hitting the man in the face until his hand went numb.

Joshua was then able to knock the other man to the ground and began to kick him mercilessly in every part of his body.

Two security men rushed over and pulled Bob off of the bludgeoned man and then grabbed Joshua and pulled him back away from the other semiconscious attacker.

Instinctively, Joshua took Bob in his arms, and the two men held each other with the unmitigated brotherhood they had shared since they met.

Nick had witnessed Bob's unbending courage, his will, and his iron control and could think of no explanation for Bob's recklessness other than moral heroism. Nick drew a parallel with Bob's late father's moral conduct during World War II. Bob's father did not have to go to war, for he was beyond the draft age limit. But when he enlisted, Bob and Elizabeth were without a father for over a year. They were in their young formative years and had suffered emotionally because of their father's patriotism.

Nick had seen what Bob was doing in light of what his father had done, and he realized Bob's actions were self-sacrifice of the highest kind. His character was beyond reproach.

This evening was most definitely Bob's defining moment! How precise a paradigm he had become for the unrelenting chivalry of our times.

There was a trail of blood leaking from Joshua's nose and a red smear darkening his scruff of beard at the corner of his mouth. He also had two eyebrow ridge cuts that were trickling blood into the line of his beard.

Bob was saturated with his own blood loss, and that of some of his attackers'. He had several minor cuts on his body, one laceration on his arm, a gash on his shoulder, and the knot on the back of his lower skull, which was still oozing blood into his already-blood-soaked shirt.

When Joshua and Bob broke their embrace, Bob led Joshua over to the van. As all the guys slowly climbed into the van, Bob grabbed one of the security men and yelled, "Get in, and drive us to the main hospital in town…NOW!"

One of the police officers heard Bob and yelled, "Just follow me!"

Without hesitation, the man started the van and quickly got behind the police car, which was running full lights and sirens. In a matter of minutes, they were pulling up to the emergency entrance to the UAB Hospital in South Birmingham. The officer raced from his vehicle inside to get doctors and nurses to come out and help the guys.

The officer told Nick and Bob, "You're not gonna find a better hospital than this… This is the University of Alabama at Birmingham Hospital, and I know they'll take good care of y'all… I'm sorry for everything that went down tonight."

Nick told the officer, "Thanks, man. It's too bad the whole force isn't like you."

Bob just glared at the officer, but he finally nodded his appreciation to him as he helped his brothers out of the van.

The nurses carefully loaded Jimmy onto a gurney and quickly moved him into an emergency room examining area.

The rest of the guys were split up among the doctors and nurses; Nick was x-rayed and told he had a sprained right shoulder and wrist. He would be in a sling for a couple of weeks. He also had some bruising and a few cuts that didn't require any stitches.

Joshua had a split lip and two eyebrow ridge cuts that needed a couple of stitches apiece. He also had bruising and minor cuts that were cleaned and bandaged.

Darnell suffered a physical wound to his left eye. After x-rays, he was told he would just have a blackened eye, along with redness and some pain, for which he would receive some pain control medication. He was also treated for bruising and minor cuts.

After Len's painful nose was x-rayed, he was told his nose was broken, so they packed it with heavy gauze and readied him for a "closed reduction surgery." A doctor would give him a local anesthetic to numb his nose, and then manually he would realign it and then bandage it.

Doug was suffering from an intense headache. After x-rays, he was told he had a grade-2, moderate concussion. The symptoms would last no more than twelve hours and involve no loss of consciousness. He would have headaches, some confusion, and dizziness, but would be good enough to go back to play his sax in about a week.

Bob's x-rays revealed he had a mild head injury, with a raised, swollen area around the main bump. There was a cut down the middle, and it took six stitches to close it. He also had bruising, minor cuts, a laceration on his left arm, and a gash on his shoulder that would have to be sutured. With a few more stitches elsewhere, he was more than ready to head north.

In the Deep South of the fifties and early sixties, the radical whites had a taste for unruliness, distortion, the unpredictable; and the lawless would take root here and luxuriate.

All the guys but Jimmy were done being x-rayed, poked, prodded, and stitched up. After they all came together in the waiting room, Nick informed them, "We haven't heard anything about Jimmy yet, but I'm going to tell the five of you right now that I'm canceling our second show in Charlotte, North Carolina, just as I canceled the second show in each of New Orleans, Baton Rouge, and most especially Birmingham. We will also have only one show in Atlantic City, New Jersey. That will give you guys a little more of a break before we play New York City. I'm going to call and cancel just our airline tickets and have Truman paged over the intercom. I'll tell him to fly into Charlotte and wait for us no matter how long it takes us to get out of here. Now you guys sit tight until we hear about Jimmy. We'll then decide what we're gonna do."

When Nick left the guys in the waiting room, he went to make his phone calls.

There were moans and groans as the five of them sat down to emotionally collect themselves. This just wasn't an eventuality that they had expected, and nowhere could any of them find solace from the prevalent gloom.

Bob sat staring at the floor with obvious abandon as his mind was struggling for purchase of his thoughts. It was purely incomprehensible violence and hate they had just experienced, and it was psychologically very disconcerting to even think about.

Half an hour later, Nick returned to the waiting room and asked Bob, "Has anyone come out yet and said anything about Jimmy?"

Bob just looked up at Nick and despondently shook his head softly from side to side. He then returned his stare back to the floor in front of him.

It was now two o'clock, Thursday morning, in Birmingham, Alabama. Finally, a tall, middle-aged, white-haired doctor approached the group of guys waiting for the news about Jimmy. He was dressed in full scrubs, right down to the floor, and wore a very multicolored surgical cap over his head. This scared every one of the guys beyond belief.

The doctor inquired, "Are all of you here for Mr. James Wisner?"

Bob and Nick answered together, "Yes. Jimmy Wisner. How is he, Doctor?"

The doctor seemed a bit anxious but informed them, "Well, I'm Doctor Gladwin, and I need to tell you we felt he had internal bleeding, so we quickly performed an emergency lower GI endoscopy procedure on Mr. Wisner. We detected where the acute bleeding was and the cause. He was experiencing left arm and shoulder pain, and his abdomen was very rigid, which means there's probably damage to his spleen. This will require emergency surgery. If not repaired or removed, the damaged spleen could be life-threatening. We're preparing him for surgery as we speak. The procedure will take two to four hours to perform, depending on the amount of damage. It's called a laparoscopic splenectomy. He'll have to be hospitalized for one to two days… Okay. I'll talk with you again after the procedure."

After the doctor walked away, Nick, without hesitation, told the guys, "Damn! Why Jimmy? I'm just going to have to cancel everything up to New York City. That will give us twelve days for rest and recuperation."

Len spoke up, suggesting, "We could just reschedule those four concerts and tell the ticket holders to just hang on to their tickets until then."

Nick agreed with Len and then informed the guys, "I'm going to stay here with Jimmy, and I'll have the plane tickets for the five of you ready at the airport. You're going to just fly into New York City and stay there until we perform at Madison Square Garden on July 5. I'll bring Jimmy with me in a couple of days."

Bob interrupted by saying, "Anyone who wants to can stay with me at the penthouse in Manhattan. There's plenty of room."

Doug turned his head toward Bob and, with drowsy eyes, told him, "We can all stay there tonight, but Len and I will probably go and visit with our families for a few days."

Bob nodded his head in agreement. "Okay, guys. You do what you need to do. You know better about how you feel than I do."

The same officer that led the van to the hospital came back in and consolingly told them, "I just got word on my radio that there are seven of those guys that will come up on charges of assault with intent to commit bodily harm and also aggravated assault… I guess there will be four of your security force that will press charges and testify against these men.

"So, I hope that brings some comfort and feelings of justice being done to all of you… Again, I'm terribly sorry for what went down."

The police officer turned and exited the hospital as the six men just stared at him with a numbness in their hearts and a burning anger in their souls.

Nick said his temporary goodbyes to the guys and then went to call Truman and the two concert venues to reschedule. Bob, Len, Joshua, Darnell, and Doug took a taxicab to the airport. They would have an hour to kill before their plane took off for New York City.

Even though it was well after midnight in Bel Air, Bob felt he needed to hear Corey's voice right now, more than anything else in the world.

EIGHTEEN

Bob located a phone in the airport lounge. He sidled up to the end of the bar and asked the bartender if he could make a long-distance call on the bar's phone as he waved a twenty-dollar bill at him.

The bartender hastened over and grabbed the twenty out of Bob's hand and told him in a relaxed manner, "No sweat, man."

Having ordered a beer earlier, Bob put the bottle to his mouth and chugged over half of it all at once. He then slowly dialed his home phone number.

On the second ring, Corey picked up, and Bob heard the most beautiful sound in the world. "Hello. Please let this be Bob!"

He threw his head back, pursed his lips, as his eyes began to moisten. He quickly regained his composure and resignedly whispered, "Hello, baby."

Corey could hear the desperation in his voice, and it scared the hell out of her. On the brink of tears, she begged him, "Why haven't you called me, darling? I have been worried sick over you. Are you all right, Bob? I heard you guys ran into a buzzsaw down there...but are you okay?"

A single tear ran down Bob's cheek as he told Corey, with his voice crackling with emotional static, "Well, Doug has a concussion, Len has a broken nose, Nick has a sprained right shoulder and wrist, Joshua has a split lip and facial cuts, and Darnell has a black eye. We all have cuts and bruises, but I'm okay…oh, yeah, and Jimmy is in emergency surgery right now to maybe remove his spleen."

"Oh my god! Baby, are you sure you're all right? Please tell me if you're not! Bob, please!"

Corey needed him to be all right, so he told her he was, even though he wasn't. He tried to play things down to Corey so she wouldn't worry so much, but she wasn't oblivious and could read between the lines.

Bob, feeling the abysmal and desperate emptiness, explained to her, "We've had to cancel our concerts right up until we play Madison Square Garden, July 5. I'm going to have a couple of the guys staying in the penthouse with me. I hope you don't mind."

Corey was now beside herself as a desperate panic seized her. Bob wasn't sounding like himself, and all of a sudden, she felt like she was talking with a stranger.

Quivering like a tuning fork and crying into the phone, she reassured him, "Of course, I don't mind. That place is both of ours, darling—and I'm coming out there this weekend to be with you. There is no way in hell I'm waiting another week to see you. I'll be there as soon as we wrap up things for this week. All right?"

"Okay, doll." Then Corey heard the phone clicking off at the other end. Her fear came out as unintelligible sobs.

As Corey sat in bed wide awake and still crying, the phone rang again. She quickly picked it up, praying it was Bob calling her back.

She answered, "Bob, is this you, darling?"

The voice at the other end of the line apologetically announced, "No, I'm sorry, Corey. This is Nick."

She interrupted him by inquisitively asking, "Oh my god, Nick. Is it true that Jimmy's in surgery right now and all of you have injuries of some kind? What on earth happened down in Birmingham last night?"

Nick explained to Corey, "I wasn't sure if Bob was going to call you, so I thought I'd let you know about the attack on us as we were leaving the music hall last night."

Corey could not control her surprise and anguish as she shouted, "Attack?"

Nick confirmed, "Yeah. There were around three dozen guys who came at us when we were exiting the hall to go to the airport. Since the police excused the hall's security force, I had to find my private security men and then told them to stay out back by the two vans. It quickly turned into pure chaos as the Owls were literally fighting for their lives."

Corey gasped, slapping her hand to her mouth, and became overcome with tears.

Nick continued, "The security guys were doing what they could, but I gotta tell you, the Owls made waste of a lot of those men who were attacking us. The downside of it all was that Doug and Bob was hit in the head with what looked like a small pipe."

Corey screamed, "In the head? Is Bob all right? He wouldn't tell me what injuries he had."

"Corey, he's got several stitches in the back of the head and here and there on his cheek and arms, but he's physically fine. However, he just doesn't seem himself right now. Last night was a very traumatic time for everyone, but I've got to tell you, Bob handled himself with extreme courage and valor. I know for a fact he saved Joshua's life and probably even Doug's and Jimmy's."

"Oh, Jesus! Oh my god! How did he do that, Nick?"

Nick tried to explain, "There was two guys on Joshua really roughing him up, and one of them had a knife out and was ready to stab him in the stomach. Bob caught sight of this before anyone else could react, and he just threw himself at the guy with the knife.

"Bob knocked the knife from his hand, but the blade caught Bob's right shoulder. He had to have that sutured."

Corey was weeping uncontrollably. "Oh, my darling man! He is just beyond belief sometimes! My dear god! I must go to him, Nick!"

Nick replied, "They should be in New York City and at the penthouse by eight this morning. All five of them said they would be spending the whole day there. Corey, you really should go and be with Bob. I think he most definitely needs you right now."

"I'll be on the next flight out of LA to New York, Nick. Thank you for calling. And I'm so grateful to you for keeping me apprised of everything. These guys could not have a better person looking over them. I'll probably be bringing all the women with me, and that includes your Charlotte, so we'll see you when you can get Jimmy out of the hospital and into New York."

"Well, thank you, Corey. Jimmy and I should see you Friday night or Saturday morning."

After Corey hung up the phone, she went in and told Haddie the entire story. Haddie was shaken and immediately asked Corey if she could fly to New York with her.

Corey not only booked tickets for herself and Haddie, but those same early morning hours of Thursday, she called and asked Alicia, Deidra, Valerie, and Nick's steady girlfriend, Charlotte, after having explained everything to each one of them, if they wanted to go into New York with her and Haddie just to be with the guys and make sure they were all all right. All four women immediately told her they absolutely needed to go and be with them.

Corey had booked six first-class passages for nine o'clock that morning. Valerie would later drive in from Burbank to Corey and Bob's estate and ride with her and Haddie over to Thousand Oaks to pick up the other three women. Charlotte would drive in to Thousand Oaks from her and Nick's place in Casa Conejo.

There would be six very worried and anxious women flying into New York that Thursday afternoon of June 23.

Earlier that Thursday morning, and before she had flown out of town, Corey raced into Jack's office at Celebrity Studios minutes after he had just arrived himself. When Jack saw how frightened Corey was, he instantly and apprehensively told her in his loud, bellowing manner, "Corey, just go! I'll have Frank [Corey's producer] stop production on the picture until you get back."

Corey looked baffled and couldn't figure out how Jack already knew about the incident in Alabama. So when she started to ask, Jack quickly informed her, "It was a big story on TV's morning news… and I've got to tell you, Corey—it was horrible to watch!"

She exhaled a huge breath as she closed her eyes and threw her head back. Her eyes started to moisten, and her heart grew large in her chest, and the fear almost became overwhelming.

Jack told her again, "Now get outta here! And take as much time as the two of you need."

Corey, without hesitating, hugged Jack and then kissed him on his cheek. She moved quickly from the office to her car, with Curtis waiting for her.

At home, she already had her bags packed and ready to go, for she knew she was leaving sometime today, and no picture shoot or studio executive was going to stop her.

The five Owls landed in New York at seven thirty that Thursday morning. They met up with Truman at LaGuardia airport. He'd been waiting two hours for them to fly in from Birmingham.

Truman had already dropped the instruments off to a storage area at Madison Square Garden, where they would be awaiting the Owls' July 5 and 6 concerts.

At the airport, the six of them were waved over to a limousine that had a sign, "Owls," in the window. Nick had called ahead and ordered the limo for them. Forty minutes later, Bob was introducing all the guys to Rodney as they entered Corey and his penthouse building at Seventy-Fourth Street and Park Avenue.

After the five Owls met Rodney, the six of them journeyed up to the penthouse suite. Doug and Len had already stayed there about a year and a half ago but were still impressed by the size, beauty, and the view from the full-wall window out onto Park Avenue.

Darnell and Joshua were totally blown away by the place when Darnell remarked, "This crib is just outta sight, man. Just way too cool, Bob."

Bob, playing it down some, slightly smiled and said mildly, "Thanks, BB… Now I'm gonna order up some food and drinks for all of us. And if you want, you can all grab a shower in one of the bedrooms across the way. You'll have to sleep two people in two of the bedrooms, and maybe Len, with his broken nose, could have a bed to himself. It's up to you guys. I'm gonna shower in the master suite, and then I'll probably just go out for a walk. I really need to clear my head right now."

All the guys answered affirmatively as they took off in the direction of the three bedrooms.

When everyone was showered and had put on fresh clothing, they threw their bloodstained clothes away—the same clothing they had worn on the plane, to the shock and terror of all the passengers on board.

The omelets, sausages, bacon, scrambled eggs, toast, and English muffins were delivered along with a pot of coffee, a quart of orange juice, and four six-packs of cold beer. The guys dived headlong into the food, and each guy grabbed a couple of beers. Bob sat and immediately chugged a beer and then grabbed another. After he drank the second beer, at a slower pace, he stood up and dutifully said, "I'm gonna go for that walk now. I'll see all of you later."

Len watched Bob leave as Len's face became filled with trepidation, not knowing exactly what was going through Bob's mind. He guessed that maybe he was blaming himself for what happened to the guys, but he couldn't be sure.

After all the guys finished eating, they all crashed in the bedrooms and on the couches and ended up sleeping for hours.

Bob wandered the streets of New York City aimlessly, trying to make sense of what had just happened to the guys. He had no particular destination in mind, except for a place he and Corey used to frequent when they were in the city together. That would be the Bow Bridge, which spanned the Lake in mid-Central Park.

The bridge's architecture made it resemble the bow of an archer or violinist; it was a masterpiece of Victorian-era design and was located not far away from the end of Seventy-Fourth Street in the park.

Bob and Corey considered Central Park their backyard because of the twenty-acre water body, the Lake, was right there, and it provided them a sense of wonder and escape from the urban life. They most especially enjoyed the sunset views the Lake showcased in the early evenings. It was always such a romantic place for them, so Bob instantly started walking to the Bow Bridge. He felt he would feel much closer to Corey if he was at the bridge.

Forty-five minutes later, he reached the bridge. After walking up to the middle and highest point on the bridge, he leaned over the side onto his elbows and bent over staring into the water. He couldn't stop from thinking of the chaotic night before in Birmingham and remembering discordantly but quite definitely about each person's injuries.

Bob thought, *Everything that's happened to me and my guys has been my fault. I promised them they would be safe, but I let them down.* A single tear began to run down his cheek as he was mesmerized by the small ripple of waves cutting through the water, while his eyes were unblinkingly stolid and frozen in time.

Corey and the other five women touched down at LaGuardia at four o'clock that late afternoon. They also brought a limo into Manhattan and arrived at the penthouse at almost five o'clock that evening.

Corey was in such a hurry to get up to the penthouse; she asked Rodney if he would bring everyone's luggage up in a short while. He nodded his head in assent.

All of the women made haste to the elevator, and immediately the button for the eighteenth floor was pushed. The silence among all the women was louder than the muffled, cranking sound of the antique mechanisms of the slow-moving elevator.

When they reached the penthouse, Corey already had her key out and promptly unlocked the door. As she and the other ladies moved quickly into the front room area, Corey saw Len and Truman sitting on the long couch not far from Joshua. Across from them, Doug and Darnell sat in the two lounger chairs. Bob was not to be seen.

Valerie quickly moved to Len and carefully put her arms around him. His eyes were both blackened from the resetting of his nose, but she managed to tenderly kiss him and sympathetically ask, "Are you all right, baby? You sure don't look very good."

With complete control, Len answered Valerie, "I'm okay, Val. I really am."

Deidra also ran to her fiancé, Joshua, with Haddie in tow behind her. Joshua stood up, and the two of them fell into each other's embrace. They held each other for several seconds, then they kissed hard and long. Deidra asked concernedly, "Are you all right, baby? I'm not liking all these stitches I'm seeing. Are you in pain, Joshua?"

Joshua, feeling like his injuries were minor compared to the other guys, told her indifferently, "They're just some cuts. It coulda been so much worse, Deidra." His mind wandered to Bob taking the guy down that was ready to knife him.

When they separated, Joshua put his hand out to Haddie, and she ran into his awaiting arms. She was already crying because she knew Bob had probably saved her son's life last night.

"Oh, Joshua, my baby boy! Thank God you're here and okay! Praise the Lord!"

Alicia was already hugging Darnell. She then kissed him and imploringly asked, "Did a doctor check your eye at the hospital?"

Darnell impassively answered Alicia, "Yeah. There's nothing broken. Just a black eye as a reminder to myself that maybe I should have ducked."

Doug chuckled in a low tone of agreement.

After Corey raced into the bedroom when the women first arrived, she couldn't find Bob anywhere. She did catch a quick glimpse of Bob's blood-soaked clothes in the bathroom wastebasket and momentarily gasped a quick mouthful of air. When she came out of the bedroom, she frantically inquired to the guys, "Has anyone seen Bob? Where is he? I can't find him anywhere."

Joshua spoke up first and, with great empathy toward Corey, said, "Corey? Bob ordered us some breakfast and, of course, some beer. He didn't eat anything, but he had a couple of beers before he told us he needed to take a walk and clear his mind. That was about nine o'clock this morning."

Corey, in disbelief, loudly asked, "THIS MORNING?"

Trying to explain to Corey the best way that he could, Len got up and walked over to her. With great concern in his eyes, he conveyed to a very frightened friend, "Corey, I've known Bob for almost six years now. From the way he was acting, starting at the hospital in

Birmingham, and right through this morning, I think he's probably blaming himself for what happened to all of us last night after the concert. If he would have come back sometime today, we were all going to sit down with him and explain that what happened, no one could have seen it coming. It really wasn't anyone's fault, but I still feel the Birmingham police didn't help the situation by dismissing the music hall's security force. We guessed it was more important that Darnell and Joshua didn't make eye contact with the white women in the audience, and the police only seemed concerned with that. They were only there to supervise and intimidate the two black guys."

Corey was stupefied and incoherent and was really just wondering and asked inquisitively, "To what purpose was the police defending anything at all? It seemed like an act of pure intimidation and hate!"

Darnell, agreeing with her, stated, "That's really all it ever is, is hate, Corey."

Len tried to help her collect her thoughts and suggested, "Do you and Bob have a place you enjoy going to in the city? A place he would find solace? Maybe a quiet, romantic place that would remind him of you… If you need someone to come with you, a couple of us could do that."

Corey was grateful, but she needed to be alone with him right now. She thanked all of them and reassuringly said, "Thanks, but all of you need to rest and relax. I'm pretty sure I know where he might be. I'll bring him home, after I try to relieve him of his heavy heart."

Doug spoke up telling Corey, "None of us are leaving here until Bob comes back."

"I thank all of you very much. Now don't hesitate to call down to Rodney and have him order whatever all of you want for dinner. Please, make yourselves at home."

Corey then raced out of the penthouse and into the elevator. When she hit the street, she headed directly for Central Park and the Lake, which was two avenues west and directly across the street from their penthouse building at Seventy-Fourth Street and Park Avenue.

From experience, Corey knew it would take about seventeen minutes to reach the Lake and her and Bob's favorite spot, Bow

Bridge. This was west of the Bethesda Terrace and connected two points in Central Park together spanning the Lake.

Corey didn't take the time to consider different shoes, and the three-inch-heeled shoes she wore on the plane were starting to cramp her feet. She nevertheless continued on.

From about a hundred yards away, Corey had a clear view from where she was and saw Bow Bridge just two minutes away. There wasn't anyone on the bridge that she could see. She still kept walking, even in pain.

She finally reached the south end of the bridge and anxiously started to walk up the incline of the sixty-foot-long cast-iron structure.

Slightly out of breath, Corey reached the apex of the bridge and saw the legs of what looked like a man leaning over, but he was hidden behind one of the eight flower urns that decorated the top of the railings. She slowly approached him, praying it was Bob. The closer she got, the more she scrutinized the figure.

Now just fifteen feet away, she recognized the man to be Bob. At that very second, her heart went quiet. For a long breathless moment, Corey stood there, and a deep silence fell over her. Her heart was now pounding as she looked at Bob lovingly, and loud enough for him to hear her, she softheartedly said, "I thought maybe I'd find you here."

Bob's heart skipped a beat as he thought he'd heard Corey's voice but couldn't believe it was really her. He didn't expect to see her until the weekend.

He raised his head slowly and prayed it was really her. He quickly jerked his head in the direction from where her voice initiated. When it registered in his floundering brain it was the love of his life, his eyes slowly closed and then reopened with a moistened gleam to them.

His voice broke as he sounded like he was pleading for her, and breathlessly, he whispered, "Oh…Corey!"

She now could clearly see the bloodied gauze taped to his right cheek and the bandage that was wrapped around his wounded right forearm. Through his light-blue rolled-up-sleeve dress shirt, she could also make out the heavy bandage that wrapped his sutured shoulder.

Corey rushed at him with enthusiasm. Her arms were wide open to embrace him. Her face was glistening with tender, heartfelt tears, and toward Bob, she ran with her unbounded love.

Bob wrapped his arms around her waist as she threw her arms around his neck.

They stood tightly holding each other for a couple of minutes. Not either one of them ever wanted to let go of the other.

Bob felt the warmth of her body encompassing him and the magic she cast over him whenever she was in his arms. Corey's body felt heavenly as he closed his eyes and could feel her breasts pressing into his heart.

Corey passionately cried into his ear, "Oh, baby! Just hold me and let me know what's going on, and if I can help you with anything…anything, darling! Just tell me!"

Bob drew his arms back from around her waist, and he lifted his hands to cup her beautifully smooth face. His eyes never left her gaze, as all he could see in her eyes was the love she felt for him. He studied her sensual lips and then moved in to tenderly kiss her.

Corey's hands fell from around his neck to holding onto his forearms. She was careful not to put a hand on any bandage. She then pulled him closer to her and kissed him long and hard. Although she took particular care of his split lip, it seemed to her like she was running through a minefield when it came to holding him, but she was lavishly enjoying every second she was with him.

Corey needed to get off her aching feet, so she suggested to Bob, "Darling, why don't we go down and sit by the water's edge, on one of the wooden benches? I wasn't thinking when I decided to come looking for you. I should have left the heels behind and changed into something a bit more reasonable."

Bob just looked at her lovingly, and with a sly but cute smile, he agreed, "Of course, baby."

When they started to slowly walk off the bridge to a wooden bench by the edge of the water, Bob scooped her up into his arms, which totally took her by surprise as she expressed a startled scream.

Corey then began to playfully laugh and was affectionately imbued with Bob's intoxicating smile. Then they kissed again, carefully, and with more tongue. As their lips separated, Corey breathlessly told Bob directly into his face, "Oh my god, baby! I just love you so much. You'll never really know how great my love is for you."

Without hesitating, Bob very self-assuredly answered, "It must be as powerful and electrifying as my love for you."

She exhaled loudly and started kissing his neck and the side of his face.

Reaching the bench by the water's edge, Bob slowly and carefully set Corey down on the seat. He then lowered himself to sit beside her as he lifted her legs up and onto his lap. He then removed both her shoes and started to gently massage her feet.

Corey smiled at him with complete adoration and lovingly told him, "Darling, you just never cease to amaze me, you delightful man."

As Bob was rubbing her first foot with both his hands, his mind flashed back to last night's dreadful incident. He sat staring at the water while his face was completely void of any facial expression.

He continued to massage Corey's foot, but at a much slower pace.

Corey could feel Bob wanted to talk about last night, but she also knew it had to be at his own discretion.

Several minutes later, while still running his hands over her foot, Bob turned to her and dolefully stated, "I know why you came looking for me today. You probably thought I was blaming myself for what happened in Birmingham…and you'd be right. That's why I needed a lot of time today to sort things out. Nick, Truman, and I tried our absolute best to safeguard this band, but we just didn't see that coming. We simply got in over our heads down there."

Corey could see Bob's eyes glistening with welled-up tears, and she began to tear up herself.

One single tear ran down Bob's right cheek and into his facial bandage. His head fell to directly looking at Corey's foot. His fingers were now lightly stroking the tendons on top of her foot as he suddenly uttered, "It could have cost some of my guys their lives, for God's sake!"

Corey could not contain a few tears of her own, as they slowly made their way down her cheeks.

Bob composed himself, and exhaling loudly, he confessed, "The decision Nick and I made to start the tour in the South carried some huge responsibilities, and we knew that possibly it could even have some momentous consequences. I've never felt that raw emotion ever before, but I just wanted to kill the men that were hurting my brothers."

Corey's face showed horrification and shock. It gave her a deep abiding chill, and in trying to pacify him, she returned quietly, "You don't know what you're saying, darling."

Bob looked Corey straight in the eyes, and realizing what he had just said, he blew a deep breath, shook his head, and with moistened eyes, declared, "Corey, I never knew a level of hate like that ever existed. I don't know where my head has been all these years, but I just feel lost when it comes to trying to understand these feelings of race-based anger and hate."

Corey tried to help him as best she could. "Life doesn't always move in a straight line, it's always complex and nuanced and contradictory. Don't ever feel alone, darling. Sometimes even grown men get lost in the fog—sometimes men get lost."

Bob sat staring into Corey's eyes as he said with great admiration and love, "What would have happened to me if I hadn't met you?"

With a very jubilant smile, she cheerfully told him, "You'd be miserable, darling!"

Bob instantly laughed out loud, and his smile could not be contained. He leaned into Corey's opened arms, and they tenderly kissed as she held him tight to her body.

With his head now resting between Corey's breasts, and lost in her arms and with tearstained eyes, he whispered, "That's why I love you so damn much, lady."

They sat silently holding each other for several more minutes, just enjoying their surroundings; the grove of oak trees behind them was beautiful and majestic in their natural state. The canopy of their branches gave deep shade for Bob and Corey, and the sun came down on the water in rays of gentled light.

It was now pushing toward the dinner hour, and as the dusk began to insinuate itself, Corey pointed out, "I think we need to get you back to the penthouse and get you something to eat. Then I'll see to it that you finally get yourself to bed and get some rest. How's that sound to you, darling?"

"I'll get something to eat and then go to bed, but only if you're there in bed with me." He challenged her to answer.

Corey broadly smiled and chuckled. "Ah, huh…well, we'll see."

Before they both stood up from the bench, Bob slipped Corey's shoes back on her feet. He then, as before, quickly whisked her up into his arms and began to carry her out of the park and away from Bow Bridge.

Corey playfully screamed, "I can walk out of the park, darling. You don't need to carry me all the way back home." She chuckled loudly.

Using Corey's words against her, Bob mockingly told her, "Ah, huh…well, we'll see."

Corey laughed out loud and resigned herself to the fact that she loved Bob carrying her in his strong arms as she wrapped her arms around his neck and lay her head on his upper chest. She was very careful not to put her arms on any of his bandaged areas.

They caught the attention of a lot of people when they exited the park and started to walk across Fifth Avenue and East on Seventy-Fourth Street. They got a few car horns that recognized them, for both Bob and Corey were world-renowned celebrities in their own right. A few people shouted out of some car windows, "Good luck, Bob, and way to go, man!"

Corey was laughing so hard, she just couldn't stop herself from turning her joyous face into his muscled chest. Tears of laughter were racing down her face.

By the time Bob reached Madison Avenue, it seemed all of Manhattan knew who they were and where he was taking her. Bob just kept smiling and continuously walking as Corey had a coy twinkle in her eye and was loving every minute while she was in his arms.

When Bob finally reached the penthouse building on Seventy-Fourth Street and Park Avenue, Rodney was standing out in front wondering what all the commotion in the street was about.

Bob came parading up to the entrance with Corey still in his arms and yelled to Rodney, "Hey, Rodney! Open the door, man!"

Rodney quickly opened the door and asked, "What in the world is going on, Bob?"

After Bob carefully set Corey down on the interior marbled floor, he raced back out and started waving to all the well-wishers and fans. The horns, whistles, and shout-outs from the street were thrilling to Bob, as Corey stood inside the front door still laughing and smiling at him while slightly shaking her head in a prideful and loving manner.

Several minutes later, Bob jogged back up to the door as Rodney held it open for him. Bob breathlessly informed Rodney, "Yeah, thanks, Rodney. Just some of our fans welcoming us home to New York…oh, yeah, and besides, Corey needed a lift home. So, of course, I was more than willing to carry my lady home."

Rodney looked a little perplexed but incredulously agreed, "Okay, I get it…maybe."

In the elevator on the way up to the eighteenth floor, Corey grabbed Bob by the shirt collar and pulled him into her body and passionately expressed, "I absolutely cherish you, Robert Brian." Then she chuckled very sexily.

They kissed once more before the elevator door opened to their floor. Bob romantically reminded Corey, "I love you to the moon and back, Alice."

After exiting the elevator, they walked to the penthouse door with their arms around each other, and Bob kissed the top of Corey's head.

Corey pushed the door open after she unlocked it, and Haddie was the first to see the two come walking in. Haddie's eyes displayed a loving relief that Bob was all right, as she moved quickly across the room to wrap her arms around his waist. She threw her head sideways into his lower chest as she cried out, "Oh, Mr. Bob! Thank you!

Thank you for saving my boy! I'll try to repay you for the rest of my life! God bless you, Mr. Bob!"

Bob was looking at all of the guys as Haddie held on to him, and then his eyes became fixed on Joshua. Joshua was slightly nodding his head in approval of what his mother was saying, and Bob smiled at Joshua with an unconstrained aura of pride about himself and his brothers.

Slightly pulling Haddie away from him, Bob looked down and into her tearstained eyes, and with his profound characteristic cadence, he made clear, "Haddie, all these men were brave enough, in one way or the other, to rise to the occasion. We all had each other's backs, and not one of them was going to let harm come to any of us… Now if you'll remember what this group of men swore to several months ago, that if one of us went down, all of us would go down. And, Haddie, that's the God's honest truth!"

Corey stood off to the side of the room as her eyes moistened with unshed tears and experienced the heartfelt and complete pride she had for this man.

"So you see, my friend, even though we couldn't have anticipated what was going to happen, we were still in it as a group of brothers would be and fought the good fight. Joshua and every other man, including Nick and Jimmy, fought with such conviction. I'm proud to say," his voice began to break, "that these men are my brothers…my family."

Tears rolled into Bob's eyes as they were running down Corey's cheeks.

All the guys quickly left their seats to come to Bob to embrace him. Each man hugged him and patted him on the back. Joshua's embrace of Bob was strong and lasted several seconds.

Joshua emotionally and quietly spoke into Bob's ear as a solitary tear ran from his eye. "Thanks, brother. I'll never forget, man!"

As the two separated, Bob nodded his head in affirmative appreciation.

Trying to lighten the moment and help dissipate the cloud of umbrage and depression that was all too prevalent in the room, Bob resignedly suggested, "Hey, what do all of you think about ordering in some dinner? It's almost seven thirty. I'll have 'em throw in some beer with our steaks and potatoes. All right?"

All the guys and ladies were on board with that.

The evening was going along quite smoothly, the conversation was jovial, the food was delicious and plentiful, and the beer was disappearing fast.

Over the din of the eleven people in the penthouse, the phone rang. Bob jumped up, telling Corey, "I've got this, doll."

After he answered the phone, Bob happily announced to everyone, "It's Nick! I'm sure it's about Jimmy. Just a second now."

Bob stood silently listening to Nick on the other end of the phone. Occasionally, he would nod his head and acknowledge, "Yeah…right."

Once, Bob exclaimed with surprise, "Really? Holy Jesus, Nick!"

The room was dead silent at this juncture of the phone conversation. Some of the guys and ladies were breathing air in shallow mouthfuls and sat in a very apprehensive state of mind as they anticipated only bad news.

Just before Bob hung up the phone, he placidly answered Nick, "Okay, man…yeah, tomorrow? All right, talk to you later, man."

Bob turned to the room of anxious faces and happily announced, "Jimmy's all right!" The yells and whoops and clapping exploded into a small thunderous roar. Bob stood brilliantly smiling, and then looking to the heavens, he took a tremendous sigh of relief. He looked over at Corey with his eyes full of unshed tears.

Corey ran to him and embraced him tightly around his waist. He kissed her on top of her head and gratefully acknowledged, "Thank you, Lord!"

With Corey's arms still around him, she resounded, "Oh my god! Yes!"

Bob began to explain, and the room quickly quieted down. "Nick said when Jimmy was taken into surgery with the possibility of severe bleeding, along with shock, both of which could have been life-threatening, he had arm and shoulder pain also, which indicated he had an injured spleen. They immediately did an emergency lower

GI endoscopy to detect where the bleeding was and the bleeding's cause."

Everyone's attention was still fixed on Bob's every word, with mouths gaped open; some of their eyes were like that of a deer caught in someone's headlights, and there was the nervous fidgeting of hands rubbing together.

"Now don't flip your wigs, but here's the kicker! You're gonna freak out about this! From the endoscopy, they decided his spleen was repairable, and they didn't need to remove it. I guess that would have left Jimmy with a compromised immune system if he lost his spleen. Well, now this is outta sight…they performed a new, minimally invasive procedure called arthroscopic exploratory repair." Very questionable looks came over most faces in the room. "They made two small incisions around the area of his spleen and then went in with small tools to repair the damaged spleen and the surrounding tissue. Jimmy will now have a faster recovery with a lot less scarring." Bob screamed, "Come on, guys, he'll be ready for Madison Square Garden and the rest of the tour!"

The guys were beside themselves with happiness and relief as they bumped shoulders and slapped each other's hands.

"Just one more note, fellas. Nick's taking him directly to his parents' house tomorrow in Queens to recuperate, as maybe Len and Doug might want to consider. Corey and I will be flying back home tomorrow afternoon. If the rest of you want to return to California, let me know now. I'll have Nick set that up for all of us."

Everyone in the room agreed, except Doug. He was leaving tonight to stay with his parents until the Owls played the Garden.

The rest of them wanted to go back to California for the twelve days of rest and relaxation. Bob immediately notified Nick about setting up the tickets for the group.

Bob finished talking with Nick and then told everyone, "I do want to get Corey back home to work on her picture. She just started it last week, and now she's already missed two days of production. So it's very important for me to get her back to doing what she loves to do. You get my drift?"

Everyone in the room agreed.

Bob looked over at Corey, who was still standing beside him with one arm around his waist. His face was illuminated with the brightest smile as he asked her, "That okay with you, baby? We need to get you back to your groove." Then he winked at her.

Corey looked at him so lovingly with those gorgeous blue eyes; they could have melted butter. Her blazing eyes were steadfast when she purred, "You're my groove, darling." She returned a slow and sexy wink back at him.

He smiled back with pure desire for this woman.

Bob hurriedly announced to the room, "We'll be ready to make tracks around noon. I'll let you know in the morning when we bug out. Okay? Right now, I need to go to bed and maybe get some sleep...if you know what I mean?"

Darnell just hummed, "Mm, huh. Oh, yeah. Right on, my man!"

Bob softly pointed his index finger in a half arc at Darnell and suavely stated, "Now this man knows what it's about. See you cool cats in the morning. And, Doug, we'll be back Tuesday, July 5. Take care of that noggin, man."

Doug smirked as he implied, "Yeah, man. Now don't you hurt yourself in there tonight. You take care."

Bob slowly walked over to Doug, and suddenly, his serious expression gave way to a shit-ass grin. He kiddingly grabbed Doug and hugged him and then shoulder-bumped him and, smiling brilliantly, told him, "Believe me, brother. You don't have to worry about that. Anything busting loose in there is purely righteous. You dig?"

The whole room uproariously laughed at both of them and clinked their beer bottles together in agreement.

Corey stood slightly embarrassed, but with a toothy grin, she showed enjoyment in their youthful jargon and rock 'n' roll banter.

NINETEEN

After Corey had quickly showered and brushed her teeth, she walked slowly out of the bathroom, dressed in a very risqué and sheer, light-yellow nightgown with a long and wide cut to the cleavage. There was nothing about it that could be left to the imagination.

Bob lay in bed, clothed only in his boxer shorts. Corey enticingly walked toward him as he watched her alluring body with high-wrought emotion in his heart.

Even though he was exhausted beyond belief, the look of love in her eyes compelled the insurmountable passion in her to ignite him.

Corey lowered herself to sit by his side, not touching or speaking to him. Her body made a half-voluntary movement toward him, and unable to stop himself, he raised his arms for her to take him into her arms. She climbed into bed on top of him, with her arms under his and her hands cupping his shoulders. Bob thought, *Oh God, it feels good, dark, and safe being held by Corey and being enveloped by her body.*

Her voice low, fervent with feeling, she quietly whispered to him, "I want you so bad, baby. I want us to make love slowly and tenderly tonight."

And the love they made that night was exactly what Corey wanted. Bob was very attentive to her needs, her desires, her entire body. She also pleasured him in every way she could. They made love into the dark side of the night and awakened the next morning, naked and in each other's arms.

Eleven banged-up, tired, and hopeful people flew out of New York at noon that Friday of June 24, including Nick, who flew Jimmy into LaGuardia and sent him to his parents' house in Queens by limo.

Upon reaching LA at five that early evening, Nick took the Thousand Oaks people home in his private limousine, and Corey, Bob, and Haddie had Curtis drive Len and Valerie to Burbank before they returned home to Bel Air.

Haddie quickly threw together a dinner for the three of them, and then Bob headed out to the pool area. He sat in a lounger with two bottles of beer on his side table.

Corey came out and informed Bob about the phone call she had just made to Jack at Celebrity. "Darling, I just talked with Jack. And he told me, to make up for the two lost days, my producer, Frank Castor, would like for me to work the weekend. He said there wouldn't be any loss of revenue or time if I could do that."

"Corey, I'll be perfectly fine until you return home. I know you want to get back to work, and I don't blame you. So go and wow 'em in Hollywood, baby!"

She slightly chuckled then leaned over his lounger and kissed him on the lips as she held his face in her hands.

Over a week later, Bob had been relaxing, swimming, reading scripts, and playing his piano. He was feeling so much better and was ready for a change of pace.

He figured he'd venture over to Celebrity and talk with Jack or anyone else he happened upon. He also figured he would take delight in sneaking into Corey's shoots and watching her greatness unfold before the camera.

From day one, Bob was always in awe of Corey's tremendous scope and professional presence when she was in front of the cameras. She was one of the most empowering and unforgettable female actresses ever to grace the screen.

Bob ran up the steps to Jack's office and fondly smiled at the spot where Corey and he met each other two years ago as they passed each other on the stairway.

With all of his bandages now removed and just the slightly-unhealed thin scar that remained on his cheek, Bob continued on into Jack's office. He ran into Deloris, Jack's same secretary that had worked there since Bob started at Celebrity Studios.

She recognized him immediately and pleasurably asked, "Hey, Bob! How are you, honey? I saw on TV and read about your band having a rough time down there in old Dixie. You okay, handsome?"

Trying to move toward Jack's office door, Bob played down the incident by remarking, "No sweat really. We're all cool now. Can you dig?"

The secretary's eyebrows raised as she answered him questioningly, "I suppose so."

Bob slightly smiled then knocked on Jack's door and let himself in.

Jack was on the phone with Kim Novak, whom Bob was going to be with in his next picture. Jack signaled to Bob to come in and sit down as he pointed at one of the leather seats sitting out in front of his desk.

When Jack hung up the phone, he bellowed with his smoke-lined vocal cords, "Bob! What a nice surprise… I've got to tell you how sorry I am for what happened to your band down in Birmingham. Thank God, all of you survived the incident."

Bob seemed bothered by having to broach the subject again. All he could tell Jack was, "Yeah, we're all healing now. Physically and emotionally. It's cool, Jack."

"I'm not going to belabor that subject anymore…so I'll tell you right now, I want you to stick around for several more minutes if you would. I was just talking with Kim Novak, and she'll be over here in a few minutes to talk to me about the picture you, Susan Hawthorne, and she will be starting in less than two months."

Bob, not wanting to interrupt Jack's meeting with Kim, suggested, "Maybe I should go and let you two talk. I feel like I'd be in the way."

"Oh, hell no! We've had her signed to this picture *Hidden Desire* for several weeks now. I'd like to introduce the two of you to one another so you can get to know each other. So come on now, Bob. What do you say?"

Bob's curiosity got the best of him, and he told Jack, "All right, Jack. I would like to meet her. I've heard so much about her."

Jack roared, "Great! Now, can I get you a drink or something?"

Bob answered quickly, "No. I'll be fine, Jack. I was going to bomb over to where Corey's shooting her picture, and I don't think she'd appreciate liquor on my breath. Especially when I tell her I'd been talking with Kim. You get my drift, man?"

"Oh, come on, Bob. Corey is fully aware of the bonds that actors make while they're working on a picture. You and I both know there's nothing in the world that could come between you and Corey. This is a business, my fine young man, not a social club. Let's just stay within the parameters of that. Okay?"

Bob nodded affirmatively and reassuringly answered, "Always have, Jack. I just wouldn't drink right now, out of respect for Corey."

Suddenly the intercom system on Jack's desk buzzed and then lit up. He pressed the button and answered, "Yes. What is it, Deloris?"

The voice came back, "Kim Novak is here to see you, Mr. Windheim. Shall I send her in?"

"Yes, of course. Send her in, Deloris."

Both Jack and Bob stood up, waiting for Kim to come walking through the door.

As the door opened, Kim walked in with such an impressive and seemingly charming demeanor. She was dressed in a high-cut, one-piece, tight white silk dress with a flowing black silk cape cut waist-high. She was glamorous and mysteriously alluring. When she spotted Bob, her smile instantly brightened to a full-facial luster.

Jack raced around his desk to shake her hand, and enthusiastically he told her, "Kim…it's great to see you again. I'm glad you could drop by. It just so happens Bob dropped in today to talk with me, and I convinced him to stick around and meet you."

Kim was smiling and laughed softly as she turned to Bob and offered him her hand. She was very refreshing in expression and of voice as she spoke to Bob, "Bob, I've heard and read so much about you. I'm just so glad to meet you. I do want to tell you your band is making such a groundbreaking and beneficial impact on society and its incongruities in race relations around the world. I think it's wonderful. You're to be commended."

As Bob stood with Kim's soft hand in his, he thought to himself, *What a staggeringly beautiful creature she is.*

He gave her the most appreciative smile, and with his slow, careful, sonorous voice, he gratuitously told her, "Well, thank you, Kim. We're certainly trying our best…and I just want to tell you how exciting it is to meet you. I've seen just about everything you've done, and it's all very powerful stuff. I think having this opportunity to work with you is just a blessing, and I honestly can't wait the almost two months to start the picture with you and Susan."

She felt she could have listened to his easy eloquence for hours. Kim thought, *His eyes alone would have done the trick, but he'd been gifted with so much more—the thick, dark, wavy hair; the beautiful face and body; and the unmeasurable talent that just flows through his veins.*

Bob had made an indelible impression on her, and she sensed it only too well that she felt a potent curiosity about him.

Jack intervened and pointed out, "Yeah, your picture is only seven weeks away and the week after the Night Owls' 21-City Tour ends."

Looking directly at Kim, Jack questioningly added, "Well, Kim. How would you like to take a walk around the studio grounds? Just to give you some familiarity with the lots and soundstages—even though in your picture *Hidden Desire*, there's going to be a lot of location shoots, and maybe some overnighters… Bob? You were going to drop in on Corey's shoot. Why don't you show Kim around the studio and maybe introduce your *wife* to her?"

Bob knew exactly what Jack was trying to do, and so he played along with a sly smile. "Of course. I can do that, as long as it's all right with Kim."

Kim enthusiastically agreed with him, "Absolutely! I'd love to meet Corey Madrigal. She is the divine queen of motion pictures. It would be a delight for me!"

Bob answered resolutely, "All right then. Let's go."

Kim turned toward the office door, and Bob followed her out, as he looked back at Jack, shaking his head with unforgivable provocation written across his face.

Bob called up to the front gate from Deloris's phone in the front office and asked the main gatekeeper, Morgan, to send a cart over to him.

After Kim and Bob slipped into the cart, Bob drove slowly around Celebrity Studios' many soundstages, sets, outbuildings, and trailers. They talked the full thirty minutes they rode around the studio acreage.

Bob talked about the movies he had made at Celebrity the last two years—the ones he had made with and without Corey. Jokingly he told her, "So you see, with the four pictures Corey and I've made together, we're now going to shoot for nine, because then we'd beat the number Tracy and Hepburn have."

Kim chuckled a very breathy response to him, replying, "Well, I hope the two of you reach your number, because I've enjoyed watching all the pictures you've made."

Bob luxuriated in her voice, the lilt of it, the easy way she laughed.

Affirmatively nodding, he gave her the most reassuring smile and gratefully told her in his low-sounding voice, "Thanks a lot, Kim. I appreciate that."

Continuing to stare at him, Kim thought this man was distractingly handsome, and he had an inveterate politeness that was totally disarming. She also knew this man was married—happily married.

A moment later, Bob pulled the cart up to the main soundstage, where Corey was working on her picture *Beneath the Sullen Sky*, with Herbert Marshall, Teresa Wright, Hope Lange, and Richard Carlson.

Stopping the cart and jumping out, Bob stated, "Well, here we are. They'll probably be shooting, but we can sneak in behind the cameras."

"Oh, all right. I'll just follow you, Bob." She was excited and quite curious to meet Corey. For she had heard, and from Hollywood legend it dictated, Corey was no pushover, that was for sure. She was strong, opinionated, easy to underestimate, and misunderstand. But what aroused Kim's curiosity was what exactly did Bob see in a woman twenty-four years his senior and had already been married three times before he came along.

Bob was met inside the door by a security guard, but he knew Bob so well, he told him to just quietly go in somewhere off camera.

Bob, smiling, looked at Kim and then placed his hand on her lower back and led her into the back of the soundstage. Bob whispered to her, "They are shooting right now, but you don't mind waiting until they take a break, do you?"

Kim softly answered, "No, not at all. I'd love to watch them shoot this scene."

Bob found a seat for Kim, but he preferred to stand and study Corey infuse her brilliance into the shot.

After two separate shots were taken of the same scene, Lloyd, the director, called out, "Okay, people. That's looking good. Let's take ten, and when we get the next scene wrapped up, we'll break for lunch."

Corey was dressed by Orry-Kelly for this picture and was wearing one of his beautiful creations of a sleek light-green formfitting rayon gown that accentuated her curvaceous figure. There was only a slight cut to the cleavage, which disappointed Bob greatly, but she was dripping with sexuality nonetheless.

As Corey began to sit down for a touch-up with her makeup man, body makeup woman, and her hairdresser, she just happened to look up and around the soundstage. Her eyes flitted right by Bob, as he was standing with his foot up against the back wall and his arms folded in front of him. She quickly took another quick glimpse to the back wall, and she realized she had seen her beautiful man standing back there.

Corey's face lit up immediately with emotional passion and heart-pounding excitement. Then she caught sight of a beautiful young woman sitting down next to him; she could plainly see it was the seductive-looking twenty-seven-year-old blond bombshell who had been cleaning up at the box office for Columbia Pictures for the last several years: Kim Novak.

The genuine smile that showcased her love for Bob slowly melted away, and the look of curiosity began to shroud her face.

Bob saw that Corey had seen him, so he motioned to her with the four fingers of his hand to come back to him.

Corey facetiously told her people, "I need a few minutes to talk with Bob. He's calling me to the back of the soundstage, and for some reason or another, he has a beautiful woman there…huh, can you beat that?"

As she walked off camera, her three groomers had looks on their faces saying Corey was acting rashly to an unknown situation. They just looked at one another very worriedly and kept a constant eye on the threesome.

Corey strode back to Bob with the cadence of her dignified eloquence and purposefully kept her gaze on only him. Without breaking eye contact with Bob, she walked directly up to him and took his face into her hands then kissed him long and passionately.

Kim was slightly embarrassed and just looked away nervously.

When their lips separated, Bob exclaimed, "Wow! That was a welcoming surprise!"

Corey was delighted with his reaction as his smile consumed her.

Bob, returning to the moment, reminded himself of Kim's presence by happily exclaiming, "Oh, Corey. I want to introduce you to Ms. Kim Novak. I just met her in Jack's office, and Jack wanted me to show her around the studio… And, Kim, this is my wife, Corey."

Kim stood up, and putting her hand out to Corey, she cordially said, "Corey Madrigal. I'm so glad to meet you. I've enjoyed every picture you've ever made."

Corey was looking her over from stem to stern, and with the absence of any notable histrionics, she smiled guardedly as she gently took Kim's hand in hers and guilelessly told her, "Why, thank you, Kim. I've seen a few of your pictures, and you did some pretty good work on them… So, you've met my husband, Bob? How do you feel about making a picture with him next month? He's really a marvel to work with. I think the both of you and Susan will work just fine together… Well, I've got to get back now."

Corey placed her hand on Bob's chest and then leaned into a shorter kiss with him.

As she walked away, she sexily added, "I'll see you later at home, darling."

Bob nodded and added, "For sure, doll."

Corey looked at Kim and unpretentiously said, "Nice meeting you, Kim. See you around."

"Yes, it's also been nice meeting you, Corey." Kim smiled, very impressed with Corey's convincing self-esteem, commanding presence, and her obvious adoration for her husband.

Bob stood looking at Corey walk back onto the set, and when she turned one last time, out of curiosity, to look at him, he smiled brilliantly at her and then winked. She smiled back, slightly shaking her head with impassioned fervor, and slowly winked back at him.

Still smiling, Bob turned to Kim and asked her, "Well, Kim. Would you like to stay a little while longer, or would you rather go find something different to occupy us?"

To Kim, Bob had a voice that came with a depth and color that any man would envy; in fact, it had an effortless professional sound to it that was charming.

With her sleepy, expressive eyes, the eyes that could burn a hole through any man, Kim looked at Bob and softheartedly murmured in her low and naturally sexy articulation, "Why don't we go and catch some lunch? What do you think, Bob?"

Trying to remain amicable, Bob mentioned, "The director said he'd break for lunch after the next scene. That way we could also lunch with Corey, but the problem with that is that scene could take ten minutes or an hour and ten minutes... So, okay, why don't we wander over to Gabby's, and I'll leave notice for Corey if she decides she would want to join us. Okay?"

Kim could see Bob had genuine affection and respect for his wife, and she found that very attractive in any man. She happily answered, "Absolutely! I would love talking with just the two of you anyway, and not the whole cast from her picture."

Bob and Kim were able to talk for a short time before they were joined by Corey, only thirty minutes after they were seated by Gabby in the quiet, reserved back room.

There seemed to be no noticeable animosity between Corey and Kim. Corey enjoyed the down-to-earth realism of Kim, and all three of them were enjoying the company and the conversation. They actually seemed to be striking up a surprisingly healthy friendship. The compatibility between the three was seamless and heartfelt.

After an hour of talking about Bob's music, the picture Corey was working on, and the picture Kim had last finished just weeks ago, *Strangers When We Meet*, with Kirk Douglas, they all agreed they would have to have a get-together sometime the week before or during the production of *Hidden Desire*.

Corey worked through the weekend on her picture. Kim returned home to Carmel, California, and her rocky-perched, stone-clad house that sat on two acres and overlooked the Pacific Ocean. She would await the start of production on her movie with Bob and Susan Hawthorne. And Bob readied himself to take off back to New York to continue the Owls tour where they had left off, playing Madison Square Garden for two nights.

The morning of Tuesday, July 5, Bob and Corey enjoyed some early morning lovemaking and a short period of pillow talk.

Bob had an eight o'clock flight to catch with the guys and left the house at six thirty, with Corey riding along with him to LAX. After they said their goodbyes, Curtis then dropped her off at the studio, and all she could think about was when she would meet up with him in San Diego, for his second concert there on Sunday, July 31.

All the Night Owls and Truman arrived in New York with the time change at three o'clock that afternoon and would stay at Bob's penthouse both nights before the two concerts. The concert at the Garden would start at eight o'clock that night, but he wanted the band to be there at seven o'clock to inspect their instruments and run a sound check on them.

Bob ordered in a huge preconcert dinner for the guys that covered the long countertops of the kitchen area. There were soft drinks and beer along with the food, and Bob felt each guy knew his limit when it came to drinking before they had to play.

Suddenly, around five o'clock, Rodney called up to the penthouse and told Bob, "There's someone I'm sending up who said he knows you guys."

Bob told him, "Okay, man, but what's his name?"

Rodney stated, "He says his name is Jimmy Wisner."

Bob yelled with enthusiasm, "Oh, hell yes! Send him up, man! He's one of my brothers!"

Bob hung up the phone and screamed to the guys, "It's Jimmy! He's coming up right now. I didn't expect to see him until we got to the Garden tonight!"

All the guys were yelling with spirited excitement and eagerness to see Jimmy and how he was doing. It had been twelve days since his spleen injury in Birmingham.

Doug opened the door to the penthouse, and all six guys waited for the elevator doors to open and reveal Jimmy to them.

When Jimmy came walking out of the elevator, the guys rushed at him, patting him on the back, and Doug and Darnell bent down and picked him up; with their arms beneath his legs, they carried him into the penthouse and carefully sat him down on the sofa.

Joshua asked Jimmy, over the commotion the guys were making, "So how's it goin', little brother? You gonna be able to keep the beat tonight?"

Jimmy was an appealing young man at five foot eight, with his lithe and slender build. He had that occasional ironic smile to his slim face, with the blue-gray eyes electric with curiosity and his teasing sense of humor.

He answered Joshua by simply saying, "Ain't no other beat-keeper gonna take my place. I'm already there, man."

All the guys yelled their affirmation and started slipping some skin to Jimmy.

They were all excited for him and ecstatic that Jimmy was back after only twelve days, when he was supposed to have taken at least two weeks before he returned to drumming.

Bob and Len slapped hands and bumped shoulders, just nodding their heads, as they smiled to one's heart's content over Jimmy's return.

Madison Square Garden was the world's most famous arena. It was colloquially known as the Garden. It was originally located on the west side of Eighth Avenue between Forty-Ninth and Fiftieth Streets. It was built in 1925 and was the only one of the four Madison Square Gardens throughout history that was not near Madison Square, but was built on the site of the city's trolley-car barns.

In 1960, the third Madison Square Garden was the multipurpose indoor arena that hosted many different events: the Ringling Bros, and Barnum and Bailey Circus, hockey, basketball, boxing, the Westminster Kennel Club annual dog show, concerts, among others.

There were three levels inside the arena for the Night Owls to play to and a capacity of 18,496 seats. However, the guys knew the sound system was state-of-the-art and powerful enough, that they would be blowing the fans right out of their seats and into the aisles with the rousing acoustics within the arena.

At exactly eight o'clock, a low voice echoed over the loud public address system, announcing, "Ladies and gentlemen. Tonight we have for you a talented, determined, and courageous group of young men who are daring to break the race barrier in rock 'n' roll music. They're coming off the first part of their 21-City Tour through the Deep South, having experienced trauma and its travails. We commend these fearless musicians and wish them great success for the rest of their tour… We here at Madison Square Garden ask our audience to give an especially warm welcome to THE NIGHT OWLS!"

The Owls were already set up out in the middle of the arena, surrounded by a full house of well over eighteen thousand people. When the spotlight hit them, the crowd went wild with thunderous applause, yells, whistles, and screaming. The young people, the black people, the women, and men alike were displaying their respect and admiration for the brave young men.

A responsive chord was struck that night with the PAS statement that would resonate with most of the concert hall.

Bob turned to the audience with his guitar hanging from his neck by the guitar strap, and he lifted both hands on high with the thumbs and forefingers joined in the gesture of perfection. He waved them around to the entire arena, and the deafening and discordant din that had encapsulated the enclosed atmosphere of the Garden only became louder.

It was at that moment Bob gave Jimmy the nod, and after the four-count lead-in, the Owls barreled into Len's composition "Stronger than You Think."

The guitars were screaming; Jimmy was punishing his drums with an accompaniment of the bass drum and the thrashing of the crash cymbal. Joshua was hitting notes sometimes that only a dog would have been able to hear. He was hitting top C, which was three octaves from reaching the highest note ever played on a trumpet—that of a quad C.

Doug's face was turning a bright red as he was melting the high notes of his alto sax and running a screaming riff in triple-time, while his fingers were moving with a lightning touch over the valves of his instrument.

The fans were mesmerized with the guys' performance, as many danced in the aisles, and there was a very conspicuous absence of any ropes or lines separating the blacks from the whites. It was a glorious view of blacks and whites sitting together, dancing together, and just plain enjoying themselves...together.

The jubilation and the self-perpetuating power of the human spirit was brilliantly mirrored in all of the guys' eyes, most especially Darnell's, Joshua's, and Bob's.

The Owls played all their more recent songs and a number of them that were produced before Joshua and Darnell joined the band. The concert lasted until almost ten thirty that night, and the arena gave them a standing ovation before they quitted the stage.

Truman had a limo outside in back of the arena for the guys, and it whisked them off to the penthouse. All of them had a couple of beers before they showered and got some clean T-shirts and sweat-pants on.

They all congratulated each other on a really great performance that night. Even Jimmy was feeling proud of the job he did, by remarking, "Yeah, my scar didn't burst open and spill my guts out all over the stage, so it was all way too cool, man."

The rest of the guys laughed, and Doug playfully threw an accent pillow off of the sofa and hit him on top of his head.

At almost midnight, Bob broke away from the guys and went into the master bedroom to call Corey. It was ten o'clock in Bel Air, and Corey picked up the phone after only one ring, as she lay in bed studying her lines for the next day's shoot. "Hello, darling. How did everything go for you guys tonight?"

With a low passionate voice, Bob whispered, "Hello, baby. Everything went like clockwork. There was no evidence of blatant discrimination, and no disturbances of any kind. It went perfectly, and over eighteen thousand people would totally agree with me."

"That's absolutely wonderful, darling. That makes me feel so much better about this tour."

Bob informed Corey, "Well, we have one more concert at the Garden tomorrow night, and then we head into Boston for a private concert at NEC. The concert at NEC, this Friday, is strictly for the faculty, past and present, and all the student body. It's a pro bono treat we're doing, just in appreciation for everything they ever did for us while we attended their school. We'll only be playing to 260 seats. It'll be a very intimate performance we give them that night."

"Bob, that sounds wonderful and a lot of fun. I hope you have a great time, but I also hope you don't run into any of your ex-girlfriends or teachers you had crushes on either." Corey chuckled her sexy laugh.

Bob smiled to himself and laughed as he exhaled a mouthful of air. He romantically tried to allay her trivial jealousies by reassuring her, "But, baby, you're my blue-eyed, auburn-haired, full-breasted pagan goddess, dancing in the moonlight, drunk on life and dry martinis, stirred."

Corey's eyes instantly started to moisten, and silence befell her end of the phone line. After a few seconds, she came back on the line, as her voice wavered forlornly, "Oh my god, Bob! I just can't handle it when you're so far away, and I can't touch you, hold you, or make love to you the way I want. I love you so much, my darling man."

"Corey, I love you beyond belief, and I will call you every chance I get, baby. Promise. I already miss you, and I've only been away from you since this morning." He slightly chuckled. "So good night, doll, I'll talk with you soon. Okay?"

"All right, sweetheart. Good night to you, my gorgeous man."

After hanging up the phone, Corey lay abed dreaming of Bob and other delightful infinitudes, as the manuscript to her picture remained beside her, opened but now ignored.

The second concert at the Garden went along just as smoothly as the first, but the structure was so old, and there was such poor ventilation; because smoking was permitted, this led to a large haze in the upper portions of the arena. It was as though the third level of seats toward the end of the concert had to view the performance through an unhealthy cloudlike distraction.

The Owls, along with Truman, headed for Boston Thursday morning, the day before their private concert at NEC. Truman delivered the instruments to Jordan Hall, where the guys would be playing to the faculty and student body of only 260 seats.

Jordan Hall was grand and exquisite and had the best atmosphere known for a concert. It was said that playing Jordan Hall was like having an out-of-body experience. There was a warm and intimate atmosphere to the hall, and it was equipped with some very amazing acoustics.

The hall dated back to 1903 and deemed a national historic landmark and was highly regarded in Boston. The landmark designation came after NEC was judged for its presence and influence in American music, its consistent engagement in broadening the appeal of music, and its historic status as an unaffiliated, independent school of music.

All the guys got out of the second van and ventured into Jordan Hall, along with Truman and the instruments. Out of the seven of them, five were alumni. The five walked around the hall remembering their recitals, plays, and live performances, on their own chosen instrument, in front of faculty for a final term grade.

That was when Bob heard two familiar women's voices behind him. The first was a soft yet distinguished voice that whose eloquence was dignified and exemplary yet still attractive. "Robert Richardson! Is that you?"

Bob turned to the sound of this inviting voice and realized it was his former teacher of four years in music theory, Ms. Phyllis Alexander.

She was tall, at five foot nine, and had an oval face that was outlined by her long dark hair, which was gathered into a French twist. Her eyes still radiated to others that gleam of greenish-brown mystery, and her body had remained sleek and trim. Her tight skirt was evidence of this as it clung to her sexy derriere. If Bob had to guess, Phyllis was probably in her late thirties.

The second woman's voice was also unmistakable, with its precise articulation and the subtle feminine delicacy it possessed. Bob noticed the voice to be that of his teacher of four years on piano, Ms. Lynelle Shepherd. "Well, if that's not Robert, I'll eat my own words."

Lynelle was around five foot six, and her facial bone structure was that of a young Katherine Hepburn—highly chiseled cheekbones that retained the high-class look of a thousand-dollars-a-day Madison Avenue fashion model. She was a plucky broad from Brooklyn who was engagingly stimulating and exciting to be around. Bob thought Lynelle must be around forty years of age by now.

Bob's face lit up and took delight in seeing these two women again. He remembered these two teachers with great fondness, for he was very attracted to both, as he worked closely for hours at a time, five days a week, with each. It wasn't as much a sexual attraction as it was an intellectual allurement. For both these women were very learned in what they taught him.

Bob smiled broadly and started walking toward them as they both stood at the back entrance to the hall.

When he reached them, he took Phyllis by the arms and kissed her on the cheek and then enveloped her in a warmhearted hug. She responded joyously, "It's just so good to see you again, Mr. Rock Star!" She had to chuckle.

Bob laughed out loud as he threw his head back. He then also kissed Lynelle on the cheek and hugged her tenderly.

Lynelle facetiously stated, "I'm so glad you stayed with your classical piano. All those hours with you for four years have really paid off!"

Bob stated, trying to convince her she was wrong, "Well, actually I have stayed with some classical piano. In February, I played to over forty people at my twenty-fourth birthday party. I laid down some stoked Debussy. It was all righteous!"

As the three of them laughed out loud, Doug yelled from the front of the stage area, "Nick! What the heck are you doing here, man?"

Everyone in the hall turned to see and greet Nick. Bob excused himself to the two ladies and started to walk over to shake Nick's hand. "Hey, brother, what brings—" Bob's attention was diverted to the rear entrance door, where Corey slowly walked into the hall and made immediate eye contact with Bob.

Instantaneously, Bob saw her but couldn't believe his own eyes. He blinked his eyes quickly and studied her closely as Corey got up exquisitely into a tiny-waisted silk dress of a smooth, high-fashion violet, with a gathering just below the bustline.

Bob's jaw dropped open; he smiled brilliantly and then loudly yelled, "What? Are you kidding me…? Corey!"

He quickly moved toward her, and she widely opened her arms to him. They embraced and kissed each other with reasonable self-restraint, as the guys were yelping their approval along with a few whistles.

When Bob pulled his head back away from Corey, he inquisitively asked her, "What a great surprise, doll? 'Cause you're the last person I thought I'd see today."

"I just wanted to be with you when you met your faculty friends again. You're not bothered by me being here, are you?" She looked up into his eyes questioningly.

Bob hugged her again and emphatically told her, "Oh my god! No, baby! I only wonder how you got away from your shoot? I know your producer, Frank, is pushing for a late July wrap on your picture. So lay it on me."

"Frank was willing to trade me today and tomorrow for both days this weekend. I, of course, told him, 'Absolutely.'"

Bob, shaking his head in disbelief, kissed Corey on the forehead and softly told her, "You're really something. You know that?"

Corey lovingly smiled at him and whispered, "For you. Yes."

Bob shook hands with Nick and introduced him to Phyllis and Lynelle. Kiddingly, Bob added, "You two got me again, didn't you?"

Nick laughingly answered, "Well, Corey said she needed to be here for you, and I needed to come out and make sure everything was in the groove… You see? No sweat. All cool."

Bob chuckled then placed his hand on Corey's lower back and told her, "Come on, doll. I want you to meet a couple of my former teachers."

Bob introduced Corey to Phyllis and Lynelle. "Corey, this is my music theory teacher, Phyllis Alexander"—and moving his attention to Lynelle—"and this is Lynelle Shepherd, my piano instructor. Ladies, I'd like you to meet my wife of less than four months, Corey Madrigal."

Corey put her hand out to both women and cordially stated, "It's my pleasure to meet both of you. I know you both did a superlative job in sharing your knowledge with Bob and nurturing all his passions for his duration here at NEC."

Phyllis answered, slightly intimidated but not afraid of Corey's publicized jealousy, "It's so nice to meet you, too, Ms. Madrigal. I've enjoyed your work throughout the years on all of your pictures. Welcome to NEC."

"Thank you, Ms. Alexander. I appreciate that."

Lynelle comically added, "It's an honor to meet you, Ms. Madrigal. It seems I read somewhere that you gifted Bob a concert grand piano on his last birthday."

Corey smiled proudly and nodded affirmatively. Bob stood with a toothy grin.

"Well, I think you need to encourage him to play more of the classics. It would be a delight if he would be willing to play one for us tomorrow night." Lynelle kept staring directly at Corey.

With her indomitable protectiveness, this statement from Lynelle made Corey's fierce loyalty toward Bob all the more touching as she poignantly answered, "I feel Bob has a masterly skill of the piano, whether he's playing Chopin, Beethoven, or rock 'n' roll. He has also been known to get through Rachmaninoff's piano concerto no. 3 in D minor, which as you, Lynelle, probably know is one of the most technically challenging piano concertos in the standard piano repertoire."

Bob stood mesmerized with Corey and totally amazed with the surreptitious musical knowledge and acumen she displayed. Lynelle was even more impressed, with not only Corey's musical knowledge, but the fact that Bob had the ability to play probably the most difficult concerto ever written for piano.

Lynelle was enthused with this information and turned to Bob, remarking, "Oh my goodness, Bob! That's wonderful to hear! So maybe tomorrow night you'll share your talent with us and maybe play just one classical piece."

Bob was still staring at Corey in wonderment as she glanced at him with a quick-witted look about her. Bob realized Lynelle had asked him a favor, and he quickly returned his focus on her. "Well, the Owls do have a set program tonight, but we'll see how the time plays out. I might just be able to squeeze something in."

Nick stepped up, and slightly raising his voice, he asked, "Well, Corey and I are ravenous. We've not had anything to eat since breakfast, which was several hours ago. Would everyone want to catch something to eat over at the Green Dragon Tavern, between Faneuil Hall and the North End? And that includes you, Phyllis and Lynelle."

All the guys were on board with that and even the two ladies. For the next three hours, Bob sat with Corey, Len, Nick, and the guys' two former teachers. They were all eating, drinking, and telling stories about their past college days and the different experiences each had with Phyllis and Lynelle, in and out of the classroom.

The other five guys sat at an adjacent table, listening and conversing back and forth with one another.

The Green Dragon Tavern had a relaxed ambience to the room that sat well with its guests. The immediate surrounding noise was just loud enough, so you could hear everyone across both tables.

The tavern originally opened in 1657 and was once a popular meeting place for Paul Revere and his revolutionary comrades. The place was steeped in history and antiquity, with the revolutionary relics and the works of art that were scattered throughout the tavern.

Doug wore his beat-to-shit black leather jacket to dinner. The same jacket he had worn on campus for the four years he attended NEC.

Darnell yelled to him across their table, "Hey, man! Isn't that the same jacket Paul Revere wore when he traveled the countryside warning the villagers loudly, 'The British are coming'? It sure as hell looks like it, brother!"

The entire bar of patrons laughed out loud, as many of them toasted Darnell by raising their steins of beer to him.

Doug mockingly became offended and returned, "Well, hell. You ought to know, old man! Weren't you riding with him, you ass?"

A lot of people in the bar and the other Owls whistled and nettled Darnell, calling out, "Oooh-h-h wee! That's a badass cut down, man!"

Darnell stayed cool, and when the kidding was over, and the din of the tavern died down, he smartly told Doug, "I've been called many things far more colorful than ass! So kiss off, hippie boy, 'cause I ain't freaked out. I'm just goin' with the flow, man!"

Doug walked around the table to Darnell, and smiling, both guys slipped each other some skin and then bumped shoulders and together started laughing at each other.

Bob leaned into a kiss on Corey's ear and inquisitively whispered, "I wasn't at all aware you knew anything about classical music. Why didn't you share that with me?"

He smiled at her as he pulled away.

Corey then kissed him on his cheek and quietly informed him, "I read a lot when you're touring, darling. It just so happens I finished a book about Rachmaninoff last night called *Sergei Rachmaninoff, a Lifetime in Music*. You must know I always like to be prepared for any situation, circumstance, or contingency that might occur. It always seems to pay off." Bob laughed to himself and then softly kissed her on the cheek. Long ago, Bob had resigned himself to the fact Corey was a professional, and she knew the art of preparedness.

Later that night, Len moved into Nick's room to allow Corey to be with Bob in his room.

Upon entering their room, Corey threw her arms around Bob's neck. He saw the fervent sexual desire in her eyes as he wrapped his hands around her lower hips. They locked into a full-mouthed kiss and began to taste each other's urgent desire.

Corey, gasping for air, breathlessly pleaded, "Take me, darling. Every part of me!" She opened Bob's pants and pushed them down.

Corey's skin was hot and delicate to the touch as she wanted to give him pleasure as much as she wanted him to envelope her.

Bob picked her up by her hips as she wrapped her legs around his waist. He then turned her and hurriedly pressed her against the wall as he slid inside of her.

Bob could feel her quivering as she pushed her hips into his body. Corey was holding him tight. The pressure, the tight sheath she could feel, it was enrapturing to her as she was breathing in a labored manner and begging him to never stop.

As Bob came in her, he loudly released an exhalation of sexual gratification, but he never quit pushing into Corey with the powerful strength of his hips and back.

She suddenly exploded into an overwhelming orgasm that just took total control of her entire body. She grabbed and held on to him even tighter as she screamed, "Oh, baby, yes! Don't ever stop!" Bob continued on for another several minutes with Corey reaching orgasm twice more.

Breathing heavily, Bob carried her over to the bed, laying her limp body onto the crumpled sheet of the unmade bed. Bob then fell into the bed with her and turned over into a deep sweet state, somewhere between sleep and wakefulness, in which their bodies enjoyed the exhaustion and knew it was exhausted from having spent itself sexually.

The ensuing pillow talk was whispered softly to each other, deep into the depths of the enraptured night.

TWENTY

The night of the concert, the Owls were tuning their instruments and running a sound check on them around seven o'clock. Jimmy was surprisingly showing some nerves when he asked out loud, "Damn, I suppose Dean Watson is going to be sitting front and center tonight. That's gonna be a drag… I don't think he ever liked me."

Len admonished Jimmy by saying, "You know, it could've just been because on Halloween he caught you and Doug egging his car. Or maybe when the two of you dropped a bag of dog shit on his front porch, wanting him to open it or step on it. And I really don't think he appreciated Doug and you dressing up like cheerleaders trying to get yourselves into the girls' locker room either."

All the guys were laughing out loud, including Corey, who was already seated out in the front row of the hall, close to the stage. She was dressed elegantly in her flowing gown that shined of a deep rustic red. It was divided by a ribbon of black under the bodice and with a cut in cleavage that any man would look at twice.

Doug then yelled out, "Hey, man! Don't worry. He's old and has probably forgotten all about those things."

Then a low, daunting voice could be heard, not far from where Corey was sitting, that resonated through the hall. "Don't be so sure of that, Mr. Peeples."

Doug's eyes widened to where you thought his eyeballs would have fallen out of the sockets, and his jaw dropped, unaware that Dean Watson was standing out in front of the stage area.

The executive dean of NEC, Mr. Charles T. Watson, was a large, hulking man with deep, penetrating eyes and a hawk nose—the kind that would easily intimidate anyone with his stare. He exuded the knowledge, professionalism, and the pure love and respect for music in the proud manner he carried himself.

Bob moved quickly down the few steps of the stage to greet Dean Watson. As they shook hands, Bob said, "It's great to see you again, sir. Don't mind Mr. Peeples up there. He just likes to have a good time."

The dean answered Bob, smiling, "It's nice to see you, too, Mr. Richardson. It seems you've put your degree here at NEC to some very good use."

Proudly Bob told him, "Yes, sir. I've certainly tried hard to do everything I love to do."

Looking back at the guys, Bob pointed out, "Yeah, and Len Perry, Jimmy Wisner, and, of course, Mr. Doug Peeples have put their sheepskins to work for them also. And the Night Owls' two newbies up there: Darnell King, a NEC graduate before the four of us, and Joshua Chambers, who used to be principal trumpet with the San Francisco Symphony Orchestra, until we stole him away this past January."

"That's all very exciting information, Mr. Richardson." Then the dean looked over at Corey and asked, "And who might this ravishing creature of stage and screen be with? Yes, Ms. Madrigal. I did notice your presence and have always held you in high esteem. You have been an extremely proficient dramatic artiste who has changed the face of Hollywood single-handedly—and I might say, for the better."

Corey stood and shook the dean's hand graciously, telling him, "Well, thank you so much, Dean Watson. I appreciate that."

Bob stepped up informing the dean, "Yes, Dean Watson. I would like you to meet my wife, Ms. Corey Madrigal. We were married this past March."

Corey smiled with such pride. Dean Watson smiled and, with a flicker of humor in his voice, stated, "I can only say, young man, I'm sorry you beat me to her… Congratulations, you two. it's been my pleasure meeting you, Ms. Madrigal. And, Bob, I'm so proud you are an alumnus of NEC. I'm looking forward to the concert in just a short time from now."

The dean shook hands with both Corey and Bob again and then ventured up to talk with his other alumni and meet Darnell and Joshua.

The faculty and students started to file in at almost seven thirty. The 260 seats were filled quite quickly. At eight o'clock, one could hear the Old North Church tower bell, over on Salem Street, striking eight times.

Dean Watson walked out onstage, and with the Night Owls standing by their instruments and ready to kick it, he approached the microphone in front of Darnell and to Bob's right.

"Tonight is a treat for all of us. For we have six young gentlemen, five of which are alumni of NEC. They call themselves the Night Owls." There were some screams and a lot of applause.

When the small audience quieted down, the dean continued, "This group of fine young men have been working hard and courageously to break down the racial barriers in rock 'n' roll music in this country. They, at times, have risked their own lives to show all people that unity, diversity, and acceptance is what civil rights is all about." The crowd yelled their approval and again clapped loudly.

Dean Watson finished by stating, "We as a people must strive to assist in the struggle for equality and an end to discrimination, not just here, but around the world. Now, I want you to listen to the lyrics of their rock songs, and then you can get dreamy about the roll songs later." There was a favorable laughter from the audience. Even the Owls and Corey had to laugh at that remark also.

"So, here for you tonight, is the internationally renowned band, the Night Owls!"

As soon as the dean walked down into the audience to sit next to Nick, who was sitting by Corey, with Truman on Corey's other side, Bob gave Jimmy the nod.

Instantly Jimmy gave the guys the four-count on his snare, and they ripped into "Conviction." Bob thought, *The band has never sounded any better than they did right now, and the cohesiveness and timing is perfection.* Or maybe just the incredible acoustics of Jordan Hall made their music sound pitch-perfect, and heavenly to his ears.

The Owls were incredible this night as they played five of their kick-ass songs right off the bat, and the audience loved that.

Bob then stepped up to the microphone after the din of the room died down. There was still a handful of young ladies who screamed in amazement, because they were actually seeing him in person and this close. Bob smiled, and with extraordinary control, he began to talk, and this quieted them down. "I have my wife here tonight."

There were a few screams from the young ladies.

"No! I love you."

"Please, marry me!"

Bob grinned and just looked at Corey as she was laughing almost hysterically along with Nick and Truman. This made Bob smile and chuckle inwardly just watching Corey laugh.

Bob yelled out to the young ladies, "But wouldn't that make me a bigamist?"

The one yelled back, "I don't care!"

Everyone in the hall was now laughing, even all the Owls, as Bob went on talking. "Well, anyway… I'd like to introduce to those very few people who aren't familiar with motion pictures my extraordinarily talented and beautiful wife, Corey Madrigal."

Corey briefly stood and took a hastened bow and then sat right back down.

There was a welcoming applause for her as she smiled at Bob pleasurably.

Phyllis and Lynelle looked over at Corey enviously and looked away despondently.

The Owls played another ten songs, including "Knowing You Were Mine." This was the song Bob composed and sang to Corey at their wedding, and now it had many people playing and dancing to it at their own weddings.

Corey emitted some emotional tears to her wedding song, as was the same reaction with many of the women in the hall that night.

Astonishingly, Bob's dry, measured voice wobbled with a wide, helpless vibrato throughout the song. It was enchanting to all just listening to that beautiful perfectly pitched baritone.

Then when everyone thought the concert was coming to an end, Bob again stepped up to the microphone, after lowering his guitar strap and placing his guitar in its stand.

He looked out smiling at Ms. Alexander and then at Ms. Shepherd, who were seated down in front only a few seats left of Corey. Corey leaned forward just a bit to see whom Bob was smiling at. She could now see it was his two former teachers she had met yesterday and talked with at the Green Dragon Tavern.

Corey looked back at Bob and realized he must now be dedicating a song to them. She had a fleeting second of jealousy, but she understood these were just a few of the faculty here at NEC that helped to mold and develop Bob's talents, which he has been reaping the benefits of ever since he graduated.

Bob surprisingly announced into the microphone, "Before we bring this concert to an end, I'd like to give just a little more back to two of my former and favorite teachers, Ms. Phyllis Alexander and Ms. Lynelle Shepherd… This is my thank-you to both of you."

The audience applauded loudly, along with some cheers.

On cue, the stagehands rolled out a big, beautiful concert grand piano. They placed it center stage, in the middle of the band, after they moved the guys a few feet away from their original spots. The piano was angled toward the audience, so when Bob began to play, he would have full vision of the entire first row.

As Bob stood in front of the piano bench, he spoke almost as if he were lecturing into the long-reaching microphone that was stretched to where his head would be when he played.

He moved the microphone close to his mouth and began saying, "You know, as most of you do, that Frederic Chopin began composing music at the tender age of eight. What I'm going to play for you tonight is Nocturne op. 9, no. 2 in B-flat minor. Chopin was twenty years old when he wrote this, and it's the second nocturne of his work and is often regarded as his most famous piece."

Phyllis and Lynelle looked at each other in amazement as they exchanged very impressed facial expressions.

An echoing sound of fascinating astonishment shot through the hall, and the surprise sensation of the audience's response to this piece gave Corey goose bumps all over her body from her absolute love and admiration she had for this man.

"This composition by Chopin reflects the moods and feelings of the nighttime. And although *nocturne* comes from the French word for *nocturnal*, the origins of the term in music were first used in Italy in the eighteenth century… When you hear the complexity of this composition, you'll be able to acknowledge why Chopin was one of the great composers of his time and how he was definitely a composer that 'wrote poems on the piano.'"

Bob then sat down on the piano bench and adjusted the microphone back in its place.

He looked over at the guys and jokingly told them as he moved his hand back and forth at them, "I won't need any accompaniment with this. Okay?"

The guys put their instruments down and gave him the sign of index finger to thumb—okay!

The audience laughed a little as Bob mentally started to prepare himself.

He took a deep breath and loudly exhaled, and then he began playing with a legato melody. Slow, methodical, he began with a subtle, timid B-flat then leapt to the distinctive major sixth and then launched into a beautiful, yearning melody.

It was expressively sweet and a piece that was homophonic (which was characterized by movement of all parts to the same melody) in texture, containing only piano for the tone color.

There was smooth transitions and crescendos and decrescendos between passages.

Bob was playing the most brilliant interpretation of the nocturne perfectly. The nocturne featured a melancholy mood and a clear melody that floated over a left-hand accompaniment of arpeggios, or broken chords.

Repetitions of the main theme added increasingly ornate embellishments that were quite noticeable in this piece. Bob truly had a rare sense of stylistic purity.

The nocturne was reflective in mood, until it suddenly became passionate near the end. The new melody that concluded the nocturne began softly, then ascended to a higher register and was forcefully played in octaves, eventually reaching the loudest part of the piece (the fortissimo). After a brilliant trill-like passage, the excitement subsided, and the nocturne ended calmly.

Bob's hands ended up high toward his face, with index fingers bent and pointed upward. Statuesquely, he remained in this position for three seconds after he concluded the piece.

The small audience gave him a thunderous standing ovation. At that point, Bob relaxed his mental faculties and rose from the piano bench and then stepped out in front of the piano and graciously bowed. The applause did not abate their tremendous approval, as Bob brilliantly smiled; and looking out at Corey, he blew her a kiss and winked at her.

Corey's eyes were moistened by the tears of pride she had emblazoned on her face and blew a kiss back to him as she slowly returned his wink.

Corey's love for him was undying and unconditional. She was lost in an overwhelming respect and the all-encompassing adoration she felt for him.

Before the applause ended, Bob signaled to all the guys to follow him. Then all six of them went down the stairs at the front of the stage and began shaking hands with Dean Watson, all the faculty they could reach, and as many of the student body that came forward.

Bob grabbed up Corey and gave her a tremendous hug as she quickly kissed his cheek and then his lips. After he softly placed Corey back on her feet, the rest of the band gave her a hug and kiss on the cheek.

Bob purposely walked down to Phyllis and hugged her and kissed her on the cheek. She, in returning his kiss on the cheek, whispered into his ear, "That Chopin was absolutely fabulous, Bob. Thank you so much for that. It's been an incredible night, and I pray this will not be the last we see of you here at NEC."

Looking directly into her eyes, he detected that old propensity she used to show that all she wanted was a quiet night with him as they lay on a blanket under the stars.

Bob smiled with a heartfelt compunction and answered her, "Maybe one day. Who knows what might open up in my schedule... Good night, Phyllis, and goodbye."

"Yes, goodbye, Robert."

Bob then hugged and cheek-kissed Lynelle. She tenderly told him, "I'm going to miss you, Mr. Richardson. You've always been a source of amazement to me, never a disappointment... Now take care of yourself, and never forget your piano. Got that?"

Bob smiled and told her, "Never, Lynelle. You worked too hard pounding all of that into me. I'll miss you also. Goodbye now."

As Bob turned to walk away and back to Corey, he witnessed a few unshed tears in Phyllis's saddened eyes. He continued to walk, nevertheless.

Corey was watching all this play out between Bob and his former teachers. However, she felt very secure in his love for her. She was not going to let this play with her mind.

Bob returned to Corey, and smiling, he inquisitively asked her, "Do we have to get you to the airport, doll? I know you have the red-eye back to LA, and it's almost midnight now. So what do you think?"

Corey, smiling, kissed him and stated, "Well, my flight is at two o'clock this morning, but I'll pick up some time flying west and be home after Curtis delivers me from the airport at around four thirty in the morning. That gives me enough time to get cleaned up and get some breakfast before I leave for the studio at six thirty."

Bob hastily told her, "Well, I'll accompany you to the Logan International Airport and sit with you until your plane flies out. I don't work again until eight o'clock Saturday night. So let's get going, baby."

"Yes, darling… I do love you, mister!"

That night, Saturday, July 9, 1960, the Owls were still in Boston but playing the Orpheum Theatre. The theater was built in 1852 and had the first American concert pipe organ installed in 1862. It was the largest pipe organ in the United States at the time; the organ had 5,474 pipes and 84 registers.

Historically known for on the eve of the Emancipation Proclamation becoming law in the north, December 31,1862, there were northern abolitionists gathered in the Orpheum Theatre to celebrate as the clock struck midnight; these people were Frederick Douglas, Wendell Phillips, Harriet Beecher Stowe, William Lloyd Garrison, and Harriet Tubman—just to name a few of the people fighting for the freedom of the slaves throughout the country.

The Orpheum Theatre could seat 2,700 people, and the Owls found it easy to play.

On their second night at the Orpheum, Bob and the other band members noticed that there were students they'd seen at NEC, along with some faculty members, in the audience that night. One face Bob did take notice of was that of Ms. Phyllis Alexander and whom he suspected was her husband seated next to her.

All Bob could do was smile and nod his head to both of them. She responded in kind.

Both nights at the Orpheum was a huge success, and as the Owls quitted the stage, Truman, Nick, and the private security force met the guys in back of the theater and whisked them off to Philadelphia for concerts on July 12 and 13.

In Hollywood, Corey was keeping herself busy with the shooting on her picture *Beneath the Sullen Sky*. She kept trying to tell herself it would only be three weeks until Bob's band was in San Diego, where she would meet him the night of the second performance.

On set that Monday morning of July 11, Corey had a scene with Richard Carlson and a bit player named Jason Brooks. Jason always played a sub-supporting actor. He was just a filler to a lot of scenes. He was thirty-four years old and was tall, lean, hard-assed, and humorless. Corey had never felt anything but mild revulsion for him.

Lloyd, the director, felt this scene was ready to be shot and told the cameras to stand by and get ready to roll.

Corey was wearing one of her original Orry-Kelly gowns that was of a lustrous yellow silk with a sedate white-marble running throughout. It also had an ample cut to the cleavage.

As Corey was readying herself for the cameras to start rolling, she glanced over at Jason, who was staring directly at her exposed cleavage. When he noticed Corey's icy stare at him, he quickly looked away expressionless.

Corey was a lady who was used to having her breasts stared at while her words most commonly went in one ear of the man doing the staring and out the other. But this was something Jason was known for doing. He had always had a dark, brooding lasciviousness about him, and Corey was never comfortable when he was on set.

When the day's shoot was over, and Lloyd felt that the cast had perfection in many of the scenes he needed done, he let them go at almost six that night.

Corey was walking out of her dressing room to leave the studio when Jason surprisingly stepped in front of her.

Corey gave out a disconcerted little cry and took a step backward. She yelled, "What do you think you're doing, Jason?"

Jason was impervious to her concern as his blood was corrupt and his spirit was seditious. "I just wanted to tell you, Corey, that I've always been attracted to you. So I was just wondering if you'd go out to dinner with me tonight?"

Corey couldn't believe what she was hearing. She thought, *The audacity of this man!* The tickle of unease had just become a sinking feeling. At that moment, she felt she had to handle this situation with diplomacy.

She told him in no uncertain terms, "I'm a married woman, Jason! And a happily married woman at that. We could never do dinner, except within a crowd of people. So, I really don't want to be bothered with this again. Do you understand me?"

Jason stood with his eyes filled with muted compassion and warned her, "I know your husband will be out of town until the end of the month. Sooner or later, this is going to happen." With pure contempt in his voice, he demoniacally stressed, "Now, are you understanding me?"

Corey stood paralyzed and felt terror stricken. She looked around for anyone that could help her. Everyone had left the immediate area.

Jason just smiled vindictively and leaned over to stroke Corey's arm. She instantly pulled away from him.

He laughed amusingly and walked away.

The anxiety came over Corey with unprecedented ferocity. She then quickly moved toward the nearest phone and called Jack, but Deloris said he left an hour ago.

She dialed her director, producer—anyone who would just talk with her and try to help allay her fears. There wasn't anyone from the studio that had arrived back home yet.

By the time she drove home, it was almost seven o'clock that night. Corey hurried into the kitchen, where she found Haddie putting the finishing touches to their dinner.

Haddie looked at Corey, and instant trepidation swept through her body. She could see Corey was emotionally upset about something. Haddie implored, "What in heaven's name has happened, Ms. Corey?"

Really shaken by this man, Corey told Haddie the entire story of what happened outside of her dressing room. Haddie insisted she call the police.

Corey told her, "The police can't arrest him for anything. He didn't assault me. He just threatened me in a hostile way."

Then the phone rang. Corey prayed it would be Bob calling her, so she darted for the phone. When she picked up the receiver, she could hear Jason's voice panting and then telling her, "I really want to be with you, Corey. Don't fight this. It's not going away."

He hung up the phone on her, and not more than a minute later, it rang again. Back in the kitchen again, Corey just looked at Haddie, and Haddie, incensed by this situation, told her, "I'll get the phone this time, Ms. Corey. This scum bucket needs to be told where to get off!"

Haddie lifted the receiver, and Bob's comforting voice could be heard, "Hello, Haddie? Is Corey home from the studio yet?"

Haddie told him what was going on, and he demanded she put Corey on the line.

After Corey explained everything to Bob, she tried not to worry him by saying, "I'm going to call Jack, Lloyd, and Frank tonight and have them keep an eye on Jason. And I figure wherever I go, I'll always have someone with me."

Bob was livid that something like this could happen on property to as big a star as Corey. He asked her, "Do I need to break away from my tour to straighten this guy out?"

Corey was emphatic in answering him, "Oh, no, darling. Please. I'm going to have everyone on this guy's case. Sooner or later, he's going to make a really big slipup, and that's when the police will pinch him. I'll get Jack and Frank to leave him in the production, because I want this guy behind bars and not in a position to do this to anyone else in the future."

"All right, doll, but I really don't like this crazy asshole talking shit to you, and most especially threatening you. You need to keep me posted on this guy. All right?"

To Corey, the bare situation was enough to delineate the conflict. She assured him, "I have the numbers of the hotels you're staying at in each city, so I'll definitely call you when this problem is solved."

Bob still wasn't pacified with what was going on at Corey's picture shoot, but to help lighten the mood somewhat, he managed to change the subject. "Isn't your picture due to wrap about the time I come into San Diego for the two concerts we have there?"

Corey, feeling a little relief for the moment, answered in anticipation, "Yes, it is, darling. It should either be that Friday, the twenty-ninth, or Saturday, the thirtieth. I can't wait for when I see you Sunday for your second night's concert in San Diego. Then you can come with me to the wrap party for my picture that Monday evening at D'Angelo's. How's that sound, baby?"

He happily responded, "That sounds fantastic, doll. I'm looking forward to that… Now I need to go with the guys and do a sound check on the instruments. I'll be talking with you soon, baby. You be careful now. Okay?"

"I will. And soon I'll be talking with you, darling. Good night, sweetheart."

"Good night, my beautiful pagan goddess." He quietly hung up the phone.

Corey laughed out loud and then took a guarded breath and sighed heavily.

The next morning on set, Corey was getting her hair styled. As she sat at the mirrored desk, while her personal hairdresser, Nina, who was providing Corey with a coiffure, she saw Jason slowly walking by and smiling into the mirror insidiously at her.

Corey watched him in the mirror and then caught Lloyd watching him. Lloyd looked at Corey, and acknowledging what he had seen, he nodded his head to her.

Throughout the entire week, Jason had walked by Corey smiling devilishly, brushing her with his body, continuously asking her if he could get her anything, trying to talk with her as she studied her manuscript, and at times, being so bold, he would even take a seat next to her, which belonged to one of the leading actors, when he noticed one to be empty.

Corey had asked him to stop his antics—it was annoying, sappy—and he kept forgetting (on purpose, she suspected), so she walked off set and told Lloyd she would be taking a break.

This whole situation was very disconcerting to Corey, and her nerves were very frayed at this point. Her anxiety came out in different ways; she was jumpy, she started to see things that weren't there, she had to sleep with a light on, and she read every night until her eyes closed involuntarily. She did everything she could to avoid feeling alone or having too much time to think about her stalker.

The Owls played Philadelphia for two nights, which was the epicenter of the rock 'n' roll industry in the late fifties and the early sixties. The first national hit records featuring the blending of country music and rhythm and blues, which was the essence of rock 'n' roll, came out of Philadelphia in 1953 and 1954.

The Owls had two concerts at the Mann Center for the Performing Arts. It was built in 1935, and it housed over 13,000 seats; 4,743 were under the roof and 8,600 outside on the lawn. It was known for hosting many award-winning artists.

Both nights were a spectacular success, because after final ticket count, Nick found out the venue had sold over fifteen thousand tickets each night. It was standing room only, and on the lawn area, one couldn't even see the grass.

The next stop in the Midwest was Detroit for two nights. The Owls would be playing the 2,900 seats of the Palms Theatre, which opened in 1925. The balcony level still contained the original theater seating that became thirty-five years old in 1960. The fans from Detroit really enjoyed the new rock 'n' roll, but the slower, more bluesy numbers of the Owls went over just as well and were highly received.

In Fort Wayne, Indiana, the band played the Allen County War Memorial Coliseum, with its 10,500 seats. It was relatively new, having opened in 1952. The group played only one concert there and then would have the next two days off, after they moved into Chicago.

Bob had been talking with Corey every night and didn't like what he had been hearing from her. He resolved himself to the fact that she had been going through a living hell.

Bob told Nick, Truman, and the guys that he was going to go home and get to the bottom of all this tumult, but he would be back Wednesday, July 20, to play the Palmer House there in Chicago.

Everyone but Bob got off the plane in Chicago the Monday morning of July 18. He would fly on to LAX, where Nick had arranged for a car to pick him up at ten o'clock that morning. He had the driver take him directly to the Celebrity Studios in Hollywood.

At close to ten thirty, he was dropped off in front of the building that led to Jack Windheim's office. Bob was ascending the stairs two at a time at a very quick pace.

When he entered the front waiting area, he hurriedly asked Deloris, "Hi, Deloris. Is Jack alone, or is he with someone right now?"

"Hiya, Bob. Jack's alone, but he asked not to be disturbed. So go on in and disturb him, honey. He'll always make room for you."

Bob smiled at her and then knocked on Jack's door and let himself in.

When Jack looked up and through the cloud of cigar smoke that encircled his desk, he wasn't surprised to see Bob standing there. Jack stood up and placed his cigar in the ashtray, saying, "I know why you're here, Bob. We've got an eye on this guy Jason. We're trying to get something on him that would stick in a court of law."

Bob, infuriated at this point, laid into Jack, "You mean to tell me you're waiting for him to hurt someone, most especially Corey? He might actually do physical harm to her, and what are you going to do at that point, Jack? Are you going to continue to sit here with your thumbs up your ass, or what?"

Jack knew Bob was extremely upset and tried to placate his anger. "Corey didn't want this guy thrown off the lot, she wants him to go to jail and for her to never have to see him again… Bob, listen to me… We're gonna get this son of a bitch, but we have to do it legally."

Bob stared at Jack with worried anger in his eyes and informed him, "I'm going over to the soundstage where they're shooting and stay far in back of the cameras. I want to get a look at this asshole and check out the whole situation. Why don't you come with me for a while, Jack? We can assess this problem in minutes and see for ourselves how crazy this bastard really is."

Jack answered resignedly, "I've watched him, along with a handful of others, and believe me, Bob, this guy is crafty, clever, and cunning… He knows exactly what he's doing. But I'll go over with you and cover up you being there. Especially from Jason. He might take the coward's way out and run, or he could become angry and try to hurt someone. So, let's go."

Jack and Bob slipped quietly into the far reaches of the soundstage. They watched a scene that was presently being shot with Herbert Marshall and Corey.

Jack pointed out Jason to Bob. Jason had a non-talking part in this scene and was standing away from Corey. Bob's eyes followed Jason's every move.

Bob and Jack stayed hidden in the back of the soundstage for the next two hours, until Lloyd called for everyone to take an hour lunch.

Bob saw Corey leave the set, probably heading for her dressing room. She had Nina following close behind her.

Then Bob and Jack saw Jason take notice of Corey heading away from the path to the outside door that would have taken her to the studio's cafeteria. Jason looked around and watched almost everyone exiting through the door in front to go have lunch.

Almost immediately, Jason headed in Corey's direction.

Without hesitating, Bob told Jack, "That's it. Come on, Jack. I don't like the smell of this. Something's up, man!"

Jack wasn't sure what they should do, saying, "All right, Bob. If that's what you feel. Let's go! But I'm going to call security first! Then I'll catch up to you!"

All of a sudden, Bob and Jack heard a female voice sharply cry out, "Oh my god. No!"

Bob turned to Jack and yelled, "Call 'em now!"

Jack started dialing the phone that was in back of the soundstage as Bob took off running toward the dressing rooms.

As he approached the dressing room area, he gasped in horror as he saw Nina's abhorrent bloodied head, as she lay on the floor in a small pool of blood. He quickly checked her to see if she was still breathing, and he found she was totally knocked unconscious, but alive.

It was at that moment Bob looked at the dressing room door and screamed, "Corey!" He turned the doorknob and found it was locked. An explosive aura of protectiveness shot through his veins that made him feel like no one or anything was going to stop him from going through that door.

He put his full weight and the muscle of his right shoulder into an abrupt strike and smashed the door open. The lock flew into the air, along with wood chips from the frame.

Bob instantly saw Corey pinned down over her vanity table by Jason's one arm while his other arm was unzipping his pants. The top of Corey's dress had been torn, to expose her bra. Jason had already lifted her gown up to her waistline and had torn off her panties.

In the span of less than a second, Bob felt like he was having a bad dream, but the reality of the situation slapped him in the face. Without thinking about anything but Corey, and Bob incensed to the highest degree humanly possible, he leapt into the air at Jason.

Bob's arms wrapped around Jason's neck as he pulled him off of Corey and then threw him to the dressing room floor. Jason landed with a thud, which momentarily took his breath away.

Jason was a big guy, a couple inches taller than Bob, but this didn't affect the way Bob was manhandling him like a rag doll.

Ecstatically surprised beyond belief, Corey shot upright and screamed, "Bob? Oh my god! Oh, baby! Thank God!"

Jack came running; as slow and encumbered as he was, he caught up and surmised what was happening. He helped Corey from the room, and then he tended to Nina, who was moaning and groaning and was almost conscious. Jack could see Bob had full control of this.

As Jason tried to get up, Bob struck him hard to the side of the head. Jason tried to hit back, but Bob was all over him, striking his head and face with both fists, one after the other. The blows were relentless, and Jason's face became reddened and bruised, and the blood was running freely down his face and into his ears. Bob had him sandwiched between the makeup vanity and a small sofa that was in the corner of the room.

Security showed up, along with some ambulance EMTs. Jack then turned his attention to the dressing room, where three security guards could not get Bob off of Jason.

Corey pleaded with Bob as she yelled, "Stop! Bob, please. Stop! Let the police handle it!"

Jack vindictively yelled at the security men, "Hey! You guys back off! Let him have at it!"

Corey turned to look at Jack in amazement. "Oh, Jack. Please make him stop!"

Bob felt the security men back away. He stood up breathless, his hands were very sore and bruised, and his clothes were soaked with Jason's blood. Bob stood over him and let Jason's limp body crumble flat to the floor. Before Bob left him, he kicked him hard to the ribs and shouted, "You son of a bitch! If you ever try this again with any-one, and I'll kill you, you piece of garbage!"

Jason lay motionless, still barely alive. The EMTs worked on him and was able to get him ready to be transported to the hospital. He obviously was in critical condition.

Nina had been taken to the hospital several minutes earlier. She would survive her head injury, where she was struck by Jason, hit-ting her with the fake military revolver he was given from the studio props.

When they pushed Jason's gurney out of the dressing room and toward the ambulance, Corey flew into Bob's arms.

Her wet, vacant, weeping eyes were looking up at him, and when he turned his face into hers, Corey broke down sobbing. She was weeping and then sobbing uncontrollably.

Bob reached over to the vanity table and grabbed a good-size towel and wrapped it around Corey's exposed shoulders.

He then held her tight to his body as his heart was pounding and his throat tight with held-in tears. He could get rid of the cause of her pain, but he knew he'd never be able to get her to forget the assault.

He softly whispered into her ear, "It's all right, baby. I'm here for you. Cry all you want. My god! I'm just so sorry this happened to you, Corey."

Bob was consoling her under his breath, which tended to give his words a confident tone that she frankly welcomed. He spoke in a humble voice, a voice that was reverent, and Corey felt so safe and warm enveloped by his body.

People in the studio's cafeteria were informed about what hap-pened backstage to Corey in her dressing room. Within minutes, many of them came running to see how she was.

Lloyd approached Corey as she still clung to Bob. Lloyd tried to comfort her by saying, "Corey, I'm so sorry about all this. Are you all right? This guy should be put away now for a long, long time… I'm just so sorry, dear."

The LAPD at the Hollywood Station walked into the back of the soundstage to get individual statements from everyone involved.

After questioning Corey, Bob, Jack, and the three security guards, the police promised they would have Jason in cuffs before the doctors could patch him up.

Over an hour later, the police told everyone that if they had any further questions, they'd be contacted, and to stay in town. Bob would have to supply the police with phone numbers and where and when he'd be at different times for the next ten days if they needed him for anything.

All the attention Corey was getting from everyone was making her very uncomfortable and very anxious. Bob knew he had to get her away from all this.

He told Lloyd, "I'm gonna take her home now, Lloyd. I'm sure she'll call you when she's ready to come back to work."

"Absolutely, Bob. She can take all the time she needs. Just let me know."

Curtis had to be called to come to the studio to pick them up and was told it was because of a problem that occurred at the studio. This surprised him as he wasn't used to coming to pick Corey up so early in the afternoon. Curtis also told Haddie, before he left to pick them up, that there was an incident at the studio and that Bob was bringing Corey home.

"Mr. Bob? What on earth is he doing in town? He's supposed to be in Chicago performing two nights from now. That's what Joshua told me last night on the phone. Oh, no! This must be something bad that's happened to Ms. Corey. Oh my god! No!"

Curtis could only shake his head and mumble, "I don't know, Haddie. I just don't know."

Less than an hour later, Curtis brought Bob and Corey home to Bel Air. They were met at the door by Haddie, who Bob told, "I'm going to get Corey into a warm bath, and then I'll come out and talk with you. Okay?"

Haddie had tears welling in her eyes as she saw in Corey's face only the shell of what was the happy, vivacious, easygoing friend she had come to love as her sister. She nodded her head to Bob in affirmation as a single tear made its way down her cheek.

Bob sat on the side of the bathtub as Corey was hidden under the amount of bubbles that was burying her. He ran a soapy loofah sponge all over her back and occasionally bent over to give her a sweet short kiss. She was responding very well to his doting over her.

When she wanted out of the tub, Bob helped her to dry off, and she moisturized her body, as Bob made one of her nightgowns ready to slip into.

As he was going to help her into bed, she boldly stated, "No. I think I would prefer to just go out to the pool area and lay with you in a lounger. Would you mind, darling?"

Bob flashed a cautionary smile to her and softly told her, "Absolutely not, doll. Anything you want... Actually, that sounds wonderful. Just give me five minutes to get these soiled clothes off and take a quick shower."

Corey managed a broken smile to him and replied, "I'll always wait for you, darling."

Ten minutes later, Bob and Corey walked into the kitchen with their arms around each other, and Haddie ran to put her arms around Corey, sympathetically asking, "Oh, Ms. Corey! Are you all right, honey? You got me so worried!"

A half an hour later, after Bob told Haddie the entire story, Haddie put her hand to her mouth, outraged yet empathetic toward Corey. In one of Haddie's rare moments in life...she was speechless. She walked over to Corey and put her arms around her, trying to comfort her, as she and Corey both had welled-up tears in their eyes.

Corey fatalistically told Haddie, "Thank you, Haddie. I think I just need a little time to process all this, but I'll be all right in the long run."

Bob then interjected, "Haddie? We're going to take our dinner out by the pool tonight. And could you bring me a couple of beers and a martini for Corey?"

Haddie complied, as Bob carried Corey in his arms out to the pool and softly placed her down into one of the double-loungers. He then lay down beside her, leaned over and kissed her on the forehead, and then told her determinedly, "Baby, I will always try my damnedest to protect you from anyone or anything. That guy had to be stopped."

Deeply touched by his tenacious protective nature, Corey tenderly told him, "Bob, you will always be my life and my salvation. I thank God every day for finding you."

Bob wanted only to soothe her, and to love her, as he leaned into her and kissed her cheek. Rampant, comforting chills shot through her. She thought, *Oh! The pure warmth of it! I'm living with one of God's angels already!*

By eight o'clock that night, they had eaten their dinner, and each had a few drinks. The evening was exquisitely delightful for them, but it was getting dusk. The sky was streaked with amethyst and burning gold, as Bob and Corey were lost in each other.

Around nine o'clock, Haddie came out to check on them, asking, "Y'all gonna stay out here all night? 'Cause I can bring out a flashlight if you want."

Bob looked at Corey, and she gave him that sly little smile she was so good at.

Bob, content with her attitude and thrilled with her demeanor, happily told Haddie, "Why don't you bring out a couple of blankets and pillows for us. I think we're going to bask under the stars and the full moon tonight. Okay, Haddie?"

"All right, then, Mr. Bob. That does sound magical."

Later, after they had all their pillows and blankets in place, Corey nestled under Bob's arm and rested her head on his chest. With her arm around his waist, she lovingly told him, "I never want this evening to end, darling."

Bob slowly kissed the top of her head for several seconds. She loved it, as she fell asleep with his arms enfolding her.

TWENTY-ONE

At quarter after five the next morning, Bob lay wide awake in the lounger, beneath the still-darkened skies, while Corey was asleep next to him. She still had her arm around his waist and her head on his chest. By the lights shining from the bottom of the pool, he looked down at her face, and she seemed angelically serene; her eyes were closed, and she was quietly exhaling her warm breath unto his chest.

He had been awake on and off all night, only to worry about Corey's safety and well-being at times when he knew he couldn't be there with her.

Forty-five minutes later was the break of dawn. The first soft strip of daylight was just touching the horizon. Bob contemplatively looked around the backyard and studied the jungle of myriad colors and the bunches of monochromatic flowers, as he felt the tender, pulsing core of Corey's heart with his arm. It was her pure heart, and he was the only one privy to that.

On Wednesday morning, the day Bob had to fly back to Chicago to perform, Corey, being the strong and independent woman she embodied, told him at breakfast, "I'm going back to work tomorrow morning, darling. I don't see why I shouldn't. It's costly when they stop shooting, and it could even jeopardize the production."

Bob looked at her, not saying a word. He was worried about her, but he also knew she was a resilient, formidable force when she put her mind to it.

Bob trusted her judgment implicitly, as he acquiesced to her wishes. "Well, baby, if you think you'll be all right, then you do what you have to do. You know I'll stand behind any decision you make, but you have to promise me, that if you have any problems at all, you'll call me, and we'll talk."

"Darling, I'll be talking with you almost every night for the next ten days, until I see you in San Diego. I'll be fine, baby. Really I will."

Curtis whisked Bob off to LAX at noon that July 20. The almost four hours Bob was flying to Chicago, he could only wonder about the fact that Corey had never wanted to initiate anything sexually with him for the two days he was at home with her. He didn't feel comfortable in bringing the subject up either, for fear she would react adversely. He hoped maybe she just needed some time to feel less stressed and to come to terms with the whole situation.

That night, the Owls readied themselves to play the Palmer House. It was built just after the civil war and had 2,263 seats for ticket holders.

The Palmer House was bedecked with garnet-shaped chandeliers, Louis Comfort Tiffany masterpieces, and a breathtaking ceiling fresco by French painter Louis Pierre Rigal.

The most notable entertainers that had appeared there were Harry Belafonte, Frank Sinatra, Louis Armstrong, Liberace, and now the world-renowned Night Owls.

When Bob arrived at the Palmer House around six o'clock, where the Owls were also staying, he explained everything to them about what had happened to Corey. They definitely were shook up about it, and each of the seven guys let Bob know they would be there for him if he or Corey needed any help in getting through this.

After catching some dinner, the Owls went directly downstairs to the theater hall and ran a sound check on their instruments. At eight o'clock, and after being given a warm and welcoming introduction, they busted into their first song, "Raging Fire."

The Owls played to a more jazz-imbued audience in Chicago, so their more saxophone-, guitar-, and trumpet-based songs spoke to the crowd. A city formerly raised on "Chicago-style jazz," from performers like Muddy Waters, Junior Wells, Sonny Boy Williamsons, Nat King Cole, Gene Ammons, Benny Goodman, and Bo Diddley, the younger fans welcomed the nontraditional sounds of the rock 'n' roll songs like "Ricochet," "Trying Hard," "No Time Out," and "Losing Track."

No longer was the New Orleans-style jazz music, with its tubas and banjos, so prodigiously influential in Chicago. Now rock 'n' roll, which was characterized with its heavy beats, simple melodies, and often contained a blues element, was poised to make its mark in the Windy City.

After a very exciting concert and sold-out performance at the Palmer House, the Night Owls took the vans and drove up to Milwaukee, Wisconsin, that same night. The hour and forty minutes it took them to drive to their hotel in the Wisconsin Center District would be their last vehicle commute. They would fly to the remaining four concert venues.

There was no noticeable trouble with protesters on this leg of the tour, until the group reached Minneapolis, Minnesota, Friday, July 22.

The protesters met them that afternoon, when all the guys went to take a look at the Roy Wilkins Minneapolis Auditorium, where they'd be performing for the next two nights.

The Owls' two rented airport vans pulled into the back entrance to the auditorium and were met with about two dozen sign-holding protesters that were yelling and pointing fingers at them. The venue's security men kept them away from the vehicles, and so there was no physical violence at all, just some very worn-out name-calling.

The population of whites in Minnesota in 1960 was 88.6 percent. Down only 0.7 percent from 1950. It seemed to the Owls that the majority of people in Minnesota wanted to keep it squeaky-white, even with the visiting celebrities who ventured into their domain.

The auditorium was built in 1932 and contained five thousand seats and came with top-class acoustics. It did draw big names—names with a white Christian ethnicity.

Tony Bennett had just played there four weeks ago. Al Hirt came in just a week prior to the Owls, and after he performed, he went straight on to appear in *The Dinah Shore Chevy Show* on NBC, broadcast from Burbank, California.

Even Elvis Presley played the auditorium in May of 1956, but to some very disappointing crowds. Parents weren't allowing their teenagers to view his bump-'n'-grind routine, so many seats went unfilled.

The two Night Owls concerts were not sellouts. The guys suspected for obvious reasons. This was one of few disappointments in Bob's life of almost constant achievements.

Directly after the second performance in Minneapolis, the Owls flew the one hour and fourteen minutes into Kansas City, Missouri. Again, they were confronted by even larger crowds of protesters and angry belligerents.

The venue's security, along with Nick's privately hired crew of twelve men, had the entire situation under control. These obvious bigots weren't allowed close to the guys.

The Starlight Theatre was only nine years old, with a capacity seating of almost eight thousand. It was a beautiful outdoor venue, and the warmth of the July evening, with a soft breeze blowing over them, was the ideal atmosphere for a traveling rock band staging an outdoor road show. And surprisingly, the one night the Owls were appearing was a sold-out performance.

The Owls stayed in Kansas City that night after their entertaining and appreciated performance. Bob needed to call Corey. He hadn't called or heard from her for two nights.

It was ten o'clock that Sunday night in Bel Air when the phone rang. Haddie picked it up on the fourth ring and answered, "Hello. This is Ms. Madrigal's residence. Can I help you?"

Bob was taken aback, because he had become so accustomed to Corey picking up the phone after sometimes only one ring.

He questioningly asked Haddie, "Haddie, this is Bob. How are you? Where's Corey? At night she usually answers the phone very quickly."

Haddie tried to explain, "Well, Mr. Bob, it's been only six days from her assault, and she's not taking calls from anyone but you. She's trying her best to get back to what's normal for her, but I think she needs a lot more time, and she absolutely needs you."

Bob was deeply concerned with Corey's welfare, but he needed to talk with her. So he asked Haddie, "Haddie, go in and tell her to pick up the phone. I really need to hear her voice right now."

"All right, Mr. Bob. I know she'll jump for joy in hearing your voice. Give me a minute now."

Haddie lightly knocked on Corey's door, for fear she might be asleep, and then she quietly stepped in and peeked around the door. She saw Corey in bed, studying her lines for tomorrow's shoot, but she looked up at Haddie and curiously asked, "What is it, Haddie?"

Haddie happily told her, "It's Mr. Bob. He says he wants to hear your voice, Ms. Corey."

Corey closed her eyes, dropped her head, and exhaled heavily into her nightgown. She threw her manuscript onto the bed next to her and immediately jumped to the phone receiver on the nightstand.

With excited anticipation, Corey purred in a low passionate voice, "Hello, darling." Bob felt overwhelming gratitude in the fact that her voice sounded warm and welcoming as always.

He responded to her with a soft and sweet, "Hello, baby. How you doing tonight?"

She answered with an element of intrigue. "I'm just laying here in bed, memorizing my lines for tomorrow, and waiting to see what occurs in the studio this week."

Bewildered, Bob asked Corey, "What do you mean, doll? Why should anything occur this week? That asshole is locked up and will never cause you trouble again."

She fatalistically implied, "Yes, darling, he may be locked up, but he will always cause me trouble. I can't help but to feel angry, anxious, sad, and most of all, scared. I distrust most people around me now."

Bob blew a cleansing melancholy breath into the phone and remorsefully told her, "Oh, Lord, baby. I'm just so sorry. So damned sorry this happened to you."

Corey tried to soothe his guilt he may have been feeling. "It really wasn't your fault, darling. I just thank God you were there for me, or I'd still be picking up the pieces to my life… I can't wait to see you later this week. Try to get to the studio when you get home. I don't want to wait until that night to hold you. All right, sweetheart?"

"Of course, I will, baby… Then I'll see you sometime Thursday morning at the studio. I promise. It'll only take two hours to get there from Denver. So, I'll see you in just three and a half days, doll. I love you, Corey. Good night, my sweet lady."

With pent-up tears in her eyes, she lovingly whispered, "Bob, hurry home to me. You're the only person that will be able to put a smile back on my face again. I love you so much, Robert Brian."

She slowly, quietly hung up the receiver of the phone.

Bob dolefully placed one hand over his eyes and forehead as his eyes became moistened.

That Monday, July 25, the Owls flew into Denver, Colorado, for concerts on Tuesday and Wednesday nights. The Denver Coliseum was a large indoor arena built in 1951. There would be 10,200 seats to fill, and Nick checked ahead with the venue's ticket sales and was informed both performances had been sold out two months ago.

The coliseum had a reputation for hosting a variety of concerts. Among the biggest celebrities who played there were Jerry Lee Lewis, the Everly Brothers, Elvis, Johnny Mathis, Fats Domino, Carl Perkins, Bill Haley and the Comets, and one of the great innovators in 1950s rock music, Little Richard. Little Richard often said that rhythm 'n' blues had a baby, and somebody named it rock 'n' roll.

Both concerts were exciting and each almost three hours long. There were Bob, Len, and Darnell up front singing; Joshua running a lot of riffs on his night mistress, the bass trumpet; and Bob dancing out in front of the audience, flirting with the young ladies and touching hands with any Owls fan that reached for him.

Pure electricity was surging through the coliseum for both concerts, but those three hours each night was the only escape that Bob had from the persistent torment of Corey's distress she had developed from the assault.

The next morning, all eight guys flew out of Denver and back home to Los Angeles for the two days they would have before the two concerts in San Diego, Saturday and Sunday.

Nick had his limo waiting for him, Doug, Jimmy, Darnell, and Joshua. Truman flew on to San Diego to secure the instruments in the Starlight Bowl amphitheater backstage area.

Bob called ahead and had Curtis meet him and Len at LAX, and after Curtis dropped him off at the Celebrity Studio, he would continue on to Burbank and take Len home to Valerie.

At ten o'clock, Bob snuck in the back door of the soundstage, with a little help from the security guard, and slowly walked up behind one of the cameras. They were actively shooting a scene with Corey, Hope Lange, and Teresa Wright, as Corey sat behind a desk professionally throwing her lines at Hope and Teresa.

Richard Carlson caught a glimpse of Bob and quietly and slowly moved toward him. When he reached Bob, not a word was said between them, as they smiled at each other and shook hands. They turned and continued to watch the shooting of the scene play out.

After another minute, Lloyd called, "Cut! All right, ready yourselves for a second take on that same scene 27. We just need to get the lighting adjusted a little differently on this shot."

Corey had scoured the areas behind the set and cameras all morning looking for Bob. Every time Lloyd called a stoppage, she waited for Bob to appear. She always seemed very disappointed when she couldn't find him.

However, on this break, Corey looked away from the camera, as though something enticing was happening out of frame. She saw Richard standing with a man that started to walk out of the darkness behind the cameras and was moving toward her.

At first, she was apprehensive, but then to her total delight and surprise, she saw the love of her life walking toward her, with a beaming smile that filled her heart.

Corey quickly rose from the desk and flew into Bob's arms, making him the envy of every man in the place.

They embraced each other very tightly as she wrapped her arms around his neck and began to inundate him with kisses to his neck, cheek, and then finally, to Bob's great pleasure, his lips. Their kiss lasted several seconds, as a single tear slipped down her face.

Hope and Teresa sat smiling and happily watched Bob and Corey entwined and bore witness to their deep, enthralling love, which was also quite obvious to everyone else.

Lloyd stood patiently waiting for Bob and Corey, for he knew Corey really needed this visceral connection with Bob. The entire production staff and crew started to lightly applaud, with a few whistles and "yeah's" thrown in for good measure.

Corey stepped back and looked at everyone smiling at her and Bob, and then slightly uncomfortable, she proudly stated, "Yes! This is my dashing husband, and I'm not sorry if I've held up production for two minutes. So, Lloyd, now that my heart is here, let's wrap up that scene."

Bob adoringly looked at Corey, smiled broadly, kissed her again, winked at her, and then he took a seat behind the cameras and off set. She kept a close eye on him at all times and occasionally cast a warm smile in his direction.

They spent lunch together at the studio's cafeteria, along with the other four actors in her picture. Emotionally, Corey seemed to be holding it all together, but Bob knew that only time would tell if she would come back to him as the woman he married.

Bob spent all of Friday with Corey at the studio and also most of Saturday. He then flew the two hours down to San Diego that afternoon for his eight o'clock concert at the Starlight Bowl amphitheater.

Again there was still no attempt by her to initiate any sexual activity with him. And even though he was a patient man, he felt that Corey might need some outside help.

As the cast and crew for *Beneath the Sullen Sky* was celebrating the closing shot to their picture, the Night Owls were at the ready to walk out onstage for the start of their first concert.

The Starlight Bowl amphitheater in San Diego, built in 1936, had 4,300 seats, and the performers and all of the seats were exposed to the weather.

The outside theater was one of the oldest musical theater companies in the country. It sat almost directly under the landing path for the San Diego International Airport. During musical performances, the conductor had a set of lights that indicated the noise level from passing planes. When the noise reached a certain level, the conductor signaled everyone to pause, and the musicians and performers froze in place until the plane passed.

The guys put on a great show that night, and as the sold-out crowd applauded and cheered their performance, they were asked to come back out and play an encore. They came back out and played two more songs for their fans.

When Bob got back to the hotel the Owls were staying at for the two nights, he dialed his home phone number to talk with Corey. There was trepidation running through him, for he really didn't know what to expect from Corey anymore in regard to anything.

Corey did pick up the phone after the second ring, which was encouraging to him, and he happily asked her, "Hello, baby. I bet you wrapped your picture up today, didn't you?"

His voice instantly started to calm her, and she warmly told him, "Good evening, sweetheart. And yes, we did wrap today. We'll be going to the wrap party Monday night, before we fly off to Hawaii on Tuesday… But how did your concert go tonight, darling?"

With emotional longing, Bob truthfully told her, "The concert went well, but I didn't see your face anywhere in the seats, so that part was very disappointing to me. So tomorrow night when you and all the Owls ladies are in the seats, I'm sure it'll go much better."

"Well, I'll try to do my part, darling." Corey softly laughed to herself.

The afternoon of Sunday, July 31, the last concert that would be on the mainland until August 12 and 13 at the Hollywood Bowl, Corey, Haddie, Deidra, Valerie, and Alicia flew over to San Diego to be with the guys for a few hours. Then they would all catch some dinner before the start of the performance.

On the plane to San Diego, Corey sat in a window seat with Haddie next to her. Corey worriedly mentioned the fact to Haddie, the one person she could trust with her most intimate feelings, that she wondered how long Bob would be able to cope with her estranged behavior and her sexual withdrawal from him.

Haddie mixed no words with Corey. She told her, shooting straight from the hip, "The only thing I could possibly tell you, Ms. Corey, is that man is the best thing that will ever happen to you in this lifetime. He's kind, generous, intelligent, exceptionally talented, amusing, and he would move heaven and earth to protect you, because he loves you more than his own life. I know deep down in my bones that he'll stay faithful to you for a thousand lifetimes. Ms. Corey, you need to be extremely careful in who you're punishing from that incident you experienced almost two weeks ago. Many men don't come along like Mr. Bob. He's your heart and soul, my friend...treat him like that."

Corey's eyes began to glisten with the sorrowful tears she now felt. After a few minutes of silence, she looked over at Haddie with a deeply renewed mental attitude, and quietly but honestly, she confessed to her, "Haddie, you know Bob has never had to say much. He'd ask a simple question or have an easy way of bringing something to light and revealed to me that he was one hundred percent aware of my feelings...and he always seemed to pick up on how I was feeling, sometimes before I did. He let me express that emotion, and most importantly, he gave me my space to figure things out for myself."

As Corey wiped a tear off her cheek with a tissue, she leaned over to Haddie and hugged her and kissed her on her cheek, gratefully saying, "Thank you, Haddie. I just needed some sense of direction from a true friend."

Haddie answered with a heartfelt "You're welcome, Ms. Corey... Now do I get a raise in pay for all this free psychiatric stuff?"

They both laughed out loud as Corey settled back in her seat and began to have dreams of reunion with the love of her life and being emotionally healed while being held in the warmth of his arms.

The five women arrived at the hotel the guys were staying at around five o'clock that early evening.

Corey raced into Bob's hotel room, and when she saw him sitting on the edge of the bed next to Len, she quickly darted to him and flung herself into his waiting arms. Landing in his lap, her momentum took them back onto the bed, where she lay on top of him.

She started kissing him long and hard as she ran her hands through his hair.

Everyone respectfully left the room and closed the door and gave Bob and Corey all the privacy they would want.

When they came up for air, Bob breathlessly told Corey, "Wherever you've been, baby, welcome home." His eyes showed pent-up tears forming.

Corey's eyes began to fill with unshed tears as she answered him almost apologetically, "I'll never leave you out in the cold again, sweetheart. You're the most important thing in my life and the biggest part of my heart."

They began kissing each other passionately while running their hands all over each other and working each other up into a sexual fervor.

They were both breathing heavily and kept probing each other's mouths with their tongues.

Bob rolled Corey over, and he now lay on top of her. He began to unbutton her blouse and exposed her sexy black bra as he kissed her neck and, with one hand, felt around her back to unhook her bra.

Suddenly and out of nowhere, a knock on the door was heard, and Truman's voice came through loud and clear. "Bob? We're trying to get the guys together to go and run a sound check on the instruments and the sound system at the theater."

Truman was totally unaware of Corey being in the room with Bob. He only knew this was the room Bob was assigned.

Out of breath, Bob forlornly looked into Corey's eyes and told her, "I'm sorry, baby. I'll make this up to you tonight when we get home in Bel Air. I promise."

Corey took a deep breath and exhaled loudly in sexual frustration. "I'll see to that, mister."

After Truman repeated himself, Bob got up and answered the door. He was still breathing kind of hard and was extremely agitated, but was able to calmly tell Truman, "I'll be there in a minute, man. Just let me get it together for a few seconds."

That's when Truman caught a quick glimpse of Corey getting up from the bed to button up her blouse.

Tongue-tied and flabbergasted, Truman tried to apologize, "Oh, man! I'm so sorry, Bob. No one gave me a heads-up. I'm just so sorry!"

Exasperated, Bob facetiously warned him, "It's okay, man. You didn't know. But I gotta tell you, you'd better not come close to my room again when I have my wife around, or I'll throw you in a box and mail you back to LA, special delivery. Got it?"

Truman totally agreed and then ran back to the shuttle van that was going to take them quickly to the amphitheater for an instrument sound check. Dinner would ensue when they returned to join the ladies.

The Owls put on a phenomenal show for their second night. The guitars were crying out with a synchronous vibration, and Bob busted a riff with a syncopated rhythm while they played "Ricochet." He stressed an unexpected part of the rhythm. The weak beats became strong, and the strong beats got de-emphasized. The riff was only two bars long, but he repeated it a few times, which immediately added a spark of new interest in the song.

Len and Darnell kept playing and were still aligned with the main pulse of the song, but Bob leaned into the backbeats (the second and fourth beats in a standard bar) and spiced up the rhythm of the underlying music.

Corey was watching Bob with an acute fascination, and as her eyes glistened, she knew she was witnessing a smooth, powerful, and brilliant young man that she loved with every fiber of her being.

Joshua was smoking the valves to his mistress-in-waiting, the C trumpet. His genius rendering of "Conviction" had him playing at least half of the possible forty-five notes available to him on his trumpet. Bob and Len turned to Joshua, smiling broadly at him, and then looked back at each other, nodding their heads in complete triumph.

Haddie had welled-up tears in her eyes as the ultimate pride she had in her son overwhelmed her with the unmeasurable talent that he possessed and displayed that night.

Jimmy even ran a thirty-second solo later in "Raging Fire" as he tore into his drums. He was playing the "money beat" (the drumbeat that was heard most often on big hits), and along with all four of his kick drums blaring, he was throwing in some open high-hat cymbals, with intermittent strokes on the crash cymbal, as he kept the lead rhythm with a scolding performance on his snare. The man may have been small, thin, and diminutive in stature, but when he ripped into his drums, no man in the theater was larger than Jimmy.

Bob threw his head back smiling profusely and just laughed with unequivocal joy. Jimmy was one of the greatest beat-keepers in the business.

When the Owls reached a part in "Maybe Another Time, Another Place," Doug opened up on his alto saxophone for a full minute with a melodious serenade.

His solo contained a lot of improvisation, which was vital in any sax solo. His expression was unique, in that when he played, he moved the sax up and down, and it was as if his horn was an extension of his body.

Tonight, the sax was the best part of the song, because Doug was bending notes downward and upward after he started them in the correct pitch.

Bob looked over at Doug and had a brilliant smile on his face, and then he turned back to his guitar shaking his head in disbelief, and then he finished the vocals with the last stanza and the last chorus to the song.

After each song the Night Owls played that night, the over four thousand fans gave them a thunderous applause, along with loud cheers and a lot of screeching whistles.

The young girls charged the stage at the end of the concert, and when security tried to return them to their seats, Bob waved security off.

Bob motioned to the guys to come down to the front edge of the stage and greet their fans. At that point, the fans mobbed the stage area. It was mostly young girls with some of their faces painted the colors of a barn owl and the snowy owl. There were also young ladies and young men trying to touch or shake one of the Night

Owls' hands or arms. Some of the young girls were crying after they touched one of the Owls' hands, but security had to be called when one of the young ladies fainted after touching Bob's face.

Corey and the guys' ladies were smiling amusingly and outright laughing, for this display of idol worship up at the front of the stage was thoroughly entertaining to them.

Corey did keep a close eye on Bob and was convinced he found great pleasure in bringing that much excitement and happiness into these young people's lives.

After the Owls quitted the stage, the guys' ladies had backstage passes, and after walking in back, Corey quickly spotted Bob among the chaos around her.

The amphitheater stagehands were breaking down the drums for transport to the San Diego International Airport, and the noise was disconcerting if one wasn't around it often.

Then the individually cased horns and guitars had to be carried to the airport van, manned by Truman, to drive to the awaiting aircraft.

After Corey spotted Bob, she ran to him. He instantly noticed her approaching and held his arms out wide to her. She raced into the warmth of his welcoming body. Then they kissed like they hadn't seen each other in weeks, which is what it seemed like to them.

All the women began congratulating and complimenting the guys on having such a spectacular performance. The whole time this was going on, Corey was still not able to let go of Bob's one arm. She held fast and tight to him, and it seemed she was not letting go any time soon.

Bob and Corey flew back home to LA that night, after the guys and their significant others, including Haddie, flew on to Honolulu, Hawaii, for their two shows that coming weekend. Bob and Corey had two first-class seats flying back to LA; however, they only needed one.

The guys figured this would give them two full days longer than Bob and Corey, who had to return home for Corey's wrap party. The party for *Beneath the Sullen Sky* was set for Monday night, eight o'clock, at D'Angelo's, after having returned home early Monday morning at two o'clock.

After Curtis delivered them to their Bel Air estate, they left their luggage at the french doors where they entered. Bob and Corey were home alone with only one thing on their mind.

Having locked an arm around each other, they moved to the master suite already kissing and then began to excitedly undress each other.

Both standing naked now, Corey took Bob's hand and led him into the bathroom and turned the shower on the warm setting.

They both stepped into the shower together, as the welcoming warmth of the water washed down over the two of them. They started kissing long and feverishly.

Corey never took her eyes off of Bob as she reached for the soap on the shower ledge and took this into her hands. She lathered her hands thickly. As she put the soap back, she reached under Bob and cupped him in her left hand and then put her right hand around his excitement.

The motion of her right hand became rhythmical, and he grew harder and harder, and what self-control he tried to retain quickly vanished. As Bob came, Corey put her left arm tightly around him and held him even tighter to her body, as she also moved her right arm around him. Bob was unable to stand for a moment, so he put his arm around Corey's neck for support.

When it was over, Bob rested back against the warm tiles, still savoring the pleasure and the water softly thundering down upon them.

He gently took Corey by the shoulders and turned her back to the tiles as they changed places. He erotically washed her torso with his lathered hands, and then just as erotically rinsed her off. He started to kiss her savagely and then moved to her breasts as he cupped each one in his hands. He began to suckle the nipple, as he sensually and tenderly bit at the excited areola. Corey began to moan loudly as she ran her hands through his head of hair and over his shoulders.

Bob then moved his head down to her lower stomach as he slowly separated her legs and started his tongue over her. He licked and suckled every part of her; Corey started to breathe unevenly with gasps of air as she moved her pelvis with his mouth. Bob kept stroking her with his tongue; when she jerked and her body became tense, she started to scream in ecstasy as she climaxed. "Oh my god! Baby, yes, yes! Oh my god, Bob!"

Minutes later, Corey began to relax somewhat and pulled Bob up to her and held him so tight to her body that the water from the showerhead could not flow between them. They stood kissing each other on the neck and shoulders, with her arms around his neck and his hands enveloping her buttocks.

When they decided to get out of the shower, they dried each other off, and then they both climbed naked into bed.

Bob closed his eyes as he held Corey in his arms. He was overwhelmed with his love for her. He never thought much about the kind of woman he'd marry, if any, and now it seemed perfectly right that she was abundantly talented as well as beautiful. And her beauty, it was natural. He had always been captivated by her.

When Corey drew her head back away from his chest, she kissed him openmouthed and lustily, and at that moment, she felt closer to him than to any other living thing in her entire life.

It was now almost four in the morning, and Bob lay back with his eyes closed, tired to the point of stupor, and she was now looking at him with such loving eyes. She pulled the sheet up over them, as Bob began to breathe heavily after he fell off to sleep.

Corey raptly stared at Bob, and her voice cracking with the tender passion she felt for him at that moment, she whispered, "Good night, my beautiful man."

Bob woke up at almost noon. As he opened his eyes and blew out a huge breathy yawn, he felt Corey lying between his legs with her hands cupped under her chin as her arms rested on his chest.

She was smiling radiantly, which made Bob slightly chuckle from her infectious smile. He couldn't help but to notice her breasts were lying on his chest. He kept staring at the beautiful way they played across his skin. The cleavage that resulted from her positioning was perhaps the most earnest invitation he had ever seen. His mouth slightly opened, and his eyes returned to look softly into her strikingly beautiful blue eyes, which were steeped with inviting sexual desire.

At that moment, Corey moved up his body and took full advantage of the situation.

Two hours later, Bob was out swimming laps in the pool while Corey was making them some eggs, sausage, and toast for breakfast.

When Corey brought the food out, Bob got out of the pool and was toweling off.

In her sexiest voice, she stated to him, "Darling, I'm surprised you had any energy left to swim today."

Her smile consumed him as he reminded her, "Well, I did sleep pretty good last night."

Corey smilingly looked at him and very sexily chuckled. "Ah-huh."

At almost eight o'clock, Corey came out of the bedroom dressed in a skin-tight, peach-colored taffeta gown. The flowing train was sheer and white and flew high and majestically behind her. Her cleavage had a sexy low cut that extended down to the base of her sternum, which showcased her voluptuous breasts. It was a sophisticated, mind-blowing gown by Emilio Pucci that came close to taking Bob's breath away. In full makeup and her hair up and beautifully arranged, she was the epitome of Hollywood glamour.

When she walked to him, as he waited for her at the french doors, he let out a loud, sexy whistle and exclaimed, "Wow! Baby! You are so badass foxy tonight!"

"Thank you, darling. Tonight I wore this for only you."

Corey then looked at what Bob was wearing and told him, "You look wonderful tonight too, sweetheart. You look so good in dark colors because of your beautiful hair."

Bob did look handsome in his sharply cut blue denim suit and a white dress shirt open at the collar. He came by that style so daringly and so naturally, thanks to some former styling by Ms. Edith Head.

Bob drove them both to D'Angelo's in his Chevy flip-top, and when the two of them walked in together, heads were turning. They were a gorgeous couple—a couple with unmatched love for each other and a power couple in Hollywood of mammoth proportions.

The din in the room quickly softened as Mario showed Bob and Corey to their table. They were, of course, seated with Herbert Marshall, Teresa Wright, Richard Carlson, and Hope Lange and all their significant others.

After all the accolades were handed out for the picture, Lloyd alluded briefly to the incident with Corey and Jason. "And I personally am thankful that Corey has been victorious in her emotional struggle with what happened to her backstage during the shooting of this picture. Kudos to you, Corey, and God bless you, my friend."

Everyone in the room stood and applauded her.

Corey simply nodded her head in affirmation with no recognizable facial expression.

When dinner was concluded, and after another drink, Bob asked Corey, "Would you dance with me, doll?"

More than willing, Corey flung the train of her dress over her shoulder and rose from her chair, answering, "Oh, of course, sweetheart. Absolutely."

The Owls song "Not Another Lonely Night" was playing in the background. Bob took her in his arms, staring directly into her face, and then he lightly kissed her on the lips for a few seconds. He pulled her very close to his body as she laid her head on his chest, whereas she could look up into his face.

Her left hand was high on his shoulder, cupping the back of his neck, as her right arm was around his waist. Bob whispered the lyrics of the song into her ear, and at that moment, it seemed to Corey that she was in her very own paradise.

The next morning, Bob and Corey flew out to Honolulu, Hawaii, for seven days. The Owls' two concerts would be that weekend, right in the middle of the seven-day stay.

The only racial discrimination in Hawaii that the Owls had to be aware of was the antiwhite bias and racial rancor directed at non-Native Hawaiians in the Aloha State.

The antiwhite sentiments had been decades and decades in the making.

In 1893, the US military forces overthrew Hawaii's monarch and placed her under house arrest. Then the US annexed the islands as a territory in 1898, and Hawaii then became a state sixty-one years later in 1959.

The resentment some Native Hawaiians felt toward whites and that trauma is qualitatively different than other ethnic groups in America. It's more akin to the American Indians, because Hawaiians had their homeland invaded, were exposed to diseases for which they had no immunity, and had an alien culture forced upon them.

The stories passed down from one generation to the next about the theft of their lands and culture were only different from the American Indians, because in Hawaii, the Native Hawaiians were far more numerous than the whites. Whereas the American Indians were grossly outnumbered by the white Europeans.

The five hours and twenty-minutes it took Bob and Corey to fly into Oahu, they managed to arrive at four o'clock that Tuesday afternoon. They were met at the airport by a limousine Nick had sent that delivered them to the Ritz Carlton Hotel at Waikiki Beach.

Bob and Corey walked through the beautiful and tropically designed lobby to check in at the front desk. They were impressed with the highly shined marble flooring, the fourteen-foot potted palm trees, the brightly colored furniture and drapes, and the circular eight-foot-wide waterfall set in the middle of the spacious marbled floor.

That's when Bob spotted Len, Valerie, Joshua, Deidra, and Haddie sitting in the hotel's bar and lounge having a cocktail.

Bob took Corey's hand, and they entered the lounge where Len, Joshua, and Haddie stood up to greet them. Len shook Bob's hand and kissed Corey on the cheek, remarking, "Hey, you two. It's about time you got here."

Joshua shook Bob's hand and kissed Corey's cheek also and remarked, "My man, Bob. You've got some catching up to do. We've been keeping busy exploring the island and the bar."

Bob jokingly told Joshua, "Yeah, man. I've been doing some exploring myself. And I bet I had more fun than you."

Joshua put his hand out, and he and Bob slipped each other some skin.

Corey stood hanging on to Bob's arm, just chuckling under her breath and looking around the lounge a little self-consciously.

Haddie came over to Corey and hugged her and Bob. After she heard what Bob told Joshua, she looked into Corey's face with anticipation and asked, "Is everything going good for you, Ms. Corey?"

Corey looked at Haddie with a huge smile and slowly blinked her eyes, joyously answering, "Everything is great, Haddie."

Haddie smiled back at her with an exhalation of thankfulness.

Valerie spoke up at that moment, and with excitement to her voice, she told Bob and Corey, "You two need to go out and buy yourself some Hawaiian-styled clothes to wear to the seven o'clock luau tonight."

Then Deidra informed them, "Yeah, Nick made reservations for all thirteen of us to go to the Chief's Luau on Waikiki Beach. It's supposed to be the best luau on the island of Oahu."

Corey looked up at Bob with those enticing eyes of hers, and looking directly into his eyes, she sexily said, "Well, you know, darling, I really love good food and expensive shopping."

Bob, lost in her cute smile, put his right index finger under her chin, slightly leaned down to her, and into her face, he said, "I guess we're going shopping, doll." Then tenderly kissed her.

Most of the dozens of people in the lounge were watching and keeping their eyes on Bob and Corey after they entered and stayed standing by the other five's table.

These two people were so publicly recognizable and world-renowned that after Bob kissed Corey so softly, the question was answered that so many people wondered about: can a young man of twenty-four find romance with a woman of forty-eight?

The answer to all of them was, *Hell yes!*

After Bob and Corey got settled in their ocean-view suite high on the twenty-first floor, they took off by taxi to the downtown area of Honolulu and the boutiques of haute couture.

Corey did almost all the shopping for both of them. She thoroughly knew high-end fashion and the designers that created them. When she finished shopping two hours later, she had silk Hawaiian-styled muumuu dresses, a sarong, and a pa'u wrapped skirt. The pa'u skirt was made from raffia, which was long palm fibers woven together.

All these dresses and skirts were created by Pierre Cardin, Givenchy, Yves Saint Laurent, Paco Rabanne, or Emilio Pucci.

She bought four silk Hawaiian-print or aloha-print shirts for Bob. For men, a nice buttoned-up Hawaiian shirt, when worn with a pair of khaki shorts or pants, went from casual to dressy.

Nick had the entourage of thirteen people meeting him in the lobby of the hotel so they could all be driven to the luau together. He was still missing four people at quarter to seven.

The elevator doors opened, and Joshua and Deidra came strolling out in their matching tropical-print outfits. The Hawaiian prints to his shirt and her muumuu were a breezy, cool ocean-blue and yellow, with exotic birds, palm trees, and pineapples throughout. The two were sleek, black, and resplendent, and the awaiting party blew wolf whistles at them as they were complimented on their eye-popping outfits.

When the second elevator opened, Bob and Corey hurried out and started to apologize for being a little slow in getting ready.

The group was duly impressed by Corey's Pierre Cardin silk, floor-length, spaghetti-sleeved muumuu dress that was richly decorated in native floral patterns of red, yellow, blue, and orange.

Bob was in a beautifully-blue patterned silk Hawaiian shirt, and along with his khaki shorts, he was a very attractive man. Both he and Corey were decked out and totally top drawer.

After everyone got done complimenting each other on their beautiful Hawaiian outfits, a limousine whisked them off to the Chief's Luau on Waikiki Beach.

There was a huge area on the beach in back of the Honolulu Royal Hilton that had luau seating for two hundred people. The Owls and their ladies were seated close to the stage, but a little right-centered. The rows of seats were all arched to face the front of the stage, and every two seats had a small table in front of them, covered in a colorful cotton cloth, for drinks and food.

As the group sat down, many people recognized the Owls and Corey, and the place was abuzz with chatter and finger-pointing. Although excited to see the Owls, a lot of them knew they would see them in concert either Friday or Saturday at the Waikiki Shell.

Bob couldn't help but notice after he sat down that the native Hawaiian band of seven guys called the Ho'onani (translated meant "to give praise") was playing authentic Hawaiian songs.

Two of them had Hilo Hawaiian steel guitars, one had a Hawaiian acoustic slide guitar, one other played the Tiki (a Tahitian drum of wood). Another drum, the Ka'eke'eke, was made of bamboo and was played simply by striking it on the ground. The remaining two guys played the soprano ukulele.

After an emcee came out and thanked everyone for coming, they also hoped everyone would enjoy the luau's food and the night's evening show.

Each row of seats took their turn going up to the luau's buffet table. Besides the customary roasted pig, there was salmon, shrimp, and pineapple kebabs and skewers, and calamari, octopus, mahi-mahi, pulled chicken, and pineapple burgers. There were many sides and dips, pineapple salads, and lobster mac 'n' cheese. For dessert, there were two huge tropical island banana cakes with buttercream frosting.

After the Owls' party of thirteen had their third drink, the floor show was about to begin.

Plates were cleared from people's tables, and then the emcee stepped up to the microphone, saying, "Tonight we're giving you a treat. We have the Hula Kahaki group here tonight, accompanying Honolulu's favorite *wahine*, Beverly Noa. They will hula to "Lonely Hula Hands."

The fifteen beautiful young Hawaiian women hurried out onto the stage colorfully dressed in matching yellow and red pa'u wrapped skirts, a yellow bikini top, along with a bright-red orchid head-wreath.

They began dancing, as Beverly Noa slowly danced her way up to the front of the stage. She was in little more than a bikini top, which showcased her luscious full breasts, and a short grass skirt that hung far below her belly button. She was a Polynesian beauty, with black hair that hung below her shoulder blades, with an orchid head-wreath of red, yellow, and white.

As the dancers were slowly moving their arms and hips in synchronized Hawaiian style, the soft, romantic sound of the song "Lovely Hula Hands" was playing.

It seemed everyone was mesmerized by the performers, most especially the men.

Corey looked over at Bob as he was drinking in the ladies' movements. Then it seemed a lot of the time, he was watching the Hawaiian band in the back of the stage and how they held and played their instruments.

Bob felt Corey staring at him, and he smiled and then leaned over and sexily asked her, "Why don't you get up there and dance like that for me?"

She took his arm into her hand, and then with the other hand, she rubbed his forearm with a hasty stroke and then lightly slapped it three times as she looked at him incredulously.

He looked at her slyly smiling at him and then laughed to himself.

Before the song was over, the emcee and Beverly went out into the audience and handpicked five gentlemen to come up and dance with her and the other dancers. Corey's human nature kicked in as she became fiercely protective about Bob going up onstage and dancing with these beautiful women, so she kept her firm hold on his arm.

Bob noticed and felt some trepidation from Corey and leaned over to allay her fears by telling her, "It's all right, doll. They never taught me this dance at NEC anyway."

Corey just smiled and kissed him on the cheek.

However, it did happen that Doug was chosen by the emcee as one of the men to go up and dance.

Doug laughed heartily and made a spectacle of himself. As he raced toward the stage, acting pretentiously about being the only one in his group that was picked, he laughed and shook his index finger at the other Owls.

The Owls party was smiling brilliantly and hilariously laughing at Doug as he quickly moved his stout yet agile body up the three steps to the stage next to Beverly.

When Beverly started back to the slow, romantic moves of the hula, the five men tried to imitate her, and the loveliness of the dance was lost.

Doug was moving his hips like he was trying to scratch himself, and when he moved both hands in synchronous strokes to his side, it looked a lot like he was wafting away an unpleasant odor.

Bob was laughing so hard, that tears started streaming down his face, and he kept his hands on his head, trying to brace it from hitting the seat in front of him. Uncontrollably, Corey was laughing at Doug and Bob when her head fell into Bob's shoulder as she wrapped her arms around his waist.

When the song ended and Doug returned to his seat acting triumphantly, the stage filled with male Tahitian fire dancers. They charged the stage bare-chested and scantily clad, with torches flaming in each dancer's hand. They began throwing the torches back and forth to one another as their feet pounded the stage, and they grunted a loud discharge of air.

By nine thirty that night, Bob and Corey were walking on Waikiki Beach with their arms around each other and intermittently stopping for a minute to hold and then deeply kiss each other.

The next morning, after they ate some incredible macadamia nut waffles at the breakfast bar in their hotel's dining area, Bob had a huge umbrella set on its side, for Corey and him, not far from the water on Waikiki Beach. The cavernous and waterproof umbrella gave them shade when they wanted it and a well-deserved full day of privacy. Once in a while, they wandered out into the shallows of the Pacific Ocean and splashed each other playfully, while getting as much of the tropical sun as they desired.

Corey would read a book, and once in a while, she'd glance over and stare at Bob, as he slept supine on a blanket next to her, only dressed in a tight black swimming suit. Her heartbeat quickened in its rhythm, her breath became labored, and her love for him was never more insurmountable than at that moment.

Thursday, the day before their first concert, Bob, Corey, Haddie, Joshua, and Deidra drove themselves around the island of Oahu in a rented car.

Corey was dressed in a Paco Rabanne wrapped pa'u skirt that was beautifully designed of orchids and ferns containing the many colors of the rainbow. There was a bright-red low-cut two-piece bathing suit beneath. Everyone else had on some kind of Hawaiian-style designed skirt, shirt, or floral-designed dress.

The group viewed the waterfalls at Ko'olau Mountain Range, the Punchbowl (a crater turned cemetery), and the other four of them watched Bob snorkel at Hanauma Bay, as he was feeding kernels of corn to the four hundred species of fish that swam in these waters.

They ended up eating dinner at the Pig and the Lady in Chinatown. After Bob and Corey dropped the others off at the Ritz, he drove the two of them back up to the North Shore, and they sat nestled together on a sand dune watching the sunset on Sunset Beach.

He sat with the back of Corey's head leaning into his chest as his legs were splayed and wrapped around her body. Bob had his arms around Corey's shoulders and his hands meeting between her breasts.

He would kiss the top of her head or her cheek and then pull her even closer to his body. They sat taking in the beautiful panoramic views of the Pacific Ocean and the beach, deeply breathing in the salty nighttime ocean breezes and holding steadfast to each other for almost another two hours.

Bob kissed Corey's temple and softly, passionately, told her, "Baby, you are totally the heart and soul of my universe. I love you madly, Corinth Beth Ann Madrigal."

Corey turned her head up to him; with glistening eyes, she gently pulled his head down, and their lips met moments later.

The first concert on Friday evening at the Waikiki Shell went spectacularly. There was a tremendous view of Diamond Head in the background, and the area was gorgeously landscaped; there were many surrounding palm trees, wild indigenous flowers about, and the lights of Honolulu were teasingly throwing tropical radiance into the air.

The outdoor shell was fairly new and had been built in 1956, with 2,400 seats under the roof, and space for another 6,000 on the lawn area. The Waikiki Shell was packed this night, and the lawn was densely covered with tourists, true Night Owl fans, and a few of the young native Hawaiians.

The ladies of the Owls attended the first performance all dressed in long, floor-length silk dresses with gorgeous tropical patterns, and a couple, including Corey's Givenchy original, had a midthigh left-leg-cut.

The Owls began with "Running Wild" and was burning down the stage with this more upbeat song and touching the hearts of most of the ladies with their soft, tender renderings of the slower love songs.

Bob played piano for "Makin' Roads Inland" and "Looking for a Lifetime with You," and the audience cheered loudly for him after those two songs had finished.

When the performance came to an end two and a half hours later, all thirteen of the Owls group headed for the Ritz's waterside cocktail bar.

Before they called it a night, at one o'clock in the morning, Corey had had a couple of the mai tai's, and Bob a couple of the Hawaiian margaritas.

As soon as they returned to their suite, clothes were being taken off and thrown about the bedroom, induced by their highly anticipated and sexually excited fervor.

The two of them slept in the next morning and awoke to a very disarrayed bedroom. As Corey moved under the sheet to position her head on Bob's chest, putting her arm around his waist, Bob awakened to her touch.

They kissed once, and noticing the clothes strewn throughout the room, they both laughed, with Bob comically stating, "Wow! They must have experienced an earthquake on the island last night."

Corey looked into his eyes, and with a tempting allurement, she professed, "I know for myself I experienced two or three, darling."

Bob lovingly smiled at her and then suddenly rolled over on her and kissed her fervently, as she feigned surprise by gleefully chuckling and amusingly smiling at him.

The rest of the afternoon, they strolled the streets of Honolulu holding hands. There was more shopping, more clothes bought, and more dining on seafood at Karai's Crab seaside restaurant in the Outrigger Waikiki Beach Resort dining room.

Everything Corey and Bob bought, they had shipped to Bel Air, because it was that or buy two or three more suitcases.

For the last concert in Honolulu, Bob wore black slacks with a brilliantly colored Cajun red-and-white floral shirt, open at the collar.

Corey was going dressed to the nines in a strapless Yves Saint Laurent original Hawaiian-style muumuu. It was a blended and flowing pattern of gorgeous green palm trees swaying to fields of multi-orange and yellow orchids on a white background. She was also wearing white open-toed Christian Dior sandals and was bedecked with the diamond bracelet and earrings Bob had given her at her birthday party in March. Her hair was up, with a stunning *okika* purple and lavender orchid (one of the most sought-after orchids in Hawaii) sexily placed in her hair behind her ear. And her makeup was subtle, yet distinctly enough to enhance her already beautiful features—most particularly those exquisite eyes.

When Corey stepped out of the bedroom and toward Bob, who was staring out at the ocean through the ceiling-to-floor window, he heard her coming and casually turned. What he laid his eyes upon was an incredibly beautiful woman who epitomized the meaning of feminine perfection.

He drank her in as his jaw slightly dropped open. He couldn't take his eyes off her.

Bob, sexually aroused, warned her, "I think I need a moment, baby. You…rather take my breath away."

Corey stood with such an elated sense of self-esteem. She never felt more like a woman than at that moment, when he made her feel like the ultimate embodiment of femininity. Her eyes became a little moistened as she looked at Bob with such love in her heart.

Corey asked, already knowing the answer, "Then you like what I'm wearing, darling?"

Salivating quite heavily, and still staring at every inch of Corey's body, Bob flirtatiously expressed in a soft and amorous voice, "Baby, you look beautiful in anything, but you look the most beautiful…in nothing at all."

Corey slowly and seductively walked over to him, and putting her face inches from his, she sexily asked, "You don't really have to go to this concert tonight, do you, sweetheart?"

Bob smiled brilliantly and placed his hand on the small of her back, then turned her toward the door, as he resignedly told her, "Come on, doll. We have a concert to go to."

Corey fatalistically exhaled, and with a slight play of histrionics, she smiled and moved for the door, kissing Bob on the cheek.

The Owls were onstage and ready to start their concert at eight o'clock. After the introduction and the audience started to quiet down from the screams and the loud welcoming applause, Jimmy hit the four-count on his snare with the handle of his drum wire brushes. They began uncharacteristically to play first the slow and sexy "Let Me Lay within Your Arms."

Len began to run opening chords on his bass guitar, Darnell and Bob blended in to play the romantic melody, as Doug laid down some soft and mellow notes on the sax. After Joshua ran a smooth riff on his main mistress, the bass trumpet, Bob took his vocal entrance.

Toward the end of the song, Bob looked directly at Corey and finished with the last chorus.

> Your magic touch is all I need
> It sets off fireworks and alarms
> So give yourself to me and

Let me lay within'...your...arms.

The entire audience applauded uproariously, with high-pitched screams from the young ladies and whistles from the young men.

Corey sat trancelike staring at Bob and no one else.

The Owls went on to play for another two hours. Then Bob stepped up to the microphone and waited for the applause and screams to abate. Even with the isolated screams he received from a few young women, he began to speak, "Thank you very much. But right now, and before we finish here tonight, the Night Owls would like to pay their respects to the island of Hawaii." There was mild applause. "We have felt welcomed here from the first moment we arrived, and remain humbled by the beauty and the pure tropical essence of your land. So in gratitude, we're going to perform a heartfelt Hawaiian song for you called 'Honolulu City Lights.'"

There was a warm applause from the audience and a surprised response from most of "Ohhh. All right."

Bob added, "Since our acoustic guitar, Darnell 'B.B.' King"—smiling, he pointed to Darnell—"knows the music theory relating specifically to the ukulele, and the similarities being a lot like the acoustic guitar, he has knowledge in playing the soprano ukulele. We know the ukulele has only four strings, but there are completely different keys on all four of them."

"Meaning you just can't transfer chords and scales from a guitar to a ukulele. Surprisingly the ukulele is every bit as complex as a guitar, but Darnell is brave enough to give it a try tonight."

The audience applauded again as Darnell put his guitar in its stand and took a borrowed ukulele from its case.

Bob moved to the concert grand piano that was to the side of the stage. He adjusted the long-string microphone in front of him and slightly nodded to Jimmy. Jimmy softly tapped his snare with the handle of his loose-haired drumstick, as he was playing extremely slow, mellow beats to the melody.

Darnell started out with the ukulele's dainty, nimble sound; it was softer than a mandolin and sweeter than a banjo. It was actually warm and mellow, yet smooth and silky.

Len played the soft melodic background chords, as Bob played the piano accompaniment to the song. Bob was playing a bass line accompaniment, with the notes in a lower register of the piano that blended in well with the ukulele and provided the rhythmic and harmonic support for the coming vocal melody solo.

Doug and Joshua had their horns at attention, propped up on their thighs, with Joshua's trumpet bell facing down, just listening to the song. Their tremendous talent on the horns would not be needed tonight for this beautiful Hawaiian love song.

Bob began to tenderly sing the lyrics to "Honolulu City Lights:"

Looking out upon the city lights
The stars above the ocean
Got my ticket for the midnight plane
It's not easy to leave again
Took my clothes and put them in my bag
Tried not to think just yet of leaving
Looking out into the city night
It's not easy to leave again.

Each time Honolulu city lights
Stir up memories in me
Each time Honolulu city lights
Bring me back again.
You are my island sunset and
You are my island dream

Put on my shoes and light a cigarette
Wondering which of my friends will be there
Standing with their leis around my neck
It's not easy to leave again

Each time Honolulu city lights
Stir up memories in me
Each night Honolulu city lights
Bring me back again,

Bring me back again,
Bring me back...again.

As the last notes to the song faded into the tropical mists, the audience gave them a rousing standing ovation. There were cheers and a high volume of screaming.

Bob looked over at Darnell and, brilliantly smiling, gave him the two thumbs up. Darnell very pleasingly smiled back, balled his fist, and enthusiastically pumped it once toward Bob.

Corey and Alicia were clapping loudly and cheering for their husbands. Corey softly shook her head, showing a heart full of pride and total respect for her brilliant man.

The next two days were spent luxuriating around the pool and resting up for the Owls' last two concerts of the 21-City Tour. They would wind it up at the Hollywood Bowl Friday and Saturday night of that same week.

Everyone left Hawaii Tuesday, August 9, with great memories of performing and soaking up the tropical sights on Oahu. The beauty of the island made it worth the over-five-hour flight.

TWENTY-TWO

A full day and a half after everyone arrived back home, Nick asked the guys to meet him at the sound studio in Thousand Oaks that Thursday. He told them he wanted to discuss some future concerts with them, and they could utilize the rest of the time working on any new material they had been working on throughout the 21-City Tour.

When the six Owls and Nick sat down in the studio at nine o'clock that morning, Nick started the conversation by asking, "I don't know if you guys have ever entertained the possibility of a Canadian cities tour. Because your records definitely are selling in all ten provinces, and even the Eskimos are buying your stuff."

All seven guys laughed or smiled after that comment.

Bob knew he had to address this sooner or later and found now was the perfect time to inform everyone, "That sounds great, Nick, but in all honesty, man, I have to tell you, I really don't want to be away from Corey now for more than a week to ten days at a time. In a while, it may not have to be limited to that short of a time, but right now, she needs me to be around. I know she's still having some apprehension about her incident in mid-July, so I'm sorry, guys…but she'll always be my first priority. I hope all of you understand."

Len immediately spoke up, defending Bob. "Hell yes, we understand, Bob. I think all of us are willing to help you two for as long as it takes."

As Len looked at the other guys, he loudly and entreatingly asked, "Right, guys? We're all on board with Bob. Right?"

Every one of them nodded affirmatively and loudly responded back, "Absolutely, man. We're with you, brother."

"One of us is hurting—all of us is hurting," Joshua responded with loving camaraderie. This mutual cohesiveness represented their lives, their brotherhood, their collective soul.

After they all bumped shoulders and slapped hands with Bob, in support of him and Corey, they got down to business working on five different songs that had lyrics written, but just ideas on the melodies.

Nick left the guys to their business of composing music, as he tried to figure out how they would logistically tour Canada only two or three cities at a time, or even one at a time.

Bob returned home from the studio at almost one that afternoon and spotted Corey sitting by the pool studying her next movie manuscript.

He continued walking over to her as she watched him approach. She loved to study the movement of his body and the cadence of his strides. With a gladdened smile on her face, she asked him, "How did your session go today, darling?"

Bob, loving the fact Corey was even interested, pleased him and made him feel even closer to her, if that was possible.

He leaned over and kissed her tenderly and then sat with her in the same lounger and told her, "Well, Nick wants us to do a Canadian tour next year, but he wasn't sure when."

This greatly disturbed Corey, and instantly she began to worry about the pending separation from Bob. Trying to remain calm, she asked, "How long a tour was he thinking, darling? I certainly hope not a prolonged one."

He quickly answered her, for he felt her anxiety and the fear in the tone of her voice. "Oh no, baby. I told him, and all the guys agreed with me, that now any tour can't be longer than seven to ten days."

Corey exhaled heavily, and instant relief shot through her body. "Thank God, and thank you so much, baby. I appreciate you and the guys for sacrificing your time for me."

"Oh my god, Corey! I would do anything for you."

She gently put her hand on his face, and they leaned in together to kiss.

Corey then mentioned matter-of-factly to Bob, "I really hate to kill this moment, baby, but I hope you remembered I needed twenty-five tickets for your second night on Saturday at the Hollywood Bowl—that night being the last performance of your 21-City Tour. A dozen of my friends wanted to be there, and they'll also be bringing their spouses or dates with them."

Bob took Corey's hand from his face and kissed the palm as he looked into her eyes and told her, "Never worry, my lady. Nick secured us a row of seats months ago. And they're in the Pool Circle Seating, which is the closest seats to the stage, just in back of the big pool of water. Nick has the ladies and Drake sitting in this area also. So it should be a fun night for everyone."

Bob was in the living room playing his piano after breakfast that Friday morning. He was playing the Piano Sonata in B minor by Liszt. It was one of the best-loved and most-performed piano works ever. Most sonatas had four movements; however, this one was one unbroken stretch of music.

Corey was helping Haddie in the kitchen when she heard the piano echoing the beautiful notes of a classical piece of music. Haddie turned to her with a whimsical look on her face, and Corey brilliantly smiled back at her.

Corey momentarily closed her eyes and then fancifully opened them, as she slowly made her way out of the kitchen to stand by the entrance to the spacious living room. She stood for several minutes just staring at Bob and watching him absorbed in doing what he loved: playing music. She knew she was his greatest passion, but with him, every aspect about music was nipping at her heels.

When the last note was still resonating through the air, Corey walked over to the piano and sat down beside him on the piano bench. After Bob's attention was diverted from the piano to her, he leaned over and kissed her.

Corey softly whispered, "That was beautiful, darling. Are you going to play some piano at the Hollywood Bowl tonight, and especially tomorrow night, when I'm there?"

Bob grinned boyishly and remarked, "I don't think there'll be any classical pieces played, but…there's three or four songs I'll accompany on the piano."

Grinning even broader, he inquired, "How's about you and I bookin' it into the bedroom and see what late morning fun we can find?"

Corey's face lit up with sexual promise, and as she smiled brilliantly at him, she took his hand in hers, and they arose from the piano and slowly walked into the bedroom hand in hand.

The first concert that Friday night was scheduled for eight o'clock, and the Owls' instruments were already set up and onstage. The guys arrived early to run a sound check on them before ticket holders started to arrive.

The Hollywood Bowl was known worldwide for its band shell, which was a distinctive set of concentric arches that were set against the backdrop of the Hollywood Hills and the famous Hollywood sign to the northeast. It was a natural amphitheater located in a shaded canyon that was chosen for its naturally perfect acoustics and its proximity to downtown Hollywood. The Owls would be playing to 17,500 seats, and all of them were sold out months ago.

At eight o'clock, an announcer's voice came over the powerful sound system. "We'd like to welcome everyone to the Hollywood Bowl tonight. It is our pleasure to have this group of men performing here tonight and tomorrow night. They are ending their 21-City Tour here, and we couldn't be more proud to have them. They've traveled a bumpy road at times to get through their tour, and not all of the time were they unscathed by the relentless discrimination, bigotry, and ensuing violence that sometimes occurred. So, let's give these bravehearted crusaders a warm welcome. NOW HERE IS THE NIGHT OWLS!"

The six Owls came jogging out, waving and smiling to the loud and thunderous applause their fans were giving them. They immediately picked up their instruments, and when Bob saw every guy was ready to go, he gave the nod to Jimmy.

Their first song dictated the way the entire night would go. For after Jimmy's four-count, he tore into a twelve-second drum solo, followed by Joshua's mistress-in-waiting, his C trumpet. His horn was loud, and he played a run of notes that made it look so easy and sound so smooth.

The guitars mixed in while Doug jumped in with a riff during the second bar. The Owls were burning down the house with their newer arrangement of "Ricochet."

It was one song after the other for an hour and a half. Then Bob put his guitar in its stand and took the microphone in his hand. He approached the front of the stage and walked down a five-foot plank that was placed across the 100,000-gallon pool that was directly in front of the stage. There were three rows of seating called the Pool Circle Seating that followed the arc of the pool around the stage front. There were approximately fifty seats in these three rows.

When he approached the center of the pool seating, there was a lot of the screaming and high-pitched whistles filling the air. He then began to sing "Maybe Another Time, Another Place."

The young women charged the stage trying to touch him, while they screamed and came close to fainting right there on the spot. Bob kept singing with his beautiful baritone voice and then started to put his one free hand out to a some of his fans. The women loved this, and after touching him, a few were hanging on to their hands like they were on fire.

The concert ended shortly after ten thirty that night, and after talking with the guys for a short time, Bob drove the thirty minutes on the US-101 home to Bel Air.

When he walked into the bedroom at a quarter to midnight, he found Corey wide awake and studying her script for Monday's start of her new picture, *Lead Me Astray*.

She looked up, and now seriously staring at Bob, Corey ordered him in a stern yet unemotional tone, "Come here."

Bob was totally exhausted and thought maybe he had heard wrong, so he implored, "What did you say, doll? Did you order me to come to you?" He smiled playfully.

Her facial expression did not change.

With a cold stare that felt she was burning a hole through him, his smile faded from his face. He actually became more attracted to her with this unusual behavior. Ignoring his better judgment, he began to slowly walk toward the bed.

When he reached her, he looked puzzled yet somewhat amused. He continued to study her unflinching facial expression.

Corey issued another order as straight-faced and demanding as before, "Take everything off and prepare to take a shower with me."

There was still no change in her demeanor.

Instantaneously Bob loudly chuckled and lit up with a huge, loving smile. His eyes were sparkling with the enormous amount of love he was feeling for her at that moment.

Without hesitating, he slowly and pleasurably began to do a striptease dance for her. As he removed a piece of clothing, he would wave it at her and then sensually dance around and then throw the piece of clothing over his shoulder. He was now getting his almost naked body very close to her.

It took every ounce of willpower for Corey not to smile or laugh, but then being a trained professional actress served her well this night.

When Bob removed his final piece of clothing, his boxer shorts, she arose from the bed and lasciviously studied his body. She put both her hands on the side of his head and gave him one of the sexiest kisses she possibly could.

They were locked in on each other as they probed the other's mouth and was biting each other's tongues.

Corey, now in a passionate fervor, took his hand and led him into the warm shower. There they washed each other with a soapy loofah sponge, massaged each other's bodies, and ended up making some very torrid love for the next hour while they were still in the shower.

The next morning, she let Bob sleep in. She knew he had a very long and tiring but fun-filled day yesterday, most especially last night.

Around ten o'clock that Saturday morning, Bob heard Corey and Haddie talking in the kitchen, so he meandered in dressed only in some sweatpants and tee shirt.

He stood at the kitchen entrance, and when Corey looked up smiling a toothy grin, she asked, "Darling, are you all rested up for your last concert tonight?"

Bob stood staring at her with a stolid look on his face. He kept his eyes fixated on her, and with a voice that was dark and grim, he ordered, "Come here."

After Corey heard his command, she was beside herself with laughter and almost fell off of the barstool she was sitting on while having coffee with Haddie. Tears began to run down her face, and Haddie was confused as to what was going on between the two of them.

Bob kept a cold look in his eyes, and his face was devoid of any emotion at all. He then began to slowly walk toward Corey, and Haddie, caught in the middle of this, felt like she was being entertained by two of the best in the business.

Corey was still laughing hard, but when he reached her seat, she flirtatiously hit him in his arm and on his chest and feigned self-defense. He then grabbed her around her waist with both hands and lifted her straight up into the air. Her head was now far above his.

Bob jokingly admonished her, "When I tell you to come to me, young lady, I mean exactly that, and don't you ever laugh at me again."

He started to slowly lower Corey's head down to his face and as he beamed a huge smile at her. She stopped smiling and became enraptured by his sparkling green eyes. She wrapped her arms around his neck and moved his head into her hands as they kissed long and hard.

Haddie sighed with relief and facetiously stated, "I'm sure I don't know what goes on in your bedroom every night, Ms. Corey and Mr. Bob, but I can tell you right now you never ever have to tell me."

The Night Owls were all at the concert venue around seven o'clock. And what Nick hadn't told them yet was the fact that Duke Ellington, Ella Fitzgerald, and James "Bubba" Miley were given tickets for the Owls' last performance of the 21-City Tour.

Closer to the concert start at eight o'clock, Corey's entourage, the Owls' ladies, Elizabeth and Drake were slowly filing into their seats in the Pool Circle Seating. Corey was center orchestra, first row, with Jack on one side of her and Susan Hawthorne on the other. The rest of her group filled in both rows mostly on the right side.

The crowd in the Garden Section behind them started to point at the celebrities that they recognized, and the buzz of voices circulated throughout the amphitheater.

The crowd again started to jump up and point fingers as Duke, Ella, and Bubba were shown their seats in center orchestra, first row, next to Jack.

When Corey saw the three sit down next to Jack, she got up and walked the one seat over to them. Smilingly, she told them, "Good evening, Duke, Ella, and, Bubba. It is so nice to see all of you again. I know the guys will love the fact you're here."

Duke shook Corey's hand and told her promisingly, "We really didn't want to miss this one tonight. And it's just great seeing you again, Corey."

Corey introduced everyone around her that she could to Duke, Ella, and Bubba. They were gracious enough to thank her and say hello to most of her group.

After the announcer came out and made the same introduction of the Owls that he had made the previous night, the six Night Owls again jogged out onto the stage.

They were met with a tremendously loud ovation, high-pitched screams, a lot of whistles, along with yelling that echoed down from the packed house.

When Bob saw the guys were ready to rock 'n' roll, he gave Jimmy the go-ahead nod.

Jimmy gave the four-count and ripped into his crash cymbal and then ran his signature twelve-second lead solo on his snare, along with his bass, high-top cymbal, and kick drums.

The three guitars jumped in, and Bob's lead guitar sounded full of reverb, and his lead tones were heavily distorted with more sustain than Darnell's rhythm tones.

Bob definitely had his treble, mid, and bass balanced. He was an awesome guitarist and could play anything put down in front of him.

On this new arrangement of "Raging Fire," Joshua started to sizzle on his main mistress and screamed a series of notes that sent goose bumps up many people's arms and necks. Bubba smiled brightly and was delighted in Joshua's explosive delivery. The purity and cleanness of the bright penetrating tones was thundering loudly into the electricity that was already collecting in the Hollywood night air.

When Doug rolled his alto saxophone into the mix, the stage became almost combustible. The energy level was intense. He started wailing, and it was powerful and strong, sharp and strident with a fluctuating pitch that repeated itself. Doug had a dynamic sound with his sax that allowed him to inject his own emotion into the song and project his own style and creativity.

The styling, written by Bob and Joshua, that was arranged on "Raging Fire" made it a uniquely structured slice of pop that would serve as a major influence on the rock 'n' roll bands that were new and old.

After Bob had sung the vocals to the song, and the last notes were played out, the audience roared with their approval. Jimmy had to wait for the screaming and applause to die down before he could start the lead-in to their next song.

Bob was used to standing somewhat sideways to his band members, so he could see and hear, to make sure everyone was playing with the same tempo and timing. When their song had ended, he turned to the audience and smiled down at Corey, Jack, and Susan.

The whole group of celebrities were applauding and smiling wildly. Corey's face was swollen with the unmitigated pride and love she felt for him.

As his head was starting to turn back to the guys, he caught a quick glimpse of Duke, Ella, and Bubba. He was sure of what he saw but instantly turned his head back in their direction anyway.

When it registered that he actually saw them sitting in the front row, he brilliantly smiled and pumped his right fist twice on his heart. He then turned to the guys and yelled, "First row, left of center!"

Smiles broke out on all their faces, and Darnell even waved to them. Duke laughed, and Ella blew a kiss that she threw into the air to all of them. Joshua was beaming from ear to ear and blew a kiss back to her.

Corey could see the excitement and pride in Bob's eyes as he motioned to Jimmy to go ahead and start the roll-in to their second song.

After the drum's wire brushes were put to the snare, Len's and Darnell's guitars entered in softly and smoothly. Doug began his romantic legato notes in a smoother manner, and even though the song started out instrumentally, it sang of passion.

Joshua played a relaxed yet very heart-touching bass trumpet with a metal straight mute attached to the bell of his main mistress. It slightly altered the trumpet's pitch and created a brighter sound and a bit more buzz.

While the five guys were playing a newer arrangement to the lead-in of "Long Journey Back to You," Bob was slowly walking out toward the Pool Circle Seating on the plank that connected the stage to the audience. After he completely crossed over the arced pool, he sat down on the end of the plank and looked directly at Corey.

There were a lot of young ladies screaming and holding their arms out to him, but his stare was completely focused on her.

With his sexy eyes penetrating Corey's eyes, and the new wireless microphone in his hand, he started to softly sing the lyrics with his velvety baritone voice.

As the song progressed and Bob sang the last stanza and chorus to her, Corey already had a stream of tears running rivulets down her cheeks.

When the song's last note dissipated into the night air, the crowd just roared with wild applause, screams, and high-pitched whistles.

Bob rose up, walked to Corey, and with a slightly provocative smile on his face, she stood up, and they quickly embraced each other. After they stopped kissing each other's necks, they kissed for a couple of seconds on the lips. Before he let her go, he told her, "Love you, baby. Always will."

This made her cry that much harder.

Bob then shook Jack's hand, went over and kissed Susan on the cheek, and then reached over to Debbie, and they grasped hands for a few seconds. He waved both his hands to Richard, Cornell, Shirley, Alex, Robert Ryan, Hope, Sterling, and Ann Sheridan.

Before Bob went back up onstage, he shook Duke's hand and thanked him for coming. He skipped over Ella and then shook Bubba's hand and thanked him also. But he went back to Ella and kissed her on the cheek and leaned over and asked her if she would come up onstage and sing with him.

Ella was taken by surprise and told Bob, "Oh, I don't think so, Bob. Maybe another time."

Bob was persistent and told her, "It doesn't have to be one of our songs. We'll sing 'Let's Do It.'"

She relented and began to rise out of her seat. Bob helped her up onto the plank, and the audience went nuts. A thunderous applause ensued, and Bob followed Ella as she walked toward the stage.

When they reached the stage, Bob had the piano brought closer to the pool area. He asked Ella if she wanted to stand beside the piano or sit with him on the piano bench. She said her voice would seem less restrained if she stood beside the piano as he played.

Before he started playing, Bob stood with the wireless microphone in hand and told the audience, "As if you didn't know by now, this is the First Lady of Song, Ms. Ella Fitzgerald. She has been gracious enough to join the nest tonight and sing a song for us."

The audience applauded loudly as Bob motioned to Doug and Joshua they could jump in at any time. Then Bob ran a short introduction of notes to "Let's Do It (Let's Fall in Love)."

He leaned over to Ella and said, "Straight up, and let's add *baby* after 'Let's do it.'"

Ella smiled and nodded her head affirmatively.

Bob started to play full notes as they both started singing together:

> Birds do it, bees do it
> Even educated fleas do it
> Let's do it, baby
> Let's fall in love
>
> In Spain, the best upper sets do it
> Lithuanians and Letts do it
> Let's do it, baby
> Let's fall in love

Joshua rolled in a sequence of accompanying notes.

> Some Argentines, without means, do it
> People say in Boston, even beans do it
> Let's do it, baby
> Let's fall in love

Bob yelled, "Take it, Ella."

> Romantic sponges, they say, do it
> Oysters down in Oyster Bay do it
> Let's do it, baby
> Let's fall in love

Doug ran a short riff of up-tempo notes.
Bob rejoined Ella, singing,

> Cold Cape Cod clams, 'gainst their wish, do it
> Even lazy jellyfish do it
> Let's do it, baby
> Let's fall in love
>
> In shallow shoals English soles do it
> Goldfish in the privacy of bowls do it

Let's do it, baby
Let's fall in love

(Loud finish)

Let's do it, baby!
Let's do it, baby!
Oh, let's do it, baby
Let's...fall...in...love!

There was a quality to Ella's voice that was fascinating, with the subtle ways she shaded her voice and the casual yet clean way she sang the words.

When Bob hit the last note on the piano, the crowd started to roar their approval. The applause was nonstop, and Bob came around to the front of the piano and hugged Elia and kissed her on the cheek. They stood with their arms around each other, and their smiles couldn't have been more prodigious in projecting their excitement.

The Owls all came down to hug and cheek-kiss Ella, and then Bob escorted Ella back down the plank and to her seat. After she sat back down, Bob jokingly and loudly told her, "Your check's in the mail."

Everyone within earshot started to laugh hilariously, as Bob quickly ran over to Corey and hastened another kiss from her. She found herself drowning in her love for him, and the heartfelt pride she had growing inside of her could not be contained. Corey sat gently shaking her head and tried to answer the question, How did she become so blessed to have such an incredible man like Bob to be the focus of her life? A single tear ran down her cheek.

Sunday morning, both Bob and Corey were out by the pool, and they were throwing lines from Corey's upcoming movie, *Lead Me Astray*. Corey would start her picture that Monday; Bob wouldn't start his picture, *Hidden Desire*, until the following Wednesday.

Corey was taking a drink of her coffee, when she set her cup down and inquisitively asked, "Darling, I know Susan and Kim are going to be in your picture *Hidden Desire*, but who else is involved? I don't think you ever told me."

Bob said matter-of-factly, "Well, there's Lew Ayers and Clint Walker. I've yet to meet Clint, but Susan tells me he's one of the good guys on lot. Now tell me again, besides Anne, Arthur, Dane, and Lee Marvin, who this Hugh Logan is."

She took another sip of her coffee and discouragingly exhaled, saying, "He's probably one of the biggest pain in the asses anyone has ever worked with. He's in his mid to late thirties, about six foot two, has an angry disposition, has always been a supporting actor, and doesn't take direction very well… So you tell me why anyone would ever want to have him on payroll."

Bob answered concernedly, "Well, he must be bringing something to the table, or Jack wouldn't have a guy like that close to you. Maybe I'll just have a talk with Jack myself and remind him what you just went through with one other jackass."

"No, it'll be all right. After all, I have Dane and Lee on set with me. They're both like you, but only in the protective mode, of course. They'll handle this guy. I'm counting on it, darling."

Bob cutely hinted, "I may just have to come by once in a while to make sure everyone is playing nice together."

Corey smiled lovingly and softly purred, "I'll look forward to that, sweetheart."

They were running read-throughs Monday morning for Corey's picture, and the friction started to ignite when Hugh Logan started questioning his lines with the director, Hal Holcomb, and even with the producer, Jules Glassman.

Hugh questioningly asked, "You have me telling this woman I love her, but you never have me with her in the entirety of the picture. How does that happen, man? It just doesn't make any sense, Hal."

The read-through had already been interrupted by Hugh three times, and the entire cast was getting a little impatient with him.

Hal explained for the fourth time, "Hugh, your character is enamored by Corey's character. If you read the script, you'll see she doesn't feel the same way about you. We're not changing the entire direction of this film just to make you happy. So either play the role and read your part the way it's written…or not."

Corey could see Lee, Dane, and Jules were staring daggers at Hugh, but Hugh was not fazed. Corey decided to let the brass handle this one.

That evening Corey complained to Bob about the disruptive nature of Hugh, how he treated everyone with disrespect and how unprofessional he was.

Bob tentatively looked at Corey as they were sitting in the kitchen with Haddie getting ready for dinner. He confessed to her, "Well, I hope you're not mad, doll, but I called Jack today and asked about this guy Hugh Logan. Jack told me Hugh is a nephew of Joseph Means, the studio executive of Destiny Studios over in Burbank."

Corey exhaled an exasperated breath of air and almost yelled, "That's it! There had to be a reason a hack like him was dumped on us. But why did Jack sign off on this guy?"

Explaining as best he could, Bob told her, "Joe is a good friend of Jack's, so after Hugh created so many problems at Destiny, Joe asked Jack if he could work him into a picture over here at Celebrity. It didn't have to be any great part, but Hugh said he had always liked Corey and wouldn't mind working with her."

Corey shot a look of grave concern at Bob. He tried to allay her fears by telling her, "Jack imperatively informed me that once rehearsals start and if this guy continues to create havoc, he will be bounced. Friendship with Joe or not, he said he wouldn't condone any loss of production on this picture."

Corey got up from her chair and went over to sit in Bob's lap. They kissed and then sat holding each other for several seconds.

Haddie could be heard over by the stove singing, "There's a somebody I'm longin' to see, I hope that he turns out to be someone who'll watch over me."

Corey smiled appreciatively to Haddie and then wrapped her arms around Bob's neck, holding on to him until dinner was ready a couple of minutes later.

The Owls' sound studio rehearsal times were moved back to evenings, now that Bob's motion picture was beginning Wednesday morning.

Bob asked the guys to bring any new songs they may have been working on after they started their 21-City Tour. Bob had three of his own, Joshua had two, and Joshua and Darnell had one.

The three Bob had contained a start on the melody, but needed the input from Doug and Joshua pertaining to their horns. Two of his songs were written to a guitar groove and were named "Kill Me with a Lie" and "My Constant Need." The last one written to a drum groove was "What More Can I Lose."

Joshua's two songs had prevailing verse structures that were emboldened with the compelling words of struggle and personal freedoms. His songs were "We Bleed the Same Blood" and "Never Wanna Look Back."

The romantic song Joshua and Darnell wrote was called "Every Bit of You Is Part of Me."

Halfway through the Owls' jam session, Nick walked into the studio. The guys were just trying to finalize the melody to one of Bob's written songs but knew Nick would only be here on pressing business matters. So they put their instruments down, and Doug asked Nick, "Hey, man! What's crackin'?"

Nick asked them to come together and excitedly told them, "I just thought I'd run the idea by you guys tonight, because Irving Green, at your Mercury Label, wants to put all your taped songs from the 21-City Tour into an album."

The guys yelled with excitement and started slapping each other on the backs and were slipping skin to one another.

Nick warned them, "Have a name ready for the album by Thursday, because it goes into production next Monday. That would give the designers a few days to create the front and back covers. I've already given them a handful of pictures of you six guys singing and playing your instruments. That should help them a lot."

Doug piped up and volunteered, "We could call it *Bouncing Around with the Night Owls.*"

There were a few chuckles, until Darnell spoke up and seriously suggested, "I think *The Night Owls Playing with Change in Mind.* What do you guys think?"

Bob said loudly, "Oh, oh, man! That is so in the groove, B.B. You hit the nail right on the head, my man!"

Every guy in the studio agreed that would be the name of their next album.

Nick then mentioned, "All right. I'll get that to 'em today, and that album should be on the market before September."

Len jokingly added, "Okay, more money for diapers this November. Yeah!"

All the guys started to crack up with laughter, and then Jimmy humorously said, "Yeah, and you may even have some leftover for booties."

After Nick quit chuckling, he mentioned rather businesslike, "And now that Bob will be shooting another picture starting tomorrow, I thought on weekends we'd perform at one or two different venues and start working your newer songs into the mix."

The guys were nodding their heads affirmatively and saying, "*All right, that's cool!*"

Then Nick, chuckling a little, announced, "Okay! Now the fun thing I wanted to tell you about was that Mr. Green thought it would be a full-blown gas if you guys could pick out and record twelve Christmas songs you like best by late November. This would be your first Christmas album, and he'd be able to start marketing that in early December. What do you say, guys?"

The Owls all laughed out loud, but after they thought about another album hitting the market this year, and the money that would bring in, Len asked, "Would we be given enough leeway to put our own arrangements to them?"

Nick answered quickly, stating, "As long as someone else has already made a recording of a song, the Owls can cover it, and you can add your own personal touches. Just remember that melody and lyrics are protected by copyright, but key and tempo are not. If you're going to change the melody or lyrics, that requires direct permission from the song owner. That will also cost you more than the compulsory mechanical license you pay royalty fees for."

Len resignedly noted, "So the answer to my question would be no."

Nick nodded his head and just smiled.

Joshua enthusiastically spoke to the group, "My mama's favorite Christmas song is 'O Holy Night,' and I know for a fact she would want Bob singing that for her."

All the guys agreed with that. But Bob had a little bit to add, by mentioning, "Well, I think if I were to ask Ms. Lady Ella to sing it with me, that would be some crazy kicks."

The guys went nuts with Bob's idea and then started rattling off some songs and the female singer they would want to sing with to that song.

Nick calmed them all down and encouragingly told them, "First, I want you to make your song list for this album, then go back and assign a couple of songs to any female singer you want on the vinyl with you. I just want you to know that your fans will want to hear you guys, and not female singers with you on every song. Get me that list as soon as possible, because Truman and I are going to have a little work in contacting, writing out a payment contract, setting a date, time, and place for each artist to meet and record each song before the middle of November. It should only take up to two weeks after all that to get this album to record stores around the world."

Len assured Nick, "We'll have that list for you by this Thursday, Nick."

Darnell spoke up and said, "We should be able to put that together before we leave today. What do you think, guys?"

Everyone was in agreement. Len conceded amiably, "All right, let's do it, guys."

Wednesday, August 17, Bob rode into Celebrity with Corey. They kissed, and she went to her first walk-through rehearsal, as Bob headed to a completely different soundstage than Corey for his first full-cast read-through.

When Bob walked in and up to the stage area, Susan met him with a huge smile and said, "Hello, Bob. I absolutely loved your concert Saturday night at the Hollywood Bowl."

Then they hugged and cheek-kissed each other. Bob thanked her for attending the concert and told her how much he enjoyed having her there. He then turned and introduced himself to Clint Walker.

Clint was thirty-three years old, six foot six, handsome, and had a good physique. He was coming off of the TV series *Cheyenne*, and now he was just picking up supporting roles here and there.

As Bob and Clint were shaking hands and exchanging small talk, Kim Novak walked up behind Bob and tapped him on the shoulder. Bob quickly turned around, and to his surprise, Kim was smiling that sexy smile when he returned that sly little smile he had and exclaimed, "Hey! It's been too long since we last seen each other. How have you been, Kim?"

He then gave her a full body hug and cheek-kissed her maybe a second too long.

She was again taken by his masculine beauty and his inviting smile. To her, Bob was conspicuously and ingratiatingly tactful and well-mannered, a man of suave, well-bred equanimity.

Kim answered with a slight smile that softened her lips, "It has been a while, but I've been just fine. Thanks for asking, Bob. I've been waiting for the start of our picture together, so I'm glad today has finally come."

Bob, agreeing, told her, "Yeah. I've been wanting to make a film, because it seems like all I've been doing lately is touring and making music. Right now this will be a needed respite from that, and how much fun are we gonna have with Susan, Lew, and Clint?"

He apologized for his forgetfulness, and Bob quickly said, "I'm sorry, Kim, but this big hunk of a man here is Clint Walker. Clint, this is Kim Novak. We're all going to be working on this film together and having tons of fun, along with Lew and Susan."

The two shook hands and were cordial to each other.

The read-throughs for their film, *Hidden Desire*, went very smoothly; and the director, Victor Trudeau, felt it seemed like every actor and actress was well versed and ready to go.

This film was centered on the inner and outer conflicts of the central protagonist, Bob. The anxieties of the main figure was that he was torn between the temptations of women and celebrity on the one hand, and authenticity and intellectual engagement on the other. This is what formed the core of the narrative.

Meanwhile, Corey's cast and production staff were getting pretty fed up with the obstreperous conduct of Hugh Logan. The tension on the set was so visceral, that Corey felt it gathering in her back, neck, and shoulder muscles.

When Hal, the director, asked Hugh to hit his mark at a certain point in the dialogue, Hugh screamed at him with downright impudence, "You really don't know what you're doing, Hal, because I should be way the hell on the other side of the room!"

Hugh grinned almost maniacally at Corey as he cocked his head in a way that rendered the ugly almost charming.

Corey started to experience the same fear she felt just before she was attacked in July by Jason Brooks. The atmosphere on the cavernous soundstage was like the moment before a big storm breaks. The tension was straining everyone's nerves.

Hal gave Hugh one more stage direction and told him to start his read. Hugh's gestures were exaggerated and imperious. Hal suggested to him to play it down with no more of his overbearing histrionics.

Hugh, being aloof, bristling, and short-tempered, feigned toughness by starting to cuss at Hal and even pointed to the cameramen; his foul mouth was unceasing.

It was lunchtime for Bob, cast, and crew. So Bob thought he'd wander over to where Corey was running through the rudimentary rehearsals for her picture and check things out. He asked Clint if he would want to wander over to Corey's rehearsal with him, and Clint liked that idea. Clint had always respected Corey's work and her talent in motion pictures, and it had always inspired him with awe.

Lee Marvin and Dane Clark, standing in back of the camera angles, were having a lot of trouble not putting their fists into this guy's face. Lee told Dane, "I think this asshole needs some real direction. What do you think, man?"

Bob and Clint walked up behind them and caught Lee's and Dane's attention as Bob seriously suggested, "I think you're right, guys. If you need any help, we're right here."

When Lee and Dane turned around to face Bob, they both smiled broadly and put their hands out to both men to shake.

After listening to the torrent of obscenities Hugh was throwing around at everyone, Bob and Clint moved up closer to camera depth, along with Lee and Dane, thinking of somehow to shut him up.

After watching for a minute or two, Clint swore he would help with anything they proposed doing about this man.

All three guys shook his hand and thanked him.

Lee boldly said, "Well then, gentlemen. Follow my lead."

Lee and Dane took the lead, with Bob and Clint right behind them. They slowly, and with menace in every step, walked on set and straight toward Hugh. All four guys looked like the front line for the Chicago Bears football team; not one of them was shorter than five foot ten, and they were with sturdy, muscular physiques.

Hal noticed them walking toward Hugh and exhaled a breath of relief. He thought maybe they were just going to scare him a little.

Corey looked up from her script and saw Bob walking with the other three men, and she quickly put her hand over her mouth and heavily sighed. Her eyes began to glisten with pride.

Hugh was watching the men walking toward him, and he not only silenced himself, his thoughts were thrown into disarray and confusion.

Lee walked up to get in Hugh's face and contemptibly yelled, "We're telling you right now to cut this shit out! Everyone is fed up with your actions, and they all are willing to throw you off of this picture, man!"

Hugh didn't say a word for a moment. Then Bob moved up toward him and sternly added, "You could at least have respect for the ladies on this set. We're pretty sure you don't have any respect for yourself, but you'd better find some respect when it comes to Corey and Anne."

Hugh chuckled and then sarcastically stated, "Oh yeah. You're Madrigal's boy, aren't you? You're not even on this picture. So get the hell out of here!"

Bob feigned a punch at him, and in reaction to that, Hugh took a swing at Bob, and he ducked, with Hugh's fist hitting Lee directly on his jaw. Lee fell to the stage floor in pain, holding his jaw.

Bob casually looked down at Lee and then back at Hugh. With lightning speed, and not giving Hugh a chance to defend himself, Bob threw a blistering blow to the side of Hugh's face, immediately dropping him to the floor. He was out cold.

There were a few cheers, and someone yelled to get an ambulance.

Clint and Dane congratulated Bob, as Clint boasted, "It looked like self-defense to me. How do you see it, Bob?"

Bob adroitly answered, "I'm pretty sure it was, man. That's all I've got to say!"

Corey moved quickly to Bob and opened her arms out to him. He took her by the waist and pulled her into him as she wrapped her arms around his neck. They stood holding each other until they heard the ambulance and police sirens screaming.

After the initial investigation by the Hollywood Police Department, Hugh Logan was arrested for assault, and it made Jack's job a lot easier in having to tell his uncle, Joseph Means, that Hugh would no longer be working on a Celebrity film ever again.

Bob and Clint ended up going to lunch with Corey and her cast of a bruised-jaw Lee, Dane, Arthur, and Anne. This group of actors really hit it off, and everyone seemed to be forming a seamless friendship with one another. So Bob took the liberty to invite the full cast from both Corey and his picture to the cast party for *Hidden Desire* that Saturday night at Susan's home. Bob did call and warn Susan, and she was more than happy to have the extra people at her party.

That Saturday night at Susan's house, the party was loud, with a lot of laughing, drinking, with just instrumental contemporary music playing in the background.

All the actors, actresses, directors, producers, and the main crew from both pictures were there, along with Jack Windheim and his secretary, Deloris. Deloris's duties at Celebrity had long extended beyond the purely secretarial.

Corey had on a slinky black cocktail dress and murderous high heels. She appeared dark and mysteriously provocative this evening. Bob got Corey up to dance with him a few times, as she always loved to slow dance with him; for being in his arms made her feel so safe and secure from the unexpected.

Corey watched each time Bob danced with another woman, but she closely watched when he and Kim danced together. She felt while watching them that Kim was a little different from the others Bob had ever danced with; there wasn't that much talking going on between them, and her eyes were shut as she rested her head on his shoulder. And he seemed momentarily lost in the short time the song played.

Corey was scared to death.

At midnight, the party started to wind down, and people were beginning to leave. Bob said his good-nights to Susan and thanked her for hosting, but turned to tell Kim good night, but she had already left the party.

When Bob and Corey were getting ready to go to bed that night, she asked him, not really wanting to know, but asked anyway, "Darling, what's going on between you and Kim?"

Bob turned to face her and knew Corey would pick up on anything that was peculiar to his normal behavior, and truthfully he answered her, "I just feel sorry for her, Corey."

Corey astonishingly rejoined, "Sorry? What on earth do you mean, Bob? She is a beautiful blonde with an hourglass figure and has eyes that are sexually corrupting."

She caught her breath and tried to calm herself. Then she slowly gathered the courage to ask, "Do you love her?"

Bob was flabbergasted with the thought that Corey could actually have asked him such a question. Incredulously he stood staring at her, and while breathing shallowly, he poured his heart out to her. "I just told you how I felt about her, and that's exactly what I meant."

Corey started to interrupt him, and Bob demanded, "Now you listen to me!"

She felt her heart now beating in her throat. She was shaken and afraid but had to trust what he was going to tell her.

"Corey, I have talked with Kim at the studio and when we ate lunch at the cafeteria and during breaks on our read-throughs, and to sum it up...she's just frustrated with making pictures anymore. She told me a person can get lured into loving themselves too much in Hollywood, and she didn't want to get into all of that. She didn't want to lose herself, and she needed to leave Hollywood to save herself. She said she liked who she was, and the studio system wanted to change all that."

Bob sat down on the bed as Corey stood on the other side. He added, "She is such a powerful presence on screen. She seems earthbound and ethereal...ordinary and extraordinary, all at the same time. My god, she was born for the colors of the films of the fifties—that kind of lighting, production design, and staging. Just yesterday, Victor had told me he couldn't believe the luminosity and brilliance Kim brought to the cameras. And now she just wants to walk away from her career and live what she calls a normal life. Corey, I am just a man. Flesh and bones. I find her desirable and different, but you ask, do I love her? Corey, I just feel sorry for her and what she's been through these last six years."

Corey resignedly told him, "I'm sorry, Bob. I didn't know that she was that unhappy. I know I overstepped in asking you such a question, but from everything I've seen of her and you, what more could I have thought?... I'm truly sorry, darling...please forgive me?"

Bob stood up and slowly started to walk for the bedroom door. Before he exited, he turned and told Corey, "Corey, you've got to stop this jealousy thing you have... I'm going outside to clear my head and get all of this in perspective. I want to be alone right now."

He kept walking as Corey slowly closed her eyes and lowered her chin into her chest, realizing the enormity of her mistake.

TWENTY-THREE

The next morning, Bob awoke from sleeping all night in a double pool lounging chair. He stretched his cramped body and yawned heavily, when he caught a glimpse of Corey sitting next to him in the adjacent lounger.

Her eyes looked as if she had been crying recently. Bob smiled at her, and softly he asked her, "Come here, doll."

Corey couldn't move fast enough to get into the double lounger with him. Bob moved over and made room for her, as he leaned over and kissed her on the forehead.

She had both of her hands on his right arm, which was wrapped around her waist, when he looked deeply into her eyes and reverently told her, "Corey, if the impossible ever happened, and I fell in love with another woman, I swear to you on my parents' gravestones you would be the first person I would tell… I just can't love you enough, lady."

Corey placed her hands on the side of his face and pulled his lips onto hers. They lay kissing for several seconds, when Haddie came down the landing steps toward them.

Haddie jokingly announced, "Okay, I'm relieved you're both not in your birthday suits."

Bob looked into Corey's eyes and smilingly whispered, "I wish we were."

Corey smiled lovingly and placed her head on his chest and sighed.

Haddie added, "Well, okay then… You had a phone call, Mr. Bob. It was Joshua. After I talked with him for a short while, he asked you to call him back sometime today."

Bob kissed Corey on top of the head and then told Haddie, "I'll call him back as soon as Corey and I finish up here. All right, Haddie? Thank you for letting me know."

"You're welcome. Now you two can resume the mischief you were getting into."

Bob and Corey chuckled at each other like a couple of love-starved teenagers. Then Bob kissed Corey on the lips once more and asked, "So, is it all cool with us, doll? Are you okay with Kim and I having a friendship? Because that's all it is, baby."

Corey sat up in the lounger and swore to him, "I'll always trust you, Bob. I'm just never sure about the women you cross paths with and their intentions. I guess I'll just have to let you handle all that. I again am very sorry, darling. I find I love you far too much for one lifetime."

He kissed her once more and told her, as he began to stand up, "Now, I'm going in to call Joshua, catch a shower and then something to eat… I'll see you at breakfast, babe."

Joshua had asked Bob to sing the new song Bob had written, "My Constant Need," at his wedding next Saturday. Joshua wanted that song to be the one he and Deidra would dance to for the rest of their lives. With great pride, Bob had not one problem telling him he would love to sing that song at his wedding. The Owls would just have to record the instrumental version with no lyrics for the wedding.

At breakfast that Sunday morning, Bob informed Corey, "Joshua wants me to sing one of the new songs the Owls are going to record this week. However, when I wrote 'My Constant Need,' I only had you in mind, Corey. So I will be singing that song to Joshua and Deidra, but also to you, babe."

Corey slid off of her counter stool slowly and sexily. As she stepped near him, she was staring at him showing all the love in her heart. She bent over and pressed her breasts into his chest as she gave Bob a long and wet kiss.

When she pulled away, she breathlessly told him, "Thank you, sweetheart. I can't wait."

That Saturday, August 27, the wedding of Joshua Elijah Chambers and Deidra Esther Franklin was ready to commence at two o'clock at the United Methodist Church of Thousand Oaks.

The music started after everyone was seated by the five ushers—Doug, Jimmy, Len, Nick, and Truman. The music playing was Canon in D by Pachelbel. It was a timeless classic that Joshua had always wanted to hear playing at his wedding ceremony. The violins and the piano were at a slow methodical pace that made it easy for both the bride and escort to match steps.

The minister and Joshua stood at the altar. Joshua was resplendent in his black tuxedo, with an ascot, cummerbund, handkerchief, and boutonniere of brilliant orange (Deidra's favorite color).

The procession started with Darnell and Alicia walking down the aisle first. Her bridesmaid dress was a strapless, floor-length, satiny gown of a beautiful shade of violet, with Darnell in his orange-accessorized black tuxedo.

Bob, the best man, escorted the matron of honor, Haddie, down the aisle. She looked stunning in her violet gown. Her eyes were a bit moistened, but she was glowing with pride.

Bob looked over at Corey when he and Haddie passed by the row she was sitting in, and he smiled and winked at her. She immediately gave him a toothy smile and winked back.

Then after Haddie stood nearest to where Deidra would be standing, Alicia and Haddie exchanged cheek-kisses. Bob walked up and stood by Joshua's left arm, and then the three guys all shook one another's hands.

Corey sat fixated on Bob and how absolutely gorgeous he was in his tuxedo with the orange accents. To her, he was the epitome of handsome manliness and courage. She felt very blessed to have this man loving her and owning her heart.

The music became just a little louder now, as Deidra and her father, Randall Franklin Jr., began to slowly walk down the aisle. Mr.

Franklin was a stately-looking black man, with a thin mustache and a full head of glistening, combed-back hair.

Deidra's right arm was wrapped in and around his left arm, and her beautiful bouquet of interspersed orange and white roses and orchids was in her left hand.

Deidra's floor-length, white sheath, strapless chiffon wedding gown had a sweetheart neckline that resembled the curves at the top of a heart and accentuated the low cut of the cleavage. The romantic neckline was extremely flattering and was a classy look on her. The gown had a center slit, with a cinched waist of intricate threading of hand-sewn lace. The coup de grace of her gown was the sweep train, which was six inches longer than the rest of her skirt and attached at the back of her waist. She had a small, shoulder-length white veil of lace. Deidra was an extremely beautiful bride.

Everyone was standing as the bride made her way down to the altar, where her groom stood mesmerized with her exquisite beauty.

During the ceremony and the exchanging of rings, Bob got to hand Joshua his ring to put on Deidra's finger. When Joshua reached toward Bob and took the ring, he leaned over and sincerely told Bob, "It's only because of you, brother, that I'm here today and able to marry the woman of my dreams. I will never forget, man. Love you, brother."

Bob immediately became choked up, and tears raced into his eyes. They quickly hugged each other, and with moistened eyes, Joshua turned back to Deidra. Bob stood with a couple of tears running down his cheeks and was trying hard to fight back more tears that were welling up in his eyes.

Haddie witnessed the exchange between her son and Bob, and she knew what it was about and started to drop tears into Deidra's bouquet she was holding for her.

Corey had a pretty good idea what was going on, and when she saw tears running down Bob's face, she instantly started to cry herself. Nick and Charlotte were sitting next to her, and Charlotte handed a tissue to Nick to give to Corey. Nick patted Corey a couple of times on the shoulder after handing her the tissue.

Corey thanked him and then dabbed her lower eyelids and nose.

After Joshua and Deidra were pronounced husband and wife, the entire church stood up and applauded and cheered for them. After they had kissed, they both hurried back down the aisle and left to get to their reception.

Joshua had secured the Malibu Room at the Four Seasons Hotel-Westlake Village in Thousand Oaks. It was located in Agoura Hills, which lay in the Santa Monica Mountains, just a few miles from the church.

All of the guests were able to drive there, and with the wedding party, they filled most of the 125 chairs. The chairs were surrounding linen-covered tables, with a fresh-cut flower arrangement of orange and violet roses and orchids placed in the middle standing in stylish vases.

There was also violet backlighting on the walls and ceiling. The entire atmosphere of the room was sophisticated, dressy, and exuded a subtle romantic ambiance.

Joshua and Deidra sat at the main table in front of the room, with Haddie next to him and the Franklins next to Deidra. Bob and Corey sat close to the bride and groom's table, with Nick, Charlotte, Len, Valerie, Darnell, and Alicia. Everyone else sat in back or across from them.

After an initial drink, everyone ate either steak or lobster dinners. The couple cut their cake, and while that was being served to the guests, Joshua rose from his seat with a cordless microphone he had been handed.

To the room, he lightly tapped his champagne glass with his fork, and then announced, "I'd like to thank everyone who made it to the wedding today. Especially Deidra's parents, Randall and Georgina, for driving down here from San Francisco."

There was a small round of applause.

"And thanks to my mama for coming all the way from Bel Air… that's like right around the corner, isn't it, Mama?"

Haddie smiled and kiddingly nodded her head in agreement. That brought laughs from a lot of the people.

"Well, Deidra and I are gonna be moving into our own home right here in Agoura Hills in a week, and, Mama, you'll be coming to live with us. How's that sound? You'll never have to work again, Mama."

A lot of the guests applauded, but Haddie was taken by surprise by all of this and could only stare at Joshua questioningly.

Corey looked at Bob and, with extreme trepidation in her voice, asked him, "Did you hear anything about this before today, Bob?"

Bob was as surprised as Corey as he answered her, "Not a single word, Corey."

Haddie looked over at Corey and Bob with a look of saddened disbelief on her face. She knew she was going to have a sit-down with her son next week, when they returned home from their honeymoon in the Bahamas.

"Okay, now I want everyone to meet my best man. For you very few people who don't know who this multitalented man is, I first need to tell you I owe my very life to him."

There were a few gasps from some and "Oh my god's" from others. Bob just sat quietly and unemotionally staring at Joshua. Corey placed her hand on Bob's hand as Joshua continued.

"He's not just a brave and brilliant musician and actor, he's my friend and my brother. Bob Richardson, everyone."

The entire room loudly applauded as Bob stood up and took the microphone from Joshua. The two shook hands and gave each other a shoulder bump.

As the room quieted down, Bob kiddingly stated, "Who's giving who a toast today?"

All five at the bride and groom's table smiled and lightly chuckled.

The guests also laughed as Bob continued, "I've only known Joshua and Deidra seven months now, but I can tell you she's a beautiful dancer and a gorgeous woman, and Joshua possesses one heck of a mean right uppercut punch."

The guests thought that was hilarious, then Bob smiled and chuckled to himself.

"When the Owls band was touring down in Birmingham this past summer, the bunch of us guys had a disagreement with some good ole boys down there. You see, we thought we had the freedom to play our music and entertain our fans and just have some fun, but they thought we didn't even have the right to be alive."

The room became solemnly quiet and cheerless. Corey swallowed heavily and dropped her head. The entire room was absorbed in thought about what he had just said.

"All six of us Owls knew this was going to be a long and hard struggle. I can't tell you how much Joshua and Darnell have opened so many eyes and so many hearts to the blatant discrimination and bigotry in this country. I mean, just by writing the songs they compose that are addressing this problem, and the fearless way they tour the country getting the word out, that this epidemic of hate has to end someday, somehow. The first day I met Joshua, he brought this remarkable and charming young woman with him. And when he started to refer to his different horns as his mistresses, most of us freaked and thought he was a complete square and was just flipping out."

There was some quiet laughter and chuckling.

"But I knew. I knew by the way he played his main mistress, the bass trumpet, he had the gift. He has displayed that gift his entire life. He fell in love with music, like myself, at a very early age. He wanted nothing more than to have that horn bring happiness and content to people everywhere. But then a little kink in the armor happened when he met the love of his life, Ms. Deidra. At that point, he wanted only to please and make happy this woman that absolutely turned his life around. The Lord blessed us the day he decided to play with the Owls, and also the day he would marry this smart, exceptional, and beautiful woman."

Bob looked directly at Joshua and Deidra and reached for his glass of champagne and lifted it high into the air and lastly stated, "So I want to now make a toast to this couple who could not be more perfectly matched to one another. May you live long, prosper always, and love powerfully. To my friends and to my brother… God bless you both."

Everyone took a sip of their drink, as there were many "Hear, hear's" from the room.

Bob came back over the microphone and informed everyone, "I think it's time these two got up to dance their first dance as a married couple. What do you say?"

The entire room began with loud shouting and applause for Joshua and Deidra to get up to dance. The couple slowly made their way to the dance floor.

Bob looked down at Corey sitting in her chair and smiled and winked at her. Not hesitating at all, she smiled and slowly winked back with a very moistened eye.

Nick started to pipe in over the sound system the instrumental version to "My Constant Need," for the Owls hadn't recorded it yet with Bob's vocals included.

As the slow romantic music started to play and Doug's soft alto sax and Joshua's bass trumpet carried the main melody, Bob began singing:

> Meeting you sent chills through me
> You unlocked my heart without a key
> For my direction and welfare you took the lead
> And when I finally woke up, you became my
> constant need
>
> You say you'll never let go of me
> I keep telling you I'll never leave
> I can always feel your love when I'm away
> For coming home to you is where I'd love to stay
>
> Let me lead you into my midnight's ecstasy
> I'll take your hand and keep you close to me
> You shook my world when you planted love's
> eternal seed
> I now dream only of you and when you became
> my constant need

I feel your touch and you're not even in the room
Don't ever leave me, baby, for it would spell my
doom
Others would cut me just to watch me bleed
But you healed my wounds, and became my con-
stant need

Lay with me and let me feel your loving touch
Your heart and soul is what I need so much
"Always sharing, always trusting" is two lovers'
creed
When you stole my heart and owned my soul,
you became...my...constant...need

When the last note of the song filtered into the air, there was a tumultuous and thundering applause from everyone, including Joshua and Deidra.

Bob lovingly looked over at Corey, and she was practically sobbing into a tissue. He turned to her, and she stood up throwing her arms around his neck. Bob wrapped his arms around her waist and started kissing her on her right cheek and neck.

Corey kissed his ear and almost inaudibly she whispered, "Just hold me, sweetheart."

The following Monday at Celebrity Studios, Bob's director, Victor, told everyone he liked what he was seeing in rehearsals, so they were going to commence the shooting on many of the scenes of the picture. Bob and Kim got a location shoot over by Malibu, so this gave Bob the chance to talk with her on the hour drive over to the coast about her fast exit from Susan's party a week ago.

With one of the prop guys driving, Victor sat in front with him, and Bob and Kim rode in the spacious backseat of the sedan.

Bob started the conversation, for Kim had been quiet and withdrawn since Susan's cast party. He asked quite concernedly, "You know you haven't seemed yourself since Susan's party last weekend. Is it anything I've said or done?"

She lightly chuckled to herself, and after a few moments, she confessed to him, "I guess I'm just envious of the relationship you have with Corey. You two seem madly in love with one another, and that's exactly what I want someday soon. I guess it's just hard for me to be around you, because it's someone like you I want to end up with."

Bob sighed heavily and thought long and hard, and he finally was able to tell her, "Kim, you're the kind of woman that's going to find that perfect man just for you. It may not be today, or even tomorrow, but you'd be bringing so much good and truth into any relationship that's based on love. I just don't see you without that special man in your life someday."

"I certainly hope you're right, Bob." Kim just sat staring out of the car window.

Bob tried to set her mind at ease by stating, "I am crazy in love with Corey, and I don't ever see another woman coming between us, so why don't you and I just be the best of friends and keep all of this Hollywood stuff on a professional level and have some fun with it. No pressure from me, no double-meaning innuendoes, no one trying to get you into bed."

"Oh, why not?" She started to laugh out loud, and he laughed along with her. Then they smiled at each other and gave each other a big reassuring hug.

Bob affirmatively conveyed, "All right! Let's do it up right, Kim. Everything will be cool."

One of the shoots that day was to have Bob and Kim on a date and playing down in the water by the ocean's edge. After they finished trying to splash each other, she'd run back up to their blanket that was spread out in a secluded spot on the beach.

Bob's cue would be to follow her, as he's dressed only in a swimming suit. She fell onto the blanket and rolled over on her back, wearing a low-cut two-piece bathing suit. He was on his knees next to her and stared into her eyes when he started to breathe a little faster.

Bob's character slowly lowered himself, from the waist up, to lie across her chest, and then he passionately kissed her. Kim's character began to whimper and told him, "Yes, yes, oh, God, yes!"

They kissed each other for at least ten seconds, as Victor had three mobile handheld cameras on them. Two shot both side angles, and the last zoomed in on a close-up.

Victor then called out, "Cut… All right, let's check our lighting again, guys, and then we'll adjust our cameras accordingly."

Kim and Bob slowly separated as she continued to stare into his eyes. Bob returned to his position on his knees but never broke his eye contact with her.

Victor called for another take with only one up-close camera, but just for the blanket scene. When the crew finished shooting six other scenes with them, Victor advised them they were done for the day. Victor told both Bob and Kim, "Nice work, you two. That was some very convincing stuff today."

The ride back to the studio that evening was a pretty quiet one for Kim. It seemed Victor and Bob were the only ones in the car talking.

When their car arrived back at Celebrity, Corey was waiting with her driver, Curtis, to take her and Bob home that evening. Bob spotted her standing and talking with Jack as they stood by the side of her Cadillac.

Bob walked up to her, and she opened her arms wide to him. They kissed, and she asked him how the shoot went. He matter-of-factly answered, "It was cool, doll."

Jack shook hands with Bob and asked him, "How are you and Kim getting along, Bob? She's a pretty good actress, isn't she?"

Bob thought about it for a few seconds and convincingly told Jack, "She's a damned good actress, Jack. One of the best."

Bob looked over at Corey, and her face revealed a slight jealousy and a touch of suspicion. Then with some awkwardness, he quickly added, "Oh, well, of course, present company excluded."

The three of them had a good laugh with that comment.

That Tuesday night at the recording studio, the Owls recorded "My Constant Need" with full vocals by Bob and backup by Darnell and Len. Nick was there and told the guys this single should be on the market by next Monday, September 5.

Meanwhile, the Owls worked quickly, but creatively, on all the arrangements to the twelve songs that were going to be on the Christmas album playlist.

After Nick had received the six women's approval that the Owls wanted to record with, he started to set up recording times, places, and dates with them. These were the six female singers the group decided upon from a list of thirteen.

Darnell's wife, Alicia, was one of those ladies, and she was very excited to record "Let It Snow, Let It Snow, Let It Snow" with her husband, but warned Darnell it would have to be soon; their baby was due in mid-October. This project wasn't going to be that hard for Alicia, as she sang in the same nightclub in Southern LA that Darnell played his guitar at, after he graduated from NEC. The two had begun dating, and later that same year, they were married.

Ann Sheridan was scheduled to sing "Baby, It's Cold Outside" with Bob. When she was contacted by Nick to record this, she jumped at the idea. She told Nick this was something she had always wanted to do for the past two years—sing with Bob Richardson.

So Nick set up the first recording session for Tuesday night, September 6, at the Thousand Oaks recording studio. Alicia lived right there in Thousand Oaks with Darnell in Bob's house, and Ann was under contract with Celebrity Studios and lived in Los Angeles County. This wouldn't be a tough commute for either one of them.

Doris Day had told Nick she would be more than happy to reprise her rendition of "Silver Bells" with Bob. She informed Nick that they could record that song right there in LA anytime before she started rehearsals in New York for the reprisal of *Oklahoma!* in early October.

Debbie Reynolds agreed that she would love to make a recording on the Night Owls' first Christmas album and sing "The Christmas Song" with Len. But it also would have to happen before October and her rehearsals for the musical play *Oklahoma!*

Nick got both Doris and Debbie to record at the studio in LA, the same studio that Mercury Records would intermittently send the Owls to record at. Doris and Debbie's time slot to record would be Thursday night, September 8.

When Ella Fitzgerald was contacted and asked to record on the album, she thought the idea of singing with Bob again on "O Holy Night" and with Joshua and Darnell on "Have Yourself a Merry Little Christmas" would be tons of fun. She also informed Nick that she would get Sarah Vaughan on board with the project, since they were good friends, and both lived in New York. Sarah was asked to sing "Silent Night" with four of the Night Owls, as their last song on the album. Doug and Joshua would be needed on their instruments, so it was just the three guitars and Jimmy singing with her. She was overwhelmed that four of the band members would be accompanying her.

However, Nick had to set up the recording session in New York, because that's where both Ella and Sarah lived, and they would only be free for October 3 and 4.

Ella and Sarah separately toured the States and internationally with well-known bands, anywhere from forty to forty-five weeks per year; this didn't leave a lot of time for recording music for either one of them.

The remaining five songs on the album would be upbeat Christmas standards, and Bob, Len, and Darnell would be harmonizing together on those. They would be recorded in the studio at Thousand Oaks before the Owls flew out to New York to record with Ella and Sarah.

It just so happened that Bob would be in New York on Sunday, October 2, getting ready to start his rehearsals for the play *Oklahoma!* on that Tuesday. The Owls were scheduled to meet with Ella and Sarah in Brooklyn at the Verve Record Studio on Monday morning, October 3. All three songs would have to be rehearsed and recorded in the same day.

Wednesday, August 31, Bob was to shoot a couple of scenes with his other costar Susan Hawthorne. These scenes would be shot on one of the smaller soundstages, because this compelling drama had Susan portraying Bob's put-upon wife and was filmed inside their home. Of the three scenes, one of them was a very steamy one that took place inside their bedroom, with both in bed.

This scene would be pushing the limitations of the Motion Picture Production Code, which was the industry's guidelines for the self-censorship of a movie's content. However, the guidelines in 1960 were becoming hazy as to what was acceptable and unacceptable in the production of a motion picture. Jack Windheim was aware they'd be walking on thin ice when Victor directed Bob and Susan in this controversial and quite steamy love scene.

Corey had knowledge of these on-property shoots between Susan and Bob and would be looking in from time to time, when she had breaks or had finished her scenes on another larger soundstage close by.

The first scene Victor shot was Susan and Bob having an argument in their bedroom, where Susan eventually slapped Bob's character hard across the face. He would then grab her and throw her onto the bed.

Susan was a little apprehensive about hitting Bob, so she asked Victor how he wanted her to play that.

Victor told her to just skim his face with her opened hand, and sound effects would dub the rest into the scene.

Bob was standing just a few feet away from Victor and Susan, and he spoke up immediately, saying, "Victor, let's make this about as real as we can and have Susan really slap me. It'll certainly help the quality and realism of the scene."

Susan was aghast. "Are you sure, Bob? I've got a pretty good right cross."

Bob smiled and assured her, "It can't be any harder than a lot of the hits I've taken lately."

Susan cautiously smiled at him and then ran a hand down the side of his face.

It was at that moment Corey was able to steal away from her shoot and sneak into the back of the soundstage. She was in time to see Susan's hand sliding down the side of her husband's face.

Kim and Clint were sitting in canvas-backed studio chairs next to the cameras, but Corey stayed farther back and away from the set lighting.

Victor yelled, "All right, places, you two. Start rolling the cameras. Action!"

Bob and Susan loudly exchanged a few lines with each other. She tore the front of his shirt, exposing his chest, then she hauled off and slapped him hard and convincingly. The crack of skin-on-skin stunned Bob momentarily, but he was still able to grab Susan and throw her onto the bed.

Corey's eyes registered complete disbelief after the real slap Susan gave him. She kept watching Bob and could see the side of his face was beet red and with the imprint of Susan's hand clearly showing.

At this point, Victor yelled, "Cut! That was sensational, you two! That just may be the only take I'm going to need of that scene. Great work!"

Susan got up from the bed and hugged Bob and then gave him a gentle cheek-kiss on the reddened cheek she had slapped.

Bob chuckled and told her, "By God, you really do have a great right cross! That was well done, Susan. Good job!"

She sympathetically sighed and hugged him again.

Corey felt Susan was smothering him with her histrionics and with feigned compassion. She also felt the steamy, highly-talked-about bed scene probably would be shot next, so she decided to hang around a little while longer.

Word quickly got out that Victor was readying the set with his stage production manager to shoot the controversial bed scene. Jack wandered over from his office; producer Samuel Ashburn was also present; and actors from other pictures filed into the back of the soundstage, where Corey was standing, just to get a peek of the scene.

Jack and Samuel wanted to see just how far Victor was going to take the original scene, the way it was written in the screenplay. The two men would have final say on the matter.

Twenty minutes later, Victor called for Bob and Susan to come up to him, as all three now stood by the bed. Victor was telling them exactly what he expected out of this scene. Then moments later, Susan lay on the bed with her dress disheveled and on her back. Bob would be standing from the spot where he had thrown her onto the bed.

The clapboard was held up in front of Bob's face, with the number of the take, name of the picture, director, and cameraman, and then it banged shut. A man shouted, "Take one!"

The two cameras whirred—one on Bob, the other on Susan. Then Victor yelled, "All right, roll the cameras. Action!"

The tempestuous look on Bob's face, and the scared but sexually bothered look of Susan drew the cameras in for close-ups.

When Bob reached the bed, he tore the rest of his shirt off, exposing his muscular chest and arms. Susan looked as though she really was sexually bothered, and she started to breathe heavily and threw her arms over her head and succumbed to his wanton lust.

Bob pinned her arms down with his hands, after he tore her dress down in front, exposing all but the nipples of her breasts. He then half lay on her, after he placed one leg between hers, and began savagely kissing her. She was moaning and thrusting her body into him. He would reach down, to what the camera would think he was removing his pants. Although it didn't show them from the waist down, he would be moving like he had entered her. Susan's character was loudly sighing with great sexual satisfaction and screaming, "Oh my god! Yes!"

Bob's character would show the cameras his head between her breasts, and the belief he was kissing them, as she moaned loudly. After another ten seconds of him kissing at her upper chest and neck, Victor called out, "Cut! That was tremendous, you two. Very realistic!"

As Victor scanned the set, he jokingly stated, "Anyone need a cold shower?"

There was some sedate laughter and mild applause, but not from Corey. She headed back to her picture shoot trying to tell herself, *They're just acting. It's just too bad Bob and Susan are so damned good at it.*

That evening at home and out in the kitchen, Bob, Corey, and Haddie were eating dinner. Corey spoke up and confessed to Bob, "I was witness, along with many others, to your bed scene with Susan today, darling."

Bob glanced over at her and inquisitively asked, "Yeah, I knew you'd be there. Well? Did it look convincing to you?"

Corey answered quite stoically and confident, "I felt it did, but I'd have to see the final edit on it, and then I could tell you more accurately. However, I know there would be no question in the fact that if it were the real thing, there would be so much more passion involved."

She gave him that sexy, attractive look, and Bob, staring directly into her bedroom eyes, slowly began to smile that sly and alluring smile he possessed. Without breaking eye contact with Corey, he asked Haddie, "Haddie, do you think you could keep our dinners warm for a while? Corey and I have some business elsewhere."

Bob stood up from his chair and took Corey's hand in his and led her to the bedroom. They heard Haddie—not surprisingly—remark as they walked out of the kitchen, "Of course. But you've got to know by now I always leave the stove on a warming temperature when you two are in the house."

Haddie called Joshua early Monday morning, the day after he and Deidra returned home from their honeymoon. Joshua answered after a few rings, "Hello."

Haddie interestingly asked, "Hello, Joshua. This is Mama, baby. How did your honeymoon go in the Bahamas? I know you both probably had the time of your lives, didn't you?"

Joshua informed her, "Yes, yes, we did, Mama. But I know what you're really calling about. And Deidra and I would really like for you to come and live with us."

Haddie rejoined by stating, "Joshua, I love that you two would want me to live with you. But honestly, baby, deep down inside of me, I feel at this stage of your life with Deidra, you need your privacy and the time to get to grow that God-given love for one another you two have been blessed with. And besides, baby, I enjoy living here with Ms. Corey and Mr. Bob. I love both of them, and they take better care of me than I take care of them."

Joshua sharply pointed out, "See… *Ms.* Corey and *Mr.* Bob! That's what I want stopped! You sound like a nineteenth-century house slave, and I somehow can't overlook that, Mama!"

Haddie now became incensed and retorted, "Now you just hush your mouth, boy. Ms. Corey had told me many years ago, when I came to live and work for her, that I could just call her *Corey*. But I told her I was brought up better than that. I was taught to respect anyone I was working for, no matter what job I was doing. Mr. Bob calls me *Ms. Haddie*, 'cause I know he cares and respects me, and he's fully aware of how well I take care of Ms. Corey. So don't let me ever hear you talk about that nasty and evil slave business again that you referred to, 'cause I'm my own woman, Joshua, and I've taken care of you and me for many years now without being a slave to no one."

Joshua, realizing the error of his ways, quickly apologized and could actually understand what his mama had told him. "I'm so sorry, Mama. I know Bob and Corey are good people, or I wouldn't be making such incredible money right now. I wouldn't be traveling around in a band with five other brilliant musicians, and I sure as heck would not be buying a beautiful new house with my wife, Deidra. I guess I was just being selfish in wanting my two best girls living comfortably with me… If you're happy, Mama, and I now know you are, then don't pay no never mind to me. But when you become a grandma, I hope to see you a lot more often, 'cause you know we're gonna need a babysitter sometimes." Joshua laughed weakly.

Haddie chuckled and lovingly answered, "That's right, baby. And I better never see anyone else with my grandbaby. Uh-huh, you know what I mean."

"I get your drift, Mama."

The Tuesday night of September 6, Nick asked the guys if they could come to the studio ahead of Alicia and Ann Sheridan, who were to arrive at six o'clock to rehearse and record their Christmas song with the Owls. Bob said he would get there from his picture shoot as soon as he could, so he drove himself in to Celebrity that morning instead of riding in with Corey.

It was just minutes past five thirty that evening when Bob had arrived and all the guys sat down with Nick to talk. Nick excitedly began to tell them, "Okay, guys, we've been invited to play the Beacon Theatre in New York City for two weeks in October."

Anyone who knew anything about music knew about the Beacon Theatre. It was a historic theater at Broadway and Seventy-Fourth Street on the Upper West Side of Manhattan. The capacity seating was 2,894, with three tiers of seating. It opened in 1929 as a motion picture and vaudeville palace. It now hosted only bands with notoriety that were capable in packing the house with paying ticket holders. The Night Owls were very capable of doing that.

The guys all yelled with excitement about performing at the Beacon. A couple of soda bottles were clinked together, and hands exchanged some skin.

Nick further informed them, "Now this engagement will run for two weeks, from October 7 through October 21…it will be four days after you record with Ella and Sarah, and then end the day before we fly out to Charlotte. North Carolina for that makeup concert October 22."

"That's too cool, man! We gonna have two weeks in the same house. This is just too crazy and groovin', Nick," Darnell enthusiastically expressed.

Nick chuckled a little, and before he thought he would bust open from the excitement, he also told the guys, "And believe it or not, the Beacon told me they would put it in writing in our contract that we would be compensated one million dollars for the two-week gig. How's that jumping up and kicking you in the ass, fellas?"

Every one of the guys jumped up and started screaming and hugging each other, patting each other on the back, and slapping hands. It took a few minutes for them to come down from their euphoria.

Nick informed them, "That's gonna be almost a hundred and forty-three thousand apiece—of course, before taxes."

The guys were beside themselves with unbelievable exuberance and ardor.

Alicia and Ann walked into the studio at that moment, after they had met each other out in the parking lot. Darnell explained to Alicia what Nick had just told them about the Beacon Theatre. Alicia hugged and kissed Darnell while Ann walked up to Bob and hugged him and cheek-kissed him, saying, "That's great news, Bob. Wow! You know, my ex-husband didn't make as much money as one of you are going to in the five years we were married... What a lucky girl that Corey is."

Bob could only smile disconcertingly. Then the guys got down to work with Joshua and Darnell, going over Alicia's song with her, and Bob and Len working with Ann on hers.

After three and a half hours rehearsing, both songs were then recorded, which Nick took with him when he left. Afterward, everyone went out for a nightcap at a local cocktail lounge, except Alicia and Darnell. She was very tired and only six weeks away from delivering her baby.

Bob and Ann sat talking for another hour with the other four guys, which didn't get him home until almost midnight.

Bob quietly took a shower and then climbed into bed snuggling close to Corey. She responded by taking his hand and placing it on her breast. They loved going to sleep like that.

Corey's picture was moving along quite smoothly, now that Hugh Logan was behind bars and out of the motion picture business for good.

Bob wandered over to her set one afternoon, after he returned back at the studio early from a location shoot with Kim, Clint, and Lew Ayers. They were instructed to take lunch and meet back at the soundstage in an hour for some close-ups that had to be shot.

Bob skipped lunch and went to watch Corey work some of her magic in front of the cameras. She was shooting a scene with Dane Clark, who was playing her lover. His character was in love with a married woman: Corey. Arthur Kennedy played Corey's husband, who knew she was cheating, and he was ready to kill anyone he caught with her.

Bob stood off set and away from the cameras. He stood there for almost an hour, unnoticed to all. He had watched Dane make love to his wife and then stayed to watch the scene when Arthur's character caught them, and he shot and wounded Dane's character.

Bob stood thinking, *It's too bad he didn't kill him, because I would have.* He then chuckled to himself and started to walk out of the soundstage.

That's when Corey spotted him. Hal called for a ten-minute break, and Corey hurried over to him. Just before he walked out of the building, Corey grabbed his arm and breathlessly told him, "What a pleasant surprise, darling."

He declared in a low sensuous voice, "Hey, baby."

She gently pulled his face down to hers, and they warmly kissed for a few seconds. Bob's thoughts were playing in his head, *How passionate and exquisite is this woman?*

When Bob moved his head away from the kiss, he slightly nodded his head and confessed to her, "I understand now, Corey, and I don't enjoy it either, doll."

Corey stood confused and questioningly asked, "Whatever do you mean, Bob? I'm not understanding, sweetheart."

He uncomfortably admitted, "I just saw you making love to Dane, and I was not very comfortable at all watching you two mixing it up over there."

Corey smiled comprehensibly and then fervently kissed him again. She then cupped his face in her hands and told him, just being inches from his lips, "Now you see what I go through ten times more often with you and your many costarring women."

Bob apologetically swore, "I'm so sorry, baby. I won't agree to any more pictures with me physically being with any other women."

Corey instantly shot back, "Nonsense! For you see, darling, I get to go home with you, shower with you, and actually make love to you. All the others just don't stand a chance."

They lovingly smiled at each other and then kissed long and hard. This drew a lot of attention to them, but they really didn't care, as they luxuriated in each other's love.

As everyone was called back to the set, Corey alluringly told Bob, "Then I'll see you tonight when I finish, darling."

He adoringly answered her as he started to move out the door, "Yes, you will!"

Corey smiled with such brilliance in her eyes.

Bob walked back to his building thinking, *To be that in love, to know that frenzy of the heart.* He had never dreamed that he would know such consuming happiness was possible.

At the recording studio in LA that Thursday evening, the Night Owls met with Doris Day and Debbie Reynolds to record their two Christmas songs for the Owls' album.

Knowing Debbie very well, Bob walked up to her and hugged and cheek-kissed her. Then Nick, who walked in behind the two, introduced Debbie and Doris to the guys. "Everyone, this is Debbie Reynolds and Doris Day. I'm sure I didn't have to introduce either one of them, but why don't all of you go up and introduce yourselves to them."

The guys did just that, with Bob waiting until after the last guy met Doris. After Doris was through shaking hands with all the guys, except Bob, he walked up to her, as she was now pleasantly staring at him.

Bob smiled charmingly, and putting his hand out to her, he graciously told her, "It's great to finally meet you, Doris. And thank you so much for wanting to join us on our first Christmas album. This is just some crazy stuff happening here."

Doris laughed and replied, "Thank you for wanting me on one of your tracks, Bob. It's also nice to meet you and all of your band."

Doris had certainly heard of Bob and his multitalented abilities, but for the first time and in person, she had noticed how invitingly handsome he was. She was awakened by his beautifully wavy hair and his piercing and glowing green eyes. The solid build and the sexuality that just exuded from him was mesmerizing to her.

After meeting Doris, Bob found her to be a breath of fresh air. A woman now thirty-eight years old, married with a child, and beautiful in a down-home comfortable way. She had some striking bright-blue eyes and was tremendously talented in all aspects of music and acting.

Debbie worked with Len, with whom she was going to be singing "The Christmas Song." Doris was working with Bob on "Silver Bells." Both ladies liked the written arrangement and tempo to their songs and were excited to get to the recording phase of the process.

If anything, the songs sounded a bit more jazzy than their original releases inferred. The guys had written in Doug's soft and rich saxophone and Joshua's mellifluous muted bass trumpet.

This group of musicians had an enjoyable time reading, singing, playing, and laughing to the music. At ten thirty that evening, they started the recording process. They didn't finish until after midnight, and then all but Darnell went out for a drink to socialize some more.

Leaving that night, Bob happily told Debbie and Doris, "I'll see you in New York in just three and a half weeks for *Oklahoma!* All right? Oh, and if you come in early, you could catch the Owls down in Brooklyn, at Verve Record Studio. We'll be recording our final two songs of the album with Ella Fitzgerald and Sarah Vaughan Monday morning at nine."

Doris was deeply excited about that and emphatically stated, "Oh my god! That's fantastic, Bob. I'd love to be there watching and listening to those voices. You know, early in my career, I styled my singing after Ella. I would love hearing her again!"

After Doris drove off to her home in Carmel-by-the-Sea, Debbie had her awaiting driver take her back to her home in Beverly Hills.

Nick put the two tapes of recorded songs in his car, but then he casually told the five guys before they got into their cars, "Hey, maybe I should inform you guys that your album *The Night Owls Playing with Change in Mind* is tearing it up in record stores everywhere, and your single 'My Constant Need' is incinerating the charts. Right now it's the number one song on the National Top 10 here and abroad and on *The Hit Parade*… I'm positive we're looking at platinum right now."

The guys were extremely excited about how well their music was selling but was getting very used to their popularity and the money that kept coming in hand over fist.

Nick reminded them, "Before we go into New York to record with Ella and Sarah, I'm gonna need you guys to put the finishing touches to your other four rock singles. That way we'd be able to have a lot more music to draw from when we're at the Beacon Theatre."

Bob arrived back home at one thirty in the morning. Again, he had to quietly take his shower and then climb into bed. This night, Corey rolled over to him and began to kiss his bare chest and neck. As tired as he was, Bob responded to her, and they made some very tender love that early morning, until they both fell asleep in each other's arms.

TWENTY-FOUR

After a very tiring day at Celebrity Studios, Bob had to head to the recording studio after he sat down and had dinner with Corey and Haddie.

The last three weeks of September, Bob and the guys worked hard at finalizing the four remaining rock songs they had composed. A lot of work went into arranging the melodies, horn placements, rhythm, chord progressions, and then coordinating all that to the lyrics.

Corey's and Bob's pictures were nearing their conclusions by the end of September. Both producers, Jules Glassman and Samuel Ashburn, were looking to wrap their pictures on the same day of October 1. They were thinking of just having one huge wrap party for all the people involved with both films that same Saturday night when production on the two pictures would be shut down.

Corey thought that was a great idea, for now she would be able to fly into New York with Bob on that Sunday morning of October 2. He was going to fly in early to get ready for the Owls' recording session with Ella and Sarah Monday morning.

These last three recordings would complete the Night Owls' Christmas album titled *The Night Owls Christmas with Hoooo's Hoo*, and it would go on sale after Halloween in early November.

By the end of September, Nick released only two of the Owls' new songs. He didn't want a glut of the Owls' records hitting the market at the same time; he wanted their fans to have time to digest them. Right now he felt the market had reached the saturation point.

So Nick decided to release the Christmas album November 18. He would then wait until after New Year's to release two more singles because the Owls wouldn't be producing any more recordings with Bob for a while; Bob would be staying busy with his Broadway play in London until January 10, 1961. Then the very last single would be released in mid-February.

Nick and Irving Green at Mercury Records thought that it would be a great idea to release another live performance album with the Owls' future two-week gig at the Beacon Theatre. Nick and the guys thought of naming the live performance album, *The Night Owls Beakin' It at the Beacon*. This album would not be released until March.

The wrap party for *Lead Me Astray* and *Hidden Desire* was a huge gathering of actors, actresses, directors, producers, Jack Windheim, and the major players of the production design team.

The party was loud, brightly lit, fun, and was the atypical glamorous Hollywood social get-together for that month. No one ever knew exactly what to expect at one of these parties. It really just depended on which celebrities were there that night to dazzle and entertain everyone.

Bob and Corey stayed only until one o'clock in the morning, for they had to get up and fly to New York at eight o'clock that same morning. They both tried to say their goodbyes to their costars, when Bob caught view of Kim standing with Susan. She was listening to Susan but staring despondently at him. Bob approached Kim while Corey was saying good night to Arthur Kennedy.

As he walked over to Susan and Kim, Bob hugged Susan first and told her, "I can honestly say, Susan, that I thoroughly enjoyed working with you. We really should give this another try sometime in the future."

Susan held him and cheek-kissed him, saying, "Yes. I really love working with you too, Bob. It was an enjoyable time…and how's your jaw where I slugged you?"

Bob flashed a huge smile and laughed as he rubbed his jaw, saying, "Oh, I think I'll survive."

Kim smiled demurely, watching Bob the entire time.

He then turned his attention to Kim. Bob took Kim in his arms, and he could feel her hug him tightly around the neck and shoulders. They both cheek-kissed each other, as the kisses lasted a bit longer than usual. Susan was feeling somewhat uncomfortable and in the way; she slowly walked away, leaving them to whatever was going on.

Bob pulled away while still holding on to Kim's hips and looked directly into her saddened eyes and professed, "I think I'm going to miss you the most, Scarecrow…"

Kim threw her head back and sexily laughed, only to bring it back down with that look she possessed of sexual want and intrigue.

Bob continued with a smile on his face, "I wish you all the best in the years to come. And when you leave this town, I pray you find what you're looking for, Kim…maybe another time, another place. Goodbye, lady."

Kim's eyes moistened as she quickly kissed him on the lips, saying, "Goodbye, Bob."

Corey stood across the room watching this scene play out between Bob and Kim. She felt helpless and knew there was nothing she could do but trust that Bob loved Kim as a concerned friend, and nothing more.

They asked Haddie to come with them to New York, which would give her another chance to spend an afternoon with Ella and meet Sarah for the first time. Haddie jumped at the idea of seeing Ella again, meeting Sarah Vaughan, and then spending eight days in New York City with Bob, Corey, Joshua, Deidra, and Darnell.

Alicia had to stay home with her mother looking after her, because she was too close to her delivery date. Len, Jimmy, and Doug stayed with their families out in Queens and Northern Jersey.

Haddie would return to LA with Corey, the day before Corey had to start her new picture, *Mystery in Her Eyes*, October 11. Haddie and Corey would be in New York just long enough to see the Night

Owls in concert at the Beacon Theatre for their opening performance on Friday, October, 7.

Monday morning Bob, Corey, and Haddie walked into Verve Records recording studio a little ahead of the nine o'clock scheduled session.

All the Owls and Truman already were there, along with Ella Fitzgerald and Sarah Vaughan. Joshua took Haddie's hand and led her over to Ella and Sarah. He introduced his mother to Sarah. "Mama, I'd like you to meet Ms. Sarah Vaughan, and you know Ms. Lady Ella already."

Haddie smiled and put her hand out to Sarah, as her eyes were registering a profound reverence toward her. "I know I've died and gone to heaven now, 'cause here I am standing with Ms. Lady Ella and Ms. Sarah Vaughan. Oh, Lord, don't nobody wake me up now!"

Sarah brightly smiled and chuckled and took Haddie's hand, saying, "How do you do, Haddie. It's a pleasure meeting you, and don't worry, I'm not going to wake you up."

After Ella hugged Haddie and told her how glad she was to see her again, Haddie walked into the soundproof booth like she was walking on air.

A minute later, Doris Day and Debbie Reynolds walked in. Everyone was taken off guard, including Ella and Sarah. Bob, who wasn't sure if they would show up or not, happily walked up to them and exclaimed, "Both of you did make it here today. That's great!"

Bob then introduced Doris and Debbie to Ella and Sarah. Ella emphatically stated, "Oh, Bob, you didn't have to introduce these two talented women to us. I believe we'd know them anywhere."

The four women shook hands, when Doris spoke up, saying, "Well, thank you, Ella, but I'm sorry, we didn't mean to intrude on your recording session with the guys. But when Bob told us you two ladies were going to be recording on their Christmas album this morning, Debbie and I just had to come to hear in person these two great voices once again."

Ella responded graciously, "Thank you, but you're not intruding at all. Just take a seat in the booth, along with Haddie, Deidra, Corey, and Truman."

After all the introductions were out of the way, the Owls got down to business.

The next two and a half hours were spent on rehearsing and changing up a few vocal placements in the three songs. By noon, Bob and Ella were recording "O Holy Night." When the two of them hit the highest crescendo note together in the last stanza, it was bone-chilling and a note dripping with reverent emotionalism.

Haddie, Deidra, Corey, Truman, Doris, and Debbie seemed swept away by the beautiful tone and the melodious, dulcet of their voices blending together so beautifully.

When Bob and Ella ended softly and smoothly and hung on to the last note so tenderly, there were a couple of glistening eyes that were sitting up in the booth and behind the technician recording this song.

Ella then recorded "Have Yourself a Merry Little Christmas" with Joshua and Darnell. The two guys had looks on their faces like this whole happening was surreal, and they couldn't actually be singing with the greatest female jazz singer in the world, yet they were.

When Bob, Len, Darnell, and Jimmy sang the final song on their Christmas album, "Silent Night," with Sarah, her voice was soft and mellow, the harmonies were flawless and warm, and everyone was pitch-perfect.

The moment became just so spiritual, as all five of them sang with such beautiful harmony and synchronicity. No one, not even little Jimmy, was flat or off-key.

All three songs that were recorded this day would be the most popular ones on the entire Night Owls Christmas album.

At close to two o'clock that afternoon, all fourteen people decided to go out to lunch and celebrate the conclusion of the Owls' album. Sarah suggested the Loft Steakhouse down on Fortieth Street. It was a chic five-star restaurant that served anything from steak to sushi. Everyone agreed to go, and Bob and Corey picked up the tab, even though there were some who mildly objected.

The next morning, the rehearsals started for *Oklahoma!* at the St. James Theatre on West Forty-Fourth Street, which was just a four-minute walk from Times Square. The St. James Theatre contained three tiers of seating, with over three thousand seats. It was one of the biggest theaters in New York. The proprietors of the theater were able to give Stanley the seven weeks he wanted for his limited engagement, from November 1 through December 20. After that, on December 26, the popular play *Do Re Mi* was coming in to play the St. James.

Stanley Kabrinski, Bob's director in *A Casual Affair*, notified everyone involved with the play that he wanted them at the theater at eight o'clock that morning.

Arriving early was the production staff, backup dancers, wardrobe, and musicians, not to mention Stanley, who was again directing and producing this second revival of *Oklahoma!* The first revival was back in 1951.

Angela Lansbury walked in by herself to a warm and welcoming applause. A thirty-five-year-old Lee Landon, one of the supporting actors, came in after her to the same applause. Arthur Stuart, the other supporting actor, was already there and seated.

Then the door to the theater opened, and Doris, Debbie, and Bob walked in together, after they coincidentally met out in the parking area in the back.

There was a rousing applause for the three main players. They all smiled bowing their heads in appreciation and kept walking toward some empty seats by Angela. Everyone introduced themselves to people they didn't know and smiled and hugged those they already knew.

Angela shook Doris's hand and asked her, "Doris, I'm glad to meet you. You've made some very good pictures. Aren't you coming off of *Midnight Lace* with Rex Harrison?"

Doris, proud and smiling, answered, "Well, thank you, Angela. And yes, I just finished that picture a few weeks ago. Rex was just so charming to work with."

At that moment, Stanley's voice came roaring out at everyone, "All right, people. Let me have your attention. I want to welcome everyone here to the St. James Theatre, and four weeks of some pretty tough rehearsals. As all of you should know, this revival of *Oklahoma!* is only going to be a limited engagement running for seven weeks after its initial opening on November 1. We will then move the entire production to the Adelphi Theatre in London, England, on December 28, and it will run for two weeks, through January 10, 1961. The Adelphi is a London West End theater that's located on the Strand in the city of Westminster. It seats 1,500 and specializes in comedy and musical theater and has had many musicals held there through the years. The English know their musicals, and we're going to give them a revival that will surpass even the original debut this play had in 1943."

Stanley perused the room and took inventory of everyone there, then added, "Starting right now, I want all my cast of characters up on the stage in a few minutes. Wardrobe will have their turn with everyone that will be performing, and background dancers will get with our choreographer. Musicians will get with our musical director. I will have one run-through with everyone who has any spoken dialogue in the manuscript...that will be today. All right, let's make this worth the money all those seats will be paying to see this play. Let's go!"

Stanley propelled everyone into concerted action, and for the remainder of the day, there was unceasing activity throughout the theater.

While Bob was at rehearsal, Corey, Haddie, and Deidra went sightseeing and shopping around Manhattan. They hit Saks, Macy's, Bloomingdale's, Nordstrom, Chanel, and many of the boutiques along Fifth Avenue. Everything that was purchased, the ladies had the stores ship at a future date when they would be home.

Joshua and Darnell spent the day at Madison Square Garden III, watching a basketball game between the New York Knicks and the Philadelphia Warriors.

All five of them were back at the penthouse before Bob was finished with his rehearsal.

When Bob returned to the penthouse, he opened the door and found all five of them leisurely having a drink. He jokingly asked, "Why wasn't I invited to the party?"

Darnel kiddingly answered, "You gotta get here earlier than six o'clock, man, or you miss happy hour."

Corey moved quickly from her seat, and setting her martini down on a table, she hurried to Bob and threw her arms around his neck. They remained by the door and warmly kissed for several seconds.

Bob drew his face away from Corey and looked at her excitedly and stated, "Now that's what I've been waiting for all day." They lightly kissed again.

When he began to move into the living room, Corey raced to get him a beer and then returned to sit down beside him on the sofa, handing him the beer.

"Thanks, baby." Bob took a quick sip of his beer and then focused on Joshua and Darnell, and as they were chuckling a little, he asked, "I bet you two can't wait for Friday night when we open at the Beacon?"

Darnell quickly responded, "I just hope Alicia waits till I get home to have our little one. That is, after our two weeks at the Beacon and that makeup concert the next day down in Charlotte."

Haddie spoke up and humorously commented, "I don't think that's up to Alicia, Darnell. You gonna have to have a talk with that little one inside her belly."

Everyone started laughing, as Darnell smiled and nodded affirmatively to Haddie.

On Friday evening, everyone was getting dressed and ready to head over to the Beacon Theatre for the Night Owls' opening night concert.

Bob arrived back at the penthouse after his rehearsal with less than an hour to get showered and dressed. Corey had some casual dress clothes laid out for him, but she and the ladies wore beautiful evening dresses that had shoulder wraps the color of their own dress.

As the audience was filing into their seats at the Beacon, the Owls were behind the curtain running a sound check on their instruments. Truman and Nick were both there and backstage helping out as best they could. Nick would start the recording tape as soon as the Owls took the stage.

Corey, Haddie, and Deidra sat in third row, center orchestra, as was expected.

At almost eight o'clock, the stage manager walked out, as many in the audience cheered along with some energized screams. They were excited in knowing the concert was ready to start and the Night Owls were only a minute away.

The stage manager started to talk over the din in the theater. "Tonight we have a rare treat for you. This band has the credentials of a band that's been around for years. In less than two and a half years, these guys have thirty-two singles and four albums out, with a Christmas album being released next month."

The audience screamed their approval, and the applause was loud and boisterous.

"They've toured Australia and Europe and just finished their 21-City Tour right here in the States just six weeks ago." More whistles and applause. "Their music has always had a purpose and a powerful message to all people—that hate and discrimination will not be tolerated anymore. They've overcome crowds of hate-mongers, evil and vicious language, and violent actions, but they have survived and have gone on to become one of the most entertaining, purpose-driven bands in the world. They have developed a personal bond between them that will never be broken."

The audience now cheered very loudly and riotously, as Corey sat in her seat with a single tear slowly running down her cheek. Her eyes, still welled up with tears, showed her incredible pride she had for all the guys.

The stage manager yelled, "Now here's one of the best! The Night Owls!"

The curtain opened, and Jimmy quickly gave the four-count. The guys ripped into "Raging Fire," with the guitars loudly stroking the chords. In between each of Bob's and Len's vocals, Joshua let loose a thunderous rage on his C trumpet, and Doug's saxophone was just screaming the notes as the clarion was explicitly brilliant.

After the Owls played "Courage for the Fight" and "Stronger Than You Think," Bob stepped up to the microphone and waited for the screaming to stop. He began talking, and the noise really lessened. "Tonight we're going to play two of our newest songs… As a matter of fact, we just released them yesterday."

There were a few screams, and he finished, "This song is called 'Every Bit of You Is Part of Me.' After this, we'll get back to some badass stuff, all right?"

Bob looked out at Corey, smiled brilliantly, and then sexily winked at her. She gave him a toothy grin and slowly winked back at him. He watched her and then turned to nod at Jimmy.

Jimmy began slow and romantically with his loose-haired sticks on the snare. The guitars were warm and mellow, as Doug rolled in the seductive and sexy sound of his saxophone's smoky notes. Joshua was whispering very soft notes with his muted bass trumpet.

Bob's perfectly pitched baritone took its vocal entrance, while Len and Darnell sang backup for him:

Every day I live for your love
I can't give you up, for I don't want to be free
Our love has survived the test of time
Because I find every bit of you is part of me

When our hearts blended into one
You opened my eyes so I could see
You showed me how true love would feel
And how natural and close it could be

Stay with me, baby, and take me in your arms
For to my heart and soul, you hold the only key
I could never leave you, you're my everything
God even knows, every bit of you is part of me

A lifetime with you will never be enough
I want you now and into eternity
You give me life and my every breath
For you have proven that every bit of you is
part…of…me

As the last note faded and Doug's sax ended the song with a warm, rounded sound, the audience roared with an unabated applause, accompanied by cheers and whistles.

All the guys waved to their fans and were smiling broadly. Bob looked down at Corey again and mouthed the words "I love you, baby."

She instantly teared up and blew him a kiss, as she mouthed the words "I love you so much, darling."

Bob turned to Jimmy and gave him the nod. The Owls played fourteen more songs, and it was almost eleven o'clock; when everyone thought the concert was coming to an end, Bob stepped up to the microphone.

"We want to thank all of you for coming tonight, and with our complete gratitude, we'd like to sing one more song for you."

The audience cheered loudly, and there was a resounding applause.

When the theater quieted down, Bob solemnly added, "This is our second newest release, called 'What More Can I Lose?' This song addresses slavery and bondage from the viewpoint of a man who had experienced it at one time. I hope it strikes a chord with everyone here tonight and around the world...thank you."

Bob just had to look at Jimmy as he began playing quarter-note grooves as slow as possible on the snare, accompanied by the bass drum. The guitars were articulating the dark and muddy chords to a heartbreaking song of man's inhumanity to man.

Joshua played the bass trumpet as it dolefully cried out the pain of human depravity and the maleficent wickedness of morally corrupt individuals.

Doug ran an unobtrusive, low-key riff in the background, as Bob sang lead to Len's and Darnell's unpretentious backup:

> The time has come to burn the evil to the ground
> It's been a long time coming and they're not goin'
>   to like the sound
> Let's chain their hands and take away everything
>   they love

Then let's celebrate their misery and later ask for
redemption from above
I'll never know how it feels to be whole, 'cause
I've been gettin' by on my tears
When the day comes when I sleep deep again, I'll
know that death is near
You've taken my family, my love, and my life,
what more can I lose
For at your hands came darkness and death, and
great amounts of wicked abuse

I've come back from the grave to make sure you
are exacted a price
I can get my revenge, and I'll be happy knowing
that I can't die twice
So now I'll dance on your grave and mourn for
my lost love again
But you haven't learned yet, that what you do
must come to an end

Centuries have passed and many have died,
because you have no soul
Let me pray for you to stop your evil ways, for
your kind has taken a great toll
If I see you again, there will be blood spilled, I
fear
For I am no longer bound to the chain, just all
the lost lives and the years

As the song came to its mournful ending, there were many wet eyes in the audience; and Corey, Haddie, and Deidra were three of the many.

The applause was earsplitting, and the cheers and screaming were thunderous and roared with their fans approval. The guys all gathered down in front of the stage and were waving, blowing kisses, and shaking hands with a lot of the young women and men who stormed the front of the stage.

Corey could see the total fatigue that showed on Bob's face as he looked down at her. She could also see the unmitigated pride and love he had for his band of brothers.

The group of six got back to the penthouse close to midnight. They went directly to their own rooms and showered and got ready for bed.

Bob got into bed wearing only his pajama bottoms and watched Corey as she walked very provocatively across the bedroom floor. Her hair fell down around her shoulders in a way he would never forget.

She climbed into bed, and he instantly pulled her over on top of him. Her breasts were hot beneath her sheer, snow-white negligee; her auburn hair was everywhere in his eyes and against his heart, and her naked legs were smooth and beautiful to his touch. Their kisses were long and lingering and drunkenly sweet.

Bob ran his hands all over her body, and in the most intensely heated moment, he entered her.

After several minutes, his totally exhausted body surrendered to her, and he came; all strength, all energy, and all dreams went out of him.

Corey held him tight to her body as she started to climax. She threw her head into his neck and fervently began kissing his neck and the side of his face.

Minutes later before she rolled off him, while breathing heavily and with an impassioned resonance to her voice, she expressed, "Oh, darling, I love you passionately and undyingly, my beautiful man."

Bob kissed her once more, and he solemnly swore to her, "Always and forever, baby."

They kissed again, and as soon as Corey rolled off him, leaving one arm wrapped around his waist, he was asleep and breathing hard.

She propped herself up on one elbow and stared at him with such love in her eyes. Lovingly, she whispered to him, "Go on and sleep, baby. Men want to sleep when it's over. Women want to talk… at least sometimes."

Bob didn't have rehearsals for the play on Sundays, so he asked Corey to book a later flight back to LA for her, Haddie, and Deidra. He didn't have to be at the Beacon until seven o'clock that night for the Night Owls' third performance, so everyone sat around that afternoon talking, drinking, laughing, and eating ordered-in food.

Nick sent a limousine at six o'clock that evening for all of them. The ladies would be taken to LaGuardia Airport, where the guys would send them off, and then the three guys would be shuttled to the theater to perform.

Bob and Corey sat in the farthest seats in the back of the limo. Bob had his arm around her and kissed her on the side of her head, smelling the tropical flavor of her shampoo. While others were talking, he leaned over and concernedly asked, "Are you gonna be all right, doll, for the three weeks you'll be alone at home, until you come back for opening night of the play?"

Corey looked up into his anxious eyes, and smilingly, she assured him, "Oh, darling, thank you for caring so much, but I'll have Haddie around, and the cast of my next movie are total professionals and formidable actors. Gig Young, Jack Carson, and Patricia Neal—I mean, my god! You couldn't ask for a more balanced array of actors."

"All I'm saying is that if anything happens at all, you call me, doll. And we'll talk every night, if we can. Okay?" Bob reassured her.

"I'm counting on it, sweetheart!"

The two solid weeks the Night Owls performed at the Beacon Theatre was a total triumph, and they had standing room only all fourteen days.

Bob and Corey talked every night after he arrived back at the penthouse with Joshua and Darnell. The night of October 21, the Owls' last night at the Beacon, Corey apprehensively asked him, "Tomorrow night when you guys fly down to Charlotte for that makeup concert, I pray that all of you stay safe and watch out for one another. Could you do that for me, darling?"

Bob answered her with trepidation in his voice, "Baby, we knew going into this that there would be an endless need to watch out for one another. So yes, we're playing there tomorrow night and going in with our eyes wide open. I don't want you worrying about anything. I'll call you before we fly out of Charlotte. Okay?"

Corey, seeming somewhat pacified about the situation, answered, "I'll try not to worry, but I can't promise you anything, darling."

Bob smiled and tentatively chuckled into the receiver of the phone. "You know, doll, I was just sitting here imagining those fine gams of yours wrapped around me—your feet crossed at the small of my back and pointing like clock hands. I can't wait to see you again, baby."

Corey sexily laughed into the phone, and smiling sweetly, she lovingly rejoined, "Oh my god! You're torturing me, Robert Brian! I won't see you for ten days, and now you've made me in extreme want of you… I should fly back there and have my way with you. What do you think about that, sweetheart?"

"I'll take a nap and leave the light on," he whispered temptingly.

Now sexually bothered beyond belief, Corey resignedly told him, "Good night, baby. I'm now going in to take a very long and cool bath."

"Good night, doll."

Nick had the guys flying down to Charlotte, North Carolina, early that Sunday afternoon of October 23. Trying to prepare for every contingency, Nick called ahead to confirm his private security force would be present that night at the concert. He even double-checked with the Bojangles Coliseum the guys would be playing that night and ascertained everything was in order and good to go.

After the guys had some dinner, they headed for the coliseum for a sound check on their instruments. Ahead of the Owls arriving, Truman had taken the instruments for setup, with some help from the crew at the coliseum.

The Bojangles Coliseum in Charlotte, built in 1955, could seat up to fourteen thousand people and was the largest unsupported dome in the world and the first free-spanning dome in the United States. It was huge, a modern technological wonder, and the guys would be playing there with that night in Birmingham recurring at every pivotal moment.

It was closing in on their eight o'clock concert start, and the crowd was filing in and filling the thousands of seats. From behind the curtain of the temporary stage, located at one end of the coliseum, the cacophony wafted into the air from the instruments being tuned simultaneously. There was an illusion of order and coherence that seemed discernible.

As the emcee announced the group, the Owls stood behind the curtain with some apprehension, but they had resolve to get their message out there to their audiences anyway.

When they heard, "Now let's welcome the Night Owls!" the curtain flew open, and Jimmy immediately ripped into his opening run on his drums with the song "Conviction."

At this point, the band was sadly aware that the audience was still being segregated; blacks on one side of the main floor seating and whites on the other. Blacks in the upper-tiered seats and whites in the lower tier.

After the rest of the Owls brought their beautifully tuned and balanced instruments to the proper pitch, everyone was playing loud, full notes; and Bob, Len, and Darnell were singing the lyrics very strong and aggressively.

As the song progressed, the beat got faster, and the Owls were delighted to see blacks and whites dancing in the aisles to their songs all over the coliseum—until dozens of white police officers came charging down the aisles, waving their arms to the guys, stopping their music. They then commenced to stretch ropes down the middle of the aisles, separating the whites from the blacks.

Bob turned to his band of brothers, his eyes both fierce and infuriated. Sweat stood out on his forehead in large perfect drops. He tried to restrain himself from doing anything rash.

In the era of Little Richard, Elvis, the Night Owls, and Chuck Berry, a curious thing started to happen: rock 'n' roll shows became so boisterously biracial that it was sometimes impossible for officials to fully segregate the people. The Owls had heard that some people could recall the cops simply throwing up their hands in resignation in trying to keep them separated.

When the cops left the coliseum, the Owls again pounded out their signature songs of rebellion and anti-discrimination, and the kids got up and danced together not caring who was dancing next to them. The Owls watched this and joyously let it happen.

Young whites and blacks found ways to breach the separation. As the Owls kept playing their music, the kids just kept getting up and dancing down the aisles and up around the stage area; they were closely packed together.

The police returned to check on things, and when they saw the kids mixed and all over the place creating a tumultuous scene of noisily exuberant rock 'n' rollers, they just shook their heads in disgust and left the coliseum, after they rolled their eyes in a mocking gesture.

The more brave and courageous musicians, whether they were white or black, or mixed, like the Night Owls, contributed to concert desegregation, which continued in some places even after it would be outlawed by the Civil Rights Act in 1964.

At almost eleven o'clock that night, the Owls quitted the stage to a resounding din of applause, screaming, cheers, and whistles. They had blown kisses and waved their arms to their fans, after they had shaken many hands down in front of the stage.

Truman would transport the instruments to the airport and take them on to Atlantic City, New Jersey, where the Owls would be playing their last makeup concert the following Sunday.

When Darnell called Alicia to tell her the Owls concert in Charlotte went very well, Alicia's mother told him to get home; Alicia was in labor.

Nick and Bob got him and Joshua out on the next flight to LA. Darnell and Joshua planned on flying back the following Sunday into Atlantic City.

Bob then went to the nearest phone in the airport and called home to Corey.

It was almost nine o'clock in Bel Air when Corey picked up the phone after the first ring, knowing it would be her life's love. She murmured, "Hello, sweetheart."

When he heard her voice, it just sent chills down his body. He smiled and lovingly asked, "How you doin', baby?"

Corey questioningly asked, "The better question would be, How did your concert go, darling? Did you guys have any problems at all?"

He proudly boasted, "At first the police roped the aisles down the middle trying to keep the black and white kids apart when they got up to dance. When the police came back to check the crowd, they gave up and left again, seeing even more kids mixing with each other... Corey, it was just a beautiful thing to see. I wish you would have been there, baby."

Excited for him, she exclaimed with delight, "That's wonderful, darling! I'm so proud of all you guys...it really does seem that times are changing. A bit slow for most people, especially the blacks, but changing nonetheless."

Having just remembered, Bob was anxious to tell her, "Yeah, and another exciting thing is about to happen. Darnell called Alicia earlier after we finished here, and Alicia's mother told him to come right home. She was in labor—not Alicia's mother, but Alicia!"

Corey laughed heartily, and still chuckling, she answered, "Oh my god! That's fantastic! I'll have Haddie keep me abreast of the situation, because right now I wouldn't want to bother them."

Bob affirmed, "Yeah, you may be right... Have you begun shooting yet, or are you still rehearsing? Everything going smoothly on set?"

Corey, very relaxed and reassured, tried to allay any fear he had. "Everything and everyone is just great, and we started to shoot last week. Our director, Anthony Towner, told us we could possibly bring this one in a few days early. That way I could fly into New York and maybe be with you for the closing night of your play."

Bob was excited about that; he exclaimed, "Oh, baby! I would really love that."

He could hear her gently chuckle as she stated, "I would love that too, darling."

He laughed sexily and then sadly told her, "Well, you foxy chick, I have rehearsal early tomorrow and for the next six days, so

I'm gonna call it a night, doll. I'll talk with you every night, until next Sunday, when we go to Atlantic City to make up that last concert. All right?"

"I look forward to that, sweetheart. Now get some rest. You're going to need it before I get there on the first of November for your opening night… Good night. my darling man. I love you so much."

Bob brilliantly smiled and exhaled heavily into the receiver of the phone, telling her, "I'm just gonna have to survive until then… Good night, baby. I love you to the moon and back, Alice."

He could hear her exhale and sigh heavily as she softly hung up the receiver.

Bob flew back to New York arriving at the penthouse at three in the morning. After taking a quick shower, he went straight to bed until the alarm clock jolted him awake at seven.

Darnell called Bob that evening and informed him, "Hey, man! I'm the father of an eight-pound, two-ounce baby girl! What do you think of that? I got me a beautiful daughter!"

Bob excitedly told him, "That's outta sight, man! She could only be beautiful, with a mother like Alicia, because I know she'd better not look like you!"

"Oh, hell no. She's the picture of Alicia, thank you, Lord!"

Bob interjected, "Well, do you two have a name for her?"

Darnell sweetly let her name roll off his lips. "Lisa Shantell."

Bob exhaled loudly into the receiver, "Oh, man. That's as beautiful as her mother."

"Amen, brother."

At rehearsal the next morning, Stanley was calling for a complete run-through of the play, with orchestra in its sequential musical numbers.

After the overture ended, there were eleven numbers sung, danced, or both. There was intermittent dialogue between some of the songs, and they wrapped act 1 in one hour and twenty minutes.

Stanley called for a short break, and all seven men and five female actors, along with orchestra and stage crew, sat amongst one another, talking, drinking water or coffee, and snacking at the catered table of fruits and goodies.

As people were conversing, Bob noticed every time Doris laughed, she had a very infectious smile. He was witness to it when they recorded their Christmas song in LA, and now throughout every rehearsal, he again took special notice. She also had a soft, lilting voice when she not only sang her songs, but when she would speak. He felt she was a highly put-together blonde; she was not only talented and beautiful, but was intelligent and kind. The type of woman he may have pursued, if it wasn't for the fact she was married and had a child and he wasn't insanely in love with Corey.

Stanley started dress rehearsals that Friday, Saturday, and Monday, the eve of opening night. He was quite pleased with the end product of his musical production.

That next Sunday in Atlantic City, all the guys met at the Jim Whelan Boardwalk Hall, which was located right on Atlantic City's Boardwalk. It was the primary convention center that hosted sporting events and musical acts and seated 10,500 fans.

Everyone congratulated Darnell on having his baby girl, Lisa Shantell. Of course, he had pictures in his wallet he would probably be carrying for the rest of his life.

The concert was uneventful and a lot of fun for the guys, as well as their faithful fans. They sang as many of their songs as they could, and most especially the indelible two or three they had that really spoke loudly of rebellion and discrimination.

The guys knew they probably wouldn't be performing for a while since Bob's opening night was coming up. Then on to London he would go with the *Oklahoma!* production, so they played for three hours to their clamoring audience. They didn't quit the stage until eleven o'clock that night.

Every one of the guys flew back to LA after the end of their last concert, except Bob. When they left, Len explained to him, "I'd stay for your opening night, man, but Valerie is due to have her baby sometime this week. And I really want to be there. Catch you later and good luck, Bob. We'll see you in January when you get back, man."

"Hey, I totally understand, Len. Now get outta here and let me know when Valerie and you get the new ankle biter," Bob wistfully stated with a small degree of infused jealousy.

"Absolutely, man." Len started to walk away and then looked back at Bob, not knowing if he envied or felt sorry for him. What he did know was that Bob was his favorite brother, and whatever decisions he ever made about the band or having children, he would respect them.

Tuesday, November 1, Corey told Bob she would be flying into New York but wasn't sure of the time. Although she did know it would be quite early, she wanted to surprise him and spend most of the day with him, before they had to leave for his opening night in the play.

It was six o'clock that morning when Corey turned the key to open the door of the penthouse. After walking in, she didn't hear any noise at all. No radio, no running shower, no bustling about…nothing. She set her purse and suitcase down in a chair. Being so early, she quietly headed for the master suite, figuring he must still be sleeping.

When she slowly pushed the door open into the room, her face lit up with loving excitement. She stood staring at Bob's half-naked body as he lay prone stretching from one corner of the bed to the other, being only covered by the one top sheet. The quilt lay crumpled on the floor.

She slipped her shoes off and quietly walked toward the bed. Her heart began to race as she drank in his bare and highly developed back muscles. She could see the top of his pajama bottoms protruding from the sheet as she stood next to the bed.

Corey first slipped her coat off, then everything else, besides her panties and bra. Being as quiet and agile as she could be, she slowly crawled onto the bed and moved up close to him. As he still slept, she lightly started to kiss him on his shoulders and back. He slightly moved and then felt the touch of someone's lips on his body. Bob was now wide awake and quickly turned his head to see who was awakening him with their morning kisses.

He was praying it was Corey and felt very sure those were her lips and her kisses. After a couple of blinks, he focused his eyes and became ecstatically overwhelmed with joy when he was looking into the very familiar, warm, and loving eyes of his greatest love.

Bob exhaled with complete sexual arousal written across his face. He took Corey in his arms and kissed her long and hard. She was moaning with delight, and in between kisses, she breathlessly whispered, "Oh, darling. Just love me. Just hold me and love me."

He looked deep into her eyes and earnestly promised, "I will always love you, Corey, and I will never let go of you, baby."

Bob got on his knees, after he reached around and unhooked her bra, and then picked her up into his arms, and gently, he lay her down and kissed her lips, and then he bent and kissed her breasts. After he slowly removed her panties, he lay between her welcoming legs, and they made love for the next two hours, before either one had even thought about wanting breakfast.

After they showered together, Corey ordered in some breakfast and a pot of coffee. They sat beside each other on the long sofa, just talking, kissing, laughing, but always kissing.

Bob casually suggested, "What do you think about us taking a walk and then catching a late lunch somewhere? I want to take my foxy chick out and strut her around town."

Corey's radiant and affectionate facial expression showed her love for him as she tenderly answered, "As long as we're together, darling, I would follow you to Mars. Just know that I have to leave tomorrow at three o'clock. Anthony said he could shoot around me today and tomorrow, but I'd really have to dig my heels in when I get back Wednesday."

"Mars, huh? I'll have to work on that for our first wedding anniversary." He smiled whimsically. Corey chuckled with such happiness. Bob surprisingly wrapped his arms around her, and they fell back onto the sofa in a deep kiss.

At six thirty, Bob and Corey were picked up by Nick and his limousine. After they were seated inside with Nick, he informed them, "I thought since I was coming to your opening night, Bob, why not pick the two of you up, because Corey and I will be sitting together in third row, center orchestra?"

Corey gratefully spoke up, "Yes, Nick. I can't tell you enough times how well you handle the business of Bob and the Owls band. You're very good at what you do. Thank you."

"Right back atcha, Corey," Nick replied as Bob proudly smiled at both of them.

When the overture started to play, Corey and Nick were firmly in their seats, and Bob was dressed in his cowboy outfit of blue jeans, solid light-blue, long-sleeved shirt, a black Texas ten-gallon hat, and light-brown rattlesnake-skin cowboy boots. He was standing downstage in his spot waiting for the curtain to go up.

The overture started to wane, the lights lowered almost to a pitch-black, and the curtain started to slowly rise. Bob, playing Curley McLain, one of two men courting Laurey Williams, took his cue from the orchestra as he came strutting out of the set's ranch house. When he ended up close to the front of the stage, he began to sing his only solo, "Oh, What a Beautiful Morning."

He was showcasing his beautiful perfectly-pitched baritone voice to the over three thousand playgoers. He even had a thirty-second dance routine, where he was soft-shoeing in his snakeskin cowboy boots.

After his solo ended and the audience loudly applauded him, Debbie Reynolds, playing Laurey Williams, entered stage left, and dialogue between the two lasted for over a minute.

Seconds later, Angela Lansbury, playing Aunt Eller, entered the stage riding in a surrey with a real horse, driven by a man in the production company. The three of them began to sing, with a little prompting from the orchestra, "The Surrey with the Fringe on Top."

Corey was delighted in watching Bob, Debbie, and Angela having a lot of fun with the song and seeming to work so effortlessly together. It was obvious to her Bob was in his element and loving every moment.

The audience again gave their unmitigated applause when the number ended. After the three rode the surrey offstage, it was Doris Day's moment to sing her solo.

She was playing the flirtatious Ado Annie and singing "I Can't Say No." Her part was in the secondary romance with Will Parker, played by Lee Landon, a thirty-five-year-old who was known for his supporting roles in Broadway and off-Broadway plays.

Doris's voice was rich and clear. She didn't use a falsetto or try to scat like Ella. There was a freshness and vitality to her sound. In her career, she had traversed genres of music like jazz, easy listening, Hollywood musicals, and even the bossa nova.

Tonight her backup included a strong brass section, a gentle piano, and a few of the company's women dancers, who slowly moved to a representational style of balletic dance in the back of the stage.

Doris and the accompanying dancers were dressed in bright Western wear: skirts with a cowhide fringe around them, long-sleeved blouses, cowboy hats set to the back of their heads, and the ever-present cowgirl boots.

As Doris hung on to the last note of the song, the audience loudly applauded her.

Midway between the first act, Bob and Debbie sang "People Will Say We're in Love"; Corey thought only of the night she and Bob had danced to this song, and he softly sang the lyrics into her ear. This was before they got together as a couple, but she would never forget that moment and that dance.

The first act finished with a fifteen-minute "Dream Ballet," with Debbie singing "Out of My Dreams," accompanied by an ensemble of Dream Figures.

The audience loudly applauded Debbie's performance, as the curtain slowly lowered and came down to obscure the players onstage. The audience kept applauding even after the curtain had come down.

The orchestra's entr'acte (a musical intermission and an overture for act 2) played for fifteen minutes. Then the lights went down, and the curtain opened to a huge production number, "The Farmer and the Cowman." There were nine of the twelve characters, plus an ensemble of all the subsidiary dancers onstage. The characters sang and danced while the ensemble danced around and in back of them.

Bob had danced with Debbie, Doris, and Angela before the spectacle ended with a loud, rousing finish. The audience loved this boisterous display of raw talent and interaction between the players.

This part of the play showcased the phenomenal abilities of the four main actors and highlighted the great choreographic sophistication of the Western dance numbers.

Corey applauded loudly after the finish to the musical number and proudly shook her head to the astounding amount of talent Bob possessed in all aspects of music and dance.

Bob and Debbie then had a reprisal of "People Will Say We're in Love," where Bob had to dance without running out of breath and hit his stage mark, the musical notes, and his key light all at the same time. At one part of the number, Bob slid into a backstep, extended his arm, and spun Debbie around. On the first beat of the next bar, he caught her in his arms and reversed direction, spinning them both toward the bench they sat on. Debbie's body was as quick and gracile as a deer's, and Bob thoroughly enjoyed dancing with her.

His and Debbie's characters were in love at this point, and they sang and danced the number creatively, romantically, and flawlessly.

There was a thunderous applause as they ended the number with a lingering kiss.

Moments later, seven of the actors with the same ensemble of dancers performed the title song "Oklahoma." It was another great stage spectacle. The colors in the wardrobe, the backdrops, and the scenery were eye-popping. And the singing and dancing were intrinsically captivating. The troupe was having a ball with this last number, and the audience felt it.

As the song ended, the orchestra started to play the *finale ultimo* (the big finish), "Oh What a Beautiful Morning" and then "People Will Say We're in Love."

The entire company of actors and dancers filed out onto the stage. Everyone was singing to the abbreviated versions of both songs. They stood in one long line with their arms interlocking with the person next to them. Bob was center stage with Debbie locked in his one arm and Doris in the other.

When the final note dissipated into the air, everyone in the company raised their arms with their hands locked to the person beside them. It was at that point the audience stood and broke into a thunderous applause, with shouts and whistles directed at the entire company. The whole line of actors and dancers bowed to the audience simultaneously.

Everyone was smiling brilliantly, as Debbie stepped up and leaned into what seemed a ceremonious kiss with Bob. Then Bob turned to Doris and kissed her also. He let go of Debbie's hand temporarily and stood in front of Doris to lean over and kiss Angela. He then hugged her and then hugged Doris, as he returned to his place in line.

Bob, still with a broad smile, located Corey in the standing crowd and winked at her sexily. She lovingly smiled at him and then returned her slow, alluring wink to him.

The curtain started to slowly fall. Then moments after it rose up again to an empty stage, the dancers came running out and took their bows to the constantly loud applause, cheering, and whistles.

After the dancers moved to the back of the stage, the six secondary actors ran out to the same greeting. Then Angela quickly walked out to a loud, appreciative applause; and as she moved back, Doris jogged out to an even louder applause. She waved and blew kisses and slowly moved back beside Angela.

At that exact moment, Bob and Debbie came out hand in hand, and the theater went nuts. The thunderous applause, which had started with Angela and Doris, had not abated since they came out onstage, but now it was deafening.

Bob and Debbie were overwhelmed with the appreciation and love they were feeling from the audience. Bouquets and large vases of flowers were brought up onstage, as both Bob's and Debbie's smiles never ceased. They hugged and kissed each other once more, as they waved and blew kisses to the crowd.

The final curtain came down, the orchestra's music was no longer wafting through the theater, and Nick and Corey started to make their way back to Bob's dressing room.

When Corey found an opening into Bob's dressing room, she ran to him with opened arms. He spotted her immediately, and an enormous smile consumed his face. He wrapped his arms around her as she proclaimed, "Oh, Bob, you were just fabulous, darling!"

"Thank you, baby. I'm just so damned glad you're here." Their kiss was long and lingering.

After they separated, Nick shook hands with Bob, and they gave each other a shoulder bump. Nick informed him, "You were pretty damned good out there tonight, man. Sorry I can't go to the reviews party with the two of you. I have to get back to LA—on business, of course. But I'll see you when I come back into New York, okay?"

"Thanks, Nick. I'm sorry you have to get back to LA. I'll catch you later, man."

Bob and Corey did go to the reviews party, but not for very long. Bob wanted to spend as much time as he could with Corey, before she left at three the next afternoon.

However, the play did open to wonderful reviews and box office receipts—the best kind of news an actor could get. Stanley was quite proud with the laudable reviews from the critics for his four main actors. All four were very bankable stars.

Bob and Corey returned to the penthouse around twelve thirty that night.

Bob was lying in bed on his back, shirtless after his quick shower, when Corey got into bed and cuddled close to him, putting her arm around his waist and her head on his chest.

Bob had one arm around her back and deeply sighed, telling her, "I don't want you to leave tomorrow, baby. Just stay here with me in bed every day. We can order in anything we need. Food, beer, dry martinis, stirred, and, of course, new sheets. What do you think about that, doll?"

Corey chuckled and laughingly told him, "That sounds wonderful, darling. But I'd never get my picture shot, and then they'd sue me for breach of contract."

Bob rolled over to come face-to-face with her and then intriguingly warned her, "They'd have to find you first."

She laughed loudly as he slowly lowered his head down to kiss her passionately on the lips. Corey responded by wrapping her arms around his neck and pulling his body on top of her. They didn't get to sleep until after two o'clock in the morning.

After a leisurely morning spent talking, eating, taking a short walk over to Bow Bridge in Central Park, and then returning to make love one more time, Corey had to fly back to LA to finish her picture.

Bob rode with her to the airport and stayed long enough to watch Corey's plane disappear into the clouds, taking away from him the only woman he would ever love so deeply and intimately.

They called each other every night after she returned home, and that Friday, November 4, Corey called him at eleven o'clock that night, feeling sure he'd be home after his performance.

With great excitement in her voice, she happily told Bob, "I have some very good news for you, sweetheart. Len and Valerie are the proud parents of a seven-pound, one-ounce baby girl!"

Bob was thrilled with this news and answered, "That's fantastic, doll. When did the baby arrive?"

"Earlier today. Len called me and asked me to tell you."

Excited, he asked Corey, "Did they have a name ready for her?"

Proudly, Corey told him, "Oh, yes. They've named her Isabella Margaret Perry. Isn't that middle name of *Margaret* after your mother?"

His eyes instantly moistened; he choked back a tear, and clearing his throat, he whispered, "Yes, it is. Yeah, that was my mother's name, all right, and I think *Isabella* is Val's mother's name. I'll have to call and thank them."

Corey complimentarily said, "It is a strong yet beautiful name for a little girl."

"Yeah, now I'm just waiting for Elizabeth's baby to come later this month. I sure hope it's a boy. We're getting outnumbered pretty fast by all you females." Bob chuckled.

Corey laughed out loud, saying, "That's the plan, darling."

They talked a while longer, and then they said their good nights.

TWENTY-FIVE

The play's seven-week run at the St. James Theatre had been completely sold out since the ticket release in early September. With every packed house, there seemed to be no complaints or disappointments from the theatergoers.

Bob was getting along about as smoothly as could be expected, being alone and just talking with Corey, Elizabeth, or one of the guys on the phone each day. But things started to change when he talked with Elizabeth a week after Corey had left to go back to LA.

He asked her that night on the phone, "Are you getting excited about the baby's arrival? And how are you feeling these days? Probably very tired, I would imagine."

Breathily Elizabeth answered, "You know, Bobby, I'm not so tired as much as I'm nauseous and dizzy all the time. But I'll be seeing my obstetrician tomorrow morning, and maybe I'll have a better idea of what's going on."

"That's a good idea, sis. Just keep me updated on what's crackin'…no pun intended." He chuckled loudly.

Elizabeth chuckled as well, saying, "That's funny, Bobby. I needed that little laugh. So I'll talk with you later this week, when we get things figured out."

"Okay. We'll talk later. Take care of yourself. I love you, sis," he said worriedly.

"I love you, too, Bobby. Goodbye now."

Elizabeth did call Bob back two days later, informing him that she was diagnosed with preeclampsia, which, she explained, was when pregnant women have high blood pressure, protein in their urine, and a swelling in their legs, feet, and hands.

Bob called Corey that same night after he talked with Elizabeth. He asked her if she knew anything about preeclampsia.

Corey told him with no reservation, feeling he should know the seriousness of her condition, "Bob, I don't think Elizabeth and Drake have told you everything there is to know about what's going on. Preeclampsia can lead to eclampsia, which is very serious and can have health risks for her and their baby. If she happens to have any seizures, that would tell them she has eclampsia."

"Seizures? My god!" he loudly stated.

Corey tried to allay some of his fears by saying, "The only cure for preeclampsia is to give birth. Even after delivery, her symptoms could last at least six weeks. But, darling, I just want you to be prepared for anything that could happen."

There was a silence from Bob's end of the phone, which worried Corey tremendously. "Are you all right, baby? I'm so sorry that this is happening, but let's pray Elizabeth is strong and that she and the baby will come out of this successfully."

After he cleared his throat and swallowed and then blinked the onset of tears out of his eyes, Bob heartbreakingly told Corey, "I pray to God they both survive this, Corey. I don't think I could bear it if I lost Elizabeth or her baby."

"I wish I could be there for you, sweetheart. This whole thing is just terrible. I will keep you posted as quickly as I receive any further information about Elizabeth and the baby."

Bob exhaled heavily into the phone and firmly told Corey, "You call me here or at the St. James Theatre, or if you have to, you leave a message with Rodney downstairs. Okay, Corey?"

Without hesitation, she pledged, "I swear to you, darling, I will find you if you need to be advised of any changes. Now you get to bed and get some rest. I know it'll be hard, but you need to stay strong for Elizabeth and Drake... Good night, my love."

"Good night, Corey. I love you."

Corey started to cry, and with a trembling voice, she whispered, "I love you, too, baby."

For the next two days, Corey religiously kept Bob updated about Elizabeth and the baby. Not much had changed until late the Friday night of November 18.

Bob was coming in the building to the penthouse, when Rodney stopped him, saying, "Bob, you have a message from Ms. Madrigal. She told me to tell you this is an emergency and for you to call home immediately."

Bob quickly ran into the elevator and hastily punched the eighteenth floor's button. He paced around the inside of the elevator like a caged animal, and when the door opened, he bolted for the penthouse door. Once inside, he rapidly dialed and phoned home.

It was eight o'clock in Bel Air that night when Corey picked up the telephone after the first ring. She instantly inquired, "Bob? Is that you?"

He promptly answered, "Yes, Corey. What's going on?"

As quickly and to the point as she could be, Corey informed him, "Bob, Elizabeth has suffered a seizure, and the doctor is inducing labor."

Bob cried out, "Oh, God, no!"

Corey had to continue telling him, "You need to come home as soon as you can. Elizabeth has been asking for you… Nick has already booked you on a flight from LaGuardia to LA at midnight tonight. Get yourself to the airport right now. Curtis and I will meet you at the airport. Okay, baby?"

"I'm leaving right now!" And as soon as he hung up the receiver, he called down to Rodney to have a cab waiting for him. Without showering or eating anything, Bob ran from the penthouse; and when the elevator opened its doors to the lobby, he raced into the awaiting cab. He caught his flight with just minutes to spare, and five hours later, his plane touched down in LA.

Corey was anxiously standing outside of her car at arrivals. In the car, Curtis was also nervously awaiting. A few moments later, Bob came running out of the terminal and toward the car.

After spotting Bob running toward her, she opened her arms to him. He quickly hugged and kissed her, and then they both jumped into the car; Curtis hurriedly drove them to Los Angeles County and USC Medical Center in the Boyle Heights neighborhood of LA.

When Bob asked at the desk for Elizabeth's room number, the floor's head nurse heard him and asked, "Are you Elizabeth Bennington's brother?"

Bob was puzzled, but asked anyway, "Yes, I am. Why?"

The nurse came closer to him and Corey and regretfully told him, "Elizabeth has been asking for you. But I must tell you she's suffering from eclampsia, which causes acute pulmonary edema. Hemorrhagic shock has developed, and due to the internal bleeding she has, there's an insufficient oxygen delivery to the cells. If this bleeding doesn't stop, the inadequate oxygen supply will lead to her death. It really is out of our hands now… I'm so sorry."

Bob was stunned to hear this, and he turned and ran to Elizabeth's room, with Corey in tow.

It was now one thirty in the morning when Bob and Corey located Elizabeth's room. Bob walked in first and saw Drake sitting beside Elizabeth's bed holding her hand. He looked very tired and disheveled, and it was quite noticeable he had been crying.

Bob slowly walked over toward the bed, and when Drake spotted him, he stood up. Bob started to cry and then moved toward him. They woefully hugged each other, with Bob painfully telling him, "I'm so, so sorry, Drake. This can't be happening."

Corey stood back crying into her tissue as Drake moved toward her and hugged and thanked her for being there.

Bob sat down in Drake's abandoned chair and took Elizabeth's hand in his. He stared into her colorless face and then leaned over and kissed her on the cheek. While his face was still near hers, she strained to open her eyes. With an exhausted and glazed-over look in her eyes, she smiled briefly and quietly whispered to Bob, "Bobby, you did come… I just want you to know…we're naming our baby boy after you. We want you to be a big part of his life…"

Bob lost it hearing that and began shaking and then sobbing into his hand. Breathlessly, after wiping his eyes and nose, he looked his loving sister in the eyes and heartbreakingly told her, "Elizabeth, I will always help Drake look after him... I love you. But now you have to go to Mom and Dad and tell them they have a grandson."

Drake moved to the other side of the bed, holding Elizabeth's other hand, when he kissed her and then sadly told her, "Goodbye, my darling."

A serene and incandescent light shined in her eyes, and for an instant, everything in the room seemed a spiritually divine and heavenly moment for everyone. And then it was over. Elizabeth slowly exhaled her last breath.

Drake cried outright while holding her limp body close to him.

Bob stood with tears running down his face, but expressionless. He was paralyzed with the dark and mournful truth of his sister's death.

Corey quickly moved to him; with tears racing down her cheeks, she wrapped her arms around his waist while standing in back of him. "I'm so sorry. I'm just so sorry!"

Bob still had the icy stare of disbelief on his face as he felt he had just lost a piece of his heart.

A nurse then came into the room and took Elizabeth's heart monitor off and any intravenous lines she had in her arms. She pronounced her death at 1:47 a.m. She then left after conveying her condolences.

Nick, Deidra, and all the guys stood outside of the door, realizing they had just arrived when Bob's sister, Elizabeth, had died. All eyes became moistened when the nurse gave notice of time of death.

Drake remained with Elizabeth and climbed into the bed with her and just held her, trying to get the warmth back into her body.

After several minutes, Corey tried to coax Bob away from the bed, as she slightly pulled at his waist, but he wouldn't budge. He stayed fixed on staring at her with his wet eyes and his mouth slightly agape.

Corey tried talking to him as she grievously pleaded, "Bob, she's gone. Can I get you to come home with me? There's nothing anyone can do for her now... Come with me, baby."

Bob slowly looked around at Corey, and she could see the pain and emptiness he was feeling at that moment. He turned back and bent over and kissed Elizabeth one last time on the cheek. Standing up again, he moved toward Corey; and unable to contain his feelings, again he wept openly and unguardedly and fell into her awaiting arms.

As Bob was sobbing onto Corey's shoulder, Len walked over to Bob; and weeping himself, he waited for Bob to bring his head up. When Bob saw Len, he heartbreakingly cried to him, "There's no one now to call me *Bobby* anymore!"

Len just grabbed Bob and hugged him tight. Corey was now sobbing and rapidly wiping tears away from her eyes with her tissue.

Len told Bob, as he still held him, "Elizabeth loved you so much, man. I wish I would have had a sister that cool."

Bob pulled away from Len's hug, looked back at Elizabeth's pale and lifeless body once more, and walked over and whispered to Drake, "If there's anything, and I mean anything, you want me to do, don't you ever hesitate to ask..." He patted Drake's shoulder a few times, and after taking Corey's hand, he slowly moved toward the door to the hospital room.

When he got outside the room, everyone took their turn and hugged him. Deidra hugged and kissed him on the cheek as a tear ran down her face. When it was Doug's turn to hug Bob, Doug hugged him tightly and even kissed him on the cheek. Bob's reaction to this made his body shake with uncontrollable sobs as he felt the love from one brother to another.

In watching that, Corey just lowered her head, and at that moment, her flood of tears began to drop from her eyes to the tiled hallway floor and began to form a small puddle.

Starting to walk away from Elizabeth's room, Bob demanded to see her baby in the same-floor nursery. Corey didn't hesitate to take him there.

As they approached the huge glass window showcasing all the newborns, Bob and Corey perused the dozen or so babies that were on display. A nurse standing by one of the hospital cribs noticed

Corey pointing at one of the babies. The nurse came over and slowly rolled the crib down and in front of the window.

On the front of the crib was printed on a blue card that read: *Robert Brian Bennington, eight pounds, two ounces: 11/19/60.*

Upon having read this, Bob put his hand over his mouth and began to shake as he cried heavily, never taking his eyes off the baby.

This just tore at her heart seeing him like this. All Corey could do was put her arm around him and proudly tell him, "He's beautiful, Bob…he is the picture image of Elizabeth. He's absolutely breathtaking, darling."

Bob got a hold of himself, and after several seconds, he slightly smiled; and as his lower lip quivered, he boasted, "He's gonna be a hunk and a chick magnet. That's for sure!"

Corey, sensing his mindset improving somewhat, quipped, "Just like his uncle."

He turned and looked at Corey with his red, swollen eyes, grinned pleasingly, and with a hint of pretense, he crowed, "As fine as wine in the springtime! Totally boss, man!"

Corey chuckled, and Bob feeling a blessed moment had just been given him, he leaned over and kissed Corey. Her heart a little unburdened now, she moaned gently as they kissed.

Bob and Corey didn't get home until three o'clock that unforgettable morning. He just quietly walked into the house and then into the shower.

Haddie came out of the kitchen wearing a robe and, with sleepy eyes, caught Corey's attention as she walked by, asking, "Ms. Corey…?"

Corey simply shook her head and informed her, "No, Haddie. Elizabeth died a little bit before two o'clock this morning. Her baby is fine. And what a gorgeous child he is."

Haddie was tearing up as she looked down the hall to the master suite and concernedly inquired, "And Mr. Bob? Is he gonna be all right, too?"

Now feeling more sure about him, Corey resignedly told her, "It's going to take some time, but he's very strong, and I'm sure he'll come to terms with this eventually… A big part of his life was just torn from him, Haddie. But the flip side of that is a new, fresh part has just been added. He now has a beautiful nephew who's his namesake."

Haddie rejoined joyfully, "Hallelujah! Praise the Lord. If there's anything I can do, Ms. Corey, you just let me know. All right?"

Gratefully, Corey smiled at her and said, "I'll do just that, Haddie. Thank you."

Corey was up and showered by seven o'clock that same morning. She called Jack at the studio and explained the entire situation to him. She told him she would return to work after Bob's sister's funeral and that she also wanted him to handle the PR on all of this and not allow the press to denigrate or take out of context anything pertaining to her death.

Jack assured Corey everything would be handled and to let him know where the funeral was going to be held, because he absolutely wanted to attend, for his surrogate son's sake.

Corey also took it upon herself to call Stanley Kabrinski in New York and apprised him of the situation. She promised him Bob would probably return to the production after the funeral and just as soon as he could, because he was such a professional.

Stanley conveyed his condolences and assured her Bob's understudy could go on that night and Sunday. Then he asked for her to let him know, if Bob could return Tuesday, after dark Monday. Corey thanked him and told him she would keep him abreast of the situation.

Bob got out of bed at nine o'clock. Not able to sleep anymore, he got up and dressed himself, then sat back down on the bed. His mind was trying to convince himself Elizabeth's death was just a dream he had experienced...but then he came to the realization that it was real and had really happened. His eyes moistened, and he forcefully choked back his unshed tears and got on his feet and headed for the kitchen, and hopefully Corey.

He sighed with relief as he heard both Haddie's and Corey's voices wafting down the hallway, enshrouding him in the love and appreciation he felt for each one of them.

Bob entered the kitchen, and Corey, concerned for him, got out of her chair and slowly moved to him. She wrapped her arms around his neck and lay her head on the lower part of his shoulder, not saying a word. He took her in his arms and kissed her on her temple.

He noticed Haddie standing by the stove, looking dolefully saddened, and he walked to her with a wounded look in his eyes and tightly hugged her.

Haddie told him with such sorrow in her voice, "Oh, Mr. Bob. I'm just so sorry for your loss. I know words just can't describe what you're goin' through right now, so you need to lay all your grief at the altar of Jesus Christ and know Elizabeth is being taken good care of now."

This brought tears to Bob's eyes. He graciously responded, "Thank you, Haddie. That was very comforting."

At that moment, the phone rang. Bob turned to the sound of it in the corner of the kitchen as Corey quickly moved to answer it. "Hello... Oh, yes. Just a minute."

Corey held the phone out to Bob and informed him, "It's Drake, darling. He needs to talk with you."

Corey and Haddie looked at each other with anxious concern, as Bob, with trepidation, took the receiver from Corey. "Hello, Drake. Are you doing all right this morning?"

Drake, disconsolately and with a soft tone to his voice, told him, "I'm doing the best I can, Bob...but what I called for is something Elizabeth asked me to do before you got to the hospital last night."

"What's that? Anything I can do to help you."

Drake asked as his voice was breaking, "She wanted you to give her main eulogy."

With the receiver still in his hand, Bob's upper torso bent over, and his body shook with each exhalation as he started to cry.

Corey moved to him and put her arms around him as he fought to catch his breath and his composure. Exhaling loudly, he solemnly told him, "Drake, I would be honored."

Drake also informed Bob, "There will be a showing tomorrow before the actual funeral proceedings, from nine to one o'clock. And during those proceedings, there will be short individual eulogies from her closest friends. You would end the funeral with your eulogy, Bob."

"All right, Drake. I'll see you at the church tomorrow. We'll talk more then…goodbye."

Bob hung up the receiver, and with his moistened eyes, he turned to Corey and grievously told her, "Drake wants me to give Elizabeth's main eulogy. It was one of her last wishes… I may not be able to get through it, but it most certainly will be done."

He then turned and walked out of the kitchen toward the piano in the living room. The next thing Corey and Haddie heard was Debussy's "Clair de Lune." Its rolling piano keys in the middle section was a melancholic masterpiece that Bob used to great effect in trying to commemorate the passing of his sister.

Corey suddenly realized this was the classical piece of music Elizabeth requested Bob to play at the restaurant where his twenty-fourth birthday party was held in February. Instantly, tears came into Corey's eyes.

Elizabeth's funeral was at the United Methodist Church of Thousand Oaks. The same church at which Joshua and Deidra were just recently married. And as dark irony would have it, the same clergyman, Reverend Timothy Burgess, would reside over this funeral, as he was the one who last said, "And now I pronounce you husband and wife."

At almost one o'clock, everyone took their seats as the reverend began with his short eulogy of Elizabeth and then the first prayer. There were a couple hundred people in attendance, including all of the actors Elizabeth worked with at the Los Angeles Center for the Performing Arts, Drake's parents, the Owls with their wives or girlfriends, Nick and Charlotte, Truman and his date, and then the many people from Celebrity Studios, including Jack Windheim, who sat next to Bob in the front row (Bob insisted on that). Corey sat on the other side of Bob, with Haddie next to her.

"Amazing Grace" and "Abide with Me" were the two songs sung by the chorus, and the two hymns that were sung by the guests were "Jerusalem" and "The Lord Is My Shepherd" (Psalm 23).

There were three short eulogies given by Elizabeth's closet friends from LA. The reverend finished with the last prayer; and the choir's last hymn, "How Great Thou Art," ended; and there was a calming silence that reverberated throughout the church.

The minister again took to the pulpit and soothingly announced, "At this time, Drake has requested Elizabeth's brother, Bob, to say the final eulogy."

The minister stepped down and took a seat beside the choir. Bob rose up from his pew as Jack also stood and hugged him and patted him on the back. Bob was expressionless and feeling numb, like he was floating above all the people in the church. He moved with leaden limbs toward the pulpit.

Corey had touchingly released his hand from hers, and she felt such trepidation running throughout her body for him. She couldn't be sure Bob would be able to give his last tribute to his sister without breaking down and losing his composure, but she prayed for him nevertheless.

Bob reached the pulpit, but he had no speech written out to lay down in front of him. For a moment, he stood just staring down at the highly varnished oakwood top of the pulpit.

He slowly and determinedly raised his head and scanned all the pews from one side of the church to the other. After swallowing heavily, he began his eulogy. "Elizabeth Margaret Bennington, my sister, played many roles in my life. She was my tormentor when I was ten, eleven, and twelve. She insisted she knew more than I did about everything. I argued she didn't, but I knew very well she did."

There was a faint chuckle that echoed through the cavernous walls of the church.

"She was my babysitter, at times, when she wasn't on a date with one of her many suitors. And, oh, how she ruled with a steel fist. She wouldn't even allow me to take a peanut butter and jelly sandwich to bed. She said it would stain the sheets. But I told her there was already stains on the sheets from the night before, when I took a grape popsicle to bed with me."

More of a quiet laugh came from the people now.

Bob swallowed again as his heart rate quickened. More solemnly he continued, "Elizabeth was also my surrogate mother. For when our parents died, I was only fourteen, and she was nineteen. Being my replacement mother was suddenly thrust upon her and at such a tender age. She could have given me up to the foster system, but she reassured me that that would never happen. So she put her own life on hold for four years, working at getting me through high school and ready for college when I graduated. When I saw her working so hard for me, I started working hard for her. I cracked the books every night, practiced the piano when I could, after she prompted me to learn the piano, and I began to help around the house whenever I could. She told me once the most important thing in her life, at that time, was me and getting me a college education. So she became my mentor, my protector, and my guidance counselor. But, you know, to me, the best thing she was, was my best friend."

Bob slightly bit his lower lip to keep it from trembling, blinked his moistening eyes, and heavily swallowed again.

Corey, and many others, kept dabbing under their eyes and at their noses, trying to catch the flow of tears.

"I honestly cannot remember a time when she wouldn't just drop everything she was doing and come to help me out. She was so kind and loving. So soft-spoken and empathetic. Intelligent and strikingly beautiful. That could be why I married a woman just like her."

Corey let out a faint cry; as she began to cry so hard, her body began to jerk. Jack slid over to her and put his arm around her as she fell into both of his arms that he had wrapped around her.

"I'm going to desperately miss my sister, Elizabeth, but will never ever forget her. I find it tragically sad she'll never see her son take his first steps, see him graduate high school, then college, or marrying the love of his life, and having grandchildren for her and Drake."

He looked over at Elizabeth as she lay so peacefully still in her open coffin, and as his voice began to crackle and break, he promised her, "And this child...will never want, sis. And we will never let him forget the wonderful and loving mother he had...and how lucky he was to have been born from the incredible parents he had come from… I'll never hear you call me *Bobby* again…" He cried out loud for a moment. "But I know I'll always hear that and see you in my dreams."

Bob started to outright cry and finished by telling her, "Good night, sis. I love you, and may God be with you on your journey."

Bob stepped down the two steps from the pulpit, and Drake walked to him, and they embraced each other tightly as Drake whispered to him, "Thank you, Bob. That was beautiful and very heartfelt."

Bob reassured him again, "If you need anything at all, please, please call me."

Returning to his seat, Corey flung herself into his arms, and they both stood crying their eyes out. There wasn't a dry eye in the entire church upon watching them.

Haddie cried out, "Poor Mr. Bob! Oh, and that poor little baby! God bless that child, and take good care of his mama, Lord."

As the guests started to rise from their pews and start to exit the church, instead of a lament expressing mourning, Drake had requested an Elizabethan song from Shakespeare's play *As You Like It.* It was a glorious celebration of young love in the springtime, reminding Drake of the day he had met Elizabeth six years ago.

Bob, Corey, and Drake stayed in the church, after all the guests had exited, to view the closing of the casket by the funeral director and his assistant.

Being one of the pallbearers, Bob helped to carry Elizabeth's coffin to the hearse and then again to the graveside committal service at the Valley of Peace cemetery in Thousand Oaks.

Corey stood with Bob and Drake at the gravesite for a while, after the guests had slowly filtered away and drove back to the church for the funeral luncheon.

Bob stood near the open grave until the casket was lowered into the ground. This grave was very near Bob and Elizabeth's parents' gravesite; and after a few moments, Bob began to feel peaceful and serene in knowing they would take good care of her now.

That evening, Bob called Stanley and told him he would be returning for Tuesday's performance. Stanley concernedly asked, "Are you absolutely sure you can do this, Bob? I don't want you to be sorry about rushing this—but I will tell you, we had a few very disgruntled ticket holders this weekend not seeing you in the play, but seeing a barely known understudy trying his very best, but coming up a little short."

"No, Stanley. I'll be all right. I really need to do this... I need to get my mind on something else right now. So, I'll see you tomorrow."

Bob and Corey lay down in the same chaise lounge for a couple of hours after Bob talked with Stanley and before he had to fly back to New York late that night.

Corey lay with her arm around Bob's waist and her head on his chest and tried to ease the burden of his pain by telling him, "Oh, darling, I wish I could go back with you tonight, but Dack Jacobsen, our producer, is really putting a push on the production right now. Which is actually a good thing for me, because the sooner we can wrap this picture, the sooner I can come to New York to be with you."

Despondent, he took his free hand and softly placed it on the side of Corey's face, kissing the top of her head. He then turned her face up to him, looked into her glistening, tentative eyes, and tenderly kissed her on the lips. She responded by taking her arm from around his waist and placing her hand behind his head. They were now kissing forcefully and long.

The comfort he was deriving from the touch and the sensual feeling of Corey's body was consoling and welcoming. His mind dictated to him he physically and emotionally needed to be with her because of the solace she brought to him at this time.

They walked with arms around each other into the house and straight for the bedroom. The love they made that evening was slow and tender. The aura that encompassed them was a beautiful and divine radiance of the God-given love they possessed for each other.

That late night, Corey went to the airport with Bob to sadly send him off on his way back to New York. Before he disappeared down the jetway and into the aircraft, he held her tight and kissed her and imploringly told her, "Now you come to me just as soon as you can, baby. We'll talk each night after I get back to the penthouse. Okay?"

"I'll be there sooner than you think, darling. Take care of yourself. I love you, mister."

As he started down the jetway, he turned back around and smiled and then winked at her.

Corey winked back, slowly shaking her head with the irrevocable and consuming love she would always have for him.

Tuesday night, Bob arrived at the theater an hour and a half before curtain, and everyone was very consoling toward him. He was handling himself quite well and trying to keep his mind busy with the play, and not so much with the passing of Elizabeth.

For weeks, the play was his only thought, besides that of Corey and infinitely missing her. But at times, he, Debbie, Doris, the supporting actors Lee and Arthur, and sometimes Angela would go out together for a late dinner or just to relax and have some drinks. It was a great release for him and bolstered his spirits immensely.

After Sunday's performance, Bob invited the main actors and actresses, along with a handful of the backup dancers, to the penthouse the next day for a get-together in the early evening.

That December 19, a dark Monday, it was a week before Stanley would take the play to London for two weeks; and four days before, it ended its limited engagement on Broadway.

The penthouse was rocking by five o'clock that night. Bob had eighteen people eating catered food, drinking wine and beer, dancing to some of the songs playing on the radio, laughing, and generally just having a good time.

A slow seductive song was now playing on the radio, and Bob was in the kitchen getting himself another beer while Doris was at the entryway to the kitchen, sipping her drink and talking about closing night of the play coming on Friday.

At that precise moment, Corey let herself into the penthouse and came eye to eye with Doris, who was totally taken by surprise by Corey's presence. When it finally registered in her mind that Corey also lived there, Doris smiled, and she cheerfully said aloud, "Well, Corey! It's so nice to see that you could come to the party."

The song "At Last" by Etta James was playing in the background; a beautiful blonde was with her husband, and all of this playing out at their penthouse, Corey's heart was now clearly beating in her throat. She had never felt a threat to her marriage this great before, and it left her standing at the door blanched, speechless, and paralyzed with fear.

Suddenly Bob popped his head around the corner of the kitchen, after hearing Doris mention Corey's name.

When Corey saw Bob's gleaming eyes and brilliant smile, gradually the warmth and the expression returned to her face. She now felt immeasurable relief.

He came bounding out of the kitchen and scooped her up in his arms. He excitedly told her, "Hello, baby! I'm just so jazzed you're here this soon. How totally cool is this?"

They exchanged a full open-mouthed kiss and momentarily embraced each other.

Bob took Corey's hand and led her into the living room area as he introduced her to everyone there. "I want all of you to meet my main squeeze…and yes, this is the most talented dramatic actress on the planet, Ms. Corinth Madrigal."

Corey laughed and blushed a little, but she was greatly relieved to now realize that this was just a party, and not a private party for two.

Bob left for a minute to get Corey a drink and brought her out a dry martini, stirred, and they kissed again very softly.

The wave of relief that swept over her was so enormous; her heart returned to her chest cavity, and she could once again breathe easily.

Bob looked at her with excitement and anticipation showing on his face and asked her, "Your picture must have wrapped a week early. I love it that you're here, baby."

Corey leaned into another kiss, and looking him directly in the eyes, she softly told him, "Six days to be exact, darling. I didn't call you because I wanted to surprise you. You know we love doing that to one another… I'm not going to the wrap party, which is tonight. I just wanted to come to New York, and then on to London, and be with you."

Bob took both their drinks and placed them on a table. He then took Corey in his arms and started to dance slowly with her to the Owls' "My Constant Need." As they moved salaciously and then barely at all, he kissed her ear and whispered, "I will personally thank you later tonight, baby."

Corey chuckled and gave him a toothy grin. At that moment, she felt Bob was almost back to his old self and who he was before Elizabeth's passing. Corey had prayed for weeks that he would survive Elizabeth's death with staying busy and the passage of time. It was working; they spent the next three days getting reacquainted in the bedroom.

The play closed that Friday night of December 23. Corey attended this night wanting to be at the final curtain party with Bob and Stanley at Sardi's.

The audience gave another standing ovation to the troupe, just as all the other nights, going back to their opening night of November 1.

Bob and Corey had two full days before they would fly out of New York to London. So on Christmas Eve, they caught a play and then dined at Carmine's Italian restaurant in Greenwich Village.

Christmas morning, they ate a filling breakfast and then took a walk down Park Avenue, enjoying all the businesses' holiday decorations and window dressings.

That night, Bob and Corey sat in front of their grayish stacked-stone gas fireplace, which was built on the biggest wall of the living area. It was rarely used, but to them, Christmas night seemed appropriate for a warming fire, drinks, and your love sitting next to you.

There were gas fireplaces in both of the top two penthouses, and both were vented by a chimney on top and through the roof of the building.

As they sat together with their arms wrapped around each other, and their drinks on small side tables, Bob reached into his pocket and brought out a small box wrapped in Christmas foil with a very small red bow.

Corey looked at the box in his hand and exhaled a breath of loving surprise and delight. She looked into his proud and gleaming eyes as hers moistened. She softly pulled his head to her and kissed him passionately on the lips.

She then took the present and carefully tore the wrapping away, to find inside, in a small box, a beautiful pair of diamond earrings. Corey looked at Bob with such love in her eyes and suddenly wrapped her arms around his neck, professing, "Oh my god! I can't even tell you how much I love you, darling. And here I didn't get you a present, because what would I get a man that already has everything?"

He answered smooth and sweetly, "You're right, doll. At that moment in time when I found you, I had everything I would ever need."

Corey's face winced with her love for him, and she began to drop tears down her face and started to kiss him long and hard.

When they separated, Bob still held her tightly to him, and he sexily expressed, "I think maybe you left my present in the bedroom for later tonight. Right?"

She could not have smiled any more brightly than she did at that moment.

"Absolutely!"

Monday morning, the entire cast, crew, costumes, sets, and director flew out of New York, and six hours and fifty minutes later, they landed at Heathrow Airport in London, England.

Everyone involved with the show was staying at the five-star Beaumont Hotel, which was less than a mile to Her Majesty's Theatre in London's West End.

The Adelphi Theatre, where Stanley's production of *Oklahoma!* would be playing for two weeks, was a West End theater, located on the Strand in the city of Westminster. The Strand and Covent Gardens specialized in comedy and musical theater and had hosted many musicals there for decades.

Bob, Corey, and a handful of the actors ventured around London that night they arrived, experiencing the changing of the guards at Buckingham Palace, Big Ben, Westminster Abbey, the Tower of London, and finished their evening at an English pub in Piccadilly Circus.

All agreed Piccadilly was London's equivalent to New York's Times Square; there were neon lights advertising plays in the West End, a lot of shopping; and the eye-catching and most striking building was the London Pavilion, which was a former music hall, and its peak was located at the corner of two streets, and the length of the building ran down both streets.

Stanley used the day before opening night to have his troupe of actors at the Adelphi Theatre for a run-through of the play, familiarizing themselves to the surface of the old and declining condition of the wooded stage.

The show was met opening night with much ardor and enthusiasm. The British audience loved the Western genre of cowboys, and most especially, singing cowboys and cowgirls.

The show received rave reviews from the English critics. The *English Herald* remarked:

> The chemistry was incredible between Ms. Reynolds and Mr. Richardson. The whole story was beautifully crafted, exquisitely acted, and magnificently wardrobed.
>
> Straightaway, this is the best play the Brits have lately been entertained by.

The two-week run of the play broke box office records for a brief limited engagement of a musical play. Tickets were being scalped for as much as twenty times the ticket's price.

During the days of the play, Corey and Bob took advantage of the amenities of the Beaumont Hotel; they swam and played together in the swimming pool, as though they were at home in Bel Air, and also had daily massages. Corey had the full-spa experience, with the facials, steam room, pedicures, and so on.

The closing night of the play, there was a great and thunderous applause for the entire troupe of actors and dancers. Flowers adorned the front of the stage, and it seemed each person onstage had a bouquet tossed to them.

Stanley came out onstage and began to wave his arms up and down, trying to quiet the tumultuous din of the theater. After less than a minute, he smiled and began to speak to the audience, "Thank you so much—I must tell you how much we love the English playgoers. They know their musicals and appreciate a quality cast of players when they see one, like I have here in *Oklahoma!*" There was an appreciative applause and cheers. "Maybe we'll be back sometime in the future, with a production even more entertaining and for a longer run."

The audience showed their appreciation with a resounding applause, shouting, and loud whistles, until the troupe took their last bow and the final curtain came down.

Bob said his goodbyes to those not flying back right away after everyone had exited the stage.

London was shrouded in fog when most of the troupe flew back to LA, but Stanley headed back to New York looking for his next big long-term Broadway production.

Bob and Corey had Curtis pick them up from the LA airport at eight o'clock the next morning. Having slept on the plane most of the way home, both agreed they wanted to shower, get some breakfast, and then head over to Celebrity to talk with Jack.

The minute Bob and Corey stepped into the house, through the back door, Haddie met them. Corey immediately hugged her and asked, "Hello, Haddie. Have you missed us? It's been over three weeks since I've seen you, and almost two months you've not seen Bob."

Excitedly, Haddie answered, "I have truly missed you, Ms. Corey…" Haddie let go of Corey and turned her attention to Bob, and when she moved to hug him, she enthusiastically said, "Well, Mr. Bob, I almost didn't recognize you. It's been way too long. How have you been?"

Bob smiled and chuckled and graciously told her, "It's great to see you, Ms. Haddie. And I'm doing just fine, thanks. How the heck have you been without me around to tick you off or bug you?"

Haddie joked back with a playful look in her eyes, "Without you around, Mr. Bob, I think I have come completely unglued." Corey stood laughing and was enjoying the amusing exchange between the two of them. "You know? I just may need a shrink after all this."

Bob smiled brilliantly and hugged her again and then kissed her on the cheek and quipped, "You know, at times I've felt that you're more sane than anyone else I know, Ms. Haddie."

He smiled once more, kissed Corey, and then headed toward the master suite to take a shower and change into fresh clothes to go to the studio with Corey.

Haddie whimsically stated as he walked away, "Well, you keep reminding me of that as I grow older…'cause I'm gonna need it."

Corey laughed out loud and then followed Bob into the bedroom. They ended up taking a shower together and lingered several minutes longer in the shower than usual, enjoying each other's company.

Two hours later at the studio, Jack was told Bob and Corey were there to see him. Jack promptly told his secretary, Deloris, to clean his slate for the next hour—no phone calls, no visitors, and no whiny actor or producer let in to vent to him.

After their initial greetings, Corey got down to business in asking Jack, "Well, Jack, you know Bob and I are starting that picture, *Rufous Eyes of Fire*, January 23, and we just wanted to know if your producer has finalized his director, and so on and so forth?"

Jack answered her with that guttural sound of smoker's lungs; and with his thickly-coated vocal cords, he croaked, "Corey, you should be pleased to know Trent Voight said he would be excited to work with you and Bob again. He stated he really thought the two of you were complete professionals and worked hard at getting it done on first takes, saving him time and money."

Corey pridefully smiled as Bob looked at her with such high esteem in his eyes.

"I guess Trent has chosen Victor Trudeau to be his director again. I mean, they did such a tremendous job on *Love's Wicked Lies* that I know they're excited to start this project with both of you again. I'm told that everyone from casting director to makeup will be exactly who worked with the both of you on *Lies*."

Corey's eyes enlarged, her mouth slightly dropped open, and she loudly asked, "Jack, are you actually telling me that Edith Head will be our costume designer again?"

Jack answered, after choking and coughing up a laugh, "That's absolutely correct, my dear. I talked with Ms. Head over the phone weeks ago, about Trent wanting her for this new picture, and she told me that she would categorically be thrilled to work with Trent, Victor, and the two of you again on any picture."

Corey was ecstatic hearing that. "Oh, yes, yes, yes! I can't wait for this picture to start." Turning her head to Bob, she excitedly asked him, "Doesn't that sound exciting, darling?"

Bob smiled broadly, and chuckling a bit, he told her, "If that makes you this happy, doll, then I'm all onboard with it and happy as hell for you."

She chuckled, then Jack informed them, "As far as your supporting actors, the casting director, Dennis Upton, has signed on Ann Sheridan, Reginald Gardner, and June Allyson, who is on loan from MGM. It cost me a lot to get her, but the story needs a woman who is the stereotypical wife to the put-upon protagonist. She seemed excited to work with us."

Corey looked at Bob with an amused concern. Talking directly to Jack, Bob earnestly stated, while nodding his head, "This sounds outta sight, Jack. I'm finding the casting to be top-grade people. I'm sure I'm gonna learn something from this project. Most especially from that lead actress, Madrigal, you have under contract. I've heard she's a fox."

Bob facetiously smiled, and Corey stood up and leaned over him, smiled, and then kissed him full-on with her hands cupping his face.

Jack sat taking a puff of his cigar and coughed out a hearty laugh. "All right, you two, be ready for your read-throughs Monday morning, the twenty-third of this month. You can pick up your manuscripts from Deloris out there on your way out."

Corey felt so exhilarated now knowing she would not only be working side by side with Bob, and again having first-class actors in supporting roles, but she would once more be working with the most prolific and celebrated costume designer in the business. "Oh, you bet your life we'll be ready, Jack. This ought to be great fun!" Corey chortled, as she and Bob began to walk toward the door.

Corey walked ahead of him, as he looked back at Jack, who smiled contently. Bob raised his eyebrows showing great satisfaction in Corey's excitement, then smiled gratifyingly and walked to the office door nodding his head affirmatively. "We'll see you then, man."

Bob asked Corey if she wanted to drive down to LA with him and visit little Robert Brian. She absolutely wanted to see him also.

Although Drake had hired a nanny to be with the baby while he worked, Drake's mother, Alice, was there at the house also.

Robert Brian was now almost two months old, and Bob kept him smiling as he held him in his arms most of the time Corey wasn't holding him. They stayed for almost two hours talking with Alice about how Drake was and if there had been any health problems with the baby. When they found out everything was running smoothly, they kissed Robert Brian and headed home to dinner.

That night of January 11, Nick called Bob and congratulated him on such good performances in *Oklahoma!* and the critical acclaim that was lauded upon him in both New York and London. He welcomed him home and then asked, "Hey, man. Are you ready for an overnighter up in Canada? I have two concerts set up for this coming Friday and Saturday nights in Vancouver, British Columbia. What do you think about that, man? That sound doable for you? You ready to get back into the Night Owls groove?"

Bob's heart started to race with excitement thinking about performing with the guys again. It had now been entirely too long. He answered Nick almost immediately, "Oh, hell yes, man! That sounds boss! Have you checked out the atmosphere of this place? I mean, are Joshua and Darnell gonna have a problem?"

"The general manager of the Orpheum assured me they have had no major problems of any kind with discrimination or violent actions, but they always have a handful of security standing by for anything at all, just in case."

Bob seemed okay with that and advised Nick, "All right, let's pop the lid on this. Make room for Corey in my room. She doesn't know it yet, but she'll be traveling with me."

Corey walked into the front room at the tail end of his conversation, and when Bob hung the phone up, she inquisitively asked, "Where am I traveling to, darling? I thought we'd be home now for a while."

Slightly surprised, Bob looked up and informed her, "I know we just got home, babe, but this Friday and Saturday night, Nick has the Owls playing the Orpheum Concert Hall in Vancouver, Canada."

Corey's eyebrows rose, and her eyes widened with the unexpected news. "Canada?"

"Yeah, it's less than three hours from here. We'll fly up Friday afternoon, and then we'll fly home right after the second performance Saturday night… I'd really love for you to come with me. We'd have all day Saturday together studying our manuscript, having breakfast, lunch, and dinner with one another. And of course, you'd be the dessert that night, doll." He smiled.

Corey stood admiring her beautiful man, then slowly walked to him, as he sat at the end of the long couch. Standing directly in front of him, she gently pulled his head into her body and told him, "I would love to go with you, sweetheart. I really want to be with you, too."

She sexily and slowly lowered her body down to him, and they kissed open-mouthed, moving their lips and tongues together savagely. After a few minutes, Bob placed his arms under her legs and around her back, carrying her into the bedroom, to Corey's total delight.

Bob and Corey greeted all the guys and Deidra at the airport Friday afternoon. It was exciting for Bob to see everyone again and to know he would be back in concert that same night in another country.

After reaching Vancouver at five o'clock in the evening, everyone got settled into their hotel rooms, and then the ten of them went out to dinner then onto the concert hall from there.

At seven o'clock, everyone entered the opulent Orpheum Theatre. The ostentatiously rich and luxurious interior of the theater really impressed everyone. It had plush golden carpeting throughout both levels of seating; there were nineteenth-century crystal chandeliers that hung from the lobby's ceiling and the main floor; and the color scheme of ivory, moss green, gold, and burgundy ran throughout the entire structure.

The guys ran a sound check on the instruments for several minutes from behind the stage curtain. At this point, Corey, Deidra, Nick, and Truman took their seats in the third row, center.

The Night Owls would be playing to almost three thousand people and were made aware by the stage manager that there had been some venerable names that had played the Orpheum, like a young Judy Garland, comedian Jack Benny, Lena Home, Ella Fitzgerald, and the Duke and his band.

The guys were really impressed with that. And now with adrenaline running high, the emcee introduced them, and then the curtain began to open to thundering applause from a packed house of Owls fans.

After Jimmy's four-count, he ripped into his drums with the lead-in to "We Bleed the Same Blood," which was just released to the public ten days ago.

Len and Darnell entered with their guitars, as Bob played a throaty run in the second bar. Joshua's C trumpet jumped in with screaming notes of a disconcerting nature. Doug played his sax with powerful and strong notes that spoke in a sarcastic vein.

As soon as the band relaxed the loud, earsplitting start to the song, Len, Darnell, and Bob made their vocal entrance.

The Owls played several of their more popular songs of rebellion and discrimination for a solid hour, then Bob stepped up to the microphone after putting his guitar in its stand.

When the audience quieted down, he earnestly spoke to them in a deliberate and subdued manner. "Now we'd like to play one of our newly released songs for you. 'Kill Me with a Lie.'"

There was more loud applause and cheers coming from the boisterous crowd of fans.

"This song speaks of a person who has had their heart ripped out by the person they had loved for a long time. Then they finally realize they had to come to terms with it. We hope you like it." Bob stepped out in front of the microphone on the stand, carrying a cordless one in his hand. He was preparing to sing the lyrics by himself in the front of the stage.

Jimmy started a soft and mellow beat on his snare with his loose-haired sticks. The beautiful melody began to be played out by Doug's warm and smokey alto sax, along with Joshua's mistress, the muted B-flat trumpet.

When Len and Darnell played the second and third bars with a fluctuating pitch, Bob took his vocal entrance to the song:

> Promise me you'll say good-bye before you walk away
> I can only give you my heart and beg for you to stay
> You were all my dreams come true, and I'd have you forever and a day
> But you let someone else in to love you, and it's a price we'll both have to pay
>
> (Chorus)
> Never speak my name again, and I'll try hard to forget this aching pain
> For now I'm by myself, but I'll never forget us always walking in the rain
> I'll go on living, although I know I'd rather die
> That was one thing I thought you'd never do, was kill me with a lie.

Shut the door and don't look back, for you'll see
me no more
I'll find someone, and their love will make my
broken heart soar
So when you hear that I have died, don't weep
your empty tears
Just think about what you had lost and the love
we shared for years

(Chorus)

Let me go from your thoughts, as you have let me
go from your life
Try to forget that we were one, and eliminate
your strife
I'll never forget you, as you have long forgotten
me
Don't fight for answers, just accept things as they
are, and let them be

(Chorus)

When Bob finished the last chorus with "kill me with a lie," the audience went crazy with a thundering applause and a deafening roar of shouts and whistles.

Bob's eyes happened upon Corey, and since he didn't write that song with her in mind, he didn't specifically look at her while he was singing, but her eyes were huge with unshed tears. She was staring at him like she was tormented with fear.

After the Owls had performed as many songs that the audience clamored for, they quitted the stage at almost eleven o'clock that night.

Having showered, Bob climbed into the hotel's queen bed with Corey close to midnight. Before he could fall asleep, he looked over at her and questioningly asked, "Did that song 'Kill Me with a Lie' upset you for some reason, doll?"

Corey was staring out into the empty atmosphere of the sterile room then slowly turned her head to face him. With melancholy dripping from her voice, she in turn asked, "What exactly did you have in mind when you wrote that song? I just couldn't wrap my head around whatever was going through your mind at that time and where you could have been."

Bob, nodding his head and now understanding her reaction, was greatly relieved. He exhaled and compassionately began to explain, "Corey, it's something I've had to deal with for about four years now."

Corey quickly sat up in bed and stared at him with great concern and apprehension.

As he sadly stared down and into his lap, he told her, "I knew this guy, Isaac Gibson, in my first year at NEC. He was an extremely talented classical piano player. His downfall was falling in love with a third-year skirt who played him along for several months until she shot him down like a dog…she just left him. She quit talking to him, quit seeing him, and really just kissed him off. Well, he was devastated, and he came to me thinking I could explain it or maybe talk with her and have her change her mind about him. But nothing I could say or do was helping to get her back to seeing him again."

Corey interjected, "Was she interested in you, darling?"

Bob blew a disconsolate breath into the air and rejoined, "She was interested in every guy that attended NEC. She had no preferences. And it seemed she didn't care what destruction she caused to anyone along the way either. About a week before final exams that spring, Isaac committed suicide in his dorm room… He hung himself in the shower with a bedsheet."

Corey inhaled a breath of surprise and was aghast with the outcome of Bob's story. "Oh, darling, I'm so sorry. You must have been beside yourself with anger for that girl."

Corey put her arms around him and kissed his neck.

Bob resolutely answered her, "No…I was more angry at myself, because I felt I didn't help him enough. But from that day on, I promised myself one day I would write a song for him…so there you have it. Baby, don't you know that if that song was written with you in mind, I would've been staring at you for the whole performance and thinking what mischief we could get into later." He gave her a wide toothy grin.

He took her in his arms, and while kissing her, he slowly lowered her unto her back, sexily saying into her face, "Why don't we get busy with some mischief?"

Corey had an alluring smile on her face and seductively purred, "Let's."

TWENTY-SIX

After their second concert in Vancouver, Bob and Corey arrived home very early Sunday morning. Corey seemed to have enjoyed herself, but she was glad to get home nonetheless.

Nick had already advised the guys that the next weekend of Saturday and Sunday night, they would again venture into Canada, but to Edmonton, Alberta, this time.

The following weekend, the two concerts in Edmonton were played at the Northern Alberta Jubilee Auditorium. They performed for 2,538 seats located on three different levels.

There was no segregation in the seating to be seen, much to the relief of the guys. The auditorium was fairly new, having just been built in 1957. Both nights were standing room only, and both concerts went exceptionally well.

Corey chose to stay home for these two concerts; she just wasn't used to traveling so much and as often as Bob. She loved her house and adored her husband, but she wanted to stay home to study the manuscript for her and Bob's next picture together. Corey knew he would only be away for just shy of two days. The separation would only make her want him that much more.

The Night Owls returned Sunday night, from two concerts in Edmonton, Alberta, at two o'clock Monday morning.

The read-throughs for the picture *Rufous Eyes of Fire* started Monday morning at seven o'clock in the number 1 soundstage reading room, located in back of the main stage.

Bob walked in on time along with Corey, but he was extremely exhausted, with only having had four hours of sleep that night, after getting back from Canada so late.

Bob met Reginald Gardiner and June Allyson as soon as he walked in and was impressed with their easygoing personalities and their film history. Both were highly publicized and accredited dramatic actors.

Corey sat next to Bob at the long, rectangular table, and Ann Sheridan was seated on his other side. Bob was conversing across the table with Reginald, when Victor, the director, got everyone's attention by saying, "All right, people. Let's get underway. You should be familiar with not only your part in the manuscript, but every other starring role in this film. It'll give you a better understanding about where we're going. As you know, this is a love story, but with a twist."

Ann only met Bob when they recorded a Christmas song for the Owls' album back in early September. At that time, she had taken instantly to his clearheaded, generous, and gracious nature.

Ann interrupted Victor by stating, "I had been imbued with the notion that love stories are best when they are ambiguous and low-key," she then slowly turned her head toward Bob and provocatively and seductively whispered, "but passionate."

Corey couldn't believe what Ann was obviously insinuating to Bob. She leaned forward from her seat and cast a rapacious glare at her.

Bob stared at Ann and found the moment to be quite amusing. As she was still looking at him, he kiddingly asked her, "You know, Ann, the cameras aren't rolling quite yet, but I hope you're aware that"—pointing his thumb with cupped fingers at Corey—"this lady is my wife?"

Ann became a little flustered, and with a tenable response, she stated, "Why, of course! I was just throwing a line out there."

Corey facetiously stated, not even looking at Ann, "As long as that's all you're throwing, dear."

At this point, Victor interposed, "Moving right along. We'll only have read-throughs today and tomorrow, because Wednesday we'll begin our rehearsals. I'll keep all of you posted day-to-day on the location shoots each of you will eventually have when we start shooting—hopefully sometime within the next two weeks."

The Friday of that week, Edith Head was present and talking with Victor and Trent. She was informed by them of the colors, styling, and overall fashion they wanted in the costuming. She inquired, "Well, do you want smart, snappy, swank, showy, sleek, suave, or smooth?"

At that moment, Victor and Trent felt she was the grand dame of costuming, and so they let Edith have carte blanche with the picture's costuming. They were convinced, with her having read the script, she would just feel what the characters should be wearing. They put their absolute trust in her and knew they would not be disappointed.

Rehearsals eventually got underway; and Bob, June, and Ann had just finished a scene with June's character, as Bob's wife, confronting him about his affair he was conducting with Ann's character, who portrayed his mistress. Corey and Reginald sat in canvas-backed chairs off-camera watching and studying the chemistry these three were displaying to everyone.

While everyone was taking a coffee break, the producer, Trent Voight, walked quickly into the soundstage, immediately notifying everyone he had some great news for them. "I'm glad you're on break. We've just received the Academy Awards nominations for this year!"

Victor looked at Trent with mild apprehension, but anxiously asked, "All right, Trent. Lay it on us. Tell us what gives."

Corey was excited about this year's nominations, but not for herself; she was mainly concerned about Bob getting the nomination for Best Actor in a Leading Role. She felt he had matured so much in the last two years performing before the cameras, that he definitely had earned a nomination.

"Oh, I'm praying you get the nomination, darling. You were just marvelous in *Love's Wicked Lies*," Corey proudly and excitedly told him, then kissed him.

Bob beamed with anticipation and nervously replied, "You too, doll."

Trent straightened his sheet of paper with both hands and then started to read, "We've received six nominations for *Love's Wicked Lies*."

Victor shouted out, "All right, okay. That's great!"

Reginald, June, and Ann applauded and were delighted for them.

Bob balled his fist and pumped it once, sharply responding, "Yes. Way too cool!"

Corey was brilliantly smiling at him and took his hand in hers and admiringly kept her gaze fixed on him.

Trent then read, "We have been nominated for Best Costume Design in Color for Ms. Edith Head." Everyone applauded that.

"Best Director, Victor Trudeau."

Bob jumped up yelling, "Hell yes. Way to go, Victor!" They then shook hands. Corey hugged Victor, and the others came to him and shook his hand.

"For Best Actress in a Leading Role, Corey Madrigal." Bob was now beside himself as he grabbed Corey around the waist and spun her in a circle, landing her back on her feet, while he yelled, "Baby, I knew it! You are the best, doll!" Each person congratulated her by either hugging her or applauding while everyone was still standing.

"And now." Corey held her breath in nervous anticipation. "For Best Actor in a Leading Role." Corey knew at that moment Bob got the nod for Best Actor and threw her arms around his neck, kissing him all over his face, and then lastly gave him a long and emotion-packed kiss on the lips.

Trent screamed anyway, "Bob Richardson!"

When Corey dropped her head from Bob's face, she could see his eyes were slightly moistened, but he was smiling at her with the unconditional adoration he had for her.

June and Ann came over and hugged him excitedly, while Reginald, Victor, and Trent shook his hand and gave him a shoulder bump; all were telling him congratulations and good luck.

Trent then read, "And for the Best Motion Picture. *Love's Wicked Lies*! Trent Voight, producer!" Everyone gave him a rousing applause. There were a lot of hugs and handshakes after that announcement. "And lastly, Jeffrey Stewart for Best Screenplay Written for the Screen. Wherever you are, Jeff...congratulations, man."

Bob slightly nodded and enjoyed Victor and Trent displaying their satisfaction in knowing all the hard work everyone put in on *Love's Wicked Lies* was now paying off.

Corey stood next to Bob with her hands wrapped around his arm as she contentedly buried her head into his sleeve. He lovingly stared at her and then kissed her on top of her head. She purred with complete fulfillment.

It was now Monday, February 6, and shooting commenced on *Rufous Eyes of Fire*.

There were still some scenes that Victor wanted shot on the soundstage, because of the cruciality of the lighting in some close-ups, but most of the picture would be shot at as many as fifteen different locations around and in the Southern California area.

Victor was focused on getting some of the close-ups shot the first week of running film. He had Bob and June (his stage wife) in an intense conversation about her questioning his fidelity and then the two falling into each other's arms and kissing after he convinced her of his innocence.

Bob had a bedroom scene with Ann, his mistress in the film. Victor moved the cameras in very close to capture the passion they would be displaying. The scene went well, until Bob was to move away from Ann and get out of bed. At that point, Ann held their last kiss too long, keeping him in her grasp, probably knowing Victor would have to reshoot the scene.

Corey was looking on from behind the cameras, and her glare became laced with doubt and suspicion toward Ann's performance.

Reginald was seated close to Corey and amusingly shook his head in disbelief. He had been aware of Ann's immediate attraction she had to most of her leading men. He turned to Corey and, in a low-toned voice, resignedly told her, "You shouldn't pay any attention to Ann's ploys. She has this uncontrollable urge, ever since I've known her, to try and enthrall and mesmerize her leading men. She rarely succeeds. And I don't see her succeeding here either. You and Bob seem extremely close."

Corey determinedly answered, "Yes, we share an absolute, unshakable trust in one another. But I will tell you right now she's not going to have carte blanche with my husband. We're here to do a job, not shop around for a new mate."

Victor called, "Cut! Ann? Don't hold the last kiss so long. Let Bob leave the bed… Now we'll have to shoot the scene again. Bob, you get back in Ann's embrace, and we'll run tape again… Roll the cameras… Action!"

The second time was perfection, as Bob walked away from the bed and released a huge sigh of relief after Victor stopped running film.

As the stage manager was setting up the next close-up scene between Corey and Reginald (her character's husband), Corey caught Ann several feet behind the placement of the cameras and asked her to step away with her for a moment.

Expecting Corey was feeling a bit jealous over the love scene, she followed her to the back of the soundstage. Ann tried to placate her by saying, "You don't need to be jealous, Corey. We're all just playing a role here. I have no designs on your husband."

Corey immediately shot back, "The hell you don't! If you think you can conquer any man you desire just by throwing your seductive feminine wiles at them, you'd better think again, Ann… Bob's not, or ever will be, on the market for salacious women like you."

Trying to defend her actions, Ann challenged Corey by stating, "You know, Corey? If Bob's all that 'pure as the driven snow,' nothing will ever come from any woman's flirtations. But there's no harm in a woman testing his parameters of fidelity. Men are human, and they have their wants and needs. He may not be interested now, but give him time. He's a man."

Corey became incensed with Ann's statement and stepped closer to her, and in her face, she forcefully warned, "I know you're not used to having a man who loves and adores you from sunup to sundown. As a matter of fact, it seems you can't even get a man who can honestly tell you he loves you…and mean it. So I'm just going to feel sorry for you, Ann, and hope someday you find someone who can stomach your theatrics, unfaithfulness, and the sullen attitude you display to others. But let me tell you this. You keep your distance from my husband, and for the sake of your own personal health, don't ever let it get back to me that you've tried to seduce him or spirit him away to your dark and lecherous hole in the ground. You know, Ann, I really had more respect for you, until now."

Corey sorrowfully turned and walked away. Victor was calling for her to shoot her scene with Reginald, as Ann stood in the same spot focusing on the floor and lost in her own thoughts of realizing what Corey had said did ring with an element of truth.

That night, Bob and Corey were having dinner at the kitchen bar, with Haddie joining them. Corey told Bob of the exchange between her and Ann at the studio. He looked at Corey inquisitively, and seeming a little befuddled, he jokingly stated, "Well, it must be because of my beautiful ears that she's attracted."

Haddie jumped in, and with her hand covering her mouth full of food, she muttered, "I seriously don't think that's what she's attracted to, Mr. Bob." She laughed uproariously, still holding her hand over her mouth.

Bob and Haddie were having a good laugh over Haddie's remark. Corey saw how much fun they were having, and she began to laugh right along with them.

That weekend, the Night Owls flew to Winnipeg, Manitoba, to play two concerts at the Seven Oaks Performing Arts Auditorium. It was a three-and-a-half-hour plane ride to play the four thousand seats of the auditorium. Both concert nights were sellouts, and the Canadian fans loved them. Bob didn't get home until three in the morning, but Corey kept a light on for him.

One week later, Corey had a twenty-fifth birthday party for Bob at the estate. She held it on the Sunday before his birthday on Monday, February 20. She had invited around fifty people, including all the close friends from Celebrity, and anyone affiliated with the Owls, which meant Len's and Darnell's babies would be there with the couples. And Drake happily accepted the invitation and also brought little Robert Brian with him.

It was a catered affair, with plenty of food, alcohol, and diapers. There was a huge blanket spread out over the grass in a more shady part of the lawn, but close to where the new parents were seated. Lisa Shantell King, Isabella Margaret Perry, and Robert Brian Bennington were all placed on the blanket, as Alicia, Valerie, Drake, and Bob were sitting and watching over the babies.

Corey loved to watch Bob interact with the babies. It looked like he was having the time of his life, playing with them and trying to make them laugh at the faces and noises he was making. When he picked up Robert, Corey noticed Bob's eyes were glistening with pride. She could tell he saw Elizabeth in Robert's face, and Bob's face reflected that love for him.

Jack Windheim, sitting on a seat closer to the pool area, had noticed Bob holding little Robert in his arms and loving every moment with him. With his gravelly-throated voice, Jack yelled out, "Bob, you really look like you're loving that. Why don't Corey and you adopt a child? You look and act like you'd make a great father."

Corey and most others heard Jack's comment, and quickly she turned her attention to Bob, as her heart started to beat faster, and her breathing was choked with apprehension. She would love to have a child, even this late in life, but she wasn't quite sure if Bob was ready.

Not taking his adoring eyes off of Robert, he propitiously answered, "You know, Jack. We may just do that."

He leaned down and kissed Robert on the forehead. Bringing his head up away from the baby, Bob slowly glanced over at Corey. Seeing unshed tears in her eyes, he winked at her and displayed a wistful, loving smile.

Corey winked back, with a single tear running down her cheek. She placed her hand over her mouth and began to outwardly cry. She raced over to him, and quickly sitting down next to him, she put one hand under the baby, covering Bob's arms, and the other arm around Bob's neck. They kissed deeply and emotionally, as everyone at the party began to applaud with great pleasure and happiness for them.

The two of them would talk off and on about adopting, but nothing just yet was set in stone.

The shooting of the picture was now moving along very smoothly. Location shoots with Ann and Bob were uneventful. She had decided for the betterment of the film and her relationship with Corey that everything had to remain all business, and she needed to be more of a professional. Ultimately, Ann responded with some of her best work.

Again Nick had the Owls flying off to Toronto, Canada, the weekend after Bob's birthday party. They played the five thousand seats in the Ontario Convention Centre. The concert venues were getting farther and farther away, and this time the four-and-a-half-hour plane ride got him home at four in the morning. Nevertheless, Corey left a light on for him.

Bob and Corey's first wedding anniversary, March 20, was getting close, so Bob okayed it with Victor, Trent, and Jack that he and Corey would take the Friday through Sunday before the twentieth and fly down to Acapulco until Sunday night. They would then finish the last two weeks of the film when they returned.

Flying into Acapulco, Mexico, around noon that Friday, Bob and Corey left their five-star hotel to walk the Acapulco Bay beach. Being a beach resort town located on the Pacific Ocean, it was set on a large bay and backed by high-rises and the Sierra Madre del Sur mountains.

All the jet set went there for its high-energy nightlife and beaches. There also was the iconic La Quebrada cliff, where professional divers plunged forty meters into a small ocean cove during the day and the nighttime hours.

Bob and Corey went to see the divers on Saturday morning, and in one of the walls of the cliff, there was a path and a restaurant where people gathered to watch the men divers and also the pelicans dive for fish.

As they sat at a table in front of the full ceiling-to-floor glass, watching the divers, Bob kiddingly mentioned to Corey he would like to try a dive like that. She looked at him like he was crazy and told him, as she held his one arm with both hands, "Don't you even think about doing that, mister! We've been through so much, and I wouldn't want to lose you now to the dark depths of the Pacific Ocean… I want you to always be with me, darling."

He saw the concern in her eyes, smiled, and then softly kissed her.

That early evening, they sat on the beach only a hundred yards from their hotel, and both agreed the view of the ocean was amazing during the sunset.

Both nights they were in Acapulco, the lovemaking was fervidly laced with the seemingly unending physical and emotional desire they possessed for each other.

Neither one wanted to return home Sunday night, but they were tried-and-true professionals, and they anxiously wanted to finish their picture. The almost-four-hour plane ride got them home to LAX at one o'clock Monday morning, March 20, the actual date of their anniversary.

When they got out of bed and ready to go to the studio the next morning, at almost seven o'clock, Bob inquisitively asked Corey, "What do you think about coming home tonight and getting dressed and going out to that French restaurant in the Hollywood Hills, Tu Es Mon Monde? After all, today is our anniversary."

Corey knew she would be totally exhausted when they arrived home from working on the picture, so she lovingly took his face in her hands and kissed him sensually and whispered, "How about we take our dinner out by the pool, and then afterward, while we're laying in a lounger together, you can hold me in your arms the rest of the night, telling and showing me just how much you love me, sweetheart?"

Bob kept staring affectionately at her lips and then her eyes. He gave her another kiss on her lips and romantically murmured into her face, "Whatever you want, baby. You're just so damn lovable, and every day I thank God for you."

Corey's eyes started to moisten as she quickly responded to him by throwing her arms around his neck and then kissing him full-on and deeply. She slightly pulled her head back and lovingly warned, "Oh my god, Robert Brian! You can't say that to me as we're walking out the door. Tell me that when we're alone and out by the pool tonight, darling… I just love you so much that it actually hurts sometimes."

They did spend that evening out by the pool, drinking martinis, eating some of their wedding cake, which Haddie had thawed out for them, and enjoying each other's company.

The next weekend, the Owls were booked for two concerts in Quebec City, Quebec. This would be the last of the Owls' Canadian concerts for three weeks. After five and a half hours flying into Quebec, they played the Grand Theatre De Quebec and its 3,500 seats. They finished the two concerts with packed houses and a lot of good press from the *Quebec Chronicle-Telegraph.*

Bob didn't arrive home until it was time for him to go to the studio that Monday morning. He quickly showered, and in a daze, he managed to get to the studio with Corey, remember his lines, and not fall asleep during any filming.

The picture's shoot was winding down the first full week of April, and Victor felt they should have this in the can early next week.

Ann had two more scenes with Corey that were to be shot on the soundstage. As the cameras were rolling, Victor loudly yelled, "Cut! Let's take that one again, Ann. You looked like you were in the shadows."

Victor gently pulled Ann to one side and reminded her, "The *key* light is the light that's yours, set up for you, aimed at you. All you have to do is be aware, feel it, and hit your mark. If you miss, even by an inch, you wind up in the shadows, if not total darkness. Okay, Ann? Let's try it again."

Ann was in an almost incoherent torrent, her voice shaking with indignation and hurt; she told him, "Victor, I know how to hit my mark! You don't need to lecture me on that. I'm also painfully aware that I don't enjoy name-above-the-title status, but you could treat me with a little more respect than this."

Victor apologized and had to adjust to Ann's eccentricities as an actress. He would even leave the camera running before and after each take to catch some of Ann's wonderful improvisations.

The Sunday of April 9, Bob and Corey celebrated her forty-ninth birthday with Jack and his secretary, Deloris, the Widmarks, the Wildes, the Cobbs, the Carlsons, and the Ryans at the swank bar and grill, Leon's Corner, in West Hollywood.

This was a high-class bar and grill where celebrities hung out in their downtime, and tonight would be no different. Corey wanted to just have a relaxing evening with friends, drinks, and good food. Being surrounded all night by other actors at Leon's helped her to unwind and allowed her to let down her hair, which Bob took inordinate delight in seeing.

When Bob and Corey arrived home after her birthday party, they were both slightly inebriated. As Corey was starting to put on her nightgown, Bob gently took it out of her hands and threw it onto an adjacent chair. He stared her directly in the eyes and sexily placed one arm under her legs and the other around her back. Corey started to breathe heavily and started to kiss him on the neck as he carried her to the bed.

She could hear his breathing was a little labored when he lustfully and savagely kissed her with full force. After having carried her to the bed, he placed her down upon the sheets, and then he lay on top of her. As they were kissing with wild abandonment, Corey rolled him over on his back, and at this point, she took over the entire sexual conquest.

Bob was loving every moment of Corey showing this forceful and sexual assertiveness. He knew she loved him to be the more dominant aggressor in bed, but once in a while, she felt she needed to show him physically just how much she wanted and loved him.

The night was a demonstrative expression of wanton lust and enthralling love. They continued on into the impassioned and heavenly lit moonglow shining through their bedroom window those early morning hours of Monday.

Two days later, the cast and crew of *Rufous Eyes of Fire* brought the production in a week early, saving Trent thousands of dollars.

Trent and Victor decided to have the wrap party at Lacey's Place in West Hollywood the night they wrapped. Victor wanted the party at a place he had not been in over a year and wanted some place a little different from D'Angelo's.

Bob and Corey danced together most of the night. He only let go of Corey to ask June if she would dance with him. She accepted, and while they danced, June told him how much she enjoyed working with him and Corey.

June did mention, "Maybe if I can get Louis B. to get you on loan to do a picture at MGM, we could pair you with Katharine Hepburn, Hedy Lamar, Elizabeth Taylor, Loretta Young, or even Marilyn Monroe. I wouldn't even mind being a supporting actress to any of them."

Bob answered her with an air of curiosity, "That sounds like an enticing invitation, June. I probably would be interested in something like that. I'll have my agent and manager, Nick, look into that. I've been nominated twice for Best Actor, maybe that'll hold some weight."

"You mean, when you win your first Academy Award this year, that will definitely hold some weight, and a lot more money for your motion picture contracts from that day on."

The next of the Night Owls' Canadian concerts was in Saskatoon, Saskatchewan. This would only be a three-hour-and-fifteen-minute flight. They left the afternoon of Friday on April 14, which was only three days before the Thirty-Third Academy Awards at the Santa Monica Civic Auditorium in Santa Monica, California.

The Owls played the Amphitheater at Rivers End, which was built along the south Saskatchewan River bank. It was a beautiful and breathtaking location. The seating capacity was 2,780, with another 200 in standing room only.

The guys enjoyed themselves at both concerts, and the fans showed their appreciation by dancing down the aisles, standing ovations, and flowers thrown up onto the stage along with a few stuffed owls.

Bob walked into the house at almost three on Sunday morning. Corey had left a light on in the bathroom for him. Bob quietly went into the bathroom and took a quick shower. Corey didn't budge an inch.

When he came into the bedroom and climbed into bed shirtless, she stirred. When Bob wrapped his arm around her waist, she awakened to his touch. She responded by turning her body into his and running her hand behind his neck.

Feeling her awake, he ran his hand all over her back and down her buttocks while kissing her warm lips and pulling her closer to him. "Hello, doll. I've missed you, baby."

Corey sensually moved her lips toward his after she whispered, "I love you, darling."

After they enjoyed a lingering kiss, Bob turned his head and his one arm behind him, and a moment later, he brought something out and handed it to Corey. In the darkened room, she didn't have the slightest idea what this creature was; it was small, soft, and very smooth. Bob lovingly told her, "This is for you, baby."

She immediately reached over and turned on the nightstand lamp. When she turned back around to get a good look at what Bob had placed in her hand, her face was consumed by one continuous smile.

Corey could now see the feathered object he had given her was a toy stuffed owl. She comically asked, "Where on earth did you get this? It is very cute, darling."

Bob's voice took on a more earnest tone when he looked into Corey's eyes and suggested, "The fans threw a handful of these up onstage last night, and I thought I'd bring one home and show it to you. I also thought maybe this could be the first toy our child would play with and the first one to go into their toy box…what do you think about that, baby?"

His eyes became a little misty as Corey shook her head from this very emotional surprise, and she began to cry outwardly; and almost inaudibly, she tearfully said, "Oh my god, Robert Brian! I am absolutely ready to have a child in our life! Just hold me, darling! Just hold me!… I'll never be able to put into words how much I love you!"

They held each other very close the rest of the early morning hours of Sunday.

Corey arose from bed long before Bob did, and while she was out in the kitchen drinking her coffee with Haddie, as Haddie prepared them some eggs, she described the entire story to her about how Bob had presented her with the toy stuffed owl and its significance.

Haddie was beside herself with happiness for them. She now knew Corey would have her second lifelong need answered, after her first need was met: meeting and marrying the love of her life. Haddie excitedly asked Corey, "Well, do you know if you wanna have a boy or a girl?"

Corey answered her quickly by stating, "It doesn't matter to me. Whatever my darling husband wants is what I want."

Bob came strolling into the kitchen at that time and kiddingly told both Haddie and Corey, "What I want is a child who is healthy, smart, musically inclined, funny, good-looking, and wants to make something of themselves. That's all. I'm not demanding anything."

He walked over to Corey as she and Haddie were still laughing, and he bent over and kissed her on top of her head. She slightly moaned with content.

Haddie asked Bob with great curiosity, "Well, Mr. Bob, I'm glad you came to this decision 'bout havin' a baby. You're gonna love everything 'bout it. Now what do you want? A boy or a girl?"

Bob hesitated a moment as his gaze drifted out of the kitchen window for a moment. He then turned to look at Corey with his loving eyes. She was still sitting down on the barstool as her welled-up tears began to glisten, waiting in anticipation for his answer.

While still having eye contact with Corey, he resoundingly answered Haddie, "You know, Ms. Haddie? I don't know what our child looks like. I just know when we see them, we're gonna know that instant that this is the child we're gonna love the rest of our lives."

Corey's welled-up tears began to spill down her cheeks as she moved quickly to throw her arms around Bob's waist. He enveloped her with his arms and then slowly moved his hands to hold her face and leaned down into an emotional kiss with her.

The bulk of the day was spent out by the pool—with Bob doing laps, he and Corey taking their lunch out there, and them talking about tomorrow night's Academy Awards ceremony.

Corey had a custom-designed gown made for her in early February by Ms. Edith Head. For when Edith heard that Corey was nominated for this year's Oscar as Best Actress, she volunteered her services to her. Edith and Corey had always gotten along and enjoyed each other's company after they worked together on *Love's Wicked Lies*. Of course, Corey was ecstatic about having her gown made for the ceremony by one of the most renowned and prolific costume designers in Hollywood.

As Corey sipped on her coffee, she mentioned to Bob, "You know I had a gown made for me months ago by Edith, and you said you didn't need another tuxedo made for you, so what tux are you wearing tomorrow night, darling?"

"I'm probably going to wear the one I wore last year, but with a light-blue shirt, cummerbund, and handkerchief." Teasing her now, he added, "I don't think I'll embarrass you, because I did have it sent out to be cleaned… I'll try hard to look like a movie star, babe, but next to you in that gown, I'm gonna look like an accordion-player's monkey."

Corey chuckled, put her cup down on her small table, and moved sultrily out of her lounger to lie with Bob in his lounger. She wrapped her arms around the back of his head and pressed her breasts into his bare chest then seductively told him, "You're absolutely going to be the best-looking man there tomorrow night, darling. You could never embarrass me, you beautiful man. I am always proud of you and in awe of just how attractive you are. And I will always be aware of the many women that would just love to be with you, sweetheart."

Bob reassured her, "All that really matters to me is that you're the woman walking in with me tomorrow night, and later the woman going home with me, to share my bed… I love you, doll."

They fell into a long and lingering kiss.

Monday night, April 17, 1961, Bob was handsomely dressed in his black tuxedo, with the light-blue accompanying shirt, handkerchief, and cummerbund. He awaited Corey in the kitchen as he talked with Haddie. Bob wanted to drive them to the awards ceremony in his Chevy, for he had plans afterward, and he wanted to be alone with Corey—no chauffeur.

At seven ten, Corey slowly moved into the kitchen, showcasing her Edith Head gown. Haddie caught sight of her first and shouted, "Oh, Ms. Corey! You look like a million dollars in that gown. It's beautiful!"

Bob turned his head to see Corey after Haddie had shouted. He couldn't speak for a few moments. Corey's gown was absolutely breathtaking. It was an off-the-shoulder, floor-length, sheath columned evening gown. It was dusty lilac with a sequined bodice mesh and a tall thigh-high left-leg slit. It was made of a shimmering chiffon, with beaded and embroidered areas around the deep V neckline. She carried a light-lilac-colored shoulder wrap and wore strappy slingback evening sandals with a three-inch block heel and made of silver leather.

Bob was mesmerized with her beauty; the show of skin from her leg to her shoulder and cleavage was unbelievably enticing to him. Her auburn hair was up and looked professionally arranged in a coif, and her makeup was glamorous and impeccably applied.

He was finally able to breathe normally again as his heart was still racing with the absolute pride and unprecedented love he had for her. "Corey"—gently shaking his head—"you are exquisite. There are no words that would describe how stunning you look tonight. So I'll drive us to Santa Monica tonight, but not in the Chevy. I'll take the Cadillac, babe. You deserve the very best."

Corey walked over to him, and with her elbow-length dusty-lilac gloves cupped in her one hand, she took his face in both her hands and solemnly told him, "We're going to take your Chevy, darling. After all, I will be accompanied by the very best."

He broke into a huge smile as they lightly touched lips so as not to mess Corey's lipstick.

She then told him, "Now let's get going, or we'll be the last to walk the red carpet."

The '52 Chevy flip-top pulled up at seven forty in front of the Santa Monica Civic Auditorium in Santa Monica, and a valet who was always available to those very few who didn't have a chauffeur came running down to the car. Bob got out and handed him the keys, which was wrapped in a fifty-dollar bill, and then thanked him as Bob went to open Corey's door.

As he opened her front passenger-side door, he helped her to step out, taking extreme precautions not to let her gown get caught on anything metal. When she was completely out of the car, with no mishaps of any kind to her or her gown, he smiled brilliantly and chuckled at her, as she stroked the side of his face with her gloved hand and looked him straight in the eyes with that confident loving smile of hers.

Corey took Bob's right hand, and as they turned to face the auditorium's front entrance, he placed his right arm around her lower back, and they commenced to walk the red carpet.

As they were walking closely together, the cameras simultaneously began flashing an endless number of bulbs at them. They were one of the most accomplished and popular couples in Hollywood at the time. Bob waved to his screaming fans and smiled at them, but he never let go of Corey's waist.

Just as last year, Bob and Corey were stopped by the Hollywood columnist for *Variety* magazine, Army Archerd. When Army waved Bob and Corey over, Corey looked up at Bob and had to get his attention by running her hand across his chest. He had been waving with his free hand and smiling at his fans, who were screaming for him to come over to them.

When he felt Corey's glove moving across his chest, it startled him. He concernedly leaned into her face as she informed him, "Army would like to talk with us, darling."

Relieved a bit, Bob answered her, "Oh, of course, doll."

Corey smiled and walked over to Army, with Bob following but still waving to his fans.

Army excitedly asked both of them, "Corey Madrigal and Bob Richardson. The two of you have been quite busy as of late. Do you see that slowing down any time soon?"

The flashbulbs were still going off like mad from the mass of photographers in front of the platform Army was interviewing celebrities from.

Just moments before, Army had interviewed Jack Lemmon and his fiancée, Felicia Farr, and then Deborah Kerr and her husband, Peter Viertel.

Corey loved this atmosphere of movie star adulation, the press fawning all over them, and being interviewed by a columnist on ABC television, while millions of people around the world were watching all this from the comfort of their own living rooms.

"We have both been very busy, Army, but in Hollywood, that's very good news," Corey proudly answered.

Looking straight at Bob, Army inquisitively asked, "And, Bob? You've had great success in touring with your band, playing Broadway, and now receiving your second Oscar nomination for your work in *Love's Wicked Lies*. Tell me, how do you juggle all of this and your marriage to your beautiful wife, too?"

Bob's face reflected pure provocation at the question.

Corey could see Bob was annoyed with Army's question, just as he was at last year's interview with him. She started to excuse them from the interview, when Bob answered the question, talking over Corey's first words. "Mr. Archerd...you know, it's not really a juggling act at all, because when you love something so much, you make time for it. That's why I tend to prioritize my loves, with my incredible wife as my number one priority. All the rest is like dogs fighting for kennel space. They either find the space or they don't... Such is life."

Corey abruptly told Army, "I think we'd better head inside now. It's getting close to the time they're going to start. Thank you, Army. Maybe we'll see you later."

Army, being kind of mystified by Bob's response, answered, "Well, okay, Corey. Good luck to both of you."

Walking down the remaining twenty feet of red carpet, Corey hooked her arm through Bob's and explained to him, "You really shouldn't take to heart anything a columnist or critic asks or writes about you. They're just trying to sell copies. They're doing their job, darling… Now you come inside and sit with your number one priority, and let's have a good time."

He leaned over and kissed her on the side of her head. He then smiled cutely, and now more cheerful, he told her, "Absolutely, baby. Let's enjoy tonight."

Once inside, Bob and Corey were escorted to their seats in the front row, down from Trevor Howard, Shirley MacLaine, Greer Garson, and Jack Lemmon on one side of them, and Deborah Kerr, Melina Mercouri, and Laurence Olivier on the other side. This was the row of seats designated for the top nominees for that year. Some of the nominees of less notoriety were assigned seats on the aisle near the stage. The seats behind, but still in focus, are given to celebrities not in contention but still hold the star power.

Corey, now with ten nominations and two wins for Best Actress, and Bob, with two nominations and a flourishing young career of always displaying his incipient talent with every movie he made, were seated center front row near the orchestra.

After everyone seemed to be in their seats, the music became softer, the ABC cameras started to roll, and an announcer's voice began to echo through the auditorium. "Welcome to tonight's Thirty-Third Academy Awards presentation. And now your host for tonight, Mr. Bob Hope."

Bob Hope came out from behind the huge curtain, wearing a black full-dress tailcoat tuxedo with white bowtie. When the applause died down, he began his twelve-minute dialogue of jokes and witty one-liners. As the program went on, he had introduced all the presenters in the less-known categories. Over an hour into the program, the Big Five awards were now ready to be presented.

The Oscar for Actor in a Supporting Role had already been awarded to Peter Ustinov in *Spartacus*. Actress in a Supporting Role went to Shirley Jones in *Elmer Gantry*. And costume design in color was awarded to Ms. Edith Head for *Love's Wicked Lies*.

At the announcement of Edith's win, both Corey and Bob got out of their seats to meet her, before she went up onstage to receive her Oscar. They hugged and congratulated her. After Edith hugged both Bob and Corey, she leaned into them and quickly stated, "Thank you so much, but now it's your turn."

Corey smiled broadly and answered, "I hope you're right, Edith."

As Edith received her Oscar and began her acceptance speech, Bob and Corey sat back down in their seats.

When Edith ended her speech and exited the stage, Bob Hope came back out and introduced last year's winner for Best Actor in a Leading Role, Charleston Heston. He was to announce the nominees for this year's Best Actress in a Leading Role.

There was a little nervousness showing on Corey's face, so Bob reached over and embraced her hand in his then lifted it toward his lips and gently kissed the top.

Corey looked at him with such love in her eyes, and then Heston began speaking, "It's my honor tonight to announce the nominees for Best Actress in a Leading Role. And I have to tell you, these five actresses are five of the best in the business. The first nominee is Greer Garson, *Sunrise at Campobello*. Deborah Kerr, *The Sundowners*. Corey Madrigal, *Love's Wicked Lies*." There were a few yells and whistles that came from the upper tier of seating; whereas, each year, there were 150 seats available to the general public.

"Shirley MacLaine, *The Apartment*. And Melina Mercouri, *Never on Sunday*. And the winner is..." The envelope was handed to him, and the tension that built in the air of the auditorium was so thick, it could have been cut with a knife.

Heston looked up, smiled, and loudly announced, "Corey Madrigal, *Love's Wicked Lies*!"

Instantly Bob jumped from his seat straight up and into the air, with his arms raised high above his head and screamed, "Oh my god! Corey! Yes! Yes!"

Corey was brilliantly smiling and laughing as she watched Bob's reaction to her win. She then threw herself into his arms, and they kissed joyously and excitedly.

Bob reluctantly released his embrace of Corey as she started her triumphant walk up the few steps in front of the stage to the podium. Heston met and cheek-kissed her and then handed her the Academy Award he had been holding.

Bob was still standing until Corey approached the microphone, then he sat back down, in respect for those sitting behind him.

Corey held her Oscar in one hand, resting it on the surface of the podium, and just stared at it, shaking her head in disbelief. When the loud applause and cheering quieted down, she breathlessly began her acceptance speech. "I want to thank the Academy for this great honor. I really didn't think I would ever see another one of these young men again"—looking at her Oscar—"but I also never thought I'd be married to one of these young male gods, either."

The audience began to laugh, and Bob's facial expression said it all; he laughed out loud as he rocked back and forth in his seat. It seemed the audience was soon laughing with him, and even Corey heartily laughed at his reaction to her comment.

It took several seconds, but Bob got himself under control as he wiped at one of his eyes. His smile to Corey was beaming with the deep love he felt for her as he blew her a heartfelt kiss. She slowly and lovingly blew a kiss back to him.

The laughter quieted down, and Corey then declared into the microphone, "I'm dedicating this award tonight to my love and my life, Robert Brian. I love you, darling!"

She then lifted the Oscar into the air and aimed it at Bob. Bob balled his fist and patted it against his heart. They stared at each other with such loving adoration.

Corey ended her speech and looked out at the audience and said, "I want to thank all of you again. I will never forget this night."

There was a loud applause for Corey as she walked offstage with her arm locked in Heston's arm.

Bob Hope came back out onstage and introduced last year's winner of the Academy Award for Best Actress in a Leading Role, Simone Signoret, to announce the nominees for Best Actor in a Leading Role.

When the auditorium and the applause died down, Simone quietly announced, "Tonight it's my privilege to announce the nominees for Best Actor in a Leading Role. Jack Lemmon, *The Apartment.* Spencer Tracy, *Inherit the Wind.* Trevor Howard, *Sons and Lovers.* Laurence Olivier, *The Entertainer.* And Bob Richardson, *Love's Wicked Lies.*" There were a few yells and whistles cascading down from the general public seating.

Simone then dramatically whispered into the microphone, "And the winner is…"

Corey left the press corps, the TV interviewers, and the photographers standing and waiting so she could go and stand just offstage and out of the view of the cameras. She wanted and needed to hear what actor would be announced as the winner of Best Actor in a Leading Role.

As she stood there impatiently waiting, with Oscar in hand, her mind wandered into thinking there wasn't a married couple who had both won Academy Awards in the same year. All Corey knew was that she desperately wanted Bob to win. Not so they'd be the first married couple to win together in the same year, but because of the hard work he put into his role and the outstanding portrayal he enacted of the pathetic yet conniving protagonist.

She felt his abilities as an actor had improved exponentially with every picture he made.

She began to pray, as she had her eyes fixed on him, while he sat in the front row of the audience not seeming uncomfortable or nervous. He was just staring at Simone and her tearing open the envelope with the winner's name enclosed.

As she opened the envelope, Simone gave a small nod of effectual surprise and then happily said aloud, "Bob Richardson, *Love's Wicked Lies*!"

The Santa Monica Civic Auditorium went nuts with thunderous applause, cheering, and whistles. Corey instantly started to cry and could no longer stand upright. Involuntarily she lowered herself to a stooping position and just wept with a happiness that took over her entire body.

When Bob heard his name called as the winner, he buried his face in his hands and fell forward onto his thighs with his face still covered. The next thing he knew, Jack Windheim was patting him on the back and told him, "Congratulations, Bob! Now you're really part of the 'in' crowd. Way to go, my boy!"

Bob stood up and hugged Jack and tried holding back his tears. Then Victor and Trent ran up to him and hugged him and shook his hand excitedly.

Jack Lemmon even came over from several seats away to congratulate Bob. Bob returned Jack's compliment by telling him, "Thanks, Jack, but you were just fantastic in *The Apartment*!"

Jack rejoined by resignedly stating, "Thanks. Maybe next year."

Bob started to make his way up the steps to meet and hug Simone. She cheek-kissed and congratulated him and then handed him his Oscar statuette. All he could do was stare at the statue, and then he slowly made his way to the microphone.

Before he could say anything, he looked to the stage wings for Corey. He could see her being helped to a standing position by director Billy Wilder. Bob waved to her with his hand to come out and join him.

Without a moment's hesitation, Corey walked very quickly toward him, even in her strappy slingback evening sandals. When Corey came back out onstage to join Bob, the crowd's applause got so much louder.

When she reached him, with her arms wide open to him, he took her by the waist as she wrapped her arms around his neck, and they kissed briefly, but amorously.

Corey told him with such love and enthusiasm in her voice, "Congratulations, baby! I'm just so damned proud of you!"

Bob made his way to the microphone while still holding on to Corey by her waist. She physically motioned him up by himself to the microphone as she dropped back a few feet. He was okay with this and understood that Corey knew this was his moment to shine, for she had her share of these moments herself, tonight and in the passing years of her career.

The audience quieted down as Bob began his acceptance speech. "Oh, wow! Thank you so much for this...you know, I've had so much time in my life to rehearse for this moment. I remember when I was eight years old, I was playing John Wayne in *The Fighting Seabees*, and I'd stand in front of the mirror with my mother's brush in my hand as the Oscar and proudly say, 'I want to thank the Academy for this award."

The audience started to laugh, with an appreciative applause accompanying that.

"I mean I won, along with Susan Hayward, who was in this picture with me. How could you go wrong and not win with that lineup?" Bob just shrugged his shoulders and mocked surprise.

Everyone was laughing now. The cameras even caught a close-up of Susan Hayward, as she was just rolling with laughter. Corey stood behind Bob and laughed with a huge toothy grin and lightly shook her head in disbelief.

When the laughter subsided, Bob sounded of a more serious nature. "I really would like to thank the person who kept me under their wing when I first came to Celebrity Studios and advised me not to just walk away and pursue my other interests, but to stay and learn, watch and study, incorporate and execute. This person was first, my best friend; second, my mentor; and third, the absolute love of my life. She has shown me that love has no age barriers. Love is always constant, and my life would not be the same without her... Corey? If I know anything at all about love, it's because of you."

Bob turned around to Corey as tears were streaking down her cheeks. He then turned back to the audience and shouted, "Thank you again! From the bottom of my heart!"

He picked up the Academy Award and pumped it three times at the audience, and they clapped even louder. Bob took Corey by the waist and kissed her. He then placed his hand holding the award around Simone's waist, and the three of them quitted the stage as the cameras kept rolling and the music played on.

Backstage the camera flashes were constant as Bob and Corey stood in front of a light-blue-and-white wall decorated with pictures of Academy Awards and the year 1961 splashed throughout. They were answering questions from the UPI, AFP, AP, and Reuters press corps, along with the *Hollywood Reporter* magazine and the *Variety* newspaper.

When the Best Director Academy Award was about to be declared, Corey was made aware of this by hearing last year's best director, William Wyler, say, "And the winner is…Victor Trudeau, *Love's Wicked Lies*!"

Bob and Corey ran from the pressroom to the stage wing. Victor was starting to give his acceptance speech, so they stood waiting for him to finish. When he ended his speech by saying, "Directing this picture with such an outstanding and talented cast of actors and actresses, such as Madrigal, Richardson, Hayworth, Carson, and Ryan… It wasn't work at all. I enjoyed it. It was fun and exciting and so fulfilling. I should have been paying for the honor, not the other way around. Thank you again so much!"

Victor started to exit the stage, and Bob met him halfway. Bob shook Victor's hand and then gave him a big bear hug. They both were all smiles, as Corey raced to hug Victor also. All three of them walked arm in arm offstage, as the audience gave them a loud and lingering applause.

Love's Wicked Lies would not win Best Picture, but *The Apartment*, with Billy Wilder, producer, taking home the Oscar. And Best Screenplay Written for the Screen would not be Jeffrey Stewart in *Love's Wicked Lie*s, but Richard Brooks for *Elmer Gantry*.

It was a good night for Jack Windheim and Celebrity Studios, for Trent Voight's production of *Love's Wicked Lies* would take home four Academy Awards out of the six it was nominated for that night. And at the one-year mark from the release of *Love's Wicked Lies*, the picture had garnered fifty million dollars in global box office revenue.

Bob and Corey were invited to just about every after-Oscar party that was in the LA area. They first attended the party of good friends Cornel Wilde, Richard Widmark, and Lew Ayers at Cornel and wife's home and stayed for less than an hour.

Susan Hawthorne had her perennial party with a showcase of stars from every studio in Hollywood. Jennifer Jones, Jason Robards, and Joan Fontaine were there from Twentieth Century Fox. Geraldine

Page, Ingrid Bergman, Paul Newman and Joanne Woodward, and Stuart Whitman from Metro Goldwyn Mayer. And a countless number of star powers from Celebrity Studios was present.

Bob and Corey were schmoozed, hugged, and cheek-kissed all night at every party they attended. After a sip of a drink at their third party, Bob asked Corey to dance with him to a slow song by the Night Owls, "My Constant Need."

Corey loved to dance with Bob, and when he asked, she looked at him with such pride and admiration, that her brightness and cheerfulness and the vigor in her eyes displayed her intense passion and love she felt for him. She sexily answered, "Why, of course, darling. I would love to."

While he held her close with both his hands, Bob was kissing her on the side of her face and ear. Corey gave a soft moan, and then he whispered into her ear, "What do you think about letting me take you somewhere I don't think you've ever been?"

Corey inquisitively gazed up at him and asked, "What do you mean, darling?"

Bob suggested, "Let's get away from all the people, all the noise, and let's just be alone for the rest of the evening. I want you to myself for the rest of the time tonight. What do you say, doll? Just you and me. It's only thirty minutes away from here."

Corey was intrigued and pleasurably told him, "Anywhere you want to go, sweetheart. As long as I'm there with you."

Bob leaned into a kiss with her and then quietly whispered, "All right, babe. Let's move slowly and slip out of the back door. No one will even know we're gone."

"I'm following you, darling," Corey whispered back.

Before they knew it and anyone at the party noticed them gone, Bob had started up the Chevy, and they were both on their way up US 405 toward Hollywood.

At about ten thirty that night, Bob was driving Corey up the very winding and twisting scenic road of Mulholland Drive north of LA and only a few miles from Bel Air. He was pointing out the different homes that were hidden away in the Hollywood Hills of the Santa Monica mountains; he showed her Marlon Brando's hideaway,

Ida Lupino's estate, Eddie Fisher's house he had built for Elizabeth Taylor, and Joan Fontaine's huge home.

After a short while, Bob parked the car on one of the pullovers where the young kids would go to neck and watch the lights of the city below. It was the best view in LA, and on clear evenings like this one, you could see the ocean; and if there was a concert at the Hollywood Bowl, the music would waft up to the road, sweetening the night air.

Bob turned the car off and got Corey out and walked her around to the front of the car, where he boosted her up onto the hood, which was pointed directly at the iconic "Hollywood" sign that stood on the far side of the hill.

He sat down on the hood next to her with his arm around her back and gripping her side.

It just so happened that night the Tommy Dorsey Band was playing the Hollywood Bowl. The band was playing "I'm Getting Sentimental over You."

Bob turned to Corey and stated, "You hear that music, doll? That is the life essence of that band wafting up to us and letting us revel in the definitive soul that they bare every time they perform that song."

Corey sat mesmerized by Bob's description of the ethereal experience a musician feels when they perform their music.

He turned his gaze on Corey and explained to her, "You see, baby. When you make a motion picture, your life's essence is captured on film forever for people to watch over and over again for many years to come. You have given a part of your soul to your performance, and you let your viewers revel in your mastery of the dramatic arts. How is a musical artist rewarded and shown appreciation for sharing their life's essence and baring their soul on vinyl? Their record goes platinum...that's how. And how are you, the consummate professional actress, rewarded and shown appreciation for sharing her life's essence and baring her soul to the camera?"

Bob took his Academy Award out from behind him and placed it on the hood of the car between them.

"This is how. You first are acknowledged after being recognized for your achievement in being nominated, and then you are ordained into sainthood by being given this golden statuette to proudly retain for the rest of your life."

Corey could not stop from staring at Bob. She had to tell him, "My god, darling. You just make everything we do sound so magical and poetic... I will always love you too much, Robert Brian."

Bob leaned over the hood of the car, moving the statuette toward the windshield, and looked directly into Corey's beautiful eyes and gave her a slow, lingering kiss. As they separated, he sexily winked at her, and she gave him that adoring look of hers and slowly winked back at him. Bob definitively told Corey, "It will never be too much, doll."

As they wrapped their arms around each other, they could hear the smooth-toned trombones to the song "So Rare" as the Dorsey Band kept a slow steady beat to the song, and the music played on.

ABOUT THE AUTHOR

Ms. Soucie, having completed her first novel in 2020, *The Right Music for Dancing*, was convinced by her senior publication consultant that there was plenty of room to write a sequel to her first novel. So she set out to accomplish this, while still helping to edit her first novel.

Almost a year and a half later, she has come up with an even more compelling answer to her first novel. She's hoping this leads to a continuing story with these enjoyable and incredible characters.

CPSIA information can be obtained
at www.ICGtesting.com
Printed in the USA
LVHW100728191022
730904LV00026B/19

9 781684 985388